Library of Congress Cataloging-in-Publication Data available on file
Library of Congress Control Number: 2013920551
ISBN 978-0-9911713-0-9

10 9 8 7 6 5 4 3 2
Printed and bound in the USA

The Touchstone Diary

Connie Bickman

Dedication

~ To Miyah, Michael, Joshua and Maryum, who came to me in my sleeping dreams, brought me their story and then guided me to put it to paper.

~ To the brave women and men who lived through events of the past and left their mark by chronicling traces of their lives.

~ To the men and women of my own bloodline in honor of their stories, especially my parents, Al and June. They always encouraged me to follow my dreams and develop my talents—particularly my mom, who always nudged me to look beyond.

~ To my own tribe of women—my daughters, Cris, Kelli and Nicole; grandgirls, Jennifer, Cassandra, Taylor, Paige, Devin and Isabella; and great-grandgirl Stella—who will all carry on the stories of our bloodline.

~ To those who proofread parts or all of the manuscript, offering their own expert advice in areas where I needed specific details.

~ A special thank you to a great part-time travel partner, my daughter Kelli (and occasional travel partners - grandgirls Jenn and little Izzy) while I researched in France, India and Scotland. These journeys were adventures I will always cherish.

touch-stone, n.   - benchmark, gauge,
                  measure, proof; any criterion for
                  determining genuineness or value; a
                  test of quality or ability; a stone
                  formerly used in testing the purity
                  of gold or silver

Preface

Several years ago my dreams led me toward a path I couldn't avoid. Night after night I saw pages play out like a movie on a screen. I couldn't blink it away and will admit that I didn't want to. It was entertaining, addictive. . .and strangely, the dreams continued almost every night.

Finally, I sat down at my computer and started to write. I closed my eyes and typed what I saw—it was as if I were watching a movie, just like in my dreams. The words seemed to be writing themselves.

After completing a few more chapters, I decided to title my manuscript. I thought "Miyah's Journey" would be a good choice and I proceeded to type that on my keyboard. But when I looked at my screen, that's not what was written. I looked down at my fingers to see if they were on the right keys. . .they were. At that point, I pushed my chair back from the desk and looked up into the ethers. I had goosebumps. I shook my head and said, "All right. I'll be your messenger. Whatever you want. Just guide me through this."

I felt a tingling sensation, as if I were receiving an answer to my request—an invisible agreement was written. "They" would guide me through the story and information. I would do the work—write, research. . .believe. I felt a light surrounded me in a cocoon of unconditional love. I knew at that instant that all I had to do was trust and keep writing. The rest would take care of itself.

When I looked back at the screen of my computer, the title was still there glaring at me in bold letters, "The Touchstone Diary."

Over the course of the next few years I wrote, researched and traveled. Even though I was convinced I was being used as a "tool" to write this book, I felt I needed to check facts that were coming to me from all directions. I wanted details. Through past and current travels to India, France, England, Nepal, Turkey, Jordan, Israel, Scotland and other places around the globe, I was able to add the smells, sounds and feelings evoked during my experiences. I compiled mounds of notes regarding anything that might possibly pertain to my "fiction-based-on-historical-events" story. It was also through these journeys that I realized misconceptions I had about the foundation of organized religion and how often times people in other countries and cultures had much different perspectives on not only Christianity and conflicting biblical translations, but also on the original Christ story itself.

I knew what I was writing would be controversial so I needed to first convince myself that some of the details I uncovered could be factual. I cross-referenced everything. Like Michael in the story, I was amazed as I uncovered information that many others had considered common knowledge, especially during my travels to France and India.

It's been an incredible journey since I began those first chapters. Yet, whenever I think back at my time writing these books, I feel that warm love and light surrounding me. I can say with all my heart that I am proud to be the messenger of "The Touchstone Diary."

Connie Bickman

Table of Contents

BOOK I – *The Red Thread*

BOOK II – *Bloodlines and Promises*

The Touchstone Diary

The Touchstone Diary
Book 1
The Red Thread

1 The Promise

Miyah could see the dim light from a single lamppost reflecting off the cobblestone. A hint of moonlight saturated the crude stones with a mysterious blue shadow, while a thin mist shrouded the evening air. Silence surrounded the city. Yet within the stillness, Miyah's footsteps could not be heard as she followed the winding street. Some said she floated like the mist, or hovered like an angel. Miyah would simply smile and say she walked in her grandmother's footsteps.

It had been like this since childhood. Miyah would be sleeping deeply when dreams filtered into her mind, altering her state of peacefulness. She'd see faceless people whose souls were calling to her, reaching out for her help. She would be urged to awaken, dress and run out into the night. She had long ago given up having to know her destination.

Tonight, as she walked swiftly and silently through the sleeping city, she recalled when she first became keeper of a powerful Touchstone—a secret so holy, even she was not fully aware of its impact. She only knew this package she carried deep inside her grandmother's ancient medicine pouch had shaped the fate of her family for many generations. It was her duty to carry on the Touchstone destiny.

Even now she could feel her grandmother's heavy breathing. She could hear Nona's raspy, yet gentle voice calling out to her, guiding her. "Go faster, my child. Time is running out. Hurry!"

Miyah picked up her pace, blindly following Nona's map unraveling in her mind. By tuning in to her own instincts and her grandmother's voice, she knew she was being guided to the right place, to the person who needed her medicine.

Before her death, Miyah's mother, Junia, often watched from an upstairs window as Miyah disappeared into the darkness. She understood, sending prayers to the spirits to guide her only child. Junia had carried the Touchstone before her daughter was born and for a brief time after. As a child, Junia, too, would awaken in the night and travel through the city, hand in hand with Nona until they reached their destination. She watched every movement, heard every word her wise mother imparted. In her youth, Junia wasn't sure if this knowledge was a gift or a curse. She often longed for a normal life where responsibilities were less. Yet she knew it was an honor to be a chosen apprentice. She felt such love whenever she watched Nona selflessly administer healing to those in need—the same love Miyah felt as a child when she watched and listened to Junia sharing her magic. Grandmother to daughter to granddaughter, the cycle had continued throughout generations.

Light shown dimly through an upstairs window as Miyah stood in front of a well-kept English-tudor home. She knocked on the door and a young woman answered, quickly inviting Miyah inside as if she were expecting her.

"Are you the woman they call Miyah? I prayed you would be coming tonight," the woman said, leading Miyah up a shadowed stairway to the bedroom. "I hope there's still time."

Miyah no longer questioned how people knew she would be arriving. It was as casual as if they had called her on the telephone and asked her to drop by. Perhaps they did, only it was in another dimension of which even they weren't aware.

"My brother, Michael, is very sick. The doctors have given him no hope. You are the only one who can help him."

Miyah nodded and offered a slight smile. "They only call on me as a last resort," she thought. "Don't they know they could avoid so much suffering if they contacted me sooner?" Yet she also knew each soul had a reason for their physical body to experience suffering and pain. Many lessons needed to be learned and sometimes sickness and coming close to death were the only ways to get their attention and open their senses to what lies beyond. One often finds truth in dying.

The young woman escorted Miyah into a stuffy bedroom and left, closing the door quietly behind her. Miyah sat down on a chair next to the bed and watched this dying man for a few minutes. He was feverish and very pale. She reached out and folded his hand into hers.

"Hello Michael. My name is Miyah," she said softly, as she glanced at the row of drugs and medications lined up on his night stand.

"You look quite peaceful," she offered. Miyah had never met Michael before, yet she felt as if she knew him.

"I'm not peaceful," Michael said in weak voice. "I'm dying. I know my sister sent for you. Can't they just let me be?" he asked.

"Are you ready to die?" Miyah asked bluntly.

"Is anyone ever ready?" Michael shot back.

"You have a choice. You can choose to live," Miyah's voice was almost a whisper. "However, a price comes with that choice and you must make promises."

Michael turned to look at Miyah. He half expected to see the devil bargaining for his soul, not this gentle woman sitting calmly by his side. He looked into her eyes, and despite his skepticism, he saw a light that drew him in. He felt a warm flow of love flush into his shivering, yet feverish body. He could not look away from the intensity of her gaze. It was as if she controlled his every thought, as if she was inside every fiber of his entire being. Yet, he didn't feel afraid. An uncommon calm came over him and he managed a slight smile.

"Are you bargaining for my soul?" he cynically asked.

"No, not your soul," Miyah replied. "What I'm asking for is more than that."

"What. . .?" he began.

"Don't ask me now. I have something I'd like you to have while you sleep. It will begin your healing and make you stronger. You'll understand more in the morning."

Miyah reached for her medicine pouch – a tattered, old cloth bag with embroidered symbols, little bells, tiny mirrors and gemstones embedded into the fabric. It was made by a Gypsy woman many generations ago and had existed in Miyah's family "forever." Nona had told her granddaughter the bag was hundreds of years old, yet, even though it was a bit tattered, it didn't show signs of ever wearing out. Nona said it was sewn with magic and love, and whenever love is woven into the texture of life, it never wears out. Miyah liked that.

She folded the fabric of the bag back to reveal a brown linen bag containing a thick diary, which she set aside. Inside was also a crude, hand-made box. She placed the box on the bed next to Michael and laid her hands on the lid, pausing a few seconds, as if in a prayer. Miyah then pulled her long hair to one side, revealing a necklace with a narrow, leather strap. Attached was a worn, washed-leather pouch from which she retrieved a small, ankh-shaped key. Unlocking the box, she slowly opened it to reveal a bundle of old cloth. Michael watched with interest, wondering what could be so important about an old box, a book and a heap of shredded fabric.

Miyah carefully began to unwind the cloth. When layers of fabric were peeled back, a large black stone was revealed. It was a rounded, long pyramid shape, embedded with sparkling bits of crystals. Miyah picked up the stone and held it in line with the moonbeams shining through the window. Tiny crystal specks reflected in the light and seemed to bring the stone to life. Miyah ceremoniously ran her hands around the entire surface of the stone while whispering a prayer, words that were foreign to Michael. Then she touched the stone to her heart and held it there for a few seconds before she gently placed it in Michael's hand.

"Look at this closely and tell me what you see," she commanded.

Michael reluctantly accepted the stone, fitting it into the palm of his hand. He felt a little foolish reading the face of a stone, but as he examined it closer he saw clear detail.

"It looks like the shape of a woman bundled up in a blanket," he slowly responded. "I see an old face peeking through an opening in the robe, yet I can't make out the features clearly. It definitely feels feminine."

"What else?" asked Miyah. "Look deeper."

He turned the stone over in his hand a few times, studying the features.

"Well, first of all, it's either heavy or I'm damn weak," he said as he examined the stone. "I see tiny crystals sparkling in the stone. And there are long lines, surface cracks, that cross each other and wrap around the circumference of the stone. Does that mean anything?"

Miyah held out her left hand, palm up. "Look at the life lines on my palm," she said. "Now look at the lines on the surface of this stone."

Michael placed the stone next to Miyah's hand. His eyes traced the lines on her palm and then the lines on the stone.

"The lines are exactly the same!" he exclaimed. "I'll be damned."

"It's not so unusual when you consider the lines on this stone also match the palms of my mother, my grandmother and all the women of our bloodline who came before them. It's our birthright. Some say our curse." She smiled, looking directly into Michael's eyes. "The markings on our palms are from the source of our healing. The Touchstone of our lives."

"I don't understand. . ." Michael started.

"You don't have to understand right now," Miyah interrupted. "You will know soon enough. Just try to remember everything you see tonight in your dreams and tell me about it later."

Michael stared back at her, feeling exhausted from their brief conversation. "I need to sleep now," he said. "But I don't feel like death is so near with you here. Will you stay with me through the night? I'm not ready to die. Hell, I'm barely 40 years old. I should be planning my life, not my death. I want another chance. . ." his voice trailed off and he sounded weary.

"Yes, I'll stay the night," Miyah replied as she put the key into the necklace pouch and tucked it back under her blouse. "But I want you to keep this stone with you as you sleep. You can place it under your pillow or hold it in your hand. It has strong healing medicine."

Michael curled his hand around the stone and laying on his side, tucked his hand under his pillow.

"I don't understand the healing magic in your stone, but I need all the help I can get. The doctors have given up on me. I've come home to die. Damn cancer," he swore. "What have I got to lose?"

"You have nothing to lose, Michael, but much to gain," Miyah said as she placed the cloth back into the wooden box and gently closed the lid. She kept her hands on the box for another prayerful moment and then placed the box next to Michael on his night stand.

"Miyah, it may seem strange, but I've seen you in my dreams. I knew you would come. Thank you for finding your way to me, especially tonight when I needed you most," Michael said as he curled his body into a fetal shape, his usual sleeping position these nights. "I've heard about your powers. I didn't mean what I said—I really am glad my sister sent for you. I don't want to die yet."

"It's not strange," Miyah whispered. "Good night, Michael. May you find peace in your dreams."

Michael watched this mysterious woman settle herself into the oversized chair next to the window. Bathed in moonlight, her features revealed a delicate profile with thick, dark hair falling to her shoulders. Her eyes were wide open, staring at the moon, as if conversing, giving and receiving messages.

"She looks so peaceful," Michael thought, as he slowly drifted off into a deep sleep, the healing stone tightly clasped in his hand.

Miyah looked over at Michael's weak body as she listened to his shallow breathing. She wondered what work he had been chosen to complete. When she was called in to heal the dying she knew they still had things they must achieve in this lifetime. Often they just needed to know they had one more chance to make new life choices. . .and a chance to make positive changes in the world. Sometimes she was called in to help make the transition from life into the next dimension. But this case was different. She could sense it. She watched his eyelids flicker and knew Michael was off on a journey. In a few days he would be healed. . .and his life would never be the same.

This she promised.

2 The Smell of Cedar

Michael slept comfortably for the first time in many weeks. Visions raced through his mind in the depth of his sleep, yet he was aware of the heavy stone clutched in his hand, smothered under his pillow. It was as if it were an anchor weighing him down into a deeper reality, into a world farther and farther away. The stone's tiny crystals seemed to glimmer through the fabric of his feather pillow, blinking brilliantly, like thousands of tiny stars bursting into the evening sky. But there was another sensation that keenly sharpened Michael's senses. It was the distinct odor of cedar. Unmistakably cedar.

Michael knew his body was asleep, but he felt an image of himself roll over to look at the old box Miyah had placed on the night stand next to his bed. It was eye level now, inches away from his face. He tried to make out the design of the rough-hewn carving on the front panel. His eyes couldn't focus completely and he blinked away thoughts that raced through his head. It was as if he were watching a play acting out, figures moving. . .slowly moving.

The smell of cedar intensified and made him dizzy. He thought he was dreaming, but it seemed so real. Images of vivid sand-swept deserts with mud brick houses and clear, blue skies rolled past him. He covered his face as a whirlwind of dust swirled around him, and after a few moments, he opened his eyes.

At first everything moved in slow motion. Michael looked down at his bare feet and felt the hot sand sifting under his toes. The intense heat of the sun beat down on him as he regained his senses. He could hear the sounds of men laughing in the distance and dogs barking as they chased after a squawking chicken. Sweat dripped from his brow and he wiped it with his hand. He stood looking at the droplets of sweat on his fingers and was startled at the reality of being somewhere else.

"Is this a dream? Will I awaken? Am I dead?"

Suddenly three young boys dressed in light blue tunics raced past him, so close Michael thought they didn't see him. He followed them into the dusty streets of an ancient village. He could hear the boys talking and laughing as they playfully tossed a pomegranate back and forth. Michael knew they were not speaking his language, but he seemed to understand what they were saying.

"Excuse me boys," he called out. "Can you help me?" But when the words came out of his mouth they didn't sound the same. It was as if they were being translated as they entered the air. It didn't matter, because no one acknowledged him. Michael reached out to touch one of the boys on the shoulder to get his attention. He felt the fabric and the bone of the boy's body, but his hand seemed to go right through as if it had touched nothing but air. Michael quickly jumped back, startled. He raced over to a woman drawing water from a nearby well.

"Excuse me, Miss. Can you help me?" he frantically called. She didn't look up as she poured water from the wooden bucket into her earthen vase.

"Miss. Miss. Please!" he yelled. She settled the jug on top of her head and gracefully walked past him, the fabric of her skirt brushing against his leg. She was so close he could smell the oil of her perfume and she didn't even see him.

Michael looked up at the blinding white light of the sun, allowing its glare to penetrate his eyes. "I'm dead!" he shouted, dropping to his knees. "I'm dead!" Michael beat his hands on the hot sand, closed his eyes and sobbed.

After several minutes he wiped away his tears with his sleeve and got up. Shoulders drooped, he slowly walked down a narrow, dirt street. Wandering aimlessly he came across an open door and walked in.

"It doesn't matter where I go," he mumbled. "No one will see the ghost I've become. Why have I deserved this destiny, and why here in this place? Why not among my own family and friends?"

He wearily sat down on a wooden bench. Bent over with his hands covering his face, Michael somberly weighed his situation.

It was a familiar smell that jerked Michael out of his gloom. The smell of cedar. He looked around the room for the first time. It was a carpenter's workshop, simple and neat. Three workbenches were placed around the room. Tools were neatly arranged in a row along one of the benches. At Michael's feet were wide-flaked shavings of wood—chippings of ash, long spirals of pine and short brown-pink curls of cedar. All of these different types of wood, yet the sweet fragrance of cedar reached out to tantalize Michael. The thought of a cedar box flashed into his memory. It seemed important, but he couldn't quite grasp it.

Michael arose to look around. Wooden wheels and yoke for oxen in various stages of construction leaned against one wall. The room was small, but brightly lit by a large window framed above the longest workbench. Beyond the open window was a narrow valley lined with trees—Lebanon cedar, shining like silver, leading straight toward the setting sun. Along the slopes of the valley he saw wheat fields and gardens, hedges of cactus and orchards of pomegranates, oranges, figs and olives.

"I should be hungry," he mumbled. "I don't think I've eaten for days."

A voice came from a shadowed corner of the workshop, startling Michael.

"Oh, excuse my manners. I should have offered you some bread and fruit. Come, sit here and be my guest," the man commanded as he placed a wooden stool next to one of the workbenches and walked from the room to fetch some food. Michael looked around to see who the man was speaking to. He saw no one else. He stood dumbfounded as the man returned and motioned for him to sit.

"You. . .you can see me?" Michael asked with astonishment. Again he was aware of the seemingly translated words coming from his own mouth and his understanding of the man's strange dialect.

"Of course I can see you. What do you think you are? A ghost!" the man laughed.

"I. . . I don't know," Michael stammered. He didn't want to reveal too much in case the man thought he was crazy. At this point, Michael doubted his own sanity.

"It seems that no one else has noticed me," he reluctantly added.

"I understand," said the man as he placed a bowl of figs and fresh bread in front of his guest. "You must have met Miyah."

Michael's jaw dropped. "You know Miyah? How? Where? I don't understand." Michael gestured to the landscape outside, then back inside to the workshop with a dramatic sweep of his arm.

"Where am I? How could you know of Miyah? This is another world." Michael was ranting now, as if he were delirious. "I remember I was dying. I had a high fever, but I was home in my own bed. She said she came to heal me. God, I must be mad. Am I dead? Who are you?" He was spinning out of control.

The man placed his hand gently on Michael's shoulder. This simple gesture brought a huge sigh from a tearful Michael and with that sigh came a wash of unexpected calm. Michael looked up into the man's deep brown eyes and recognized the same intensity he had seen in Miyah's gaze. He felt the same warm flow of love flush into his being.

"Who are you?" he repeated.

"I have many names, but you may call me Joshua. You are in the land of Palestine, the Holy Land—Israel. Come. Break bread with me. Replenish your body and we will talk." The man poured wine into a wood-hewn goblet and handed it to Michael.

"You are not dead. You are in another reality. . .one you would know as ancient times. You are here to learn and after a time you will return to your world. This may seem as a dream to you, but know that it will mark a significant change in your life. You will not be the same man as when you came to me. Only good will come from this journey. You will learn much. I promise."

"Promise. There's that word again," Michael said. "Miyah spoke of a promise, but she never explained. I know I've not always made the right choices in my life, but I'm not a bad person. Why do you think I must change? What's wrong with me the way I am? I didn't ask for this."

"Didn't you?" the carpenter questioned. "You said you weren't ready to die. You asked for another chance. It may be hard for you to understand all at once, but know that you are safe, you are well and you have not gone mad. Be assured that you have been given a gift. A gift offered to only a few."

"A gift?" Michael repeated, shaking his head. "A gift. . ." His voice trailed in defeat. "Some gift."

"Isn't life a gift?" asked the carpenter. "Your life—a chance to live a longer, more meaningful life—isn't that a gift?"

Joshua tore a piece of bread from the loaf and handed it to his guest. Michael ate in silence, sorting through his thoughts.

"I'm alive," echoed through his mind. "I'm alive!" He rested his eyes on the figure of the man called Joshua, whose words and mere presence calmed him.

"Yes," he thought. "This must be a dream. Joshua said I'll return to my home. It's just a dream." Michael found his appetite and reached for some figs on the plate. He gulped down a swig of the bitter wine.

"I'm alive," he repeated out loud to convince himself.

Michael watched cautiously as Joshua moved around the room. This man was about 5'11", 170 pounds, muscular and well-proportioned. He had long, dark hair, the color of new wine, that parted in the middle and curled past his shoulders. His beard was the same color as his hair. His skin was fairly dark. Perhaps he was of Egyptian, Armenian or Jewish decent, Michael thought. He seemed to exude everything positive. Even his posture said this man was very sure of himself. Michael noticed that Joshua had large hands with long, tapering fingers, and thought it curious that he had one longer fingernail on his left little finger. Michael knew that in Buddhism this was considered an auspicious sign to bring longevity of life.

"I see you have regained your appetite. That is good," said Joshua. "You will need the nourishment for your lessons."

"You keep speaking of lessons. What are these lessons?"

"They are truths about the universe, about compassion and life. They are lessons of the oneness of God and nature and self. Lessons about miracles." Joshua paused for a moment, wondering how much Michael could absorb.

"In your world, a miracle is defined as an event that is unexplainable by the laws of nature . . .or unexplained by science. It is believed to be a supernatural happening, or an act of God. Yet science is a chronicle of man's growing awareness of the laws of nature. Your flying machines and transportation network, electricity, music, medical instruments, the list is long, are all results of man's science—of what can be achieved. People of my time would think these to be miracles—things that are unexplainable by our limited knowledge of science. However, there are many mysteries of my time that we have awareness of, that your world would still consider a miracle. Things your society knew at one time in history, but has forgotten."

"How do you know of our transportation networks and science?"

Michael asked. "What miracles?" He was suddenly full of questions. The lesson had begun.

"I have traveled through your world many times—sometimes unnoticed, as you are now in this dimension, and other times as a person gaining insight and knowledge of how the world is progressing in its various stages of growth."

"You've time traveled?" Michael asked in wonder.

"It's not really time travel," Joshua explained. "I have been taught by ancient yogis who explored the mysteries of the universe through their sense of inner awareness." He continued, "Your scientists expand their knowledge with instruments and tools. Yogis work with intuition, manifestation and with the interchangeable nature of matter and energy. We can move between worlds in deep meditative states. Our souls can leave our bodies and we are able to restructure ourselves in another area to whatever degree we desire. People in your day would consider this a miracle. In ancient time it is common practice for those who believe."

"Believe. Believe in what?" Michael questioned.

"Yogis experience the world reflecting a mirror image of even the smallest fragment of creation. They believe the core of human existence, the only changeless aspect of a human being, is the soul—the part of an individual that is one with God—that *is* God. The part of myself that is God."

"You're saying you're God!" Michael exclaimed.

"Yes. I am God," Joshua said smiling. "But you are also God. We are all a part of God. We are one."

Michael stared at Joshua, trying to sort out what he was hearing. These were certainly not the lessons taught to him as a child in religion class. His church would have called it blasphemy. Others would have called it ego.

"Writing is one of your talents, correct?" Joshua asked.

"But. . .how did you know. . ." Michael started.

"You must know of the works of Emerson. He once wrote: 'The universe is represented in every one of its particles. . . The world globes itself in a drop of dew. . . The true doctrine of omnipresence is that God appears with all His parts in every moss and cobweb.' You see, God appears in everything. That includes you and me and everything you can see. . .and much you don't see."

Joshua waved his hand in the direction of the carpenter's shop and through the window to the outside world. "Everything. We have been sending messages to the world through generations of scholars and writers and artists. Sadly, many have been persecuted through the ages for trying to spread the truth. It is often difficult to go against those who have much to gain from smothering the wisdom of the ancients."

Michael stared at Joshua in silence, absorbing what he was hearing, not quite knowing how to respond.

"Alas," Joshua said. "You have only been here a short time and I am already preaching to you! For you see, I only do carpentry work as a pastime. My true calling is that of a teacher and a healer. Please forgive me for getting ahead of myself and partake of this meal with me."

Joshua brought more food and the two men ate heartily as they turned their attention to the workshop and talked about the carpentry trade and the various stages of completion of projects in the shop. Michael complimented Joshua for his superb workmanship as he toasted with a wooden goblet carved by Joshua.

"It's just an enjoyment for me, although I come from a family of carpenters," Joshua acknowledged. "They were proud of the craft. In this day being a carpenter is more like being an architect in your time. In Greek the word is tekton, meaning a skilled carpenter of cabinets and furniture, but also a designer, construction engineer and architect. A tekton can build a house, construct a bridge or design a temple. The work can be very complicated and the tools are sometimes crude, yet it is still considered a lowly occupation."

He picked up a wooden box that rested in a pile of shavings. "I am particularly proud of this box I am carving," he said as he blew the sawdust from the lid. "It is soon to be a gift for my companion. I gave a similar box to my mother when I was 12-years-old. She has used it all these years to hold her herbs and healing stones. It is her prize possession. She says it holds her magic."

Michael stepped closer to look at the box. It seemed familiar to him, but before he could examine it closer, a woman entered the room. Her perfume mixed with the fragrance of cedar and Michael reeled at the sight of her. He wondered for a moment if he would be invisible to her—like he was at the well. He stood silent as she approached Joshua with a welcoming smile. Joshua's eyes lit up as he watched her cross the room. Her small hands folded into his as they met and embraced.

"I thought I heard you in here," she said as he gently kissed her on the lips. "And who were you talking to?"

"Oh, let me introduce you," Joshua said as he led her toward the workbench. "Michael, this is my companion, Maryum. Maryum, this is Michael."

Maryum gave Joshua a smile and Michael froze. He didn't know if she was just humoring Joshua or if she was acknowledging the introduction. Finally, Maryum said, "It's nice to meet you."

"Likewise." Not wanting to seem disrespectful, but unable to resist, he added, "I think we may have met earlier today. . . at the well."

Maryum looked directly at Michael, and said, "You are a stranger here and must not know that women are not allowed to speak with unrelated men when they are in public places, like the well. It's the law. We could be stoned as harlots for this simple act. But I am sorry, for I truly did not see you at the well today."

"No one saw me," Michael blurted. "My hand passed right through a boy playing in the courtyard. The men, even the dogs. . .no one seemed to notice me. How is it that you can see me now?"

Joshua stepped forward. "Maryum can only see you now because of our connection, because I introduced you to her. She understands my receiving visitors from other dimensions and I often share these visits with her. It's one of our secrets."

"Do you mean this has happened before? You often have people appear as I did—from other lands, other time periods, other realities?"

"Oh, yes," Joshua responded. "There are many seekers who come to me. Miyah and the women of her bloodline have sent many for healing over the centuries. I am afraid there will be many more. There is a lot of work to be done."

"But, you didn't tell me how you know Miyah," Michael said, looking from Joshua to Maryum and back.

"She is of my bloodline. She is of the future as I am of the past. She is, or will be, a descendant of mine. . .of ours," Joshua said, gesturing to Maryum with a smile. "As I said before, you are visiting ancient times now. You have stepped back into our lifetime. As I have come from a family of healers, so do my children and the children who follow. Our bloodline has carried through for generations with a mission of healing and teaching. It is our Touchstone."

Michael gasped. Touchstone. He recalled Miyah speaking of her Touchstone. He had a flashback of the cedar box Miyah had placed by his bedside. He walked over to the box Joshua had been carving. Examining it carefully, his fingers outlined the ornate carvings beginning to take shape on the panel of the box. . .carvings of figures. . . figures that seemed to move and come alive, as in a play. The smell of cedar intensified and suddenly made him dizzy. Michael looked back at Joshua and Maryum who were quietly conversing about their upcoming wedding.

"We have been given a wedding gift of spikenard oil," Maryum said to Joshua. "I tried to resist it because it is so expensive," she said humbly. Joshua smiled as he lovingly kissed her forehead.

Michael could vaguely hear their voices in the distance and tried to respond, but everything seemed to move in slow motion.

"Joshua," he called. "Joshua, don't let me leave yet. I have so many questions. You said you would teach me. . . I have to know more. . ."

And just then Michael's world went black as he lost consciousness.

3 The Diary

Bathed in the light of a full moon, Miyah slowly turned brittle pages of her worn diary and began to quietly read out loud. She knew the pages by heart, but never tired of reading the wisdom that women of her bloodline had shared through the ages. She loved the smell of the book, the feel of each crisp page, the loop of the penmanship and the sheer energy of hearing her own voice speak each sacred word. And she loved the family secrets woven into the ink throughout the diary.

Entries were written in the book in several languages. Among them were Aramaic, Hebrew, Greek, Latin, French and English. Miyah could read every word of each story since she was a small child, just as she had been taught. Sometimes the pages flowed as an actual diary of events, written in hurried handwriting, as if the writer was anxious to get it all out before she would forget, or before she would burst with the passion of her words. And sometimes healing remedies, herbal recipes and spells were jotted down as a notebook of powerful medicine for generations to follow.

— To increase the effectiveness and power of healing, you must remember to align your energies with the lunar cycle and tap into the natural tides and currents of life. Our bodies are mainly composed of water and because the moon turns the tide, we must wax and wane with the moon.

— Healing energy is highest when the moon is becoming full, or waxing, and weakest when it is waning. The new moon is dark for three days before it appears as a crescent. Tune into the natural flow by working when the moon is waxing from new to full.

— The most important ingredient of any healing is love. Thought and prayer are powerful, but faith and love work magic. You must first believe before your wishes will come true, and always cast your healing spells from the heart.

The leather diary was scarred and weathered with time, soiled with the oils and marks of hundreds of fingerprints of the women who were its caretakers. A simple brown linen bag, ragged at the seams but sewn sturdy, was its protector, keeping the pages safe through the years. An emblem initialed both the corner of the bag and the cover of the book. The symbol was a talisman of sorts, "charged with magical energy," Miyah's grandmother, Nona, had said.

Miyah knew this symbol well. It was a family crest, as ancient as the diary itself. Hidden within the design was a double M. Every women in

Miyah's family had one or two M's somewhere in their name. Miyah's M's were in her first two initials—Miyah Maria.

"It's a tradition," she was told as a child when she questioned everything. The answers to her questions always led to more questions, but Miyah never ceased asking and her patient mentors never tired of her curiosity.

"This girl. This girl is special," they agreed, as they smiled in their wisdom, knowing what would be Miyah's fate.

"Special" in Miyah's family meant only one thing. She was gifted. She was a healer. That fact would shape her destiny and rule her life. But often in the bloodline a generation or two was skipped, so the birth of a new "special" child was always a celebration.

Miyah's grandmother, Nona, was the wisest healer Miyah had known. Miyah's own mother, Junia, was also a healer, but she was a frail woman and seemed to resist her powers. She was happy to have Nona take over the teachings of Miyah, and when the time came, she passed the candle to her eager young daughter.

"You already know more than I can teach you, my child," Junia said when Miyah was only ten. "I have other work I need to complete."

That same year Junia died peacefully in her sleep. Miyah was devastated. How could the sisterhood let her mother die so young? For a few days Miyah rebelled against the insight she had inherited. It was her way of protesting her mother's death. But the power was too strong to evade her for long and she knew the special bond she and her mother shared would never be broken. Her mother would always be with her, helping her from the other side. Miyah knew there is no real death, that the physical body is just a vehicle for a hundred years or less while the soul is on the earth plane. She found some solace in that.

Having never known her father, Miyah lived with her grandmother, Nona, and continued her apprenticeship, learning herbal remedies, magic spells and ancient healing rituals. They spoke of Junia often, bringing her to life in their stories and their love. Laughter overcame sorrow and loneliness. Being with Nona was a happy time in Miyah's life.

When Miyah was 18, Nona told her it was time for herself to leave the earth for another dimension. She had important work to do and her mission on earth was finished.

"You can't leave me," Miyah cried, knowing her tears would make no difference.

"I will never leave you, my dear child," Nona soothed her, stroking her granddaughter's long, curly hair. "I will always be here when you need me. We are bound together. Our hearts will always beat as one. Our family's love flows through the bloodline and we will never be far apart. All you need to do is ask for me and I'll be at your side."

It was a difficult time for Miyah, but soon after Nona's death she began to appear in Miyah's dreams at night, and also in her waking dreams. Miyah learned that she could connect with souls who have passed and gain insight from them when she needed their help for healing. She could tap into their knowledge any time she needed their energy. This was comforting to her and she called upon Junia and Nona often. It was also a turning point in her life, as death seemed to become her calling card. Sometimes she was called upon to help the dying pass over peacefully—to celebrate moving into another dimension of time. And sometimes, as with Michael's case, she was called in to help extend life—to give people another chance to make better use of their earth time—to redirect them into fulfilling their soul's purpose, the mission they accepted when they were born.

~ ~ ~ ~ ~

The years passed quickly as Miyah found herself immersed in healing work. She often wondered where the last years had gone since Nona died and she inherited the family's "doctor bag" – a medicine pouch holding healing stones, a cedar box and the diary, among oils, crystals, and other healing tools. She had always been satisfied to be completely devoted to her healing practice, but tonight as she sat in Michael's room she wondered where the next 20 years would bring her. She glanced at Michael and wondered just who this man was. Why did she somehow feel differently about him than she had her other patients? Did they share a past? A destiny?

She brushed away these thoughts and reached for her medicine bag. Taking out a blue candle and a pin, she inscribed Michael's name on the candle, writing from the bottom to the top. She then stuck the pin into the base of the wax, placed the candle on a tray in the windowsill and lit the wick. She would let the candle burn until it extinguished itself and would retrieve the pin for future use. This old healing ritual, used to alleviate pain, had been scribbled on the edge of a page in her diary.

Miyah covered herself with a quilted, white blanket from the back of the chair and settled in for the night, immersing herself into the diary. Sleep never came easy to Miyah and reading often provided any answers she sought.

– Many illnesses are affected by the mind. Thinking you are healthy can actually make you healthy. Sending love to a sick person, whether the person is aware of it or not, can improve that person's condition.

Miyah knew about the power of love. It was the glue that bound her family together over the ages. It was the foundation, the Touchstone, of their healing powers.

There was an early entry in the diary that Miyah could close her eyes and envision, as if she were present herself when it was written. She could feel the pain and anxiety of this ancestor as she felt the urgency to journal her message. Perhaps the compassion Miyah felt for this woman was the reason she, herself, had been chosen to work with the dying. Perhaps her destiny had been cast hundreds, even thousands of years ago. Perhaps she had been there, perhaps.

— I am saddened that I must leave my homeland and seek refuge in Egypt. The safety of my family is most important for the future of our people. My husband, daughter, brother, sister, uncle and others, will leave with me under the cover of darkness this night and travel in secrecy until we are safe. I mourn leaving friends and family behind, yet know their hearts are with me, with us, as we flee —

It was signed. . . *Maryum*

4 *The Healing*

Michael awoke abruptly from his sleep. He was disoriented, not sure where he was. That was strange, as he knew he had been bedridden in his house for weeks. Things seemed even stranger when he noticed a woman curled up in a chair by his window. He couldn't recall awakening to a woman in his bedroom for a long, long time. He watched her for a while, her body flooded by the light of the morning sun. And then it all came back to him.

He looked over at the cedar box still settled on his bed stand. "My God," he said, as he recalled his dream.

"Miyah! Miyah! Wake up! I have to talk to you."

Startled by his urgent words, Miyah's eyes flew open. She jumped out of her chair, nearly tripping over her blanket as she ran to his bedside.

"What? What's wrong? Are you OK?"

"I, I'm not sure," he stammered. "I may have just come back from the dead."

Miyah felt a little light headed from awakening with such a start. Brushing thick curls of unruly hair from her face, she pushed a chair next to Michael's bed and sat down.

"What are you talking about?" she asked.

"Maybe it was a dream. I don't know. I remember falling asleep while looking at the carvings on the side of that cedar box. . ." He pointed toward the box and his sentence stopped in mid air.

"Impossible," he said.

"Michael, what are you talking about?" Miyah repeated.

"This box! This box had carvings around the front of it. They were pictures of an ancient village, a village with people and trees and. . ." his voice trailed off again as he turned the box from side to side, rubbing his hand along the finish of each surface.

"Impossible," he repeated. "There's nothing here." Sweat beaded on his forehead as he laid back on his pillow in confusion. "It must be the fever. I'm delirious."

"No, Michael. You're not delirious," Miyah consoled. She reached over to retrieve the stone that was still clutched in his hand. Michael had forgotten about the stone that seemed to conform naturally to his palm. He reluctantly handed it over.

"What have you done to me?" he asked, needing answers. Just then his sister, Elizabeth, entered the room with a tray of hot, herbal tea.

"I thought I heard you two talking in here. I figured you might like to start the day with some tea. Or would you prefer coffee, Miyah?"

"No, tea will be fine, but I would like to freshen up a bit first. Can you direct me to the bathroom?"

"Yes, of course. I'm sorry I didn't take the time to show you around when you arrived last night. I was anxious to deliver you to Michael's bedside. How do you think he looks this morning? Do you think he is better?"

"Look at me for yourself!" Michael weakly shouted. "Don't talk as if I'm not here. Ask me how I am, not her."

Elizabeth lowered her eyes to the floor and stammered a quiet, "I'm sorry, Michael," as she backed out of the room. Miyah followed her, looking back over her shoulder at Michael with a disappointed glance.

"If that's the way you treat others, perhaps I should just leave now. You may not be worthy of saving after all." She closed the door behind her, leaving Michael exasperated with himself and at the thought of not seeing Miyah again. He had more to tell her.

"I'm sorry. Don't leave." She heard him through the closed door as she continued down the hallway.

"Miyah, please forgive Michael for being rude. He wasn't always like that. I think it's the medication. He's always been a loving brother. He's taken care of me ever since our parents died. Michael is all I have." Elizabeth broke into a flood of tears. "I can't bear the thought of losing him. Please tell me you can help. Please don't leave us now."

Miyah put her arm around Elizabeth's shoulders. "Don't worry, dear," she calmly said. "I never abandon my patients. But medication or not, you don't deserve to be treated like that and Michael owes the apology to you, not to me. Please stand up to him and make him respect you. You are a much stronger woman than you realize.

"You also must also think about finding a life of your own. Even though Michael has taken care of you in the past, you are not bound to be his nursemaid forever. I know you've taken good care of him while he's been ill, but it's time for you to discover the things *you* want. You must find your independence, your freedom and in that you'll find your happiness. Sometimes we hurt people more by helping them. They rely on us too much and take us for granted. Michael needs to find his own strength and can't continue to use you as a crutch when he is healed."

"How do you know this?" Elizabeth asked. "How do you know I've put my life on hold for him? I mean, it's not that I mind. He's my brother and I love him. It's just that even before his illness he was very demanding. Sometimes I felt like I was his mother. I'm sorry. I don't mean to complain. I shouldn't have said that," she rambled.

"Don't worry, Elizabeth. It's OK. You can talk to me. I don't know how I know these things, but I do."

Elizabeth took a deep breath and released her fears. "I've been so afraid to think about myself, especially now, with the thought of my only family member dying. I don't want him to die—but I don't know if I'm afraid for him, or because I don't want to be left alone. I feel so selfish, like such a hypocrite. Everyone thinks I'm so good, giving up important things in my life to take care of Michael—to help him, but what if it's for me so I won't be left alone? What if I'm just thinking about myself? I don't want to live a lonely life like Michael has. I don't want to be alone. I want to be loved."

Elizabeth stared at Miyah for a moment and then broke into tears.

"There is a man. His name is Robert. I haven't known him very long, he just came into my life one day, but I loved him so much. Michael is my family and he needed me so I had to make choices. I. . .I had no choice."

"But you do. If you love this man as much as you say, you need to tell him. Would it help if I told you that Michael is going to get better? He'll have a second chance at life and, believe me, he will no longer expect you to stay around to take care of him. He's going to awaken to many things that will change his outlook on living and dying. So think about what you want in your own life and reach for it. Michael will be OK. I promise you that. But will you?"

Miyah placed her hands on top of Elizabeth's head, releasing healing energy into her body. Elizabeth sobbed, feeling the heat coming from Miyah's throbbing hands. And then, as if a weight had been lifted off her shoulders, she stood tall, taller than she ever knew she could.

"I can't tell you how I feel at this moment," she said. "I've heard you were a powerful healer and I thought you were here for Michael. . .but I think you have also been sent here to heal my wounds. Thank you Miyah. Thank you for your kindness and for your words of encouragement."

For the first time in weeks Elizabeth smiled. Brushing the tears from her eyes, she gave Miyah a big hug, kissing her on both cheeks. Never in her life had Elizabeth been spontaneous—until this moment. She reached for her jacket. "Do you mind if I leave for a while? I must see if I still have a future."

"Go. Follow your dream. I'll be here if your brother needs anything." Miyah waved her hand toward the door. As Elizabeth left, Miyah headed into the kitchen to see what she could find for breakfast. She was famished and she knew Michael had a lot to share with her when she returned to his room. They would both need all their strength to get them through the next few days.

~~~~~

Miyah took her time with breakfast. When she returned to the room with a tray of oatmeal, toast, freshly squeezed orange juice and sliced pears, she was surprised to see Michael sitting on the edge of his bed. His focus was outside, peering through the window at a sunny world that had become practically unknown to him these last few months as he fought his battle with cancer.

"I'm sorry," he said. "I saw Elizabeth leaving. She was running. I hope I didn't hurt her. I don't intend to be mean to her. It's just that I'm impatient. We've been through a lot together and sometimes she gets on my nerves. I don't know what will happen to her when I die. I've taken care of her for so long. She's been my responsibility. I'm her only family. She's OK isn't she?" Michael had the most painful look in his eyes as he spoke. It was a sad mixture of contempt and deep love.

"Yes, she'll be alright. But, Michael, I wouldn't expect her to be around to take care of you as much now. She has her own future to think of."

"What do you mean? I've taken care of her all these years and now, when I'm sick and dying, she's going to abandon me? What kind of gratitude is that? I need her here to help me now."

"Haven't you been listening to anything I've told you? Why did you send for me if you didn't think I could heal you? You must believe in me. Don't you see, Michael, you are going to be healed. You don't need Elizabeth here and Elizabeth no longer needs you to take care of her. You must set her free."

Michael stared at Miyah. "I didn't send for you, Elizabeth did. How do you know so much about our personal lives?" he questioned. "How dare you come in here and turn our world around. Healing my illness is one thing, but messing with my family life is entirely another. It's none of your business."

"But it is my business, Michael, if I'm to heal you. It's all interconnected, tied together like family. You can't simply heal what's on the outside. Healing must come from within and all around. There are often deep-rooted causes for illness and every strand that is connected must be considered. You must break your control over Elizabeth to free yourself and. . ."

"How dare y. . ." Michael shouted, but he stopped. His anger quickly passed as flashes of last night's dream crept back into his memory. Suddenly nothing else seemed important—not Elizabeth's leaving, not Miyah's stern words, not even the thought of him dying. Nothing was as important as these fragments of a dream.

Michael put his hands over his eyes to lessen the jolts of memory flashing through his brain. Wincing, he called out a name, shouting it over and over. "Joshua, Joshua," he called. "Joshua, don't let me leave yet. I have so many questions. I have to know more. . ."

Slowly Michael lowered his hands and looked at Miyah in complete bewilderment.

"What just happened?" he asked. "What I just said was involuntary. I mean, it just came out of my mouth as if I had no control. But I know what it was about. Oh, my God, Miyah. I know what it was about. I just remembered my dream from last night. It had to do with the cedar box. Remember I tried to tell you about the carving, about the movie on the panel of the box. I went inside, inside the movie and you won't believe this, but I went back into another time, into an ancient time and I met this man and his companion and. . ."

Michael emotionally poured out the story in his dream, recalling each detail of his vision. When he was finished he looked into Miyah's eyes.

"And he said he knew you. That you were of his future generation, of his and Maryum's bloodline. How could that be? How can any of this be?"

Exhausted, he looked to her for answers, forgetting the argument of the morning. His voice was gentler, softer, even compassionate. He was beginning to understand what Miyah had been trying to tell him. Now he was ready to listen.

Miyah was silent while Michael spoke. She nodded her head and even smiled a few times as if fondly remembering a loved one. Michael appreciated her attentiveness, but at times thought maybe she knew exactly what he was going to say before he voiced it, as if she had been there or had lived the story herself. She was a good listener and now Michael sat silently, looking at her, waiting for her response, waiting for an explanation.

Miyah got up and poured herself a cup of tea, offering him some. Anxious to hear her story, he took the cup and then, fatigued, settled himself back against his propped-up pillows. He needed answers and was confident Miyah had them. A type of melancholy washed over him. Why had he doubted her? Why hadn't he respected her abilities? How could he be so stupid, so macho, even in his weakened state?

"Before you start," he said sheepishly as she settled into the chair next to him. "I owe you yet another apology. I'm grateful you're here and for what you've done for both me and my sister. I can feel my strength is already returning just from last night's healing. Everything is happening so quickly and it's beyond my grasp of understanding. I'll try to be more patient—and I really do trust you. Please forgive me."

"I didn't expect you to be so difficult, Michael, but your apology is accepted on the condition that you also apologize to Elizabeth when you see her, and make a vow to treat her with the respect she has earned. She's your sister and she loves you. Someday perhaps you will understand the importance of family, the bond of blood. You're so lucky to have each other. Cherish that, Michael. Cherish that."

Michael nodded his head, a bit ashamed. "Yes, I hear what you're saying. I will apologize to Elizabeth. She's been through a lot. I do love her. I don't think I've told her that in a long time. Thank you," he said. "Now please tell me what all this means, this dream. . .if it was a dream."

Miyah took a deep breath. She placed the cedar box on her lap. Her outspread hands rested on the box. She sat for a brief time with her eyes closed in silent meditation, asking for the correct words. Then she began her story. "A very long time ago. . ."

5 The Cedar Box

Michael tried to listen as Miyah began her story. He knew how important this was, but soon found he couldn't concentrate on her words. His eyes wandered to the box in her lap. Again, he thought he could see carvings on the long panel and soon was absorbed within its movement. His mind carried him back into another dimension. He wanted to hear Miyah's story, but he had no choice. He closed his eyes in the dizziness and when he awoke he was again in the carpenter's shop. But this time it was different.

The faint fragrance of cedar came to him again. He saw a sturdy boy of twelve, with brown eyes and skin bronzed from the sun. The boy was dressed in a knee-length, white garment rounded at the neck, tied at the waist with a knotted cord. His feet were as brown as the dirt under the cedar shavings on the floor. He turned an oblong box over and over in his hands, running his fingers along its sides and joints in search of the slightest imperfection. The box was made without nail or peg. The sides and bottom dovetailed into one another in a way that commanded skill and long, patient labor. The boy's hands were strong, yet delicately graceful and gentle with their touch. A rag bandage was tied around one finger on the left hand, previously nicked by a carving tool. Pride shown in his eyes as he examined his craftsmanship.

A voice from an adjoining room beckoned him. It was a foreign dialect, Aramaic, Michael thought, but still, he understood each word. "Come in to supper, my son. Your father and I await."

"In one moment, Mother," he replied, smoothing a spot on the box. "I am nearly finished."

"Finished with what?" His mother appeared in the doorway. She was almost thirty, wearing an outer robe of plain brown over an under-dress of deep blue. Her hair was shoulder length, silhouetting her eyes—brown, like the boy's.

Quickly hiding the box behind his back, the boy smiled. "It will be finished soon."

The woman smiled at her son's mysterious manner and replied as she left the room, "Put away your tools now and finish later. A meal awaits."

The boy blew sawdust off the box and admired his work. He gently wrapped the box in a white linen cloth and walked toward the door, holding his gift in front of him with pride. Michael followed him and peeked into the dark, hearth-lit room. He heard the boy say, "It is finished, Mother, just in time for your birthday." He placed the package in her lap.

The boy's mother smiled at him lovingly, then gingerly unwrapped the cloth to reveal the cedar box.

"It is a marvelous box for one so young," she exclaimed.

"Father taught me," he said, nodding a thank you to his father who was seated at the head of the low stone table.

"It has taken me many weeks to make. I put my heart into it because it was for you, for your special day."

"Thank you my son for your labors and your thoughtfulness, and thank you my husband for being such a fine teacher. This is the most beautiful box I have ever seen. Surely there is not another like it in the land." She turned it over and over, examining each side. She gave an extra nod of approval as she pointed to her son's name carefully chiseled in Hebrew, in the bottom right-hand corner, inside the lid of the cedar box. It was a final touch, a signature of the craftsman, but more importantly, a symbol for a mother to always remember her son's love.

She read the letters aloud, from right to left, *"Yod (y),* ישוע *Shin (sh), Vav (oo), Ayin (a).* I shall use this box every day so I will always be reminded of you." She hugged her son closely to her breast and ruffled his unruly hair. "Thank you, Yeshua, my son. Now sit so we can thank the earth for our meal."

Before the boy sat down he looked directly at Michael who was standing in the shadow of the doorway. The boy smiled at him, then turned to take his place at the table with his two sisters and five brothers, including the baby, Amos.

~~~~~

Michael bolted up, dripping in sweat. He shook his head.

"No it can't be," he said. He looked over to see that Miyah had stopped telling her story and was watching him. He reached for the cedar box on her lap and hesitated before he opened the lid. The lamps were off in the room and the dim window light wasn't enough to allow Michael's eyes to focus. He reached his hand inside to feel if he could detect etched letters or a symbol. It was there. His fingers traced over it, slowly at first, and then they fumbled quickly in a panic of discovery. Michael couldn't make out what the letters said. They were more like symbols. He wanted to get up and turn on the light and look inside. . .but then again, did he really want to know? Could he handle it if this was truly the same box?

Michael fell back on his pillow. He couldn't look at Miyah. Was this some sort of cruel trick being played on a man who was supposed to die? Exhausted, he closed his eyes, trying to regain his composure, but a recent memory quickly flashed into his mind:

— *Joshua picked up a wooden box that rested in a pile of shavings. "I am particularly proud of this box I am carving," he said as he blew the sawdust from the lid. "It is soon to be a gift for my companion. I gave one similar to this to my mother when I was 12-years-old. She has used it all these years to hold her herbs and healing stones. It is her most prized possession. She says it holds her magic."*

Michael opened his eyes. Miyah's silence answered his question. He leaned against the wall, needing its support to hold himself upright. Pulling his legs up close to his chest and hugging them for comfort, he said, "You know what I've just seen, don't you? How the hell do you know?" His voice was gentle, not speaking in anger, rather in awe.

"How the hell do you know?" His voice trailed off, but his eyes kept contact with hers.

"Are you ready to listen to me now?" she asked. "I wouldn't be here if I wasn't supposed to share this with you. I'm not sure why. . ."

Michael laughed out loud. "What! Something you don't know!" It felt good to laugh, even though it was more like hysteria.

Miyah laughed with him. "There is much I don't know. There are also things I do know that are just as much a mystery to me as anyone else. My family calls it a gift. I've just accepted it. So, please don't question me about my 'sources.' Just trust me. What I'm sharing with you is very important. Not many people have been allowed access to this knowledge. It's sacred, Michael, very sacred. I must trust you'll use it well, for whatever tasks you've been chosen to carry out. What Joshua and Maryum told you is true. I am of their lineage. Isn't that enough to make you trust me?"

Michael nodded. He knew he had been difficult. Wouldn't anyone in this situation? It was as if a magnet had been pulling him into places he wasn't sure he wanted to go. His entire body sighed as he relinquished control over his destiny.

"I seem to keep apologizing to you," he said. "But now I'm ready to hear your story. You have my attention," he nodded to her. "Share your wisdom."

Miyah retrieve the cedar box from him. She nestled it back on her lap and began her meditative ritual once again. She took a deep breath and began to speak slowly and clearly.

"It is true, Michael. You've seen the makings of this cedar box in Joshua's workshop. There are only two of these boxes in existence. Joshua made them both. One for his mother and one for his bride. Both women were healers, just like Joshua. They used the boxes to keep their herbs and medicines.

"This was a very long time ago, before we had today's calendar to count our days. This was a time when the world was a much simpler place in which to live. Medicine was offered up from the earth, from plants, roots, seeds, stones, and from communing with the spirits to seek answers and knowledge for healing potions and remedies. The wisdom of how to use these medicines was held in the hands of those who sought it. They were called many things: shaman, bush doctor, Gypsy, priestess, herbalist, alchemist, prophet. . .and witch. These were the doctors of the ages. Healers. Saviors of life. Often they were leaders and goddesses of pagan rituals and ceremony. They were honored for their knowledge, for their vision seeking, for their ability to heal with pure God energy and for their dedication to life. They were also respected for their reverence in assisting in the dying process. For as you know, death is simply part of the recycling of life."

Shifting in her chair, Miyah continued, "But times were changing and those who came into power and ruled the country knew how strong women were and feared them for their power. False accusations were made against many women, causing some to be banished from their homes, stoned in public and even burned at the stake. A new religion was forming. It was a religion ruled by men. Women, especially women healers, needed to be separated, to be put in a place of low esteem so they would no longer be trusted for their healing. They were said to be possessed by demons, that their healing was evil. It became blasphemous to think that anyone other than a man possessed the God-given ability to heal. People became ruled by fear.

"But that didn't stop women from continuing their healing work. They went underground, so to speak. People who lived in the country were called pagans. The word had no other meaning other than 'country dwellers,' but the new Church used the word 'pagan' as if the people were ignorant heathens, a cult. They condemned ancient pagan rituals of honoring the earth with fertility ceremonies, full moon offerings and prayers to the elements. Pagan rituals had to be held secretly in forests, in private fields and homes. Some men, like Joshua, continued to support the powers of the women and assisted them in every way possible. These men held the truth in their hearts and boldly protested against new rulers governing the people. These rulers were more concerned with power, wealth and position. They were unlike the former kings who respected the earth and held ceremony in tune with the cycles of nature, honoring solstice, equinox and the earth's seasons."

Miyah looked at Michael. He was watching her intensely, listening to every word. He knew this was no ordinary story. This was ancient history.

"But what about Maryum, and Joshua's mother," Michael interrupted. "Were they safe?" His journalistic background kicked in. He thought his innate sense for details had been buried a long time ago when his health began to fail. He'd lost interest in recording other people's stories, a talent that had come naturally to him. But now he felt a resurgence of strength, and of curiosity. He wanted details.

"What happened to the cedar boxes?"

"I'm getting to them," Miyah replied, amused at his sudden child-like interest.

"As events unfolded, the safety of the women and of both cedar boxes was of grave concern. Because Joshua and Maryum lived in the house of Joshua's family, both boxes had always rested side-by-side in an alcove near the hearth when they weren't in use. Although not identical, they were very much alike. Both carried the signature of their craftsman in the bottom right-hand corner, inside the lid: *'Ayin (a), vav (oo), shin (sh), yod (y).'* Hebrew is read right to left, so you get 'yshooa', Yeshua, or Joshua.

"Mother Mariam's box was worn from years of use. The corners had rounded some and the wood had settled itself into a darker sheen, taking on the life of the many oils and smoke traces used while its mistress carried out her healing work. Maryum had received her box as a wedding gift from her husband a few years before this political and religious upheaval. Yet it bore the marks of a healer, the odor of herbs and oils blended with the sweet smell of cedar.

"There's too much to tell you now about the plight of these two women, but I will say that Mariam later ended up traveling to Ephesus, on the Aegean coast of present-day Turkey, where she lived much of her life. She was in her fifties by this time and carried the cedar box with her. Ephesus was then capital of the Roman province of Asia and one of the greatest cities of the Roman Empire. It was a civilized, modern city, however Mariam preferred the countryside and moved to a stone house on Nightingale Mountain soon after her arrival. She continued to use her box of potions, often secretly, in her missionary work. Some say she is buried in Ephesus, but our family history says she left there about AD 43 and traveled to other lands with Joshua and Maryum."

Miyah paused. "My diary says she died near Murree—then called Mari—and was buried at a place which is now called Pindi-Point. Her tomb there is called 'Mai Mari da Asthan'—the resting place of Mother Mariam. It's near the Kashmir border."

Michael twitched, realizing that Miyah's story dated back thousands of years. Mariam, as well as Maryum, would have been Miyah's great, many times great, grandmothers. That also meant his dreamtime experience had brought him back into that time period.

"This gets pretty deep, Michael. Are you sure you want to hear it now?" He nodded and she continued. "Mariam's wish was for her cedar box to be kept in the family, if at all possible. Joshua had many brothers and sisters, but they were scattered far among the lands."

"What about Joshua and Maryum?" Michael interrupted. "They would seem the logical heirs."

"The circumstances at the time made it unwise for them to keep the boxes together for safety reasons."

She slowly continued, "However, family and extended family were one in the same in those days. Mariam's cousin, Salome, was married to Zebedaeus. Their son John was a healer, friend and caretaker to her for many years. John inherited the cedar box and all its medicine. He used it well until it was time to pass the box on. He left the box under the care of one of his close and trusted friends, Isaac ben Isaac, son of Abraham. When Isaac ben Isaac died in AD 97, the box stayed within the protection of his family. They were the guardians of the box for generations. Even though many family members suffered persecution and death for their healing methods, someone always survived to protect and carry on the safety of the cedar box.

"When the last of the Isaac lineage died in Great Britain, the box was inherited by a Scottish doctor who used it wisely until 1924. The location of the box became a mystery with the sudden death of the doctor in a fiery car accident. My family searched for this box and found many people who had been healed by the doctor. Each spoke kindly of him and told many stories of miracles, using the powers of the box, but no one could find a trace of that cedar box. I can only pray it's in good hands, or at the very least, is still hidden, waiting for the right person to discover it. Perhaps some day it'll be reunited with its companion box." Miyah caressed the box. "Perhaps, some day. . ."

Michael felt a pang of sadness. After all, hadn't he met Joshua, the maker of both cedar boxes? Hadn't he seen both boxes and the two women they were carved for—the women Joshua loved? Whether they had been dreams or not, Michael felt the connection.

"And what about this cedar box?" he asked. "Has it been in your family through all these years?"

"Yes," Miyah replied. "It's been handed down through the generations. I can tell you more about that later. It's complicated. I might add that there's something special about the protectors of this cedar box. The magic within the box and the box itself, has mostly been guarded by feminine energy, not entirely, but mainly by the female members of our family."

Miyah stood and placed the box back on the nightstand. Shaking the wrinkles out of her dress, she walked toward the door. "I'm going outside for some fresh air. Do you think you're strong enough to take a walk with me?"

Michael hadn't been out of his room for weeks. The thought of taking a walk exhausted him, yet at the same time it sounded appealing.

"Tell you what. Let me try my land legs in the house before I venture outside. A hike down to the kitchen would be a good first outing. But maybe I should have a little nap first. This morning's conversation has been very intense."

"All right," Miyah said, as she crossed the room to open the window. "But we can at least let some air into this stale room. Fresh air will be good for you." A warm breeze circulated into the room, billowing the white, cotton curtains like a flag in the wind.

"One more thing," Michael said. "Could you please take the box with you out of the room for awhile. I really need to sleep and am afraid of what dreams may come if you leave it here. I just want some quiet, peaceful sleep."

"Are you sure?" Miyah questioned. "Usually patients don't want to be away from the energy of the box."

"I, I guess I'm a little afraid of what it has to show me next." This was a big admission for Michael—to say he was afraid. "It's so much to process. I need to think about it all. I need to recharge. And. . ." he hesitated, "I prefer you're in the room with me when I'm dreaming. I feel an element of protection when you're here. You must understand that."

"Of course I do," Miyah replied as she reached into her medicine pouch and retrieved a clear quartz crystal about the length of her little finger. She held it up to the window light to reveal its many facets.

"What is that?" Michael asked.

"It's a quartz crystal. Crystals are sometimes used to increase health and vitality to a person."

"How?" he asked, not doubting the probability of it.

"Quartz crystals release a frequency of energy, a vibration, that's been used for centuries as healing tools. Here, take this and hold it in both hands. Close your eyes and imagine being bathed in white light. Visualize your illness and point the crystal to that area. Imagine a stream of light flowing from the crystal and bathing you in its pure rays.

"When you're finished with your visualization, place the crystal under your pillow while you sleep." She smiled as she read his immediate thoughts. "Don't worry. It won't take you 'away.' It'll help you sleep peacefully while the white light you envisioned works its healing powers."

Michael took the crystal, saying nothing.

Miyah then placed a sprig of rosemary under his pillow. "This is to keep unpleasant dreams away."

"Is that what I'm doing—dreaming?" Michael asked.

"In a sense," she replied. "The world of the unconscious mind is revealed to us in our dreams. It taps into the collective unconsciousness, knowledge that can be accessed by everyone. Unfortunately few people realize the importance or the power of their dreams. So pay attention, Michael. This is part of your healing."

Miyah walked over and collected the cedar box and her medicine bag.

"Sleep in peace Michael." She gently patted him on the shoulder. He looked tired.

~~~~~

Michael heard the front door shut and watched Miyah through the open window as she walked down the sidewalk and through the gate, her medicine pouch with all its treasures slung over her shoulder. For a moment he felt a panic. "What if she doesn't come back?" But just as quickly he released the thought. She was a healer. Her job wasn't finished here.

He looked down at the crystal clutched in his hands. Holding it up to the light he noticed the prism-like colors reflecting through the glassy stone. Visualization was new to him but he was willing to try anything to be healed. Following Miyah's directions he closed his eyes and imagined a white light surrounding him. A mist, a cloud of white, diffused light enveloped his body and he visualized the crystal scanning his body from top to bottom, washing him with its rays. He felt a rush of calm surround him.

Laying down on his bed, with the crystal safely tucked in his hand, Michael instantly fell asleep, deeply and peacefully. He knew he was being healed. He was no longer afraid of death. . .or of life.

6 The Medicine Bag

Miyah stepped out into the fresh air, welcoming the deep heat of the sun on her face. Crossing the street she glanced back at Michael's house and at the upstairs window that for the past few months had closed off the outside to his pain. The curtains danced into the breeze as a sign of renewed life.

She positioned her medicine bag around her neck and shoulder, securely tucked it under her arm, and headed toward the park. Making it a habit to live by her instincts, Miyah clutched her precious bag a little tighter as she felt a wash of discontent pass over. She felt she was being watched and silently called upon Nona and Junia to protect her from this shadow of uncertainty.

Miyah reached the park and settled into an ornate, cement bench where she felt she could evaluate this sudden emotion with a clear view of her surroundings. The bench backed up against a stone wall that formed the base of a massive bridge. To her left and right were beautifully tended flower gardens, fragrant in the morning air. A walking path stretched east to west, crossing the park. In front of her were rows of ancient oak trees lining the walkway she had just followed.

A couple strolled along the path, walking hand-in-hand while their young son ran ahead, chasing a gray squirrel up a tree. The boy laughed, skipping and jumping as he played in his own magical world.

Beyond the couple, Miyah saw a man leaning against a shade tree, shrouded by its deep shadow. He drew long drags from a cigarette as he surveyed the park. She tuned inward, into her senses, and could detect anxiety, jealousy and greed vibrating from this man's energy field. She clutched her medicine bag. Taking a few deep breaths, Miyah centered her chakras and called again for protection from her strong sisterhood of ancestors.

The man nervously glanced her way several times. Miyah decided to meet him head on. She stared directly at him, challenging his glances while sending messages with her mind that she was not a victim. He couldn't help but feel the energy of her powerful gaze. Surprised at her boldness, the man betrayed his own intentions. Cursing, he threw his cigarette to the ground and crushed out its light with his heel. He glanced back over his shoulder at Miyah as he walked away.

Miyah knew Nona and her guides were protecting her, but at the same time she wondered what this encounter signaled. She could feel a change in the air—a warning, awakening of sorts—that the balance of her life was about to tip. Knowing all things happen for a reason, she did not ponder her thoughts or try to evaluate the situation. She simply reminded herself to listen carefully to the voice of wisdom—the voices that had guided her and her ancestors for generations. She reached into her medicine bag and touched the cedar box, a reassuring gesture that all was safe. Miyah knew the contents of this bag were powerful healing tools, yet used in the wrong context could be very dangerous. This is why she was never far from her treasure. It was like protecting a child—a child that was 2,000 years old.

Instead of heading back to Michael's house, Miyah turned the direction the mysterious man had walked. She was curious about her brief encounter with him and intuitively let her mind follow her feet, as if they were a divining rod on a magnetic path. Now the stalker was being stalked. Even though the man was a few minutes ahead of her, she caught up with him near a sidewalk café. She stopped with a gasp. The man she had seen in the park was standing next to Elizabeth, talking excitedly, using his hands to accent his tone. Elizabeth responded to him with a sweet, giddy smile and soon she was in his arms in a full embrace. Was this the man she had so urgently needed to see? Was this Robert, the lover she had brushed aside to care for her brother? If he had arranged to meet Elizabeth, why had he been following her? This was not a coincidence and Miyah knew it. She wondered how pieces of this puzzle would fit together, and again felt the urge to tuck her precious medicine bag safely under her arm. Before Elizabeth and Robert could see her, Miyah turned and headed back to Michael's house. She knew all would be revealed to her in due time, yet felt the sooner she could assist Michael through his healing process and be out of his house, the better.

Miyah's "Gypsy" blood always kept her yearning for new experiences. She had been told that through Maryum's ancestors, before migrating to Egypt and Syria, flowed the blood of the Romanies, a tribe of nomads who originated in the Hindu Kush region of Kashmir, a flesh and blood link with the roots of civilization. They were skillful storytellers, musicians and fortune tellers. Often traveling in vardos, horse-drawn wagons in caravans, they were gifted practitioners of palmistry, crystal reading, divination, tarot card reading, clairvoyance and healing with herbs, oils, flowers and minerals. Through the ages many were mistrusted and persecuted and eventually incorporated Christian, Hindu and Buddhist traditions into their culture. Some adopted non-Gypsy names, becoming skilled tinsmiths, coppersmiths, blacksmiths and carpenters. But for many, like Miyah, the ability to heal was so deeply embedded within their DNA that their destiny could never be changed. It was literally written in stone.

The family's medicine pouch came from that tradition. Miyah had always admired the craftsmanship of the bag itself, although somewhat tattered, the warm colors of the earth mixed with bright and bold embroidered symbols, little bells, tiny mirrors, and gemstones that were embedded into the fabric. She remembered the special day when she was given the bag and told that whenever love is woven into the texture of life, it never wears out. Junia and

Nona told her about each of the patches and symbols that had been added to the bag over the many years since it was first sewn, and encouraged her to someday add her own "signature" to the fabric as each of them had done. But Miyah hadn't yet decided what symbol she wanted to add to the bag. Perhaps when the day came when she had a daughter to pass the Touchstone legacy to, she would know what was most significant.

Junia had embroidered two small roses, one red and one pink, in a corner of the bag. To her the rose was a feminine symbol of hope, joy and an expression of beauty and grace. The pink blossom was for happiness, gentleness and sweetness—all the things Miyah felt described her mother. The red blossom was a symbol of martyrdom—a sign of the family's Touchstone destiny.

Nona added a small piece of mirror, carefully tucked into the fabric and sewn so there were no sharp edges.

"This is so we always remember to stop and reflect what our purpose is in the world," she said. "And to remember that everyone you meet is a mirror image of yourself. What you see in them is also a part of yourself."

This seemed a bit confusing to Miyah at the time, but as she grew in experience and wisdom, she understood its meaning, looking often into the tiny reflection of herself. Sometimes she saw Nona's face in the mirror—an image of strength and courage shining back at her.

Miyah especially loved the smell of the bag's tapestry. She knew it held a family history within its threads that would never be unraveled. Sweet aromas of healing oils, trace odors of campfires, the sweat and tears of many women ancestors who spent hours working their healing rituals, the smells of Nona's magic potions. . .and the familiar scent of her mother's perfume. Simply possessing the medicine bag gave Miyah mental power, knowing that it was not only her proud destiny to carry on the family's healing tradition, it was also her passion. The medicine bag was as important to her as its precious contents inside, each containing its own history and power. The medicine bag was Miyah's warm, fuzzy blanket of comfort, but it was also her rock of confidence.

~ ~ ~ ~ ~

When Miyah arrived back at the house, Michael was watching out his bedroom window, anxiously awaiting her return. He managed his way downstairs and opened the door, welcoming her. The sheer sight of her brought strength back into his body and a feeling of lightness heightened his senses.

"I was worried that you'd left me," he admitted. "You were gone several hours."

Amused by his observance and anxiety, Miyah smiled. "Oh was I?" she asked, knowing full well how long she had been gone. "I must have lost track of time. I stopped by the market to pick up some fresh fruit and vegetables. I hope you don't mind me taking over your kitchen," she said, adding, "You look like your rest did you good."

"Yes," Michael replied. "This is the first time I've been out of my room in days. I have to say it feels good. I even made some tea. Will you join me?"

"Of course," Miyah answered, as she walked past him into the kitchen. She knew Michael was on a fast physical path to recovery. She also knew he had many lessons he still needed to learn before her job was finished and before he would be fully back into the world. But now she had some questions for him.

"Michael," she began as she put groceries away. "Have you met this man that Elizabeth was dating? I believe his name is Robert."

"I met him once, but briefly," Michael said. "He came by the house to pick her up for dinner one night and she introduced us. I don't know much about him, other than I had a strange feeling and later when I questioned Elizabeth about his background she got defensive and told me I was being judgemental without even knowing him. That sent up red flags for me right away, but I backed down because I knew she wouldn't listen to me, and I didn't have the strength to fight with her. I thought I would do some investigating later when I was feeling better, but until now that just hasn't happened. Why do you ask?"

"Oh, I just wondered. Elizabeth mentioned him and I was curious about who this man was," she said casually, trying not to betray her thoughts.

"I'm surprised she said anything about him. I thought she broke up with him weeks ago. I know she did it because of me, to take care of me, but I didn't care because I was glad she wasn't seeing him anymore. I guess that was selfish of me."

"Perhaps," Miyah said. "But maybe you were simply being protective because you love her."

"I still owe her an apology. I know," Michael replied. "And maybe I also owe them both a thank you, because I believe Robert is the one who suggested she connect with you to help me."

Miyah was a bit bewildered at Michael's statement. "That's odd. I've never met Robert before. Did Elizabeth say how Robert knew about me?"

Michael smiled. He was quite charming when he smiled. "Are you kidding? You're an angel icon. Elizabeth said that people tell stories of how you suddenly appear and help them. She said you're famous, a miracle worker. . .like Jesus! I'm sure Robert heard about you and told Elizabeth." Michael added, "Thank God he did. That's why Elizabeth contacted you."

"You don't understand, Michael. People don't contact me. Elizabeth didn't call me on the phone or send me a letter or an email. I just get an inner sense when I'm suppose to connect with a person in need and I go to them. I suppose Elizabeth could have summoned me through telepathy."

"Hell, no," Michael responded quickly. "Elizabeth is a simple woman. She doesn't know about stuff like that."

"Stuff like that is simple," Miyah said. "In ancient times people communicated with telepathy all the time. There are so many things today's culture has forgotten. So many things. . ." her voice trailed off.

"Did *you* know about me before Elizabeth told you?" Miyah asked.

"Well, no," Michael stuttered. "And I have to confess that I didn't believe any of it when she told me about you being a miracle worker. . .that is until I saw you in my dreams. I had given up all hope of living."

Michael studied Miyah's sudden pensive mood. He was learning a lot about her—that behind that beautiful, delicate face was a wealth of accumulated knowledge from ancient teachings. He was grateful he was going to learn from her. . .to have time. He shook his head and let go a long sigh, signaling the end of the conversation about Robert and Elizabeth.

There was a lapse of silence as they drank their tea. Miyah always loved the silence. She listened for the small sounds in between the stillness— the dripping of the water in the kitchen sink, the tapping of the teaspoon touching the side of the cup as it stirred, and the sound of the tea bag as it sloshed onto the plate. She could hear her own breathing and Michael swallowing as he gulped his tea. She loved that her senses were fine-tuned to be able to enjoy all the half-notes, the skips and beats between the lines of life.

Finally Michael spoke. "Look here," he paused. "I know this is some sort of miracle. It's too outlandish for me to think anything else, so I've accepted your magic. I don't understand it, but obviously you've worked your healing wizardry on my cancer and I feel stronger already, I know I'm on my way to being well. Hell, I don't even want to know how this works. I'm just grateful you're here and that I'm not dying. . .well, not dying today anyhow." He waited for her to respond. She was silent.

"When you first came you said something about a promise I had to make. I know I was feverish and I didn't quite follow you. Then I had the dreams—maybe they were hallucinations, I don't know, but they've brought me into a deeper realization of other realities and I need to have you explain more of this to me. I feel anxiety, fear, excitement and all sorts of emotions when I think about what you've shown me these last two days. On one hand I'm scared to death of exploring this further. Yet I have a thirst for it that I just can't quench. I want more. . .I need more. . ." His voice lingered and all he could do was look to Miyah for answers, for guidance.

Their eyes locked for a few moments and Miyah finally broke the trance. During these brief seconds she saw a glimpse into what was to come. What was revealed was surprising to her—unexpected events that would not only change Michael's life, but would also alter hers. This she did not foresee before, and she was a bit shaken by this new revelation. Taking a deep breath to center her thoughts, she lowered her tea cup to its plate and then looked back at Michael.

"I don't know everything. Things are revealed to me as I need to know them. I just follow my intuition or my gut feeling. We're all on this earth at this time for a reason and if we allow ourselves to tune into our inner voice, our guides, spirit, God, whatever name you prefer for the Universal Force, we'll find that so much more exists in this realm than we're aware of. It's beautiful. It's mysterious. It's exciting. But most of all it's powerful. This Force that guides us is ancient. It's truly the voice of God. It's available to everyone, but few are able to open their hearts and their minds to receive this gift—to understand the peace and compassion of spirit. This is where I want to take you, Michael. But it's not going to be an easy journey. You'll discover things that go against what you've been taught. You'll doubt what you see and hear. You'll curse me for exposing you to this beam of light that will blind your thoughts and shine a new path. And most of all, you'll experience the loneliness and scorn that others will impose on you for your new discoveries and beliefs. It's difficult to change the way people think after being filled with teachings of the past 2,000 years."

Michael felt a twinge of remorse as he recalled his "dreams" into the past. "So what you're saying is that the imagery I experienced, what I called dreams, is real. People can travel back into the past. Is that the Touchstone secret, time travel?"

"Oh, no Michael," Miyah shook her head. "That's only a small part of it, a vehicle for teaching. There's much more. . .so much more. You'll see—but only when you're ready. You'll need all your strength to get you through this. You thought the cancer was bad. Just wait for what lies ahead for you," she laughed.

Michael's first response was anger at her scoffing him, but this quickly passed as he realized the adventure upon which he was about to embark. He hadn't felt this way for years.

"Do you mean I'm cured? I've traded my cancer, perhaps my soul, for this promise I made to you in a feverish fit?" Now he smiled, but just slightly, not knowing for sure if he was making light of the situation or if he had truly traded his own soul for a promise—whatever it was.

Reading his thoughts, Miyah's expression darkened. "It's very serious, Michael," she said. "You haven't traded your soul for anything. But the promise is not to be taken lightly. It's an honor to be given this opportunity. In time you'll see. . .in time you'll see many things and you'll understand how important this is. You'll know why you've been chosen and just what you are to do with this information—how you'll fulfill your promise. You'll know when the time is right. That's all I can tell you."

Michael said he understood, even though he didn't. What he did know was that he would find out eventually. That was good enough for him. He also knew that he trusted Miyah completely. He trusted her with his life. . . with his very soul.

"I'm going to take a shower," he announced. "I think that'll do wonders for me. You're staying again tonight aren't you?" he asked.

"Yes," she answered. "You have more work to do with the cedar box tonight and I need to be present."

Michael felt excitement and dread at the same time.

"Whatever you say," was all he could stutter, a cold sweat beginning to bead on his skin.

~~~~~

While Michael showered, Miyah put fresh linens on his bed and smudged his room with sweetgrass and cedar sage to clear the negativity that had accumulated while he was sick. She collected the crystal she had let him use and brought it out to the garden to wash it in a bucket of rainwater. She held it to the sun for cleansing and thanked the Universe for its abundant healing powers before she wrapped it and placed it back into her medicine bag. She knew Michael's own inner physician would continue to heal him over the next few weeks and that he would have a lot of explaining to do on his next doctor's visit. She wondered how Michael would explain himself, but then realized he most likely wouldn't even go back to his doctor. After all, his doctor had let him go home to die. He didn't really expect to see him again.

Michael felt refreshed from his shower and settled into a favorite chair in the library with a book he had started months ago. He felt comforted being in this room again, surrounded by old friends—books filled with history, religion, travel and cultural photographs, art, self-help antidotes and just good stories, information he mainly used for research when he was writing. But he soon tired of reading and felt pangs of anxiousness as thoughts of the cedar box trailed through his mind. He almost felt as if it were an addiction, a fix he couldn't wait for.

He went upstairs to his room and began to look around for Miyah's medicine bag. He knew the box would be inside. Her sweater was laid neatly over the chair next to the window. The bag was nowhere to be found. He could smell a trace scent of her perfume on the pillow where she had slept the night before. He remembered how beautiful she looked bathed in the moonlight. He was becoming intoxicated by this mysterious woman—or was it the cedar box? Michael was confused by his emotions.

He was suddenly very tired and welcomed the fresh bedding Miyah had prepared for him. He closed the window part way, just enough to shut out the breeze, yet keep the air circulating. He had appreciated Miyah airing out his room and realized how much he missed being outdoors in nature. He vowed that tomorrow he would venture out into the garden—one step at a time to recovery.

"I'll rest my eyes for awhile until Miyah comes," he thought as he crawled into bed. He looked over to his nightstand where the cedar box had beckoned him into another reality earlier that day. He felt a sharp pang of longing. He shut his eyes and drifted off to sleep. It had been a long day.

~~~~~

Miyah finished her rituals in the garden and went back inside. She found her way to the downstairs bathroom, locked the door, closed the shade and drew a warm bath. She undressed and loosened the tie around her hair, letting it fall upon her shoulders as she brushed it in long, caring strokes. She loved the way her long hair felt on her bare back, gently caressing her skin as she moved her head. Thick, healthy hair was another thing she inherited from the women of her bloodline. When she was finished brushing she lit a candle in a bowl on the counter, cleaned the hair from her brush and rolled it into a small nest, which she placed into the fire. It was a sign of long life if the hair flamed up vigorously and an omen of ill health if it simply smoldered away. Miyah got down eye-level with the candle and watched it burn into a tall, golden flame. A good omen.

Taking advantage of the quiet time, she lowered herself into a warm bubble bath with some lavender oil for a relaxing soak. She knew she would need to be refreshed for all the work she had before her, but she didn't mind, as this was her path, one she diligently followed without question. She knew her soul's purpose was her connection with the Touchstone. She closed her eyes as she said a prayer of thankfulness to all who guided her and to those who loved her. This simple gesture filled her heart with joy. She reached over and her fingertips gently caressed the medicine bag on the floor next to the tub. She traced the outline of the cedar chest through the fabric and thought of Nona, Junia and all her ancestors who were keepers of this special box. Meditative peacefulness spread over her, for Miyah knew how to live in the moment.

And this moment was good.

7   The Land

Michael could smell the lavender perfume of Miyah's bath the minute she entered his room and he slowly shook the sleepiness from his nap. His eyes followed her as she moved across the floor.

Miyah quietly carried her medicine bag to the big chair by the window and began to sort through it for the "tools" she would need for the night's healing. She lit a candle and began to whisper a mantra to prepare herself for what was to come. She knew that whatever is sent out mentally or verbally, repeated over and over, adds power to the spell.

Miyah also knew that mantras—"yoga for the mind"—brings blessings to the chanter. Nona had told her that mantras were common forms of prayer in many religions. She said that just as "Om mani padme hum" is a mantra of Hindu and Buddhist tradition, the "Hail Mary" or "Our Father" prayers are Christian mantras. Miyah also learned that reciting the beads of the Catholic rosary, or using a mala—a string of 108 beads in Eastern traditions—are ancient tools used in chanting mantras. She found it interesting that the original Catholic rosary had 108 beads, but was later pared down to 59.

The translation of the word mantra is "instrument of thought." Nona had explained that when a mantra is chanted you are recharging your breath. Sound waves travel from your voice and summon powerful cosmic forces. Your energy, together with the energy of the mantra completely engages the mind and allows you to go within.

"There are 108 main nadia or veins, that go from the heart to all the extremities. After reciting a manta 108 times, the body becomes purified. Each syllable is filled with spiritual power as it vibrates with blessings."

Miyah looked out the window to see the sun beginning to disappear over the landscape. She knew the best time to recite a mantra was during transition periods of a day, such as sunrise and sunset. She closed her eyes and again melodiously recited the words her ancestors had repeated thousands of times over the centuries, "Yango ketso pu, yango ketso pu, yango ketso pu." Her voice deepened with each chant and she began to rock back and forth as the words flowed from deep within her and time passed without notice.

She gradually came out of her trance and ended her mantra with a nod of gratitude to the Universe for all her blessings. Before she turned to check on Michael, she saw a small, brown bunny in the center of the yard, sitting and looking up at her. Associated with the Moon Goddess, the rabbit is a messenger of lunar deities. It represents death and rebirth, rejuvenation and resurrection and is also a fertility symbol. Miyah took this as a good omen. The ground work Michael had before him was certainly fertile with rebirth. It was fitting. Michael was on his way to a new and healthy life.

She ended her ritual with a long, whispered "Ommm" —the first sound of the universe, perfectly symbolizing the moment.

As Miyah placed the cedar box on the nightstand next to his bed, Michael sat up.

"What were you doing over there?" he asked. "I know you were doing some sort of ritual, but what does it mean?"

"I hope I didn't disturb you. I thought you were still asleep," she replied. "I was asking my ancestors for wisdom and blessings," she added, "and also strength and protection for both of us during these times of healing."

"Protection. From what do we need protection?"

"Oh," Miyah said slowly, choosing her words carefully. "There are forces out there that would very much like to tap into the energies we're working with," she nodded toward the cedar box.

"Do you mean evil spirits?" Michael asked, a bit unnerved.

"I'm more concerned about those on the earth level right now," she replied. "But don't concern yourself with any of that. All you need to do is concentrate on getting well. You have a lot of important work ahead of you, whether you realize it or not."

Michael started to ask what she meant, but Miyah waved her hand toward the cedar box.

"Shall we begin?"

Michael took a deep breath and slowly let the air out, as if he was biding for time. "I want to. . .I'm anxious to see what will happen. . . but I feel a bit apprehensive, a little afraid," he stammered, looking at the cedar box. "It's very mysterious and unusual, you certainly must understand what I'm feeling." He looked to Miyah for some reassurance. "Where will I end up this time? Will I be safe? What if I can't get back one of these times? I can't help these thoughts."

"Your thoughts create your reality, Michael," Miyah said. "Don't you know that you draw to you what you fear? If you go into your dreamtime with all of these fears, you may just draw those kinds of experiences to you. I've done preparation work around you and I want you to know that whatever work we are doing here is done with the highest levels of protection. Love and light surround you. You've been chosen to be given this gift of insight into past worlds by ancestors of light, not of dark. You'll be safe. . .and you'll come back each time. Didn't you hear me say you have a lot of work to do here ? It all ties together. You may not understand it now, but it'll be clear to you someday. You must learn to have faith. Trust in me, Michael, and trust in yourself."

Michael nodded. "I trust you completely, Miyah. I do."

"If you need to feel more secure during your travels you can carry this stone with you." She placed a half-dollar-size, flat, oval stone into his hand.

"Draw your courage from it and if it helps, think of me as an affirmation that I'm holding you safe while you journey."

As she spoke, Michael couldn't help but bring his attention to the cedar box. It was as if it was in sync with their conversation and signalling for him to begin his journey. Feeling that familiar dizziness he stared at the panel, which was forming into shapes and shadows. Soon Michael was gone, lost to the mercy of the mysterious cedar box.

~ ~ ~ ~ ~

Anticipating a welcoming reunion with Joshua and Maryum, Michael looked around at an unfamiliar landscape. Again he was alone in a strange place. A pang of fear crossed his mind and he remembered what Miyah had told him about his thoughts creating his reality. He opened his hand and looked at the stone Miyah had given him.

"Courage," she said.

An image of Miyah crossed his vision and he took a deep breath, dissipating any fear he felt. With Miyah by his side in any shape or form, even a stone, he had courage to step into this new dreamtime adventure. Yes, he should look at it as an adventure. . .an adventure of a lifetime.

Now, acutely aware of the elements of his surroundings, Michael could feel the hot sun bearing down on him and the heat burning through to the soles of his feet. He understood why Miyah insisted he wear a pair of sandals before he began his journey. But he felt quite silly standing in the desert in a pair of white, cotton pajamas. Feeling the barrenness of his location, Michael looked around to search for familiar signs from his last "visit" to point him in the right direction. There were none, only rolling hills of desert sand giving rise to more of the same. He began to walk, not knowing where his footsteps would lead. After what seemed like hours had passed, he began to call Miyah's name, deeply questioning the purpose of this trip. Had he gotten lost somewhere in the abyss of his time travel? Would he ever be found again?

He tried to hold Miyah's words in his mind and find faith to believe in them as he fingered the flat stone in the palm of his hand. "Draw your courage from this stone and if it helps, think of me as an affirmation that I'm holding you safe while you journey."

"Is my doubt creating my reality?" he wondered.

"Faith, faith, faith," he began to chant over and over again, rhythmically with each step he took, hot sand washing and burning through the leather of his sandals.

Finally he reached the top of a high dune. He saw something moving in the distance. It's a mirage he thought, squinting his eyes to focus on the dot of an image moving through lines of heat waves. Michael could make out the form of a man riding a camel. He began to run toward the traveler, waving his arms to attract attention. The man and beast stopped in their tracks. Michael must have seemed a strange apparition coming from seemingly nowhere, stumbling down a hill of deep sinkholes of sand. The camel rider edged forward as Michael, stricken by the dry heat, slowed his pace.

When they finally met, Michael's mouth was so dry he couldn't speak. He put his hands on his knees and bent over, his chest heaving to catch his breath.

"No need to bow to me, my friend," a voice from above him said. "I am not your king."

Michael slowly looked up, seeing only a dark silhouette against a bright, white sky. He straightened up and shadowed his eyes with his hand, trying to focus on the figure's features. Again, he didn't know the language of this man but he understood it and knew his words would be understood, if he could ever speak again. He tried to swallow, but not a trace of saliva lubricated his throat.

"Ah, you have no water," the man said, as he reached for a goatskin bag and tossed it to Michael. After fumbling with the lid, Michael finally opened the bag and drowned himself with a surge of hot, but welcomed, liquid. As he was doing this, the traveler touched a stick to the side of his camel and the animal lowered itself to its knees, first jerking forward and then abruptly backward. The traveler swung his leg around and dismounted, leaning against his beast, observing this strange man.

"Thank you," Michael said as he handed the canvas of water back to the man.

"You keep this," the man said. "Never go to the desert without water."

Michael wondered how he could explain his presence here. Where was he? What year was it? And who was this man who was saving him from becoming desert bones?

"Your friend has sent me to fetch you. He said you are foreign and would not know of our ways and that I should be patient with you." He spoke as he unraveled a piece of white cloth and proceeded to wrap it around Michael's head for protection against the sun. "Do you know how to ride a camel?"

"Err, no," Michael stuttered, looking over the colorful roping, tassels and tiny bells that adorned the camel's head gear. "Who did you say sent you?" he questioned.

"Your friend. We will join with him soon. Now, climb on and remember to lean way back when Ishmal stands up, otherwise you will plummet over his head and end up where you began."

Grateful for the ride, Michael stretched his legs over the back of the camel and settled behind the man.

"What is your name?" he asked.

"I am Ahmad," the man replied.

"Thank you, Ahmad. I am Michael."

"I know," he replied. "Lean back."

Ishmal rocked forward to unfold his long, rear legs from beneath him, raising his back end in the air, putting his body at an angle that, if his riders were not leaning back, they would surely be thrown over the camel's head as Ahmad had indicated. Then the animal surged backward to straighten out his front legs and the men leaned forward. Michael felt like he was on a bucking bronco, being thrown to and fro, until Ishmal finally stood tall. Michael was grateful for the directions Ahmad had given him and now squirmed around to find a comfortable niche on the camel's back.

Ahmad turned to take a closer look at Michael. He reached over and touched the fabric of his white, pin-striped cotton pajamas. "Who is your tailor?" he asked earnestly.

"My. . .my tailor?" Michael said.

"Where did you get your kurta?" the camel driver insisted.

"Ah, Macy's, I guess," Michael replied, feeling a bit silly that the man thought his pajamas were his everyday attire.

"I like," the man said, as he switched the camel to begin their walk.

They rode in silence through the desert. A streamlined trace of a single camel and two riders mimicked a long, dark shadow drawing across the white sand floor.

"Faith, faith, faith," Michael continued his mantra quietly to himself.

~~~~~

After a while the atmosphere began to change and Michael could smell the dryness of the desert give way to the humidity and mustiness of salt air. In the distance he could see green palm trees and shapes that looked like buildings, but he was afraid to get too excited, fearing it was a mirage. As they neared, he realized the desert sands did indeed give way to lush, green patches of trees and grasses, surrounding a large, busy village. Beyond that a vast ocean of water sparkled in the sunlight. The thought of submerging himself in that cold, refreshing water sustained Michael as they made their way to the village.

Riding down a dusty street, he looked for anything that might look familiar. He saw women dressed in colorful fabric draped around their bodies to form a dress. Balanced on their heads were large baskets filled with goods. He watched a Gypsy woman as she gracefully squatted, scooped up a pile of camel dung and tossed it into her basket. Then she walked over to a campfire and dumped her basket of dung into a larger pile. Animal dung was a good resource to supplement scarce firewood. It fueled their fires, which in turn gave them light, heated them on cold nights and cooked their food. Nothing went to waste. The culture was much different than Michael expected—but then, he really didn't know what to expect.

Soon they stopped by a mud house with a thatched roof made of palm and reeds. A man came out to greet them and grabbed the camel's reins.

"Ahmad," the man shouted. "I see you found the visitor." He walked around the camel, eyeing the likes of Michael.

Just then Ishmal lunged forward, folding his fore legs beneath him, and then rolled backward as he bent his rear legs underneath. Michael, unprepared for the sudden movement, nearly fell head over heels on top of Ahmad. Both desert men laughed and grabbed hold of Michael to help him dismount, steadying him firmly on the ground.

Ahmad showed off his new friend and tugged the fabric of Michael's pajamas. "Macy's," he said.

"Ah, Macy's," his friend repeated. "I like. Where is this tailor, Macy's?"

Michael chuckled and simply said, "Far, far away from here." Looking around at the dusty village oasis, he asked, "But where are we and can you take me to my friend, Joshua?"

"I do not know a man named Joshua, but I will take you to Issa. He is waiting."

"Issa?" Michael questioned.

"Yes, Issa. He is the one who sent me to find you." Ahmad walked away, and turned into a narrow alleyway. Michael quickly stepped up to follow, not wanting to get lost in this foreign place.

Ahmad stopped in front of a small, adobe house on the far edge of the busy village. There were several other mud houses connected to it, all surrounded by a low fence made of the same brick as the houses, which Michael realized was also made out of recycled dried animal manure.

"Issa is here," said Ahmad as he swung open the heavy, wooden door and motioned for Michael to enter.

The room was simple with a wood table in the center, three chairs with no backs and a long bench against one wall. Sleeping mats were rolled up in one corner of the room and the other corner had a slightly raised mud platform with a four-inch lip around it to hold in the ashes from the cooking fire. The ceiling and walls around the primitive campfire were stained with dark soot and the room smelled like smoke. Michael wasn't sure what to think, as he was expecting to be reunited with Joshua.

Michael heard Ahmad speaking to someone outside and soon a young man entered the room.

"Michael, my friend. It is good you found me again," the boy said.

Michael just stood looking at this boy named Issa. He was almost as tall as Michael, yet was still young—early twenties, Michael guessed. He seemed very confident and as he came closer, Michael stared at him.

The lad said. "It's me, Joshua—only here in this land they call me Issa Natha, or just Issa."

"Joshua!" Michael said with surprise.

"Issa," the boy repeated.

Michael didn't care what his name was, he just wanted to hug him, he was so happy to see him again. He fidgeted, and sensing his thoughts, Issa stepped forward and gave him a strong hug, clapping his hand on Michael's shoulder.

"What took you so long to get here?" he asked.

"Get here?" Michael replied. "Where are we?"

"We are in Jagannath Puri, Orissa," Issa said, and seeing the blank look on Michael's face, he added, "India."

"India!" Michael exclaimed. "India! But how did you get here? Why are you here?"

"I left my family when I was in my thirteenth year, not long after you visited me when I was carving the cedar box for my mother. It was the age which traditionally I should accept a wife and many fathers were coming to our home seeking a husband for their daughters. How could I carry on the mission for which my mother said I was born, if I was betrothed so young, living in a small village with little knowledge of the world?"

"But this is so far from your home. How did you get here?" Michael asked again.

Picking up a stick from the fire box, Issa drew a map on the dirt floor of the house.

"My Essene teachers in Egypt arranged for me to travel with merchants on a camel caravan over the main East-West trade route, what you call the Silk Road. The trade route from Jerusalem goes to Damascus, through Babylon to Kharax. We journeyed through Assyria and Chaldea—Mesopotamia— and from Kharax, I proceeded toward Sindh by ship." He drew concise lines in the dirt, connecting place to place, recalling the maps he had studied on his voyage.

"I stayed in Sindh province for a brief time and there I came in contact with the Jain priests. It was interesting to learn of their beliefs. Their teachings stress leading a pure life through non-violence, noble actions and thoughts, and by kindness to all beings. Like the Essenes, they also do not eat meat."

"Did you stay with them? What did you do there?" Michael was full of questions, still in disbelief that this young man had actually journeyed so far from his home.

"Yes, I stayed with them for a brief time. I also spent some time with the Sindhi fishermen. They have a way of fishing I had never seen before. They catch fish in the Indus River by floating earthen pots on the surface of the water. I thought this to be very clever!"

Issa continued to draw on his map in the sand. "After I left Sindh, I crossed the Indus River and moved across Southeast India, traveling with another merchant caravan until I reached Jagannath Puri, here in the province of Orissa. On my journey I visited temples and met with priests and wise men. For these many years I have been learning works of healing. I have also journeyed beyond to other holy cities—Rajagriha, Varanasi and Benares."

Michael was flabbergasted. It seemed so brave for a mere boy to have traveled all that way. Looking at Issa's map, Michael realized he had traveled through what is now Syria, Iraq, Iran, Afghanistan and Pakistan to reach India.

"And you traveled alone? You must have a lot of courage, Josh. . .err, Issa."

"I was never alone," Issa replied. "There were many merchants in the caravans who travel this way to trade their wares on a regular route. It is their life. My uncle Joseph and Essene brothers made sure I was well cared for."

"But why are you here?" Michael asked.

"My thirst for knowledge never seems to be quenched," Issa said. "I came to learn. In Varanasi, the holy city of Hindus on the banks of the river Ganges, I was introduced to the Vedas, Hindu scriptures, by the priests. Pilgrims go there from all parts of India for prayer and meditation and to bathe in the water. Did you know that the dead are cremated on the banks of the sacred Ganges River right out in the open, and the ashes are thrown into the water—the same water where the people bathe?!"

Issa continued, "Here in India I have been welcomed by the white robed Brahmin priests and have spent almost six years being taught to read and understand the Vedas, to heal by prayer. I have learned to teach and explain the Holy Scripture. These priests have knowledge of how to cast out evil spirits from the body and have many other healing ways. They have shared with me the Achar Samhita, their code of conduct. This teaches truthfulness, mercy, charity, serving others, compassion and ethics. If you like, I can introduce you to some of my teachers: Chetan Nath, who is a Nath Guru, and Kahjian, who has taught me about cleansing of the body in preparation for physical and mental strength."

Michael was without words. This young man he met in a simple carpenter shop was here in India, far from home, embarking on an adventure which Michael himself would never have considered in his own adult life. He seemed so wise for his years and so eager to share what he had learned, even though Michael did not understand much of what Issa said about his teachings. It was all foreign to him.

Just then Michael remembered his first meeting with Joshua in the carpenter shop.

"But I met you with Maryum when you were much older, so that must mean you return to your home."

"Oh, yes, I will return, but not until I have gained the knowledge necessary for me to carry on my life's mission. There are many mysteries of life, Michael, and I am privileged to have been chosen to deliver these messages to the people. It will be an honor to become such a great teacher, but it also requires much work on my part."

Michael sat and stared at this man for awhile, until Issa broke the silence.

"You must be weary from your journey."

Michael laughed. "My journey here was nothing compared to yours! But next time can you maybe drop me closer to you? The ride through the desert was nice but I wasn't really prepared for it."

"Are we ever prepared for what lies ahead? You learned to ride a camel. You conversed with local people. You saw some of the country. You must remember to always enjoy the moment and take in the beauty of your surroundings. You will be surprised. Sometimes the journey is just as important as the end result. Come, let's go for a walk. There is something I would like to show you. . .but first, let's get you out of those pajamas and into something more fitting." Issa fetched a white cotton robe from a hook on the wall and handed it to Michael.

"You may not be accustomed to the dress here but it is very comfortable and cool under the hot sun."

Michael remembered the turban Ahmad had made for him in the desert and began to unwind it. He never thought he'd actually be glad he wore his hair long, tied into a ponytail. His sister, Elizabeth, had always wanted him to cut it. Now, he removed the pony tail binder and combed through his hair with his fingers. He never wore his hair down at home and it felt good. Stripping down to his boxer shorts, he donned the robe and let it hang casually to his ankles. He looked like any of the other men in the village with his robe and long hair.

Michael saw Ahmad through the open door of the house. He neatly folded his pajamas, along with the cloth for the headpiece, went outside and gave them to him.

"A gift from my tailor, Macy's," he said, with a smile.

Ahmad graciously accepted the gift, bowing his head again and again.

"Thank you. Thank you. Such a gift I have never received before."

Issa nodded in approval.

~ ~ ~ ~ ~

Michael and Issa talked about the land as they walked through the white sands along Puri beach on the nearby waters of the Bay of Bengal. Waves rolled and crashed against the shore.

"This country is beautiful, is it not?" Issa said, lifting his head to let the salty mist wash over his face, as the waves sent a fine spray of water through the air.

"Yes, but how do people survive here? What do they do?" Michael asked, also enjoying the refreshing mist.

"Agriculture is the mainstay of this land," Issa replied. "Mostly farmers grow rice, but they also plant legumes, cotton, tobacco, sugarcane and turmeric. They process their sugarcane here as well."

"I saw livestock when I arrived," Michael said, "water buffalo and other cattle, sheep, goats."

"Yes, we have animals," Issa acknowledged. "We also have many talented weavers of fine textiles, woodcarvers, sewers of fishnets and makers of paper, soap and baskets." He pointed to racks of colorful silk fabric hanging in a waterfront market stall.

Michael appreciated the craft of fine art and admired the wares. He sensed the fragrance of a variety of smells—aromatic, sweet, tart, vinegary and flowery, as tall baskets of colorful spices and herbs lined a row on the edge of the nearby marketplace. He could also detect the penetrating smell of sweat from bodies clustered too close together in the heat and the pungent, powerful odor of urine. He watched a child squat next to a nearby pile of woven baskets to pee.

Issa saw Michael's reaction to the child nonchalantly urinating in the open.

"This is India," he said, shrugging his shoulders, as if that would explain it. He then directed Michael away from the market and brought him into a wood building. From there they entered a back room, shutting the door behind them.

"I want to show you something of much importance," Issa said to Michael, opening the ornate door of a large, wooden cupboard. There was a false panel inside the top shelf of the cupboard and Issa pried the panel open to retrieve some ancient manuscripts.

"These are rare collections of manuscripts that tell of the rich, ancient knowledge of Orissa," he said. "They are made of twenty-seven sections: the Veda, Tanra, Darsana, Silpa Sastra, Abhidhana, Ayurved and such." Issa rolled out some of the manuscripts which were designed in rare, garland-shaped, sword-shaped, fan-shaped, rat-shaped and parrot-shaped papers. Some were made from palm-leaf, others of bamboo leaf, hand-made paper, bhurja bark and kumbhi bark.

Michael didn't understand why Issa was showing him these manuscripts, other than being a writer he would appreciate their beauty.

"They are unique," he said, reaching out to touch the fine workmanship.

"I have also left my mark with these manuscripts," Issa said. "So people will know I was here and that I studied with the great teachers. I have written about my life in this place and of my studies. I will do that in all my travels—leave my mark, so those who come after me will know I was there. I want you to know this."

"But why?" Michael asked.

"Because some day it will be of great importance."

A noise from the other room hastened Issa to roll up the papers and return them to their sanctuary. Pressing his finger to his lips, he motioned for Michael to be still.

After a few moments, Issa peeked through a crack in the door to see if it was safe to leave. Walking out of the building, Issa looked from side to side to see if they were being followed. When he was sure all was clear, he motioned for Michael to follow him.

"Is there a problem?" Michael asked. "Something I should know about?"

"Nothing for you to worry about at this moment," Issa replied, leading Michael off into the crowded street.

"Come this way. There is a famous shrine I want to show you. It's a pilgrimage destination—the temple of Jagannath."

"Jag-a-nnath," Michael repeated, slowly breaking the word apart for pronunciation.

"Yes," Issa explained. "The word Jag means Universe, and Nath means Lord—Lord of the Universe."

Issa explained further as they made their way through the growing crowd. "The wooden temple of Jagannath, which honors Lord Krishna, was originally a Buddhist shrine representing the Buddha, Dharma and Sangha—The Buddhist Holy Trinity. Because Hindu traditions absorbed practices of other faiths, including those of Buddhism, into their beliefs, Krishna, his brother Balarama, and sister Subhadra, make up the Hindu Trinity."

"Wait a minute. You've lost me here," Michael said. "You're talking about Holy Trinities of Buddhism and Hinduism, yet you are a Jew from Palestine. And what about Christianity?"

"Remember," Issa reminded him, "you're in a time right now where Christianity as you know it has not yet been fully developed. The concept of the Buddhist and Hindu trinities have been around for thousands of years already. To confuse you further, when you are back in your home, if you research this temple of Jagannath you will see that a new temple was built in your 12th century." He gestured at the structure in front of them.

"What you see before you is the original wooden temple. This was a stupa that contained the holy relics of Buddha and later was absorbed by Hindu tradition and became the temple of Jagannath.

"See the ceremony over there?" he pointed to a procession of Brahmin priests carrying an ornate box in what seemed to be a ritual. "Every twelve years a small casket containing asthi, or ashes, of Lord Krishna is inserted into the wooden body of Jagannath."

Michael watched the priests enter the temple. The sights and sounds of their procession overwhelmed him and he wondered how he would keep all of this straight.

"You may find it interesting that the Hindus and Buddhists say the world was created when God uttered the sound 'OM,'" Issa noted.

Michael replied, "I know the Bible says 'In the beginning was the word.'"

"It is the same," Issa nodded with a smile. "The word was OM."

Issa and Michael stood before the temple admiring the massive structure.

"Traditionally, pilgrims are required to offer worship first at a Shiva temple, then at the sacred Banyan tree and the shrine of Balarama before proceeding to worship Jagannath," Issa explained. "But I think it will be all right if we enter the temple for a few minutes so you can appreciate its beauty. It may be difficult for you to get beyond the concept that Hinduism worships many gods, yet in fact it acknowledges one God who is boundless in manifestations—that everything in creation is God's manifestation."

The two men took off their shoes, went inside and sat together in silence.

~~~~

Upon leaving the temple, Issa was approached by a young boy who delivered to him an urgent message. The boy pointed through the crowd to Ahmad, who was leaning against a building across the busy roadway. Issa and Michael crossed the street. Issa and Ahmad stepped into an alley where much discussion followed. Michael couldn't hear what they were saying, but knew by their body language that it was important. After several minutes, Ahmad, in a brotherly gesture, laid his hand on the young man's shoulder. Issa motioned for Michael to join them and they quickly walked down the alley toward another part of the village.

"The great chariot festival will begin soon. The streets are already crowding with people so it will be easy for you to slip away," Ahmad said, looking around to see if anyone else could hear them. "I will go and make the necessary preparations for you, my friend."

As Ahmad left, Issa pulled Michael into a small room, closing the wooden, window shutters of the door, leaving only a thin stream of light to enter through the cracks under the shuttered frame.

"What's wrong?" Michael asked anxiously. "What has happened?"

"I am sorry you are here during this time my friend. But don't worry, you will be safe and return to your home unharmed. It is me they are looking for."

Michael stared at this gentle young man, wondering what he could have possibly done to find himself in danger.

"For these many years I've lived here in peace with the Vaisyas, the yellow race and the Soudras, the black race. I believe God establishes no difference between his children. We are all equally dear to him and I've preached the holy Hindu scriptures to the lower castes—the farmers, merchants and laborers. My mission is to teach love, truth and purity of heart to all God's children. The Brahmins oppose this and it has enraged the Brahmin priests and Kshatriyas warriors that I've taught their sacred words to the lower castes. Because of this, they are threatening my life."

"What? That can't be!" Michael exclaimed. "Why would they want to harm you for teaching the people, no matter if they are rich or poor. What difference does it make?"

"You don't understand the caste system here in India. Yes, it is very unfair, but that is their tradition. I hope it will change some day so everyone will be viewed as equal. I thought that by teaching them, it would make a beginning. I am sad I must leave my work here. I only hope there will be no repercussions on those whom I have taught." Issa slumped against the wall.

In his agony he said, "The Brahmins have taught me the use of their herbs and medicines, mathematics and religious doctrines. We had many philosophical discussions and they became my friends. I cannot believe my teachers have any part in this. How can the teaching of God's word cause so much discontent in the lives of those who wish to live simple and pure lives? Power. It is all about power and greed." Issa seemed to talk to himself, feeling a sense of desperation for his fellow people.

"Where will you go?" Michael asked.

"Ahmad has been expecting this and has mapped out a route for me. I will head toward the Himalayan foothills in Nepal, to Kapilavatsu, the birthplace of Gautama Buddha. The Buddhist monasteries will take me in."

Then regrouping his composure with a sigh, Issa sat up straight and added, "Just as I told you Michael, I too must look at this as another adventure. My work here is done, my studies are finished. I must move on to the next lesson. Come, we must go now."

As Ahmad had predicted, the streets were crowded with hundreds of thousands gathering from all over the country for the celebration.

"What is this festival?" Michael asked as they made their way, shoulder-to-shoulder through the crowd.

"They have as many as 24 elaborate festivals here every year. This is the most important, the Rath Yatra—the chariot festival. There will be a procession through the streets of three colossal chariots that resemble temples and bear the images of the Trinity of Jagannath, Balarama and Subhadra. Everyone's attention will be on the chariots so it will be a good time for me to escape." Issa added, "Jagannath's chariot is a giant. There will be much activity going on, so be careful."

Being tossed to and fro by the crowd, Michael made a quick decision to stick close to Issa.

"It is truly a spectacle," Issa yelled over the noise of the crowd. "They make new chariots every year and it takes more than 4,000 people to drag them." He pointed toward a distant hill where people had gathered to begin moving the chariots.

"First the giant carts were pulled to the deity's summer home where the deities were worshipped for a week. Then they were brought back here for this procession." Just then Issa recognized one of the warriors coming toward him.

"Come, this way," he said as he quickly pulled Michael deeper into the crowd. Michael tripped and temporarily lost sight of Issa. He began to panic as the crowd closed in around him, pushing him along with them. The scene was insane with bullock carts racing through the center of town, turning up dust and nearly running people over. People were jeering and circling around rings of squatting men betting on cockfights. In the distance Michael could see the frenzy of horse and camel races. Above him flew falcons, being released to return to their masters in games of sport. He began to feel dizzy when suddenly someone grabbed onto him and linking arms like a chain, dragged him into a narrow alley. Almost afraid to see who had either kidnapped or saved him, Michael was relieved to find Issa, calmly asking if he was OK.

"I thought I had lost you," Michael said with a sigh of relief. "Let's get out of here!"

Relieved to be out of the crowd, Michael followed Issa down a dark, musty passageway. They wound their way through the village in a series of small alleys until they reached the edge of the desert through which Michael had first entered the village. Ahmad waited with provisions and two camels. Michael walked over and prepared to mount one of the camels. Issa put his hand on Michael's shoulder.

"No, my friend. You must stay here. We will join with a caravan across the desert and will travel for many weeks to reach our destination."

"But, but, I want to go with you. You can't expect me to stay here!" Michael pleaded as he gestured toward the mayhem of the crowded streets in the distance.

"Oh, no, you won't have to stay here," Issa said. "Never fear, you will return soon to your home."

"But where will I find you again?" Michael said, not wanting to leave his friend.

"I don't know where, but rest assured you will find me again. We still have much work to do together. We will be reunited soon. Have faith."

The camels rose to their full height with their riders intact and Michael, looking up into the sun at them, could only see a silhouette of Issa, sunshine rimming his body like a halo.

"Be safe," Michael called to Issa, already feeling an empty place in his heart for this young man.

Ahmad just smiled and raised a package in his hand, waving it at Michael, nodding his head.

"Macy's!" Ahmad shouted as he rode away into the desert with Issa.

After Issa left, Michael didn't know what to do. He wandered back to the house where he had first seen Issa and sat for a time reflecting on where he was. He grabbed a nectarine from a bowl on the table, peeled it and ate a bite, realizing how hungry he was. Michael wondered if he could find his way back to the house where Issa had shown him the scrolls. He hadn't examined them closely and was curious about the writings Issa said he left there. He picked up the water vessel Ahmad had given him and opened the top to take a drink, but as he drew the flask to his lips he saw a group of men heading toward the house. "Of course," he thought, "if the warriors were looking for Issa, they would surely be watching this house."

Not knowing where he was going and remembering Ahmad's words, "Never go to the desert without water," Michael slung the leather strap of the goatskin water bag around his neck. Stepping up on the bench, he quickly forced his body through a small, open window in the back of the room and fell to the ground outside. Michael didn't know which direction to head, but he knew he didn't want to face the Hindu warriors or the crowds of people celebrating the festival. He ducked behind adjoining houses and jumped over the earthen fence. He could hear voices of the men chasing after him and all he could think of was to head for the dark shade of a nearby alley.

Sliding down behind a large, clay water vessel, he pulled his legs into his chest and tried to make himself invisible. Grasping his arms around his knees and tucking his head down, he noticed the stone Miyah had given him was still tucked where he had put it for safe keeping, inside the cording of the water canteen. Michael grabbed the stone, as if just touching it would save him and bring him back to his world. He quietly chanted, whispering the name "Miyah" over and over. He could hear the shuffle of feet coming down the alley, getting closer and closer. Michael closed his eyes and tried to hold his breath, firmly grasping the stone in his fist.

"Do you see him?" someone shouted to the man searching the alley. "Is he there?"

The warrior stood over the pottery vessel and thrust his sharp banyan spear into the shadow of the jar.

"Ha!" the warrior snorted, squinting his eyes as he aimed his spear into the shadow again. He reached down and scooped up a nectarine with a piece out of it, laying on top of a crumpled white robe.

"No," he grunted. "There is only a pile of cloth." He walked away, eating the fruit.

8 The Healing Stone

"Michael, Michael, it's OK." Miyah sat on the bed next to his shaking body, cradling him in her arms and rocking back and forth, calming him like she would a frightened child.

"It's alright. You're safe. You're home," she soothed.

It took some time for Michael to uncurl from his fetal position. He opened his eyes slowly to be sure he was not still cowering in the alley with the silhouette of a large warrior looming over him with a spear. He found comfort in Miyah's arms, yet felt a bit embarrassed that she saw him in this condition.

"Just hold me," he whispered.

"As long as you want, Michael. I'm here for you," she replied softly, rocking gently.

After he regained his composure, he slowly lifted his head and straightened his back.

"Miyah," he said, gently. "Miyah," is all he could say.

"I've seen you in your dreamtime, Michael, and I'm sorry it took so long for you to come back," she said. "You're safe now."

"I know," he said. "I'm safe now."

"You had quite a traumatic experience this time."

"Yes. I'm not sure why things ended so dramatically, but I sure as hell was scared," he admitted, as he moved over and leaned against the wall.

After sitting in silence for a few minutes, Michael finally spoke. "I don't want to talk about it just now. I'd rather distance myself from it for awhile, if you don't mind," he said, as he stretched out his legs, suddenly realizing he was dressed only in his boxer shorts. . .his boxer shorts, sandals and a goatskin water flask around his neck.

"Are you going to get in the habit of bringing souvenirs home with you?" Miyah teased, making light of the situation. "And where in the world are your pajamas?"

"Where in the world, indeed?" Michael said, thinking of Ahmad and his new Macy's suit.

~~~~~

While Michael showered, Miyah chopped fresh vegetables to prepare dinner. She always knew what Michael was encountering on his vision quests. To her it was like watching a movie unfold, but she never let Michael know that. She wanted him to tell her of his adventures in his own words. Sometimes verbalizing the experience brings out realizations and understandings that a person wouldn't always get during the actual event.

When Michael didn't come into the kitchen after such a long time, Miyah went to find him. He was in his study searching for a map.

"I still can't believe that young boy traveled all the way across country like that," he exclaimed. "I need to see for myself. . .to follow that route. . .if I can remember what he told me."

"You just might want to pin that map up on the wall," Miyah suggested. "I think that lad is headed for many travels in his time. Just remember that many of the old cities and provinces have changed names over these hundreds of years."

"Yes, but *you* know, don't you? You can show me."

"Yes, I can, Michael, but can't it wait until later? Dinner is ready," Miyah said as she turned and walked back into the kitchen.

"You must be famished," she yelled over her shoulder.

Michael hesitated. He still had his mind wrapped around his visit with Issa and wasn't ready to let it go. "I'll be there in a few minutes," he called.

He found an old world map, unrolled it and as Miyah suggested, pinned it up on the wall. He grabbed a yellow highlighter and began to map out the general path Issa mentioned.

"I'll be damned," he said. "It works. There are variations in some of the names, but it works. Syria, Iraq, Iran, Afghanistan, Pakistan, India. . ." he traced his finger along the map. "Incredible."

He grabbed a dictionary off his bookshelf. "Issa kept talking about his Essene teachers," Michael said. The dictionary's description was brief.

> Essene: i s n; es n – noun - a member of an ancient Jewish ascetic sect of the 2nd century BC –2nd century AD in Palestine, who lived in highly organized groups and held property in common. The Essenes are widely regarded as the authors of the Dead Sea Scrolls.
> ORIGIN from Latin Esseni (plural), from Greek Ess noi, perhaps from Aramaic.

"I need to find more information," he thought. He scribbled himself a note, but his mind gave in to his stomach as the aroma of food floated in from the kitchen.

Miyah handed him a glass of cranberry juice as he entered the kitchen.

"Thanks," Michael said as he pulled his chair up to the table. "Today was pretty intense. It's funny how I begin to worry about that boy just as if he were my own child. It was really hard to see him ride out across that desert, not knowing what was ahead of him. The only thing that gave me some peace is knowing he does eventually return to his home safely. I know. I've seen him with Maryum.

"I'm trying to figure out what this journey was about. Issa told me a lot about his studying with other religious teachers, the Essenes, Jain and Hindu priests, Buddhist lamas, and of his mission. He says he has to teach the world. He's an ambitious one, that boy. He also started to tell me about hiding some of his personal writings with other manuscripts. He said they would be important in the future. I didn't find out more because someone interrupted us, but he was very secretive about it. Do you think now is the future he was talking about?"

"Now you're getting it," Miyah said. "And yes, this is definitely the time he meant. Information is being revealed to you in pieces because it would be too much to receive all at one time. Take notes. You'll want to remember all the details."

They talked about Michael's adventure while they ate their meal, with Michael giving Miyah a detailed description of the temple and of his clothing exchange with Ahmad, which brought a laugh from both of them.

"And Issa was right when he said Jagannath's chariot was a giant. I saw it being pulled through the crowded marketplace by hundreds of people. It was over 45 feet tall with 16 wheels, each at least seven feet in diameter. It's a wonder no one gets killed during the festival. . ." Then, pondering his last statement, he added, "I suppose that's why they were searching for Issa on that day. It would have been a perfect cover-up—crushed by that massive crowd."

Miyah patted his hand as she got up to get some tea. Michael noticed she had placed the stone he had carried with him next to his plate on the table. Picking it up, he said, "I was so happy to have this stone with me. Is that what brought me back at just the right time?"

Miyah thought for a moment before she answered. "The stone is what gave you focus and intention, but it isn't what brought you back. I do want you to keep this stone with you, though. Consider it a talisman to always remember how fortunate you've been in your own healing. And as I said before, you can use it to think of me as an affirmation that I'm holding you safe while you journey."

"Well, it certainly worked today," Michael said as he turned it over between his thumb and forefinger.

"It looks a lot like a smaller version of the large stone you had me hold when I was sick. Where did it come from?"

"It's not an ordinary stone," Miyah told him. "Look closely and see the crystal specks embedded into the surface."

"It's covered with them," Michael said, as he held the stone up to the light, making the crystal-like specks sparkle in their own reflection.

"Each of those specks represent a person who has been healed by a woman of the bloodline," Miyah noted. "A stone like this has been given to every person who has been healed."

"But that would be thousands," he replied.

"We've had a lot of time to work on it," Miyah smiled.

"Just what is the endless source of these stones? Where do you find them?" he asked.

"Well, that's a more difficult question to answer," Miyah said. "I guess you could say it's magic. I've never questioned it. When it's time, I simply reach into my medicine bag and retrieve a stone."

"That must be some heavy bag," Michael teased.

"I like that you understand that not all things have answers in my world. Thank you for that."

"And just how many stones have you given out?" he questioned.

"I've never counted," she answered.

"Have these patients all worked with the cedar box, too?" Michael asked, almost jealous that he may not be the only one.

"Some, yes, but not in the way you have," she told him. "Usually if someone was sent back into ancient times, it was to receive healings for specific illnesses. When they returned they had no recollection of their journey."

"You mean they got to work with the cedar box without making you a promise in return?" he asked. "Why was I different?"

"You, like Issa, have a mission. You've been chosen to spread the word to people of the world. Be patient. . ."

"Yeah, yeah, all will be revealed to me in time," he interrupted. "I know, I know. "

"Well, yes," she replied. "And thank you for understanding. Now, I don't know about you, but I'm tired. I'm going to take a hot bath and go to bed. I suggest you get some sleep too."

"Do you want me to help with the dishes first?" he asked.

"No, they'll wait until morning. Just help me clear them," she responded.

"Is the cedar box still in my room?" he asked, as he stacked their dishes.

"No, I've removed it. You'll sleep soundly tonight."

"It's funny," Michael said. "I already have a love/hate relationship with that box. Sometimes I can hardly wait to be absorbed into its mysterious theatre. Yet other times I'm afraid to even be around it, fearing it'll suck me in and I'll never return."

"I keep telling you that you'll always return," Miyah responded. "Perhaps when you fully trust that, you'll be more relaxed when you're traveling. Just knowing you won't be harmed, that you'll always come back and I'll always be waiting here for you, should give you a different outlook on situations while you're in these foreign lands. It's all about faith, Michael. You must learn to have faith. . .for many reasons."

"Yes, I'll try to remember that the next time a vicious warrior is standing over me with a spear," he laughed. "And then I'll have the stone to give me courage, as you said." He flipped it into the air and caught it, grasping it firmly in his fist. "Maybe I could have it made into a necklace so I wouldn't worry about losing it."

"That would be a good idea," Miyah agreed. "Especially if you keep giving away your clothes! Leave it with me and I'll do that for you."

Michael walked over and placed the stone in her hand. "Take good care of this—my Faith Stone," he said, and he bent down and gently kissed her on the forehead.

"What was that for?" Miyah blushed.

"Why. . .I really don't know. I just had the urge," Michael responded, a bit embarrassed. "It, it just felt natural–a thank you for all you've done for me, even though I sometimes wonder if this is really happening or if I'm going mad. Either way, it's the most exciting time I've had in my life and I'm grateful for that—no matter what the outcome." He stood there for a few moments, just looking at Miyah, until it seemed awkward.

"I. . .I think I'll go to my study and type out some notes," he quietly said as he made his exit. "I have a lot of notes to make. . ."

"Good night, Michael," Miyah responded, watching him back out of the room. Surprised at her own emotions, she quickly turned and busied herself with cleaning up the kitchen. Working with her patients in the past had been so routine. She knew her work with Michael was different, a turning point for the Touchstone of her bloodline, but she hadn't stopped to think how it may involve her.

She fingered the smooth outline of the healing stone, Michael's "Faith Stone," and a smile slowly spread across her face.

9 Elizabeth's Curse

Miyah returned to her house to pack some clothes and a few personal items. She hadn't realized this job would take so much time and was not prepared for an extended visit. Both Michael and Elizabeth insisted she stay with them until Michael's healing sessions were complete.

Elizabeth cleaned out the spare room for Miyah. The room hadn't been used as a guest room for many years and had become more of a storage room for old memories. While packing up odds and ends into boxes bound for the attic, she came across an old photo album of when she and Michael were children. It was a scrapbook of happy days when their parents were alive and life was an endless day of play and togetherness. She sat on the bed and turned page after page of old photographs, grateful her mother had taken time to assemble their lives in such order. Her fingers outlined her mother's handwriting beneath each picture and Elizabeth couldn't hold back her tears. Tears for the loss of her childhood, her parents and of the difficulties life had dealt to her. . .and to Michael.

Michael heard her sobbing as he came down the hallway and at first hesitated, wondering if he should intrude on her, but his brotherly compassion took over and he sat on the bed next to her, putting his arm around her.

"Lizzy, Lizzy, what's the matter?"

Elizabeth looked up at him, wiping her tears. "You haven't called me Lizzy in a long time. . .Mikey," she said. They both smiled in recognition of their pet sibling names.

"I know," he said. "What's happened to us?" And after a short pause he added, "You know how much I love you, don't you? You're my little sister and you'll always be important to me. I'm sorry I snapped at you and sometimes acted ungrateful. There's no excuse for that. Please forgive me."

Elizabeth put her arms around Michael and gave him a lingering hug. "I've missed you," she said. "I can see you're nearly well. It truly is a miracle. I've missed the old Michael. Have you come back to me?"

"Yes, I believe I have," he responded. "I really hadn't thought about it, but now that you mention it, I think I have. I know I still have some recovering to do, but honestly, Sis, I haven't felt this good in months—maybe even years. Whatever the medicine Miyah has brought to me is, it's miraculous."

". . .and do I sense a bit of attraction on your part, too?" Elizabeth teased.

"I don't know what you're talking about," he quickly replied. "She's a powerful healer and I'm finding I have a lot to learn from her. She's also a good teacher. . .and she's a good listener. . .and. . ." His voice trailed off.

"Nevertheless, thank you for bringing her here. I would be dead without your intervention."

"I think you should thank Robert for that. He's the one who suggested her. He seemed to know all about her," Elizabeth replied. "I thought it very kind of him to help me in praying to 'attract' her, being he knew you didn't even like him." Elizabeth watched Michael for his reaction.

"Yes, I suppose I should be grateful to him. But I still don't like him. I don't know why. There's just something about him that didn't sit well with me. And it isn't because he's interested in my little sister here. I really do want you to be happy, Lizzy. I just didn't think Robert was the right person for you."

Elizabeth pulled away. "Well, you certainly ruined that brotherly moment," she said coldly, closing the photo album and tossing it on top of the bureau. "I was hoping you would feel differently, because I'm seeing Robert again and I'm planning on spending a lot of time with him. I ask that you act civil toward him when he's here."

"What do you mean, when he's here?"

"This is my house too, Michael. Mom and Dad left it to both of us. I have just as much right to have Robert visit me, even stay overnight if I want him to, as you do having Miyah here, even if it's for different reasons. I have rights too." She walked away.

Michael followed her down the hall. "Yes you do. I'm only thinking about you, Lizzy."

"Who I see is not your decision, Michael. It's mine," she retorted.

"Do me a favor then and give me advance warning when he's going to be here so I can make myself invisible. I'd rather not see him."

"I'd rather he not see you either and know what an ungrateful S.O.B. you are. Maybe he shouldn't have sent for Miyah at all. Then where would you be?" Elizabeth slammed the door to her bedroom and threw herself on the bed.

"Why does he have to be so difficult?" she asked herself. "Why can't everything just be easy?" She decided not to tell Michael that Robert was coming by later to pick her up and they were going away for the weekend.

"It's none of his business."

~~~~~

Miyah could sense the tension in the air the minute she walked through the door. She brought groceries into the kitchen, put some of them away and arranged a fresh bouquet of flowers on the table. Looking around she didn't see Michael or Elizabeth. She instinctively knew that something had transpired between them. Not wanting to interfere, she brought her suitcase to the guest room and unpacked. She didn't bring a lot, just enough to get her through the next few days. She hadn't been in the guest room before and was happy to see it had its own bathroom. She so loved her evening bath—a time to relax, meditate and read her diary.

On the bureau was a note, scrawled hurriedly from Elizabeth.

"Robert is coming by later to pick me up. We're going away for the weekend. Michael and I had words. He doesn't need to know." Elizabeth

Miyah held the note in her hand and wondered if it had been wise to encourage Elizabeth to re-connect with Robert. Why hadn't she foreseen what problems this would cause? Why hadn't she picked up on the shortcomings in Robert's character? For some reason she knew this was all playing out exactly the way it was supposed to, but still, she wondered what the outcome would be. Who is this mysterious man and what was the real reason he wanted Miyah to come to this house? She knew Robert and Michael despised each other, so really didn't think it was, as Elizabeth thought, to heal Michael. There was more to it. She knew she must be cautious around him and said a quick prayer for guidance.

Heading downstairs to finish putting groceries away and prepare something to eat, she noticed Michael in his library with the door partially closed. Choosing not to disturb him, she closed the door to the kitchen and began chopping fresh vegetables. Neither Elizabeth nor Michael had much interest in cooking, so they welcomed her presence in the kitchen. Before she came, most of their meals were from a can, boxed dinner, frozen package or take-out.

Miyah had always prepared meals for herself as if she were a special guest, right down to cloth napkins, candles and a pretty centerpiece. She enjoyed it and why not? Why not treat herself as she would any other dinner guest? She made preparing the meal as much of the experience as eating it and enjoyed every moment. Tonight she was making a big spinach salad with grated carrots, fresh avocado, cucumbers, sliced red grapes, apples and Mandarin oranges, topped with soy nuts and goat cheese. Fresh asparagus and sliced tomatoes, broiled with a thin slice of mozzarella cheese would be served on the side. That's it. Just a jolt of vegetables and fruit. . .her favorite foods. Part of Michael's healing process was also in the food she had been preparing for him. He admitted he was a bit reluctant to try some of her concoctions, like seaweed soup, but he was game for everything. He never complained, rather praised her cooking. Elizabeth as well said she had never felt so healthy and had much more energy as a result of all of the fresh food in the refrigerator.

Miyah was so involved in her food preparation that she hadn't heard the kitchen door swing open. She turned around, startled to see Robert leaning against the door frame staring at her.

"What are you doing here?" she responded, wiping her hands on her apron. "How long have you been here?"

"Long enough to see you enjoy being in the kitchen. What was that tune you were humming?" he asked.

"Where is Elizabeth?" Miyah responded, not answering his question.

Looking past him, she could see that Elizabeth and Michael were in the study, in a full-blown, heated argument, resuming their conversation from earlier that day. Her suitcase sat in the hallway near the door. Michael walked over and shut the study door to help drown out their voices.

"You seem to already know, but let me introduce myself. I'm Robert," the man said. "Liz's boyfriend."

"Yes, I know who you are," she replied, deciding to take this opportunity to quiz Robert about his intentions with Elizabeth, and also to avoid them overhearing Michael and Elizabeth's booming conversation.

"So, how did you meet Elizabeth, and how long have you two known each other?"

"You get right to the point, don't you," he replied. "Not that it's any of your business, but I met her at the library. It seems we both made frequent trips to the land of books and knowledge, and that we also enjoyed the same books. I find Elizabeth a very attractive and interesting woman. I also think she deserves a life of her own, away from her overpowering brother. It would do wonders for her."

"Oh, you don't care for Michael? Then why did you suggest I come here to heal him? " she asked.

"I didn't do it for Michael. I did it for Elizabeth. She was so worried about him, and besides, she would never leave him if he was sick."

"And if he had died?" Miyah questioned.

"Well, that would be another story now, wouldn't it," he replied. "But he didn't die and he looks like he's well on his way to recovery, thanks to you."

"How did you know about me?" Miyah pressed him further.

"Your name just keeps coming up. I was losing patients because of you."

"What do you mean?"

"I'm a therapist and when four of my patients canceled their appointments and didn't reschedule, I got curious and contacted them. Three of them had been visited by you and were miraculously healed. So of course, I asked questions about you."

"And what happened to the fourth person?" Miyah asked.

"Oh. He committed suicide. You can't fix them all," he casually stated.

Miyah wondered what kind of therapist would make a flippant remark like that.

"Elizabeth tells me you have worked wonders with your book of potions." Looking around the kitchen, he added, "Where do you keep your magic kit? Can I see it? You ought to patent it. You'd make millions."

Miyah had all she could do to hold her composure. "First of all, if that's what you think, you don't know anything about me. Second, Elizabeth couldn't have told you anything about what I do, because she hasn't been around when our healings were in session. So I'd like to know where you've gotten your information. Why does it matter to you? Or is that why you've seduced Elizabeth, so you could get a closer look at my work?"

Miyah could feel her blood pressure rising, and took a slow, deep breath to calm down. She seldom got riled up, but could see right through Robert's intentions and it made her blood boil. Especially the part about him using Elizabeth to get to her.

"You're even more beautiful when you're angry," Robert replied. "Smart and beautiful. No wonder Michael wants to keep you around. You and your magic tricks."

Miyah's impulse to slap him was stopped when the study door suddenly opened and Elizabeth bolted into the kitchen.

"Come, Robert, let's get out of here," she shouted. "Miyah, I'll come back for the rest of my clothes in a few days. I'm not staying here with that man any longer. He's selfish and pious. He's no longer any relation to me. I hate him! I don't ever want to see him again."

"Elizabeth, you don't mean that," Miyah tried to soothe her.

"Yes I do!" she shot back. "He can go to hell for all I care. I curse the day I called you. He'd be dead and I'd be free."

With that Elizabeth tugged at Robert's arm and pulled him out the door, grabbing her suitcase on the way. Robert seemed reluctant to go, as if he didn't have all he came for. He grabbed a carrot from the counter, waved it at Miyah and with a cocky smile, said, "I'll be seeing you. Aabracadabra!"

Miyah wanted to throw something at him or at least kick him in the pants on the way out the door, but she knew it would do no good. Her concern was for Elizabeth. After the way Robert had spoken to Miyah, she knew he didn't love Elizabeth. He was using her as a pawn in some great scheme. But what was it? What did he know about the cedar box and the power of the diary? She would have to consult with Nona and Junia to see if the Touchstone was in danger. But now she walked to the door and watched Robert and Elizabeth drive off. She wondered when she would see her again and how Robert would play off of her emotions. Michael stood next to her. She had no words for him. She just put her hand on his shoulder to let him know she understood. He shrugged and went back into the study, closing the door.

10   Return to the East

Little was said about Elizabeth after that. Both Michael and Miyah harbored large doses of guilt. Miyah for suggesting Elizabeth get back in touch with her old boyfriend before knowing anything about him, and Michael for feeling he had driven her away while trying to protect her.

"You were acting out of love," Miyah said to console him.

"You can't know everything," he said to console her.

There was nothing else to say. Miyah prayed for Elizabeth's safety and well-being and asked Nona to watch over her. Michael retreated to his room for two days and wanted to be left alone. He hoped his only sister would come back one day and reconcile. He thought about trying to find where she was, but at this point, knew she wouldn't see him. "Just wait it out," he told himself, as he sunk deeper into depression. "She'll come home."

Miyah respected Michael's privacy for those two days, putting trays of food outside his door, but on the third day she couldn't bear it any longer. She burst into his room, drew back the curtains to let the sunlight in and settled a cup of tea on the nightstand.

"Either you're coming out of this room today or I'm leaving. I can do no good to you on the other side of the door. Get up, take a shower and come down to breakfast, or shut the door and feel sorry for yourself. It's your choice." She headed toward the kitchen to cook breakfast.

Miyah was sitting down to eat when Michael slipped into his chair at the table.

"I'm sorry," he said. "I just didn't expect this. I know I need to put it behind me and trust she'll be safe. It's just hard."

"Yes, it is," Miyah replied. "It's hard for everyone. But that doesn't mean you shut down and close yourself off. You need to move on, Michael. Your cancer is nearly gone. You're getting stronger every day, but you still have a long way to go. Again, you have choices. You can choose to move ahead, continue working with the cedar box or shut yourself in and possibly face a relapse with your self pity. What will it be?" She set a plate of scrambled eggs, wheat toast and sausage in front of him.

Michael knew she was purposely being tough on him. He also knew she was right. He slowly picked up his fork and began to eat. That was a first step. They finished their breakfast in silence, washed and dried the dishes together and put them away. Then Miyah suggested they go into the garden and continue their sessions. It was a beautiful, sunny day and she couldn't bear to stay inside.

"You could use the fresh air after these days of being shut in," she commented.

"You're right. I know," he gave in. "I hope I have the strength to journey today. I've missed it. It's interesting that no matter how emotionally or physically weak I feel in this world, I'm stronger and completely fit on the other side. I guess I should think about getting off my ass and start a workout program."

"I think that's a good idea," Miyah laughed. "You'll feel better once you get some muscle back on those bones."

Michael looked at his thin physique reflected on the glass of the patio door.

"You'd never guess I was a star athlete at one time in my life. . ." he sighed. "I'm going to take a shower and I'll meet you out back."

Miyah gathered her medicine bag and headed outside to set up a comfortable spot on the garden patio. Her chair faced the sun so she could soak in the rays and observe Michael while he journeyed back into the unknown. Michael came out dressed in a casual sweater, jeans and tennis shoes, and settled into a soft cushioned lawn chair in the shade. Miyah covered him with a light blanket. There were no close neighbors and the patio garden was closed in with a tall fence to keep deer and rabbits out when there was a vegetable garden. The yard was also fortified by giant oak trees so they had plenty of privacy. When Michael's parents built the house years ago, they had expected the area to turn into a large housing development, so they also purchased the adjoining lots on each side and in the back to keep their seclusion. They fenced the entire property and landscaped it for minimum maintenance. The property looked as beautiful as the park across the street.

Miyah pulled a small, round table next to Michael's chair and began her ritual of unwrapping the cedar box and placing it next to him.

"I just wish I knew where I was going to end up each time," Michael said.

"Remember, I'm holding your energy, so you need not be afraid. You must look at it as an adventure. Where's your sense of daring, your Indiana Jones wild spirit? You must find it and embrace it! Do you realize how lucky you are to have these opportunities to receive these teachings? This has never happened before. Ever," she stressed.

"Oh, one more thing." Miyah reached into her pocket and brought out a familiar stone, which now had a small drilled hole with an attached chain. She put it around his neck.

"Here's your Faith Stone. I thought you'd like to keep it with you."

"Boy, does this bring back memories!" he said. "Thank you for making it into a necklace. I'm sure it'll be a source of strength for me while I'm gone."

She nodded and sat back into her chair.

"I have music going through my head today, so I'm going to hum a song my mother used to sing. It'll also help to relax you, being we're doing this outside in a different atmosphere than we're used to. I hope you don't mind."

"That's fine," he replied, closing his eyes, listening to the sounds of nature around him.

Miyah began to hum, but the smell of cedar quickly overtook Michael's senses and he didn't hear her sweet melody for very long. It was as if his spirit was anxious after all these days to travel—to re-connect with an old friend.

Michael saw figures moving on the panel of the box, but there were no palm trees and desert sands. This time he disappeared into a fog of rolling hills, framed by tall, snow-capped mountains.

He immediately felt the chill of the air and was grateful that the blanket Miyah had tucked around him was still intact. He wrapped it over his shoulders like a cape and looked around to evaluate his environment. He didn't see any roads or main trails. To his right was a river with a wide, rocky beach and to his left was a tall hill. Part way up the hillside he noticed a cave in the barren landscape. After walking down river about five minutes, he saw a smaller cave. Just as he was deciding if he should attempt to climb up and explore, he saw what he thought was a familiar figure appear from the shadows of the cave. Waving his arms to attract attention, Michael called out, "Joshua, Issa. . .down here."

The man quickly disappeared back into the cave. Wondering if he had mistaken the man for Joshua, Michael looked around for a safe place in case he would need to retreat quickly. But, soon another man appeared and shouted down to him, waving his arms in a welcoming gesture.

"Michael! I didn't expect to see you. Come up. Be careful, there are lose rocks. Climb over this way," he directed Michael to a pathway that had less vegetation and many of the rocks had already tumbled away. Michael climbed and was breathless when he reached the cave opening. He sat on a boulder to catch his breath, wiping sweat from his face with the blanket.

"Aw, you are enjoying the spectacular view of the Himalayas," Joshua said as he clapped Michael on the back. "And the sacred Ganges River below. It is breathtaking, is it not?"

"The Himalayas!" Michael exclaimed. "Where are we?"

"Oh, we are still in India, northern India, about an hour up-river from Rishikesh. These caves have been known to yogis for centuries."

Michael looked around. Joshua was right. Set in the side of this sheer cliff on the banks of the Ganga, the cave had a spectacular view of the river and the surrounding peaks of the Himalayas.

"Come in. Come in," Joshua motioned. Michael followed him inside the cave. It was not very deep and a single torch provided light inside, casting eerie shadows on the rock wall surface. The man Michael had first seen from below nodded politely and walked past him, settling himself on a large boulder outside the cave as if he were a guardian.

"What are you doing here?" Michael asked. "Are you in hiding?"

"Oh, no," Joshua said. "I am here to concentrate on yogic practices. The first cave up river is called Vashishta Guha cave, made famous by the ancient sage, Vashishta. The yogis there have invited me to stay and meditate with them. This is one of many sacred places in India."

He continued, "I've been to the holy city of Hardwar and also lived in

Benares for a time since I saw you last. It is the spiritual heart of India, dedicated to the worship of Shiva, and is the major center in all of India for Vedic learning and spiritual philosophy."

"Shiva?" Michael questioned. "I still don't understand why you're so interested in all these different religious studies."

"I keep telling you, I am preparing myself for a return to my homeland," Joshua replied. "How can I become a great teacher if I have limited knowledge? By studying the ancient wisdom of great teachers of many traditions, including the Buddhist and Hindu dharmas, I will be better equipped to share my awareness with others. These teachings all honor the same God, but mark my words, people will reject that. They will be fearful of what is unfamiliar to them. Of course, you already know that. You have the advantage of knowing both past and future."

Michael shrugged. "I don't know if I would call it an advantage."

"Remember when we first met and I told you of what you termed time travel? This is where I learned how to do such things, from the Masters here in India."

Joshua continued. "I have been aware of the purpose of my life since a young age, but it is my Indian teachers who have made everything clear to me regarding my life. I know what my life's purpose is and how it will play out in the eyes of the world. I know there will be many untruths told until the real truths are made known. There will be many wars fought over the name of religion. That saddens me. But I can make a physical contribution while I am here. Knowledge that comes through education is, and always will be, the only way to set people free from what burdens them. It is the only way to achieve peace and balance."

"But what religion are you?" Michael asked.

"Love is the only pure religion, Michael. There is no real name for my spirituality as yet. I was raised Jewish, but *my* religion is to establish love, truth and purity of heart in the world. God is not remote from us at some mystically infinite distance, but rather is inside each one of us. We should be inspired to lead our lives in harmony with the Infinite—to recognize our existence here on earth as a part of the whole, in oneness."

He paused. "Here I am preaching to you again. But do you understand what I am saying to you?"

Michael looked at Joshua earnestly. He could see this young man had grown and matured since he saw him last in Puri.

"I don't know who you are, Joshua, or do I call you Issa? I don't know who you will become. But I do know that you are a man with integrity and honesty and that you are marked for greatness. I'm proud to have met you."

"You can call me Joshua if that is easier. And, Michael, my friend, you know me better than you think," Joshua answered, with a laugh, walking out of the cave into the sunlight. "You have known me all your life."

"What do you mean?" Michael questioned.

"You will see. . ." Joshua answered as he motioned for Michael to join him on the cliff. Michael followed, eager to see where this intriguing conversation was leading, and glad to feel the warmth of the sun on his body.

~~~~~

Michael suddenly bolted upright as the echoing sound of ferocious, barking dogs brought him out of his trance. He instinctively reached for the Faith Stone around his neck and as he yanked it, the chain broke and the stone fell to the ground.

"What?" he said, looking around. "Where am I?"

Miyah waited a few seconds for him to gather his wit. She was afraid this sudden jolt on this end of his journey could affect him in a negative way, and wanted him to get his bearings first. He looked at her and said in confusion, "Miyah?"

"Yes, Michael," she responded. "I'm sorry you landed back here that way. It sounds like there's a dog fight in the park across the street. Perhaps I should have given you earplugs. Are you OK?"

"I guess so," he replied. "But I wasn't ready to come back. It was such a short time. We were in a cave in the Himalayas and Joshua was just saying that I knew him better than I thought. I was going to ask him what he meant and those damn dogs started barking."

Michael reached down to collect his necklace.

"Here, let me have that," Miyah said.

"I'm sorry," Michael replied. "I guess I must have really jerked at it when I awoke. I didn't mean for it to break. I hope that's not a bad omen."

"No, it's not," Miyah assured him. "It's just a bad clasp. I can easily fix it. Let's go inside. If you want to continue we can go to your study."

"Yes, I would like that. You mean I get to travel twice today? I must really have a lot of lessons to learn. But let me get a jacket. If I go back there, I don't want to be shivering my teeth out. I'll meet you in the study in half an hour." He gave a longing look at the cedar box on the table. "Don't forget your tools."

"Oh don't worry," Miyah said, as she collected the cedar box into her medicine bag. "You don't have to remind me of that."

Michael went into the bathroom and splashed his face with water. He looked into the mirror and was surprised to see how healthy he suddenly looked. His face was thin, but he had a rosy glow to him that was a good sign. He would never scoff at the word "miracle," as he was living proof. In just a short time, Miyah had transformed his physical and mental body to health. He had something to look forward to each day—his lessons with Joshua. He was impatient with himself for losing two days moping around in his room over Elizabeth's departure. He grabbed his jacket off the hook in the hallway and headed to his study.

Miyah arrived with a tray of sandwiches, sliced vegetables and some ice tea. "I know you probably aren't hungry, but you need to keep up your strength. And," she added, "I've filled up your flask with water in case you need it. It should probably be returned to its era anyhow."

"Why?" he asked. "I was hoping to keep it as a souvenir. I did exchange it for my pajamas, if you remember?" he chuckled.

"Yes, I know," Miyah replied. "But I should tell you that things that are brought back from the past have a short 'shelf life.' They only last a few days, sometimes only a few hours and then poof, they're gone. I think it's a protective feature."

"Protective of what?" he asked.

"Not everyone who has traveled back has been as honest as they should have been," Miyah said. "Many years ago someone brought rare coins back, hoping to sell them and make his fortune. He made a deal, collected his money and when the recipient went to view his treasure, there was nothing. Unfortunately, the man met an untimely demise. Our initial efforts to heal him were wasted. That's why people are carefully screened now—why only a select few are allowed into the veil of the past."

"So I was screened?" Michael questioned, biting into a sandwich.

"No, Michael," Miyah said, looking directly into his eyes. "You were chosen. Shall we begin?"

Michael slipped into his jacket and got comfortable on the leather sofa. Miyah placed the cedar box next to him on the lamp table and sat down at the desk with her diary in hand.

"So what happens if I leave things on my journey?" Michael was curious. "Does that mean my pajamas disappeared on Ahmad?"

"Well, that's a good question. A lot of it has to do with intent. If you're bringing or giving something with good intention, that will not alter the course of the world or harm others and your gift is given in respect, then it's probably going to be OK. But if you take something back with any kind of malice in mind, such as a dangerous weapon, you won't get very far. . .and your lessons will end abruptly."

"Who makes those decisions?" Michael asked.

"Does it matter? Just use your best judgement, Michael. Keep it simple."

He dug into his jacket pockets and dumped out the contents on the table. A matchbook, some change, a pen and grocery receipt, a pocket knife and car keys. He left the car keys and coins and shoved the rest back into his pocket.

"Tools," he said. "They might come in handy."

Miyah handed him the water flask. "Be sure to drink plenty of water."

Michael settled back into his chair and closed his eyes as Miyah began again to hum her hauntingly melody. Soon the cedar box grabbed onto Michael and he was lost into its spell.

~ ~ ~ ~ ~

Michael stood on a hill overlooking a beautiful valley of running streams. The countryside was covered with red roses, violets and narcissus growing in fields along with sweet-scented herbs. In the village below, the gates, walls, courtyards and roofs were rimmed with torches of tulips. In the distance, mountains with snow-capped peaks and glaciers rose over the valley like guardians of their treasure. The air was chilled and Michael could tell by his breathing that he was at a very high altitude.

"These are my people," a voice from behind him said, startling Michael. He turned around to see a much older Joshua, bearded, with long, untidy hair.

"Joshua!" Michael exclaimed. "I'm always so glad to see you!"

The two men shook hands. "You look good, my friend," Joshua commented. "It has been many years since we met last."

The time thing was always confusing to Michael because in his mind, he had just been with Joshua an hour ago. Obviously, in Joshua's time, many years had passed. He looked older. Wiser.

"Where have you been, old friend?" Michael inquired.

"Well, let's see," Joshua thought a moment. "Since we last met I've been many places. I spent six years studying with Buddhist monks in a monastery in Kapilavastu, Nepal, and traveled to Tibet for further studies. Now I am here in Kashmir. I will continue through Persia on my way back home."

"Six years!" Michael exclaimed.

"Actually it has been more than that," Joshua corrected. "I have been traveling for many years, learning and also teaching. It has been a most beneficial journey. I was always aware of the purpose of my life, but as I told you before, it has been these Masters who made everything clear to me regarding this purpose. I carry their kind teachings in my heart."

"Is that what you mean when you said these are your people?" Michael asked.

"Oh, no. I meant the people in this area," he said, pointing to the village and beyond. "They are what you call the Lost Tribes of Israel."

"Here? In Kashmir?" Michael replied. "Why are they here, so far from their homeland?"

"Oh, you don't know your Bible stories very well, do you Michael?" Joshua teased.

"Of the Twelve Tribes of Israel, named for the twelve sons of Jacob, only two remained in Palestine—those of Judah and Israel. Some of the tribes who were cast out migrated eastward toward Afghanistan, Iraq, Kashmir and India. Many markings of their heritage can be found in their food, their songs, dress, customs and language. This was their Promise Land."

"The Promise Land," Michael repeated. "Kashmir?"

"Yes. In Hebrew the word kasher, kashir, or your English pronunciation, kosher, means 'approval.' Kashmiris call their country Kashir, and its inhabitants Kashur."

Joshua continued, "Kashmir is known among the local Muslim population as Bagh-i-Suleiman, the Garden of Solomon. See over there," he pointed, "on the mountain overlooking the city. That small temple is called Takht-i-Suleiman, the Throne of Solomon. . .King Solomon, son of David."

"So you can make connections of the Israelites settling here through similarities in their names and also through references with King Solomon," Michael understood. "Didn't the Silk Road trading route also pass through this region?"

"Yes, the spice route. There are thousands of rock inscriptions in this area, many written in Hebrew. It's been documented by many, including an identification society in London, that the Kashmiri population is of Israelite descent. Hundreds of names of geographical features, towns, regions and estates, as well as of tribes, clans, families and individuals in the Old Testament can be attached with similar names in Kashmir. I know I am jumping time tenses here, but I do have a pretty good handle on the future. Your time."

Joshua laughed as he thought of how confusing much of this must sound to Michael. But Michael was following him pretty well.

"There must also be similar customs," he wondered as he pulled the pen and grocery list out of his pocket. He turned the paper over and began to take notes, making a mental note to start carrying a notebook with him.

"Yes, of course," Joshua was pleased to answer. "Their way of life, behavior, morals, character, clothing, language and habits are all described as typically Israelite. Like Israelis, the Kahmiris use only oil and no fat for frying and baking. They like boiled fish, called *fari*, eaten in remembrance of the time before their exodus from Egypt. Butcher knives are made in the half-moon shape, typical of the Israelites, and even the rudders on the boats on Dal Lake are of the same heart shape. You'll find that men wear distinctive caps on their heads and the clothing of the older women is similar to that of Jewish women. The women also wear headscarves and laces. Like young Jewish girls, the girls of Kashmir dance in two facing columns with linked arms, moving together forward and backward to the rhythm of their songs, which are called *rof*."

He continued, "As in Jewish custom, a woman of Kashmir observes forty days seclusion for purification after bearing a child. And here's an important connection," he added. "Many older graves in Kashmir are aligned in an east-west direction in the Jewish tradition, whereas Islamic graves normally point north-south. Some graves are inscribed in Hebrew. There are many signs. Too many to mention. Just know that this is a truth and this place is very special. You will come back to this country at another time and learn more about my life here."

"I look forward to that and thank you for pointing all of this out to me. I'll have to do some research when I return home. I had no idea there were biblical links to Kashmir, or even to India. I guess I never gave it a second thought when I read things in the Bible that said 'from the East.' It does add an entire other dimension to religious studies. I can understand now why you're traveling through this land and getting to understand the people. I'm forever in awe of you, Joshua, and your commitment to knowledge."

"Come, I want to show you one more thing before you go back," Joshua said. "It is a distance away so we are going to energy travel. Hold on to my arm and close your eyes. Sometimes the light can be blinding."

Michael grinned. He completely trusted Joshua, and besides, hadn't he been doing just that as he crossed dimensions to Joshua's world—energy traveling? He linked arms with Joshua. Even with his eyes closed he could see an intense light through his eyelids. He had the sensation of movement, yet knew his feet weren't moving. It was different from his transformation between future and past. He was moving in the same time period, simply changing locations. He liked this mode of transportation. It certainly beat the high cost of gasoline.

"You can open your eyes now," Joshua said. "We are close, but I'd like to walk so we can talk more. Over there is Mount Nebo and the Plains of Moab."

Michael looked in the direction Joshua pointed.

"Do you know of Moab?" Joshua asked.

"I've heard of it. Moab. I know it's talked about in the Bible, but can't really recall why. Tell me," he requested.

"Ah, the Bible verse you may be referring to is Deuteronomy 34. *'So Moses the servant of the Lord died there in the land of Moab, according to the word of the Lord. And they buried him in a valley in the land of Moab, over against Beth-peor.'"*

"Are you saying this is where Moses is buried?" Michael exclaimed.

"Let's walk," Joshua simply replied.

The two men climbed westward along a barely traceable path for nearly an hour. The mountain's shape and vegetation reminded Michael of the hills he had hiked as a boy. He was enjoying the exercise.

They stopped for a rest and Michael pulled the water vessel out from under his jacket.

"I think I'm supposed to return this," he said after he took a sip of refreshing water. He handed the bag to Joshua.

"Thank you," Joshua replied, taking a drink. "I can use this on my travels."

Michael offered Joshua the matches and jackknife also, but, turning the knife over in his hands and admiring it, Joshua admitted it might be more of a burden than an asset, being neither had been invented yet.

They continued their walk on a path that crossed several fields before finally reaching the small hamlet of Buth, directly beneath the barren plateau of Mount Nebo. They hiked to an area above the village that resembled an unfenced garden which contained a small, wooden, cabin-like shrine.

"This hut is the tomb of an Islamic saint, Sang Bibi, a female recluse, and two of her followers," Joshua said. "And that stone column in the shadow of the wooden building, is the tombstone of Moses. The *rishis* have been reverently tending the grave for more than 2,700 years."

"This is it?" exclaimed Michael. "No big religious shrine, no fanfare, not even a plaque?"

"None needed," Joshua replied. "There are also other places that honor Moses in this land: The Springs of Moses, The Place of Moses, The Cornerstone of Moses, where he rested. On the riverbank south of Srinagar, is Moses' Bath-place. There is also a magic stone called Ka-Ka-Bal or Sang-i-Musa, Stone of Moses. They say that stone rises by itself and remains suspended if twelve people, representing twelve tribes of Israel, touch it with one finger while chanting the magic spell 'Ka-ka, ka-ka.'

"There are many references to Moses in this land. In your current time there is a restored basilica on Mount Nebo, in the village of Siyagha, with mosaic floors and monastery rooms. It was originally built in honor of Moses and serves as a memorial to him, a sanctuary where there is unity and a symbol of hope among Christians, Moslems and Jews. From that site you get a bird's-eye view of the Holy Land and the southern Jordan Valley. You can see a panorama of the Dead Sea and the desert of Judah to the south, and the mountains of Judea and Samaria to the west. On a clear day you can see Bethlehem, the towers and buildings of Jerusalem and the Mount of Olives."

"Wait a minute," Michael said. "What country is this?"

"Jordan," Joshua answered as the two men stood looking over the valley.

Just then the *wali rishi*, the official guardian of the tomb, approached the two men, waving his arms in the air.

"What are you doing here?" he shouted looking at Michael's unusual dress. "You should not be here without my supervision. I am the protector of the tomb and you did not ask permission to step on this holy ground." The man took his position as guardian serious and was upset that these two trespassers had slipped by him.

"I am sorry," Joshua said, putting his hands together as if in prayer, and bowing to the man. "We meant no harm. We will leave."

The man turned and pointed down the hill. "You must go now!"

"Come Michael, take my arm," Joshua said quietly, and as he did so, the two men disappeared into thin air. The elderly guardian turned back to where the men had stood and saw no one. He rubbed his eyes to clear his vision and shook his head. He walked over to see if the men were hiding somewhere and to check the site to be sure nothing had been damaged. Seeing nothing, he returned to his station on the hillside, mumbling as he went.

~~~~~

Michael awoke slowly and was disappointed to find himself back on his sofa in the library of his home. Miyah was sitting at the desk watching him as he returned to his world.

"That seemed to be a gentle transition," she said.

"Yes, it was a very educational journey. I'm never certain why things are revealed to me, but know there's always a good reason."

He stood to take his jacket off and his pen and grocery list fell out of the pocket.

"Ha," he laughed, as he picked them up and looked at the notes he had made. "I guess this is my answer. Joshua suggested I do some research. You know, Miyah, I always thought I was a pretty educated guy. But I feel like a child who is just learning to speak, or walk or think. I've read and studied a lot in my lifetime and now I wonder if I really absorbed much of it at all. I had Bible studies in church when I was a kid and thought I was an average religion student. But I really don't know anything. Oh, by the way, did I tell you I was just in Kashmir? Yes, Kashmir. . .and Jordan! And Joshua was showing me where the Lost Tribes of Israel settled after their exodus from Egypt. He said it was their Promise Land. Kashmir! I had no idea. Hell, I don't even know anything about Kashmir, except that it's part of India and borders China, Pakistan and Afghanistan. Why would Joshua even want me to research the Israelites in Kashmir? For what purpose?" he babbled on.

"That's a good question," Miyah responded. "One you can only answer by following Joshua's suggestion and doing some research. And, I might add, I think you'll really enjoy it. You probably noticed that I brought a box of some of my favorite books the other day. It gave me something familiar to read while you were closed off in your bedroom. I think you'll find a lot of information in them as well."

"I suppose I better get to work." Michael gazed at the rows of books on the shelves in the room and at the pile of books Miyah referred to. He reached over and turned on his computer.

"Do you know how fortunate we are to have these resources so readily available at our fingertips?" he asked, eager to dig in. "I don't quite know where to begin. . ."

"Let me know if you need my help," Miyah said as she left the room. "I'm going to brew a pot tea."

11 Revelations

Miyah brewed a pot of tea and brought it to Michael in his library.

"I'll be in my room if you need help," she said.

"Thanks," Michael replied, without looking up. He was still trying to figure out why Joshua wanted him to research Kashmir and the Israelite connection. He began to sort through the collection of books Miyah gave him.

She went to her room and closed the door, knowing that what Michael was about to discover would be the beginning of new revelations for him. Even though he may not put all the pieces together right now, he would be building a foundation for future writings that were important to not only him, but to the destiny of the Touchstone.

Miyah thought a dose of positive energy might be needed, so she gathered a handful of high vibrational stones from her bag. She cleared a corner on her bedroom floor and carefully placed each stone to form a circle—white for peace and tranquility, green for love and money, red for passion and to avoid arguments, orange for luck, yellow for wisdom and lessons, brown for possessions and gifts, and black to avoid negativity.

Once the seven stones had been arranged in a circle, she fixed the clasp on Michael's necklace and placed it in the center of the stones. Miyah then placed rune stones atop each stone of the circle. A rune stone to accomplish impossible deeds was placed on the orange stone. A rune for possession of tangible objects stacked atop the brown stone. The black stone balanced a rune for protection. A rune representing healing was placed on the white stone and the rune stone representing love was put in place over the green stone. The yellow stone, representing wisdom and lessons needed some powerful energy, and on this Miyah gently placed a clear crystal for clarity and knowledge. She looked at the remaining stone—the red stone for passion and arguments. She stacked the rune of comfort on top as she thought of Elizabeth's actions earlier in the week. These added amulets would strengthen the power of the spell and empower the necklace with those specific energies. The circle would need to remain unbroken with the stones in place for at least 24 hours for them to work their magic, sending strong, positive vibrations into the necklace.

Miyah lit a candle and placed it in the circle of stones, next to the necklace. She quietly chanted words of wisdom, evoking the stones to do their work.

~~~~~

Michael had been busy for hours, typing notes relating to the similarities in the Israelite and Kashmiri names. He cross-referenced everything, reading out loud as he wrote – "In an area on the border of Pakistan, called Yusmarg

(Handwara), is a group which to this day calls itself B'nei Israel, meaning children of Israel. Many of the inhabitants of Kashmir say this is the ancient name of all the people of Kashmir. Events of Kashmir have established, without a trace of doubt, that the origins of the Kashmiri people are to be found in the people of Israel.

". . .one of the tribes of Kashmir is called Asheriya, which in Israel, is Asher; the tribe of Dand is Dan; Gadha is Gad; Lavi is Levi; The Tribe of Shaul is the Hebrew name of King Saul; Musa is Moses; Suliamanish is Solomon.

"There is the tribe of Israel, the tribe of *Abri* which is the tribe of *Hebrew,* and the tribe of *Kahana* which is the word for Jewish *priest.*

"I see how the tribes can be identified in Kashmir," Michael mumbled. "It's interesting, but why am I copying this stuff?" He questioned himself.

Then he came across something that pretty much blew him away.

"Christ!" he exclaimed, calling out for Miyah.

"Come down here and look at this," he yelled upstairs.

"What is it?" Miyah asked as she responded to his call.

"Christ," he repeated, pointing to a passage in a book that was originally published in 1894.

"In Kashmir it is a believed that ***Jesus did not die on the cross,*** but in his search for the Lost Tribes of Israel, he reached the Kashmir Valley and lived there until his death and was over 100-years-old. His grave is at a place called Rozabal on Khanyar Street in Srinagar, Kashmir!"

Michael sat down on the chair by his desk. He stared at Miyah.

"Do you suppose this is what Joshua was leading me to discover? That Jesus didn't die on the cross? That Jesus lived in Kashmir and eventually died there? This is revolutionary information. You know that don't you?"

"Yes, I know," Miyah replied.

"But of course, you do know all of this. You knew exactly what he was getting at. That's why you brought all of these books for me to research. Why couldn't you just tell me and save me some work?"

"Some things are better discovered yourself," she stated. "There's more for you to uncover. Keep researching and you'll find a lot of sources to reference. It adds an entirely new dimension to religion, Michael, and one that's not easy to swallow. Read for yourself, go as deep as you can. Use the internet if you don't want to trust my source books. Do whatever you wish, but read carefully. This is very important to all of us. . .and don't believe everything you read. Cross reference everything!"

Michael was a step ahead of her with his hands on his computer keyboard, Googling his book findings. "Wow!" he exclaimed. "A search through the search engine about Jesus in Kashmir came up with a few *hundred thousand* websites on the topic! How could *everyone* not know this?"

"Looks like you have your work cut out for you," Miyah responded.

"Do you realize that establishing facts about Jesus living—and dying—in

Kashmir could generate a huge influx of visitors to Kashmir? The numbers of tourist traffic there would go into the millions," Michael calculated. "Not to mention the political and religious complications."

His excitement was escalating. "Look at this!" he pointed, as he began to read. "This pertains to the missing years of Jesus between ages 12 and about 30. It says he visited Kashmir, India and Tibet during those years. Joshua must have met him in his travels. That's why he told me about the Lost Tribes of Israel in Kashmir. I would guess that to connect Jesus to Kashmir, the first step was to show Kashmir's connection to the Israelites. . .this is amazing!"

Miyah sat and watched Michael. He was like a child with new toys and she knew he was just beginning. She wanted him to find as much as he could on his own before he came to her for answers or for verification. It was important he knew that much research had already been done over many years on the life of Jesus, beyond the original Roman Church version of the story, and that what he was about to discover was not meant to diminish anyone's belief in religion. It would enhance it. For that reason, she needed Michael to come to his own conclusions first, based on his own discoveries.

"Look here Miyah!" Michael couldn't contain himself. "It also says that he went to Kashmir to trace the Israelites, who had been exiled by the Assyrians in the years 722-721 BC, and to connect with the Ten Tribes of the northern Kingdom of Israel who had been dispersed all over the world after the destruction of the Second Temple by Romans."

Michael scrolled down the page. "There's documentation of his travels, recorded in a Tibetan manuscript in Ladakh, in a famous Buddhist monastery called the Hemis Monastery. It says the originals were compiled in the old Indian language of Pali, during the first two centuries AD and kept in the monastery, which was affiliated with the Potala Palace of the Dalai Lama." Michael stopped.

"There's more to Jesus's teachings and healing work than the mere three or four years recorded in the Bible. He was even greater than you can imagine," Miyah said. "Not in a power-driven, dogmatic way, but as a true healer, a prophet of prophets, a gentle role model for peace and love. The simplicity of his pure existence is more powerful than any church. Can you imagine how many lives he must have touched in a positive way, living to be over a hundred-years-old?"

Michael sat back in his chair to collect his thoughts.

"But why. . .why would the early Church write that he died on the cross? Why would they make that up?"

"Remember, Michael, the Christian Bible wasn't compiled until around three hundred years after the crucifixion. Mark, Matthew, Luke and John were written between AD 60-110 and the early Church councils, mainly the First Council of Nicea, changed much of the doctrine in AD 325. The

Romans wanted a way to control people. What better way than through religion? Incorporate old pagan beliefs into a mold that can be sculpted to fit your desires. 'He died for your SINS,' meaning you are not worthy, you are tainted, you were born bad, evil, a sinner, but the Church can save you, if you believe them. 'We offer the *only* way you can be saved because Jesus died for your sins. . .and this gave us, HIS Church, the power to save you.' Does that sound familiar? Somehow the teachings of love and peace that Jesus preached got mixed up with a fear-based Church that the Romans molded to suit their own power-controlling needs. I know it sounds harsh, but you'll discover this for yourself as you dig into the beginnings of early Christianity."

Miyah added, "Don't get me wrong, Michael. I'm not saying religion is bad. Not at all. I'm a firm believer in God. I'm just urging you to study the history of the Church and come to your own conclusions as to what you wish to believe. I don't know what your religious upbringing and background is. For me, the pure teachings of Jesus—peace, love, kindness, sharing, respect and gratitude are my Church, and that wins out over dogma any day."

"Wow," Michael replied. "It just seems quite unusual for someone who can trace her bloodline all the way back to biblical times, to speak out against the Church like this. I'm a bit taken aback by it."

"I'm not speaking out against the institution of Church, Michael. I believe the spirit of community a church offers for its congregation is important. And there are many churches that speak more of the positive aspects of Jesus' life, honoring his miracles and healings, stressing the values of living a pure life. There are many churches whose mission is to help the poor and support and uplift others. But, there are also many who use the life of Jesus as a monetary tool and a means for power and control.

"Have you been to the Vatican? The entire complex, from the museum and vaults below the ground, to the building and the altars themselves, drip with riches—gold, silver, jewels—while there are people starving on the streets outside, begging for food so their families can merely survive. What good are all the riches in the world, if it does not serve all the people? Is one person better than the next? Is the priest better than the pauper? The injustice of it all, especially in today's world, is something I can't understand. It certainly isn't anything Jesus would have tolerated. He championed the poor and challenged the wealthy. How do you think he would react to the wealth of some of our churches today? I'm grateful the Vatican protects precious art and artifacts, but there is much to be disclosed about the sources of their wealth—the Vatican Bank, and other Vatican-affiliated banks, share in big industry and corporations, stock and bond holdings and even ties with the mafia. A lot of these things are coming to the surface now, and it's not a pretty picture. I'm not picking on Catholicism. There are many religious branches that are multi-million dollar businesses. It's the core business practices and ethics of those in higher ranks of the Church that bother me. The true message of Jesus is overshadowed."

"I didn't mean to get you so riled up," Michael said. "I see this is a very serious subject for you."

"It's very serious. The corruption began a long time ago. Vatican wealth wasn't built in a day. Its roots began in the early fourth century when the Roman Emperor Constantine converted to Christianity and gave a huge amount of riches to the Pope. In 1929, Mussolini's Lateran Treaty gave the Roman Catholic Church privileges and protection. Both the regime and the Church benefited financially. Vatican Incorporated is a business."

Michael piped in, "I know the Vatican is a Sovereign State, has their own law as an independent state and is exempt from paying taxes for properties, investments and citizens. They don't pay duty on imported goods either. I seem to remember reading something a long time ago about their ties to Hitler. Something about taxing German wages. . ."

"Yes," Miyah said. "It's called the Kirchensteuer, the Church Tax—a state income tax, eight to ten percent, deducted from all wage-earners in Germany. I believe it still exists and the only way people can avoid paying is by denouncing their religion. The tax was given to Protestant and Catholic Churches, but the Vatican received a substantial amount, especially before, during and even after World War II—100 million dollars in 1943.

"Cardinal Pacelli was the Vatican's Secretary of State at the time and he sealed a treaty with Nazi Germany. When he became Pope Pius XII, he declined to excommunicate either Hitler or Mussolini. Imagine that—a person could be excommunicated for divorcing, but not for murder and shocking crimes against humanity! There is much injustice in the power of the Church."

Michael thought it might be a good time to lighten the conversation.

"If it makes you feel better, the church I attended as a young boy was an old, wooden building, quite humble, and the congregation and preacher always helped each other and the poor in one way or another. My dad was a volunteer maintenance man there, which meant, among other chores, my sister and I got roped into helping polish the pews and wood floors, which he waxed two or three times a year. My mom made all the angel wings and costumes for the Christmas pageants and other decorations needed for events. I don't recall seeing any jewels in that church. . .except maybe my folks. I hope there are still churches like that out there. . . there must be."

Michael paused. "As we got older our family stopped going to church. I haven't really thought this deeply about religion before."

Miyah apologized. "I'm sorry. I didn't mean to preach to you. I just got carried away. It's very complicated."

"Yes, I'm beginning to see that," Michael said.

Miyah got her second wind. "To complicate your studies even more, you should know that there were as many as <u>29 savior-gods before Jesus</u> – some real, some mythical, and they all had a common story—virgin birth, born in a cave or stable, were healers, overcome by evil powers, slain, arose from the dead, founded religious institutions, expected to make a second coming.

"Christian doctrine can even be traced to incorporate pre-Christian beliefs that were common during the time of Jesus. Beliefs that were popular with people were used by followers, such as Paul, to create an updated version of an ancient theme for the purpose of converting people to the new religion.

"I would like you to look up 'Mithros' or 'Mithra.' It's the religion, a pagan belief system, that a large majority of people were following around the time of Jesus. I think you'll have a better understanding of where many of our biblical writings stem from, including crucifixion. It may also help you to understand that even though I'm connected by my bloodline back to the time of the very core of religion, I prefer to say I am a spiritual person, rather than a religious one."

Michael appreciated Miyah's revelations. He made a note . . .Mithros, Mithra.

Unable to resist, Miyah added, "Just to give you a brief summary—the religion of Mithra preceded Christianity by roughly six hundred years. Mithraic worship, at one time, covered a large portion of the world and flourished as late as the second century. The Messianic idea originated in ancient Persia and this is where the Jewish and Christian concepts of a Savior came from.

"And listen to this. . .Mithra, the sun god of ancient Persia, had the exact same life as Jesus—all the way from the virgin birth to being crucified on a cross. The Orthodox Christian hierarchy is nearly identical to the Mithraic version: rituals, communion wafer, water baptism, the altar and liturgy were adopted from Mithra and earlier pagan mystery religions. I know you'll find it interesting and it'll give you a better understanding of what was going on during the lifetime of Joshua. I think you'll have a lot of questions for him the next time you meet."

Michael underlined the word Mithros on the note he had made.

"Well, Joshua did steer me in this direction for one reason or another, so it looks like I had better get busy," Michael said. "Do we have any coffee? I think I'll need large doses of caffeine. Looks like a long night ahead of me."

"I'll brew some. . .but don't expect me to stay up with you," Miyah said. "I'm looking forward to a hot bath and a good night's sleep. Don't stay up too late. You need your rest. You have much to do and need a sharp mind."

"How do you expect me to sleep at all with what I've just discovered? I need details, facts. . .I need answers! I'm expecting you to fill in a lot of the blanks, so you go and enjoy your bath and a peaceful night's sleep. I'll be grilling you in the morning. Isn't that why you're still here after all?"

"Yes, I suppose you're right," Miyah responded. "Coffee it is."

She quietly placed a carafe of coffee on a tray next to Michael before retreating upstairs. Michael, his desk already buried in a pile of opened, bookmarked books and notes, was absorbed in his research. The light from his computer screen illuminated his face, as his fingers flew over the keyboard, stopping only to grab the pencil out of his mouth now and then to jot down another fact on his notebook.

"This is amazing," he mumbled. "I can't believe it! The cave I met Joshua in is called the Jesus Cave! Joshua is leading me on a path that follows the footsteps of Jesus through the East. This is incredible! I need to go back. . .I need to talk with Joshua, I have so many questions.

"I need a system," he muttered. "I need to organize this information so I can access it easily. I need a system. . ."

He was obsessed.

~~~~~

After a long relaxing bath, Miyah snuggled into the fluffy comforter warming her bed. She propped the pillows up behind her, took her diary from the medicine bag and hugged it to her chest. She had never shown its contents to anyone, and hadn't intended to do so until the day came when she would read it to her own daughter, teaching her all the details of the family's legacy. But she knew there was information she may have to share with Michael. Even if he discovered most of the story himself through his research over the next few days, there would still be pieces of the puzzle she may have to put in place—information written in the pages of the diary centuries ago by the women who lived in that time.

She carefully turned the pages until she came to the passages she wanted to read. It was written by a distraught woman, recounting events.

> — Information was obtained by Nicodemus in the high court and he secretly sent a letter to me. The letter was meant to warn Yeshua about a planned attack on him when he traveled to Ephraim. We discussed this at length and I begged him not to complete these travels. I could not bear the thought of what would happen to my beloved.

Words had been underlined and notes were scribbled in the margin of the diary by someone much later in time to help understand some of the details.

Joseph of Arimathea — Both Yosef and Nicodemus have told us that a trial has already been laid out for the third hour on the day before the Sabbath, which will result in crucifixion. They had tried to sabotage the orders, but sadly confessed that it could not be averted, so they have conceived a plan to avoid the plot from ending in the death of our Master. They would not tell me nor any family members or the disciples of this plan, lest it be foiled. I must trust them, as they have both been good confidants to us. Yosef, Yeshua's Uncle, is highly respected as a member of the Sanhedrin - the 70 member high council of the supreme Jewish authorities for all affairs of state, judicature and religion. Nicodemus is a Jewish Councilor and some time ago was secretly initiated by Yeshua under cover of night. I must say nothing to the others. I pray for the safety of my husband, the father of my daughter and of the child yet in my womb.

Pages of the next entry had wrinkles and water stains that had remained folded within the diary over the years. The entry was unusually graphic as if the woman wanted to preserve exact details as a record. Miyah emotionally read. . .

— The pain I bear is as if I were being stoned and lashed upon myself. What have they done to my beloved? How could this be? My heart has been torn from my chest and stomped upon. I must remain strong for Yeshua's mother and for the others, but I do not know how I, myself, can survive Yeshua's torment. They have tortured him with whips and metal scourges. They mocked him, forcing him to carry a *patibulum* and paraded him through the streets. He walked past the Sheep Gate and the pools of Bethesda and just outside the city wall, when he started downhill into the white stone and dust of the Kidron Valley, toward the hill of *Golgatha*, he faltered and collapsed. Simon, a Jew who

patibulum- crossbeam of at least 70 pounds

Golgatha- Skull's Place in Aramaic

Cyrene-
North
Africa

nails from <u>Cyrene</u> picked up the patibulum and carried it the rest of the way. Soldiers dragged Yeshua to his feet and pushed him along, up the Kirdon's eastern slope. Many crosses clustered across this hillside as signs of the daily torture performed by the Romans. It is brutal.

- At Golgatha, the soldiers stripped Yeshua naked and laid him on his back. They held him down and at the sixth hour they took a heavy, oak mallet and drove nails through his wrists and into the patibulum. Then Yeshua, on the patibulum, was hoisted onto a thick upright post that was sunk deep into the ground. The notched post and patibulum were lashed together with a thick, flax rope. Soldiers held his sagging body against the cross so his weight would not rip his wrists away from the nails and they hoisted up his legs and pounded long, iron spikes through the tops of his feet into the post. His feet were just inches above the ground and if not for the spikes holding him there, he could have stretched out his limbs and stood to relieve his pain. I fell to my knees and cried out in agony for Yeshua. He was silent in his pain.

- Close to the ninth hour, a captain named Longinus raised a sponge of <u>vinegar</u> <u>water</u> and hyssop to the lips of Yeshua, from a bowl left at the base of the cross. That being the only kindness shown, as hyssop is used in rites of purification. I quivered with Mariam and Yeshua's sister Ruth, as we observed this tragedy. My own daughter, Sera, was being cared for away from the city, to protect her from this brutal day. The unborn child I carry in my womb must also be protected and I am grateful that few others know of my condition.

vinager
- wine

Abba be with us all in this time of great injustice. . .and not let my faith in Yosef and Nicodemus waver.

The next entries were not as legible. The writer began to journal and then crossed out her words and began anew. This happened several times, until the attempt to put words to the events that were unfolding around her were abandoned or somehow disrupted. Two pages were also left blank, as if the writer had planned on leaving space to come back when she was less distraught to fill in her notes. Then it was simply written:

— "Yeshua was pronounced dead at the ninth hour."

. . . a thin line was drawn to the bottom of the page, as if the pen had slipped and trailed off the paper.

Miyah knew that during ancient times among Jews, a day was counted from sunrise, so the third hour (trial) would be 9 a.m., the sixth hour (crucifixion) was 12 noon and the ninth hour (supposed death), 3 p.m.

Throughout the diary there were notes made in the margins to clarify many of the ancient names and ways. Miyah was grateful for these notes, which also added another personal element to the beauty of the diary, with several different handwriting styles. She turned the page and translated the next entries, which were almost written matter of factly.

— It is the day before the Sabbath and the day of preparation for the Passover, which begins the 14th day of Nisan - the time of the full moon of Nisan. Bodies should not remain on the cross on the Sabbath, a high day, so a sense of urgency prevails to remove bodies of Jewish men before Shabbat, so Jewish law will not be broken. Men on their crosses who were still living, had their legs mercilessly broken by soldiers. Removing the support a man had from his lower body causes him to sink downward, crushing his lungs with his ribcage, so he could die quickly and be taken away. But when the soldiers came to Yeshua, the captain, Longinus, said he was already dead, so they did not break his legs. Instead, a soldier pierced his side to see if Yeshua was truly dead and receiving no reaction from the body, except blood from the wound, they

left him there.

— Yosef had requested to take Yeshua's body down from the cross and planned to place him in his family tomb, which had recently been completed. We mournfully assisted him with this task and took Yeshua away. A portion of wood from the crossbeam, the nails, the crown of thorns and proclamation written by Pontius Pilate were also collected and brought with the body. Because Jewish custom does not allow burial rites to be performed on Saturday, we did not place the body in the tomb of Yosef, as many had expected, but instead in a place hidden away, not far from the tomb. A large stone was rolled in front of the tomb to seal it so no one would know it was empty.

The character of the next writing had changed to a seemingly bolder penmanship. Miyah continued to read, translating the Aramaic paragraphs.

— In my sorrow and anger, I could not place my eyes upon either Yosef nor Nicodemus. I faulted them for failing to save Yeshua. The other disciples had gone into hiding for fear of persecution themselves, but I could not leave my Master. In Traditional Jewish Law the body is not to be touched, except by giving it a ritual bath, a Takara, for purity.

— Embalming, or the use of spices, is not a part of our Jewish custom. The body is traditionally put into the ground or tomb in the quickest way, with only customary burial shrouds. Therefore, my heart began to beat wildly when I saw Nicodemus go to Yeshua that same night and bring with him a mixture of a hundred pounds of myrrh and aloes. I peered through the door as he began to apply these herbs. I entered the room and questioned him, and since we were among no others who could hear, Yosef and Nicodemus' plot was revealed to me. They thought if they managed to take Yeshua down from the cross early enough, and everything was well planned, it would be possible to keep him alive.

— "Why," Nicodemus asked, "do you think that after only three hours Yeshua appeared to have died, when it usually takes two or three days for a man to die in this fashion?" He informed me that many men have survived their ordeal on the cross and lived to breathe another day. I was too numb to understand what Nicodemus was telling me.

— He explained that while on the cross, Yeshua was in shock with low blood pressure from his torture and from a blow to his head, which earlier had caused him to collapse while he carried the patibulum. He lost consciousness because of little blood supply to the brain. His ashen skin and motionless body gave the appearance of his death to bystanders, including myself. The vinegar water given to him contained not only hyssop, but also was laced with opium, which is widely used here, and a mixture of herbs to be sure Yeshua would remain unconscious. The opium was also for pain. The captain who kept Yeshua's legs from being broken, and who also gave him the vinegar, was Longinus, a secret follower of Yeshua, who assisted Yosef and Nicodemus in their plans.

— When Yeshua was taken down from the cross and laid on the ground, circulation to his brain was restored. A darkening of the sun occurred at the ninth hour overshadowing the land and putting a great chill in the air. This coldness helped to maintain Yeshua's blood pressure.

— I could not believe my ears and rushed

eclipse

to the side of my beloved, who still had the appearance of lifelessness, but as I put my head onto his chest, I could hear his slight breathing and I rejoiced with all my heart!

— I proceeded to assist Nicodemus in bathing the body clean of the blood and filth from his ordeal and together we applied olive oil, myrrh and aloes to heal the wounds.

— Yeshua remained unconscious, but was alive so we were not breaking any Jewish laws. He no longer needed burial preparation. We wound his body loosely in linen clothes so the wrapping would not be soaked in blood and seeping fluids. I stayed with Yeshua all of the night, raising water to his lips, tending to his wounds and praying for his healing.

— Yosef returned toward morning and told me it was of the utmost importance that I do not share this joyous news with anyone until after we were certain of his recovery. He said it would be devastating, especially to his mother, if she thought her son was alive, and then did not, after all, recover from his injuries. I knew how difficult it would be to play the role of a mourning wife after what I just discovered, but I vowed my silence. They plan to take Yeshua away as soon as he is able, so he can heal properly and can continue his mission, unobserved by those who would harm him again. Praise these men — Yosef, Nicodemus and Longinus for their devotion to Yeshua.

Miyah marked her page. Because she felt such sadness and agony each time she read these pages, she had avoided them for many years. Perhaps that is why they were written in such detail. It was important to the writer for those who followed to have a true sense of what Yeshua and his family and followers experienced. It may also have helped to ease the woman's anguish as she carefully put her story to paper.

— Because we did not want to come under

suspicion of the Romans, I was careful to keep our secret by continuing the role of a widowed woman. On the first day of the week, when it was lawful to do so, I went to the tomb in pretense to prepare Yeshua's body for burial. I am grateful that Mariam, his mother, did not have to participate in this ritual. In Hebrew tradition, the duty of anointing the body for burial is reserved for the wife, unless he died unmarried, then it is the duty of his mother. I was joined by Miriam of Yaagov and Shalome, who also brought spices, but would not participate in the actual preparation. The sun was dawning and Shalome asked who would roll the boulder away so we could enter. But when we arrived, two men dressed in white robes, were standing by the tomb. The stone had already been moved. I recognized these two men as Yeshua's Essene teachers and knew they must be a part of Yosef's plan to save Yeshua. The Essenes are well known for their knowledge of herbs and healing. We entered the tomb and to the disbelief of the two women, it was empty.

 — "Why are you here looking for a living person at a burial site?" the men asked, referring to the fact that Yeshua was still alive. But Shalome and Miriam did not understand their words, and ran out of the tomb in fear.

Miyah laid her diary aside, got up and stretched. She hadn't realized how late it was. She felt chilled as she got out from under her warm comforter and reached for her robe. She checked the candle in her ring of stones to be sure it was out and went into the hallway. Seeing the light in the library, she tiptoed down the steps and saw that Michael had fallen asleep, his head resting on a pile of books on his desk. Miyah took a blanket from the couch and placed it over his shoulders. She shut the light off in the library and went back to her room to read one more diary entry before retiring for the night. Miyah opened the book to one short sentence. . .

 — Yeshua lives! My Yeshua lives!

12   The Awakening

When Miyah went downstairs the next morning, Michael was already working.

"Good morning," she said, "You're up early."

"Oh, I was up before the sun," he cheerily replied. "I can't believe I even fell asleep. This is all so incredibly revealing." He made a wide sweep of his hand over dozens of books with little pieces of pink and yellow sticky papers sticking out of them to mark passages he wanted to record. He could barely wait for Miyah to awaken so he could share his findings with her. He had to talk to someone or he would burst.

"Thank you for bringing these books to me for references. It's absolutely amazing to find that the escape of Jesus from death on the cross is so well documented as a common theme. It's in Christian and Muslim scriptures, old medical and historical books, including ancient Buddhist records. Evidence is also provided about his journey to India in search of the Lost Tribes of Israel *after* the crucifixion!"

Michael almost tumbled over his words. "Did you know that scholars have known for years that all Bible translations are based on the same Catholic version issued by the early popes of Rome? Some scholars have even refused to accept the content of the Bible for this reason alone. And, get this, by the third century AD, there were more than 25 different versions of Jesus' death and resurrection and most of these have him *not* dying on the cross! There's nothing about an ascension in the original texts. That was added later, around AD 200. The concept of him 'coming again' simply meant that he was going away, traveling, and would return to his homeland. The 'second coming' phenomenon was added later, and only as a Christian idea. It didn't appear in any other religion's transcripts. Do you know what all of this means? This truth would destroy the basis for organized religion, or at least diminish their fortunes!"

Miyah quickly replied, "No. The real truth does not make Christianity any less significant. In fact, it could strengthen the ties that lead to the original purpose of Jesus' message—love and peace. And just as important, it could be the base that unites all religions, instead of fighting in the name of religious beliefs."

"Where did these books come from?" Michael asked. "Some of them are very old."

"Most of them have been in my family for many years," Miyah answered. "But some of them are fairly new. Our ancestors have been sending messages through selected people and working to get this knowledge out into the world for a long time. It's been done on a gradual level, a gentle awakening. It's happening in many aspects, through authors of spiritual books, revealing movies, modern prophets and other ways."

"Am I another of those proposed authors chosen to write another revealing book?" he asked, unsure of the answer.

"It's not just another revealing book. You have no idea how large your task is. Now is the time to gather all this information together and bring it forward. What you're doing is compiling the complete story, some of it from sources never revealed before, like information you're learning from traveling back into the past and. . ."

". . .and from your diary," he finished her sentence, gesturing to the book in her hands.

"Yes. I've never been asked to share passages from the diary with anyone before. It's a very sacred book. It holds extremely personal information about the history of my bloodline, written by the women themselves as events happened. Do you understand the importance of that? A personal journal through a time in history that has been riddled with speculation and false translations. If these secrets are meant to be revealed in this day and age, it must mark a religious milestone in our history. I can't begin to tell you how important that is."

"Does it frighten you?" he asked.

"No, it doesn't frighten me because I have complete faith in the wisdom of my ancestors and the spirits who continuously work behind the veil to heal this world and its people."

"It sounds like a spiritual revolution is coming," Michael said, only half serious.

"It isn't a revolution. It's an awakening," Miyah stated.

"But why me?" he asked. "Why have I been chosen to carry out this huge undertaking?"

"That I don't know. Perhaps it's because you've come into this completely unbiased. You've most likely questioned religious dogma as a youth and have had a lot of interest in other religions of the world. You seem to respect other religions and, although you believe in God, you don't favor any one belief system. You're a good writer with a curious mind and know how to research," she said as she pointed to his messy pile of books and papers. "And maybe, equally as important, because you're an honest, caring man. It's not for me to know why."

She continued, "When I first came here I thought it was only to heal you of your illness. Once that was established, I found that my job is now to keep you on task and lead you through your journey of discovery. I know I keep telling you this, Michael, but you must realize how honored you should be to have these opportunities to travel back into ancient times. Something important has to come out of this. Something significant."

"Do you think we're nearing what they call the 'end time?' I read that all truth would be revealed in the end time."

"If that's so, Michael, then these revelations need not challenge your faith, but rather strengthen it. I don't know what lies ahead. I just know what is necessary now and that we have a lot of work to do. So, first things first— I'm going in the kitchen to make breakfast," she said, with a slight wave of her hand. "You must have worked up an appetite with all your writing last night. I'll call you when breakfast is ready."

Michael noticed as she left the room that she had her medicine bag with her. That usually meant he was going to be off on another journey. He looked over his pile of work and for a brief moment, he wanted to stay in his study all day and keep up his fact-finding mission. But he knew it would still be there waiting for him when he returned. Anticipation mounted as he thought of all the questions he would have for Joshua when he saw him again.

"What a trip!" he thought, and dug back into his work to finish some notes before breakfast. Miyah was right. He was famished!

~ ~ ~ ~ ~

Michael brought his notes with him to breakfast and read fact after fact of what he had found. He was so overwhelmed by this new revelations and the many references to back it up, that he couldn't believe he hadn't known this before.

". . .but I never even thought to question the fact that Jesus may not have died on the cross," he told Miyah. "It never entered my mind to question it."

Miyah listened, pleased at his enthusiasm, but finally shooed him out of the kitchen, commanding him to get back to work. He took his coffee cup and settled back into the library. This study had always been Michael's favorite room in the house. There were long, oak-framed windows that went almost ceiling to floor, flooding the room with morning light. Rich, oak trim and bookcases accented the walls. Old, worn, Persian rugs covered large areas of the wooden floor. The room was masculine, but it also had a warm feeling to it. Perhaps Michael liked the room so much because it surrounded him with books that had belonged to his parents.

Both were quite scholarly and his father, an archeologist, spent a great deal of time in this room. His father commandeered the big, L-shaped, mahogany desk that took up a large portion of the room, but it was his mother's special touches that warmed the room. She had her own half of the room and filled her shelves with personal book preferences. Her favorite place to read was a large, linen-covered chair, where she could curl up with a soft afghan and get lost in her books. Next to the chair was an antique table with a curious, bronze giraffe/palm tree lamp she brought back from one of their travels to Africa. Michael remembers his dad telling the story over and over, of how difficult it was to get it home in their suitcase, teasing his mother in his animation. She would quickly add that once they got it home, he insisted it matched his desk better and tried to steal it away from her. She would laugh and say she kept it on her side of the room just to spite him.

His mother maintained a small, tidy desk in the opposite corner of the room and it is there she did her writing. She had authored several mystery novels and children's books and it was through her animated storytelling and use of words that Michael obtained an interest in becoming a writer. His talents had so far been limited to newspapers and magazine writing, but he had made quite a name for himself. . .until his bout with cancer. At first he had received letters and calls encouraging him to keep writing and offering wishes for his recovery, but as the year wore on, no one seemed to have missed his columns and articles anymore. Of course, it was Michael who stopped responding to any correspondence, wanting to be left alone in his misery. He always was a solitary person. The life of a writer can be lonely. Other than his sister Elizabeth, doctor appointments and hospital visits, he had little contact with the outside world. . .until Miyah entered the picture.

How things had changed so drastically in such a short time. Once in a while he received a card from an old colleague and wondered what they would think now if they knew of his miraculous recovery and of how his life had turned, yet he never responded to any of the correspondence. Sometimes he even wondered if he was just in a feverish state of delirium and none of this was really true. . .but then Miyah would enter the room and he knew that the light of the world had touched him and he was truly blessed. He was not only healed, he was in the middle of a mystery his mother would have been proud to pen. He wondered if the spirit of his mother was there looking over his shoulder, along with that of his archeologist father, guiding him in his research. Last night, as he scoured through mountains of material, he thought he could feel their presence. He even thought he could smell the faint aroma of his mother's perfume. God he missed them.

Michael sat down at his desk, his father's desk, and looked at the mass of notes and information he had accumulated in just a day. He was so excited about his findings that he hadn't taken time to organize a system and realized the subjects of his note-taking ranged from Bible verses and quotes from the Koran to portions of historic articles. Along with the entries he had written in his computer, he had stacks of details copied from books.

"I need to put everything in one place," he said to himself, as he grabbed a tablet with pages of scribbled notations off the pile. He then made several files in his computer: **JESUS, ISRAELITES, KASHMIR, JESUS IN INDIA, THE LOST TRIBES OF ISRAEL, CRUCIFIXION.** It was a good start. He wished he had done this the night before, because now he had to type all of the notes he made. He looked at one of his lists and started a file in bold letters:

CRUCIFIXION. Behind it he added a description from the dictionary:

"crucifixion kro s fik sh n - noun chiefly historical; the

execution of a person by nailing or binding them to a cross."

Michael began to type, numbering his notes.

1. There were many crucifixions of biblical time. A man was put on the cross and his hands and feet were nailed to it. It was possible that after a day or two, if the man was still alive, it was decided to forgive him and spare his life. The punishment already received was sufficient. If it was decided to kill him, he was kept on the cross and water or bread was not allowed. He was left in the sun for three or more days, then his bones were broken and he died.

2. According to Jewish custom it was unlawful and a punishable crime to let anyone remain on the cross on the Sabbath day, the feast Fasah of the Jews, or during the night previous to it. Jews observed the lunar calendar, sunset being regarded as beginning the day.

3. While Pontius Pilate presided at his court, his wife Claudia sent word to him not to have anything to do with Jesus. She had a dream that troubled her. Because of this vision, along with his own doubts, Pilate found a way to rescue Jesus: first, he fixed Friday for the crucifixion, only a few hours before sunset, the night of the Great Sabbath. Pilate knew the Jews, in accordance with the commandments of their law, could keep Jesus on the cross only until the evening and after that it was unlawful, so Jesus was taken down before evening. Thieves who were crucified at the same time as Jesus were still alive, but Jesus supposedly died within three hours. Soldiers broke the legs of the thieves to ensure death, but thinking Jesus had already died, they instead pierced his side and he bled. Blood, however, congeals after death, yet Jesus still bled, proving he was not dead. Saying Jesus was already dead was an excuse made up to save him from the process of leg breaking.

4. Among the testimonies of the gospels are words of Pilate himself, recorded by St. Mark: "And now when the event was come, because it was the preparation, that is the day before the Sabbath, Joseph of Arimathea, an honourable counsellor who also waited for the kingdom of God, went in boldly unto Pilate and craved the body of Jesus. And Pilate marvelled if he were already dead." This would show that at the time of the crucifixion, a doubt had been raised whether Jesus had in fact died so soon, and the doubt came from a person who knew from experience how long it took a person to die on the cross—Pontius Pilate.

5. Joseph of Arimathea was a friend of Pilate and a notable person. He was also an uncle and secret disciple of Jesus. He presented himself at the right time and the body of Jesus was given to him. Joseph was a big man and arriving at the scene he carried away Jesus as if he were a corpse.

6. Evidence of great value with regard to the escape of Jesus from the cross is a medical preparation known as Marham-i-Isa or the "Ointment of Jesus" recorded in hundreds of medical books. Some of these books were compiled by Christians, some texts by Magi of ancient Persia, by Jews and some by Muslims. Most of the texts are very old. Investigations show that in the beginning, the preparation was known as an oral tradition among hundreds of thousands of people before it was recorded. In the time of Jesus, shortly after the event of the cross, a pharmaceutical work was compiled in Latin with mention of this preparation, along with the statement that the medicine had been prepared for the wounds of Jesus. This work was translated into several languages, until, in the time of Mamun-al-Rashid, it was translated into Arabic. It is a result of divine intervention that eminent physicians of all religions—Christian, Jew, Magi and Muslim—have mentioned this preparation in their books and have stated it was prepared for Jesus by his disciples. A study of books on pharmacology shows this preparation is useful in cases of injuries due to blows or falls, arresting immediately the flow of blood, and as it also contains myrrh, the wound remains aseptic. The wounds of Jesus healed in a few days by the use of this ointment. Within three days he recovered sufficiently to be able to walk seventy miles on foot from Jerusalem to Galilee. *There are over 1,000 books that record this fact.*

7. Matthew, chapter 28, verses 7 to 10. These verses say the women who were told that Jesus was alive and was going to Galilee, were also told they should inform the disciples. They were pleased to hear this, but they went with a "terrified heart" (because they were afraid Jesus might be caught again.) The ninth verse says, that while these women were on their way to inform the disciples, Jesus met and saluted them. The tenth verse says that Jesus asked them not to be afraid, (i.e. of his being caught); he asked them to inform his brethren that they should all go to Galilee; that they would see him there, (i.e. he could not stay where he was for fear of being captured.)

8. According to the Bible: On Sunday morning Jesus first met Mary Magdalene, who at once informed the disciples that Jesus was alive, but they did not believe her. Then he was seen by two of the disciples who were going toward the village of Emmaus on the way to Galilee, which was 3.75 miles from Jerusalem. Jesus had planned to travel on, but they did not want him to go, saying they should be together that night. He then dined with the eleven disciples and during the meal he showed them his hands and feet which were wounded, and they thought he was a spirit. Then he said: "Behold my hands and my feet, that it is myself; handle me and see, for a spirit hath not flesh and bones, as ye see me have." He took boiled fish and a piece of honeycomb and ate in their presence. All of them spent the night at the village of Emmaus and he reprimanded them for their lack of faith.

9. **In spite of the fact** that accounts of the gospels differ, the texts clearly show that Jesus met his disciples in the mortal human body, showed his wounds to the disciples, dined with them, slept in their company and made a long journey on foot to Galilee, a distance of seventy miles from Jerusalem. Jesus himself showed his disciples the flesh and bones of his body, and had hunger and thirst—necessities of the mortal body. If he had been resurrected after death, how could his spirit body still have the wounds inflicted upon him on the cross? What need would he have to eat? Jesus fled secretly from the country to save his own life and asked his disciples not to tell others.

Michael started his next file and began to transfer notes into his computer, weeding through his scribbling and side notes, trying to put them in order. Miyah stood at the doorway with her diary in her hand, watching him. She didn't want to disturb his concentration, yet felt it was important for him to hear what some of the writings revealed. He had been working for several hours and she finally decided he might like a break.

"Do you have time for tea?" she asked.

Michael looked up from his work and let out a big sigh. He was reluctant, but, yes, he could use a break.

"Tea and a stretch would be good," he replied, getting up from his chair and following her to the sitting area near the window.

"I love the way the light bathes this room," Miyah said. "No wonder it's your favorite place in the house. It's becoming mine also."

"If you like, you may use my mother's desk. She insisted her desk be next to the window for that very reason. She loved the sunlight streaming through the windows."

"Thank you. That's kind of you," Miyah responded. "I may do that."

Michael did some stretching to get out the kinks from sitting too long at the computer and then sat down across from her in the large, leather chair. Taking his teacup in hand, he said, "I see you have your medicine bag with you. Does that mean I'm heading out for another adventure today?"

"I think your travels for today will be of a different nature," she replied. Before he could question her statement, she placed the diary on the coffee table between them. Her hand remained on the book as if to protect it.

"Do you mean you're actually going to show me pages of your diary?" he asked in amazement. "You know it's something I would never have asked to see, knowing how important it is to you."

"Yes, and I thank you for that. But because of all the information you've just discovered regarding the crucifixion and the continued life of Jesus, I thought you would like some verification of your facts."

"Only if you're sure you want to share it with me," he said softly.

"Yes, it's time," she said, and motioned for him to sit by her on the sofa.

He eagerly moved over and sat next to her.

"Before I open the diary, I want to tell you that it's written in many different languages. The passages I'm going to read to you are in Aramaic, and sometimes mixed with Hebrew. I'll be translating them into English as I read. But instead of just listening to me read, I want you to follow along, to see the handwriting. Notice where the ink flows smoothly and where it is heavy, sometimes with blotches, where the pen rested too long while the author thought, or pressed too hard in a moment of anguish or even anger. The soul of the diary is not just in the words. The story is also in how the words are written. There are smudges from healing oils and traces left from magical potions, even stains from tears. . .and blood. My heart beats within the pages of this book. If you listen to the sound of my voice, you'll hear the breath of the hundreds of women who have left their mark in this journal. The DNA of my family lives in this diary."

Michael was silent. Reverent.

Miyah placed her hands on the diary, like she had on the cedar box, and whispered a prayer of thankfulness before she opened the book. Michael leaned closer to get a better look at the pages. The writing was beautiful, sometimes flowing as she had said, and other times as if it were an effort to get the words on paper. The pages were yellowed and stained, but the ink did not seem faded on any of the pages he saw. Miyah carefully turned to a section she had marked. She began.

> —Information was obtained by Nicodemus in the high court and he secretly sent a letter to me. The letter was meant to warn Yeshua about a planned attack on him when he traveled to Ephraim…

The words looked foreign to Michael. "How can she read this so smoothly, as if it were written in English," he wondered. But he quickly vanished his own thoughts and was absorbed into the words Miyah was reading.

She read the same passages she had read to herself the previous night, feeling they gave some clarification to Michael's notes and not only verified his findings, but also made the events human—not just words recorded in history. Michael listened intently to the words as Miyah read page after page of diary entries.

> —The pain I bear is as if I were being stoned and lashed upon myself. What have they done to my beloved? How could this be? My heart has been torn from my chest and stomped upon.

Michael stared at the words on the page and it was as if he could see the drama unfold—like the scene on the side of the cedar box right before he traveled. It was as if the diary gathered him inside its pages and he was there with the writer. He could feel her pain and misery. . .and then her joy.

— I felt as a stranger in their eyes and asked where was their faith? I beseeched the disciples not to repeat my words to anyone, lest Yeshua's safety be endangered. Yet my joy could not be made less. . .Yeshua lives! My Yeshua lives!

They sat in silence for several minutes. Then Miyah read on.

—Yeshua's brother James did not join the other disciples in their resumption of fishing by the Sea of Galilee. He instead returned to Nazareth to tend his fields and be with his wife. As head of the family he is obligated to care for his mother and Yeshua's other brothers and sisters. It has been a very difficult time for them all, especially for his mother. She wept when she heard her son was alive and saw that his wounds were healed. She clung to him and did not want her first-born son to leave her sight again. But alas, he reminded her that he has a mission to accomplish and that she of all people, should understand his life's purpose. He sent her to her home in Nazareth to care for his siblings, telling her that when he was safe he would make arrangements for her to join him. I, too, cannot bear to release him, but he has reasoned with me that it is the only safe choice for both of us, for our daughter and for our unborn child. I am joyous he is alive and cherish our remaining time together, yet I am sorrowful that he must leave. I pray for the day we unite again.

There was a gap on the page, indicating a time lapse. Michael could see by the penmanship that the woman who wrote this was troubled.

— There is talk of more than 500 people who have seen Yeshua in Galilee and report that he is alive. It is becoming unsafe for him to remain in this place and plans are being made for us to travel to Egypt. We will be together and safe in the protection of the Essene community.

Miyah gently closed the diary.

"It's so beautiful," a somber Michael said. "I felt like I was right there with her. I could hear her breath. . ." he stammered. "I could feel her intense love for Yeshua."

"Yes," is all Miyah said.

"Her words also give me a better understanding of what you were saying earlier about faith and religion. There are so many layers. I know so little.

"Will you read more?" he asked. "I mean, is it possible for you to read more to me? What happened next?"

Miyah hesitated. "I can read more to you, but later. By revealing this now I wanted you to go about your research with a compassion for what unfolds in those notes and not just see them as mere facts on paper."

"I understand," he replied. "I do have a few questions though, about what you just read," he began. "I'm wondering why this is in your diary. I know you trace your roots back to that time period, but how does this relate to you?"

"Oh yes, I knew you would have a lot of questions," she quickly replied, avoiding a direct answer. "We'll have plenty of time for me to answer them. But not just now. I think you should finish organizing what you've already uncovered. I'm sure that will lead to even more questions. I know we'll have a lot to talk about."

"But. . ." he objected, having some very important things he needed clarified. He didn't finish his appeal, realizing she was finished and his curiosity would not be relieved today.

As Miyah got up to leave, Michael reached for her hand. He held it for a few seconds and tenderly said,

"Thank you. I want you to know I have the utmost respect for you. I mean it."

"You're welcome," she said quietly.

They looked at each other for an awkward second and then Miyah pulled her hand away, collected her diary and placed it safely inside the medicine bag.

Michael stood up and motioned toward the stack of books. "Well, I better get back to the books," he said shyly. "Yup, I better get to work."

He clumsily walked back to his desk. "Work. . . yes, more work."

13   The Lost Tribes

Michael knew he had to shake the thoughts that just went through his head. He didn't want to do anything that would compromise his relationship with Miyah. He meant it when he said he respected her. He looked at the mess on his desk and tried to concentrate. He grabbed another stack of notes to transfer into his computer files knowing it was important information that needed to be done while his mind was still fresh.

"Concentrate," he told himself. "Concentrate."

He tapped his pencil on the desk for a few minutes, wondering just what he would do with all these facts once they were compiled. The writing process had many stages. He knew the research was necessary but he couldn't help but wonder about the outcome. He weeded through the marked books and his written notes and slowly began transferring what he had read and cross-referenced into a semblance of order. He glanced at a stack of books he hadn't even opened yet, wondering what jewels he would discover beneath their covers. First things first, he reminded himself. One thing at a time.

He typed **KASHMIR** at the top of his page in bold letters and behind it added a dictionary description:

"Kashmir - ka sh mi r - a region on the northern border of India and in northeastern Pakistan. Formerly a state of India, it has been fought over by India and Pakistan since partition in 1947. The northwestern part is controlled by Pakistan, most of it forming the state of Azad Kashmir, while the remainder is incorporated into the Indian state of Jammu and Kashmir."

Checking the notes on his tablet he began a numbered list and consolidated facts from sources he found about Jesus in Kashmir:

1. **There are manuscripts**, such as the Qanun Bu Ali Sina, handwritten in the time of Jesus in the years after the crucifixion. These books are with Jews, Magi, Christians, Arabs, Persians, Greeks, Romans, Germans, and the French, as well as in the ancient libraries of other European countries and Asia. In Rauzat-us-Safa, a well-known book of history, there is an account in the Persian language which translated, says: "Jesus (on whom be peace) was named the Messiah because he was a great traveler. He wore a woolen scarf on his head, and a woolen cloak on his body. He had a stick in his hand and used to wander from city to city and country to country. At nightfall he would stay wherever he was. He ate jungle vegetables, drank jungle water and traveled on foot. During one of his travels his companions bought him a horse. He rode the horse one day but as he could not make any provision for the feeding of the horse, he returned it. Journeying from his country, he arrived at Nasibain, a place between Mosul and Syria. With him were a few of his disciples who he sent into the city to preach. In the city there were

wrong and unfounded rumors about Jesus (on whom be peace), and his mother. The governor of the city arrested the disciples and then summoned Jesus. Jesus miraculously healed some persons and exhibited other miracles. The king of the territory of Nasibain, with all his armies and people, became followers of Jesus. The legend of the 'coming down of food' contained in the Holy Quran is from the days of his travels."

2. **There are eighteen books** of the Hindus called the Puranas. The ninth book, the Bhavishya Mahapuranna, written in AD 115 when Jesus is said to have been still alive, mentions Jesus' journey to Kashmir, meeting with King Shalivahana in AD 78.

3. **History** – After the rule of David and Solomon there was mutual fighting between the tribes of Israel. As a result each tribe became separated from the rest. This continued up to the time of Nebuchadnezzar, who launched an invasion and killed 70,000 Jews. He sacked the city, taking the remaining Jews with him to Babel as prisoners and settled them in Persia and Media. They later escaped to the East and settled in the Ghaur hills, living there for a long time. Water and land were scarce, so many eventually migrated to India.

4. **The Encyclopaedia of Geography**, (London, 1856) – the Afghans trace their genealogy to Saul, the Israelite King, and call themselves the descendants of Israel. Afghans say they are of Jewish origin; that King Babul captured them and settled them in the territory of Ghaur, northwest of Kabul; they continued in their own Jewish faith, but that Khalid bin Abdulla married the daughter of a chief of this tribe and made them accept Islam that same year.

5. **Starting his journey from Jerusalem** and passing through Nasibus(450 miles from Jerusalem) and Iran, Jesus is known to have reached Afghanistan and to have met the Jews who settled there after bondage from Nebuchadnezzar.

6. **There are maps** showing the route Jesus took in his journey to Kashmir. In maps published by Christians, Media is shown toward the south of the Sea of Khizar (Azov), where Persia is today. The eastern frontier of Persia is adjacent to Afghanistan. The sea is toward the south and the Turkish Empire is toward the west. By traveling to Nasibain, Jesus intended to come to Afghanistan through Persia and to preach to the lost Jews who had come to be known as Afghans. The word "Afghan" appears to be of Hebrew origin. It means "brave."

7. **Jesus took a route through Afghanistan** so the Lost Tribes of Israel, Afghans, could learn from his teachings. The eastern frontier of Kashmir touches Tibet. From Kashmir he could easily go to Tibet. Having come to the Punjab, the land of five rivers, he wandered through important places before going to Kashmir and Tibet. Old historical records of this area show that Jesus was seen in Nepal, Benares and other places. He went to Kashmir through Jammu or Rawalpindi. It is certain he stayed in these

territories only through winter and by the end of March or the beginning of April, he started for Kashmir, which resembled Sham (Syria and its surrounding country.) He lived there, where other Israelite tribes had settled. Most of these Israelites had adopted Buddhism, but after a time the Tribes who came to be known as Afghans and Kashmiris, eventually became Muslims.

8. **The Kashmiri people are the descendants of Israel**; their dress, their features and some of their customs point to the fact that they are of Israelite origin. *"The natives are of a tall, robust frame of body, with manly features - the women full-formed and handsome, with aquiline nose and features resembling the Jewish."* Among the Afghans, as among the Jews, the younger brother marries the widow of the elder brother.

9. **Isaiah 9:6 -** *". . .the multitude and camels shall cover thee, the dromedaries of Midian and Ephah, all they from Sheba shall come and they shall bring gold and incense."* Strings of camels still travel with merchandise from Kashmir, Kabul, Khokand, Keetay and Orenbough. Near Samarcand there are gold and turquoise mines.

10. **The name Afghan is** not used by the people themselves. They call themselves Pooshtoon, and in the plural Pooshtauneh, from which comes the name Puten, given to them in India. They trace their origin to Saul, King of Israel, calling themselves Ben-i-Israel. They were transplanted by the King of Babylon from the Holy Land to Ghore, lying to the north west of Kabul, and lived as Jews until AD 682, when they were converted to Mohometanism by an Arab Chief Khaled-ibn-Abdalla, who had married a daughter of an Afghan chief. The people differ strikingly from the neighboring nations and have among themselves a common origin. They are said to resemble Jews in form and features and are divided into several tribes, inhabiting separate territories and remaining almost unmixed.

11. **The Books of Hadith** show the Holy Prophet Jesus was 125 years old when he died. *"Sects of Islam believe Jesus traveled in many parts of the world and was called the 'traveling prophet' because of his long journeys."* Not only are these reports found in the Books of Hadith, but they have been well-known among Muslim sects. It says in Kanz-ul-Ummal (Volume 2, a comprehensive Book of Hadith): *"God directed Jesus (on whom be peace) 'O Jesus! Move from one place to another - go from one country to another lest thou shouldst be recognized and persecuted.'"* In the same Book, on the report of Jabar: *"Jesus always used to travel; he went from one country to another, and at nightfall slept wherever he was. He used to eat the vegetation of the jungle and drink pure water."*

Michael noted that #11 verified the Persian records, #1 on his list.

12. **Hundreds of thousands of people** have been to the tomb of Jesus in Srinagar, Kashmir. *"Just as he was crucified on*

Golgotha, (at Gilgit, or sri in Kashmiri) so has his tomb been found at the place of sri (now Srinagar)." The place where Jesus was crucified was called Gilgit, and the place where in the latter part of the nineteenth century the tomb of Jesus was discovered, was also called Gilgit, a local memorial to the event of the cross. This word is of Hebrew origin and suggests the city was founded in the time of Jesus.

13. **"There has been discovered** *recently a coin in this very land of the Punjab, on which is inscribed the name of Jesus in Pali characters. This coin belongs to the time of Jesus. This shows that Jesus came to this land and received kingly honour."* The coin must have been issued by a king who had become a follower of Jesus. Another coin was found with the figure of an Israelite which is also believed to be the figure of Jesus.

14. **"And we made the son of Mary,** *and his other [his wife], a sign and gave them shelter on an elevated land of green valleys and springs of running water."* The Quran

15. **Generations of followers of Jesus in the East** call themselves Muslims and inhabit a number of villages scattered throughout the western area of Afghanistan, whose center is Herat. There are thousands of these "Muslim Christians" and their chief is Abba Yahiyya (Father John), who can recite the succession of teachers, through nearly sixty generations, back to Issa the Kashmiri (Jesus, son of Mariam of Nasara). Their holy book is the "Traditions of the Masih" (anointed one). Father John believes that Western Christians have read and repeated only part of the story and have completely misunderstood the message. He says that some of the events in the Bible are true, but a great deal was put in for less than worthy reasons. He says they have the true story told to them by the Master Jesus himself, who lived many years after biblical materials stated.

16. **Even though they are in different parts of the world,** the Gnostics Christians, the followers of Jesus in Afghanistan, and the Buddhists of Tibet share an understanding of the teachings of Jesus that are exactly the same, with Jesus stating that personal acts involving prayer, self-purification, the practice of truth and justice and the practice of meditation, would bring human beings to know God. However, today's Western version of Christianity places Jesus as the intermediary between humans and God.

17. **Common names for Jesus in the East** were Isa-Masih, Issa, Yuz Asaf, Esa.

Michael stopped typing and rubbed his eyes.

"Issa. That's interesting," he thought. "Joshua said they called him Issa too, when I met him on one of our journeys. Does this mean they also revere Joshua as a prophet? I have so many questions to ask him."

Michael looked over his list. As exciting as all this was, it was also becoming overwhelming. It was confusing to gather so much information with names he had never heard of and most he couldn't even pronounce. He felt he had enough facts to establish for himself that there were descendants of the Lost Tribes of Israel in the Afghanistan, Kashmir region. The history was so vast and so foreign that he could never do it justice. His immediate mission was to establish facts about Jesus' survival of the crucifixion, how, why and what happened after, and where he went—and to find a link between Kashmir and the Lost Tribes of Israel that Joshua had told him about. He found more than he could ever have imagined, and knew where to go for more if need be.

So much had been revealed to Michael in a short time, but of all the information he had just researched, he realized that the most controversial of this entire story may be the fact that today's generations of faithful followers of Jesus in the East are Muslims, whose religious books tell stories of Jesus' life in their countries *after* the crucifixion. With the world in such turmoil as it is in these times, Michael thought that may indeed be a hot topic for Christians of the world to consider.

Michael had been working for almost four hours and had not seen Miyah since she read from her diary. Getting up to stretch, he walked over to the window to enjoy the sunlight and looking out into the garden, he saw her there, on her knees, working in a bed of flowers. He watched her for a while and couldn't help but wonder about her life. Was she happy in her mission? Was she lonely? Did she have friends?

One thing Michael did know—that she was beautiful, even with dirt up to her arms. He felt a tenderness toward her that surprised even himself. What is to become of this, he wondered? Dare I hope for any more than she's already given me? He continued to watch her for a few more minutes, then went to the kitchen, poured a couple of glasses of lemonade and went outside to ask if he could help. He needed fresh air and Miyah certainly was a breath of fresh air to him.

14 Michael's Secret

"It's such a beautiful day. What am I doing locked inside the house, while you're out here enjoying the sunshine?" Michael asked as he handed a glass of lemonade to Miyah, refraining from talking about the research swimming around in his head. He had so many questions for her, but thought they both could use a break.

Miyah looked up from her work and gratefully took the drink from his hand. "You should get out here for at least an hour each day," she said. "It's amazing how being in nature has the ability to heal just about anything."

He watched as she continued to pull weeds.

"Here let me help," he said, as he knelt beside her and started clearing leaves from around some flowers.

"The landscaping in your yard was carefully planned," Miyah noted. "It looks like it doesn't require much maintenance–just light weeding, watering, and mowing now and then."

"Yes," Michael replied. "I have my mother to thank for that, although caring for the yard was a family affair. It was something we enjoyed together and we all spent a lot of time out here. I remember as a boy playing baseball with my dad in the back yard. When Elizabeth was little we had a swing set over in the corner, and a big sandbox that we all played in. Mom and Dad used to help us build tall sand castles in it, just as if we were on a beach. We were a close family and I always assumed we would have them to depend on up into their old age. Their car accident was a complete shock."

"I'm sorry," Miyah said.

Not wanting to talk more about their death, Michael continued, "We had a big swimming pool right here where the patio is now. After I went off to college and Elizabeth was busy with her school friends and activities, no one used it much, so my folks had it covered over and landscaped this patio above it. They loved being out here.

"After my folks died I did all the mowing and watering in the yard. It took quite some time. When I got sick, we hired someone to mow and Elizabeth took over weeding and watering. I suppose I'll be able to tend to things again myself now."

They worked side-by-side for a while, enjoying each other's company as well as the fresh air. Miyah, always in tune with nature, loved the warmth of the sun on her back and the chorus of birdsong in the trees.

Michael suddenly blurted out, "I have a secret, too! Elizabeth doesn't even know, but for some reason I feel I can share this with you." He laughed, "You've revealed so much to me, now I'd like to tell you my secret."

Amused, Miyah asked, "If it's a secret, are you sure you want to share it?"

"I'd forgotten about it until just now," he admitted. "I've never told anyone. It's really a family secret."

"I'm intrigued," Miyah said. "What sort of secrets are you holding in your family closet?"

"Family closet," Michael laughed again. "That's pretty close. It's nothing as revealing as your family secrets, but it's all I've got." He continued, "I told you my folks covered over the swimming pool when they built the patio. They covered over it. They didn't fill it in. They made it into a type of bomb shelter in case we were ever invaded or needed to hide or something. I'm not really sure why. I just thought it was another whim of my parents and didn't pay a lot of attention to it. With Mom being a mystery writer and Dad having spent time in archaeological digs in Egypt, France and other countries, I always thought of it as their own private hideaway. They were a bit eccentric after all. I haven't been down there in awhile, but remember it was quite elaborate.

"See these large, glass block tiles that are placed around the patio? They act as a type of skylight to let natural light into the rooms. There are air-oxygen portals that vent through some of the statuary in the gardens. We have a natural artesian well on the property that feeds the fountains you see around the patio, so there's even a system for fresh filtered water. It's really quite brilliant."

Miyah listened intently, wondering if there was another reason for this shelter.

"How do you get into it?" she asked.

"They built a tunnel to the house and a false door in one of the closets," he said. "That's why I laughed when you asked about secrets in the family closet. There's also an entrance here on the patio. . .Ah!" Michael had a thought. "Now it's my turn to make your brain work. If you can find both entrances, I'll let you see the shelter. How's that for a challenge?"

"It sounds like a wonderful game—and a diversion from your work. But we can both use some fun," Miyah readily agreed, looking around. "Let's see. It shouldn't be too difficult out here to find something that would look like an entrance."

"We'll see about that," Michael doubtfully responded.

Miyah walked around the patio looking for a trap door that could look like it went into a cellar. She found several clusters of glass blocks, but peering into them, could not see anything below. She looked for false plants or flowers that could be guarding an entrance. She searched around the stonework grill and the obvious, a stone facade tool shed covered with ivy, at the edge of the patio. Then she walked the circumference of the courtyard, searching for clues. Michael grabbed a hose and began to water the flower beds as he smugly watched her, amused at her thought process. Now she was the one searching for treasure. He was enjoying the role reversal.

Miyah fingered the seams of the thick slate pathway that wound through the garden, thinking the entrance may be off the patio courtyard, angling into the hidden room.

"Should I tell you if you're hot or cold?" Michael called out.

"No thank you," she shouted back. "I can manage on my own."

So like her, he thought with a shrug, thinking it was impossible for her to find the entrance by herself.

For nearly half an hour Miyah circled the trees and the statues and even searched along the foundation of the house. She wasn't about to give up. She wondered if it was cheating if she used her "powers" to give her a clue. She closed her eyes. The vision of a white statue came into her mind. A white statue and a fish.

She looked around and wandered over to the small pond in the yard, not far from the patio. The pond, filled with koi fish, was surrounded by four medium-sized, marble statues. She walked around the first two, but intuitively stopped at the sculpture of a nude woman with a jar at her feet, spilling water into the pond. Circling the pool of water was a sidewalk of large slate tiles. Directly to the right of the nude statue was a slate sidewalk that connected back to the patio, about 12 feet away. Two sets of tiles in the center of this sidewalk were at least three feet square, unusually large, Miyah thought, for a sidewalk, especially in comparison to the other slate tiles. As consistent as Michael's mother had been in design detail of the garden and courtyard, it was peculiar to have these tiles differ so drastically in size. She bent down and felt around the edges of the tiles and discovered that they were connected underneath by a piece of wood—the door, she thought. But how could it be opened? It would be too heavy to open like a hatch door. It must slide. But she noticed it was the same height as the adjoining slate, and the grass on either side was also cut at the same level. Maybe she was wrong.

Again, she saw a flash of the nude statue in her mind. She walked over to examine it closely. Her eyes traced the curves and lines of the body, but nothing seemed unusual. Its marble tones and height were the same as the others, but the jar at the feet of the statue drew her attention. Flowing from the jar was a stream of water. Michael had said that artesian wells fed the fountains and also supplied fresh water to the shelter hidden below.

Miyah gently pushed away the tall bushes around the base of the vase, noticing a stamp of some sort. At first she thought it was the signature of the mason who made the statues. The letters were ornate and not easy to read. She traced her fingers along the lines of each letter, e-n-t-r-e-r. "*Entrer*," she whispered. "French for enter."

The word was enclosed within an oblong border and was raised slightly from the bottom of the jar. Miyah pushed on the symbol. She looked around. Nothing happened. She took a stick and traced around the border of the symbol to clean off the moss. She tried turning the symbol clockwise.

It didn't move. Then she tried turning it counter-clockwise. Immediately the water flowing into the pond from the jar slowed to a trickle. Miyah heard a grating noise behind her and turned quickly to see the two larger slate tiles rise up about three inches and then slide over to the left, revealing a stone stairway. She let go an uncharacteristic squeal of accomplishment.

"Is this it?" she called out to Michael. "Is this the entrance?"

"I'll be damned," Michael replied. "I'll be damned."

He turned off the hose and strode over to Miyah and the uncovered staircase.

"I can't believe you found it," he said, still in astonishment. "Wait a minute. You had help didn't you? That's not fair. I didn't expect you to bring in the troops!"

"Should I be offended that you don't have enough faith in my abilities to think I could do this on my own? I'm a rather good detective, if I do say so myself," she retorted, adding coyly, "I had just a *little* help."

"I knew it!" he exclaimed. "It doesn't matter. I'm impressed. This was no easy task."

"Can we go down and take a look?" Miyah asked impatiently, peering into the opening.

"Ah, but you have only accomplished half of our little game," he responded. "You first have to find the entrance from inside the house—and no help this time!" he laughed. "Besides, the door at the bottom of the stairs is locked."

"What, no secret buttons to push to unlock the door from the outside?" she teased.

"Possibly," Michael said, enjoying keeping the intrigue. He reached over to the fountain jar and turned the symbol clockwise. The grate slid back over the opening and lowered itself down into place. Water began to flow at its normal rate into the pond. He carefully pushed the bushes back around the base of the jar to hide its secrets. Michael was enjoying having the upper hand for once. For some odd reason it made him feel masculine again.

Miyah was also enjoying this game. Since she had been on her own, her life had been so serious. She loved her work, was dedicated to it and would never complain, but she also knew that her life lacked playful moments. She enjoyed laughing with Michael and delighted in this "game" he was playing with her. It seemed to lighten the load for both of them.

They collected the tray of lemonade glasses and went inside. Then Michael laid down one more rule.

"This time I want to hear your thought process. I'm tagging along with you. I want to be sure you don't get any outside help," he explained.

"How will you know?" she asked, smiling.

"Ha," he said. "Because it's a rule. None of your magic. OK?"

"OK," she said. "I'll prove to you that I can do this on my own."

Standing in the kitchen she began her deductions out loud.

"OK, you said the entrance was through a closet. I would immediately eliminate the upstairs closets; too far to connect. Logic would say that if a tunnel was built to connect the old pool structure to the house, it would adjoin through the basement, which would be at about the same level. I haven't been in your basement but that will be my last searching point, because you said 'closet,' and that to me would refer to a room in the main part of the house. There must be at least half a dozen closets on this level. The kitchen has a large pantry, the dining room has a linen closet, the entryway has a coat closet, and the sitting room has a nice storage closet, but they're all at the front of the house, so logically could be eliminated. That leaves the rooms at the rear of the house, which are the bathroom, a hallway, a bedroom and your library study. How am I doing so far?"

"Fine," Michael said with a blank expression, not wanting to give her any clues, even though he thought her logical deductions were brilliant.

"My guess would be your library. It's where your parents spent most of their time and it opens up onto the patio."

Miyah headed to the library. She really hadn't noticed before, but there were two closets in the library; one on each side of the room and both were on an outside wall. She went over to the closet on Michael's father's side of the room. Opening the door she saw rows of deep shelving lining the space. Rectangular, wicker baskets neatly organized everything from magazines to office supplies.

"Wow," she said. "I don't think I've ever seen such an organized closet before."

"Yeah," Michael replied. "My folks were sticklers for being able to find things when they needed it."

"May I?" she asked, referring to removing some of the baskets to closer examine the shelves.

"Of course," he answered. "Do you need help? I don't know if any of them are heavy or not."

"Thank you. Could you take down the ones from the top shelves?"

They removed the baskets from the closet. Miyah knocked on the wood panels for a hollow sound, checking to see if there was a false wall behind the shelves or perhaps another door. Michael lost himself in the contents of the baskets. One was filled with trinkets collected on family travels. He picked up a small metal version of the Eiffel Tower, a souvenir from a visit to Paris when he was about ten-years-old. Turning it over in his hand brought back memories of the months his family had spent touring France. He was just a boy, but remembered well the amazing adventures they had on that trip. He realized how fortunate he was to have traveled so much with his family. His parents believed travel was education and supported that through yearly vacations to other lands. Often these trips coincided with his father's work as an archeologist and he brought the family along, always finding time to spend with them. Michael rummaged through the basket and was filled with sentiment, until the sound of Miyah's voice brought his attention back to her mission.

"I don't see anything here," she announced. "But can we leave the baskets out for a while in case I come across something?"

"Huh, oh, of course," he said, replacing the memories in his hands with reality. "Sure."

Miyah went to the closet on Michael's mother's side of the room. It too, was lined with baskets, carefully organizing their contents. They pulled the baskets off the shelves and Miyah began the same routine of knocking on the wall and listening for variances in sound. She felt around the perimeter of the shelving and looked for anything out of the ordinary; a latch, a hinge, or even a worn piece of wood that would indicate something opening and closing. But she found nothing.

"I don't understand," she said. "I thought this would be so much easier than outside."

"Yes, I knew you did," Michael replied, with a slight mock in his voice.

Together they replaced the baskets in both closets. When they were finished she went over and picked up a dictionary from Michael's desk. She went to the definition of "closet," reading out loud.

". . .a clothes closet, cabinet, cupboard, wardrobe, armoire, locker."

Looking at Michael she said, "I may have taken you too literally." He followed her and stood leaning against the doorway while she searched the hall closet, the bedroom closet and wooden wardrobe. Again, she came up empty.

"Well, I guess it's the basement," she admitted, heading back down the hallway. But just as she was about to open the basement door, she turned and went into the bathroom. She opened the linen closet door and peered inside. Trying to be logical, she reasoned, "If someone wanted to keep a doorway secret, they wouldn't first want to have to remove everything from the shelves before they could open it. That would leave clues that something was going on. No, the entire shelving unit would have to open, or rotate or something." She pushed on everything she could find that might open a concealed door, but nothing happened.

As she closed the door, she noticed hinges, indicating that next to the closet was a cupboard. A long, framed mirror completely covered the cupboard door, including the hinges, that were set in at least an inch from the edge of the mirror's wide frame. The edges of the frame were beveled in the opposite direction as usual and on the backside of the mirror, just enough so the edge would clear the wall if it were to open. She'd stopped in front of the mirror before and straightened her dress or brushed her hair, but hadn't looked any further than the mirror itself. Looking for a way to open the cupboard, she wedged her fingers behind the mirror, trying to pry open the cupboard door.

It wouldn't move.

"There must be a release here somewhere," she said, running her hand around the outside of the mirror. When she got to the lower right side, she felt something. It was a button, flattened against the bottom of the frame. Gently pushing the button, she released the lock on the door. Miyah pulled at the edge of the frame and it opened.

Seeing that Miyah was heading in the right direction, Michael went to the front and back doors of the house, as well as the kitchen door, and locked them all. He seldom had company, but certainly didn't want anyone walking into the house at this moment. He hurried back to the bathroom to watch as Miyah discovered the second secret doorway.

"Bravo," he clapped. "I'm impressed. But it wasn't as easy as you thought, was it?"

"I'll admit it," she said. "I was a bit overconfident at first. Point taken. I learn lessons every day too."

Miyah slowly opened the door the rest of the way to reveal a stairway.

"It really is clever, isn't it? No one would think to look for a secret door in a bathroom, and what better way to have an escape. . .no one would follow you into the bathroom. All you'd have to do is open the window and if you didn't come out, they would have thought you escaped through the window. Excellent! But why, Michael, would your parents feel the need to have an escape route? From what? From whom?"

"Oh, don't go jumping to conclusions," he quickly replied. "I never said anything about needing escaping or having a hideaway from anything other than a place for themselves. They called it a bomb shelter and if there was any reasoning at all behind finding shelter for safety, that would be it. They did joke though about hiding from FEMA to stay in their home if Marshal Law was ever declared. I think a lot of people had bomb shelters years ago."

Miyah was sure there was more behind this than Michael thought. She would have to be alert for signs. . .and keep it to herself, as Michael obviously was very protective of his parents.

"You won the prize! After you, my lady," Michael motioned down the stairway, switching on a dim light. "They even had a backup lighting system in place, with a series of batteries, solar—from the glass tiles on the patio, and candles and lanterns, just in case of a power outage. They thought of everything."

As Miyah began to descend the stairway, Michael pulled the mirrored door closed and she heard the latch click behind them.

~~~~~

There was another door at the bottom of the steps. Miyah watched as Michael reached down to the end of some moulding underneath the last hinge. He slid a small piece of the wood to one side and retrieved a key. He unlocked the door and replaced the key.

"Go ahead," he said. "Go on in. Make yourself at home."

Miyah turned the doorknob and walked in. Michael reached around her and flipped on the lights. The door opened into a kitchen-family room area. Miyah had expected one huge cement-lined room. After all, it was at one time a swimming pool. She was quite surprised. The walls were still cement, but had been painted white and the cement floor had been leveled out and was covered with carpet. The glass tile skylights from the courtyard above streamed in light that was illuminated throughout the room by panels of reflective material placed strategically around the ceiling. There appeared to be panels that could be slid over the skylights if the room got too hot, or needed to be darkened so light couldn't be detected from above through the glass blocks. Maybe that's why she didn't get the feeling of being claustrophobic surrounded by cement walls. The glass tile skylights brought the outside world in. She could even see outlines of the trees above.

An abundance of kitchen cupboards lined the walls and a snack bar divided the kitchen and family area. The kitchen had a sink with faucets, but next to it was a hand levered water pump. The built-in stove resembled more of an outside grill with a griddle on one side and propane tanks stored below. There was also an electric double burner unit on the counter with a toaster oven and a microwave built into the cabinets. A refrigerator in the corner was supplemented by several heavy-duty, stainless steel coolers that resembled the old fashioned ice boxes stacked on top of each other. The empty refrigerator was unplugged and the door was slightly ajar. Miyah opened the cupboards. They were filled with canned and boxed food. A hand towel was draped over the sink and a vase of silk flowers brightened the countertop.

"I told you they thought of everything," Michael repeated. "It has all the usual electrical appliances, plus back-up devices in case of a power outage." He picked a can of beans out of the cupboard. "I wonder what the expiration date is on some of this stuff?" he said, looking at the label. "I suppose I should come down here some time and weed through this food." He put the can back on the shelf and shut the cupboard door.

"It's like a grocery store," Miyah exclaimed. "I don't think I've ever had this much food in my house at one time!"

Michael continued the tour. Near the snack bar was a long, wooden table with 12 chairs around it. The furniture was practical and looked comfortable. There were three couches placed in a horseshoe shape with a large coffee table in the center. Michael said all the couches folded out into beds. One wall was completely lined with shelving filled with games, puzzles, books—lots of books, and family photographs. Miyah walked over and picked up one of the framed pictures.

"Who is this?" she asked. Michael took the photo from her.

"That's my mother," he said, looking at the photo tenderly. "That's my dad," he said, pointing to the man in the photo. "The other two were their good friends." He picked up another framed photo.

"This is Elizabeth and me. It was taken a few weeks before the accident." He put the frames back on the shelf and walked away.

"Let me show you the rest of the shelter," he said, changing the subject. Miyah lingered a moment, looking at the picture of his parents and their friends to ingrain it into her memory bank. The face of the other woman in the photo was not clear, shadowed by a large hat, yet it somehow stirred something in Miyah. . .a memory.

Michael motioned to four doors. "They're left open to keep the circulation flowing down here," he explained. The two doors across from the family room led into bedrooms. They were each lined with six bunk beds on one side. The opposite side was designed wall-to-wall with shelving, hooks, clothing rods, an elaborate open closet system that was filled with, what else, wicker baskets for drawers. There were blankets, pillows, sleeping bags, and blow-up mattresses. Jackets, robes and assorted clothing filled one section of the closet rods. Beneath it were warm winter boots, slippers and shoes. It was almost as if the occupants of this place had just stepped out for a few minutes and would be back soon. Miyah found it a bit creepy.

"I know," Michael said. "At first I gave them a hard time about storing all this stuff here. I told them that homeless people on the streets would give anything to have a warm jacket and a blanket. But they said that some day I might be glad they prepared all this. They said I didn't understand the state of the world as well as they did and that the powers that be, what they called 'the government behind the government' were running our world into ruin. They said our environment couldn't hold out forever the way we abused it, and that everyone should have a shelter like this for the survival of their families. Then they would say not to tell a soul, not even Elizabeth. She wasn't very good at keeping secrets. And they said not to worry about any of this because they had it all taken care of. Yeah, the sky is falling but don't worry, we have food and warm coats and puzzles to pass the time. I thought they had gone over the deep end, but, as I said, they were both a little eccentric. . .remarkable and brilliant, but eccentric. . .and I loved them for it, so I pretty much ignored all of this and let it be.

"And that's not all," he motioned Miyah toward the other two doors. "One leads into the bathroom, which is fully stocked with all of the toilet paper and any of the toiletries anyone in the entire town could ever need, and the other leads into the storage room."

Miyah followed him down a short hall into a room that was filled wall-to-wall and down the center with shelving. It was like a general store. Everything from maintenance and building tools to vitamins and medical supplies, to boxes marked garden seeds, rice, oatmeal, flour, sugar, salt, water purification tablets. There were six bicycles hanging from racks in the ceiling. Almost buried in supplies was a desk-like area between some of the shelves. Books and journals were stacked on one corner and reams of paper on the other. An old typewriter sat between the piles. A basket marked, "typewriter ribbon, pencils, office supplies, parts" rested on a shelf above the desk. A clear sheet of plastic covered the typewriter to keep the dust out, although Miyah didn't see much dust anywhere. It must be because of the filtration system Michael mentioned. She had also expected the place to smell musty, but that wasn't the case either.

"This is all so amazing," Miyah said as she pushed through the plastic on a couple keys on the typewriter. "I haven't seen one of these in years."

"My father kept all of his field journals down here for safe keeping. Most of them are over there in that vault. It was his life's work and he said it was his biggest treasure, next to his family." Michael motioned to an area hidden behind a panel of clothing.

"Either they were both completely crazy or they were very perceptive. I just don't quite know what to say."

"I know," Michael responded. "I decided to leave it as it was. It's sort of a shrine to them. . .and who knows, it may just save lives some day, as they said. How am I to know? It's hidden away here and not bothering anyone. I checked once in awhile to be sure there is no water leakage or anything like that. So far, everything seems to be perfect. We don't even have mice. I know I keep saying it, but they thought of everything."

Michael pointed to a door on the end of the family room. "That leads up into the garden."

"Thank you for sharing this with me, Michael," Miyah said earnestly. "It really is a family secret that clearly, no one else could have."

"You know when I got sick I thought I should tell someone, but for some reason I just didn't want to tell Elizabeth. She was the logical person, but I don't know what held me back. Then in my battle to stay alive, I forgot about it, until today. I'm glad I told you. Someone other than myself should know. I feel a sense of relief because of telling you."

Michael shut off the lights and locked the door and they walked down the short hallway to the steps that led back to the house. Before they reached the stairway he steered Miyah into a space to the side of the steps.

"What?" she questioned, as he pushed her aside.

"I'm sorry," he said. "There's just one more thing to show you." He pointed to another door under the stairway, which appeared to be a closet. Producing another key from a hidden niche in the frame, he unlocked the door and slowly opened it. Miyah could feel her body stiffen in the temporary moment of darkness as Michael switched off the light in the hallway and reached around into the next room to turn on a light.

"You see, you would have been correct also if you had headed here to search for a passageway. We're in the basement of the house," he said, closing the door. The basement side of the door was a panel of shelves filled with tin cans that had been nailed to the wood to keep them from falling when the door was opened. The tins were filled with various nails and such, so it wouldn't seem out of the ordinary for them to be in a secured container.

Miyah looked around. There were racks of tools and miscellaneous building supplies and parts, and more shelves of supplies: food, cleaning supplies, everything imaginable. Among the cob webs were a few sealed wooden crates in the corner and a large wine and liquor cupboard on one end of the room.

"I imagine they put that on this side of the shelter so they could access it easily. My parents weren't heavy drinkers, but liked a glass of wine now and then," Michael said as he picked a bottle of wine from the shelf and blew off the dust."

"Let's get out of here." He steered Miyah toward the stairway. Brushing the cob webs away from above her head, she admitted she would be glad to get back into the sanctity of the house.

～～～～～

"Whew," Miyah said. "That was quite a tour."

"I hope you enjoyed it," Michael said. "I think we both needed a break."

"Yes," Miyah agreed. "I suppose we can wait until tomorrow to continue our work. It's almost time to make dinner."

Michael interrupted. "I'm heading right back to my desk. I still have a lot to do. For some reason I feel refreshed. Maybe it's finally being able to show someone the shelter. It really takes a load off. Let me know when dinner is ready though. I'm famished!"

He rested his hand on her shoulder a moment and then headed into his library. He looked out the window, staring over the garden for a few minutes and then reached over to unlock the French doors that opened onto the patio—but the door wasn't locked.

"That's strange," he said to himself. "I thought I locked this door when we went into the shelter. Hmm. It must have already been locked and I unlocked it instead. I'll have to be more careful." He opened the door and filled his lungs with fresh air. With renewed vigor, he turned on his computer and began to page through another pile of books.

Miyah washed her hands, took some vegetables out of the refrigerator and began to chop. She wondered if Michael's parents had insights into some future event she was unaware of. A flash of memory brought up the photograph of Michael's parents and their friends.

"Why do they seem so familiar?" she wondered.

15 Journey to Another Land

Michael worked into the night and slept late the next morning. When he awoke Miyah was not there. At first he wondered if he had frightened her away after revealing his outlandish family secret. He made himself some oatmeal and toast and brewed a pot of coffee. Miyah came in with an armful of groceries an hour later.

"I hope you're using the household account I set up for groceries," he said taking the bags from her. "I don't want you to spend your own money feeding me."

"I'm eating too, Michael," she reminded him. "But don't worry. I have no problem spending your money, especially if it means you are eating healthier. I hope you don't mind that I threw out some of the processed food you had in your cupboards. . .most everything contained MSG, aspartame or high fructose corn syrup. That's all bad for you, no wonder you got sick!" she said. "I bet you never read a label in your life."

"You're right, and obviously neither did Elizabeth. I appreciate your healthy diet and your attempt to teach me to make better food choices," he replied, adding, "I know we really got side tracked yesterday and I still have a lot of things I want to discuss with you. I have so many questions about the things I'm reading, and one detail in particular. Do you think we can set some time aside today to talk?"

"Yes, I think it's nearly time," she said,

"What do you mean—nearly?" he replied.

"You haven't journeyed for a few days and I think it's time for another adventure. It just may answer a few of your questions."

"Where am I going? You know don't you? Can't you give me a clue so I'm prepared?" he begged.

"You'll have everything you need," she assured him. "Why don't you work on your notes while I put groceries away? I'll meet you in the library in an hour."

Anxious to see Joshua again, Michael quickly agreed. He skipped up the steps to take his shower and get ready for the day.

When he returned, Miyah was in the library waiting for him, her medicine bag at her side. She was curled up in a chair, reading her diary.

"Remember you promised to read to me again," he said when he saw her.

"Yes, I will," she said. "There's more you need to hear. Are you ready to get started?"

"I am," he answered, settling himself on the couch across from her. This time he had a notebook.

"I want to give this back to you first," Miyah said, reaching over to hand him the repaired necklace. "It should hold fast now."

"Thank you. I wouldn't want to leave home without it," he joked as he put it around his neck. "Seriously," he looked into her eyes. "This Faith Stone, as I call it, is my connection to you when I'm traveling. It gives me faith that I'll return."

"I know," she acknowledged. "You don't really need it to return, but if it gives you confidence, that's all that matters."

Michael laid down on the couch and watched Miyah unwrap the cedar box. She placed it on the table in front of him and settled back into her chair with her diary. She began to hum like she had the last time Michael traveled. Michael closed his eyes and listened to her serene voice, but he couldn't resist the calling of the box on the table and turned his head to look at the panel. Figures began to form and shape within themselves and soon Michael was again lost to the mystery of the cedar box.

~~~~~

Michael began to cough and shielded his face to keep the dust from his eyes. He was in some sort of mine. Men were working with picks and crude hammers on the walls of a cave. He looked around for Joshua and saw a light from outside. He made his way to the opening and stepped out. There were many men working, loading donkeys with baskets of minerals. He walked around surveying the operation and spotted Joshua talking to another man, using precise hand motions, as if he were explaining some sort of process. Michael waited until he was finished and approached him. In a welcoming gesture Joshua clapped him on the shoulder as if he had been waiting for him.

"Ah, and here is my friend!" he said.

"I'm always happy to see you Joshua," Michael replied with genuine pleasure. "But where are we?"

"We are in Caledonia," Joshua answered. "A land you would call Scotland."

"Scotland!" Michael exclaimed. "You've traveled from your home to Egypt, India, Nepal, Tibet and Kashmir to Scotland! I never would have imagined it all possible. How?" he asked.

"My uncle, Joseph of Arimathea, is a great merchant. He owns many ships and travels the world with his business. He learned the tin and copper trade from the Phoenicians, which is as important as steel in your time. The Phoenicians have been transporting ore from Britain for centuries. Joseph is a member of the ruling political body of the entire country. His official title is 'Nobilis Decurio,' a minister of mines for the Roman empire."

"Is this the same Joseph of Arimathea who saved Jesus from the cross during the crucifixion?" Michael asked.

"Yes," Joshua answered, smiling at Michael. "I am pleased you have done some investigating and discovered much that has been hidden about those times. That is good. We will talk more about that before you leave me this time."

"I've noticed you're taking me on the path that follows the travels of Jesus. You must have known him?" Michael inquired. "I have so many questions for you."

Joshua smiled, seemingly amused. "First let me tell you about my uncle," he said, getting back to his conversation. "He has been called one of the richest men in the world. Joseph is a man of refinement, well educated and one who possesses many talents. He has keen political and business ability, which has made it possible for him to gain close contact with many of the Kings: Beli, Lud, Llyr and Arviragus. King Arviragus gave Joseph 12 hides—let's see, to you that would be about 160 acre parcels, or 2,000 acres—of tax free land."

The two men walked around the encampment while they talked.

"This is one of my uncle's mines. I journeyed here with him a few times many years ago when I was a boy and am pleased to return. Maryum and I have a small house near what you would in your time call Glastonbury, Somerset. In this period of time it is an island that is completely surrounded by marshlands. In your studies you will find it sometimes referred to as the Isle of Avalon, from an old Welsh word *abal*, meaning apple."

"Avalon," Michael repeated. "Isn't that from the time of the King Arthur and Guinevere legends?"

"Yes, and that is a most interesting tale. You may want to examine that history as well. This land has many legends. When I speak with you, we talk of names in this time, as well as in future times. Those names are ones which you will more easily identify. You must tell me if my mixture of past, present and future bewilders you."

"No, I'm interested in it all," Michael said. "I'll take notes and what I don't remember I'll be able to research when I return. Please continue."

"In Welsh it is called 'Ynys Afallach,' which means the Island of Apples, as you can see an abundance of fruit grows here. It has also been called 'Ynys Gutrin,' the Island of Glass, and from these words the invading Saxons will later coin the place-name Glastingebury, which still later will be pronounced Glastonbury."

Michael looked around. The hilltops were clothed with wandering grape vines and nature seemed to provide a bounty of vegetables and grains. Groves of apple trees grew along the edge of the woods that led to the high, tapered peaks of the Tor.

Joshua spoke again, "My mother, Mariam is also with us. This has been a good place for quiet study, prayer and meditation. I'm studying with the ancient Druids of this land, sharing my wisdom with them and at the same time gaining their insights."

"Druids?" Michael questioned. "What could you learn from the Druids?"

"You don't know much about Celtic culture, my friend," Joshua responded. "Druids are members of the learned class among the ancient Celts. They serve many functions, among them priests, teachers, judges, seers, doctors and philosophers, and are highly respected by many in the ancient world. The name Druid, or in the case of a woman, Druidess, itself translates to a wise man or priest/priestess. I have come to discover that these Druids are especially gifted at poetry and philosophy."

"And what are some of their teachings about?" Michael was curious.

"They teach that souls do not suffer death, but after death pass from one body to another and they regard this as the strongest incentive to valor, since the actual fear of death is disregarded. They have also much knowledge of the stars and their motion, of the size of the world, wisdom of the earth, and of natural philosophy. The Druidic elite are divided into three parts: the Bards—lyric poets, musicians; Vates—diviners and seers; and the Druids—priests/priestesses, philosophers, theologians. They enjoy a high status within Gallic society, a rank akin to the knights, who are the highest nobility below the tribal chief magistrate or king.

"In the Celtic world, the priesthood is a separate, highly respected and important grade of society. Some compare them to the Indian Brahmins, the Persian Magi, or the Egyptian priests and priestesses. They were generally seen by the Romans as priests, seers, healers, prophets and magicians—even called the 'Magi of the North.' They believe in one divine spirit, yet honored the sun, moon, stars and nature spirits. My grandmother, Anna, spent much time here and became one of their priestess."

Joshua continued, "They don't write their secret wisdom, preferring instead on memory and oral teachings, shared only with specially prepared candidates. So you see, I am honored to follow my grandmother's footsteps and be enfolded within their circle of wisdom to learn their truths and beliefs."

"It's good to hear you're continuing your quest for knowledge," Michael said, looking around at the men working the mine. "I wondered for a moment if you were giving up your studies to become a merchant or a miner!"

Joshua laughed. "I am always eager to learn and I find the smelting of tin from ore an interesting enterprise, but it is only a slight diversion. I will continue my studies, my teaching and my travels. Life is a great teacher, do you agree?"

"Yes," Michael concurred. "I've learned more since I've met you than I have in my entire years of education. You're a great teacher. Thank you for all you've shown me."

"It is because you are a good student," Joshua reciprocated.

"We have explored much of this land, teaching and learning the ways of the people here. It's a pleasant country. Some of the places we've traveled to are known by the names of Penzance, Falmouth, St-Just-in-Roseland and Looe, which are all in Cornwall, as well as many of the Isles. Joseph and I have overseen the building of an abbey so our teaching can continue. Students come to me here and I share many of the principals I have learned from other cultures, but my destiny is that I begin my travels again, and I must return to India and Kashmir where we once met, to teach my people. I have much to do before my time is finished.

"Come. I invite you to my house and to see the abbey. We shall partake of a meal together while you are here." Joshua reached out and took Michael's arm and in a flash the two men were transported to a small cluster of wattle huts, mud plastered over a framework of sticks woven with branches.

Maryum was sitting at a wooden table outside the house, writing in a leather-bound book when they arrived. Michael glanced at the book and was about to comment on it, when she stood up and greeted him. He was surprised to see she was expecting another child.

"Congratulations," he said, making a gesture toward her condition.

"Thank you," she confidently replied. "You have found us again."

She smiled. "It is a pleasure to have you visit our humble home. It's good you are here now. In only two days time we will be leaving with Joseph on a merchant voyage to the north islands, to what in your time is called Iona, and back to the land of the Druids. It's my hope our child won't be born until we return back here," she said, glancing at her husband.

Joshua embraced his wife.

"I have no fear for your safety, my love. Nor that of our child. Are we not great healers?" he laughed and she laid her head against his chest.

Soon Mariam came out of the house, wiping her hands on the apron of her dress. Along side her was a young girl holding a little boy on her hip.

"This is my beautiful daughter, Sera Tamar," Joshua proudly announced, playfully tousling the top of her hair. "She's the image of her mother. And this is our son Joseph David, who was born in Alexandria." He took the boy from Sera and held him high in the air. The boy squealed with laughter.

"And my mother, Mariam" Joshua said as he settled Joseph in one arm and put the other arm around the older woman. "I don't believe she met you in your previous visits. I know you saw her when I carved that box for her birthday."

Mariam smiled, nodding a greeting toward Michael. "It is a pleasure to meet you," she said politely. Then turning to her son, she added, "It was a most beautiful gift my son," she said. "I have used it all these many years to hold my herbs and spices."

"Yes, mother," he said tenderly. "I know."

"As do I with the box he carved for me as a wedding gift," Maryum joined in. "We are both so fortunate to have such a talented man in our family."

"And now," Joshua said, "I have gone from wooden boxes to mud monasteries!" He motioned to a structure in the distance. "You must see the abbey before you return. But first let us dine together." Joshua and Michael followed the women into the modest, mud hut.

After a meal of figs, nuts, fruit and a tasty vegetable stew, the two men walked a distance to the abbey church built by Joseph, Joshua and the men of the area.

"It was Joseph's design, and even though it's only made of mud, it serves us well. It also has become an important library for manuscripts we hold as important. Some day they will bring to light the happenings of these days when myself, my family and Joseph lived upon this land. As for the structure itself, you will find that later, as history progresses, the building will endure many additions, destructions and will finally be made strong by rebuilding with stone. But this day I am proud that we are the first to put down the base of this church and establish the roots of our teachings here. It's part of my mission."

Michael had been fairly quiet all evening, soaking in what Joshua was telling him and writing in his notebook, being glad he remembered to bring it along.

"Your mission. Can we talk about your mission?"

"As you like," Joshua said.

"It's taken me a while to map this out and research a lot of things I never in my life would have thought to seek out," Michael said, getting right to the point.

"What things?" Joshua shrewdly asked.

"Things that Miyah told me, and things I researched—about Jesus traveling to the East as a young boy to study other cultures and not dying on the cross. About him marrying and having children. . .and living to be over a hundred years old and going back to Kashmir to preach. . .and that he is buried there. My journeys with you through the cedar box have followed the footsteps of what I've researched is the path Jesus took during the 'lost years,' as a boy, and later as an adult. Help me to understand this. Your life seems to be patterned after him, or parallels his journeys. You talk about your mission and of Joseph being your uncle. Wasn't he also Jesus' uncle? Are you related? Cousins? You must have known Jesus personally, yet you have never once mentioned his name."

Joshua was silent.

". . .except one time, when you said they also call you Issa. I read that Issa is one of the names they called Jesus in the East. . .Issa. . ." and Michael's voice trailed off as he listened to his own words. His legs weakened and he had to sit down on a large rock to keep from collapsing. His notebook fell out of his hand and he broke out in a cold sweat, lowering his head so he wouldn't faint.

"Yes. What you are saying is true," Joshua said, as he put his hand on top of Michael's head. "And what you are thinking at this moment is also true. I am Issa."

Michael couldn't bring himself to look at this man he had come to know as a friend and a wise teacher. He couldn't believe what he was hearing. It wasn't possible that he could have been on all these journeys, had all these conversations and not have known. He was not a stupid man. How could he have not known? And now—what should he do now? Be respectful and get down on his knees to this holy man? To Jesus!

Feeling Michael's body shake, Joshua consoled him, sending healing energy to him.

"I'm your friend, Michael. Please do not treat me any differently than you have been. Who do you perceive I should be now? Can I be any different than who I have been on our journeys together? We have traveled through many stages of my life and I am the same person as I was then. Yes, I am a prophet. I am Jesus. But I am human. Stand up and look at me. I am your friend."

Michael slowly rose and looked into Joshua's eyes. His own eyes swelled with tears and he broke down and cried while Joshua embraced him and held him to his chest. They stood there in the shadow of the abbey for quite some time. When Michael finally regained his composure he apologized for his actions.

"I'm sorry I overreacted," he said, wiping his face with his sleeve. "I was so overwhelmed at this revelation and at the same time feeling dim-witted for not recognizing who you are. I should have figured this out a long time ago. I'm sorry. Please forgive me. . .err. . .I mean. . ."

Joshua laughed boisterously. "I forgive you!" he said loudly. "I forgive you!"

"But what do I call you now?" Michael asked.

"Call me Joshua, as you always have," he replied. "My given name, Yeshua, is the same as Joshua. Come, my friend," he said as he put his hand on Michael's shoulder. "It is time we began our walk back. The women are waiting." He collected Michael's notebook from the ground and handed it to him. "You will see me again. We are not finished yet."

Michael sighed with relief and then laughed, almost hysterically.

"Why don't you just zap us back to your home? Why do you walk so much or sail so much when you can just materialize yourself and your family anywhere you want to?"

"Why?" Joshua humored him. "Why would I want to do that? Have you not heard that the real adventures. . .the true lessons in life. . .are in the journey, not the destination?"

The sun was beginning to set and everything glowed with that edge of evening perfection. Michael turned to see a golden halo of light surround the peaks of the abbey and in an instant he too, became light.

~~~~~

Michael lay on the couch with his eyes wide open for several minutes, not moving at all. He was digesting all he had just experienced.

"I can't believe it," he finally said. "What I just learned, how can it be? My friend, the man I've been so anxious to visit each time. . .my friend Joshua. . . Yeshua . . .Issa. . .Jesus. My friend is Jesus! I've been hanging around with Jesus! Jesus!" he repeated, shouting. "The real Jesus!"

Slowly he rolled over to his side and looked at Miyah. She was watching him with a smile on her face.

"Of course, you knew this," he said.

"Isn't it beautiful?" she replied.

"And you. . ." Michael hesitated a moment. "You, who claimed to be a descendent of Joshua and Maryum. . .you are of the bloodline of Jesus and Mary Magdalene. My God! How could I not have put this together—figured this out myself?" He rambled, sitting on the edge of the couch.

"Of course, it all fits together so obviously now. I was so enthralled with the whole time traveling thing with the cedar box, and in awe of what was happening to me that I didn't see it from any other standpoint. Then the diary readings. . .and the research. . .and the name Issa. . .the questions I had for you. . .that never got answered. You were waiting for him to tell me himself. I can't believe I was so naive and didn't see it. . ."

"Don't be so hard on yourself, Michael. If you knew from the beginning you would have been too in awe of the legend of Jesus to absorb all the lessons you needed to learn. It wasn't meant for you to know until now. You wouldn't have seen the 'boy' Jesus and the 'man' Jesus as he lived through turmoils just like any other person. You were shown the human side of the prophet."

"Not only that! I've talked with Mary Magdalene—and the Holy Mother Mary!" he exclaimed.

"Miyah! I saw Maryum writing in your diary! I know it was the same book. How incredible is that!? Your diary was there, 2,000 years ago—and here it is with you now, handed down through all those years. I understand why it's so precious to you. I actually saw her writing in it." He was still having trouble digesting it all.

Michael stood up and paced the floor for a few minutes. Miyah watched him, wondering if this was too much for him to process. He sat back down, across from Miyah and stared at her, searching for understanding.

He finally spoke. "I've respected your role as a healer and accepted your magic without question. After all, you healed me. That was a miracle. I know I gave you a hard time when you first came here, and I sincerely apologize for that. But now, how do I see you? You are a descendent of Jesus, for Christ sake—oh, excuse me, I should choose my words more carefully from now on." he almost laughed.

"Do I look upon you now as a saint? As a daughter of Jesus? As what? I thought I was getting to know you, and Miyah, I have to admit that I have very strong feelings for you. But, now it seems that you may be unapproachable. Who are you?"

"Michael. First of all, I am not a saint. I am a healer who comes from a long line of healers. I take my work seriously because of my lineage. I'm honored to be chosen to do this work. There have been many of us throughout the ages and I'm nothing special, just one of them. My task is to carry on the tradition—the Touchstone—the standard of healing that was set by Jesus. . .Joshua. . .and his followers. My work is who I am. But, I'm also human. Please don't see me any differently than you have. I'm a woman with feelings and emotions, just like any other."

They sat in silence for a moment looking into each other's eyes, each of them wondering what would become of this awakening. Then Michael stood up, reached out for her hand and walked with her to the window.

"I've so much to process right now," he said with a sigh. "My head is so full of the knowledge you and Joshua have communicated to me. I see I've much more to absorb," he motioned to the books on his desk. "And, yes, I'm willing, anxious, to continue all the studies made available to me. I'm honored. Really. But, if I seem a bit confused now and then, please understand. My feelings are so mixed up right now."

"I understand," Miyah replied.

"No, you don't really," he said. "All I've wanted to do for the last few days, Miyah, is to hold you in my arms. I've never felt this way before. And now, because of your. . .your status, I'm not sure if I'm thinking appropriately. I don't want anything to happen that would stand in the way of continuing my lessons with Joshua, and I respect you too much to offend you with my, my lustful thoughts."

Miyah listened through this most revealing declaration and surprising even herself, she raised up on her tiptoes and gently kissed Michael on the cheek.

"I am a woman, Michael. I have feelings too," she whispered. The two of them embraced, holding each other in the frame of sunlight that radiated through the window.

Michael didn't want this moment to end, but Miyah pushed away gently and said, "Michael, I wanted to tell you before, but I have to go away for a couple of days. It has nothing to do with anything you just told me. I have some things I need to take care of at my own home. I've been going back and forth while you work, but need some time to finish a few things. You shouldn't mind. You have a lot of work to do yourself."

"Of course I mind," Michael responded. "I've grown accustomed to having you here and I like it. I'm selfish. But I know you have your own things to take care of. Of course, do what you must. Just promise me you'll come back. You will come back won't you?" he questioned.

"Yes. I'll come back," she replied.

"Before I go, we'll have another journey. That is if you're up to it tomorrow."

"I'm always up to it," Michael quickly said. "Tomorrow is good. I need time to make a few notes first. I'm still reeling from my travels in Scotland!"

"Of course," she said and attempted to walk away. Michael pulled her back and hugged her gently, kissing the top of her head as he held her. They both enjoyed the tender moment.

"Now, get to work!" she laughingly ordered, slipping out of the library, closing the door behind her. Michael just shook his head, unable to wipe the smile off his face. He sat down at his computer and stared at the screen for a while, trying to refocus his thoughts. It wasn't easy. Refocusing.

Finally he typed two new headings: **JOSEPH OF ARIMATHEA** and **JESUS IN SCOTLAND** and began compiling his research into a folder of notes.

1. **A traditional story in Scotland** is that of Jesus teaching the miners of Cornwall how to make tin from ore.

2. **Old Cornwall mining ordinance maps** show two interesting names: "Corpus Christi"(Body of Christ), and "Wheel of Jesus"(wheel is a Cornish name for mine.) Also found in abundance in Cornwall's mining area are "Tunic Crosses." These crosses picture a Christian cross on one side and the image of a young boy dressed in a short tunic; obviously not a picture of a crucified or risen Christ.

3. **"Traditions among the hill folk** of Somerset say that Joseph, after first seeking tin from the Scillies (Islands) and Cornwall, came to the Mendips and was accompanied on several occasions by Jesus. At the parish Church of Priddy, high on top of the Mendips, they have an old saying: 'As sure as our Lord was at Priddy. . .' And a carole sung by the children of Priddy begins: 'Joseph was a tin merchant, a tin merchant, a tin merchant,' and it goes on to describe him arriving from the sea in a boat."

4. **Jesus' uncle, Joseph of Arimathea** became his guardian (by law, as next of kin) when Jesus' father, Joseph, Mary's husband, died early in Jesus' life. He took Jesus with him on his journeys to Glastonbury, England. The place was also called Avalon; the King Arthur Avalon.

5. **St. Augustine wrote to Pope Gregory** saying he'd discovered a church in Glastonbury, built by followers of Jesus. But the

historian St. Gildas (a 6th-Century British cleric) said the ancient church went back before AD 37 and was built by Jesus himself. He said *"Jesus ministered on this island during the last year of the reign of Tiberius."* Tiberius retired to Caprae in AD 27.

6. The historical records called the "Doomsday Surveys," witness Jesus' family presence in Glastonbury, stating that Glastonbury contained 160 acre parcels of land that "have never paid tax." This was because the King Arviragus gave these parcels to Joseph of Arimathea on one of his trips to England in AD 37.

7. Ancient carvings on the stone arch of Place Manor Church include an insignia of an anchor, a lamb and cross. Pictographs tell the story of Jesus and his uncle coming to Place for tin.

8. Joseph of Arimathea is venerated as a saint by the Catholic, Lutheran, Eastern Orthodox and some Angelican churches. His feast-day is March 17 in the West, July 31 in the East. The Orthodox also commemorate him on the Sunday of the Myrrh Bearers — the second Sunday after Pascha (Easter)— as well as on July 31. He appears in some early New Testament writings, and a series of legends grew around him during the Middle Ages, which tied him to Britain and the Holy Grail.

9. DICTIONARY — "Druid - noun - "a priest, magician, or soothsayer in the ancient Celtic religion. A member of a present-day group claiming to represent or be derived from this religion. A number of early writers acknowledge that druids were masters of philosophy, of problems secret and sublime and of religious matters. They were renowned for their astronomical knowledge and for their healing abilities. Christian author Hippolytus says Druids were capable of foretelling certain events by means of Pythagorean reckoning and calculation. Druids believed in the immortality of the soul, and in reincarnation. They also highly revere the number 'three,' and it is believed they may have taught much of their philosophy in poetic, triadic form. Many early Celtic beliefs have similarities with early Indian Vedic culture and beliefs. This is because of a common Indo-European heritage."

10. "Joseph of Arimathea arrived in Glastonbury by boat over the flooded Somerset Levels. He stuck his staff into the ground and it flowered miraculously into the Glastonbury Thorn, or Holy Thorn." This is the explanation of a hybrid hawthorn tree that only grows within a few miles of Glastonbury, which flowers twice annually, once in spring and again around Christmas.

11. Glastonbury - *"Along the Brue River and into the lake is the presupposed route of travel. At its center lay the fabled Isle of Glastonbury. It is accepted that Joseph of Arimathea, Jesus, and some of the disciples returned here after the crucifixion and spread Christianity to the locals. Many origins of the King Arthur tales sprout from this region. Some suppose a few of the knights, if not the legendary King Arthur himself,* *are descendants of Joseph."* The lake is now gone, replaced by wetland growth, fill, drainage and developments.

Michael added one more note to his file, facts he found while researching Scotland that he knew were of significance to the Jesus story, given the fact that Miyah's last name was Sinclair.

12. Rosslyn Chapel has been described as the "Church of the Holy Grail." It's located along the "Rose Line" (ley line) three miles south of Edinburgh. Created by Templar Knight, Sir William St. Clair, Rosslyn Chapel is a Masonic Temple. The Sinclair (originally St. Clair) family is descended from what has been referred to as the Jesus Holy Bloodline, a Rose line or lineage, the "true vine." The rose is everywhere in the chapel. According to Walter Johannes Stein (a pupil of the Hungarian mystic Rudolf Steiner): *"There are two spiritual traditions which found each other and united in Rosslyn Chapel. These two traditions appear also in the history of the Holy Grail. Both of them deal with the secrets of Christianity; but one deals with the subject from the macro-cosmic point of view, the other from the micro-cosmic aspect. That these two traditions have united in Rosslyn Chapel can be seen in the symbols used there, which indicate both paths: how man can strive to become Divine, and how the Divine became flesh. Christ as the corner stone of cosmic and human evolution, is shown in the Chapel."*

Michael turned off his computer. Enough, he thought as he looked over his notes. There is just too much to consume. Enough for today. He folded his arms over his desk and put his head down on them. He closed his eyes and almost instantly drifted off to sleep.

16 The Wedding Feast

Sometime during the night Michael had stretched out on the sofa. He was still sound asleep when Miyah came downstairs. She didn't wake him, knowing the previous day had been quite traumatic, but it wasn't long before he wandered into the kitchen.

"Good morning," he said. "Man, I really slept last night. I don't even remember getting up and moving to the couch. My body must have shut down for awhile."

"Good morning," Miyah replied. "I brewed some good strong coffee. I've already eaten, so if you still want me to read from the diary after your breakfast, let me know. I'll be on the patio."

"Right to work," he chuckled. "I can't think of anything I'd rather do."

When Michael finished eating, he joined Miyah outside. "It's a beautiful day. I must remember never to take anything for granted," he stated, stretching his arms to the sky.

"I want to read a few pages that may help fill in some of the details about Joshua and Maryum in Great Britain," Miyah said.

Michael sat next to Miyah on the lounge chair so he could clearly see the pages, hoping he wouldn't be too distracted sitting so close.

Miyah paged through the diary to the passages she wanted and then began, translating as she read.

> — I have heard there are many legends and stories about my life. Let this make clear one of them. After the crucifixion of Yeshua it was difficult for me to leave my home — the home of my family. As one of the 12 female disciples, and as the wife of Yeshua, I knew we would be watched. We also knew our daughter — next in the sacred lineage — may be in danger.
>
> — Fleeing Judea was our only option. And so we left on a journey to Egypt, back to our ancestral land, to the sacred protection of the Isis clan. After our departure we sent out a rumor that the people had banished us on a boat without oars or sails, to be rid of us by death at sea, so our absence would not be questioned.
>
> — We traveled together with Yosef of

Arimathea on one of his ships. Among our group were my sister Martha; my brother Lazarus; Yeshua's mother Mariam and her sister Mary Jacob; Mary Salome, mother of James the son of Zebedee; Maximinus; and Sidonius, a blind man from Jericho; a faithful hand-maiden Marcella; Yeshua's brother James; Phillip and other disciples; my beloved husband, Yeshua and our daughter, Sera; and Yeshua's sisters Ruth, Martha, Mirium and their families. Yeshua's other brothers, Joseph, Simon, Jude and Amos, had already taken asylum with their families. Yeshua's elderly grandmother, Anna, was safe at Mount Carmel.

— Our second child, a son, Yosef David, was born in Alexandria. He was named after his grandfather Yosef and his uncle, Yosef of Arimathea, with his second name, David being a link to the Davidic lineage.

— After we lived several years in Egypt, arrangements were made for some of us to journey with Yosef of Arimathea on his ship. From Egypt we landed at Râ, near <u>Marseilles</u>, in the Vienoise province of the <u>Gauls</u>. We were received there by <u>Gipcyan</u> and cared for. Our children were given special protection and were revered as the children of Yeshua, the great prophet. After a time we traveled north with Yosef to <u>Britannia</u>. Yeshua's mother, Mariam, traveled with us, as this was the birthplace of her own parents, Anna and Joachim, and many of her family. Anna's sons — Andrew, Josephus and Noah remained in this land. Yosef of Arimathea, Anna's son by a first marriage, is Yeshua's uncle.

<u>Marseilles</u> – a Phoenician trading post

<u>Gaul</u> – France

<u>Gipcyan</u>, – Gypsy, short for Egyptian, originally from Egypt.

<u>Britannia</u> – Great Britain

Miyah paused for a moment. "Maybe I should have explained this line of family to you first. As you may know, Anna and Joachim are the parents of Mariam, or Mary, the mother of Jesus. Both the maternal and paternal grandparents of Anna, and the paternal grandparents of Joachim were born and lived at Fortingall, Scotland, as did several generations before them. Joachim's grandparents moved to Galilee at a young age, but Anna's grandparents remained in Fortingall. Anna's maternal grandmother, Heline, was a direct descendant of Helen of Troy. Heline's daughter, Elmyra (whose temple name was Faustina) was Anna's mother. Anna was born at Fortingall, but moved with her mother and father to the Mt. Carmel region of Galilee and then later to Nazareth."

"It helps to follow the connections back," Michael said as he made an outline in his notebook of the genealogy of Mariam's family. "Until the journey I had yesterday and your diary reading and explanation, I had no idea of the biblical family's roots in Scotland."

"I have a couple other entries to read to you," she said as she turned the pages.

> — Mother Mariam, Yeshua and I, along with our children and some of the disciples, have traveled with Yosef across the lands of Mariam's ancestors and have been *Cambrea later renamed Eilean Isa, Island of Jesus* welcomed with open hearts. It is on the Island of Cambrea where we stayed with the Druid monks for a time, as I was heavy with child and unable to travel far. Then we sailed to a nearby island that had *Island of the Druids - the Isle of Iona* a larger Druid community so I could receive better care, and our son John was born there on Innis nam Druidneach. When the baby and I are strong enough we will travel again to where Yosef has business with the royal family, who is related to him and Yeshua. But for now, I am content on this peaceful island with our friends.

Miyah turned a few pages, skipping to one last passage.

> *Glastonbury* — We have settled here among family and friends for many years now and I do love this beautiful land. Our sons are growing in the likeness of their father and Sera is in her twelfth year. It is time for her to expand her knowledge and

receive her priestess initiation into the mysteries of the Temple of Isis, so we will begin a journey back to Gaul. Yeshua, Yosef David, and John will remain here for a time so the boys can receive required teachings from their father as they grow. They will return to *Innis nam Druidneach* for further teachings with the Druid priests. Our sons' education is of utmost importance. I know they will be well cared for, but my heart aches to leave my young sons and my husband. Yeshua assures me we will be reunited again and reminds me that the future of our children lies in cultivating their own wisdom. I honor my husband's wishes, and trust in his judgement. It is the nature of our calling that makes us sacrifice so dearly. Yeshua has much work to accomplish. He will continue his teachings and I will return with our daughter, Sera, and mother Mariam under the faithful guidance of Yosef and his men.
—Blessed be the day when my husband and children are united together with me. I long for that day.

the Isle of Iona

"I don't understand," Michael said. "What is the Temple of Isis and what does that have to do with religion?"

"Oh," Miyah quickly responded. "It has a lot to do with early religion, pre-Christian religion. Isis was known as the Queen of Heaven and the Mother of the Gods. She's the Egyptian goddess of the mystery religions, wife of Osiris, whom she resurrected from the dead, and mother of the pharaoh Horus. Her name literally means 'she of the throne.' Worship of Isis was dominant and spread as far as Western Asia, Greece, France, Spain, Germany, Portugal, Africa, Britain, Rome and beyond, and continued until its suppression in Christian times."

"I really don't know anything about Isis," Michael admitted.

Miyah smiled. "Isis was worshiped as a protector, mother, wife and the patron goddess of nature, fertility and magic. She was also known as the protector of the dead and the goddess of children. Maryum was raised in the understanding of Isis Energy. She was from a wealthy family, whose ancestral heritage covered the land surrounding the holy City of David. Her father, Syrus the Jairus, was a chief priest, and her mother, Eucharia, was from Egypt and was an Isis initiate. When Maryum was twelve-years-old she was sent to study with a secret sisterhood of initiates under the wings of Isis. Here she was trained in the secrets of Egyptian rituals and ceremonies, the alchemies of Horus and the healing mysteries of the Isis cult. Joshua's mother, Mariam, and her mother Anna, were also high initiates of Isis. Mariam was trained in Egypt and also at Mount Carmel. She was a highly advanced soul, the holder of an energy stream directly from Isis. She became a great teacher to initiates at Mount Carmel."

"That sounds almost blasphemous!" Michael exclaimed. "To say that Mary, the mother of Jesus, was a priestess under the Isis cult! Christians would be outraged."

"Remember, Isis was *before* a new religion called Christianity came into force. Egyptian mystery faiths were considered a pagan religion to the Romans at the time they compiled the Bible and any reference to them was left out. Do some research," Miyah advised. "I think you'll find Egyptian mythology fascinating."

"But isn't mythology compared to fairytales?" Michael asked.

"A myth is a collection of cultural stories, beliefs or traditions, and yes, some are exaggerated and fictitious. . .but not all. In the story of Isis it's more of a sacred narrative explaining accounts of her time. Should the story of Isis resurrecting Osiris from death be any less believable than Jesus raising Lazarus from the dead? They were both healers."

Michael made another note in his book. "Isis. Egyptian religious mysteries. I'm overwhelmed with all the research I've done, and have yet to do," he said. "There's so much out there to learn. I'll never remember it all."

"That's why you write it down," Miyah laughed. "You don't have to remember it. It'll all come together, don't worry. But don't you think it's fascinating? The history of our past is so vast, we'll never recapture it all. We can only hope to gain from its wisdom and be like Joshua—always thirsting for more."

"Yes, I suppose you're right. There will always be more. . ." Michael said. "But what happened to Joseph David and John? Were they ever reunited with their mother?"

"Yes, they were reunited with their mother and sister, Sera Tamar, in France. Maryum had her wish and her family was together for a time. As adults, the three children—the trinity of Joshua and Maryum—carried on the bloodline and many of those offspring became known as Touchstone carriers, preserving and protecting the original teachings of Joshua and Maryum, and holding the truth of Johsua's long life of prophethood.

Sera grew up to become a great leader among the Cathars in France.

She had many children, all of whom were healers. Some stayed in France, others traveled to Italy, where Sera's brother Joseph David and his family lived.

Joseph David, although young, was remembered in Glastonbury, along with his father and Joseph of Arimathea, as founding the first church settlement in Britain. You saw it—the abbey Joshua brought you to. Eventually Joseph David traveled to Italy, teaching the sacred principles taught to him by his father. Settling there, his family grew, spreading the bloodline throughout Italy.

John ended up back in Glastonbury and other parts of Scotland spending most of his life there, also spreading the words of Joshua and Maryum, under the adult name of John Martin. He married, but his wife, Elisabeth, died while giving birth to their daughter. John named her Sara, after his sister. He later married again and his wife, Muriel, had two sons, Thomas and Germane. Thomas had a son named Simon, who went by the name of Simon of Merian, in honor of his great-grandmother, Maryum, AND his great-great grandmother, Mariam. It's all recorded in my diary.

"John's daughter, Sara, had a daughter who was named Sara Bernice. This daughter traveled to France, to the Rennes region in the south and lived there for 26 years. She was buried there and a shrine, the Magdalene Chapel, now stands in this place. The sacred ground in that area was first blessed by her great-grandmother, Maryum, and later by her own grandfather, John. You should travel there sometime, Michael. I don't mean time travel. I mean go and visit this era. A lot of history exists in the Rennes area and I know you'd be interested."

"Maybe we could travel there together some time," he replied.

"Perhaps," she said, closing the diary, gently put it back into its brown linen pouch and then into the medicine bag. "I'd like to go back there someday. But for now, are you sure you're up to another journey? You went through quite a lot yesterday."

"Absolutely," he eagerly replied.

"I won't tell you where you're going, but I will tell you that it's a time before Scotland. Back several years, in fact, to a time of celebration—back even before the crucifixion, so you'll have to temporarily discard those things that haven't yet happened in this time period. You've had some pretty heavy stuff these last few days, maybe it's time for some fun."

"Fun, hmmm," Michael thought. An idea formulated in his head. "Let's do it. I'm ready!"

~~~~~

They went inside and Michael stretched out on the couch, watching as Miyah retrieved the cedar box and completed her prayer ritual.

"Can you sit closer to me?" he asked, gesturing to a chair next to the couch.

"I suppose," she said, moving over by him, keeping the medicine bag with her. "You don't have to worry. I'll be here the entire time," she reminded him.

"I know, but I just wanted you closer," he made a lame excuse.

She placed the box on the table near them, sat back and closed her eyes to hold the energy for Michael's safe journey.

Michael lay on his side, staring at the panel on the cedar box, waiting for it to come alive. Just as it began to move and a flash of light appeared to draw him into its story, he quickly reached over and grabbed Miyah's hand, taking her with him! They were both absorbed into the light of the vortex created by the cedar box and whisked away together, into the past.

～～～～～

Clearing her vision and looking around, Miyah yelled, "What!? What just happened?" She screamed at Michael. "What did you do?"

"I. . .I did this with Joshua and we traveled together. I thought you were entitled to some fun too. . .and would be glad to visit your ancestors. Did I do something wrong? Are you OK?" he asked.

Miyah put her hands over her face, rubbing her forehead with her fingers as if she were trying to uncloud her thoughts.

"I don't know. I don't know how. . ." she answered, facing Michael. "Don't you know that while you're traveling I'm sitting by you, holding the energy and watching over you. There's no one there on the other side right now to protect us and to guard over the cedar box while we're here. Michael! What have you done?!"

He had never seen her so distraught and was beginning to worry.

"I. . .I'm sorry. I'm sorry! I thought you'd like to come with me. It was an impulse. I should have asked you first. What can we do? Does this mean we may not be able to get back?" he asked, touching the Faith Stone around his neck.

"I don't know," she said abruptly. "This has never happened before. I have to think."

Michael backed off and sat down on the ledge of a stone wall. He observed as Miyah stood in the center of a lush garden and seemed to talk to herself. He knew she was calling on her grandmother and mother for council and that he shouldn't interrupt. Finally, she reached into her medicine bag, which thankfully had been on her lap and had made the journey with them, and took out something, stones he thought, and placed them in a circle near the base of a willow tree. She scattered some herbs in the center of the circle and walked around it three times, while she recited a chant. After what seemed like a long time, she turned and walked toward Michael. He wasn't sure what to prepare for. He felt sick to his stomach at what he had done and had no idea how to make it right. He seemed more worried about making up with Miyah than the fact that he may be lost here forever. Wherever he was, at least he was with Miyah.

She took a deep breath before she spoke to him.

"First of all Michael, I can't believe you did that. You obviously don't yet realize how serious our work is and how it applies to the dynamics of what you would call magic. I've called upon my grandmother, Nona, and she'll hold our energy for a safe journey while we're gone, and even more importantly, will protect the cedar box.

"Secondly, I'm sorry I screamed at you the way I did. I've just never encountered anything like this before—where I lost control during a spell. It was so unexpected. Promise me that you'll never do anything like this again."

"I promise, cross my heart," he quickly replied, making the sign of a cross over his chest. "I'm so sorry, Miyah. I thought I was doing something good for you. I didn't mean anything harmful. When you said 'fun,' well, I just thought you deserved some fun too, whatever it is."

"I admit, that's just what Nona told me when I called upon her. She scolded me for overreacting. Can you believe that? She scolded me!" Miyah exclaimed. "So, I suppose it's all right that I'm here with you on this journey. Come, let's see if we can find Joshua."

Michael let out a sigh of relief and took Miyah's hand.

"She scolded you, really?" he teased.

"Drop it, Michael," she warned, and they walked through the garden toward some mud houses in the village.

~ ~ ~ ~ ~

It was Joshua who saw them first, followed by Maryum—both of them reaching out to greet the travelers.

"I am so happy you've come to our wedding celebration," Joshua said, as he gave Michael an embrace. "Welcome."

Maryum and Miyah likewise exchanged loving embraces and expressions of pleasure that she would be present at the ceremony. Joshua enclosed Miyah in his arms, kissing her on each cheek.

"Miyah. Our Miyah. What an honor it is to have you here. It's been too long since you've come back to see us. We're always connected, but it's better to have you with us in the flesh. Welcome. Welcome!"

Michael had never seen Miyah smile so brightly. She was with family, her own people. She was home. No matter how this episode had begun, he was glad he brought her along.

It was early in the morning and the countryside was blooming with spring flowers. Farmers were between harvests of barley and wheat, so the demands of their fields were lessened. Joshua and Michael walked around the village where sheep, goats and a few cattle roamed freely. A donkey brayed as it pulled a mill wheel for grinding barley and wheat into flour.

"You are very quiet this time," Joshua said to Michael. "You must feel like a yo-yo."

"What do you mean?" he asked.

"The last we met was in Scotland, many years ahead of this day, and now we have come back to the past," he explained.

"I'm so relieved you know that," Michael breathed a sigh. "I was afraid you were just in 'now' time, and wouldn't know of our conversation in Scotland. It does get confusing, doesn't it? I'm also a little embarrassed that I didn't know who you really were in our other rendezvous. I should have known."

"No, I did not want you to see me as anything other than your friend, and a man in search of his mission. I want you to continue to see me in that light, Michael."

"Thank you," is all Michael could think to say. "I'm honored."

"It is I who am honored," Joshua replied. They continued their walk as Joshua pointed out places of interest in the village.

Meanwhile, Miyah was in one of the houses with the other women, helping Maryum prepare for her wedding ceremony. The previous night, one of the women had applied henna in abstract patterns with a thin, feathered reed on Maryum's neck and hands. This morning they laughed and sang traditional songs as they wove Maryum's hair into braids combed with olive oil scented with cassia flowers and aloes. They wound the braids into a crown on her head and covered them with a handcrafted hair net. An expensive Phoenician dye, made by simmering Murex snails for nine days, had produced a purple-blue indigo dye that was carefully applied to the lids of Maryum's eyes. Her dress was simple, yet elegant. She was draped with two sashes, one to accentuate the curve of her hips and the other wound beneath her breasts.

Miyah stepped back to admire her. "You look so beautiful," she said to Maryum.

"I'm truly pleased you're present for this occasion," Maryum replied, embracing her.

Joshua's mother, Mariam, brought Miyah a soft linen dress with a thin, flax sash to tie around her waist, along with a hooded cloak. Nodding her head in approval, Anna carefully handed Miyah the medicine bag and helped her re-adjust it around her neck, draping a sash over it to avoid drawing attention.

"Thank you," Mariam whispered to Miyah. "Thank you for carrying on our Touchstone." Miyah embraced the Holy Mother. Anna smiled, pleased with this gathering of powerful women of the bloodline.

Michael and Joshua arrived at the house where the ceremony would take place and Joshua greeted the guests as they entered the courtyard. His brothers, disciples, his uncle Joseph of Arimathea, and the other men all greeted him with "Rabboni." Joshua responded each time with, "Shelama."

Michael looked around at the structure of the houses surrounding the courtyard. They were made of stacked limestone and basalt, mortared with mud, then coated with a stucco made from a mixture of mud and clay. He imagined these houses needed constant repair as water corroded the stucco and worked its way into the crude mortar between the stones. It looked like a never ending job. He was grateful for his comfortable house back home. He had been given a proper tunic to wear and with his hair long, untied from his usual pony tail, he blended in with the other men. He watched, making mental notes of details as each guest arrived and greeted Joshua.

Soon the women of the wedding party arrived and entered the courtyard to the music of flutes, harps and drums. They removed their outer cloaks and joined their families. Michael didn't spot Miyah among the crowd. Just as he was about to go searching for her, he felt a tug on his sleeve.

"My," she said with a smile. "I hardly recognized you with your long hair. You look like one of the disciples!"

A bit embarrassed, Michael attempted to pull his hair back.

"No leave it," Miyah said, fingering his dark curls. "I like it. I like it a lot."

He smiled at her. "Really? You don't know how many times I thought about cutting it all off. Here, I'm glad it's long," he laughed nervously. "But look at you! You're glowing. You look beautiful Miyah. Have you forgiven me for bringing you with me on this journey?"

"I should be thanking you, Michael," she replied. "I had forgotten how wonderful it is to come back to my roots. I haven't done that for a very long time. Maryum has been such an inspiration to me. Look what a beautiful bride she is. I'm very happy to be here."

The music softened and the bride and groom stood before the assembled guests. The ceremony was simple, with the *ketuvah* being recited by an elder, followed by singing of psalms. Maryum approached Joshua and preceded to anoint him with the spikenard oil they had been given as a wedding gift. The essential oil had been extracted from the stems of the plant and sealed in vials. Now, Maryum broke open the seal and poured the thick contents into her hands, then massaged the pungent oil into Joshua's head, hair, hands and feet. She proclaimed her love as she dried his feet with her long mahogany-red hair. Joshua smiled at the gesture. Everyone around them could feel the love radiating from both of them at this ceremonial act.

Portions of the *Shir ha-Shirim*, also called the Song of Songs, originally written by King Solomon for his beloved Sheba, were quoted.

"As the lily among thorns, so is my love among the daughters," Joshua recited.

Maryum answered, *"As the apple tree among the trees of the wood, so is my beloved among the sons. I sat down under his shadow with great delight, and his fruit was sweet to my taste."*

More of the Song of Songs were recited as the vows continued, and even though it was a simple ceremony, because of the intensity of their love, it was also quite sensual.

Michael and Miyah glanced at each other during the ceremony.

"I can't believe I'm standing here witnessing this," he whispered to her. "I can't believe I'm standing here with you!" he said, enfolding her hand into his.

The music resumed and Joshua and Maryum had their first dance as husband and wife. The feasting and drinking began and Miyah and Michael joined in the dancing and merriment of the day. Tables were filled with bowls of fruit, including dates, almonds, apricots, pomegranates and walnuts, along with salted fish, flat bread and a stew of dried meat and vegetables. Large vats of wine appeared and were consumed. By late afternoon everyone was well fed and dizzy with too much drink. Clay oil lamps were brought out to light the festivities for those who would stay into the night.

Michael had never seen Miyah laugh so much as he watched her dance and interact with her ancestors. He couldn't take his eyes off her.

Knowing it would soon be time to return, Miyah sought out Joshua and Maryum and spoke with them at length. Michael, standing nearby, tried to hear their discussion but there was too much noise. When their conversation looked as though it was coming to an end, he joined them, knowing it would soon be time to leave. He humbly thanked both of them for including him in their wedding celebration.

"I hope to see you again soon," Joshua said with a wink and a clap on the back. "Safe journey."

"Ha!" Michael laughed. "Safe journeys to you too, my friend!"

Miyah embraced both Joshua and Maryum and said her goodbyes.

Tearfully she said. "It's time for us to return," and gave Maryum a lingering hug.

"My love and presence are always with you, my dear granddaughter," Maryum held her in her arms. "No need for tears."

Michael followed Miyah back into the garden from where they first came. She collected her stones from beneath the willow tree and placed them back into her bag. She walked over to him and took his hand. He knew he had too much to drink and couldn't resist any longer. He took her in his arms and kissed her passionately, just as a shield of white, crystallized light surrounded them and transported them back to Michael's home.

"Whew!" he said, as he let go his hold on her. "That was a lightning bolt of a kiss! Literally!"

Miyah caught her breath and laughed nervously. "How much wine did you drink? I think you had better sleep this one off. "

"Not much. Too much," he said, laughing. "I had too much to drink. But wasn't it grand, Miyah? It wouldn't have been the same without you."

"I suppose I should thank you again for tagging me along. I really enjoyed it too. It's been a most special day for me. But now," she said, as she collected the cedar box from its place on the table, "It's time to get out of these wedding clothes. . ."

Michael finished her sentence, ". . .before they disappear on us!"

"That's not what I was going to say," she blushed. "But good idea." She slipped away to her room to take a shower, locking her door behind her.

By the time she came back downstairs, Michael too, had showered and was on his second cup of coffee. He had sobered up some and was sitting back at his computer.

"I hope I wasn't out of line today," he said when he saw her. "It's been a long time since I've had even one glass of wine. What was I thinking? I guess I just got caught up in the moment. Forgive me if I did anything to offend you in any way."

"Not at all," Miyah responded. "I saw another side of you tonight that I hadn't known. You literally let your hair down. And I didn't know you were such a good dancer."

"Neither did I," he replied.

It was then that he noticed her suitcase on the floor in the hallway.

"Where are you going?" he said, almost in a panic. "What's wrong?"

"Nothing is wrong, Michael. Don't you remember? I told you yesterday I needed to go to my house to take care of a few things? It's still necessary, and you should be able to concentrate on your research better while I'm gone. Don't worry, I'll come back. Our work isn't finished."

"Is that the only reason you're coming back?" he asked. "To finish our work?"

"No." Miyah blushed. "I think I have plenty of reasons to come back."

She walked over and lightly kissed Michael on the lips and then walked out the door.

17 Planting the Seed

Miyah sat in front of the mirror in her own room, thoughtfully brushing through her long hair. She was glad she had inherited the beautiful, thick mane of her mother. It was, she thought, one of her best features. She finished brushing her soft curls and then wound them around into a neat bun on the top of her head, tucking the ends under to hold them firm. She looked at herself in the mirror for a long time and let her hands rub over her breasts and down to her belly. A frown wrinkled upon her brow. She leaned forward and took a closer look at herself in the mirror.

"Is it time?" she asked. "Is it time?"

Normally Miyah had little trouble with her "seeing." She simply asked what she wanted to foresee and it was shown to her. That was a part of her vision. But occasionally things weren't as clear as she wanted. Often in these times her grandmother, Nona, appeared and conversed with her, giving her council to the answers she sought. But this time she felt the need to surround herself with the light of wisdom from a wider circle of the women of her tribe. The question she needed answering was the most important decision she would make in this lifetime, and it affected her entire clan. She longed for a reunion of the sisterhood who loved her. She needed to be reassured that she was walking her path in the manner demanded of her, and just as important, that they were all right there beside her. A gathering ceremony was in order.

After bathing in a hot bath of rosewater for purity, she filled her medicine pouch with items she needed for the ritual. In the garden she found lavender, wild rose hips, a small piece of hazel and boughs of juniper, taking only a few branches. She gathered small twigs and wood and started a fire in a ring of stones in a private area under a secluded archway of trees.

The sun was fading into the west and the sky was brilliant with a fireball of colors. Miyah took off her shawl and spread it on the grass. The light of the sunset rimmed her naked body with the golden hue of a goddess. She reached up and undid her hairdo, her hair falling around her shoulders. Standing naked beside the fire she cast the juniper on the flames and as the smoke rose, she touched the branch of hazel to her forehead. She laid fruit and flowers before the fire and touched the salt and oil in sequence to her chest.

As if in communion, she broke a piece of bread and ate it, and then poured wine into an old wooden goblet, a family heirloom. She closed her eyes and raised the goblet of wine first to the sky, then toward the flames. She took a sip and touched her closed hand to her chest in gratitude. Miyah then took a worn, heirloom scrying mirror out of her medicine pouch. She sat on her shawl and positioned the mirror in front of her so the flames of the fire reflected on the glass. She took a jar of rainwater out of her medicine pouch and poured water across the silver surface of the mirror.

Miyah leaned into the pool of mirrored water, her hair framing her face, and whispered, "By things common and uncommon, by water and fire, salt and oil, bread and wine, by fruit and flowers of the earth offered to the goddess, bring together the tribe of my ancestors—the women of sight who have gone before me, who gather around me, who send light and love to me in this lifetime."

Then she began to softly chant the words of songs her mother and grandmother had taught her. Music of the Gypsies, the saints, sages and crones, and of the priestesses. She rocked back and forth as she honored the earth and the four directions and sang ancient words that cast spells of love and life, and bring the light of the future into the souls of the living.

Miyah stopped her incantations just as the sun lowered itself into the earth and in the darkness, reds, oranges and blues of the fire reflected off the scrying glass and through the still water. Slowly, the surface of the water began to move. The blurred face Miyah saw in the mirror was first her own, then slowly it shifted, changing to the peaceful face of Junia, then Nona, and others in her lineage, and finally to a woman with a ring of rowan berries bound about her forehead.

"What do you seek, dear Miyah?" the goddess asked. "What cannot you find within yourself that you need to council with your tribe?"

"I believe I'm ready to have the seed planted to carry our Touchstone legacy into the next generation. I seek the approval from my ancestors that I've made the right choice," Miyah said with reverence. "I must be certain the time is right and the man I've chosen is right."

"Ah," the goddess smiled. "Do you think your choices are yours alone? We are always here, guiding and guarding over you, my child. That is part of our Touchstone duty. Our bloodline is bound so strongly by love and light that you are never alone. Every particle of your being is a part of each of your ancestors. We are your collective thoughts. Your goodness is our goodness. Your bounty is ours.

"Prepare your love potion, my dear," the goddess continued. "Look, you will see."

Miyah leaned closer and looked through the water and flames, deep into the center of the mirrored image. As it cleared, images of a little girl appeared, giggling and running through a garden of flowers, her long, unruly hair blowing in the breeze of a summer day. At first glance, Miyah though it to be herself when she was young. But, behind the child was a woman, Miyah, walking hand-in-hand with a man. They were laughing and he stopped to pick a pink rose and tucked it clumsily behind her ear. Then he leaned down and gently kissed her on the lips.

Miyah squinted, leaning closer to see who the man was. She needed to be sure.

~ ~ ~ ~ ~

Michael stepped out of a cold shower. He thought it would help. It didn't. He couldn't get Miyah out of his mind. He dressed quickly, pacing in circles and finally bolted out the door and wound his way through the streets until he stood in front of her house. He slowly crossed to the park and sat on a bench, staring at her window, thinking of what he would say to her. He thought it strange that he had never been to her house before or had recollection of her talking about it, yet he seemed to be led directly here, and he undoubtedly knew this was where she lived. Michael finally went to the door and rang the bell. No answer. He rang again and knocked, gently at first, then louder, almost frantically. He had to see her!

He followed a path to the back of the house and opened a squeaky, iron gate. He was about to knock on the back door when he saw smoke and flames rising above a clearing in the trees beyond the garden. Seeing no one around, he walked toward the wooded area to be sure nothing was wrong.

Michael stopped suddenly in his tracks as he came around a giant oak tree near the pathway. Brilliant orange and golden light of the sunset shown through the trees as a gateway to heaven. . .and in its path stood an angel. A naked angel. Colors of the sun rimmed Miyah's body, wrapping their fiery fingers around every curve of her breast and outlining the roundness of her hips.

Michael broke out in a cold sweat, feeling his manhood rise. He couldn't help himself. He moved closer, unable to take his eyes off her. She was the most beautiful creature he had ever seen. He watched, taking in her every movement, absorbed in her beauty. . .in the beauty of this moment. He watched as the sun disappeared and the light of the fire took its place, caressing the lines of her body. He had seen her perform her "magic" before in the healing rituals she worked, but he never imagined anything like this. He wondered what she was doing? What she was singing? Why was she naked?

He quickly pulled himself into the shadow of the tree.

"What am I doing?" he thought, closing his eyes and letting out a long sigh. "I shouldn't be watching her. I shouldn't be here."

Leaning into the rough bark of the tree, he took a few more deep breaths, trying to calm his emotions. All he could think about was running his fingers through her hair, smelling her perfume, touching her. He was lost in the mere thought of making love to her. But he respected her too much. He owed her his life. He would never force himself on her. He should leave. Yes, he should go home, take another cold shower. Still. . .he had to take one more look before he left.

Peering around the tree, Michael looked back toward the fire. But Miyah was gone. He scanned the area. She was nowhere in sight. He knew it wasn't a dream. It wasn't like when he gazed at the carvings on the cedar box and became lost in their dimension. This was real time. He leaned back against the tree, closed his eyes, and took another deep breath.

"I have to go," he said softly.

"Go where?" a familiar voice asked.

"Jesus! You scared me!" Michael said, jumping away from her. "I'm sorry. I'm sorry. I just came to talk to you and then you didn't answer the door. . . and I saw the smoke. . .and I wanted to be sure everything was OK. . .and, God, Miyah, I didn't mean to spy on you. I'm sorry. I shouldn't be here. I'm sorry."

He was ready to turn and run away as fast as he could. "She should just slap me now and I'll never see her again," he thought as he felt the pain of his embarrassment.

But Miyah wasn't upset. "It's OK Michael," she said, lowering her eyes to the ground. "I called you here to me."

"You what?!" he exclaimed, feeling a mixture of emotions arise—anger for being manipulated and at the same time immense joy at the thought that she beckoned him to her.

"You called me here? How? Why? For what?" His voice was high pitched in confusion.

"For this," she said, as she stepped closer and rising up on her tiptoes, she brought her lips to his, in not quite a kiss, but close enough so he could taste, almost swallow her breath.

"For this," she repeated.

The sensation of her body so near, wrapped only in a thin shawl, overwhelmed him. He put his arms around her and pulled her body into his, so close he could feel her heartbeat, or was it his, or were they beating as one? He didn't know, didn't care. He slipped his hand around her back, under the thin shawl and he felt the softness of her skin. He tried to be gentle when he kissed her, but the madness of his passion gave him away. His hands wandered over her body, he wanted every inch of her. His kisses were urgent, lustful.

Suddenly she pulled away. "Michael, slow down," she gasped. At first he was confused, wondering if she was playing a cruel game on him, but as he looked into her eyes he could see that she too was filled with passion. She wanted him too.

"It's been a long time. . ." he started to apologize.

She cut him off. "We have all night," she said, "I just didn't expect you to be here so soon."

She snuggled against his chest to keep warm.

"There is something we should talk about first."

"I don't want to talk . . .I can't talk now," Michael said as he picked her up and carried her back to the fire, kissing her, gently this time, all the way to the campfire. He took her shawl from her shoulders and spread it on the ground.

"But we do have to talk about this," she protested, unaware of how her naked body glowed in the light of the fire.

"Shhhh," Michael said, pressing his fingers against her lips. "Not now. God, you're so beautiful," he whispered, reaching for her.

"But. . ." she started. Michael's mouth on hers drowned out her protests and she gave in to their desire. As they kissed he removed his shirt and shuddered at the sensation of her soft skin on his. She felt the hot, sensual pounding of his chest beating his heartbeat into hers.

"Let me do it," she whispered, and continued to undress him, slowly, gently kissing his body as she removed his clothing, her long, thick hair brushing against his skin. Michael's body had taken its toll during his illness, but now his muscles stood taut, unavoidably flexing at her touch.

Miyah had been schooled in the art of lovemaking. She had been taught that the blending of two bodies was a beautiful act and should be treated reverently, letting the mind step aside and allowing only the senses to explore the pleasures that came natural to both beings. No thinking, just feeling, touching, responding to each other with blind abandonment, enjoying each moment in complete ecstasy.

Michael stood hopelessly helpless, like a child, and obeyed her every command, feeling like he would explode at any moment.

"Take a deep breath," she suggested, smiling knowingly. His hands twitched and he needed to touch her body, her hair, caress her shoulders, kiss her neck, lie with her. . . his will gave out and he recklessly pulled off the rest of his clothes, threw his shoes and socks in the air and pulled her down onto the shawl. They kissed with a passion neither of them had known before, their hands exploring every inch of each other's nakedness, entwining their bodies with a rhythm that made them one.

When the campfire burned to embers, the fire within kept them warm throughout the night, their bodies, silhouetted by the light of the moon, rising and falling passionately in union to the beat of their own hearts.

~~~~~~

Sometime in the early morning hours they made their way back to the house and into Miyah's bed. Neither of them really remembered when. It didn't matter. Their lovemaking continued, feverishly, between short naps and sultry showers, throughout the day. They couldn't get enough of each other and time wasn't of any importance.

Finally Michael said tenderly as he ran his fingers along the curve of her hip, "Miyah, I need to rest. You're wearing me out, little witch. I don't want to have a relapse."

"Ah, you've had your way with me and now you cast me aside," Miyah teased. "Sleep, Michael, we need you well." She kissed him on the tip of his nose and lay her head on his chest. "Sweet dreams," she whispered.

They both fell into a deep sleep and it was Miyah who awoke hours later. Her first thought was to be sure her medicine bag was safe and not forgotten back by the stone fire pit in the woods. She sighed in relief when she saw it was back on the peg in the room where it belonged. Then she lay in silence, looking at this man beside her, the man in the mirror. Remembering the council she had with her tribe, she knew it was right, but she hadn't had a chance to tell Michael anything. Things hadn't happened the way she expected. Her love ritual must have been more potent than she thought. Everything moved so quickly. She wanted to speak with him first of what the consequences of their lovemaking would bring, of what was ahead for them. Was he going to be angry? She didn't want to hurt him, or for him to think she had taken advantage of him. Was it too late? They had to talk.

She watched him for awhile. He slept deeply, with a smile of contentment on his face. Miyah smiled too. The tender emotions washing through her senses surprised her. She hadn't expected to fall in love with Michael.

She kissed him gently and got up, pausing naked in front of the mirror.

"What a sight," she thought, running her fingers through her tousled mane of hair. She pondered there for a moment as her hands rubbed the flatness of her belly.

She smiled. "The ancestors are happy—our bloodline is strong."

18   The Deception

It was late afternoon before Michael awoke. He looked around, disoriented. He lay in bed, not moving, listening to the silence that surrounded him, hearing only his own breathing. He could feel the warmth of the sun on his back coming through a window behind him and leaving a cross pattern of light in the center of the wooden floor. His eyes scanned the room. A night stand next to the bed held an earthen vase formed into a lamp, topped with a ecru linen shade. The night stand was covered with a textile runner that looked old, maybe hand-woven by some indigenous native. The walls were painted a rich terra-cotta that made the room earthy and warm. A sepia photograph of women and children hung on one wall next to a row of hooks holding a silk robe, a wide-brimmed straw hat and Miyah's medicine bag. The room was simple, yet elegant.

Michael's senses were heightened by the steady sound of dripping water . . . drip. . .drip. . .drip, and he focused beyond a doorway into the sunlit bathroom. He watched the crystals of water as they formed perfect droplets and released from the faucet in a rhythmic dance. He noticed the sheer curtains in the bedroom, pulled to one side of the French doors that opened to a small balcony and revealed a world of giant trees and blue skies beyond. A smile gradually crossed his face. He rolled over, expecting to see Miyah next to him, snuggled under the fluffy, white down comforter that half covered the bed and trailed onto the floor. He was disappointed she wasn't there, but knew he hadn't dreamt the last 24 hours. It was much too vivid to be a dream.

Eager to find her, he stretched and got out of bed. Seeing his clothes neatly folded on a chair in the corner, he grabbed them and headed to the bathroom, grinning.

~~~~~

Miyah had been up for hours. She never did need much sleep and because she had been staying at Michael's house for such a long time during his healing and ultimate travels, she had a lot of work to catch up on at her own house. This was her refuge—RoseVine—the home of her family, which in itself was a house of secrets and mystery. This is where she felt safest, surrounded by complete love and support of the energy of her ancestors. It was literally a house of spirits. Family spirits.

She needed the comfort and wisdom of her elders now. The events of last night happened sooner than she had expected and she still hadn't talked with Michael about the outcome and consequences of their lovemaking.

She so wished they had spoken earlier, before their rendezvous. She hadn't expected Michael to show up at her house the way he did, realizing that her love ritual was a spell far more powerful than she had intended. She didn't even know if Michael wanted to father a child with her. She knew she had a potentially emotional conversation with Michael ahead of her, yet she couldn't help but smile when thinking of their night of romance.

~ ~ ~ ~ ~

Michael wandered around the house, which seemed an endless maze of rooms and doors. He counted at least four bedrooms on the second floor, along with a stairway leading to a third level. A couple of times he thought he saw movement out of the corner of his eye, but when he brought his attention to the area, no one was there. It was eerie. Taking the stairs down to the first floor, he ducked in and out of several rooms, again feeling the presence of "something." It made him feel uneasy.

"I'm not really snooping," he finally said aloud. "I'm just looking for Miyah." He accepted the fact that there were most likely spirits or ghosts lingering in this mysterious old house. After all, it was Miyah's house.

When he came across a massive library, he felt at ease and temporarily lost himself in the collection of books lining the shelves. Bookcases surrounded the room on all four walls. The room had high ceilings, low-hanging chandeliers, and old wood. Antique rugs covered the wood floors and furniture graced the center of the room. Two fabric-covered, high-back chairs with an end table between them faced an ornate oak desk covered with papers. Michael lingered in the room, fingering through some of the books, feeling the feminine energy of the space. It felt powerful, yet soothing. He hoped he would be able to spend more time there, but right now he needed to find Miyah.

"How come I knew I'd find you in the kitchen?" he asked as he entered the room. "I hope you don't mind, but I've been wandering around enjoying the house in my search for you. You have quite a place here. I almost got lost in your library until I was forced to follow scent of this enticing aroma."

He felt a little awkward. Theirs had been such a different kind of relationship up until a few hours ago and he wasn't sure how to behave with her now. It had been a long time since he was involved with a woman and was not real confident in himself. Still, he walked over and kissed her lightly on the lips and playfully tousled her hair.

"God, you're beautiful," he said, pulling her to him in a tender hug.

Miyah, too, felt awkward, but responded to his affection.

"Thank you," she gently said. "I'll show you more of the house later if you like. I don't have a bomb shelter like you have, but there is some pretty interesting history regarding the house. But you must be hungry. You haven't eaten since yesterday."

Thank goodness for good food, she thought. It's always an excellent catalyst for conversation.

"I made a pot of soup and some fresh bread," she said as she opened the oven to reveal two golden loaves of wheat bread she had started rising the day before.

"Hmmm, that smells incredible," Michael said. "Here, let me help you." He grabbed a pot holder and removed the pans from the oven, placing them on top of the stove.

They each dished up their own soup into pottery bowls and buttered slices of fresh bread, eating in silence for what seemed like ages. Finally, Miyah spoke.

"I want you to know how special last night was to me," she started.

Michael let out a big sigh. "You don't know what it means to hear you say that. I was thinking I may have been out of line, coming to your house and into your yard like that. I wasn't spying on you last night. You know that don't you? I'm not even sure how I got here. And honestly, Miyah, I'm sorry, but I never even thought about using protection. I wasn't prepared at all for what happened."

"No, no," Miyah stopped him. "You don't understand," she said. "I tried to talk to you last night, but we both got caught up in our passion. We should have talked before this happened. There are some important things you need to know."

"I don't know what you mean," Michael replied, sitting back in his chair. "What things?"

"Things I should have asked you before we got to this point." She hesitated.

"Miyah! You didn't have to ask me about making love to you. I've wanted to do that for a long time."

"It's more complicated than that," she said.

"Yes," he laughed, "I'm getting used to the fact that with you there will always be things that are complicated. It's OK, Miyah. It's OK. I accept that. I do. It's actually exciting and refreshing, and you've brought so much into my life—even before last night." He reached out to grab her hand, but she slowly pulled back.

"I hope you'll always feel that way," she said, grasping for words.

She slowly continued. "Michael, do you remember when we were at Joshua and Maryum's wedding ceremony? I was talking with them for quite some time about some very important things."

"Yes, it seemed rather intense so I waited until you were finished before I joined the three of you. What does Joshua have to do with this?"

"Everything, really. He told me that a crucial period of events will soon happen in our lifetime and that also means changes will be coming to our family traditions. He stressed that it was time to continue the bloodline."

Michael stared at Miyah, soaking in the meaning of her words. It took him a while to process what she was getting at.

"You. . .you mean, this was all planned?" he finally asked. "I thought I interrupted your ritual, and it was because of me that we ended in each other's arms. You mean you used me to try and get pregnant—to carry on the bloodline? Is that what you mean Miyah? Are you trying to tell me that you used me?"

"No, Michael, not at all. Don't ever think that. I would never have made love with you if I didn't care for you. . .and I do care for you deeply. I honestly do. More so than even I realized. I tried to discuss this with you before—to talk this through with you, but it just didn't work out that way. I didn't use you, Michael. I *chose* you. We chose you. Please understand. I wanted to talk with you about it first. . .to see how you would feel, but. . ."

Michael got up and walked to the window. He gazed out into the yard for a long time, saying nothing, a chain of thoughts racing through his head. Miyah watched him, not knowing what else to say. She had never meant to deceive or hurt him.

"I guess I just need time to digest all of this," he finally said, touching the Faith Stone around his neck.

"I woke up an hour ago feeling on top of the world, and now I feel empty, like I have this hole in my heart. I don't know how to take this," he said, not meeting her eyes. "I just don't know."

"Michael, last night was very special to me. That will never change. Believe me."

There was a long period of silence.

"I'll stop by your house in a few days," Miyah broke the stillness. "We can talk after you've had time to think about this. And if you want, I'll pack up the things I have there. I never meant to deceive you, and I certainly don't want to force anything on you."

He finally turned and faced her. She could see the pain in his eyes, and that tore at her heart.

". . .you didn't have to cast a spell to bring me to you," Michael said softly, shaking his head as visions of watching her ritual around the campfire flashed through his memory. "I would have come to you anyhow. You should have known that. You should have known. . ."

He turned and walked away from her.

Miyah watched him through the window as he walked down the street, shoulders slumped, with his hands in his pockets. He kicked at a large stone in the road, as if to relieve some of his anguish. Tears rolled down her cheeks as she watched him move farther and farther away from her.

Miyah had only cried a few times in her entire life—when her mother, Junia, died and again when her grandmother, Nona, died. But now she sobbed. Not for what had transpired the night before, of that she was glad. She realized that she had fallen in love with this man and she may lose him now forever. Is this what her mother felt when she sometimes called being a Touchstone carrier a curse? Is this why Junia wanted a "normal" life? Is this why her own father left? She turned away from the window and went to her bedroom. Curled up in her bed, she wept, not for herself, but for others in her life—for Michael, and for the daughter she knew she had conceived.

"Nona, dear Nona. Come to me and answer the questions I've had in my mind since I was ten-years-old," she cried. "We talk only of the women of our bloodline, but surely there is significance in the fathers of our women. Why aren't they recorded in our legends with the stories of our sisters? I know the powerful love story of Joshua and Maryum and a few lovers from my diary, but what of the others? Is there a curse that forbids the carrier of the Touchstone to love and be loved? Tell me of my father and my grandfather. Did you love?"

"Shhh, my child, don't cry," Nona appeared to soothe her granddaughter, gathering her into her arms and rocking her like a baby. "I'm here with you."

"Oh Nona!" Miyah wept. "I miss you so much. Can't you come back to me in the flesh and stay with me? I'm so lonely without you."

"Now, now, my dear," Nona consoled. "You know I'm always with you. You're never alone."

"I know, but sometimes it's just not the same as having you here as a real person," Miyah said, and then quickly added, "I'm sorry. I'm glad you're here in whatever form. I need you so much."

"Yes, dear, it's all right," Nona soothed, rocking her gently.

"Now about these answers you so desperately need," she said. "Where to begin?"

"Tell me about my father," Miyah asked. "Did you know him?"

"John. Of course I knew him. He was a good man. A gentle man. Your mother and father were very much in love. They had a long courtship and were very happy at first."

"What happened? What went wrong?" Miyah questioned. "Mother never spoke about him."

"Junia never told John about her Touchstone duties or of her healing capacities. He thought she was a midwife and that's why she had such an odd work schedule. But even those duties were too much for him to handle. He couldn't accept her being summoned at all hours of the day or night to help others and demanded her to quit her job. Junia thought that if he couldn't accept her as a midwife, how could she ever tell him the truth about her healing abilities. He'd never understand. He was a good man, but stubborn. At the time he was doing some research and accepted a big job that would take him overseas. He wanted her to go with him, but she told him she couldn't give up her work here. He accused her of letting that be a priority over him and they had a fight. He left Junia without ever knowing he was to become a father. He came back after a short time, pleading for her to return to France with him, but she refused. They wrote letters for a while, but eventually they stopped."

"Why didn't she tell him?" Miyah asked. "Why didn't she tell him she was pregnant?"

"There are several reasons, I suppose. Your mother was strong willed. She said if he couldn't accept her as she was and honor her desires too, then she wasn't sure if he was the right person for her, even though she loved him dearly. She also knew that if she told him she was expecting and he stayed, there would be no end to the pressure of quitting her work."

"But could she have quit? Has anyone ever quit?" Miyah asked, never considering that before.

"As long as I was here to keep the Touchstone powers going, she could have stepped back and I would have taken over her duties. I was always there for her and we often worked together. But your mother took her obligation very seriously. She saw forfeiting her powers as a failure and wasn't willing to be a weak link in the long line of family healers. Besides, even though she often yearned for a traditional lifestyle, she enjoyed being a healer. Helping people is what we do. How could she give that up?"

"Do you think it would have made a difference if she had told him the truth about her legacy?" Miyah asked.

"She tried a few times, leaving hints here and there and even starting conversations and long debates on religion and the historical roles of women through the ages. But your father always seemed to be on the opposing end of the conversation, and she knew without a doubt that he would never accept or understand where she came from. It was so difficult for her."

"Yet, she loved him," Miyah said.

"Yes, she did. She also knew the moment she conceived you and was so hoping you would not inherit 'the gift,' so you could live a normal life. She loved you and was so happy when you were born. I know she sometimes said the Touchstone was a curse, but she never really meant it. She knew it was an honor to be a chosen one and when she realized that you would be the next Touchstone carrier, she rejoiced and did everything she could to be a good teacher to you. She knew you were special.

"When she saw how quickly you learned your lessons and what a natural healer you were, she knew it was beyond her judgement to protect you from your destiny and actually became eager to pass the Touchstone on to you as soon as you were ready."

"Did she ever see my father again? What happened to him?" Miyah questioned.

"She never fully recovered from John leaving her. There were so many unanswered questions—why had he stopped writing? Had he ever thought of her? Did he ever really love her? Did he have another family? She anguished over these things. I think your mother really died from a broken heart," Nona said. "Not all women of the bloodline are strong and wise in matters of love."

"But didn't she consult the council, as is the custom, before she chose him?" Miyah asked.

"Yes, she did, and the council was split at first, until Junia pleaded with them to approve of John. I'm sure they knew what the outcome would be, but this was a lesson for Junia that could only be learned by living through the sadness. She will incarnate again, and next time she will be wiser, for her lesson was hard earned, but not in vain. There are reasons she doesn't appear to you often even now."

"Mother never told me of this. I wish she could have confided in me," Miyah lamented. "Maybe I could have eased her pain."

"Oh, you were so young, and believe me, you did ease her pain just by being her daughter. She delighted in everything you did and you were such a loving child to her. You are what kept her going all those years. But she knew that when you were ten-years-old you were destined to take over the Touchstone, and by relinquishing the Touchstone to you, she freed herself of her obligations to the sisterhood. It was then that she tried to find John and heard he had died in a car accident in France. It was quite a shock to her and she wondered if things had been different, would he still be alive? She never ceased loving him and seemed to give up after that. She knew I was here for you for the next decade, at least. She was tired and had become fragile. She knew it was her time."

Nona continued, "As for some women of our bloodline, many men were chosen without ever knowing they fathered the next visionary. They were good men, but would only stand in the way of the women fulfilling their duty as the keeper of the Touchstone. Times were much harder then."

"That seems so harsh," Miyah replied.

"It may be," Nona agreed. "But we don't always understand the ways of the ancients, and it wasn't always the case. For many of our women, life wasn't so severe, and they lived and loved and carried on their healing in secret, or with the admiration and assistance of their men. There have also been many situations of healthy, loving families living within the boundaries of the Touchstone secrets and respecting these gifts."

"So it is possible," Miyah said, "to live as a family and still uphold our tradition."

"Of course. It may not always be easy, but it is possible," Nona replied.

"And what about you, Grandmother? You've never spoken of my grandfather."

Nona was silent for a few moments.

"Your grandfather was one of those rare exceptions. He was also a healer, so he understood my mission. We often worked together, side-by-side in our healing rituals and ceremonies. I was blessed to have known him for most of my life and we were very much in love."

Miyah didn't understand. How could Nona have a man in her life and Miyah not know about it? She had been with her for most of her own life.

Nona continued. "Your grandfather knew about the Touchstone and respected every aspect of it. He was in awe of it, actually, and even traveled back with me to meet Joshua and Maryum several times. When the time came, he was honored to father a child, your mother, who would be a part of such an important bloodline. He understood completely. But our circumstances were much different." Nona spoke with a fondness in her voice.

"You see, Miyah, your grandfather was a Catholic priest. It would have been a huge scandal for him to be caught with a mistress, let alone someone who claimed to be a descendent of Jesus himself. Can you imagine! We were best friends and very discreet lovers. Though he was often in disagreement with many of the Church's philosophies, he felt that he could do more good being on the inside. His mission with the Church was his own Touchstone of sorts, and he used his leverage as a priest to do much good in the world. We were a good couple, Tomas and I. A great pair of healers."

"Nona! I had no idea!" Miyah exclaimed. "I'm so happy for you, that you had true love in your life and that you both shared a mutual understanding of our ancestry. What a gift that must have been. Did mother know about Tomas? That he was her father?"

"She knew. She loved Tomas and he came around often. We did a lot of charity work together, healing work, and your mother loved that. It was Tomas who helped her through some of her really tough times with your father. He was such an intuitive and gentle man. It was good for Junia to have that male energy in her life. You knew him when you were a child, Miyah. You called him Papa Tom when you were little. Don't you remember?"

Miyah thought for second. "Papa Tom. Of course I remember him. He was tall, very distinguished looking. He always made me laugh and brought me chocolate. He was around the family a lot when I was growing up. At one time I thought it odd that we had a family priest, yet we never went to church. But then we never were a traditional family. When I didn't see him so often I thought he just got too busy in the church to spend time with us. Papa Tom was my grandfather? What happened to him?"

"Tomas and I were together, so to speak, for nearly 50 years. It was difficult for him when I passed over, even though I often appeared to him in spirit."

"I remember him at your funeral, Nona!" Miyah exclaimed. "He was saying prayers and was so distraught that I recall going over and putting my arm around his shoulder. I remember him shaking, and I was consoling him. Oh, I wish I had known he was my grandfather then. Why didn't you tell me?"

"I couldn't Miyah. He came under a lot of scrutiny in the Church after your mother died. He was quite emotional at her funeral and spent even more time with us afterward, which drew suspicion from some of the bishops. He was reprimanded severely by the Church. His mission was as important to him as our Touchstone is to us, and we had to be sure no one else knew of our relationship. It only strengthened our love and respect for each other. Our travels to commune with Joshua and others from the past made him a better priest than anyone could imagine because he understood the human element of the Christ story better than most."

"Nona! I think we have some photographs of him somewhere here in the house. I'll have to look for them. I remember a picture of the four of us, Tomas, you, mother and me on a picnic somewhere, or was it a charity event? I don't know, but I remember seeing that photograph. Help me find it, will you?" Miyah asked.

"Yes, I know which picture you're talking about and you'll have it by tomorrow. I'm glad you remember Tomas so fondly. You were always very important to him and he loved you as much as your mother and I. So you see, Miyah, there are also strong men who are linked to our bloodline and have been instrumental in helping us carry out our mission of healing. Don't be dismayed. I believe your Michael will understand that it's a great honor to become a link in the bloodline. He'll be as important in your life as Tomas was in mine."

"I know," Miyah admitted. "He's been given access to so much of our lives already. He's traveled back into many stages of our history and it's even surprised me that so much has been revealed to him. It just never occurred to me that he would react the way he did. I didn't realize he had fallen in love with me and that emotions would be so strong. I didn't intend to hurt him. It's ironic isn't it, that we can be such great healers in the lives of others and when it comes to our own lives, sometimes we just make a mess of it. What's that about?"

"It's about being human, Miyah. We're healers, not superwomen." Nona laughed.

"I have just one more question for you," Miyah said. "What ever happened to Tomas?"

"After my death, he stayed around and kept an eye on you—from a distance, of course, because of an already suspicious Church, but I know he consoled you and the two of you met many times. It was so difficult for him not to tell you how much he loved you and to embrace you as a granddaughter. But after he realized your strength and knew you would be OK, he requested to change locations so he wouldn't be tempted to seek you out and reveal his identity. He was given a church in a small village in the south of France to carry on his mission. It was easier for him, I might add, because it's much more open there to the phenomenon of miracles and healing than in the United States. He has been very happy there."

"Wait!" Miyah exclaimed. "You said 'has.' You mean Tomas is still alive? I have a relative that is still here? My grandfather?" She was ecstatic!

"Yes, my dear, you do, and I'm thinking it may be time for you two to reconnect after all these years," Nona said, giving Miyah an endearing hug.

"Is he here? Is he coming here?" Miyah could barely contain her excitement.

"Not that I know of," Nona replied. "Maybe you should take a journey and discover some more of your ancestry."

"Me? Go to France. . .?" Miyah questioned.

". . .to meet your grandfather," Nona finished her sentence. "Just think about it. Anything is possible. You can start by writing to him. I know he would be thrilled to hear from you."

"I would love that—but would it still cause problems for him in the Church? I mean, isn't that why he left in the first place?"

"Tomas is getting old. He's retired and has gained a reputation as a powerful miracle worker over his lifetime. I don't think the Church would want to cause any waves now because he's so loved by the people. Write to him and see how he feels. I'll leave you his address."

Nona kissed her granddaughter on the forehead and stood up.

"It's time for me to go, dear. Thank you for calling on me and know that I'm always here for you. You know, it's not for me to tell you these things until you ask about them yourself. I'm very happy to have answered your questions. It's time you knew."

Miyah jumped up and clung to Nona.

"I never want you to leave," she said. "I'm so grateful for you. . .for you and mother. I love you both so much."

"We know, Miyah. We know. Goodnight my dear. I'll see you again soon enough."

Miyah took a step back. "Goodnight Nona. Thank you."

She watched as the image of her grandmother dissipated into the air.

19   The Family

Michael wandered around aimlessly after leaving Miyah's house, caught up in his ego and self pity. After a while he realized he was completely lost. Not only did he not know where he was, but he had no idea where he had come from—where Miyah's house was. He finally found a main thoroughfare and hailed a taxi.

"13 Park Drive," he said to the taxi driver.

"You're a long way from home, mister," the man replied. "Good thing I came along. I'm not on my regular route."

"Huh? Oh, thanks," Michael mumbled, and settled back into the seat. He was so absorbed in his thoughts that he still didn't watch to get his bearings. He was just glad to get home into the safety and security of his own surroundings. He had only been away from his house a couple of times in the last few months, other than his time travels, and he was exhausted from his excursion. He knew that a big part of that was emotional fatigue and all he wanted to do was sleep. That had always been a good escape for him in the past. He went straight to his room, kicked off his shoes and crawled into bed, clothes and all. He didn't want to think anymore or face any kind of reality. He just wanted to block himself off from the world.

But before he closed his eyes, he couldn't help but glance at his night stand and the place where the cedar box would rest when he was on his journeys. He reached out and ran his hand over the empty space and let his fingers linger there a while. He was so confused. Maybe he would feel better in the morning. He rolled over and faced the wall, putting his pillow over his head to block out all reality. In his depression, he instantly fell asleep.

The next morning Michael woke with a jolt.

"Oh my God, what have I done?" he exclaimed. "What was I thinking?"

He slipped into his shoes and headed out the door. Running down the street, he soon realized that he had no idea where he was heading. It must have been her spell that led him directly to her the night before. Now, he slowed his pace and tried to reason, looking for markers he could remember. He had lived in this city for years and thought he knew his way around. Where was her house? What street did she live on? He walked for what seemed like hours, trying to retrace his footsteps to no avail. He finally made his way back home.

"It can't be that difficult," he said, pulling out a city map to try and pinpoint the park across from her house. He located his block and with a yellow highlighter, traced his way to every park within ten miles. Grabbing his car keys, he set out to locate each one, even the parks he knew well. He drove around and circled each park, looking to see if he could recognise Miyah's house. One park seemed familiar to him and he thought for sure he had located the right place. He drove around the block several times looking for a house that could be Miyah's. He looked for the tall oak trees in the back yard and an old, three-story Victorian house with a wrap-around porch and window dormers. He parked his car and walked into the park to get a different perspective, sitting on a park bench as he had done that night when he was getting up the courage to ring her doorbell. But where he thought her house should be, contained only an empty lot—a large lot with oak trees in the back. It looked so familiar, but there was no house. He circled it on his map anyhow.

"Have I lost her forever?" he asked himself as he drove back home and parked in his garage. "What have I done?"

Michael moped around the rest of the day, feeling angry at himself for being so insensitive. He remembered Miyah telling him several times that she needed to speak with him first, that they had to talk, but he hadn't wanted to talk. He only wanted to make love to her. It wasn't her fault. He should have listened to her. And the ironic thing, he realized, is that the end result would have been exactly the same. They would have made love, and knowing he was going to be a part of this illusive bloodline would have made him love her even more. He would still be there in her arms today.

He went to the bedroom she had been staying in and stood there for awhile, wanting to soak in her energy. He took her bathrobe off the hook on the door and holding it to his face, he breathed in her perfume. Hugging her robe to his body he sat on the edge of her bed and vowed he would make this up to her. She was the best thing that had ever happened to him and the thought of having a child with her made him ecstatic. Why had he reacted the way he did?

"Forgive me, Miyah," is all he could say. "Forgive me."

One thing that brought him solace was remembering that she said she would come by in a few days and they could talk. He would have to find something to do to make that time go faster. He went to his study and immersed himself back into his research. It was the best solution he could find. It kept him in touch with her in an odd way.

~ ~ ~ ~ ~

A full week passed before Miyah went back to Michael's house. She had a lot of work to do before she could face him again. Some of it was regular household duties that needed attention. Other work included harvesting and drying herbs from her garden and making medicinal tinctures and poultices. She also had other patients she needed to visit. Michael had taken so much of her time, that now she was glad to be out helping others who also needed her.

True to her word, Nona had led Miyah directly to a shelf in the closet that held an old hatbox of family photos. Miyah was hesitant at first to open the box. She knew it would bring up a lot of old memories. She was young when her mother died, but those years were filled with happiness and a zest for life. A lot of Miyah's past was a blur because she had always been so devoted to her work. Perhaps this was a good time to reflect on those days and revive childhood memories. Junia and Nona had filled her life with so much joy that she never missed not having a father. Now she wondered what he looked like and wanted to connect with him on some level. After all, Junia remained in love with him until her dying day, even though he left her.

Miyah removed the lid and took out a handful of photographs. She wondered if these were the only images that recorded her family life. It didn't seem like much. She sorted through the pile, lingering at each photo: baby pictures of herself in sundresses and wild, curly hair; shots of Junia pulling her in a red wagon; photos of Junia, Nona and herself in a bed of wildflowers. And in the background of many of the photos was Papa Tom. The more she thought about Papa Tom, the more she remembered his presence in her life. He *was* always a grandfather figure, even if she hadn't realized it at the time. He was there for birthday parties and holidays. She always thought of him as the neighborhood priest and a friend of the family. Now, looking at him in the photos, laughing and enjoying himself, she knew that he was truly a part of the family. Being with her family was where he must have felt at home, where he could completely be himself—with his best friend, daughter and granddaughter.

Miyah set aside three photographs. One was of Nona, Junia, Miyah and Papa Tom together. Papa Tom was sitting on a chair in the family library with Nona and Junia standing around him. Miyah, about five-years-old, was on his lap. Another photo was of a young Junia and a man holding hands and walking on a beach—a man she knew must have been her father. They looked happy together, smiling and carefree. Miyah stared at the photo, looking at it closely. For some reason the man looked familiar to her. Was she seeing herself in him or was there something else?

The third photograph, taken in the backyard of their home, was of Miyah at age 18, photographed just a month or two before Nona died. Miyah was wearing a brown dress with a soft pattern of colorful flowers. Her hair was down, covering her shoulders, and she was barefoot, leaning against one of the old, oak trees, with a straw hat in her hand. She was laughing.. She remembered when Nona took that photo. She was teasing her, and had told her something funny. Miyah wished she could remember now what it was. She could use a laugh. That was the last photograph ever taken of her. And, looking closely she noticed Papa Tom standing by himself in the background watching over her. He was always there. Oh, how she wished she had known. He must have had many joyful times with her family, but also painful times, when he wished he could have expressed his love for her mother and herself. Thank God he had Nona and their love. Fifty years was a long time. She calculated that Tomas must be in his 80s now. Nona said he was retired and living a peaceful life.

Miyah looked inside the hat box again and saw an envelope. Gingerly picking it up she caught her breath. Her name was hand printed on the front. Just "Miyah," no address, which meant the envelope was never posted and must have been placed in the hat box for safe keeping. There was a letter inside. She slowly opened the folds of the thin paper and read.

My dear Miyah,

I don't know if you will ever read this letter, but I had to write it. I could not go away without leaving the truth behind me—without revealing myself to you. Perhaps the first thing I should do is tell you how important your family has been to me all these years. Your grandmother, Nona, and I met when we were very young and she has meant more to me that any other living soul. I have loved her my entire life. Her death has saddened me beyond belief and I know you must feel the same grief. I have been torn between consoling you and sharing my deep secret with you, or going away to safely continue my life's work as a priest in service to others. Believe me, I have struggled with this. You, as a carrier of the Touchstone, must be able to understand my decision and I hope you will forgive me for leaving you alone. We both know you have a powerful force of family in the spirit world to keep you strong.

The only other time I felt this deep grief was when your mother, Junia, died. She was my only daughter—the love child of Nona and myself. I was able to be a father to her and a grandfather to you, only under the privacy of your home and in complete secrecy. But the time we spent together was monumental to me. I want you to know how much I love you. I am proud to be a link in your bloodline. I know you have an important road to follow, carrying on your family tradition and I am so proud of you for keeping your legacy alive. The life of a healer is not always easy. I know that from my own work. I am also aware of the struggles Nona and Junia went through to fulfill their promise. It may be tough sometimes, but it is fulfilling beyond measure.

Miyah paused, blinking her eyes to keep back the tears. She continued.

I doubt I will ever return to the States, but my hope is that I will see you one more time before I die. You were such a lovely child, and as a young woman your beauty grew inside as well as out. I know you have honored your mother and grandmother in your love for them, as I honor you in my love for you.

If you ever read this letter and want to contact me, Nona will find a way to bring you to me. We both know that anything is possible.

Please continue your journey and know you are loved from across the sea.

Papa Tom

Miyah sat and stared at the letter. Why hadn't she found it earlier? All those years when she was so lonely, she could have been with her grandfather. She had family.

She set the letter and three photographs aside and returned the hat box to its shelf. Taking her medicine bag from the hook, she fetched her diary and carefully placed the letter and photos into the folds of the pages. These were important pieces of her history, a link to the men in their bloodline that was missing. She wanted these objects close to her. As close as her diary and cedar box.

~ ~ ~ ~ ~

Miyah knew she had to face Michael sooner or later, and after finishing as much work as she could, she set out to meet with him. Whatever he had decided she would accept. She was prepared if he wanted to have her out of his life completely, which meant she would need to concoct a spell for him to forget everything he knew about the Touchstone, Joshua and the cedar box. He would only know he was miraculously healed and would continue on with his life without memory of her. She would try to go to him with no expectations, but it would be difficult.

She didn't think it appropriate to use her key, so she knocked on the door. She knew Michael was home because there were lights on inside the house. She knocked again, and when no one answered she finally used her key to let herself in. She thought he deliberately hadn't come to the door, so slipped up the stairs to her room and quietly packed her suitcase with the few articles of clothing and toiletries she had left there. She searched around for her bathrobe.

"Funny," she thought. "I always left it on the hook." Shrugging her shoulders, she zipped up her suitcase and went downstairs. She looked into the study, but didn't see Michael, so she set her bag next to the door and went into the kitchen to write him a note. She couldn't just leave without saying goodbye.

"What do you think you're doing?" a voice behind her startled her.

She turned to see Michael leaning against the doorway.

"Where do you think you're going?" he repeated.

"You didn't let me in when I knocked so I thought I should gather my things. I was writing you a note," she offered.

"A note! Is that all I deserve—a note?" he questioned.

She didn't know how to read him. His voice was not stern, rather soft, as if he were playing with her.

"I didn't know. . ." she began, but before she could finish her sentence he strode across the floor and gathered her into his arms, covering her lips with his.

"Miyah, oh Miyah. I've been waiting for you to come back. Where have you been? It's been hell here without you."

He kissed her passionately and she returned his kisses just as eagerly.

"I'm sorry," they said in unison, and they both broke into laughter.

"This time," Michael said, "before we go any further, let's talk." He took her hand and led her into the study. "Sit down next to me and let's talk," he repeated.

Not knowing who should start or how to start, they sat there awkwardly for a moment. It was Michael who broke the silence.

"I'm so sorry I reacted the way I did," he began. "I was just taken aback by the way things played out. I tried for two days to get back to your house to apologize, but I couldn't find you. How crazy is that? I couldn't find you. But here you are and I need you to know that I was a real jerk, and I'm so sorry. If I'd listened and we'd talked this out like you wanted, I'd have still made love to you, Miyah. I would have told you that I'd be proud to be the father of your child. Honored. I'm telling you that now. I'm elated. Do you understand? Overjoyed!" He kissed her again.

"Michael, I'm so happy to hear you say that. I didn't know what to expect when I came here today. I was preparing myself for the worst, but hoping it would turn out this way. I know it's a lot to ask of you and there are still a lot of things we'll need to talk about when the time comes to raise a child in the tradition of the Touchstone. It isn't going to be easy for you. But I have to say that this past week I learned a lot about my family that I didn't know before and that will help prepare me to be a better mother and teacher. It also helps to clarify for me the role of a father figure in my daughter's life."

"Daughter?" Michael asked.

"Yes, I'm sure. The next generation of the bloodline has to be female."

"A beautiful replica of her mother, I hope," he said.

Miyah blushed, something she rarely did. "I'll have a lot to explain to you Michael about life in the Touchstone realm. I mean it when I say it won't be easy."

"I think we have a lot of time to talk about that," Michael said. "And I promise I'll listen to every word you have to tell me. I will. But right now I have something important to deal with."

"What is that?" she asked.

Michael got up, went to the hall and picked up her suitcase.

"We need to get this unpacked first. You're not going anywhere."

Miyah was surprised to see Michael being so assertive. She followed him up the stairs, but he turned into his bedroom instead of hers, grabbed her hand and pulled her in with him.

"And I'm insisting you move in here with me, so I don't lose track of you again." He took her into his arms and closed the door behind them.

They didn't come out until the next day.

The next morning Miyah shared Nona's story with Michael and told him about her grandfather. She showed him the photograph of Papa Tom with her family.

"I'll be damned," Michael exclaimed. "Your grandfather was a Catholic priest! Isn't that ironic?"

"I suppose," Miyah said. "But one of the beautiful things about it is that he traveled back with Nona on several occasions and met with Joshua. Papa Tom was a healer. Do you know how amazing that must have been for him? He often worked side-by-side with Nona. He must have learned a lot from her—and from Joshua. He stayed with the Church because he thought he could do more good with his connections through the clergy. He deeply believed in his work, yet he was just as passionate about keeping connected with his own family. It must have been difficult for him."

"So it is possible to raise a family together and not just be a donor," Michael half-teased. "I'm glad Nona shared this with you. It's timely, isn't it? Papa Tom must have been a great man,"

"Was? No, Michael. He still is. Papa Tom is alive." She handed him the letter Tomas had written to her.

Michael read the letter, saying nothing. He could feel the emotion in the words. He handed the paper back to Miyah and embraced her.

"That's beautiful," he said. "I could feel his struggle and his love for you."

"I need to find him, Michael. I need to see him."

"Of course you do. We can make plans as soon as you know where he is."

"We?" she responded.

"Yes, we. I want to be a part of this too, Miyah. If I'm going to be another link in your bloodline, I want us to walk all these paths together. I don't want to go back into my mundane world. How could I after meeting Joshua and Maryum, experiencing all you've opened up for me? I love you and am committed to you—and all the mystery that comes with it. And besides, I need to meet another man who has woven his way through the Touchstone web and survived." Michael laughed.

"Can I see that photograph again?" he asked.

Miyah handed the family picture to him, along with the photo of herself and Tomas in the background.

"I think I may have met your Papa Tom before. He looks familiar to me." Michael said, reaching for a magnifying glass to take a closer look at the man in both photos.

"Just a minute," he said and went off to fetch something in the living room. He came back with a photo album and began to flip through it.

"I'll be. . ." he whispered. "Look here Miyah."

It was a wedding picture of Michael's parents and in the center of the photo was a priest.

"He was the priest who married my parents!" Michael exclaimed.

Miyah looked closely at the photo. It was Papa Tom. But it wasn't the priest that made her gasp and go weak in the knees. She positioned the magnifying glass over the other two people in the photograph, the best man and maid of honor.

"Michael," she whispered. "Michael!"

"What? What is it?" he asked as she sat down on the sofa.

"Do you know these other people?" she asked. "The attendants at their wedding."

"I don't remember their names. I know they were my parent's best friends for many years—the same couple in the photo we saw in the bomb shelter. I think the couple split up, because the man didn't come around after awhile, but the woman and my mother remained friends. I think her name might have been Jane or something like that. She didn't have many friends and Mom said she was different from other people. In what way, I don't know, but Mom liked her and they were together a lot. You know when you're a kid you don't pay much attention to what goes on with adults. But I do remember that Jane had a child and we used to play together now and then. Why? Do you know them?"

Miyah flipped through the album and found other photos of the two women together, and photos of the children. Michael was a couple of years older than the little girl, but there were several pictures of them playing in the sand on a beach, swinging in the park, and of Michael blowing out candles at a seventh birthday party, the little girl right beside him, with white frosting all over her face.

"Yes, that's her. Funny, I remember being fond of her, but I don't recall her name. There were always so many kids around our house when I was growing up. My mom loved the laughter of children."

"What happened to Jane and her daughter?" Miyah asked.

"We traveled a lot, and were away for long periods of time. I don't know, maybe they moved. Why are you asking so many questions about them?"

Miyah reached for her diary and took out the last photo she carried with her. The photograph of her parents.

"Do you recognize these people?" she asked.

Michael stared at the picture. "It looks like. . .the same couple. . ." he started. "Wait a minute. Where did you get this photo? Who are these people?"

Miyah took a deep breath. "They are my parents. My mother Junia and John, the father I never knew."

"Our parents knew each other?" Michael asked, comparing Miyah's photo with the wedding picture. "They were friends! Then these children, these kids, must be you and me!" he exclaimed. "I don't believe it!"

They looked at each other for a few seconds, not knowing what to say.

"What could this mean?" Miyah wondered.

"It means that we were destined to be together," Michael said. "Don't you see? Your grandfather performed my parents' wedding ceremony, our parents were friends, you and I were playmates when we were children, and our mothers must have known somehow that we would be together some day. It sounds like a love story that my mother would have written in one of her novels!"

Michael observed that Miyah's reaction was not as cheery as his.

"What is it?" he asked. "Don't you think this is an incredible discovery?"

"Yes. Yes I do," Miyah answered. "It's just that there is so much to consume all of a sudden. After all these years of having only Junia and Nona in my life, and then being completely alone for such a long time, I'm suddenly presented with family and friends who I never knew of before. Why has there been such a gap in my life? Why don't I remember having any friends growing up? How could I not have known my own mother had a best friend to confide in—that my grandmother had a lover—or that I had a playmate?"

"You were only a child, Miyah," Michael reminded her.

"But I wasn't stupid. I was ten-years-old when Mother died. Was I so wrapped up in my own world that I never paid enough attention to life around me to know what my own mother was going through? I must have been so selfish."

Michael was beginning to understand. "Or was it because you lived your life in such seclusion? Maybe you were protected for a reason, so you wouldn't be tainted by the normal worries and fears of adolescence. You should be happy to know that your mother had a friend she could laugh with and confide in."

"Yes. I know. And I am. Maybe I can learn more about my father now too," Miyah replied.

"It's funny, I never thought much about my childhood until now. I guess I didn't know anything different and I was always content. My work has been my entire life. But there has to be a balance. Nona was happy. She and Papa Tom worked it out so they could each do their own work and still have each other's love. Mother wasn't so lucky. I know she was happy in other ways, but I also know she wanted more," Miyah was thinking out loud.

"Do me a favor, Michael. Don't let our daughter be raised in a bubble like I was. I want her to have friends and live *in* this world and be a part of it. I don't want her to live in seclusion like I have. I know Junia and Nona meant the best for me always, and for some reason it was probably the best for me at the time, but I want a fuller life for my daughter. We'll find a way for her to honor the traditions of our bloodline and live a full life at the same time. I want her to remember her childhood and know her family. I want more for her."

"I want that too," Michael replied. "And as a father, I promise to see that it happens. Trust me."

"Have you ever heard of the red thread of destiny?" Miyah pensively asked.

"I can't say as I have," Michael responded.

"It's an Asian thought, similar to the Western concept of soulmates or a twin flame, where two people are connected by a red thread throughout each of their lifetimes, making them destined lovers or partners regardless of time, place or circumstances. This magical cord may stretch or tangle, but never breaks. I see it with Nona and Tomas, and with my parents, which is a good example of a tangled relationship. It means we come back lifetime after lifetime in the same circle of people, and even if it's only for a brief time, we'll connect in one way or another with our 'life partner.' Sometimes it's to work out things that were left unfinished the last time around. Other times it's to reunite two people who love deeply on a soul level and have found each other again for another round of happiness. Some cultures believe it's not always a lover situation, but can be mother/daughter, son/father, sisters, friends, any combination of personalities who need to reconnect.

"I believe, Michael Wilder, that you and I are soulmates, connected by the red thread of destiny," Mijah said. "We're probably connected in more ways than we realized."

20   The Encounter

Late that afternoon Miyah went into the bathroom and unlatched the secret door that led to the bomb shelter. At the bottom of the steps she found the key along the door frame and let herself into the underground hideaway. The rooms were bathed in patches of light from the overhead panels. Intending to take another look at the photo of Michael's parents with her mom and dad, she walked across to the far end of the room. She picked up the photograph and started back across the room, but suddenly felt a shift in the energy and stopped to look around.

"That's odd," she said, walking into the kitchen area. She observed water dripping from the faucet. She noticed crumbs of food on the counter top and a damp dish towel draped over the sink. The refrigerator, which had been turned off, with the door ajar when her and Michael were there before, was now working. She opened the refrigerator door and saw a carton of milk and some leftovers on a shelf. She walked around and noticed a magazine on one of the sofas and some Kleenex in the trash container in the bathroom.

"What are you doing down here?" Michael's voice boomed, startling her.

Miyah jumped. "Michael! You scared me."

"I didn't mean to. I just saw the bathroom bomb shelter door open so I came to see what was going on. Did you want something from down here?" He was curious.

"I came down to get the photograph of your parents and I noticed that some things seem to be a little out of order," she explained, waving the picture frame in her hand.

"Like what?" he asked.

"It looks like someone has been staying down here," Miyah replied.

"That's highly unlikely, being we're the only people who know about this place," Michael said, looking around.

"But I see what you mean," he added, looking into one of the bedrooms. "That bed looks messed up and I don't remember the extra blanket being there before. I don't like the looks of this." He walked over to be sure the door that led up to the garden was locked.

"Maybe I was wrong. Maybe someone else did know about this shelter," he looked around to see if anything was missing.

"The only thing of real value here are my father's things in his safe." He slid some hangers and fabric aside in one of the storage areas to reveal the safe, dialed in the combination and opened the strongbox.

"It looks like everything is here," he said, moving some drawings and papers around. "I don't understand." He closed the heavy door, respun the dial and rearranged the hangers to cover up the safe.

"Are you sure Elizabeth didn't know about this room?" Miyah asked.

"I don't think so. I know my parents never told her."

"What are you going to do?"

"I could change the locks or barricade the doors, but then I wouldn't know who had been in here. I could put surveillance cameras up, but that would take a couple of days and I'm not sure I could do it myself. I'm not very electronically savvy. You know, we do have a security system for the entire property. I guess it would be wise if I started using it again, just to be safe. But for now, maybe I should stake out the place and see if anyone comes back."

Michael walked around checking all the rooms.

"I doubt if anyone has come in through the upstairs or basement doors. I would have known that, but I *was* gone for one whole night and day." He winked at Miyah. "What does your intuition say?"

Miyah shut her eyes and thought for a moment. "I do think entrance was made from the garden. Maybe someone was watching us the day I found the secret passage. It's possible. I have a hunch, Michael, but really don't want to say anything until there's more evidence. We should sleep down here tonight and see if anyone comes back."

"Are you sure? I can do this by myself," Michael said. "You don't have to get involved, just in case there's some danger."

"No, I want to do it with you," Miyah replied.

"OK, if you're sure. I'll get some flashlights and we can stay in the other bedroom. It's pretty quiet down here so I think we'll hear if anyone comes in, especially if it's through the garden. The slate doorway grates against the frame when it slides to open. It's not terribly noisy, but can be heard from in here. We'll know if anyone tries to get in. We can come back down here after dark and see what happens. Are you sure you're OK with this? It might be a little frightening."

"Wouldn't you rather have someone with you than face this alone?" she replied.

"Yes, I guess you're right. Thanks for your support."

Michael and Miyah made sure the doors upstairs were locked and everything looked as routine as possible. Michael set a timer on a lamp in his bedroom so the invader would think he was awake in his room until 11 p.m. Just after dark they made their way back to the bomb shelter, securing the latch on the bathroom entrance. Michael unlocked the door from the shelter into the basement in case there was any danger and they would need to escape. Earlier in the day he had added some dirt near the garden entrance and watered the lawn to make a patch of mud that would catch a footprint if he needed some sort of evidence. He admitted he had read too many of his mother's mystery novels and was a bit excited about playing detective.

They settled in and waited. They never seemed to run out of things to talk about, especially now since they had recently discovered their past childhood relationship. They brought up memories both of them shared, but had long forgotten. It wasn't until after midnight that Michael heard the grate of the slate door as it raised above the stairway.

"Shhhhh" he whispered, laying his fingers to his lips. "Someone is coming."

They had left the bedroom door ajar just enough to see into the other room. Light from the solar patio blocks above reflected enough light to illuminate the center of the room, even though the edges of the room were still shadowed. They could hear the key turn in the door and it slowly squeaked open. A figure stepped into the room and quietly closed the door, locking it.

The trespasser went directly into the bathroom. Michael and Miyah hadn't gotten enough of a glimpse to see who it might be. After a few minutes, the bathroom door opened and the person went into the other bedroom. They could hear movement in there and wondered what they should do next.

"Should we wait until we think he's asleep and catch him by surprise?" Michael asked in a whisper.

Just then the person came out of the bedroom and crossed over to the kitchen. It wasn't until the refrigerator door opened and the light illuminated the intruder that Michael could get a clear look. He stepped out of the bedroom and in a booming voice yelled, "What are you doing here?"

There was a loud scream and the entire carton of milk slipped from her hand, spilling onto the floor.

Michael flipped on the light and there stood Elizabeth, wide eyed, scared to death.

"Michael!" she yelled. "God! You scared me! What are *you* doing down here?" She bent down and picked up the milk carton, throwing it into the sink. She grabbed the towel and began mopping up the spilled milk.

"How did *you* know about this shelter and why are you sneaking around down here?" he demanded.

Miyah felt it wise to stay out of sight until the confrontation was over.

"Me? I can't believe you never told me about it. I wasn't good enough. But you told Miyah. . .and she's not even family. How could you do that and not tell me? Why didn't Mom and Dad ever tell me? I guess I've never been good enough for this family!" she yelled at him.

Michael took a deep breath. "This isn't about knowing about the shelter, Elizabeth. If you wanted to come home, you could have any time. I don't understand why you're hiding down here."

Elizabeth began to cry. "I didn't want you to know. . .I guess it's my pride. I'm such a failure. Sometimes Robert and I don't get along. He's so difficult," she rambled on. "I came by the day you and Miyah were in the garden and I saw you open the staircase. And then when you went into the house I watched through the windows. I used my key to unlock the library door and watched your little game continue. I followed the two of you down the stairway. I couldn't believe there was something like this in my own home and you never told me—yet you revealed it to her. I felt so deceived, Michael. How could you do that?"

"I would have told you eventually, Sis, but honestly, after I got so sick I had forgotten about it. Mom and Dad called it their bomb shelter and didn't want anyone to know about it in case there was some sort of national emergency or something. You know how eccentric they were. You didn't tell Robert, or anyone else about it did you?"

Elizabeth nodded a negative.

Michael crossed the floor and put his arms around her.

"Now stop crying and get your stuff together. You should be upstairs in your own room. I'm happy to have you back, and relieved I don't have a serial murder living in my basement!"

Michael glanced at Miyah and motioned for her to stay put. It wasn't a good idea for Elizabeth to see her right now.

After Michael and Elizabeth made their way back upstairs, Miyah slipped through the basement door and quietly tip-toed up to her former bedroom. Michael and Elizabeth were in the kitchen putting on the tea kettle, and Miyah thought they needed to be alone to talk things out. She could face her in the morning and try to counteract some of this jealousy Elizabeth had built up toward her.

Miyah left the lights off in her room and sat looking out the window into the moonlit night. She wasn't sure how Elizabeth would react when she realized that Miyah and Michael had become a couple. It was better to take small steps in this situation.

She heard a noise and turned to see a note slipped under her door. She unfolded the paper and read, "Thank you. I love you. I'll see you in the morning."

Miyah smiled at how thoughtful Michael was, and she crawled into bed, content for the evening.

~~~~~

Miyah was in the kitchen making breakfast when Elizabeth came downstairs the next morning. She didn't seem surprised to see Miyah.

"I knew you were still here," Elizabeth said snidely. "I'm not quite sure why. Michael looks better than he has in years. Do you usually stick around this long with your patients?"

Miyah didn't say anything. She just handed Elizabeth a cup of coffee and motioned for her to sit down at the table. She slowly poured cream into her coffee, stirred it and laid the spoon down on the saucer. She took a long sip, feeling Elizabeth watching her, waiting for her to respond.

"I'm so glad you're back, Elizabeth. We've both been very worried about you."

"Have you now?" Elizabeth retorted.

"Yes. We have," Miyah said firmly.

"I suppose you're both saying, 'I told you so,'" she sassed.

"No, not at all. Michael loves you so much. All he wants is for you to be happy. And so do I. Believe me, we just want you to be happy."

Elizabeth looked down into her coffee cup.

"I suppose I shouldn't be so cruel. You saved my brother's life and have been here for him when he needed support. I just get so tired of hearing about you. Robert always asked about you. Every time I came home to get something he wanted to know about you. I think he's obsessed with you. How do I compete with that?"

Miyah stared at her for a few seconds.

"I only met Robert through you, Elizabeth. I have no connection with him at all. Please don't see me as a threat. If he's asking about me, there must be some underlying reason. I'd like to know, myself, what that's about. What sort of questions does he ask?"

"It doesn't matter anymore. I've left him and don't want to see him again."

Miyah reached over and held Elizabeth's hands in hers.

"You're such an intelligent and beautiful woman. Before you give yourself to someone else you first must find out who you are. Be the person you want to be. Love that person. Don't try to fit into someone else's mold. Life is too short to be sad or empty. Embrace yourself for who *you* are and your life will be filled with so much joy. You don't need Robert to make you happy. You only need yourself right now. True love can only come when you truly love yourself first."

"Oh Miyah. I'm so glad you're here. You're the sister I never had. I need all your wisdom right now. I feel so lost," Elizabeth felt a sudden rush of emotion.

"I'm here for you. And so is Michael."

"Yes, I know. He apologized to me last night. We had a nice long talk and I think we have things back on the right track again," Elizabeth said. "And he told me he loves you. At first I was jealous, I admit. But now I can't think of anyone else I would want for him."

The women got up and gave each other an emotional hug, just as Michael walked into the room.

"Can I get in on this?" he asked, going over and embracing his two favorite women.

"What a great way to start the morning."

The day passed quickly and Miyah watched Elizabeth and Michael work in the back yard, grooming shrubs, watering flowers and laughing as they playfully sprayed each other with the hose. She thought it important the two of them bond again. It had been too long since they'd spent healthy time together. Their relationship was so stressed when Michael was ill and now it was time to reawaken that sibling connection.

Miyah had been writing in her diary at the smaller desk in the study. Her medicine bag hung on the back of the chair and she had placed the cedar box on the desk next to her. She was using some of the stones in the box to do a gratitude ritual. They had a lot to be grateful for. She finished her ceremony and went over to Michael's desk, taking the opportunity to look over the notes he made in her absence. She was impressed with the depth of information he'd uncovered with his research.

Just as Michael and Elizabeth came into the study, laughing and playfully shoving each other, the doorbell rang.

"I'll get it," Elizabeth called as she danced across the room.

There was immediate silence and the energy shifted into a thick, dark mood.

"What are you doing here?" she demanded.

Robert stood in the doorway with a smirk on his face.

"I came to see you, Babe" he said. "I've missed you. Can I come in?"

He pushed past her, kissed her on the forehead and walked directly into the study. He nodded to Michael and Miyah, greeting them as if they were long, lost friends.

"Michael! You look wonderful. I can see that having Miyah around here agrees with you." He directed his eyes Miyah.

"Elizabeth, do you want to see Robert?" Michael stepped forward.

"Of course she does," Robert replied. "I've come to win her back. She belongs with me. Don't you know that I love your sister?"

It took Elizabeth a little while to gather her wits. Her impulse was to run to him and melt into his arms. But she was stronger now. Somehow being with her family gave her courage.

"No. I don't," she answered, motioning toward the door for him to leave. "I don't want to see you. We're finished, Robert. We have nothing to say to each other." She surprised herself with her boldness.

"Oh, come on now, Babe. You know you don't mean that. So we've had a few little quabbles. Everyone does. You don't just run away from them. You face them and work through them," Robert said as he edged his way further into the study.

"Maybe Miyah could give us some of her expert advice," he said, reaching out to touch her medicine bag on the chair. "She seems to know everything."

Suddenly his eyes rested on the cedar box and for a moment he forgot what he was saying. He found himself mesmerized and was reaching out to touch the box when Michael took charge.

"What do you want?" he said, walking toward Robert.

Robert pulled his hand back and turned around.

"Do you think Elizabeth and I could have a moment to talk privately? Please, Liz," he pleaded. "Just a few minutes."

She sighed and reluctantly said, "I suppose. But just a minute. Michael will be right here."

"Of course I will. You don't have to do this, you know," he reassured her.

"It's OK. It's time we had closure," Elizabeth said, turning and walking toward the couch.

Miyah hadn't said a word, knowing the minute Robert walked in what he was up to. She cringed when he touched her medicine bag and saw the look he had given the cedar box. She walked toward the desk, stared directly into Robert's eyes with a steel black glare, collected the box, diary and medicine bag and moved past him.

As if in slow motion, the sheer air of Miyah's movement generated a cold sensation and made Robert involuntarily shrink back. To him she looked like a dark, misty shadow, ten-feet-tall, whirling through the air like a poltergeist with a band of faceless spirits surrounding her. Saying nothing, she telepathically sent a warning to him, letting him know she and her healing tools were not to be reckoned with.

Robert suddenly felt like a dagger had been cast into his throat and his mouth went dry. At first he couldn't speak or move. When he finally regained his senses, he quickly headed toward the door.

"You're not a healer!" he shouted in fear. "You're a witch! Stay away from me, you witch!" He stumbled out, shaking his finger at Michael. "You better be careful. She's a witch! And she owns your soul." Robert got into his car and squealed rubber down the street.

Elizabeth heard him yelling, but her back was to them so she hadn't seen any of what had transpired. She ran to the door.

"What happened?" she asked. "I thought he wanted to talk to me."

"I don't think we'll be seeing him again," Michael said slowly, looking curiously at Miyah.

"Why did he call you a witch? I'm so sorry, Miyah. I'm sure he didn't mean it. Don't take offense," Elizabeth apologized for him.

Miyah took a long, slow, deep breath. "Don't worry, Elizabeth. I've been called many things before. Witch is a good thing."

They closed and locked the door and Elizabeth went into the kitchen. Michael hadn't taken his eyes off Miyah since Robert left. Finally he spoke.

"This is certainly a side of you I've never seen before," he honestly admitted. "What happened in there?"

"What did you see?" she innocently asked.

"Well, I just saw a grown man shrink down in absolute fear, simply from you looking at him. That glare was pretty intense."

"Oh. . .I just sent him a few mental images to give him some advice. After all, he did ask for advice, didn't he?" Miyah said, adding, "You know he was here to steal the cedar box don't you?"

"I was beginning to get that picture."

"He's been courting Elizabeth all along just to get to me," Miyah said.

"But how could he have known about the cedar box?" Michael asked, as they both turned their heads toward the kitchen.

"Let's go have a talk with my sister," Michael uttered.

"Remember, Michael, she knows nothing about your journeys with the box, and she mustn't find out. It's not meant to be shared with her or anyone."

"Yes, I know. Don't worry. I'd never want to endanger your work or jeopardise my chances to travel with the cedar box. It's just as sacred to me as it is to you."

"Thank you for realizing that."

"Besides," he teased, "I never want you to get mad at me like you just did with Robert! It was pretty scary."

Miyah shrugged her shoulders and followed him into the kitchen.

They sat around the table talking about Robert and Elizabeth's relationship, letting her vent her anxieties first. Then Michael skillfully steered the conversation and commented, "Did you see the way he looked at your things on the desk, Miyah. It was as if he wanted to steal them."

"Oh, how could that be?" she innocently replied. "How would he have known anything about my medicine bag of tools."

They both turned and looked at Elizabeth. She looked down at her teacup and then back to each of them.

"Well, maybe I did say something to him. Miyah, he was always talking about you, asking me stuff about what kinds of things you use for healing and all. I didn't know. I never saw you while you were working with Michael. I just knew you had this bag and carried all your things in it. Then one day I came here to get some of my clothes and no one was home. I saw this wood box on the coffee table and it looked interesting. I thought it must be yours. I reached down to pick it up and my cell phone rang. There was no one there. I reached for the box again and my phone rang a second time—and then it all happened a third time. It was getting weird. I looked at the box and got this funny feeling, so I got my things and left. I told Robert about it later and he had all kinds of questions about what it looked like and all that. I told him it was no big deal, but I suppose because it was yours and you probably used it to hold your healing stuff, he wanted to know more. We ended up in a big fight about it and I told him I didn't want to talk about you anymore."

Miyah was amused as Elizabeth spoke. It must have been when she traveled with Michael to the wedding feast. She could just see Nona sitting there in the chair, guarding the cedar box and entertaining herself while making Elizabeth's cell phone ring to keep her from touching the box. She was so grateful she had called on Nona to hold the energy while she and Michael were gone that day.

"He really is jealous of you and the healing work you do, Miyah. He's so envious it's creepy. I hope he never comes back here. I'm sorry if I caused trouble. Why do you think he wanted to steal that box anyhow. What's inside it?"

"Just some stones and herbs I use," Miyah told her. "He wouldn't know what to do with them even if he had the box. It's useless to him. The true magic isn't in the tools, it's in the hands of the healer," she added. "If only he knew that."

Elizabeth went back outside to finish her gardening. It was always a source of relaxation to her and she wanted to be alone with her thoughts.

Michael moved his chair over closer to Miyah. "There's more to this, isn't there?" he asked.

"I'm not sure. But I do agree with Elizabeth. I hope Robert never comes back here again."

They sat quietly drinking their tea.

"I think we should get away for awhile. How does France sound? Elizabeth can watch the house. I'll restart the security system so she'll be safe. Let's get out of here."

Miyah smiled and said, "I thought you'd never ask."

21 Journey to France

The next few days passed quickly. Elizabeth was happier than she had been in a long time. She had a family again, a healthy, loving family. She was content.

Michael continued his research, but also spent a lot of time making plans to travel to France with Miyah. He compared airfare, searched out hotels, car rentals, mapped out places he wanted to show Miyah, all things a typical traveler would do. Miyah let him make his plans, even though she knew their travel arrangements could be effortless.

"Just don't book anything yet," she had told him. She resumed her healing practice and every day had patients to visit. It felt good to be back working again. Of one thing she was sure—she would never run out of people who needed her healing.

As the days passed, Michael was beginning to feel distressed. He couldn't get Miyah to commit to travel dates and wondered if she really did want to go to France at all. He'd even dug out some of the old souvenirs of his parents and left them strategically around the house—the Eiffel Tower miniature replica, an alabaster Venus di Milo statue, coasters from restaurants with French names and artwork. He knew she had seen them, but still showed little excitement about the trip. Was there something holding her back or was she just consumed with her healing work? Didn't she want to see her grandfather after all these years? And neither of them had spoken of the possibility of her being pregnant. He was waiting for her to approach the subject, but she never brought it up. Deep down, it was always on his mind. He decided it was time to confront her with both, but knew he'd have to be prudent.

"I noticed that my passport needs renewing," he said to her one day. "I didn't ask you, but do you have a passport, or should we apply for yours at the same time?" He thought he was being very clever.

Miyah knew what he was up to, but decided to humor him.

"I've never needed a passport for my travels before," she said. "Do you think I should get one?"

"OK, Miyah," Michael grew serious. "I know you could just zap us to wherever we want to go, and maybe that's why you're not as excited about making travel plans as I've been. I know it would be cheaper and quicker and all of that, but I want to travel *with* you. I want to experience all the little details along the way with you. I want the journey to be just as much a part of our trip as the destination—the sidewalk cafés, the mood and music of the city, the sunsets and landscapes of the countryside, and yes, even the tedious long flights and airport transfers. I want to share it all with you. Can you see what I mean? I have the money to cover the entire trip, so if that's it, please don't worry about money."

"No, Michael, the money is not it. I may not have a traditional source of income, but it's always there when I need it. But thank you for your generosity."

"Do you have a birth certificate to apply for a passport?"

"Of course," she replied.

"Then what is it?" he moved closer and took her hands in his. "Is there something else you need to tell me?"

Miyah was silent.

"Are you reluctant to see your grandfather again? Or could it have something to do with your health?" He was searching.

"My health," she replied. "No, I'm as healthy as can be. Why would you ask that?"

"Miyah. We haven't talked about conceiving a child since you came back. You referred to us having a daughter some day and how she should be raised, but since those first few days you've said nothing, confirmed nothing. I've been waiting for you to tell me if you're pregnant, but you haven't said a word. I wondered if after the way I acted at first that maybe you changed your mind and decided I wasn't worthy enough to help carry on the bloodline. Your silence has been killing me."

"Oh, I'm sorry, Michael. I never wanted you to feel that way. I guess I just thought you knew that all the elements were in line that first night and that our lovemaking would have positive results. I was waiting for you to bring it up and thought that maybe you weren't sure you wanted to. . ."

Michael embraced her to him before she could finish her sentence. "Did you say positive results?" he nearly shouted. "You are. . .we are. . .I'm going to be a father!" He picked her up and swung her around in circles. "I'm overjoyed!" he said, smothering her with kisses. Then he gently put her down. "Are you OK, have you been feeling OK? I haven't seen you being sick or anything. Do you need to see a doctor? When? When will this happen?"

Miyah laughed. "Of course I'm OK. And no, I haven't been sick. I don't need a doctor and will have a midwife when the time is right."

"Which is. . ." he asked.

"I'm about three months along," she said.

Michael laid his hand on her belly. "I wish you would have told me. Is that why you've hesitated to travel? Do you need to be sure everything is all right first?"

"Oh no. I'm fine. Don't start treating me like a porcelain doll now. Really everything is fine. But I do have something to tell you and I don't want you to take it personal or be angry with me," she said.

"I could never be mad at you," he replied. "What is it?"

She hesitated. "I have already 'traveled' to see Papa Tom."

"You went without me?" Michael voiced his disappointment.

"Well, in a sense. Don't be upset, Michael. I didn't really meet with him. I just wanted to see him and be in his presence. He didn't know I was there, or at least didn't acknowledge if he did sense it. I just had to see him again."

"And how did that feel?" Michael asked, still feeling a bit left out.

"It was a mixture of joy and sadness. It opened a floodgate of wonderful childhood memories of when we were all together. And yet, there was a sweet sorrow knowing what he sacrificed, and also of what I missed, not having him here when I needed him most—after Nona died. I harbored a bit of resentment because of him leaving me. But I think I've worked through that, with the help of Nona of course, and I'm ready to face him."

"Does that mean we can send for our passports and get the ball rolling?" Michael asked.

"I guess it does," Miyah replied.

"I'll get our paperwork expedited so we can book our flights. It's OK that we travel the old fashioned way isn't it?" he teased. "I want you to be comfortable. You can do all the magic you want along the way to make things go smoothly. Just don't tell me about it! Feed my male ego and let me think I'm the experienced world traveler who's making all the arrangements work effortlessly."

He pulled her into his arms again and kissed her. "I love you so much and am so happy to have a child with you."

"I love you too," she said. "And thank you for being so understanding. Just because I have certain healing powers doesn't mean I have everything figured out in my own life. I appreciate your compassion and kindness. I told you it won't always be easy. Thanks for sticking with me."

"Always," he said, nuzzling her neck. "Always."

~ ~ ~ ~ ~

Miyah had to search some to find her birth certificate. She had never really looked at it before and was curious to see the name recorded for her father, or if there was a name listed at all. The certificate was in an envelope that contained other family records, in the same closet where Miyah had found the hat box of old photos. It seemed there were a lot of family heirlooms there she would have to take time and explore, but today she was on a mission to find her birth certificate. Miyah sorted through the papers and put all but one back into the envelope. She stared at the certificate for awhile before she unfolded it.

Born to Junia Maria Sinclair, and John Charles Maartin,
a daughter, Miyah Maria Maartin Sinclair
6 lbs. 8 oz, 20 inches long

As a home birth, it was signed and notarized by her own grandmother as midwife. *M. Nona Thornburg Sinclair*

Miyah was pleased to see that her father's name appeared on her birth certificate. She hadn't even known his last name, Maartin, and was surprised to see that Maartin was also a part of her own official name, Miyah Maria Maartin Sinclair. But what surprised her the most was the signature of her grandmother. She knew Nona's last name was Sinclair, that she had given that name to Junia and it was passed on to her, but she had never seen Thornburg written in Nona's name before.

Just then, she remembered the paper on which Nona had written a name and address for her. She went downstairs to her desk to fetch the note. It was written there, as clear as day: "Father Tomas Thornburg, 13 Rue Canal, Rennes-les-Bains, France."

Miyah said out loud, "So Nona included Papa Tom's last name. Does that mean they were secretly married? And was Sinclair Nona's father or mother's last name?" Miyah had so much to learn about her family. It never seemed important to her before, but now that she was going to have a child, she wanted to know more about her immediate genealogy. She wondered why Nona hadn't disclosed this when they spoke, yet knew she and Junia would provide answers to anything she asked. She also wanted to ask Papa Tom some questions. He owed her answers.

~~~~~

Michael checked all the security systems for the house so Elizabeth would be safe while they were gone. She didn't seem nearly as concerned as he was and she actually was looking forward to having the place to herself for awhile. Now that she had gotten her life back on track she was not only enjoying her job more, but was also going back to college part time. She had reconnected with some old girlfriends and had plenty to keep her busy.

Miyah packed lightly, knowing she could buy—or manifest—anything she needed while there. She realized she would have to leave the cedar box at home. She knew it would be safe under the watch of Nona and Junia at RoseVine—in a dimension "behind the veil." However, she wanted to bring the diary. She wasn't sure why, but had a feeling it was important to have it with her, maybe for reference, or to lead them somewhere they needed to be. She placed it and some of her stones, crystals, herbs and oils that she regularly worked with inside the medicine bag. Michael had given her a fashionable, lightweight travel satchel with a long, wide strap that she could wear crossed over her chest for hands-free carrying. He knew the medicine bag would fit nicely inside, along with whatever other items she felt she needed to keep next to her. She also made sure she had some family photos and other mementos packed, things she wanted to show Papa Tom.

Michael's enthusiasm was finally rubbing off and Miyah was getting excited about the trip, not just to see Papa Tom, but because of all the reasons Michael mentioned. He had insisted they start out in Paris. He knew she would have gone straight to the south of France to see Tomas if it were left to her. That's why he took over planning their adventure. She loved that he was such a romantic and she wanted to savor every piece of this journey with him.

As expected, their flight was comfortable and their luggage arrived at Charles de Gaulle Airport in Paris when they did. They hailed a taxi and checked into the luxurious Hotel Le Meurice on Rue de Rivoli.

"This looks too expensive," Miyah first objected, as, along with the bellman, they were met with crystal chandeliers framed by thick archways and the lobby's elegant French ivory accents.

"This is Paris! We need to start off with a bang," Michael said. "We'll stay here a couple of nights and then move to a cozier hotel. I wanted you to feel like a princess for awhile. Enjoy it. You deserve it."

"It's beautiful," she exclaimed as she looked around at the mix of 18th century architecture and contemporary elegance that made her feel like royalty would walk in any moment to greet them. She felt under dressed in her simple sundress with all this luxury surrounding her.

Michael checked in and they rode the elevator to the seventh floor, the top. Their room was rich in the style of Louis XVI with Italian marble in the bathroom and a view of the city from the balcony. The gilded cupola of the dome over Napoléon's tomb could be seen in the distance. A bottle of Rosé champagne, a tray of pink petit fours and a bouquet of roses with a welcome note awaited them on a silver tray at the end of the bed.

"What a splendid touch," Michael said as he reached for the champagne.

"I don't want to be difficult," Miyah said, "but you know I can't drink alcohol."

"Oh, I hadn't thought of that," Michael replied. "No problem, we'll exchange it for a bottle of orange juice, something healthy."

"Sounds great," Miyah laughed, walking over to give him a kiss. "You're so wonderful. I can hardly believe all of this."

"We're just beginning," Michael said, swooping her up into his arms. "I know it's been a long journey for you. I don't want you to get tired out in your condition, so I've arranged for us to start our afternoon here relaxing at the hotel spa with massages. I have some kinks to work out after that long flight. I'm sure you could use some relaxation. We have an hour to unpack before our appointment," he said looking at his watch. "Then afterward I thought we could take a walk along the Tuileries Garden and the Place de la Concorde, and maybe come back here for dinner—they have an excellent menu. You have to see the incredible ceiling in the dining room of this hotel!" Michael was bubbling over with excitement to finally be in Paris with

Miyah. He slowed down for a minute, "Remember, if at any time during this trip you get tired or sick of my plans and follies, just let me know. I don't want to be bossy. I want you to have the best time of your life here, with me."

"Don't worry, I'll let you know if I get tired, but honestly Michael, I love having someone else be in charge for a change. I've had to make all my own plans for so long, it's really refreshing. Thank you. This is already so much more than I expected."

Michael planned for them to spend an entire week in Paris, exploring the city. He had been there several times with his parents and was looking forward to showing the sites to Miyah. He had encouraged her to bring at least two pairs of her most comfortable walking shoes because that's what you do in Paris—walk.

The next day they became tourists, starting with the long walk uphill to the Sacré-Coeur Basilica, which dominated the hillside in Montmartre. Dedicated to the Sacred Heart of Jesus, it ironically was originally built due to the politics of monarchy, martyrdom and war. They walked up flights of steps leading to the basilica. Michael pointed out the portico with its three arches adorned by two bronze, equestrian statues of French national saints, Joan of Arc and King Saint Louis IX.

"The building is so white," Miyah noted. "How do they keep it so clean?"

"The Sacré-Coeur is built of travertine stone quarried in Château-Landon, here in France," Michael explained. "My dad told me that this type of stone constantly releases calcite, which keeps the building white, even with weathering and pollution."

They went inside, kneeling to show their reverence and also to enjoy the architecture. The light was dim, but Michael pointed out the beautiful golden mosaics glowing from the domes. One, entitled "Christ in Majesty," was one of the largest mosaics in the world. Miyah marveled at the frescos of beautiful scenes painted in the side domes of the church and watched as people came to pray and light candles. In a side alcove, Miyah lit a candle to Nona and Junia, and in honor of her ancestors and the journeys they went through to shape the core of her own spiritual life. Michael lit a candle in honor of his parents and for the future of their yet unborn child.

Sacré-Couer - Paris

They climbed to the top of the dome, 271 feet above Montmartre, for a spectacular panoramic view of Paris.

"This is the second-highest viewpoint after the Eiffel Tower," Michael said. "I know it's a climb to get up here, but I think the walk around the inside of the dome alone is worth the climb, not to mention the view. Are you doing OK?"

"I need to catch my breath," Miyah said, giving her true condition away by rubbing her hands on the lower part of her back. "Just give me a minute to rest."

Michael made a mental note to take it slower. He was so excited to show her everything that he forgot they should pace themselves.

"Looks like I'll owe you a good back and foot rub when we get back to the hotel tonight," he said.

"You're on," she replied. "And you're right. The view from up here is spectacular." They took in the vista and once again marveled at the expansive length and breadth of the city.

After they descended the dome, they walked the meditation garden behind the basilica complex, stopping to throw coins in the garden's fountain, and rested on a bench in the shade. Then they made their way over a couple of blocks to the heart of the district.

Miyah felt at home among Montmartre's narrow streets filled with art, mimes and interesting little shops. Artists working outside in the tree-lined square at Place du Tertre wanted to paint her picture or at least sell her a painting, or a cutout of a black silhouette of her head, made in 30 seconds. They watched as experts made their signature crepes in the window of a small boulangerie and enjoyed rich chocolate and banana laden crepes as an appetizer before lunch.

People-watching became a favorite pastime as they dined on linen-covered tables outside La Bonne Franquette Café. Along the cobblestone streets and sidewalks, they enjoyed the music of concertina players and acrobats performing on the streets. Later they took in the blazing neon lights of contrasting Pigalle a few streets away.

"Pigalle is an interesting place," Michael offered as they walked down the long boulevard toward its center. "It's where night erupts in red lights. It's famous for sex shops on the main boulevard, with prostitutes operating in the side streets. Some say the neighborhood's raunchy reputation led to its World War II nickname of "Pig Alley" by soldiers, and that translated into Pigalle. The world-famous cabarets, Divan du Monde and the Moulin Rouge are here." He pointed to the sails of Paris's most famous windmill, the Moulin Rouge.

"I love coming here." He quickly added, "not because of the sex shops or anything like that, but because the entire area offers a wilder, more carefree side of Parisian life. There are a lot of little coffee shops and new restaurants, and just being in the footsteps left by a generation of legendary artists is inspiring.

"Montmartre and Pigalle were the focus of a remarkable time in the history of the arts. An entire generation of artists contributed to the reputation of this place. Degas, Cézanne, Delacroix, Monét and Van Gogh all lived, suffered and painted here. Renoir and Lautrec, and twenty years later, Picasso, Modigliani and others, arrived to make their contribution to this legendary art community. Just being here makes me want to take up painting," he laughed. They wandered among the shops and bought some postcards.

The couple sat on a painted, wooden bench near the Anver Metro Station for nearly an hour, watching people come and go. Looking down the street they could see The Cabaret and in the other direction, Moulin Rouge. Everyday life of the city filled their senses: the whir of traffic, horns, a nearby siren, motorcycles, idling buses, the clack, clack, clack of a scooter over the cracks in the sidewalk, people on roller blades weaving through the traffic, and dozens of pigeons waiting for crumbs. People were everywhere, waiting for buses, discussing directions with maps in their hands, trying to find their way through the maze of streets and signs. School kids with backpacks walked alone or in groups. French, English, Japanese, German, along with British and Australian accents could be heard like a chorus of languages stirring in a pot. They saw lovers kissing passionately and openly—men and women, men and men, women and women. Love knows no boundaries in Paris.

His fascination with the street scene ended when Michael noticed a man nearby watching them. He didn't seem like a tourist, rather he seemed quite focused on them. Michael looked over at Miyah's bag, tucked under her arm, and moved his wallet inside his zippered jacket pocket for safety. He made a mental note of the man and hoped there would be no problems on this trip.

Suddenly another man approached Michael trying to sell him a gold chain, a Rolex, flowers, T-shirts. . .anything. After politely, but assertively declining the man's goods, Michael and Miyah quickly left the area. They walked downhill to the famous Opera Garnier, then over to Napoléon's Arc De Triomphe, and down the famous Avenue Des Champs Elysées to the green and gold water fountains and the red granite Obelisk brought from the Amon Temple at Luxor, Egypt.

Michael looked around to see if the mysterious man had followed them, and seeing no sign of him, relaxed a bit, telling himself he was overreacting. They stopped in front of the Obelisk to look at the hieroglyphics of owls, ravens, bulls, bees, eyes, kings and ancient symbols etched on all four sides of the 75 foot stone monument. Michael pointed out that the Obelisk was erected at that site, where from 1793 to 1795, the guillotine had brought thousands of people, including Marie Antoinette, to their death.

"That's interesting," Miyah added, "because obelisks in Egypt are usually associated with timelessness and memorials. They were usually placed in pairs in front of temples and symbolized the sun god Ra. It was also thought that the gods existed within the structure."

"All I know is that it's more than 3,300 years old and the hieroglyphics talk about the time of the pharaohs Ramses II and Ramses III," Michael replied, recalling history details from his parents. "And you're right about the pairs. Two obelisks from the entrance of Luxor Temple were given to France, but the second one ended up staying in Egypt because it was too difficult and heavy to move. This one took two months to get on board the ship 'Louxor,' and three years of traveling time from the Nile riverbanks. I think it's interesting that France made their own hieroglyphic sketches on the base here to show the process of transporting and erecting it. No wonder they didn't want to attempt a second move." He pointed to the pedestal with gilded images portraying the monumental task, including the mechanical devices that were used to erect it.

Hieroglyphics on Luxor Obelisk, Paris

"The second obelisk was officially given back to the Egyptians in the 1990s, even though it never left there in the first place. I also know that the original top to this one was supposedly stolen in the 6th century BC, and France added that gold-leafed pyramid cap to the top." He motioned toward the gold pyramid on the top of the obelisk.

Michael took a bunch of close-up photos of the hieroglyphics.

"Maybe we can get these translated somehow," he said. "You know, my dad was in Egypt years ago and I know he went to Luxor. I'll have to dig through his slides to see if there are any photos of the obelisk that remained there. Then we'd have photos of the pair. I also think Egypt gave obelisks to New York and London, but they call them 'needles' or something.

"Enough for one day?" he asked, and they headed toward their hotel. "I don't know about you, but my feet are killing me!"

"Yeah, mine are pretty swollen," Miyah said. "I should probably put my feet up for awhile, but I feel great. It's been nice to get all this exercise and history lessons on top of that. There's so much incredible architecture in this city. Everywhere you look, there's beauty—in the buildings, the statues and art, in the people, even in the food! I can't believe how much I ate today! I love Paris already and we've been here less than two days."

"Remember, you're eating for two now. Enjoy every morsel." Michael grinned. "At least you have an excuse to eat! I'm just a bottomless pit these days! I think it's because I'm so happy."

The next few days were filled with art and churches. They shopped at the booksellers—the bouquinistes—along the banks of the Seine, displaying second hand books, old prints and postcards. Michael noted that at night the books were locked into green painted wooden containers hung on the parapets (protective walls) along the river, an ancient custom that has continued over the decades.

They went to the historic Gar d Orsay, the 19th century railway station on the left bank of the Seine in front of the Louvre.

"This building was converted from a railway station to a museum in 1986 and houses the work of some of Paris's major artists from the middle of the 19th century to the beginning of World War I," Michael explained, "It gives me actual goosebumps to know we're surrounded by art of the masters."

"I didn't know you were such an art lover," Miyah stated.

"Paris did that to me years ago when I first came here with my parents. They both loved art and saw to it that Elizabeth and I were introduced to it everywhere we went. Although I don't think it left as much of an impression on her as it has me," he replied. "They always said travel was the best education and art was continuously included in our sightseeing excursions. I'm grateful for that."

"They must have been very special people," Miyah said, sensing his nostalgia.

"They were. I really miss them. Being here brings them back to me in a lot of ways." He turned to look at Miyah. "Thank you for being here with me. It means so much. It's the first time I've been back here since their deaths. So you see this trip is meaningful for both of us. Memories of my parents for me, and Papa Tom for you."

"We're both blessed," Miyah replied.

They found their way to St. Germain des Prés, the oldest and most famous abbey founded in 543, and then to St. Chapelle, St. Severin and to St. Sulpice, the second largest church in Paris. Here they discovered the repeated symbols of Mary Magdalene inside the church. Miyah stood pensively in front of the marble Pieta, the sculpture of the Holy Mother holding her crucified son in her lap—but this statue was unusual, especially for a Catholic Church—almost unorthodox. The marble was carved with Mary Magdalene seated on the ground leaning against the Holy Mother, with her head resting against the head of Jesus as he lay slumped in his mother's arms. His right arm draped toward the floor, with his finger just touching the fabric of Mary Magdalene's dress, over her knee.

"They say that more churches are dedicated to Mary Magdalene in France than to any other saint, including the Holy Mother," Michael somberly noted. "This statue may be a startling acknowledgement that the Church is fully aware of the truth of Jesus and Mary Magdalene's union."

"Thank God there are those in the Church who are brave enough to display this type of art honoring them," Miyah softly replied.

They left St. Sulpice and spent an afternoon at Notre Dame, the largest church towering on the Place du Parvis Notre Dame. They marveled at the beautiful facade of the cathedral with the Gallery of the Kings, containing 19th century statue replicas of 28 French kings. Michael pointed out the architectural elements of the building: rampant arches, spires, peaks, windows, doors, rose windows and a magical population of monsters, gargoyles—some of which were statues and others actual water spouts—and demons emerging from magnificent doorways or springing out of pillars garlanded with scrolled leaves.

He narrated, "Did you know that every wall, every stone in this building is a page from the history of France, of science and of art? It took almost 200 years to build, beginning in 1163 and finishing midway through the 14th century, so almost every event in the history of France had an affect on this cathedral, including the French Revolution. I find that so amazing. Mary Stuart was married here. Joan of Arc was proclaimed a saint here. Henry VI of England was crowned as the child king of France in this church, and Napoléon crowned himself emperor of the French here. In 1944 General de Gaulle announced the end of the German occupation of Paris right here in this church. We're swimming in history as we stand here!" he stated with exuberance. "The ghosts of over 800 years of history are alive in the framework of this massive church!"

Miyah related to a statue of the Holy Mother in front of the Rose window, but their biggest discovery was an entire stained glass window, to the right just inside the cathedral, with 22 panels of scenes dedicated to the connected lives of Jesus and Mary Magdalene.

"I've never noticed that before," Michael admitted as they stood studying the colorful glass panels.

"Why would you?" Miyah said, lingering to take in each panel. "Unless you were specifically looking for it. There are so many windows, you really have to study them to see the pattern."

He took Miyah's hand and lead her to a small door near the north tower that led to the top of the cathedral. From there they had another stunning city panorama from a different viewpoint.

"I see why they call this the city of romance," Miyah said as they stood looking out over the city. "I love the way everything is so accessible. Are you sure it's OK for us to be up here?"

Michael smiled and wrapped his arms around her. "I don't see anyone objecting, do you?"

She glanced at a human-sized gargoyle statue with both horns and wings, perched atop the railing next to the sloped roof line, looking as if he would pounce on them at any moment if they misbehaved.

"Not yet," she laughed. They stood enjoying the view of the bridges over the Seine, the lush parks and the faded rooftops below, dotted with chimneys.

"Is that the Sacré-Coeur way over there?" she pointed. "You mean we walked that far the other day! It looks like it's at least five miles. No wonder my feet were so tired!" she exclaimed. "Paris really is a city of total seduction. I'm completely lost in her mysteries."

They left Notre Dame and strolled along the sidewalks, lingering on the terrace of a French bistro in the Latin Quarter to enjoy their lunch.

"Did you know this is called the Latin Quarter because Latin was the official language used by professors and students of the area?" Michael asked. "And do, by all means tell me to shut up if you're sick of my little historic notes," he laughed.

"Not at all. I find them interesting, as long as they don't turn into volumes," Miyah replied, as they headed back to their hotel.

Earlier they had moved to the Hotel Britannique, 20 Avenue Victoria, a charming hotel in the center of the city and an easy walk to the sites they wanted to visit. Miyah loved the hotel as soon as she walked in and saw the large, ornamental, crystal globe decorating the end of the banister.

"My mother loved this place," Michael told her. "The hotel's been here since 1861 and hasn't changed much. She said the silky fabrics, velvet, antiques, old wood and soft lighting reminded her of an Agatha Christie novel."

"Well, let's not have any mysteries to solve while we're staying here," Miyah said, as she put her hand to her medicine bag, which, inside the travel satchel, hadn't left her side. "We've hopefully left all traces of that behind," she added, referring to the incident with Robert, not even liking that his name had entered her thoughts.

Notre Dame - Paris

Eiffel Tower - Paris

"Yes, let's forget about that," Michael said, with an image of the man watching them on the street flashing through his mind.

"There's still so much I want to show you in Paris," he said when they got to their room. "We need another week!"

"And another pair of shoes," Miyah said, rubbing her tired, swollen feet.

"Ah, but let me tell you of the things I *won't* drag you to see—the fifteen different medieval churches that all boast of having the relics of the foreskin of Jesus; the clay at Canterbury left over after God fashioned Adam; bones of St. James, St. Mark and several other saints;

and the most outrageous, Mary Magdalene's arm."

"Well, thank you for sparing me that!" Miyah laughed.

"We'll just have to come back again," he said, as he put her feet on his lap and began to give her a foot massage. "We'll have to make Paris an annual event, that's all there is to it. I insist."

"You won't find me objecting," Miyah agreed, enjoying her foot rub. She handed him a small bottle of essential oils to rub on the bottom of her feet.

Black Madonna-Chartes

"This smells good," he said, taking a deep whiff. "What's in it?"

"It's a blend of patchouli, tangerine, orange and ylang ylang, mixed with a little almond oil. It should ease the tightness in my feet and legs and help me get a good night sleep."

"You'll need a good night sleep," he said, carefully massaging the oil into her feet and legs. "We have to make the best of the next few days before we leave for the south. We'll take the train to see

Labyrinth - Chartes

Chartes Cathedral. That'll take an entire day, but it's such a work of art, you have to see it. You'll see the giant 800-year-old labyrinth, 42 feet across on the floor inside the cathedral, although sadly now it's usually covered with chairs. There's also a sculpted labyrinth on the grounds that maybe we can walk." Michael continued excitedly. "The stained glass window closest to the entrance of the labyrinth inside the church has 22 panels and is dedicated to Mary Magdalene. In fact, there are several hundred statues of women carved on Chartes Cathedral, more than any other church in the world. Saint Anne, mother of the Holy Mother, is represented prominently in a place of power, on the north side, the Door of the Initiates."

"I'm looking forward to spending time there," Miyah admitted. "I've read a little about Chartes and know that many esoteric symbols and designs were incorporated into the architecture of the church."

Michael continued with their itinerary. "We need an entire day at the Louvre and even that won't be enough. Let's save that for our last day. Tomorrow we'll go visit the Iron Lady, the Eiffel Tower."

"Tell me about the Eiffel Tower," Miyah requested—anything to keep him on task with her foot massage.

"Well, it was built for the 1889 World's Fair, and when it was erected it was a source of a big scandal. A petition was signed condemning the bizarre construction, claiming the beauty of Paris would be ruined by the 'ugly factory chimney.' They called it the Iron Lady because it took 7,300 tons of iron and two years to build. It's ironic because today it's symbolic of Paris and is so much a part of the city's landscape.

"But the main thing I want to show you tomorrow is La Madeleine, the Church of Mary Magdalene. It resembles a Greek temple and I think you'll want to spend some time there."

"I've read a little bit about it," Miyah said. "I love that such a monumental church has been dedicated to Mary Magdalene. There seem to be many all over France and other places in Europe as well. That says volumes, doesn't it?"

Michael was listening, but had taken more interest in the massage he was giving Miyah. She could tell he was trying to be casual about it, but his sudden silence and change of breathing gave him away.

"Did I tell you that my back hurt too?" she cleverly asked. "Do you mind rubbing some of this on my shoulders and back." She smiled as she began to undress. . .

~~~~~

The City of Light awoke with golden morning sunshine spreading across the rooftops, bringing life to everything it touched. It was difficult to crawl out of their cozy canopy bed and awaken to the world, but Miyah and Michael's time in Paris was quickly coming to an end and they had a lot planned for the day. They started with breakfast at sunrise, amid pots of sunflowers on their little patio. A basket of delicate breads and pastries was delivered to their room on a bamboo tray. The subtle aroma of Darjeeling steaming from a big, white teapot welcomed them to the morning, along with white, oversized porcelain cups with the hotel emblem stamped in gold on the outside.

Miyah sat sipping her tea and taking in the moment. It bothered her that the flash of Robert had entered her head the day before. Everything had been so perfect, and now she wondered if she should be on her guard for something. She sent out a shield of protection and asked for Nona and Junia and her spirit guides to watch over them, and also Elizabeth back home.

"Please don't let anything ruin our plans or interrupt our trip," she asked as she lit a candle for protection and placed a crystal next to it. "If there is something lingering, redirect that energy into something positive." Then she let go of any negative thoughts she may have had so she wouldn't draw that energy to her, and meditated to clear her chakras.

She appreciated Michael giving her space in the morning to keep up with her meditation and rituals. They were a part of her everyday routine and she was glad he respected that. She had offered to teach him how to meditate, but he admitted he wasn't quite ready yet. He had already come a long way from when she first met him and she would never put any pressure on him to participate in her work. Just accepting it was enough for her, even though some day she knew he would get to the point where he would want to find that place of calm meditation offers. She was patient. It would be in his own time.

They started their excursion with a leisurely walk to the Eiffel Tower, wandering along the Seine and enjoying the long boulevards, glittering shop windows and golden history of the city. They ate delicious crepes from the crepe stand on Blvd. Saint Germain and finally made their way to La Madeleine.

The church dominated the Faubourg Saint Honoré and Grand Boulevards and it was built to do just that, acting as one of the cornerstones of the westward expansion of the capitol in the middle of the 18th century.

"I told you it looks like a Greek Temple," Michael said as they admired the building. "At one time it was a temple, a memorial for the heroes and victims of the French Revolution. It has 52 Corinthian columns surrounding the building with statues of saints."

"So it wasn't originally built as a shrine to Mary Magdalene?" Miyah asked.

"Well, in a way it was. There was a small parish here in the very beginning. Then in 1492 King Charles VIII officially protected the original church and established a brotherhood of Saint Mary Magdalene. Throughout history the buildings that were here were moved, torn down, rebuilt, added on to, changed and had many uses. The first cornerstone for this building was laid in 1763 by Louis XV, but it wasn't until 1802 that the site was declared a parish of La Madeleine. Louis XVIII re-dedicated it to Saint Magdalene in 1814, and miraculously in 1832 all state funds allocated to public monuments were granted to La Madeleine. Its construction caused a lot of problems for the French state, and it took over eighty years to be completed. I find it interesting that most of the great romantic artists of the era contributed to the building of La Madeleine. I think the church is now affiliated with a Benedictine abbey."

"Do you know why they chose to dedicate it to Mary Magdalene?" Miyah wondered if there were more personal, historic details.

"I don't know. Maybe you should ask your personal guides to see if any of those kings are related? Now that would be interesting," he winked.

They walked around the outside of the building, which was surrounded by tall iron fences and gates, set on its own cement pedestal in the center of four busy flagstone streets, taking up an entire block. Twenty-eight large steps stretched across the width of the front of the building. Michael pointed out the sculptured roses in the ceiling of each of the seventeen outside bays on one side of the structure.

"There are enough statues here to fill a museum," Miyah said, counting thirty-four, as they circled the building studying the saints lined up behind the pillars.

"Just wait until you see inside," Michael said.

Before they entered the church Miyah admired the triangular upper part of the front of the building. The Latin inscription: D.O.M. SVB. INVOCAT S.MAR.MAGDALENAE was carved, which translates, "To God the Almighty, under the invocation of Saint Mary Magdalene." Bigger than life-sized high-relief carvings filled the entire triangle. Jesus was in the center with angels on each side of him. Mary Magdalene knelt to his right, looking up at him. He was looking down at her, arms outstretched. Over a dozen other figures of men, women and children, filled the immense scene.

Michael and Miyah entered the church through the gigantic bronze doors, which were themselves famous for their detailed sculptured panels.

Once inside, Miyah fell silent. She sat on one of the wooden chairs in a long row of seats and reverently said a prayer before she explored the church. Michael sat next to her, equally in awe of the energy that even he could feel in this place. Some of the references to Mary Magdalene were subtle. Arches and bows of the sidewalls were composed of rosettes on a blue background, which alternated with red panels painted with cherubs and symbols, and the letter M, for Magdalene.

Miyah and Michael walked around, looking at the icons, paying particular interest to a round-headed arch of cupolas and semi circular bays that had six scenes painted of Mary Magdalene's life. One was titled *"Praying Saint Mary Magdalene visited by the Angels,"* which included Mary reading from her book by candlelight, with a vase in the foreground, a cross in the back and Mary surrounded by angels who "came to serve her."

Another painting was *"The Conversation of Saint Mary Magdalene,"* where a richly dressed Mary stood to the right of Jesus during a sermon. *"The Meal at Simon's"* showed Jesus sitting, raising his hand over Mary as she wiped his feet with her hair after washing them with precious oils.

"You know that was part of an ancient three-day wedding ritual," Miyah whispered. "Washing the groom's feet with spikenard oil." Michael nodded his head as he recalled Joshua and Maryum's wedding ritual.

They continued to the next painting, *"Saint Mary Magdalene, a Witness of the Death of Jesus"* where she was kneeling in full light at the foot of the cross, comforting Mother Mary and Saint John. The next scene was called *"Saint Mary Magdalene at the Sepulchre,"* which was when she went to the tomb and found angels instead of the body of Jesus. The sixth painting was *"Death of Saint Mary Magdalene,"* with a skull and books by her side in the desert, surrounded by angels.

Michael looped Miyah's arm through his as they viewed the paintings. He wondered what thoughts were going through her head and how true these depictions were in the life of this woman that he, himself, had met and knew as Maryum.

"It was such a hard life for them," Miyah murmured.

"Yes, but I see it in a completely new light now. . .now that I know a different ending to their story," he offered. "A much happier ending."

They moved toward the main altar of the church and sat down on a step near one of the pillars to take in the fullness of an incredible large fresco in the dome looming high above the altar. Jesus, in the center, presided over the history of Eastern Christianity at his right, which included the first martyrs and disciples, saints, Rabbis, dark-skinned kings, Egyptian priests, a female Druid, Magi and commoners.

At his left was Western Christianity, represented by richly robed Catholic popes, saints, Roman soldiers, nobles from the crusades, important historical men, and a king with a round ball in one hand and sword in the other. In the bottom center of the painting was a black raven, with its wings outstretched, head facing toward Eastern Christianity. Even the Emperor Napoléon, his coat sprinkled with golden bees, and a company of Cardinals and Bishops were painted into the fresco, adding historical reference marking the era of painting the artwork. Standing at the top of a high stairway, with a golden staff in his hand, surrounded by the apostles, Jesus blessed the people. Mary Magdalene, robed in white, with her hands clasped in prayer, was being lifted up to him on a bed of clouds, like a high altar. The words DELIEXIT MULTIM, *"she has loved much,"* were written on a golden banner held by three angels. Both Jesus and Mary Magdalene had halos of golden light surrounding their heads, depicting them as the "King and Queen of Heaven."

Miyah and Michael looked at each other knowingly, saying nothing. They moved closer to view the magnificent white statue looming behind the white marble altar beneath the fresco. The detailed four-figure statue was titled *"The Ecstasy of Saint Mary Magdalene,"* and showed her on a woven basket, supported by three angels holding hands in a circle around her. She was raised above them, arms outstretched, palms open, and with her eyes closed had a peaceful look on her face. On each side of the exquisitely

Church of Mary Magdalene - Paris

Church of Mary Magdalene - Paris

carved altar were two kneeling angels, one praying and the other with her hands crossed over her heart. Amid all the paintings and ornate architecture, this statue of Mary Magdalene, enhanced by golden tints of the altar and from the circle of scrollwork around the frescos above, was the focal point of the church. Miyah stood in front of the statue and touched her closed hand to her own heart three times in reverence.

Evidence of Jesus and Mary Magdalene together in France appeared in a mosaic panel above the colonnade titled, *"Christ and Those Who Evangelized Gaul."* Separated by palm trees that grow both in Palestine and in Provence, France, were figures of saints, all with golden halos. The first person on Jesus' right was Mary Magdalene with the alabaster jar at her side, followed by other saints. To Jesus' left was Martha (Mary Magdalene's sister), Lazarus (her brother), Mary Jacobe, and Mary Salome, all of whom traveled to Gaul with Mary Magdalene. They were followed in the mosaic by more saints and church founders. The inscription on the left side read: CHRISTO TRIUPHANTI/ET APOSTOLIS NOSTRIS UNDEVIGINTI QUOS CUM IPSO IN TERRIS CONVERSATOS;EVANGELIUM / AB EJUS ORE ACCEPTUM / GALLIIS PRAEDICASSE; MAJORUM RELATIONE TRADITUM EST.

"Can you translate that?" Michael asked.

"It says, *'To Christ triumphant and to the nineteen apostles who are said to have lived on the earth with him. It is said they brought the gospel they received from him to Gaul. We believe it because of the tradition of our ancestors.'*"

"The tradition of our ancestors! Wow," Michael said. He thought for a moment. "Everything in this church so openly reveals not only the presence of Jesus and Mary Magdalene living in France, but also openly acknowledges their close relationship. It's so obvious. But if the church here, and I suspect many churches throughout France, are so open about this belief and even honor it, why do other churches treat it as scandalous lies? It's contradicting factors within their own religious beliefs. I don't understand it."

Statue of Jesus
Mary Magdalene Church, Paris

Miyah agreed. "It also bothers me that the Church accused Mary Magdalene of being a prostitute, all because Pope Gregory the Great misinterpreted the story in one of Luke's gospel, intentionally or not, and accused Mary as being 'the fallen woman,' a prostitute. I know the Catholic church officially apologized in the 1960s for making that 'mistake,' but it's a few centuries late. Because of Pope Gregory's accusations, it's been recorded throughout the ages with written word and art and it's hard to erase that image. The more we know about the real depth of our religious roots, the clearer the truth is to us, yet it gets more complicated at the same time. Many churches do honor Mary Magdalene as a saint, though. She has her own feast day on July 22. "

The couple walked around and viewed many statues situated along each side of the church, including figures of *"Holy Mother Mary,"* *"Virgin with the Child,"* the *"Baptism of Christ,"* and the *"Wedding of the Blessed Virgin,"* showing Mary and Joseph on their knees being blessed by a priest. They lingered before a life-sized, white alabaster statue of Jesus, draped with his chest partially bare, revealing a physically fit body. One arm was outstretched in compassion and the other touched the hooded fabric of his garment.

"This is my favorite statue of Jesus," Michael stated. "I've never seen anything like it before. It's so peaceful and such a contrast to the violence of the crucifixion statues you see in most churches. This is the Jesus I know. A man of peace, not of suffering."

He stood there for awhile, just looking at the statue and slowly reached out to touch the bare foot sticking out from under the sculpted draping of the garment, letting his fingers linger there for awhile.

"I feel like I'm looking into the eyes of Joshua," Michael said, as emotion swelled inside him.

Miyah took Michael's arm and stood next to him.

"Yes," she whispered. "I feel it too."

A middle-age priest had been watching them and walked over to hand Miyah a prayer card. On it was a picture of Jesus in the garden with Mary Magdalene kneeling in front of him. Off to the side was the crypt with the stone rolled away. A prayer to Saint Mary Magdalene was written on the back of the card in French.

"Our church may seem unusual to some," he said. "It reconciles the history of France with the Christian religion and some find it confusing. Biblical history here is not always as it has been typically portrayed." He nodded to them. "As Saint Mark said, 'Love your fellow man as you love yourself, there is no commandment greater than this.'" He hesitated a moment and then continued, "I sense you find more meaning in this church than most. Brothers in need have always been welcomed and served in this church. Bless you both on your journey." He made the sign of the cross and walked away.

"Thank you Father," is all Miyah and Michael could murmur, they were so taken aback by his impromptu message and blessing.

"That was interesting," Michael whispered. "He must have observed our interest in all the Magdalene references. Brothers in need? Was he trying to tell us something to be aware of, or just being polite?"

"I don't know," Miyah answered, turning the prayer card over in her hand. She translated some of the homage to Mary Magdalene, *". . .your love for him makes you want to serve. Help us to understand that. . ."* and the last verse, *". . . sent forth as you were to others, we must tell all that Jesus is alive. May we, in your wake, be messengers of Hope."* Miyah stared at the card for a few moments, processing the words and then tucked it into the pocket of her bag so she wouldn't lose it.

"Thank you for bringing me here today," Miyah said. "And for giving us so much time to take it all in. It's an amazing church and tribute. I'm pleased it's here, so public in the center of this city for everyone to see. It makes me feel good. I want to come back here again."

"I have to admit that it's the first time I paid so much attention to details in the church. I'm really glad we discovered it together."

Miyah added, "Now, what's for dinner? All this religion makes me hungry."

~ ~ ~ ~ ~

They headed out to explore the Louvre first thing the next morning. It was their last day in the city and they didn't want to waste any time.

Courtyard of the Louvre, Paris

Glass pyramid - Louvre

Stairway in the Louvre

They went through security and entered the museum on Rue de Rivoli, where the inverted glass pyramid drew light from a larger, external pyramid at the center of the Cour Napoléon. Miyah enjoyed the magical play of light and glass reflecting clouds and silhouettes of tourists who seemed to be suspended in mid air.

"The museum is actually housed in the original Louvre Palace which began as a fortress, built in the late 12th century. Now it's home to the largest collection of art in the world, from all eras and from all over the world, dating back as far as 5,000 BC." Michael said. "Venus de Milo, Mona Lisa and original works of Michelangelo, Raphael and Leonardo deVinci are here. We can even tour Napoléon's quarters and see his lavish lifestyle. You're going to love it. But slow me down anytime you need to sit and rest. There's so much to take in. We probably should have planned two days instead of one," he lamented before they had even begun.

"It sounds like a Michael mecca," Miyah laughed. "Where should we begin?" she asked looking at all the wings—Richelieu, Sully, Denon, with four floors in each wing.

"It's divided into ten sections," Michael opened the Louvre map he received with their tickets and showed her the layout of the museum.

"Oriental Antiquities, Egyptian Antiquities and the Greek and Roman Antiquities are three sections. We have Paintings, Sculptures, Decorative Arts, Arts of Islam, Prints and Drawings, Arts of Africa, Asia, Oceania and the Americas, and History of the Louvre. We won't make it to all the sections today. We'll be lucky to get through half. I'll get us to the places I think will be of most interest to us now. Like I said, we'll just have to come back!

"Let's start in the Sully Wing with the Egyptian Antiquities. There's an entire collection of statues of Isis you may find interesting. There's a replica of the pyramid's Sphinx, along with hieroglyphic history of the pharaohs and queens. Maybe Ramses will give you some clues to the writings on the Obelisk.

"Then, because this seems to be a quest for the feminine, we'll be sure to see Venus de Milo, Diana, The Winged Victory of Samothrace and the goddesses and gods in the Greek and Roman section. The brochure says there's a fragment of a frieze from the Parthenon Temple on the Athens Acropolis that represents the annual celebration of the sacred feminine Athena, patron deity of war and the daughter of Zeus. It looks quite impressive."

They wandered through the galleries and where it was allowed, Michael took photographs. Miyah knew they would be glad he'd been documenting their trip with hundreds of photos for them to reminisce on later.

They proceeded to the Paintings section and stood before *"The Mona Lisa,"* admiring da Vinci's famous lady in a single glass case mounted by itself on a huge wall. Nearly half an hour was spent looking at details of the largest painting in the museum, *"The Wedding at Cana,"* with Jesus and a plainly dressed woman sitting in the center of an L-shaped banquet table while music, drinking and merriment went on all around them. Miyah was impressed by the number of paintings of the masters throughout the museum that included Mary Magdalene.

"Other than the Holy Mother, she's the most painted woman in religious iconry," Michael said. "Most of the time when Mary Magdalene is shown with other women, she's the only one who doesn't have her hair covered, and in the majority of the paintings she's with Jesus. I always wondered about those paintings of La Tour and others where she had a human skull with her. Do you know what the skull represents?" he asked.

"I know those paintings," Miyah said. "It's a series of four that are very similar. The skull was used to symbolize impermanence and the inevitability of death. The flame of the candle meant enlightenment and purification. In the painting where she's looking at the candle reflecting in the mirror, it meant increased spirituality as the flames burned higher and upward. It's very revealing. The skull is a common symbol in Buddhism, a reminder of death and rebirth, but not in a dark or sorrowful way, more as a joyous remembrance that life continues after death. With all the studies Jesus did with Buddhist masters, I'm not surprised to see the symbol of the skull represented with Mary Magdalene, the closest person to him, who also studied with him."

"That makes sense," Michael said. "I'd never have made the connection if I hadn't seen him with my own eyes studying in India, Nepal and Tibet."

"Here's something else for you to ponder," she said. "What do you think of as you look at all of these paintings of her with a book in her hands?"

Michael didn't know what she meant. He thought the books represented her studying to become a better disciple. She was often painted with symbols—an alabaster jar, the skull, a book, her long flowing hair, and dressed in red, which was actually the color of female royalty in the Nazarene tradition. He shrugged his shoulders and looked at Miyah for an answer. She just smiled and patted her purse, which he knew contained her diary.

"So it's true," he said remembering seeing Maryum writing in her diary during his visit to Scotland.

"Yes. Books were rare in her time. Most writings were in scroll form. Mariam gave this diary to her as a wedding gift. It never left her side. Of course the diary has been altered through the ages with the addition of paper and mending the leather binding. Maybe she's painted with a book by her side because she often had her diary with her. She was writing, not reading."

"My God. No wonder you won't let that thing out of your sight," he whispered. "It must be incredible for you to see these huge paintings and know you have a secret connection to them in so many different ways."

"It's not just the Magdalene connection. I honor all the women who left their mark in the diary. They were wise women and played important roles in our lineage. But the diary began with her. I have such a different story of her life from the diary, so I guess that's why it's so important to me to see how the world knows her, and how she's being portrayed through these paintings. After all, they are representative of the image of her that was passed down through the ages."

"I understand," Michael nodded. "I understand, and I'm interested because of my connection through the cedar box with her and Joshua. It puts a different perspective on how I see things too."

As they walked through the gallery he put on his reading glasses to take a closer look at details in the rest of the paintings of Mary Magdalene, especially those of her portrayed with books to see if they had a similar appearance in each of the paintings, or if they resembled Miyah's diary at all. He also walked closer to Miyah, as if to guard her and their secret. How can she be so nonchalant about it he wondered and then remembered the powerful force of Touchstone spirits that were there to protect her. The diary had longevity. It had already survived 2,000 years.

They were both feeling a little overwhelmed and took a long break so Miyah could rest her back and feet, sitting at a window table of the museum's Café Mollien. They shared a *baguette poulet, fromage frais* (french bread sandwich with chicken and soft cheese) and *tarte au citron* (lemon pie), as they watched the crowd of tourists in the courtyard below.

"We'll have to come here every time we're in Paris," Miyah mused watching the sunlight play off the angles of the glass pyramid in the center of the square. "I feel we've seen such a small portion of the art represented here."

Michael agreed. "You'll never get tired of visiting the Louvre."

Afterward they resumed their tour through the galleries and room after room of priceless art. Michael could have gone on forever, but could see Miyah was getting tired.

"There's one more statue I want to show you before we leave," he said. "It's on the lower ground floor, tucked away in an alcove of 12th and 16th century Northern European sculptures."

They took the elevator down to the lowest level and wound their way to the end of a series of exhibits, which almost seemed to be hidden away in the basement. In a glass case near the end of the room was a statue of a delicately painted nude, young Mary Magdalene, her long hair cascading around her body, with both breasts revealed.

"You know the Catholic Church's legend is that Mary withdrew to Sainte Baume, a cave on a hill by Marseille. I guess Sainte Baume means Holy Cave. She supposedly lived alone in the cave, naked, for thirty years and died there," Michael said softly.

"I know. How fitting for the Church to conveniently tuck her away in a cave to sequester the feminine and dismiss her power like that. It's such an insult."

"But they get a lot of people making pilgrimages there," Michael said.

"Well, that's a cave I don't want to go to on this trip," she stated. "She's been exploited enough."

"Maybe that's why the statue is tucked away down here. Not everyone believes that story," Michael offered. "I didn't want it to upset you, I just thought you'd like to see the statue."

"Oh, it doesn't upset me, but think about it—they would never allow a naked statue of the Holy Mother!" she replied. "Why a naked representation

Mary Magdalene Statue - Louvre

of Mary Magdalene? It's demeaning. She was such an important women in religious history. Her real story is so beautiful—the healing work and miracles she continued to do throughout her life. I want everyone to embrace the beauty and longevity of that. So many people across the borders benefited by her and Jesus' teachings and healings over decades, not just those few years Christians acknowledge and revere. Their story is so much bigger than that."

"I know," Michael replied. "I know."

They sat outside the museum for a while and enjoyed the evening display of golden light that illuminated the grounds and made the Louvre's glass pyramid glow like a luminescent crystal growing out of the earth. As the sun dimmed they walked along the boulevard, discussing the events of their magnificent week in Paris and marveling at how fast the time had passed.

They lingered now and then to inhale the essence of the city to take those last breaths of remembrance home. Neither of them wanted the adventure to end. Hand-in hand they crossed the Pont Alexandre arch bridge, with its Art Nouveau globed lamps, gilded cherubs, nymphs and winged horses at each end. They stopped on the bridge to watch the lights of the Eiffel Tower sparkle, blinking off and on at scheduled intervals.

And that night, to celebrate their mutual love of the magical city of Paris, they took a romantic river cruise, dining by candle-light while peacefully floating down the Seine.

Lighted Eiffel Tower and boat on the Seine at Night

22 The Reunion

Michael rose early the next morning and slipped out to do some last minute shopping. He had something special he wanted to buy for Miyah.

Miyah packed her suitcase and settled herself on the balcony to do yoga and her ritual prayer ceremony. She didn't hear the rapid knocking or the man's voice on the other side of the door calling out her name.

"Mademoiselle Sinclair." Silence. Knock, knock, knock. Silence.

"Mademoiselle Sinclair. I have a message for you."

The door knob turned slightly back and forth as if to test the lock. Then a note was slipped under the door and the long, narrow trace of the messenger's shadow disappeared from beneath the door.

Lost in her meditation, nearly two hours had passed before Miyah realized it was getting late. "Michael should have been back by now," she thought. He had planned on coming back for breakfast before they left for Orly Airport for their late afternoon flight to Toulouse. She got a bottle of water from the night stand and made another check to be sure all her belongings were packed. She called down to the front desk to see if there were any messages for her.

"No Mademoiselle. I don't see anything here," the clerk replied.

Miyah was concerned, wondering if she should use her powers to search him out. Then she noticed the note on the floor by the door. It was the same prayer card the priest had given her when they visited The Church of Mary Magdalene. She thought maybe it had slipped out of her bag somehow and went to put it back, but then she turned it over. It had a handwritten message on the back and Miyah realized that someone had delivered this card to her earlier in the day.

"Brothers in need have always been welcomed and served in this church."

Just then she heard a key turning the lock and it startled her. The door opened and a dishevelled Michael rushed in, closing the door behind him. Breathing heavily, he went directly over to sit on the edge of the bed.

"What happened?" Miyah asked, tucking the card in her pocket, while rushing to his side. "Is something wrong?"

Michael sighed, running his hands through his tousled hair. "I just had the most harrowing encounter," he said. "A man approached me, asking for directions, I thought. I couldn't understand him and told him I wasn't from here and couldn't help. He became irritated and started to curse, shoving me around. I thought I was going to be mugged, robbed. . .or worse, so I started yelling loudly to attract attention. The man was a raving lunatic. He was shouting in French so I don't know what he was saying, and he kept shoving me. It must have been quite a scene. I guess I don't blame anyone for not wanting to get involved, not knowing who was the perpetrator and who was the victim.

"But then a priest, the same priest we met in the church the other day, came up to us and shouted something in French. The man stopped and just stared at me, then giving me one last shove as if to get in the final word, he turned and ran down the street. The priest apologized for the man's rude behavior and insisted I come to the church with him to calm down. While I was there, sitting in a small room in the back, two other priests came in and started asking me all kinds of questions. They asked about you too. I don't know why they were questioning me. I told them we were tourists. The priest who brought me there just stood in the shadows and said nothing. I'm not sure which was the most bizarre. The wild man on the street or the inquisition of the priests.

"Nothing is missing so it wasn't a ruse for a robbery," he said, checking for his wallet.

"What kind of questions did they ask you?"

"Oh, they were very polite and tried to make it look like casual conversation. They offered me a glass of water and asked where I was from, what I did for a living, if I had any friends or relatives here. I told them no, and they asked specifically about you. They wanted to know how long I had known you, where we met, things that were just too personal to be casual conversation. They said they remembered seeing us together in the church earlier in the week and wanted to know how we enjoyed the statues and imagery. Now how would they have remembered us with the hundreds of people who go through there each day? They also asked why we were so interested in the meanings of the Magdalene icons in the church, which means they probably heard our conversations that day.

"Miyah," he said, "I hate to ask, but do you think it could have anything to do with the Touchstone and the bloodline? I almost wonder if the man on the street was a ruse for the priest to 'rescue' me and get me to the church for questioning."

"I don't know. I mean, I don't know why, or even how, anyone would know who I am. I've never been to Paris before. I can't image that Papa Tom would have said anything to anyone here about us coming, and even if he did, there would be no need to interrogate you, or either of us for that matter. I'm so sorry you went through all of this," she said, fingering the card in her pocket. She decided not to show it to him now and add more anxiety to his day. . .but why would someone offer refuge unless they perhaps thought she, or they, needed it?

"We've had such a perfect time here, I hate to end with this," Michael said, reaching for her hand. "But in any case, right now I'm glad to get out of the city and head south. Do you mind if we leave for the airport now?"

"Of course. I'm ready when you are," she said.

"And could you please ask your guides," he made a circle in the air with his finger, "to help us here so we don't have anymore of these curious encounters on our journeys? That was enough drama for one trip."

"Done," she said. "But I'm sure there is a message in here somewhere and we should be vigilant none the less. Things aren't always as they may first appear."

~~~~~

They stayed that night in Toulouse, putting the events of the day behind them and early the next morning started their travels though Cathar country. The Cathars of Southern France were known to be ancient followers of Jesus, Mary Magdalene and their children, Sera in particular. They were a peaceful people, in tune with nature and the earth. Miyah immediately felt at home here. The local population viewed Catharism as a firm stand by those who wanted "freedom of religion" against "Big Brother," the Catholic Church. Catharism in France died as an organized church in 1321, but as a religion—a truer form of early Christian religion. . .it remained alive.

Cathars were known for hands-on healing and it was said they could speak with animals. The main core of their belief system was the rejection of the material world, which was seen as a trap imprisoning the soul. Excessive material possessions were viewed as evil and were to be opposed and rejected. Therefore, they didn't build churches, were mainly vegetarian, shared possessions and ate common meals. Their doctrine was appealing for its core magical rituals, but also because they thought the Pope and Catholic "corporation" were corrupt and the ultimate in materialistic values.

Cathar society also included charity, initiating a welfare system that cared for the poor, elderly, and sick. They established schools and hospitals and practiced birth control, which brought on all sorts of accusations from the Church. They firmly believed in equality of the sexes, which also enraged the male-dominated Church. The Roman Catholic Church also feared that the Cathars, who believed Mary Magdalene was the Grail Mother, possessed knowledge of the bloodlines of Jesus, which was not in agreement with their orthodox teaching of the crucifixion.

"I did a little research on the Cathars before we left," Michael said as they were driving. "The name Cathar came from the Greek word, Katharos, which means 'pure.' I found it interesting they consider themselves Christians, yet they are pretty much incompatible with most Christian doctrines. They don't believe in baptism or communion, or any of the sacraments. Their Christianity has no redeeming crucifixion story, no last judgement, no resurrection, and it seems

St. Martin's Church statue of St. Canterine, Limoux

their theology, liturgy and even moral teachings are the complete opposite of Catholicism. No wonder the Church started crusades to do away with them and with their writings."

"They do believe in a spiritual baptism," Miyah corrected. "Instead of a water baptism, it's a laying on of hands and can only be given to adults, because they believe that faith, free choice, clear and conscious consent are all necessary to receive baptism and children don't understand the meaning of that until they are older.

"The mission of Christ of the Cathars is also very different," she continued. "They believe Jesus was sent to convey a message of love and truth, in contrast to the Church's teaching that Jesus was sent by God to redeem the sins of man through his death.

"Catharism was a version of Christianity brought to Europe to preserve traditions of the pure truths that Jesus taught. Many Cathar families were descendents of Jesus and Mary Magdalene through their children Sera and Joseph, who settled in France and Italy. These Cathars were considered to be 'the pure ones.'"

"Yes, I read about that," Michael said. "They didn't honor the cross because it was used as an instrument of torture for Jesus. They said something like, 'If they had hanged your father, would you worship the rope that caused his death.' That's quite profound, don't you think!"

They drove east along A-61 and near Carcassonne they turned south about 20 miles to Limoux on the River Aude. They parked in the lot on the town square dominated by cafés, and wandered around the narrow brick streets until they found a cozy vegetarian restaurant tucked into a nearby side street. The friendly waitress spoke English with a heavy French accent and after their meal she suggested they visit the historical Church of Saint Martin, just a few blocks down the street on the other side of the square.

"It was built before 982 and later enlarged," she told them. "Outside the church there are six columns with decorations—St. Martin on horseback cutting his cloak; the meal at Simon the Pharisee with Mary Magdalene sitting at Jesus' feet; and Samson and the lion."

"Cutting his cloak?" Michael questioned, looking at Miyah. He also wondered if the reference to the church and Mary Magdalene was a coincidence, or had she overheard some of their conversation.

"Oh, maybe you don't know the story of St. Martin," she said. "Martin was a Christian, forced to enlist in the Army. He went from garrison to garrison on horseback. On a cold day near Amiens, a half-naked beggar asked him for some coins. 'I have no money,' Martin told the man, 'but I can help you.' He cut his cloak into two parts and gave one part to the poor man. The next night Jesus appeared to Martin wearing his half cloak and said to him, 'You covered me with this garment. What we do to others we do to ourselves.'

"So Martin became known as the saint of charity. If you go inside the church, you'll see a carved wooden canopy with three angels. One angel holds an anchor, the symbol of Hope, the other a chalice, an object of Faith, and St. Martin, representing Charity. I'm sorry if I'm rattling on," she apologized. "It's just such a special church and often tourists miss it. There are many revealing stories told within the art of the church."

"Thank you for the information," Miyah said. "We'll be sure to go there."

They paid for their lunch, including a generous tip to the informative waitress, and walked to the church. It was a stone structure and Michael pointed to the dozens of gargoyles perched along the corners of the tower next to the building. Inside it was cold and dark, but the stained glass windows were exquisite and the sunlight outside illuminated their colors, making them a focal point of the church.

Miyah pointed to a large double paneled window. It was titled *"The Marriage of Jesus and Mary Magdalene."* The figures, one in each panel, were dressed alike in royal blue robes, clasped at the neck with golden trim and a starburst design in the fabric. Their matching underdress was white with a scattered pattern of four dots placed in the shape of a cross, or the four directions. Their bodies were facing forward, eyes looking downward, with arms outstretched and palms down. A wide pink ribbon draped along the inside edge of their robes and was placed in the same position on both figures. Miyah realized it was a scarf used for handfasting, symbolic in early wedding ceremonies to "tie" the couple together in union. In the center, their hands reached toward each other in the space between the window panels. The pink scarf also led there, connecting the two of them together. They both had golden halos around their heads. The background looked like a red double seated throne, bordered with a series of dots and colorful designs. Miyah was struck with awe to see such a bold statement right here in a church for everyone to see. It was a silent proclamation.

But there was more. Another set of windows showed the haloed couple kneeling together before a Jewish priest who had his hand out, performing a ceremony. A young boy next to him held an open book, the pages facing outward, as if the priest had been reading from it. Mary had her hands crossed over her chest and another person in the background was shown watching over them. And yet another stained glass window showed Mary at Jesus feet, anointing them with oil, part of an ancient wedding ritual. Of the five people in the panel, Jesus and Mary were the only two with halos. A fleur-de-lis adorned the top of the window.

Michael reached out and took Miyah's hand and they stood there taking in the beauty of the stained glass window, appreciating the art and what it represented, being so public.

They soon discovered that controversial art was everywhere in the church. Michael pointed to a painting of Jesus being taken down from the cross—and his eyes were open! There was also fabric on the wall with a winged dragon wrapped around a cross.

"Do you think that represents the dragon and the sword of St. Michael," he asked.

"I don't know, but it's similar to the winged dragon and cross on the base of the apprentice pillar at Rossyln Chapel in Scotland," Miyah replied, also noticing the flowering thistle that is common in Scotland. "There are so many revealing symbolisms here, I feel there's a deeper meaning they're trying to convey," she said as Michael focused his camera in the dim light of the church. "I wonder how many people truly understand it."

Diana statue - Alet les Bains

She took note of a life-sized statue titled *"St. Anne,"* the grandmother of Jesus, with Mary a child of about six-years-old. Both were richly clad in flowing robed garments. St. Anne's robe was adorned with a pattern of fleur-de-lis designs and Celtic cross symbols bordered the edge of the fabric. St. Anne was holding a long rolled out scroll, and Mary, her hands clasped in prayer, was looking up at her mother. The alcove of the church where the statue stood was painted with a leaf-design fleur-de-lis pattern inside and between interlinking circles.

"It's a beautiful statue," Michael replied, taking a photo of a nearby statue of a woman wearing a crown, standing with her hand on a half wagon wheel. On the pedestal and embroidered in the wall design behind her were the initials SC. These initials were also painted on the front of crosses in other parts of the church.

"Do you know what SC stands for?" he asked Miyah.

"I believe that is Saint Catherine," she replied, looking at the statue. "But I see SC in several places around the church—also SB or BS intertwined in symbols."

Just then a man appeared and said the church was closing. Miyah tried to ask him some questions but he abruptly ushered them out.

"Maybe I shouldn't have taken photos," Michael said as they walked to their car. "He didn't seem to want us in there."

"I don't know. Maybe he was just in a hurry. I would think that with such an open display of the message those windows and art represent, they would expect people to be curious."

"Or maybe few people these days take the time to even notice," Michael said. "Sometimes the most obvious can be right in front of your nose."

They continued their journey south along D118, through the lush countryside, passing many vineyards that produced the white wine of which Limoux is famous. Over a hundred years ago Napoleon Bonaparte ordered the construction of the narrow road all the way from Carcassonne and had trees planted to shade his troops as they made the journey south.

Just south of Limoux they stopped in the little town of Alet les Bains, nestled into a valley of the mountainous area. Founded in the 9th century, but occupied since prehistoric times, the place was known for its thermal water hot springs. The Romans called the valley *Pagus Electensis - The Chosen Place.*

"There's a lot of history in this little village. Even Nostradamus had a house here!" Michael said, looking at a brochure he had picked up. "Legend says that early in the first period of Christianity a sanctuary was founded on the site of a Roman temple dedicated to the goddess Diana, the Roman goddess of the moon, the hunt and chastity. There's supposed to be a statue of her somewhere in a small square. Maybe we can find it."

They walked past medieval houses and felt like they were traveling back through the centuries, with charming narrow streets shadowed by the deep shade of projecting facades along the buildings. They came across the lone statue in a paved square, sheltered among two-story houses. Diana stood atop a fountain with water spewing from the mouth of a genderless face with the bodies and heads of four snakes woven through its hair. Above the fountain head was written *Liberté, Égalité Fraternité,* the national motto of France—Liberty, Equality and Fraternity (brotherhood).

Nostradamus House symbols
Alet les Bains

Alet les Bainsu

"Diana was the goddess who looked after women," Miyah explained. "She was one of the maiden goddesses, Artemis, Athena and Hestia, who swore never to marry. The daughter of Jupiter and Latona, she was born with her twin brother Apollo, on the Island of Delos. Diana preferred the mountains and oak groves and was called upon by women who wanted to become pregnant or those who asked for an easy delivery. There's a large Cult of Diana alive today, especially in the States."

"That's interesting," Michael said, observing the almost masculine structure of the stone statue. They walked further, into an area that had stone columns with carvings. He read more of the brochure.

Star of David window
in church ruins -
Alet les Bains

"Listen to this. The Benedictine Abbey of Notre Dame, fortified with a moat, was made a cathedral in 1318. Some of the carvings of the Chapter House show the Flight into Egypt; the Annunciation, or announcement of the Incarnation by the angel Gabriel to Mary; a Centaur—a creature with the head, arms, and torso of a man and the body and legs of a horse—mounted by a rider; a bear hunt and two ibex, or wild goats, fighting. That's quite a combination, religious or not. I'll bet there are some good Knights Templar legends behind those symbols," he said, pointing to a figure on a white column in the ruins of the building.

"That figure is a bear," Miyah said looking closely. "In Merovingian folklore the bear is the 'strong one' who's been asleep but is expected to awaken and return."

"Well, this one is definitely awake. It looks like it's biting the ass of the animal in front of it," Michael laughed. "I wonder what that means—there's a head on a shelf, resting on the bears back and underneath the bear, sideways, is another head. Maybe it symbolizes defeat," he reasoned.

"Look here," he pointed down a row of old houses on the narrow street. "There are Star of David symbols carved into the wood and pillars all around. They're really dominate." He referred to some symbols carved on raised pieces of wood on a beam over a door of one of the house.

"Next to that star is a fancy yin-yang sign on one side and what looks like a boat or some sort of vessel on the other side. . .or maybe it's a shield. Here's another series of three raised symbols—a crown and a cross, or maybe it is an X, and either a half moon or a fish. I sure wish I had studied more about symbolism. My dad loved that sort of thing. I bet that's why he spent so much time in the south of France. It's a mecca of icons and metaphors." Michael stepped back to take some photographs.

"Your brochure says that is Nostradamus's house," Miyah said looking over the literature. "What stories this old wood could tell. . . secrets it must hold."

"That entire house has 'X' crossbars everywhere. That seems unusual, looking at the construction of the surrounding homes," he said.

"The X was a sacred sign standing for truth and enlightenment that marked the foreheads of spiritually enlightened initiates at the Dead Sea Monastery at Qumran. The Knights Templar actually used the X, tipped, as a cross, to signify the protection of truth, which for them in the beginning, was the secret of the bloodline. It wasn't until much later that it was used by

Christians as the 'sign of the cross.'" Miyah explained.

"This house, with all of these symbols, must have been an important gathering place for the Knights Templar in their day . . .maybe even still today," Michael said.

Miyah explained further, "X's were carved into stone walls of Cathar castles and in caves that were hiding places during the persecutions. The X also indicated that Gnostic teachings were available at that location so people could pursue their teachings in a safe environment."

They walked to the ancient Cathedral of Alet, hoping to take a tour.

"Looks like it's closed already so we can't go through, but it seems like most of it is in ruins. It says that after seven or eight assaults during religious battles, a cannonball destroyed part of the cathedral roof and it eventually collapsed. Later, stone from the abbey was sold to construct the new royal road for Napoleon." Michael peered through the gates at giant stone pillars and arched windows that represented such an important period of history.

"It's a shame it's in such bad shape," he lamented. Then he pointed his camera through the open archway of a tall window, focusing on a wall on the other side.

"Look at the round Star of David windows," he gestured to Miyah. "They have the fleur-de-lis pattern inside each of the six points, and. . ." zooming in with his lens, "the triangle and inverted triangle are along each of the 18 lines that form the star. That represents something, doesn't it?"

"The triangles, one up and one down, are the foundation of the star itself—one upward triangle for the male, the blade, and the inverted triangle for the female, the chalice. The fleur-de-lis is an ancient symbol designed after the lily or iris flower, but was originally used in France as the royal arms symbol of Merovingian kings, portraying royal blood. For descendants of Jesus and Mary Magdalene it was also a symbol of the Trinity for their three children, Sera Tamar, Joseph David and John Martin. It was used so people of the bloodline, and those who protected it, could recognize each other in their travels."

". . .the blade and the chalice. . ." Michael repeated.

"Notice the shape of a rose in the center," Miyah pointed to one of the windows.

"It would take a lifetime to decipher all the hidden meanings behind the symbols we've seen scattered throughout France—concealed signs in paintings, stained glass window art, carvings, statues. . .it seems to be everywhere. It can't be denied that the artists and builders were trying to get a message across," Michael stated.

"To preserve the truth for others to discover at a later time," Miyah suggested.

Michael looked at his watch. "It's getting late. We should probably get going if we want to get to Rennes-les-Bains before dark. It's not far, and I bet your grandfather is wondering where we are."

"Yes, I know," Miyah said. "I'm enjoying our historic tour, but am getting a little anxious to see him. And I really don't feel like going through another church for awhile. I love the fact that they are so open to showing another side of the Christ story in their icons, but it's almost overwhelming."

"I didn't want to say it, so I'm glad you did. I haven't been in this many churches in my entire life!" he laughed.

They drove a few miles to Couiza and headed east, toward the town of Arques on a flat, winding road that cut its way into the steeply-wooded hills, past the village of Rennes-le-Château high atop a hill in the distance. After about ten minutes Michael turned right and drove a mile or so, greeted by steeper gorges, raked hillsides and dense, dark green woods, to the little hamlet of Rennes-les-Bains.

"Do you know much about Rennes-les-Bains?" he asked, pulling into town.

"I know the village is an old health resort known as far back as when the Phoenicians and the Romans used its water for spas. There are many water sources with different minerals in the mountains around the area. That's why alchemists in the Middle Ages stayed here. The Salz River is an unusual salty river that flows through the village."

"I'm glad we're staying with your grandfather. There doesn't seem to be a lot of accommodations in the town. The Hotel de France and other places I checked were all booked. The population here is only between 150 and 200, depending on the season. There were a few houses and private rooms for rent, but I didn't know how long we'd be staying."

"I don't know either," Miyah replied. "I guess that depends on Papa Tom."

The light of the day was just coming into its golden stage. Gray and pink houses with turquoise shutters and green trimmed yellow houses seemed to glow in the luminosity of the late afternoon sun. The town rested along the valley bottom with tall houses, several stories high, hugging the river's edge on both sides of the Salz. Some had balconies that overlooked the river.

"This must be it," Michael said, following his GPS directions, as he stopped in front of a quaint house set back off the main street, not far from the river. He turned the car off and looked at Miyah.

"Are you ready for this?" he asked. "I'm here with you, so be sure to let me know if you need me for anything," he reassured her.

"Thank you Michael, but I feel pretty good about this and think it'll be a positive reunion. I guess we'll find out soon enough," she said, nodding toward the house. An elderly man was coming across the lawn toward the car, with a smile on his face and a stride to his step.

"I thought you'd never get here," he said, as he opened the car door for Miyah, hardly waiting for her to get out before he swept her up in a big bear hug.

"Oh, Miy, you have grown into such a beautiful woman. Let me have a look at you." He held her out from him and nodded his head in approval. "Miy, Miy. I never thought I would see you again."

"Miy." She hadn't been called that since she was a child.

"Papa Tom," she said with tears welling in her eyes. "I'm so happy to be here. I would have come sooner if I had known. . ." He put his fingers to her lips.

"There's plenty of time for explanations," he said. "Let's get you inside and settled. My housemaid has dinner ready for us." He turned to see Michael getting their luggage out of the trunk.

"And this must be Michael," Tomas said, reaching out to shake his hand. "Thank you for bringing Miy to me. You can't imagine how much this means to an old man."

"It means a lot to her too," Michael said, shaking Tomas' hand.

They went inside and Tomas gave them a quick tour of the house and then showed them to their room, a nice, simple room on the second floor that had a small balcony with a clear view of the river and the tree-lined hills beyond. They quickly freshened up and then went to the dining room where Tomas was waiting.

"This is my housemaid, Lydia. She comes by every day to cook meals for me and take care of the place. I don't know what I'd do without her help. I never have been much of a housekeeper, although I used to be pretty good in the kitchen in my day. Your grandma would attest to that," he said, nodding toward Miyah.

"Pleased to meet you Lydia," Miyah said, shaking her hand. "Thank you for taking such good care of. . . my grandfather." It sounded strange saying it out loud, coming from her own lips. . .my grandfather.

"Oh, it's my pleasure," Lydia replied with a heavy French accent. "He is a pretty special man. Everyone in the community will tell you that."

Tomas humbly waved his hand at her and shook his head.

Even though he was much older, he had aged gracefully.

"You look so good after all these years. Just as I remembered," Miyah said.

"Well, I'm definitely older, but still in good health. What's it been. . .ten years or so?"

"Closer to twenty," Miyah corrected him. "I was 18 when you left."

"Twenty years," Tomas mused. "It can't be. It just can't be. You don't look a day older than eighteen!"

They ate dinner and talked pleasantly about the village, about his retirement from the Church and how he still volunteered whenever he could in the community. Miyah wanted to get to the bones of the conversation, but was being patient. She had waited this long to hear his side of the story, she could wait a little longer. It was almost as if she could feel Nona tapping her on the shoulder, holding her back and telling her to be understanding and patient.

"Oh, how Nona loved this man," Miyah thought as she watched him talking with Michael. Yet, she still couldn't help but feel deceived that she wasn't told about him when Nona was alive. She was cheated out of all the years with him when she was so lonely for family. Nona and Junia had always been there for her, but having real, living family that she could touch and love was different. There's security in just knowing that you're not completely on your own, that someone else is physically there when you need your hand held. Miyah had several conversations about this with both Nona and Junia recently and they understood how she felt. She was sure Papa Tom knew too.

"Well, it's getting late, and I know you two have had a long day," Tomas finally said. "We can talk more in the morning." He squeezed Miyah's hand.

"And I know you and I have a lot to talk about," he said, kissing her on the forehead.

"Believe me, I'm just as anxious to talk with you. I have a lot of explaining to do, but it's way past my bedtime. I'll see you in the morning. Good night Miy."

He turned to Michael. "It's nice to meet you and see that you're taking such good care of Miy. Thank you."

"Good night, sir," Michael replied, as Tomas left the room.

"He's right. I'm really tired too," Michael said. "Tomorrow is another day. Miy. I kind of like that. How come you never told me they called you Miy?" he teased.

~~~~~

Miyah got up early the next morning, grabbed a croissant and an orange for breakfast and went for a walk. Across the street from the river, she followed a winding path up into the woods. She knew this would be an important day for her and wanted to do some meditating before meeting with her grandfather. She had so many questions for him and wanted to be clear-minded.

Soon she came across a strange, large stone, nearly five feet tall, settled in the woods with no other rocks of its size nearby. It was a rounded boulder, but looked as though a chair with armrests had been crudely carved out of one side. She walked around it and ran her hands over the surface, observing the shape and mass of the stone. Looking closely, she noticed a small ankh-like symbol carved into the back of the chair. Miyah traced the surface with her fingers, knowing that the ankh was the Egyptian hieroglyphic character that represents "eternal life," and was also associated with the goddess Isis. It was considered the "key of life," "*the crux ansat,*" symbolic of the truth that a fruitful union was a gift from the deity. She smiled at that thought, touching the necklace pouch she wore, with the ankh-shaped key inside, and took this as a positive sign.

Next to the stone chair was a stone circle and a small flowing spring. Miyah could feel this was a powerful place. Looking back down the path and into the dark, eerie forest she saw no one who might interrupt her meditation, so she sat down, nestling herself into the giant chair. The cold of the stone soaked through her skirt, yet at the same time it felt warm and welcoming. She closed her eyes and said a silent prayer for protection and guidance, as she did every morning before her meditation.

But her mind would not clear and allow thought to vanish, as is necessary for a peaceful meditation. Instead, images raced through.

A movie of men on horseback rode through villages and were causing the destruction of everything in sight. Women and children were screaming and running—and being murdered as they tried to flee. Then there was a large bonfire, and men and women were willingly walking into the fire to their death, bravely praying and laying themselves down in the flames.

It was a disturbing scene and Miyah opened her eyes, not wanting to see more. She knew the vision she saw was the Inquisition—the Crusades the Catholic Church led against the Cathars. This was well documented and she felt that the spirits of those martyrs who would rather die for their faith than be forced into a religion they rebuked, were speaking to her. They, and the beliefs they stood for, didn't want to be forgotten. She knew her life was tied to the Cathars in many ways because of their strong desire, their own Touchstone legacy, to protect the secrets of Mary Magdalene.

She shook her head as if to clear her thoughts and tried to get up from the stone chair, but it was as if she was belted in and the stone wouldn't let her leave. It wasn't finished with her yet. She finally gave in and closed her eyes again. This time the scene had changed. It was long before medieval times.

The sky was dark with clouds and flashes of lightning streaked through the night. Suddenly a bolt of lightning struck a giant boulder resting on a bed of stones higher up the hill. The boulder dislodged and rolled part way down the hillside. As it rolled the lightning struck it again and again, causing portions of the stone to crumble away. It settled in a grove of trees and oceans of rain washed over it, smoothing the surfaces round. Then the sun shown and a Goddess appeared, surrounded by a court of men and women who served her. She sat upon the stone throne and a banquet was offered, not to honor her, but to praise the earth—the Mother, and all her gifts. Wine was first sprinkled upon the land before it touched the lips of the goddess. Crumbs from bread were broken and scattered for animals and birds to share in this meal. A plate of fruit was held high toward the sun and the sky, while words of gratitude were chanted in unison by all who gathered around the Goddess.

It was a beautiful, peaceful scene and Miyah felt as if she were partaking of the ceremony with the others. She was in communion with them.

Suddenly the snap of a branch and a rustle in the woods behind her broke her trance. She jumped off the boulder and almost lost her balance.

"I see you've found the Throne of Isis," Tomas said. "I'm not surprised it led you to it."

"The Throne of Isis?" Miyah said, regaining her composure.

"Yes. I'm sorry if I frightened you. I saw you leave this morning and wanted to catch up with you, but I don't move as quickly as I used to. I hope I didn't disturb your meditation," he apologized.

"It ended up being more of a revelation," Miyah said. "I saw the strangest scenes as I sat on the boulder. You called it the Throne of Isis?"

"Yes. You probably know that Rennes-les-Baines is a place of healing springs and ancient stone baths that the Romans built over Celtic sites. Many Roman statues of Isis from the 1st and 2nd centuries have been uncovered here. There's also an old legend that says the Spirit of Nodens—God of the Great Deep, a Celtic deity associated with healing and the sea—flashed himself as lightning from the depths of the waters and formed a throne in the celestial kingdoms—a seat of stone created for the Goddess. She ruled from this throne, and around her the temple of Isis came into being, which was also made of stone, hollowed out by lightning. This Seat of Stone was veiled from mortal eyes by a curtain of deep unyielding ocean and only the vision of goddesses could see through its veil."

"That's a beautiful legend," Miyah said, caressing the back of the stone seat. "The energy here is immense, like a vortex. Your legend may just explain one of the visions I had while sitting there."

"That wouldn't surprise me a bit. You have the goddess energy within you. But you said one of the visions?"

"The other was quite disturbing. I think it was from the Crusade era when the Church attempted to eliminate the Cathars."

"Understandably," Tomas said. "Back in 1908, workmen discovered a giant mass grave in this area while working on the access road to town. It was several hundred meters long and contained six to eight layers of skeletons from the time of the Albigensian Crusade. The history from that time was brutal and yet it represents an almost proud sense of martyrdom for many people who believed in the cause."

He continued, "This side of the mountain looks toward the rising sun in the east. It's a pre-Christian site, traced to the Druids and was used for ritual and earth-honoring ceremonies." He pointed toward the boulder Miyah had been sitting on.

"When Christianity swept through, the Church demonized the ceremonial site and the stone throne, saying it was a site sacred to Satan.

Of course, the Church didn't like it that a legend associated the area with a goddess, so they re-named it *Fauteuil du Diable* or the Devil's Armchair."

"Which name do you prefer to call it?" she asked. For a priest, he seemed to know a lot about goddesses and Celtic paganism.

"Oh, I would prefer the Goddess Isis to the devil any day," he said in good humor. "Wouldn't you?"

Miyah smiled and nodded her head.

"I'm not saying that the Goddess Isis isn't important," he continued, "but I think you and I have other things to discuss. Will you walk with me back toward the village?"

"Of course," she said, for the first time noticing he was walking with a cane. She linked her arm in his. "You probably shouldn't be hiking around these hills by yourself."

"Oh, I've been told that," he said. "But I don't know what I'll do when I can't go out for my daily walks anymore. I need to fill my lungs with the fresh air of nature and listen to the birds at least once a day. Getting old doesn't mean I have to sit inside and waste away. I think I've kept my health because I'm so active and keep these ol' bones moving. I'm not about to stop now."

They slowly made their way along the path back down the hill to the river. Upstream they saw three women, ankle deep in the water, holding hands, laughing and singing, swaying with the flow of the river. Miyah watched as they each produced a folded piece of paper and, placing them on a flat rock, they lit the papers on fire, saying prayers as their messages burned and the smoke dissipated into the air.

Tomas smiled and said. "I spoke with those women yesterday. They're from the U.S., staying in a chateau just outside of Castleneu Magnoc, several hours drive from here. They're three generations—mother, daughter and granddaughter, curious about the life of Jesus and Mary Magdalene in this area, and also about the Essene traditions here. You'll find many people in this country who are openly searching for religious truth. It's very refreshing."

Miyah bent down and picked up a small, flat stone from the edge of the river. She turned it over in her hand a few times, then put it into her medicine bag, which was draped over her shoulder. Tomas reached over and touched the bag.

"This bag brings back so many memories," he said. "It never left Nona's side. Seeing you with it seems so natural. It brings her back to me."

He led Miyah to a wooden bench along the river. They sat down and she faced him.

"I've been waiting for this day ever since Nona told me about you. I don't even know where to begin with my questions," Miyah said.

"Then let me," he replied. "Let me begin."

He took a deep breath and let out a long sigh. "First, I have a question to ask you. I need to know how you see me now. . .today."

"I don't know what you mean," Miyah answered.

"When you were a little girl, and even a teenager, you knew me as your neighborhood priest. Your family didn't attend the church and I often wondered if you thought it was odd that I was at your house so much. Surely you must have been aware of the interaction between myself and your grandmother, and you must have noticed the attention I gave to your mother, my beautiful daughter Junia, bless her. Didn't you think it unusual that I was always there for birthdays and every event that was important to your family, including solstice, equinox and other non-Christian rituals?"

"No," Miyah replied, recalling her childhood. "I think that because I grew up always having you around I never gave it much thought. My life was pretty sheltered and maybe because I didn't attend church, I thought this is what priests did, interact with families. I know I was always so happy to see you. You were my only father figure. It sounds ironic now, saying that. You were our family's father figure, literally. My Papa Tom."

"You're the only one who called me that."

"No, it was just short for Father Tomas. Everyone called you Father Tomas."

"Yes, Father Tomas, but you called me Papa Tom because it was short for Grandpa Tom. When you were really young I tried to get you to say Grandpa, but you settled on Papa. . .Papa Tom. Maybe you were influenced by hearing everyone else call me Father Tomas, but your 'Papa Tom' was endearing to me. So you see, Miyah, I wasn't trying to hide the fact from you that you were my granddaughter. I was always very proud of it.

"My being at Nona's house, at RoseVine, being allowed behind the veil and into your world, was the only place I truly felt I could be myself. Your grandmother, Junia and you, were my world."

"Then why did you keep our family a secret? Why did you stay with the Church?" she bluntly asked.

"That was complicated. Nona and I had many discussions about this. We were the Odd Couple, serving the same God, yet coming to the altar from completely different sides of the universe. We had such great respect and honor for each other's beliefs and even beyond that, we knew there were many ways to serve. It wasn't about serving God, as you would expect. It was more about serving the people. . .serving the people the way Jesus did. Nona could heal through mysterious ways that came from the most powerful bloodline of healing there ever was. I was in awe of that and so proud of her. But I could heal in other ways by being among God's children, and what better way to do that, than through the Church. I didn't have to agree with all of their dogma, and I know I was being hypocritical in a sense by taking vows I didn't completely believe in. But, don't you see Miyah, it was the best way I could serve at the time. Simply by being there—to listen, lend support and offer advice—it's all a part of healing. I was able to reach people who wouldn't have been receptive to me if I wasn't a trusted priest.

"I learned so much from Nona. She taught me how to incorporate some of her wisdom into my own practice. I felt like I became an extension of her hands, of the hands of Jesus and Mary Magdalene, when I was helping the sick. You, of all people, must be able to understand that feeling. I learned about many healers down through the ages, when it was commonplace to do hands-on healing, or to brew up herbs and tinctures as remedies for illness. Almost everyone had their own 'doctor' somewhere in the family line.

"Ironically, in modern times it isn't accepted as well—and that began back when healers, primarily women, were called witches and evil because they were a threat to the control of the Church. All of a sudden healing became the work of the devil, instead of the work of God. It was a sad, sad time. It still is in many ways, even today, as natural remedies are often discouraged because they compete with the multi-million dollar pharmaceutical companies which, of course, are tied to big business, which flows into the government. . .but don't get me started on that!" he laughed. "That's something I gladly left behind!

"Things are slowly changing, and many people, even nuns, are healing through alternative methods like Reiki, massage and other types of energy work that's now accepted by much of society. God willing, that will continue to flourish."

Miyah sat silent, processing all he was saying.

Tomas continued. "I was caught between my love of serving through the Church and the love I had for my family. Somehow, I felt fortunate that I was able to have it all for so long, but people saw us together frequently at events or on outings and eventually began to talk. The Church didn't like that. I was reprimanded several times and eventually only was able to spend time with you at RoseVine, where no one could see us. Yet, those were some of the happiest times of my life. We were a family there. I loved all three of you so much.

"Things changed when Junia died. It was such a tragic loss. My own parents died when I was a child and I had no other family, so hadn't really had a personal experience with death—even though I officiated at many funerals and helped families through the process. This was different. It was personal.

"I spoke at Junia's cremation ceremony, which was a small, private affair. Nona wanted it that way, but I was so emotional. I had lost my only daughter. I had a break down shortly after that. Nona was there to console me and for a brief time I was angry that she wasn't grieving as much as I was. She made me realize that it was only a transition into another form of energy. And then Junia appeared to us one day when Nona summoned her.

After that, I spoke to Junia often and it seemed as if she were right there with me. I hadn't really lost my daughter, only her physical body was gone. She was. . .is . . .still with me, as I imagine she is with you."

He patted Miyah's hand. "And Nona was always there for me. I owe so much to her. I'm only human, I still miss them both so much. . ." Tomas stopped talking and just sat there, listening to the rushing of the river.

Miyah had thought all these years that the loss of Junia and Nona was hers alone—that only she mourned for them, only she was left behind. Having them with her in spirit form gave her solace all these years, but it wasn't the same. Somehow, now, she felt comforted that she shared their loss with Tomas—someone who loved them both as much as she did. Someone who had loved them first. She brushed the tears away and put her arm around his shoulders. He seemed frail, vulnerable.

He slowly continued, "The Church discovered my secret after Junia died. I'm not sure how. It doesn't really matter. They wanted to transfer me to another state to avoid a scandal. I convinced them to let me stay and was very discreet about coming to see you after that. Even though no one else could physically see us at RoseVine, the Church kept track of my whereabouts at all times. Seeing Nona was easier, because she was able to materialize and appear wherever I was–a feat I really appreciated later when she brought me on journeys back into biblical times."

"Nona said she brought you back to meet the ancients," Miyah said.

"Ah, yes. Do you know what that meant to me, especially as a priest? I had been preaching the words of Jesus all my adult life and somehow magically appeared into his very world. I couldn't believe my eyes. Nona took me back many times and I was able to have conversations about religion and how it evolved through the ages. It changed my thoughts on the business of organized religion and reaffirmed my belief in serving the people. That was the mission of Jesus all along. It was so simple. . .to teach and heal the people. Of course you already know all of that. But personally, it made my mission stronger. It made me a stronger man. . .and a better priest."

Tomas turned and looked at Miyah. "I feel like I'm in confession!" He laughed. "Only I'm doing the confessing—confessing my life to you. A load has been lifted off my shoulders. I'm grateful to have you here. I've wanted to tell you these things for many years. You're the only one alive who can completely understand my truth."

"But then why did you leave me after Nona died. . .when I needed you most?" She finally asked the question that had been festering ever since she learned that he was her grandfather and was still alive.

"Why did you leave me alone?"

"That was one of the most difficult things I've done in my entire life," he answered. "At first I was angry at Nona for leaving me. I didn't want her to go, and didn't understand when she said it was her time to leave. Even after all she had taught me about the spirit world and such, I couldn't grasp the concept that a person would just say they have to move on, their work is done and they choose to leave the earth. . .to die. I saw it as her choosing to leave me, and that was painful. Later I began to understand, through her in spirit, that she could do so much more for others from the 'other side.' She 'visited' me almost every day and she also reassured me that you were going to be OK."

"But why did *you* leave *me*?" Miyah repeated. "We could have helped each other. I needed you."

"If you recall I did come and see you quite a lot for several months after Nona left. But, again, the Church chastised me. You were eighteen-years-old, a beautiful, young woman. They didn't want a scandal. At their strong suggestion, I was required to request a transfer to another church. Coming here to France, and to an area of the country that takes a much more open approach to Church dogma, and often an opposing view of many of its beliefs—like the life of Mary Magdalene, for instance—was the only place I could think of to live out my life. I've been able to heal others openly here, where the source of my 'powers' is never questioned. I feel as if I'm still working side-by-side with Nona in my work, that the bloodline has shared the gift with me."

"I can understand that, but why didn't you tell me you were my grandfather before you left?" she questioned. "Why didn't anyone tell me? It seems so unfair. I lost out on so much."

"We knew you would find out when the time was right. I know that sounds cliché, but it's true. If you knew I was your grandfather, you wouldn't have wanted me to leave. It would have been harder on both of us."

"But I would have come with you," she objected.

"And what about the work you were called to do there? Who would have taken care of all those people you've helped through the years? You were needed right where you were. And I could have hardly shown up here, a priest with a beautiful young woman on my arm."

"I would have liked to have made that choice for myself," she retorted.

"Sometimes choices are made for us. Maybe that's part of being a Touchstone carrier. Up until now, you seemed to have accepted your fate without question. Should it be any different now? It had been decided that you'd be told when you, yourself questioned it. Nona and Junia have always looked over you and were there whenever you needed them. You were never alone. And I always knew what you were doing through Nona. I knew you were safe and have always been so proud of you," he was grasping for words.

"Look, Miyah, I don't know if it was the wisest decision or not. At the time, it seemed the right thing to do under the circumstances. I can't change what's been done. It was meant to protect you, not to hurt you. And, I'm probably the one who owes you the apology if the decision was wrong, because it protected me and my relationship with the Church more than anything. Maybe I was the selfish one. I'm truly sorry." He added, "Surely you've spoken with both Nona and Junia about this, yourself."

"Yes, of course I have," she replied. "And I understand what all of you have told me. But I can't help but feel that I've lost out on all those years I would have liked to have spent with you. Just knowing I had family, living family, would have meant so much to me. I don't blame you or Nona or Mother. I know you always had my best interest in mind. I. . .I just feel I've missed out on so much."

Tomas reached over and hugged Miyah, wanting to comfort her. "You're my granddaughter, my blood flows through you just as much as Nona's blood. I have always loved you. And we're together now. We both have wonderful memories of our family that will always bond us together with our past. I don't have that many more years left on this earth and want to make the most of what I do have. That includes trying to make up time and being a good grandfather to you. . .that is if you'll allow me."

"It's all I want," Miyah said.

She had another question and respectfully asked, "You may be retired, but you're still known as a priest and have been in this village for a long time. Aren't you afraid that people knowing you fathered a daughter and have a granddaughter will affect your relationship in the community?"

"I lost you once because of the Church," he said. "I won't let it happen again. I'll be proud to have everyone know you're my granddaughter. So far I've only told my housekeeper, Lydia. She actually seemed pleased to learn I had a secret life that made me so happy."

"It's OK. . .you don't have to shout it from the rooftops. It can be our secret, I don't care. As long as you and I know, that's all that matters," Miyah said, giving him a kiss on the cheek.

"Oh, I'm quite sure Lydia has spread the word by now! News doesn't stay quiet for long in these small villages," Tomas laughed.

Rennes-les-Bains

Rennes-les-Bains

Rennes-les-Bains

23 Mystery of Rennes-le-Château

Michael wanted to give Miyah and Tomas as much time as they needed. He knew they had a lot to talk about. He grabbed his camera and set out to explore the village. He walked along the river and through a wooded area, and after a while discovered a busy sports area with tennis courts, miniature golf and a boules pitch. He photographed a rustic wooden sign indicating walks to some of the local landmarks: L'Homme Mort, La Cabanasse, La Source de la Madeleine and a cross-country route to the neighboring village of Rennes-le-Château, about three miles away.

He found a post office and a few small shops, a bar with snacks, a pizzeria and three other restaurants. He looked through a small art gallery in the AudeEspace d'Art that showcased talented local artists, and spent time admiring the work.

Browsing through one of the shops he was drawn to an amber necklace with copper pieces that had designs stamped into them, spaced randomly between irregularly-shaped amber beads. The shopkeeper told him that Rennes-les-Bains is currently best known for its hot springs, but the first people to arrive in the area didn't come for the healing waters. They came in search of amber. She said the deposits of amber found in Rennes-les-Bains, Sougraigne and Bugarach counted for most of the amber beads found on ancient sites throughout all of southern France.

"Unfortunately," she added, "the mineral wealth of the region, which included copper, iron, lead and silver, also attracted the Roman invaders who exploited the mines around Rennes-les-Bains. Human remains, tombs, underground caves, pottery and coins have been unearthed for centuries around here and people are still finding things. You might even find some unpolished amber stones if you know what to look for."

"I thought amber was made from the sap of trees," Michael stated.

"Yes, the source of amber is fossilized wood resin, but the soft resin forms and eventually hardens. Amber is considered resin, but they still call them stones. If you look closely you might find remnants of insects, larva, pieces of flowers or slivers of bark from the tree itself trapped inside the amber. Because it's soft, it can easily be heated and formed into beads and other shapes."

"But how does a person know if it's really amber or plastic?" Michael asked. "This is a pretty expensive necklace."

"Yes it is, but it's also handcrafted," she answered, pointing to the designs in the copper beads. "Let me show you how you can tell if it's real amber." She took a pin and held it under a lit match for as long as she could hold the match without getting burned. Then she touched one of the amber beads with the heated pin.

"Smell this," she commanded. Michael obliged. "What does it smell like?" she asked him.

"It has the odor of wood, sort of like the copal I once burned."

"Exactly," the woman said triumphantly. "Amber is a form of copal—resin. That's how you can tell—if it has that wood resin smell. There are also five types of amber and a range of colors from the yellow-orange-brown in this necklace to whitish, pale lemon and almost black. The most uncommon colors are red, green and blue amber which are very rare."

"Did the amber beads in this necklace come from the area?" Michael asked.

The shopkeeper smiled, looked directly at him and said. "But of course. And this piece is very old."

She had one more selling point. "Folklore attributes amber to having medicinal properties and the Greeks connected the stone to the Sun God."

Maybe he was a sucker for a good story, but Michael liked the necklace and thought it would be a nice gift for Miyah.

"How can I resist?" he asked. "Can you wrap it for me?" He made his purchase and thanked the woman for her interesting information.

"Be sure to come back," she said. "The village square has music and dancing in the evenings and some days market stalls are set up by local vendors. I'm sure you and your lady would enjoy it."

Michael wandered into the town square and sat down on a wooden bench, shaded by fragrant lime trees, to enjoy the peacefulness of the day. The shopkeeper said copper was mined here. He wondered if Joseph of Arimathea and his ships traded copper mined from this area. It was possible the family had history here. The coast wasn't that far away, and much closer than Joseph's copper and tin mines in Britain.

It wasn't long before the aroma of food reached him. He found a table in the outside seating area at Pizzeria de la Place and splurged, ordering a pizza with frîtes on top, and a carafe of rosé.

A large play area nearby provided a place for kids to use up energy while their parents lingered to enjoy conversation and leisurely eat their food. There were half a dozen kids in the playground, but Michael's attention was drawn to one little girl in particular. She had big brown eyes and dark hair pulled back in a pony tail. She wore a bright red sweater and blue jeans, anchored by a pair of yellow rubber boots that went all the way up to the her knees.

"I wonder what my daughter will look like?" he thought. He could hardly wait to be a father. The girl looked to be about six-years-old and was playing with a little blonde boy, who was much smaller than herself. She laughed, jumped and twirled around, just to make the little boy laugh. He was sitting on the ground, clapping his hands and enjoying the show. Soon a woman came over and picked up the little boy. It was then that Michael noticed he had a metal brace on one leg. The woman stood him up for a brief time and he balanced himself against her. She adjusted her purse across her shoulder, then hoisted him up on her hip. She took the little girl by the hand and walked away. The blonde haired boy was still laughing as he watched his sister skipping by his side.

Michael wasn't sure why he was so touched by this scene. He couldn't help but think that if Miyah were here, she could heal whatever ailed the little boy. He wondered why Tomas hadn't helped him. Then, as if on cue, he overheard the couple at the next table commenting on the family.

"Isn't it wonderful how well little Peter is doing since his accident?" the woman in a flowered dress asked. "They weren't sure he would even survive. It truly is a miracle."

"Yes," the other woman chimed in. "It just proves what the power of prayer can do. His mother is lucky to have little Mary to help. She's such an angel, being so attentive to her brother the way she is. That child has lived through a lot in her young life, and look at her, she's such a joy. God bless them both."

Michael suddenly realized that things aren't always as they seem. He was feeling sorry for the little lame boy and he finds out that the boy being alive was a miracle in itself. It was a reminder for Michael to always look for the miracles in life, and to count his own blessings. After all, wasn't his being alive and here today one of those miracles?

Just as his pizza arrived, he heard a voice over his shoulder.

"That was thoughtful of you," Miyah said, coming around to plant a kiss on his cheek.

Michael motioned to the waiter for more plates and glasses.

"What's this? French fries on pizza!" Miyah said, picking up frîtes from the top of the pizza. "Hmm, good," she said.

"That's one of the specialties here," Tomas laughed. "You'll enjoy it."

"Did you two have a nice walk?" Michael asked. "You've been gone all morning."

"Oh yes," Miyah replied, smiling at Tomas. "We had an excellent walk."

"She's a hard one to keep up with, I can tell you that," Tomas teased.

Michael was pleased to see the jovial interaction between the two of them. It meant that Miyah must have gotten the answers she needed.

"I was wondering what the two of you had planned for tomorrow?" Tomas asked as Michael poured him a glass of rosé. "I thought you might like to take a drive up to Rennes-le-Château. I'm sure you both would be interested in the legends of the village and the Magdalene Church there,"

"I would love that," Miyah said, looking at Michael for his opinion.

"Me too," he replied. "Maybe you could give us an outline of the village before we go. I've read some, but I'm sure you know a lot more details."

"Wait until I get back," Miyah said. "I need to find the ladies room." She got up and walked into the cafe.

Before Michael had a chance to ask some questions he hoped Tomas could answer, Tomas said, "Michael Wilder. . .I remember a couple named Wilder from back home."

"Paul and Kat. . .Katrina," Michael offered. "You performed my parent's wedding ceremony."

"Yes, yes, that's it. Not only that, but I believe I also baptized you. . .and didn't you have a sister?"

"I'm amazed you have such a good memory. You must have married and baptized hundreds of people," Michael said.

"Oh, but I remember your family. This is all fitting together now," he said. "The wedding wasn't in a church, it was in their back yard—as were the baptisms. Your folks called them blessing ceremonies because it really had little to do with the Church. They wrote most of the words, and I have to say I was touched by the nature of their honesty. I remember they had this beautifully groomed back yard that was fenced all the way around like a fortress, and they had a swimming pool. They were good friends of Junia and John. That's how I met them. Your mother and Junia were the best of friends, especially after John left. Kat was a great comfort to Junia all through her pregnancy. She was there when Miyah was born, one of the few people who had been allowed into RoseVine. Junia wanted her there and knew she could trust her."

"So Miyah was born at home," Michael said, ". . .and my mother was there! This seems so bizarre that after all these years we've found each other and are discovering our family had a history together."

"Isn't it wonderful how divine providence works." Tomas said. "I'm sure it isn't a coincidence. Your mothers are up there pulling the strings. They always talked about the two of you growing up and getting married some day."

Michael laughed. "Well, we had both forgotten about those early childhood days until recently when we came across some photos of our parents together. It was a bit eerie at first, realizing we had spent so much time together as kids, up until Miyah was almost ten, and neither of us really remembered each other until now."

"Yes," Tomas said. "That must have been when Junia died. Her death also hit Kat pretty hard. She was a gracious lady and wanted to help Nona with Miyah. But Miyah was pretty much kept at RoseVine, which you must know, was impossible for anyone to find, unless specifically invited. Then your family went off traveling again. Miyah had Nona and myself to console her. I think she blocked out most of her childhood after Junia died. She had some big shoes to fill, and even at that young age, understood the important role she had inherited as the Touchstone keeper. Up until that time she shared duties with Junia and was always learning. Thank God Nona was there to be her rock. It was a very difficult time for the child. But look at her now," he said, seeing Miyah walking toward them. "She's as radiant as ever and I can see you two are very happy."

"Did I miss anything?" Miyah asked. "Or was it just man talk?"

Michael smiled and got up to pull a chair out for her.

"We were just discussing how much we both love you," Tomas said, reaching for another piece of pizza. "You better grab some food before we eat it all."

"Thanks. I'm always hungry these days," she said, winking at Michael.

They ate and talked about how great the local French food was and about the lore and landscape of the country. Tomas gave them a quick outline of the area.

"There are five mountains in this region that form a perfect five-pointed star when you connect their geographical lines," he said. "And there's a sixth mountain in the precise center of the star. Medieval Templars who stayed here practiced sacred geometry. The castles and chapels were built according to alignments that formed perfect five and six-pointed stars on the land. Perhaps the most well known mountain in the area is Mount Bugarach which, among other things, is known as the site of an ancient Essene community."

"I didn't know the Essene teachings spread this far," Michael said.

"Yes, they have quite a history in this area and people are still drawn here to pull in that ancient energy."

Tomas continued, "Bugarach is sometimes called The Magic Mountain. The entire region is limestone and there are numerous caverns with large underground salt deposits, specifically here, in Rennes-les-Bains. Rennes-le-Château is said to have a large underground water tank, several hundreds of metres deep. The underground network runs for miles, with an underground river that enters into the Mediterranean basin. The river doesn't appear on any maps but it runs its course underneath the surface of the land. In pagan Celtic religion, these hollow hills were known to be entrances to 'other worlds,' specifically the realm of the fairies."

"Fairies!" Michael said with a smirk. "Now we have fairies?"

Miyah and Tomas looked at him as if he didn't have a clue that the world of fairies was as natural as the three of them sitting there. Michael read their expression and decided not to get into that subject right now.

"What do the caves under Mount Bugarach have to do with this area, other than the salt connection?" Michael asked with a more serious tone.

"Plenty," Tomas answered. "The cave systems are immense and it's believed they connect the six mountains—the five-pointed star—to the center mountain. Rennes-les-Bains and Rennes-le-Château lie among these passageways and there are many stories of treasure hidden within this labyrinth of caves. In 1645 a shepherd named Ignace Paris fell into a cave in search of one of his sheep. He found the sheep and also a large number of gold coins. He told the villagers that he discovered a room full of gold under the mountain, but when he refused to tell them exactly where, he was stoned to death on a charge of thievery."

"Oh my God!" Michael all of a sudden exclaimed, having a flash back of his youth. "I think I may have been here before with my father on one of his expeditions. I remember we were in France and he was with some other men exploring a series of caves. I wandered away, chasing a squirrel or some little animal and got lost in a maze of underground chambers. I remember the darkness of the underground but I was never afraid. I had a dim flashlight, so managed to move through the darkness. But I remember feeling like I was being led or protected. My parents were frantic because I was missing for an entire day. A series of tunnels and several stone structures had writings on them. After awhile I came across a huge lake with waterfalls and rivers flowing into it. It was amazing. I just sat there, mesmerized by that beautiful lake in the belly of the mountain.

"After awhile I wandered back out by myself, but that's all I remembered. My father didn't let me go back there with him after that. Mom and I stayed in a nearby village or sometimes in Paris while he continued his work. She was pregnant with my sister at the time. That's how I got to know Paris so well and acquired an appreciation for art. Mom and I explored the city while Dad spent his time underground, searching for. . .I don't know what. He was an archeologist. He was always searching for something."

"Do you know who he was working for?" Tomas was curious.

"There was a man he worked with on that project. I don't think he was another archeologist, but some sort of academic. I was young and don't remember his name. But I do recall that my father went back and forth to France a lot to work on the project. He got a call from that colleague some time later and they were very excited because the man said he found what they had been looking for. Dad was heading back to France to meet him and continue their exploration, but when he arrived he found that the man had suddenly and mysteriously died the day before near the site they had been excavating. There were so many different stories as to how, and exactly where, the man died that I'm not sure anyone knew the truth. My father was very upset and when he tried to complete their work in the caves, the French government, or some authority, came in and actually sealed up the entrances with cement. Dad was told to go back home and was warned that he should not try to further pursue their efforts in the area."

"Do you remember what year that was?" Tomas was very interested in what Michael was saying.

"You mean when the man died? Oh. . .it was so long ago, I really don't know. There were others involved in their expedition too, but I don't remember their names. I was preoccupied with my own stuff at the time and

Dad always had an archeological project going somewhere. I recalled this particular instance because I had that connection with getting lost in the cave and then was upset for not being allowed to go back there with him. That maze of caves was a young boy's fantasy world."

Michael was silent for a few moments. "I wonder. . ." He stopped in mid-sentence and looked around at the other people in the courtyard.

"You were saying?" Tomas responded.

"Oh, it was nothing. I was just thinking to myself," Michael replied.

Miyah put her hand on his arm as if she felt she needed to reassure him everything was OK.

"Don't worry Michael. You may be surprised to hear there are many stories similar to yours," Tomas said. "Details somewhat differ, but the gist of the story is the same. Normally, it's an animal or a small child that falls into an opening and is found, sometimes days later, in perfect health. The children usually have no memory of their adventure, so I'm surprised you remembered as much as you did about a lake and ancient writings. Sometimes the missing person was an adult—a hunter, a shepherd, and in one case a magistrate who was discovered after he was missing for a great period of time. His beard had grown long and he had no memory of what happened to him. Another story reported two men lost in the caves under Bugarach. They returned days later with completely white hair—with no memory. Some also said they felt the presence of some sort of creature who watched over them."

"Like, maybe fairies?" Miyah said to Michael, who ignored her comment.

"But what were the men looking for?" Michael asked.

Tomas leaned in and said in a very quiet voice, "Some say the Ark of the Covenant rests in these caves. Others say Visigoth and Templar treasures; gold, silver and antiquities pillaged from Jerusalem by the Roman Emperor Titus in AD 70, including the solid gold seven-branched candlestick belonging to the Jews; Cathar treasures; King Dagobert II's wealth from the wars of 650—supposedly his son, Sigisbert IV, survived the family murders and found refuge in Rhedae (Rennes-le-Château) and became lord of the region. This would mean the Merovingian bloodline survived, with a legitimate claim to the French throne. That would be incriminating. Some insist that sacred documents and important burial sites are hidden here. No one really knows.

"Here's another fact. Mount Bugarach is also the notorious center of UFO activity in France. It's rumored to be a passageway for subterranean activity of extra-terrestrials and also a landing site for UFOs, where they come to pick up pilgrims who have decoded the region's mysteries. It's even been suggested that's why people return with no memory of being in the mountain. They've been taken up and 'decoded,' shall we say!" Tomas smiled at them.

Michael laughed. "OK, I believe in UFOs, but I wasn't taken up in any space ship. I still have my memory of that day. UFOs, underground creatures and fairies? I think I prefer the hidden treasure stories."

"What I find interesting," Miyah chimed in, "is here I was thinking we were coming to France for me to be reunited with you, Papa Tom, but now I realize that it's much deeper than that. Michael's family background lies within the layers of history here in this land, just as much as mine."

"You're right, my dear," Tomas replied. "And that's precisely why things are unfolding in this way—all in the time frame they're meant to happen. Regardless of the reasons, I'm immensely pleased that you're here. I think we'll have a most interesting visit. You're welcome to stay as long as you wish."

~~~~~

That night Miyah lay wrapped in Michael's arms with the sound outside of the river rushing by as it flowed over the rocks and through the village. It was a sweet lullaby. The moon showered their bed with a bluish, yellow light and Michael played with a curl of hair on Miyah's forehead.

"What do you think of Tomas?" he asked. "You two must have had a good discussion today."

"Yes, I was glad to talk things out right away. I still want to ask him about my father, but I think I have a better understanding of why he left and of how his life's mission has shaped him."

"Do you trust him?"

"That's an odd thing to ask," she responded. "Of course I trust him. Why? Don't you?"

"I don't know. It's just that he doesn't talk like any clergy I've ever known. He seems to know a lot about pagan rituals, folklore, fairies and stuff."

Miyah laughed. "Do you think he could have any ties to our family if he didn't? Think about it, Michael. He spent almost all his life with Nona. Of course he would have knowledge and acceptance of goddesses and core earthly beliefs. Plus, just by living here, a country steeped in pagan history, Celtic lore and mysticism, he's bound to have a much different viewpoint than most religious figures in the States. He's living on the land where the Crusades murdered entire families because their beliefs threatened the power of the Church. He's bound to step back from the bonds of his religion's dogma, knowing what he does about our family. I can understand why he ended up here, in the country that protected the truth about our bloodline. In his own way, it was a means to stay connected to our roots and maybe discover more about it. He sure knows a lot about the history of the area. I'm anxious to hear what else he has to say about our family history here in France."

"You're right, of course," Michael said, holding her closer. He loved the fragrance of her hair.

"Are you happy?" he asked, changing the subject.

"Of course," she replied, snuggling closer into his arms. "Why do you ask?"

"Because sometimes I look at you and I'm so overjoyed with love and gratitude that I have to pinch myself to be sure I'm really alive and this is truly happening to me. Less than a year ago I was dying, and now I'm in France, lying in bed with a beautiful woman whom I love dearly and. . ." he put his hand over her belly, ". . .and I'm going to be a father. I'm so happy. I must be in heaven. Really." He began to kiss her neck and shoulders, but before he could go any further, he felt a thump under his hand.

"What!" he laughed. "Did the baby just kick?"

"Oh yes she did," Miyah said. "She's been quite active today."

"This is the first time I've felt her," he said. "That's so amazing." He rolled over so he could watch the movements of her stomach.

"This is so amazing!" he repeated, covering her belly with his hand.

"Yes, and in a few months, I'll be wishing you were feeling it from the inside, instead of me," she joked. "Judging by how much she moves around now, I can imagine we'll have a very active little one on our hands.

"I know my pregnancy has started to show," she said. "It's a good thing I wear skirts most of the time, so I won't have to alter my wardrobe much. I should tell Tomas soon. I think he'll be proud to become a great-grandfather."

"I'm trying not to be overly protective because I know you don't want to be fussed over, but you have to promise me you'll let me know when you're tired or need anything at all—pickles, ice cream in the middle of the night—anything!" he said.

"Thankfully my cravings have been for things like mineral water, almonds, fresh fruit, dates and apples. You've probably noticed me hoarding these things!" she laughed.

"And your daily doses of raspberry leaf tea," he added.

"Hmm. . .but now, all I need is you," she said, seductively pulling him closer.

"Your wish is my command. . ." he whispered. And they made love surrounded by the light of a full moon and serenaded by the rhythmic music of the River Salz.

~~~~~

They had plans the next morning to drive Tomas' car to Rennes-le-Château.

"Friends of mine are heading to the airport in Toulouse and offered to return your rental car," he had told them the first day they arrived in Rennes-les-Bains. "It would be doing them a favor, providing transportation to the airport, and you don't need the car. You have mine. I haven't driven much in the last few years, but have kept it in good shape. It's Miyah's car now," he had said with a grin.

They walked to the wooden shed behind the house and Tomas opened the garage door. Michael expected to see a rusty old beater. He was surprised when Tomas handed him the keys to a clean, perfectly conditioned, vintage, black, 1959 Cadillac Coupe de Ville. He let out a long whistle.

"A generous family looked at it as a donation to a worthy cause, garnering a few prayers on their behalf," Tomas mused. He offered some history of Rennes-le-Château as they drove.

"The village was originally called Rhedae, formed around 410 by the Visigoth after they pillaged Rome and took possession of a massive treasure from Jerusalem. They were talented builders and built a town flanked by two forts with all access sealed by an impassable ring of towers, linked by communication signals. The Merovingians, or Franks, led by King Clovis, later defeated the Visigoth, set fire to Toulouse, their capitol, and pushed them back to Carcassonne, which then became their frontier town.

"The Merovingians thrived in this area and many tombstones from their cemeteries have been found. During the time of the Troubadours, Rhedae became famous for its court, with Kings and Queens staying here. There are many layers to this history, but the village was destroyed and rebuilt several times, underwent raids and slaughtering of the villagers, and even plague. Eventually the city of Rhedae disappeared forever and only a small village of houses and the Church of Mary Magdalene remained, tucked away around the chateau of the Voisin family, and they named the village Rennes-le-Château."

Tomas continued, "To understand the situation of the village, you must first know the genealogy of the family who settled here. Bear with me. The last Voisin daughter, Jeanne, married Spanish Lord de Marquefave. Their daughter, Blanche de Marquefave, married Pierre Raymond d'Hautpoul and as a dowry gave him the estate of Rennes. Henri Baron d'Hautpoul took the title of Seigneur de Blanchefort. In 1732, the last Marquis de Blanchefort married Marie de Négre Dables, who came from a large family, but was left a widow 30 years later with no male heir. Her full name became Marie de Négre Dables-Dame d'Hautpoul de Blanchefort. She died in the chateau in 1781 at the age of 67."

"That's all very interesting," Michael said dryly.

"Oh, but now it does get interesting," Tomas replied. "Before she died, Lady Blanchefort confided a great secret that had been passed down in her family from generation to generation, to abbé Antoine Bigou, who had been the parish priest for seven years in Rennes-le-Château. She also entrusted him with some important documents, telling the abbé to, in turn, pass on the secret only to someone whom he deemed trustworthy. He was terrified by what he had learned and hid the documents, telling no one. Ten years later he had a large gravestone laid flat on the tomb of the Lady Blanchefort, engraved with the Latin inscription, *Et in Arcadia Ego,* in Greek lettering. The flagstone was transported all the way from the Tomb of Arques, a funeral monument on the road to Narbonne."

"Doesn't *Et in Arcadia Ego* have to do with a painting by Nicolas Poussin?" Miyah asked, remembering it from their visit to the Louvre.

Michael added. "*Les Bergers d'Arcadie – The Shepherds of Arcadia.* He painted two pieces on the Arcadia theme, the second painting around 1639, which is in the Louvre. It translates 'Even in Arcadia, I exist.' Arcadia referring to the countryside and 'I' referring to death. The first painting had a human skull on top of the tombstone, the second painting didn't."

"We'll come back to that," Tomas said, returning to his story. "Abbé Bigou had another tombstone erected which intentionally drew attention to a cryptogram which, if translated, carried a key that would lead to a secret place. This was during the time of the French Revolution, so inside the church the priest also turned face down an ancient stone sculpture of a knight and child riding on a horse together. In 1792, Bigou was declared a rebellious priest. He fled to Spain and mysteriously died there 18 months later. Some say he had approached the Church with his secret and they didn't like what they heard. But before he left, he shared his secret with another exiled priest, the abbé Cauneille, who in turn passed it along to two other priests, abbé Jean Vié, parish priest of Rennes-les-Bains from 1840 to 1870, and abbé Emile Francois Cayron, a priest in the Aude during the same period."

"What was the secret?" Michael asked.

"Well, it seems that is the question of the ages!" Tomas exclaimed. "Supposedly it was about priceless treasure buried in twelve hidden places, somewhere around Rennes-le-Château and Rennes-les-Bains. Later two more priests were given the secret information and they evidently were able to translate the cryptogram. That was abbé Bérenger Saunière, who was made parish priest of Rennes-le-Château in 1885, and abbé Henri Boudet, who succeeded Jean Vié as parish priest of Rennes-les-Bains. You may have heard the story from there. The little church was in bad shape and Saunière headed a campaign to fully renovate it, which many say was a cover to be able to tear the church apart in his search for the treasure. He received money from various sources, but a Monsieur Guillaume gave him 3,000 francs, which was a huge sum of money at the time, in return for searching for any documents that may be hidden in the church. There were many political reasons for this relating to the heir of the throne of France."

"Whew," Michael said. "It's like a scene right out of a mystery novel. My mom would have loved this. I wonder if she knew about the story."

"Oh, if they spent as much time in this area as you said, I'm sure she knew and probably did her share of researching," Miyah replied. "It might have even tied in with the work your father was doing."

"Many books have been written that included the mystery, but the first was written by abbé Boudet himself," Tomas said. "He was a very cultured man, especially in archaeology and ancient languages. While Saunière was busy tearing apart the church, Boudet published a 310-page manuscript titled, *La Vraie Langue Celtique et le Cromlech de Rennes-les-Bains – The True Celtic Language and the Stone Circle of Rennes-les-Bains*. It was completed in 1880 and published in 1886 by Francois Pomie, the printer to the Bishop of Carcassonne. Filled with humor and mystery, it was criticized from the beginning as a strange work of fantasy. Five hundred copies were produced at a cost of 5,382 gold francs, paid for out of Boudet's own pocket. Of the 500 copies, only 98 were sold, 100 were given to libraries and institutions and 200 were given away by Boudet as gifts to friends. The remaining 102 copies were supposedly destroyed in 1914, an act initiated by the Bishop de Beausejour.

"The book concealed, between the lines, the Blanchefort secret and even gave the exact location of 12 hidden chests, which could only be opened with a key of numbers decoded in a foreign language. The book may have been meant as a diversion, as Boudet was reported to have falsified grave stones in the cemetery and to have changed locations of certain stone crosses. His book got little attention. Boudet published many more texts, one named *Lazarus Come Outside* in 1890, but that book was also banned by his bishop for unknown reasons and didn't even see the light of day.

"Although most people credit Saunière for the bizarre decorating and coded artwork in the church, some say it was really Boudet, along with Marie Denarnaud, a young woman assigned as Saunière's housemaid, who were behind all the strange activities, prompting him with assignments."

"I read about Marie Denarnaud," Miyah said. "She wore the latest Paris fashions, fancy hats and unusual antique jewelry, but was quite arrogant with the other women. She was called Mademoiselle Marie, but was nicknamed 'La Madone' among the villagers."

"She was also known to visit the graveyard faithfully every night until some complaints were made of her and Saunière digging in the cemetery," Tomas added. "She died in 1953, at the age of 85, and supposedly never told anyone of the secrets she shared with Boudet and Saunière."

"But did they really find anything?" Michael asked.

"When they removed the altar in the church, a flagstone was broken, revealing a hiding place with a container filled with gold and other treasure. On one of the pillars supporting the altar was a Visigoth symbol of a 'cross of silence.' Saunière dismissed the workers and continued on his own, but it was reported that he was later seen removing a wooden tube with wax seals from the pillar. The tube supposedly contained two parchments and a manuscript, which later, decoded by Boudet, deciphered the epitaph of Lady Blanchefort's headstone, which is some of the information he later included in his book. Another strange message was also decoded and roughly translated into something like:

'Shepherdess no temptation
that Poussin Teniers hold the key, Pax 681
by the cross and chevel, or horse of God
I dispatch this guardian demon at midday blue apples.'

"What an unusual message. It doesn't make any sense. I can't fathom how he figured all that out," Miyah said. "What did it mean?"

"I don't know exactly, but when Saunière was in Paris, he visited the Louvre and bought three reproductions. The most famous was *Les Bergers d'Arcadie*, by Nicolas Poussin, of the tomb of Arques with the inscription *Et In Arcadia Ego*. The Rennes countryside is supposedly reproduced in the background, and the tomb in the painting is thought to be a copy of a real tomb that rested on a rocky knoll overlooking a bend of the River Rialsesse, near Les Pontils, just a few miles from here. However, just the base slab of the tomb remains today. The landowner got tired of treasure hunters constantly attempting to open the tomb and in 1988 he had it removed.

"As you said earlier, Michael, the painting translates as *The Shepherds of Arcadia,* and the main figure is a woman—a *Shepherdess.*

"The second painting Saunière bought was *La Tentation de St. Antoine* by David Teniers. The feast day of St. Anthony, as well as St. Sulpice's Feast Day, are coincidently on January 17, the date of Lady Blanchefort's death engraved on her tomb. Having no male heirs, she was the last marquise d'Hautpoul. I might also add to that list of January 17 dates, that Saunière also died on that day, years later, supposedly of a heart attack or stroke. But, getting back to the paintings—there were three Teniers painters: a father and two sons, and they painted a dozen or more renditions of *The Temptations of St. Anthony.* But in only one of these, St. Anthony was NOT being tempted by the devil. *'No temptation,'* might have referred to that specific painting, which had a background with a cave, similar to the background of the Poussin painting."

"And the third painting?" Miyah asked.

"There was little known about this painting at first. It was a portrait of Pope Celestine V and the artist was possibly Barthelemy Van Eyck, who was an alchemist and painter at the court of a man who was well-known within Priory of Zion. St. Peter Celestine was the founder of the Celestine Order and became known as Celestine V. He lived the life of a hermit, turning his back on material things. People flocked to him for advice and to have him pray for them. He wore layman's clothing and didn't try to attract people. He did the opposite of the Church, taking a pagan approach, much like the early Cathars, and abandoned everything material.

"He was elected pope when he was 72-years-old and reigned for five months. Not being comfortable with his new position he 'resigned' and resumed the simple life of a monk. There are reports that he was instrumental in helping the Templars carry out their secret mission.

"There are some symbols in the painting that could be hidden messages. He's holding a papal key; there are Templar style crosses in the wood trim in the background, on the floor tiles, on designs of his court's clothing, and on staffs the men are holding; there are two fleur-de-lis symbols on the floor tiles, the symbol for Merovingian royalty; there are two tiles that say 'MM' in the center bottom of the painting; the two bishops have their hands on a tiara, crowning him. The bishop on Celestine V's right is wearing red, and another bishop is wearing white, which could represent the red and white of the Knights Templar. Celestine V is wearing a neutral blue-black robe.

"It's also interesting that after he left the papal position, he was detained under careful guard in the castle of Fumone near Anagni, which some say alluded to his prior involvement with the Templars. He lived in a replica of his former monastic cell until his death on *January 17*, at the age of a 105."

"So Saunière brought the paintings back to Rennes-le-Château to study them for clues," Michael summed up. "He must have found want he was looking for, but we really don't know what the references to the paintings meant, correct?"

"Yes, but we do know the messages he found referred to Saint Sulpice in Paris, which was modeled after the Temple of Solomon and was finished around the time of Blanchefort's death. It also encouraged the person who deciphered the message to be silent until the year 1891."

"Where did they get 1891?" Miyah asked.

"Oh, that's interesting." Tomas loved puzzles and was eager to explain this one. "Remember that Bigou was putting everything into code. When he made Lady Blanchefort's tombstone, he chiseled Roman numerals. She died in 1781, so the letters should have read. . ." Tomas took out a piece of paper and wrote, XVII JANVIER MDCCLXXXI. January 17, 1781. But instead he changed a "C" to zero, which doesn't exist in Roman numerals. Tomas wrote, XVII JANVIER MDCOLXXXI. "So you skip over the zero, and it reads MDCLXXXI, 1681. Boudet translated the zero to represent the zero meridian line that passes through Saint Sulpice and Rennes-les-Bains. Many of the messages left were in reverse, so by turning the number upside down, he got 1891."

"The next line of the coded message is '*By the cross and horse of God*,'" Michael said. "Do you have a translation for that?"

"Remember the stone that Bigou had turned face down of the knight and child on horseback? When this stone was relocated by following the clues, there was also a skull pierced by a ritual incision, similar to those carried out on the dead in Merovingian times so their soul would escape toward heaven.

PAX 681 might have signified the transfer of royalty to Rhedae, in the year 681, after the death of King Dagobert II, who was a Magdalene heir. He was the only Merovingian king to be canonized and officially declared a saint, so in a sense was recognized by the Church. His second marriage was to the Visigothic princess, Gisela of the Razés, and their son, Sigebert IV, would have legally been a male heir to the French throne. After Dagobert's death, Sigebert and his sister Rathilde were smuggled from the palace to the abbey of Oereen. A year after Dagobert's death a detachment of knights, led by Merovée Levi, collected Sigebert from the abbey and, riding with him on horseback, delivered him to his Visigothic grandfather in the Razés, to Rhedae—Rennes-le-Château. The Visigoths of the area were said to have been descended from the House of Benjamin, which had fled to the Arcadia region of Greece, and then north into France a thousand years earlier."

"Whew," Michael said. "So the stone Bigou turned face-down was the carving of a knight with the boy on a horse—Sigebert IV, heir to the French throne. I sure hope we can sit down later so you can help me write all of this down. It's really confusing."

"Oh, you'll easily find it in your history books. I'm just giving you a condensed version," Tomas replied.

"Condensed!" Michael said. "Ha!"

"But what about the 'blue apples' in the epitaph?" Miyah asked. "That's an interesting reference."

"Pommes bleues. There is speculation. Some say it refers to grapes—which could refer to another wonderful Poussin painting called *Grapes of the Promised Land*, where two men are on a winding road, carrying a long branch between them with a giant cluster of grapes, even though there are no grape vines in the painting. Behind them is a man on a ladder, picking apples from a tall tree. A woman is walking to the river, carrying a basket of clothes on her head. Another woman is kneeling, washing clothes. In the far distance is a tall mountain similar to Bugarach, and closer you see a village and a castle fortress up on a rocky hill, resembling Rennes-le-Château. Blue apples most likely refers to the grapes, or the vine, which in turn refers to branches of the bloodline."

"That would make sense," Miyah said. "Fruit of the vine—the bloodline."

"Ah, but there is another explanation that directly relates to Renne," Tomas said. "At midday, noon, on January 17, the sun shines through the church's stained-glass window of *Jesus Raising Lazarus from the Dead*. Orbs of bluish and other colored lights appear and eventually shine on the base of the altar at the bas-relief of Mary Magdalene kneeling in prayer, her fingers laced into a woven pattern, with a skull at her knees. You'll see this relief when we go into the church. It could refer to a location in the area.

"I might add that Saunière also discovered a stairway that led to a vault beneath the church, which led to a series of caves."

"Caves that connected through the maze of the five-pointed star," Michael surmised. "This would make a great mystery novel."

Tomas laughed. "Oh, you don't know the half of it! Saunière went to Saint Sulpice, where symbolism of the church represents the countryside around Rennes-les-Bains, to have the parchments translated. He spent five days there and was introduced to the author of many freemasonry studies and the men, who in 1891, founded 'The Rose+Cross of The Temple and the Grail.' Many Rose Croix, or Rosicrucians, often became Saunière's guests at Rennes-le-Château. Their doctrine was built on esoteric truths and knowledge related to the inner teachings of the ancient past, which provided insight into nature, the physical universe and a symbolic and spiritual alchemy. I recall one of their writings, *The thoughts attached to the real desire of the seeker will lead us to him and him to us.*'

"Saunière's discoveries marked the beginning of tremendous wealth, and both he and Denarnaud lived as though they had unlimited funds. The restoration of the Church of Mary Magdalene was finished with huge amounts of money and inaugurated in 1897. Saunière kept meticulous accounting books, so all purchases and where they came from, were recorded.

"After the inauguration, work continued on land purchased in Denarnaud's name. The construction included a christened Magdala Tower overlooking the valley; a Renaissance style house, named Villa Bethania; a semi-circular gallery on the side of the cliff with a second tower crowning a greenhouse; a park with fountains; and even a small zoo. The Church was completely scandalized by such a display of a simple priest's wealth and from 1910 onward Saunière was under investigation by the Diocese of Carcassonne for excessive spending and failure to produce evidence of the source of his fortune. He refused to share his secrets with the bishop and was sentenced for trafficking masses, receiving money for masses he never said. It was reported that he had over 100,000 requests for masses, and at that time each request was accompanied by at least 1 to 1.5 francs. There was no way he could perform that many prayer services. The Church forbade him to carry out priestly duties any longer.

"Some say his wealth was because the Vatican paid him to turn sacred documents over to them. Two genealogy manuscripts dating from 1244 and 1644 were reportedly bought by the Vatican and they supposedly kept giving Saunière large amounts of money through their contact, the abbé Henri Boudet, to continue his search. They hoped Saunière would find the Ark of the Covenant. Others say he received a tremendous amount of money from selling other treasures in the black market. It most likely was all of these things that brought his fortunes."

"As a retired priest, how do you feel about all of this going on within the Church?" Miyah asked.

"I was fortunate to have known about many things through Nona and my travels back to the ancients that had already shaped my beliefs and opinions of the Church before I even came here. The corruption of the Church comes from inside the upper levels of the Church: the Vatican, especially Vatican bankers, and other powerful men connected with them who have been influenced by power, money and material values. There are also many moral issues that have impacted the Church and caused many of us priests to lose faith, shall we say, in the establishment."

"Such as?" Michael was intrigued by Tomas' confession.

"Well, for instance, do you remember back in the 60s, when the invention of the birth control pill was so controversial? Denouncing using the pill was a huge issue in the Church."

Michael nodded.

"What you may not have known is that among the Vatican's many bank, business and property investments, they also owned a pharmaceutical company called Instituto Farmacologico Sereno. One of their best selling products was an oral contraceptive called Luteolas, and the Church benefited greatly for many years from profits derived from that birth control pill, while during the entire time it was opposing its use."

"That's unbelievable," Michael shook his head. "It's hypocritical!"

"Indeed," replied Tomas.

"But what I discovered here in France, along with the story of Rennes-le-Château, makes my faith in the original mission of Jesus even stronger. The wealth, riches and power that have dominated the Church throughout history is a sad legacy and doesn't follow the original Jesus story. Members of the Vatican know the truth about the life of Jesus, but they maintain their external religion as a means of controlling their followers. However, thankfully, there are factions within the Church who hold very different beliefs. There are thousands of priests and clergy all around, who, regardless of the ruthless power of the Church, know and protect the same beliefs as myself. And yes, that does include knowing about the bloodline and the fact that the end result of the crucifixion was a fabrication to strengthen power over the people by the Roman Church. I was a priest, not a puppet, and I know in my heart that I have served the people well. That was my mission. That was the true mission of Jesus. And, thank God, there are many of us who hold true to that mission.

"I think Saunière originally planned to expose the secret he discovered about the bloodline, but when he presented it to the bishop, there was no way the Church would allow it. In his mind, building the Magdala Tower, selling off the treasures which may have originally come from the Church in the first place, and making his property on Rennes-le-Château a shrine to Mary Magdalene with mysterious symbols and altered artwork, he was, in his own way, mocking the wealth of the Church and drawing attention to his discovery of the Merovingian line as descendants of Jesus and Mary

Magdalene."

"Well said, Grandfather," Miyah patted his knee. "I can see why you enjoy living in this area with so much religious history and intrigue woven throughout the land."

"I have many clerical friends who share these beliefs," he said. "And there seems to be plenty of evidence in the land to prove these truths. This is a holy place."

"And Saunière, what became of him?" Michael asked.

"Oh, there's a lot more to the story, but before his death of a sudden stroke, on *January 17*, 1917, Saunière did eventually pass on his secret to his friend, abbé Rivière of Espéraza. Rivière in turn passed the secret to another priest, and so on. Marie Denarnaud remained in her house and once said that the people of Rennes-le-Château walked on gold without knowing it, and that what was left hidden was enough to feed the entire village for a hundred years and there would still be more left. She eventually entrusted all her possessions to Noel and Henriette Corbu, a family whom she let move into Villa Bethania. Corbu refurbished Villa Bethania into a hotel-restaurant, Hotel du Tour, to support his family and drew upon the history of the treasure to bring people into his hotel, all the time searching for the treasure himself.

"Denarnaud reportedly told Corbu not to worry about money, that one day she would tell him a secret that would make him a very rich man. . .but she had a sudden stroke before she could share the secret. Noel Corbu took care of Denarnaud and may have learned of something from her incoherent whispers before she died. He was killed in a terrible car crash in 1953, the same year as Denarnaud's death, pointing to the fact that someone may have suspected she told him the secret and that his death was not an accident. The Corbu family sold the property in 1960. Corbu however, is actually the one who renewed the Rennes-le-Château story, which drew international attention. People still come here to search for clues that might lead to more treasures hidden in these hills and valleys."

"Has there been actual documentation of any of this?" Michael asked.

"Oh yes. Plenty. In 2001 a team from California used echo-sounding techniques and discovered a crypt beneath the church. According to analysis of soil samples, the crypt dated to the fifth century AD. They also found an object buried beneath the Magdala Tower, which remember had been built by Saunière. It was a chest, measuring a little over three feet wide and almost three feet deep, containing documents. The group was granted permission to return in 2002, under the close supervision of the Vatican. Along with an ancient history specialist from Italy, they did more detailed echo soundings. I haven't heard anything about them since."

"Do you think there's still treasure hidden here?" Miyah asked.

Tomas nodded his head. "Ah yes, I know there is," he said, looking out the window. "I know there is."

They followed the winding road that led up the hill to Rennes-le-Château. The village was perched high on a rocky outcrop offering spectacular views over the Razès countryside, with Carcassonne to the north and the Pyrenees looming in the distance. With its natural defense location and abundant resources, this ancient site was proof of man's presence there for over 3,000 years, and it still looked archaic from below. As they drove to the top of the hill, Michael hoped he wouldn't meet another car on the curvy road. One side of the mountain rolled upward, and the other side of the narrow road dropped down to the valley.

"For years Rennes-le-Château was isolated with no road at all leading from Couiza," Tomas said, noting Michael's concern. "It wasn't until the abbé Saunière paid for a road to be constructed that one was built."

They drove into the village and parked in the lot near the Magdala Tower.

"Thank you for giving us the history before we got here," Michael said. "I already feel like I know the place."

"There's a lot more inside. It's a good thing you brought your notebook and camera," Tomas laughed. "You'll need them. It's taken me years to remember all of this and sometimes I still forget."

"How *do* you remember it all?" Miyah was amazed.

"I'm a member of an association called 'Terre de Rhedae' that began in 1989, helping to protect the communal inheritance of the area," Tomas admitted. "I help organize tours and welcome visitors to the little museum next to the church. We can stop in there before we leave. It has a large collection of documents and personal items that once belonged to Saunière and Denarnaud—and even dinosaur eggs that were unearthed nearby!"

He added, "I joined the association to be helpful. Many of the local families received objects from Sauniére, religious items, rare jewelry, gold coins. He was very generous to his parishioners and they want to protect the development of this community, which has a population of about 111 residents. It's understandable they want to support their town, guarding its interests."

Tomas walked with them through the village so they could get a feel for the town. Flowers—trios of red tulips—were blooming in thick-walled window boxes of the stone houses. Michael photographed red tiled roofs, windows with shutters, lace curtains and ornate wrought iron bars. He zoomed in on metal door knockers, paint-worn wooden doors that unlocked with skeleton keys and had brass doorknobs in the middle of the door. Tall, three-storied homes surrounded the narrow streets of the village.

"It's so quaint and clean," Miyah said. "I feel like I'm back in another era."

"That's part of why I love coming here. It's peaceful," Tomas replied.

He showed them the Château des Seigneurs De Rennes, the castle that gave the village of Rennes-le-Château its name. Originally a Visigothic

Asmodeus – the devil – greets you as you enter Saunière's Church – Rennes-le-Château

fortress, only one original room in the north section of the castle remained. The castle had been built and destroyed several times throughout history and built again in the 16th century.

"This is where Marie de Négre Dables Dame d'Hautpoul de Blanchefort lived," Tomas said. "Remember, she's the one who died January 17, 1781 and passed down the secret to abbé Bigou—the woman for whom he made the mysterious cryptogram headstone. The Magdalene Church isn't the only building in this village that has secrets. The castle has four main buildings on a central courtyard with four corner towers, one circular and three square. Twelve stones over the threshold represent the 12 apostles, or the 12 signs of the zodiac. The castle has secret dungeons and closed off underground passageways, which I'm sure join to the church and the cave system beyond.

"Are you ready for a tour of the church?" Tomas asked, heading them in the direction of the Church of St. Mary Magdalene. They didn't get very far when both Michael and Miyah stopped in front of a table loaded with books and pamphlets. Tomas quickly herded them on, telling them they could stop back later and that there was also a bookstore near the museum. They rounded the corner and stood in front of the limestone church—the Church of Saint Mary Magdalene, dedicated to her in 1059.

"The original chapel belonged to the chateau and was built in the 8th and 9th centuries," Tomas explained. "The parishioners had their own Church of St. Pierre in the village. The restoration work here lasted for nine years and believe me, you'll find everything unusual. It's like Alice falling into Wonderland or Dorothy tripping into Oz, only the symbolism of everything here is real and refers to events in history, and perhaps the future."

Two gargoyles on tall pillars, where the triangular porch roof began, greeted them outside the church. Under one was a date, 1891, the year the abbé discovered the tomb. Above the gargoyles were two large white pillars, looking like the knights of a chest board with white doves on top of each of them.

Tomas pointed above the door, just inside the triangular alcove where there was a statue of Mary Magdalene cradling a red cross in her arms. Another cross above her had several inscriptions. Tomas read one of them, *"Regnum mundi et omnem ornatum soeculi contempsi propter amorem domini mei Jesu Christi quem vidi quem amiva in quem credidi quem dilex."*

"Which means?" Michael asked.

"It means *I have scorned the kingdom of this world and all adornment of this century because of my lord Jesus Christ, whom I saw, I loved, in whom I believed and loved.*' Actually when you put *quem dilex* together, it translates as *'in whom I have taken pleasure.'*"

"Whew," Michael exclaimed. "That's revealing."

"Can you read that?" he asked Miyah, pointing to another inscription.

"*Terribilis est locus iste.* It doesn't make any sense," she replied.

"You're right! It says *'This place is terrible!'* Yes really, that's what it says. He's warning you before you even enter the church. And below it says *Domus mea domus oratorionis vocabitur*, '*My house will be known as a house of prayer.*' Welcome to Saunière's strange church," Tomas laughed.

They entered the church and Miyah gasped, grabbing Michael's arm. To the left of the door they were greeted by a large statue of a horned, eye-bulging, dark-skinned devil with long fingers and toe nails, garbed in a green tunic. He was kneeling, bending under the weight of a holy water basin, and looking toward the checkerboard floor. Two salamander-like creatures decorated the pillar above the basin, and between them was a round red seal with the initials, "B.S."

"Whoa," Michael reacted. "I don't think I'd want to put my fingers into that holy water! This isn't what I would expect for a greeter inside the church."

"Oh, I know what you mean," Tomas laughed again. "Everyone reacts that way. I'm sure that's precisely why he was placed there, to get your attention. Remember things here are often represented in reverse. The devil is the opposite of good. Some interpret this as the devil is defeated and bowing to God, and even go so far as to say the devil is the Church itself, bowing to the truth. Others refer to him as Asmodeus, the legendary guardian of treasure—remember the epitaph, *'I dispatch this guardian demon.'* In 1st-3rd century texts of the Testament of Solomon, the king invokes Asmodeus to aid in the construction of the Temple. The demon appears and predicts Solomon's kingdom will one day be divided. As you can see, no one really knows exactly why this statue is in the church, but we know that whatever the meaning, it must be a powerful clue. Maybe it's Saunière's way to reference a divided kingdom within the Church itself—those focused on power and wealth verses those who mindfully and faithfully serve the people and continue Jesus' mission of love and peace.

"In medieval cathedrals it was common to place statues of demons outside the church, usually on the north side, as a message that the way to escape evil was by entering the church. Maybe it has a reference to that," Tomas added.

"He has angels above him on the pillar," Miyah noticed. There were four angels, each looking in four different directions and each with their hand in one of the signs of the cross positions. Above the angels was a cross of equal dimensions, with the fleur-de-lis on all four points, and a rose in the center. A circle behind the cross joined its points. One angel was kneeling and pointed with her index finger to the inscription below them.

"It reads, *'By this sign ye shall conquer him,'*" Tomas said.

"By what sign?" Michael asked. "The insignia of the B.S.? The devil statue? What does the B.S. mean? Bérenger Saunière? We saw BS initials in St. Martin Church in Limoux, too."

"Possibly Bérenger Saunière, he also had connections with that church, or B.S. could mean Blanque and Salz, two rivers nearby that meet at a fork called 'le bénitier,' or the holy water basin. In 1928 a small solid gold statue, half melted down, was found in the Blanque River.

"And the angels are each looking in different directions, which could refer to the four directions," Tomas noted. "Plus the verse, *'by this sign ye shall conquer him'* doesn't in its original verse include the word *'him'* at the end, so the reference must be intentional."

"We haven't even begun and this is driving me crazy!" Michael said. "You're right, Tomas. It's like walking inside a giant puzzle."

"But there is a difference," Miyah whispered. "We already know the ending. Where the Magdalene legend leads. . .and from where it came."

Michael smiled at Miyah and squeezed her hand. "So I shouldn't get too carried away with this and just look at it as a mysterious puzzle," he said. "You have to admit it makes us use our brains. . .connecting all the dots!"

"Yes," Miyah admitted. "But this church is not at all what I expected. I thought it would be more of a shrine to the Magdalene, like the church in Paris."

"The Tower of Magdala on the edge of the grounds is really the temple that honors her," Tomas interrupted. "We'll visit there last. You must remember that this original chapel was devoted to Mary Magdalene around the first century. It was supposedly built on sacred ground that had a temple dedicated to the priestess Isis. Bigou was the first priest to learn of the hidden treasures and it was Saunière who redesigned the church as he searched. He completely altered the church to include esoteric messages, which he did intentionally, for others to find. . .to rebuke the Church. . .who knows? He placed riddles within the icons of the Church that primarily end up pointing back to the Merovingian bloodline. The material treasures he obviously wanted to keep for himself, but I don't think that all of the riches buried in these hills could be dug up in one lifetime."

Michael took out his journal and pen and began to make sketchy notes as Tomas guided them through the church, pointing out the unusual artwork, statues and symbols:

• black and white checkerboard tiles on the floor – 64 tiles, laid out like a chessboard, oriented to the four-points of the compass.

• sign of the Rose+Cross at the center of the fleur-de-lis on each side of the confessional – a shepherd looking for a sheep in an underground cave.

• a large wall fresco of the Mount of Beatitude, where Jesus gave his sermon on eight spiritual blessings – the penitence bag in the foreground has a hole in it; pomegranate leaves.

• the stations of the cross statues are in reverse order, beginning on the left, ending on the right – the Rose+Cross insignia is in each of the stations; odd items were added to each station. These odd items also relate to precise locations found in stone circles around Rennes-les-Bains:

– Station I, Jesus before Pontius Pilate, there is a golden griffin, animal with lion's head and eagle's back.

– Station VIII, a woman wearing a black veil holds a child dressed in a tartan – the son, John, born in Scotland?

– Station X, a soldier is gambling for Jesus' tunic using two dice. One shows a five, the other is tipped and shows a three and a four (total 12, adds to 3 - trinity?) – which isn't possible as those numbers aren't next to each other on dice. Is this a numeric key used to decipher the cryptogram on the headstone?

– Station XIV, a body is being carried into the tomb and there is a full moon intentionally painted into the night sky, indicating that the body could not have been dead, as Jewish law didn't permit burial or touching a dead body after sunset on Passover.

• statues of Joseph (on the left when looking at the altar) and Mary (on the right) at the front of the church, both are holding babies. Is it Jesus and Mary Magdalene holding two of their children? Both babies are naked. One has a penis, the other's genitals are draped so you can't tell if it is a male or female.

• the towns of Bethany and Magdala are both represented in the frescos.

• statue of Jesus being baptized by John the Baptist; Jesus is crouched in the same position as the devil in the church entrance, but in reverse, facing the other direction; the clothes he wears are a similar color but the patterns are reversed; Jesus also stares at the checkerboard floor; good verses evil.

• the bas-relief of the altar: Mary Magdalene, in tears, kneeling in a grotto with scenery that resembles David Tenier's painting, *The Temptations of Saint Anthony the Hermit*, one of the paintings Saunière brought back from the Louvre; her fingers are woven in a triple X pattern, a sign of concealed esoteric knowledge; open book; skull. Tomas says the inscription under the bas-relief has since disappeared. It said *"Jesu. Medela. Vulnerum • Spes. Una. Penitentium. -* second line *Per. Magdalene. Lacrymas • Peccata. Nostra. Diluas."* - *"Jesus, remedy of wounds, sole hope for those who regret, by the tears of Magdalene dissolve our sins."*

• Saunière was obsessed with portraying Mary Magdalene in ways that would draw attention to her and make people ask questions.

• a Templar cross, the letter M, and sacred heart are on the mural – M for Magdalene and sacred heart for Jesus.

- the altar has fleur-de-lis decorations and the seal of Blanchefort castle (a few miles away and connected by tunnels to the church).

- stained glass window above the altar – Mary with jar, wiping Jesus feet with her hair; four men at table with Jesus; only Jesus and Mary have halos.

- secret room behind the sacristy; a large cupboard/closet with a false back opens to a room that has a cemented-in doorway inside, which led to stairway that lead to caves; sacristy is closed to public.

- two Saint Anthony statues – St. Anthony the hermit with a "closed" book, and St. Anthony of Padua.**

- sunlight passes through the stained glass window opposite the St. Anthony the Hermit and supposedly illuminates the statue on *January 17*, the date he died, and the day of the Feast of St. Anthony – another January 17 date.

- **St. Anthony of Padua – Saint of lost things, was placed in front of the mural tomb of the last Merovingian king, Sigebert IV (boy on the horse with the knight who escaped to Rhedae), who died in Rhedae 750; his grandson had this church built on the site of a pagan temple; *ancient parchment found in a Jerusalem Bible said there was a temple dedicated to Isis, which in the reign of Titus - AD 70 - was given the name Magdala!*

The pillar - Rennes-le-Château

Skull and Cross in courtyard of the church - Rennes-le-Château

Michael couldn't write fast enough, stopping only long enough to take photos. He was so excited about what he was hearing. Again he said, "My mom, the mystery writer, would have loved this story! It's almost unbelievable." He made another note in his journal before they went outside.

- Boudet's book: using a set-square and compasses (Freemason symbols), the same zodiac can be drawn inside the church as in the surrounding countryside, but in reverse:

  – Countryside - line of Capricorn or <u>January 17</u>, goes from the Devil's Armchair (Throne of Isis) near Rennes-les-Bains to the Magdala Tower at Rennes-le-Château.

  – Inside church - from the devil statue to the altar; evil to good – opposites.

– Combined with clues of the statues and their positions, the location of 12 caskets can be found – each open with a special number based on the 12 signs of the zodiac; numbers are in Boudet's book; reference to Templar treasure in Bézu, a nearby town.

Michael made one more note on a fact which Tomas had mentioned briefly.

22 steps
– 11 on each side
Rennes-le-Château

• The Grotto in the garden, designed by Saunière, was a duplicate of The Grotto of Mary, a cave in the Vallée des Couleurs, which surrounds the village. A straight view of the cave, with its defined large, stone formation, can be seen from the narrow window of Magdala Tower. Inside this Grotto of Mary are the remains of two ancient graves. . .

Michael slapped his journal shut.

"I'm on overload," he said. "If I were a treasure hunter I would go insane with all this information. What a puzzle. There's so much history. How can you stand living here and not fall into the hands of the mystery?"

"Oh, we have plenty of lively conversations about all of it, I assure you," Tomas replied. "There are those around here who continue the search. I enjoy listening to their speculation and thought patterns regarding deciphering the clues, but I have no interest in finding hidden treasures. For me, the mystery itself is the treasure."

They walked out to the garden. On one side of the walkway was a white Visigothic pillar with Mission 1891 carved on it. Above the pillar was a statue of a praying Mary with a rosary belt around her waist, and atop the alcove was a castle replica in stone. It was badly weathered but a line of XXXXXX's bordered the entire front of the castle.

"When first placed outside from the church, Saunière set the pillar upside down making the date 1681—the date inscribed on the Marquise de Blanchefort's headstone. Some say it meant that the decoding of the clues inside the church should be worked out upside down, or in reverse," Tomas informed them. The pillar itself had a studded cross with equal lengths and symbols surrounding it. On the top was a moulding that was twisted like a rope, creating the likeness of 'croix du silence,' the cross of silence.

On the other side of the walkway was

Magdala Tower – Rennes-le-Château

the Garden of Calvary on what had at one time been the village square. Red tulips bloomed in the flower beds of this triangular shaped courtyard and in the center was a life size crucifix with an almost art deco starburst behind the entire upper body of Jesus. To the right of that was a small grotto in the point of the triangle, with a statue of Mary Magdalene inside. There was a gate at one end that led to the graveyard. The gate was locked but above the doorway was a skull and crossbones. The skull had 22 teeth. A cross above it had the initials JHS.

"I keep seeing references to the number 22," Michael said, getting his journal out. "There must be something significant about that number."

"The number 22 is a master number in numerology that aligns with psychic gifts, heightened awareness and intuitiveness," Miyah said. "It refers to living in two worlds and can contain secrets to esoteric questions. There are also 22 pathways in the Kabbala, 22 letters in the Hebrew alphabet and 22 is the number of the final Major Arcana in the Egyptian tarot deck."

"How do you know all this about the number 22?" Michael asked.

"It's numerology," she replied. "Plus my birthday is in on the 22nd!"

"How could I forget that?" Michael laughed.

"You'll also see that there are a total of 22 steps leading up to the terrace on top of the Magdala Tower and 22 battlements, or squared openings, on the top. I believe the number 22 also has to do with treachery from hidden enemies," Tomas said.

"It's also associated with power and the mastery of material things," Miyah added.

"I had no idea the significance of a number could mean so much. I've never studied numerology."

"You've also heard all the references to January 17, I'm sure," Tomas said. "That's one mystery I haven't figured out yet. I'll let you know if I ever do."

"It might relate to the number nine, the sum of 1-17," Miyah speculated.

"In numerology nine refers to endings. It's also the number of financial wealth. It seems that every time we hear of one of the untimely deaths connected to this story that occurred on that date, someone profited one way or another."

"It could be," Tomas said. "I know there's a connection somewhere."

They walked a few steps and Tomas pointed out Villa Bethania beyond the garden. "Bethania was the name of Lazarus' house, Mary Magdalene's brother. It was Saunière's plan that this residence would become a retirement home for the local priests, but things changed after his death. Instead there's a retirement home for priests in Carcassonne, which is also named Bethania."

"I found it interesting when I read that Marie Denarnaud, who lived in this house, used to hang sprigs of a broom from the window—to ward off bad luck, they said," Miyah noted. "I wonder if she had some pagan blood in her. She might have known that, representing the element of air, brooms were used for purification. Ritual circles were swept clean of negative energy and Denarnaud and Saunière did spend a lot of time in the graveyard. She most likely was using the broom sprigs as a form of purification."

They crossed the property to the site of the Magdala Tower, the tower on the edge of the plateau. It was built over the remains of the ramparts of the ancient citadel, hugging the side of a cliff, overlooking the valley below.

"There's a wonderful library in the tower. I like to sit and read some of the rare books shelved here. I'm lucky to have some special privileges," Tomas chuckled. "Here are more numbers for you Michael. The round watchtower has 12 battlements, like the 12 signs of the zodiac, and is positioned like a sundial. It was originally called the clock tower. There's supposed to be an underground passage that leads all the way to the castle at Coustaussa on the road to Narbonne, and it runs right through the Blanchefort Castle. AND the foundation stone was laid on January 17, the Feast Day of St. Anthony."

"That's too much," Michael said. "Lead me to the bookstore. I have to get some books on this place."

"And I have to find a bathroom!" Miyah admitted. "I'll meet you by the museum."

They took a short break and then Tomas gave Michael and Miyah a tour of the museum with its archaeological exhibits, artifacts, documents and written history of Rhedea, including the connection with Charlemagne. After a quick lunch in the garden restaurant, he left them grazing in the bookstore and went to visit some friends in the village. He knew he'd have at least an hour before he could pull them away from their shopping. There were a lot of books, postcards, and souvenirs to sort through, plus booths selling drawings, sculptures, engravings and graphics representing discoveries over the past years, recreated by artists of the area.

Miyah bought a sketch of the Magdala Tower and Michael purchased several books in English which he was grateful to find. The clerk, Maria Josephina it read on her name tag, said in her heavy French accent, "You must remember that the story here at Rennes-le-Château is just a small slice of the history of the entire area. You might also be interested in the Templar Castle in the village of Bézu, the white fortress with its many legends, and Blanchefort Castle. There are so many sites. You'll find ancient Celtic lore all around this area."

Michael thought she was just trying to sell him some more books, but then she said something curious. "Medicine, magic and religion are all connected here. Sometimes people come and the legends and mysteries spin, like a web, into their head, and they never leave. Sometimes they find that they, too, are connected by secrets."

Both Miyah and Michael stared at her. What did she mean? Was she warning them of something? The woman nodded to them, thanked them for their purchases and walked away.

The three travelers walked back toward the car and Miyah noticed an unusual white Celtic cross, about four feet tall. It was in a grassy patch with no other crosses or tombstones nearby, just a rusty bicycle half hidden in the bushes under a painted sign that read *La Porte de Rennes*. In the center of the cross was a handprint, palm side out—yet another mysterious symbol in the village of Rennes-le-Château.

Tomas put his arm around his granddaughter and said, "As someone once said, 'the land of the Cathars must be discovered like a good wine—in small sips.'"

Bike and sign at Rennes-le-Château

Celtic Cross Rennes-le-Château

View of valley from Rennes-le-Château

Above Entrance Mary Magdalene - Rennes-le-Château

Magdala Church at Rennes-le-Château

That night both Michael and Miyah were intellectually drained by the discoveries of their day.

"I thought Paris was intense," Miyah said, drying her wet hair, a towel wrapped around her from her shower. "But today was completely exhausting."

Michael was sitting up in bed, browsing through one of the books he bought at Rennes-le-Château. "I agree. There's so much mystery here. I'm glad I took so many notes," he said. "Tomas is a treasure of information. . .if you'll excuse the pun!"

"It seemed just last night that you were questioning me about him," she teased. "I'm glad to see you trusting him now."

"Yes, he really is remarkable. I feel he still has more to tell us though."

"I think so too," Miyah agreed. "I sensed him holding something back tonight at dinner. He probably thought we had enough for one day."

"He was right!" Michael exclaimed. "I think my brain would explode if I heard any more today. I'm sure we'll both be refreshed after a good night's sleep, and be begging for more." He watched Miyah as she put on her nightgown, the moonlight accenting the small, growing curve of her belly.

"At first I thought it strange the way the two of us came together and discovered our parents were friends and that we even shared a childhood," he talked slowly, pensively thinking about his words. "If that wasn't unusual enough, now I remember being here before as a boy with my parents and they had ties to the mystery surrounding this place. And your family is connected here from its very roots. A year ago I never would have believed such coincidences possible, but now I know it's all part of our fate, a divine plan. I can hardly wait to see where we're led next." He let out a long sigh.

"I sense a 'but. . .' " Miyah said, crawling into bed next to him.

"It may seem ridiculous, but remember yesterday at the pizzeria when we were talking about the caves and I started to say something, but stopped?"

"Yes, I knew something was bothering you."

"I was thinking about the maps and papers back home in my father's safe and wondering if any of them could possibly relate to his work here. And how could my mother, as a writer of mystery books, not have wanted to write about all of this. It even inspires *me*."

"Just because nothing was published doesn't mean your mother never wrote anything about Rennes. If your father did find something he may have wanted to keep it quiet, under the circumstances of his co-worker's death. Perhaps they did keep these things in their vault for safe keeping. You said he came to this area often."

"Yes, and I know that regardless of being told not to by the French government, the Church, whomever, he still came back here after that man died. My mom stayed home with us kids, but I remember her being concerned about him. It seems there was more than one mysterious accident even prior to that time. Now I can see why Mom was so worried. I wish I had paid more attention."

"Maybe there's a reason he didn't want you to. If there was danger involved, it would have been better if you didn't know anything," Miyah said.

"I'm speculating here, but maybe that's the real reason they built the bomb shelter. Maybe it was to hide themselves if they ever needed to. Does that sound crazy?"

"No, not at all. I have a feeling you'll find out more about your parents as our trip progresses."

"And when we get home I have to check through my father's documents. You know, I've never really gone through their things. It's pretty much the way they left them. Maybe it's time to do some housecleaning. Will you be up to helping me with that? Maybe there's nothing to it, but it keeps coming into my mind, so I see that as a message to stay alert."

"You're learning to listen to your intuition. That's good," Miyah said. "And speaking of intuition—what else is bothering you?"

Michael laughed. "I guess I'll never be able to keep secrets from you," he said, but then turned somber again.

"Tomas told us of at least a dozen people, and said there were probably many more over the decades, who had sudden strokes or heart attacks or who died in terrible car accidents. He alluded to the fact that none of those deaths were really natural causes or accidental and that all of those people were tied in one way or another with the mysteries of the treasures here. I can't help but wonder, if my parents did learn something here, if their car crash wasn't an accident either." Michael looked at Miyah to see her reaction.

"I wish I could say it was totally unrelated, Michael, but I don't know. It's possible."

"Here's another thought," he hesitated. "Is it possible, because our fathers were friends, that John could have worked with my dad, and that his death was another of those 'accidents?' You said he left your mother to do some research on a project overseas and she later learned he had died in a car crash in France."

Michael hesitated. "Miyah. . .I don't know if I should tell you this. . .but when I had the flashback of being lost in the cave when I was ten-years-old, I remembered a man who was with my father searching for me. I'm sure now, from looking at his picture, that it was John. Your father. They must have worked on the project in the caves together. Maybe he got so lost in the mysteries of his treasure hunting that he couldn't go back. The strange words of that lady where I bought my books keeps coming into my head— *Sometimes people come and the legends and mysteries spin, like a web, into their head and they never leave. Sometimes they find that they, too, are connected by secrets.*' Maybe he got caught in the web. . .and that's why he stayed."

"But if he was in contact with your parents, he must have known about me. Your parents must have told him." Miyah leaned back against the headboard to think this through.

"John wrote Junia a few letters, right? Maybe she knew how important this work was to him, and maybe she gave him his freedom by not telling him. She already knew the future of your destiny. You said she never told him about the

Touchstone legacy. Couldn't *you* have been another secret she kept from him? It would have been easy if he wasn't around, and she kept pretty busy raising you. She may have asked my parents not to tell him either."

Miyah was silent.

"On the other hand, suppose John did know and realized there was danger in what they were searching for and wanted to protect the both of you. He could have asked my parents to keep his whereabouts quiet. Either scenario would be the ultimate love sacrifice for each one of them," Michael offered as a possible explanation.

"I guess either way, my parents would have to have been involved in secrecy. Maybe it's just too outlandish to even consider," he said.

"I guess we both know who might have the answers," Michael pondered.

"I think I need to have a conversation with Nona and Junia," Miyah said. "I know they haven't told me the whole story. I just don't know why."

"Maybe because not knowing led us on this incredible journey," Michael answered, pulling her to him and rocking her in his arms.

"You keep telling me that things are revealed to us when the time is right. This applies to you too, my dear. What did Tomas say when we left the museum today—'like a good wine, things sometimes need to be discovered in sips.' I think we both need to stop gulping and take smaller sips."

"When did you get to be so wise?" she asked him, closing her eyes, relaxing in his gentle rocking.

"Since I started hanging around with you," he replied. "It's all because of you."

~ ~ ~ ~ ~

Both Miyah and Michael agreed that for the next few days they just wanted to hang around, enjoy the mineral springs, eat good food and relax. Their entire trip so far had been very fast paced and Miyah felt she needed to rest. Tomas had a few meetings and needed to catch up on his daily routine around the village, so they enjoyed a few slow paced days. Michael found internet service and checked in with Elizabeth, who said she was doing wonderfully without him. They took long walks in the woods and explored some of the natural and unnatural wonders of the area, which included "moving rocks" and stone circles. Miyah showed Michael the Throne of Isis and told him of her visions while sitting there.

They took advantage of the healing waters of the natural springs in the village. Miyah, in her condition, thought she shouldn't use the hot springs spa, so they walked along a path under the bridge to a stone circle with a natural spring area that was more private, where water flowed from a source along a stone wall. Large stones provided places to sit in the pool of luke warm water and relax in the natural mineral springs. They both enjoyed massages at the health center, and while Miyah joined in some yoga sessions, Michael worked out on the exercise equipment.

Miyah told Tomas that she and Michael were expecting a baby and he just smiled and nodded his head, "I know, dear. I'm so happy for you," he said. "I'm going to be a great-grandfather. Can you imagine that?"

People had begun to wave and greet them by name as they walked through the village. Miyah knew Tomas had spread the word about her being his granddaughter. He was very proud of her. Everyone loved Tomas and accepted his news with the same enthusiasm he had announced it. No one seemed to think anything of the fact that he was a retired priest. Quite the opposite, they enjoyed hearing the news, knowing he had experienced true love in his lifetime. They could also see how much joy being a grandfather gave him.

Lydia still brought some meals to the house and did light housekeeping, and Miyah joined her in the market, searching for fresh vegetables and fruits, but Miyah insisted on doing some of the cooking and Tomas didn't complain. They often dined on the patio outside, enjoying the music of birdsong and rush of the river. They also enjoyed evenings at the town square, listening to talented, local musicians. Tomas seemed to know everyone.

"That's what's missing," Michael said one night while they were sitting in the square, enjoying the entertainment. He was watching as person after person waved Tomas over to their table to talk with them.

"What do you mean?" Miyah asked.

"This village has a sense of community. That's what's missing at home. I don't even know my neighbors anymore. When did we get to be so busy, or so self-indulgent that we forgot to connect within our own community. Maybe that's why there's so much violence and crime in our country."

"He is very popular, isn't he," Miyah said, fondly watching him.

"But look around, everyone is interacting. It's a community," Michael stressed.

"Well, maybe when we get home you should throw a block party and get people together—maybe you'll find there is a community there, it's just you who is the lone wolf," she teased.

"You might be right about that," he admitted. "We'll have to see."

They had intentionally avoided talking with Tomas about their conversation regarding their parents, but both Michael and Miyah knew they needed to bring it up. Miyah hadn't called upon Nona or Junia yet. She knew they were there, waiting, but she wanted to enjoy some free time away from the realities of her life.

But Miyah being called upon to heal was never far away. It was just done in more subtle ways these days. While in the store one day a little girl smashed her finger in the wires of the shopping basket and began to scream and cry. Her mother was more concerned about the noise than her daughter's pain and was trying to get her to be quiet. Miyah concentrated healing energy to the little girl and her throbbing finger. Soon the girl stopped crying. She looked at her hand, as if she, herself, was surprised it didn't hurt anymore. Then she looked directly at Miyah, who was an aisle away. The little girl gradually smiled and in her childlike innocence, she knew that Miyah had healed her. Obscure incidents like these happened regularly in Miyah's life and she found joy knowing that her healing was momentous on many levels.

On a whim, they decided to drive to Saintes-Maries-de-la-Mer for a short holiday on the coast. Miyah was enjoying some semblance of a normal life.

It was only a three hour drive, first heading north, back through Limoux to Carcassonne, then east on A61 to A9, where turning south would lead them to Barcelona. Instead they went north, past Narbonne and Bézeiers, then at Montpellier they turned east, driving along the coastline and through the marshland countryside to Les-Saintes-Maries-de-la-Mer. Miyah knew the legends of this coastal city and this time she was the one to share a history lesson with her audience in the car during the drive. She read part of the same story from her diary that she had read to Michael some time ago about her ancestors, who included Joshua, Maryum, their daughter Sera and son Joseph; Maryum's brother Lazarus and sister Martha; Mother Mariam and her sisters, Mary Jacobe and Mary Salome, the mother of John and James; several other disciples; and family who fled Judea to Egypt, and later sailed to France with Joseph of Arimathea on one of his ships, landing at Oppidum-Râ.

The ancient fortress town was actually later engulfed by the sea. The area was known to have had both Egyptian and Phoenician settlements and the current village had many names over the years. It was known as *Notre-Dame-de-Ratis* (Râ becoming Râtis—boat or island) – *Our Lady of the Boat or Island*; and later as *Notre-Dame-de-la-Mer – Our Lady of the Sea;* then in the 17th century it was called *Ville-des-Trois-Maries – Village of the Three Marys*. In 1838 it was changed to *Les-Saintes-Maries-de-la-Mer – Saint Marys of the Sea.*

"The Church said they were cast out in a small wooden boat and drifted to the shores of Gaul, now France, without oars or paddles," Tomas said.

Miyah laughed. "I know. Have you looked at a map? It's a long way to drift to the coast of France in a small wooden boat with no sail, and arrive alive! It's a pretty preposterous idea. There were actually more than seventy disciples and companions who were expelled by persecutions from the Holy Land and crossed the Mediterranean to Alexandria in Egypt. Some stayed in Egypt, and some traveled to other lands. Jacob and Isaac, brothers of Mother Mariam, migrated to the Languedoc region of France on an earlier trade ship. Isaac's wife, Tabitha and their daughter Sara, along with her husband, Phillip, were all disciples. Several years passed before the Magdalene group followed their path to France. Marseille was on one of Joseph's trade routes, but due to bad weather they veered off course and landed at Râ. My diary says it was a very rough journey. They most likely did go from ship to shore in smaller boats."

Michael added, "I wonder why people haven't questioned some of the bizarre 'facts' the Church has given to explain away the real truth? Like getting rid of Mary Magdalene by saying that after arriving in France she retired to a cave in Baume on a hill by Marseille and lived by herself for 30 years, naked, to repent! Why would she have bothered to sail for months to a foreign land to hide herself away in a cave? At least the Church, in 1969, did come forward and admit there was no biblical reference to her being a prostitute and officially confirmed her as the 'Apostle to the Apostles.' It had started from a speech by a Catholic bishop, but for centuries the lie was carried on through art and books, and there's no way to change those images."

"For your information, Michael, many have questioned the Church on these issues," Tomas said. "That's why there's so much open discussion about religion these days. People are starting to examine biblical history in a more literal sense, and it doesn't shed very good light on the motives of the early

Roman Church. But don't discount the complete story of Mary at Marseille. She, her brother Lazarus, along with Maximinus and other disciples, did sail on to Marseille with Joseph. Mary Magdalene and the disciple's work there is revered by the Church as converting Provence to Christianity—Jesus's early version of the simple laws of Christianity. Also in Vézelay Mary Magdalene is known to have performed many miracles: awakening a dead knight, aiding sailors at sea, returning vision to a blind pilgrim and more. She's the patron saint of Vézelay, Autun and Marseilles and is hailed as a great healer."

"Isn't Marseille the oldest city in France?" Michael asked

"Yes, in 600 BC it was a trading port, called Massalia in Greek, and today is the largest commercial port on the coastline," Tomas answered. "It's also the second largest city in France, next to Paris. Sainte Baume is actually a bit east of Marseille and relics were found in a cave there, which were claimed to be the bones of Mary Magdalene. They were placed in the Basilica of Sainte-Maximin-la-Saint-Baume and worshiped throughout the Middle Ages. However a rival church, the Abbey of Sainte Madeleine in Vézelay in the north central Burgundy region of France, also claimed to have the remains of Mary Magdalene in their possession. They claimed that a monk named Baudillon had brought bones of Mary Magdalene to Vézelay from Saint-Maximin-la-Sainte-Baume."

Tomas continued, "In 1058 the Pope confirmed the bones to be genuine, although I have no idea how that could have been done. Possessing relics of saints was the source of all kinds of fraud in the Middle Ages. It's too bad they didn't have DNA testing back then. Anyhow, with two churches claiming the bones of Mary Magdalene, a solution was eventually offered. In 1279, Charles II, King of Naples, built a Dominican convent at La-Sainte-Baume. Supposedly the original shrine was found intact, with an explanatory note stating why the relics had been moved and hidden. Both are huge pilgrimage sites today, sponsored by the Church and are also large sources of income for the area."

"It seems there are many places in France that claim to be the resting place of Mary Magdalene," Michael noted.

"It depends on if you follow the Church's version or the stories of ancient legends," Miyah replied.

"Like the belief that she could be buried at Rennes-Le-Château," Tomas added. "Whatever the truth is, I'm happy to see that she is honored, no matter if it's as a disciple, prophet, saint, healer, wife, mother or Goddess."

"You must know the truth, Miyah," Michael said, looking at her in the rear-view mirror. "Isn't it written somewhere in your diary?"

"Yes," Miyah replied, patting her diary. "It is. But there are things that aren't meant to be revealed, simply for the protection of the site and also to honor those involved. This is one those secrets. Don't you see, it doesn't really matter where the physical place is, it's acknowledging her story, her strength, power and wisdom that's important. Honoring the sacred feminine. The same goes for Mother Mariam, who is said to be buried in both Ephesius and near Kashmir, among other places."

"Protection," Tomas repeated. "That's precisely why I hope they never find the tombs that are supposedly hidden in Rennes. Can you imagine what it would do to the area, not to mention the lives of the people who live there? It would be a circus."

"I understand what you mean," Miyah said sympathetically. "From my diary I know that at least one tomb of our bloodline must lie in Rennes-le-Château —that of Sara Bernice, the great-granddaughter of Mary Magdalene and Jesus. Their son, John Martin, who was born in Scotland, had a daughter he named Sara. Sara's daughter, Sara Bernice lived in this area for 26 years and is supposedly buried under the Magdala Chapel."

"It says that in your diary?" Tomas asked, seemingly surprised.

"Yes, I'll read it to you later if you like," she answered.

They drove through the marshy countryside along the Gulf of Lyon to Les-Saints-Maries-de-la-Mer. Surrounded by wildlands of a protected environment, the town was located in the heart of Camargue, western Europe's largest river delta. The Camargue was comprised of vast plains and lagoons cut off from the sea by sandbars and encircled by reed-covered marshes. These marshes were surrounded by large cultivated areas, making it an important farming community. There were also many *manade*, or ranches, owned by the famous Camargue cowboys, where both bulls and horses were bred. Sometimes called the Texas of France, this area was known for raising black bulls, the *taureaux*.

Lunch was the first thing on their mind and they found a restaurant that served fresh fish and shellfish dishes. Michael ordered *Terrines à la Provençale,* a delicacy made with tiny clam-like shellfish. Tomas settled on *paella,* a Spanish dish of rice, saffron, chicken and seafood, cooked and served in a large, shallow pan. Miyah ordered a healthy salad, but ate from both Michael and Tomas' plates.

After lunch they drove past the stables where some of the famous white Camargue horses were kept, and past the lagoon of pink flamingos that make the area their home. They checked into a small whitewashed inn, slightly off the main street, yet within walking distance to the downtown. After a short nap, brought on by the long drive and eating too much, they freshened up and walked to explore the village.

Strolling through the streets surrounded by white buildings with red tile roofs, proved to be a stark contrast to the quaintness of Rennes-le-Château and Rennes-les-Bains. Tomas commented on how different the culture was with the mix of French and Spanish influence, and how touristy the area appeared to be, even though the population of the city was only 2,000.

"You don't get out much, do you?" Michael teased, enjoying the fresh smell of the sea. "I saw a brochure in the hotel lobby that said they have a bull fighting arena here. It's one of their big attractions. Maybe we should check their schedule?"

"I don't think so," Tomas replied. "I mean, you could if you want to, but I'm not interested in anything violent, although I'm sure their tradition is interesting and it would be colorful."

"There are also water sports, a nudist beach, mountain biking, tennis, horseback riding. . ."

"Slow down," Miyah said. "I thought we came here to relax and enjoy the sea."

"I was just kidding," he said. "I don't think I have energy for much of that anymore. Although a few years ago I'd have tried to do it all. . .including the nudist beach."

"You're not that old!" Miyah laughed.

"I guess my priorities have just changed," he replied, putting his arm around her. "I hope I haven't turned into a bore!"

"Far from it," Miyah assured him.

"I rather like the Gypsy influence here," Tomas piped up. "I've done some studying about them in this area." He told Michael and Miyah that the French Gypsies are called Gitans, from Spanish *Gitano,* a short form of *Egiptano,* or Egyptian.

"Which makes sense, when you hear that Gypsies of the area welcomed the Marys and offered them protection. They had that Egyptian connection."

They were only spending one day in the village, so decided to enjoy the Gipsy Museum, the Baroncelli Museum and the waterfront first, and tour the church the next day before they headed back to Rennes-les-Bains.

"Here's something for you, Michael, with your interest in art," Miyah pointed out, reading from a paper in the museum. "The town at one time was quite a literary and artistic center with artists like Ernest Hemmingway and Picasso spending time here. Vincent van Gogh painted here in 1888. Maybe we can find a copy of his *Street in Saintes-Maries* painting in one of the stores."

They wandered through the shops that offered everything from art, antiques and trinkets to clothing, jewelry, handwoven baskets and purses. A market was set up near the beach and they strolled through, purchasing fresh fruit and bread for a picnic. Miyah bought a hand woven hat from a Gypsy woman and also a three-stranded silver and turquoise necklace, which to her looked very Southwestern in style, but she didn't ask what the origin of the necklace was. Michael was completely occupied taking photographs, while Tomas enjoyed speaking French to some of the local Gypsy vendors.

"You know they're wonderful tradesmen," Tomas said after one of his conversations. "Some were metal-workers, woodworkers, basket makers, fortune tellers, salesmen, artists, and musicians, but these days also do things like gardening, pruning and cutting trees and restoring houses. The economy of today has also affected their lifestyles."

Afterward they spent an hour or so on the sandy beach, nibbling fruit, cheese and crackers, with wine for Michael and Tomas. They played in the waves that gently rolled into the shore and walked along the long sandy stretch of beach to Port Gardian where fishermen moored their boats and sportsmen docked their sailboats. It was a long day, but relaxing. Miyah was happy to have the two men she loved in her life there with her, and she knew Tomas was enjoying himself more than he had in a long time. It was a perfect day.

The next morning Michael awoke at dawn to take advantage of the early morning sunlight and walked through residential streets near the hotel and along a canal that fed into the lagoon. He photographed some unusual thatched roof houses, which the hotel clerk told him were gardian's cabins. The *gardiano,* or gardians were the horsemen who watched over the region's fighting bulls for export to Spain. He also explained the imagery of the cross symbol that Michael photographed earlier. He said the Camargue cross, the emblem of Saintes-

Maries-de-la-Mer, was composed of three symbols—an anchor, a cross, and a heart. The upper cross represented the trident-shaped tool used by gardian cowboys, with its three-pronged arms. The anchor symbolized the fishermen of the region, and the heart was a reminder to love and share with those who are near and far.

After the trio checked out of the hotel, they went to find a bakery to buy some of the area's famous pastries in the shape of a boat or *navette*, referring to the arrival of the Marys in a small boat. Next they went to the Church of Saintes-Maries-de-la-Mer, in the center of the village, which from the outside resembled a stone fortress. The roof was surrounded by a castle-style walkway, which clearly served as a look-out tower at one time. Tops of the wall feature battlements, or loopholes with a guard room, now innocently described as a rooftop chapel. The fortress had been pillaged and restored over the centuries and even had a well dug inside the church so the population could hole up there during long sieges of battle. In the 9th century the original small chapel was replaced by a fortified church, the Notre-Dame-de-la-Mer—meaning Our Lady of the Sea.

"Here's an interesting anecdote," he read from a brochure, "In the year 869, when the original fortified church was being built under the direct supervision of the Archbishop of Arles, the Saracens raided the town and carried the Archbishop away. The people of Arles quickly raised the demanded ransom. The Saracens returned with the Archbishop, set him up on the throne with great respect, and parted with the loot. The grateful people only then discovered that the man was dead, and the Saracens had respectfully returned a corpse to the throne!"

He read on, "In the 11th century, the monks of Montmajour established a monastery here and in the 12th century they rebuilt the church, adding a defense system. In the 14th century, battlements were added to the top, allowing boiling oil and dropped projectiles to be used against attackers. Now, that's protecting the church!"

They went inside the dark church, where the cold stone walls were adorned with a few simple archways with columns between them. It wasn't without its demons either, as on one of the pillars was the head of a devouring monster with the head of an angel on the trim above it. Another column held the head of a satry, a man with a goat's ears, horns, tail and legs. A large wooden statue of two Marys in a small boat was on one side of the church.

"Why don't they have *three* Marys in the boat?" Michael whispered.

"Mary Magdalene was honored here in the early centuries, but when the Church took over, just the two Marys were celebrated and Magdalene had pretty much been taken out of the picture. Remember, she didn't stay here, just Mary Jacob and Mary Salome lived out their lives here," Miyah explained.

She pointed to a large painting above the boat statue that represented Mary, dressed in blue, holding a vessel or jar, not alabaster, but more metal looking.

"Mary Magdalene was usually painted holding a jar, but Mother Mary was usually dressed in blue. Which Mary is it?" Michael asked.

"Maybe the painting represents both of them," Miyah whispered.

Michael took photographs of some of the unusual icons in the church along with a wall of items randomly placed behind a large glass wall: chalices; parchment documents; a wooden head of a black madonna; paintings of black madonnas and other saints; a black Barbie-like doll dressed in a puffy red dress and ornate headgear; two golden arms; large golden candlesticks and crosses; and other paintings—a very unusual collection of relics.

In front of the church a few steps led up to where the altar was located and high above, raised out from the stone wall, was a life-sized statue of Mary and child.

"Again, which Mary?" Michael whispered.

"I don't know. Joseph was a baby when they arrived here. Sera was a little older," she replied. "I suppose it depends on who you ask, the Church or the local historians."

There were also steps that led down under the altar area to a room called the crypt. As they walked down the steps, Miyah pointed to an antique brass plate that hung above the doorway. It was of a boat on the water, and in it were not two, but three women. . .three Marys.

The crypt housed a small wooden statue of the Black Madonna, Saint

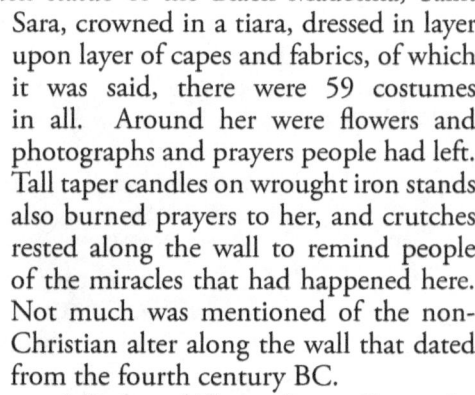

Church entrance to crypt - Les-Maries-de-la-Mer

Sara - the Black Madonna - Les-Maries-de-la-Mer

Sara, crowned in a tiara, dressed in layer upon layer of capes and fabrics, of which it was said, there were 59 costumes in all. Around her were flowers and photographs and prayers people had left. Tall taper candles on wrought iron stands also burned prayers to her, and crutches rested along the wall to remind people of the miracles that had happened here. Not much was mentioned of the non-Christian alter along the wall that dated from the fourth century BC.

Miyah and Tomas lit candles in the church and offered their prayers to Saint Sara.

"I know it's a simple church with not all the fancy statuary and gold trim that you find in a lot of our churches," Tomas said as they left the church. "But I think that's why I like it. It's humble, the way Jesus was."

"Yes, I liked it's simplicity, too," Michael agreed. "But tell me about the Black Madonna that's worshiped here. I know there are over 500 Black Madonnas in villages and towns in Europe, Britain, North Africa and the Americas, but I've never learned of their origin, or what they represent. I remember seeing a Black Madonna in Chartes Cathedral when we were there. One of Mary Magdalene's most prominent shrines centered around a statue named *'Our Lady Under the Earth,'* which I assume refers to some hidden aspect of her life."

"Yes, the Black Madonna could represent the Earth Mother," Tomas said. "But she really is a Christianized version of the Mother Goddess. It was the Churches way of accepting pagan traditions, by absorbing them into the Church and masking the magical powers that were believed to come with the Black Madonna legends. It would have been too difficult for the Church to condemn these popular ancient goddess idols, so they, along with many other traditions, were incorporated into the Church as part of their own celebrations."

Tomas explained that Black Madonnas appeared all over France as far back as the 3rd century when Cybele, who was black, was the supreme deity of Lyon, the capitol of much of south-eastern France. Ceres, also black, was the Roman Goddess of agricultural fertility. Black Madonna icons were brought back by the Crusaders from the Middle East as models of the Goddess Isis, who was always portrayed with dark, Egyptian/African skin.

"Many deities were known to have been worshiped in Provence, first by the Greeks and later by the Romans, but the earliest influence came from the Egyptians since they and the Phoenicians first used Marseille as a trading port. This all predates Christianity, and remains of temples to Artemis, Cybele, the Celtic Triple Goddess Matres, and also Isis, have been excavated in the area," Tomas said.

He added, "The name Paris, actually was derived from *Isis. . .par Isis.*"

"You're kidding?" Michael said. "I never would have guessed that. Par Isis. Paris."

"The Merovingians in France worshipped Cybele as Diana of the Nine Fires, and in 679, Dagobert II. . .remember he was the King who was canonized as Saint Meroginy. . . established a cult to Isis, who received the name of 'Our Lady.' Many cathedrals in the middle ages were dedicated to *Notre Dame – 'Our Lady'*– and it's not clear which 'Our Lady' they referred to, especially since most of them were funded by Knights Templar, the sworn protectors of Mary Magdalene," Tomas noted.

He continued, "There's strong evidence that Mary Magdalene was worshiped right along side the Virgin Mary up until the Albigensian Crusades and that she is still secretly worshiped through art and imagery in churches. Even in the Bible she's repeatedly portrayed as a visionary and leader of the early movement. In the Gospel of John, Jesus gives her special teachings and commissions her as an apostle to the apostles, although the term apostle wasn't specifically used for her until later. The strength of these literary biblical writings do suggest that historically, Mary Magdalene was a prophetic visionary and important leader within at least one sector of the early Christian movement."

"You would certainly think so, after what we've seen while we've been here, and I'm sure that's just a small portion of what's found all over France—all over Europe as far as that goes," Michael replied. "So 'Our Lady of the Sea,' *Notre-Dame-de-la-Mer*, was originally referring to Isis?"

"And later to Mary Magdalene, who with her Egyptian blood was believed to be a Goddess of the Isis order and the true Black Madonna," Miyah stated.

"And of course, the Egyptian Mother Goddess Isis was often shown with the infant Horus in her lap—the original mother and child icon."

"So, getting back to the Black Madonna in this church, could that mean when dark-skinned, Egyptian blooded Maryum and her infant son Joseph arrived from the sea, she was seen as the Black Madonna, the image of Isis and her child?" Michael asked.

"And her daughter Sera was eventually adopted as the Patron Saint of the Gypsies. If you noticed the different spellings of Sera. In my diary it's spelled S-e-r-a," Miyah explained. "In the church it's spelled S-a-r-a-h, and the Gypsies spell it S-a-r-a. Three spellings for the same person, so you can see how stories easily change from culture-to-culture and generation-to-generation. There was also a large Jewish community already established in the area, and they would know that the name Sera in Hebrew, means princess. . .of royal blood."

"How did the Gypsies of the area adopt Sara as their patron saint?" Michael asked.

"Ah, the Gitan were known to have a naturally religious soul and adopted the religions of the countries they traveled to. At the time of Sara, they worshiped the Goddess Ishtari or Astarte, the Goddess of love and war. Once a year they carried a statue of her on their shoulders into the sea to receive blessings. This ritual may have roots in India where during a celebration of the Goddess Durga, also called Kali, a statue or carving was immersed in water. Kali also means 'black' in both Sanskrit and Romani, the language still spoken by a lot of the European Gypsies who originally came from India and Kashmir, many through Egypt."

Miyah continued, "Kali, the Hindu Goddess of creativity, sickness, death, and destruction is associated with eternal energy and is considered the Goddess of Time and Change. In the 1st century she was known as a Goddess of War, thus the translation from Ishtari, Goddess of War and Love, is possible. It's interesting that more recent movements conceive Kali as a benevolent Mother Goddess. But Sara-la-Kali wasn't adopted as the Black Madonna of the Gypsies until the 15th century. Some say that in order to appease the Catholic Church, the Goddess Kali was hidden inside another version of the sacred feminine—that of Sara.

"What would the Catholic Church have done if they knew the Goddess of Destruction was being housed inside their church? So Sara-la-Kali or Sara the Egyptian, may have become the Patron Saint of the Gypsies as a reminder of their original roots.

"They were nomads, but their society is founded on family. Gypsies have always had a connection with the earth, water, fire and the outdoors. Their faith is strong, but joyful and festive. I've always admired their nomadic spirit."

"I was talking with some of the Gypsy, Gitan, yesterday in the market," Tomas said, "and asking about their big celebration here in May. I might like to come back some time for it. They told me that it's a three-day festival, and for them it means family reunions, trading, song and dance, and a lot of guitar playing. They come from all over Europe in their colorful caravans, which these days are trailers pulled behind their cars. They're still painted and decorated in traditional styles and the insides have shrines and icons that represent their lifestyle. Some of the traditional wooden Gypsy wagons are also brought here. One of the men I talked with said they look forward to it all year long."

Tomas went on to share what he had heard from the Gitan men in the market. "They said that on May 24, Sara-la-Kali is carried on a platform by four Gitan and taken down to the sea. She's dressed in all of her 59 capes of bright, embroidered, gold-decorated fabrics with only her face visible. She slowly emerges from the church, escorted by the gardians and girls who come from Arles dressed in traditional costumes. The gardians on their white Camargue horses lead a parade through town and then line up in the water along the sea, extending their long lances toward the sky. They told me that people reach out to touch Sara's clothes, throwing kisses to her and the children are raised up to receive protection from her. Everyone sings, prays and shouts praises of '*Vive Sante Sara.*' Then she's escorted into the sea with her porters entering the water up to their waists and slowly, with the singing continuing, she's returned to her crypt under the church."

"It sounds like a very symbolic ritual," Miyah said.

"That's just the first day," Tomas replied. "They said this is a three-day festival. On the second day, the statues of the two Marys in their boat are taken to the sea in the same manner. And on the third day bulls are driven through the streets by gardians on horseback and the crowd tries to make them escape, complete with a '*bandido*' and other theatrics. They said the three days are filled with games, folklore, bullfights, traditional dancing and singing. You don't suppose you could come back in May and escort me to this lively celebration, could you?"

"I'll put that on my calendar," Miyah laughed.

"It sounded so much more exciting hearing it first hand from the people I spoke with," Tomas said. "I checked a church program before we came. It simply said, 'Mass to celebrate the pilgrimage and a ceremony parading relics of the Marys and Sarah to the sea.'

"But the Gitan men also said that the third day is important because it commemorates the Marquis de Baroncelli with a ceremony at his tomb. Evidently he was born in 1869 of an aristocratic Florentine family and developed a love of bulls. He settled in the Camargue in 1895, organized the activities of the gardians, started the Camargue horse races and promoted minority rights. The Gitan and gardians say they attend his ceremony and remember him for his humanity and generosity because he also fought for, and won, the right for the Gitans to honor Saint Sara publicly."

"Aren't there more festivals here during the year too?" Michael asked.

"Yes, the last Sunday in July—*Les cavaliers de la Nacioun Gardiano*. Villagers from Arles attend with young women in traditional dress. There's more bull running, gardian equestrian games, traditional medieval dancing and other festivities. And on the Sunday nearest to October 22, there's a second pilgrimage featuring the gardians and the Marys, but not Sara or the Gitans."

"I'm still a bit confused with the Gypsy, or Gitan, and Catholic Church connection," Michael admitted. "You're saying this Marquis got permission to honor Saint Sarah as their more pagan Sara-la-Kali, an Egyptian Goddess? That sounds unorthodox."

"From what I understand, the first processions of Sara-la-Kali escorted by the Gypsies in traditional costume weren't associated with the Church. But after WWII when hundreds of thousands of Gypsies perished in concentration camps, during a little known holocaust, the National Gypsy Chaplaincy was founded in France under the Catholic Church. Starting in 1953, priests officiated at the procession of Saint Sarah's parade to the sea—combining the Marys into it and making it more of a Catholic celebration than that of its original Gypsy roots."

"You know the bathing of sacred objects is found in a lot of cultures," Miyah added. "Once a year the Romans bathed their Goddess Cybele in a river, the Buddhists bathed baby Buddha in tea on his birthday, Christians used to bathe statues of Mother Mary in wine on Good Friday. A lot of people bathe their holy images in water to purify them—and how about baptism?"

"It's just that the Gitan with their colorful lifestyle and love of music and dance, make the celebration a lot livelier than the Church would have it," Tomas said. "I rather like that."

"So maybe you don't mind the touristy aspect of this town anymore," Michael teased. "It sounds pretty exciting here, at least part of the year. Can you imagine the crowds? They say more than 10,000 pilgrims!"

"That would be the only thing to keep me away," Tomas laughed. "The crowds."

Mary Magdalene - Les-Maries-de-la-Mer

Church of Mary Magdalene - Les-Maries-de-la-Mer

Beach at Les-Maries-de-la-Mer

Orbs in Church of Mary Magdalene - Les-Maries-de-la-Mer

25 *Secrets Unfold*

Tomas was somber for a few days after their return from Les-Maries-de-la-Mer. When Miyah asked, he insisted he was all right. He just had a lot on his mind. Michael and Miyah decided to give him his privacy and did some day trip site seeing around the area, enjoying the beauty of the countryside.

"You know we should think about heading back to the States pretty soon," Miyah said one afternoon. "We've been gone almost two months."

"Yes, I know. I just don't want this time to end. It's been such a wonderful journey together," Michael said, hugging her tenderly.

"We still have a long journey ahead of us," she replied, patting her belly. "It's going to change our lives in ways we can't even imagine."

"I'm so looking forward to becoming a father. I only hope I'm half as good at it as my own parents were. It's too bad our daughter will grow up without knowing her grandparents."

"Well, she'll have Tomas, and we'll have to make an effort for the two of them to spend time together before he leaves us. At least she can have some memories."

When they arrived back at Tomas' house early that evening, he seemed unusually solemn and he told them he needed to share something with both of them. He sat them down, brought a tray of tea and biscuits and proceeded. He took his time, as if pondering how to present his story. Finally, he settled back and started. . .

"Did I tell you that I was priest here at Rennes-les-Bains?" he asked, not waiting for an answer. "I acquired the position from an elderly priest who, on his death bed, called me to him. I assumed it was for last rites, but when I arrived, he had a lot to tell me." Tomas looked directly at Miyah and then to Michael.

"He had been left, by a previous priest at Rennes-le-Château, with an important secret."

"Not the secret of Boudet and Saunière?" Michael jumped ahead.

"Precisely."

"You. . .you are a holder of the secrets of Rennes-le-Château!" Miyah exclaimed in disbelief. "No wonder you knew so many details of the area's history."

"Oh, I didn't at the time. I've made it my business to know. But it presents an interesting scenario, doesn't it? That the very secret I was given custody of, through this priest of the Church, is part of the same secret I was entrusted with when I met Nona, which, as your grandfather, I am in a sense, a part of—the holy bloodline."

"So that really IS the secret of the treasures of Rennes-le-Château!"

Michael declared. "The bloodline."

"That's only part of it," Tomas replied. "You can tell by the stories I've told you that there were also many valuable items that were confiscated, sold or given away. And there is more, but I don't want to get into that just yet. Because of the bloodline, more information will be passed on to you, Miyah, in due time."

"Isn't it ironic that priests of the Church hold such important secrets *against* the Church?" Miyah related.

Tomas came to his own defense. "It does make sense that the Church has been involved, being the secret was passed from priest to priest—usually exiled or renegade priests who had challenged the history, dogma, intentions and wealth of the Church. The irony is that much of the treasure that was sold, now lies hidden beneath the Vatican itself, in their vaults.

"The priests who knew, honored their belief in the bloodline in discreet ways, fearing the wrath of the Church. It's been like that through the ages, hiding secrets in art and icons. That's why you see so many stained glass windows and churches honoring Mary Magdalene throughout France and other parts of Europe. It was their compromise. The Pope rescinded the ancient Church accusation of Mary being a prostitute and made her a saint, even gave her her own saint day—but that's as far as they would go. To admit to the world that she was the wife of Jesus and they had children would counteract their celibacy rules for priests and elevate the role of women they so carefully had worked to downplay. And to admit that Jesus didn't die for your sins on the cross, but lived to be a ripe old age, teaching generations of God's children a gentler message of love, peace and honoring nature and your neighbor—not preaching about guilt, fearing the Lord, and tithing to the riches of the Church, well, that would have been impossible. It would have crumbled the very belief system on which the Roman Catholic Church presented their religion."

Tomas stopped pensively before he continued. "Much of that is changing now. It's a new age. You already know all of this Miyah, but I need to put it into perspective. Messages have been sent out, some subtle, some more subliminal through the last decades. The mass population has been reading about religious untruths in books and articles, and has seen it in movies and documentaries. Changes can even be translated in warnings from the earth itself in weather patterns and world events. The largest portion of the population is looking for a change, searching for a bright light ahead in their future. It'll be difficult for the Church at first. Remember, the Bible was complied around AD 300 and was shaped to benefit the Romans at the time. Religious leaders have accepted that for years, but certainly without questions themselves. The true story *is* much of the same story. . .only with a different ending, not a brutal, tragic ending, but rather a happy, human story that can be related to. It's filled with life, family, healing, teaching, joy and everlasting love. It doesn't really matter who the descendents are, where they live or what they do, if they have royal blood or not—just the fact that they exist, and that they hopefully have continued the healing and teaching that carried them through the generations. That's what's most important."

Tomas paused and took a sip of his tea. "Forgive me if I sound like I'm on the pulpit preaching. I get carried away when I think of all the injustices that have been done in the name of the Church—in God's name—and how it should have been so different."

Miyah reached over and took Tomas' hand. "You're truly a saint, Tomas Thornburg. You've been blessed with being a link that connects the bloodline on two levels—the secrets carried throughout history and your personal connection with the bloodline."

"Do you have any idea how difficult it's been to carry that on my shoulders?" he asked. "Oh, there are many others who know, not just myself. But now that I'm able to share all of this with you, I'm finally feeling the burden is lessened." He took a Bible from his bookshelf and retrieved a small card from it. Handing it to Miyah, he asked, "Do you recognize this?"

"Yes!" she quickly responded. "It's the prayer card the priest gave me in the Church of Mary Magdalene in Paris." She turned it over. "I thought the last line was rather strange, unless I read it wrong."

She translated ". . . *sent forth as you were to others, we must tell all that Jesus is alive. May we, in your wake, be messengers of Hope.'* And then I received another card, slipped under the door of our hotel room." She looked at Michael. "I didn't want to worry you," she said apologetically, "That card said, *'Brothers in need have always been welcomed and served in this church.'* I tucked it in my purse with the other card and forgot about them until now. What does it mean?"

"It's a way that some of us renegade priests, and there are hundreds now as the times are changing, use to communicate. I'm sure the first card was given to you as a concealed way to welcome you into our fold. The version you read is an altered copy of the usual verse. The second card was to let you know that if you are ever in danger while here, you can take refuge in the Church of Mary Magdalene, or Saint Sulpice for that matter. There are brothers there who know the secret and are pledged to protect the bloodline."

Michael told Tomas of his encounter on the street and being rescued by a priest and brought to the church. "I felt as if I was being interrogated."

"I'm sure that was to be certain of your intentions with Miyah—to be sure you wouldn't endanger her in any way," Tomas explained.

"I felt like we were followed at other times too," he admitted, turning to Miyah. "I'm sorry I didn't want to worry *you!*" he said apologetically. They both smiled, realizing their instincts to protect each other.

"It may have been our people. I'm sorry if you felt uncomfortable. Miyah's safety will always be of the utmost importance. Everyone is very happy to have you here," he said to her. "You just can't imagine."

"Are you saying we're in some sort of danger being here?" Michael asked.

"Oh no, not at all. The story of the bloodline, especially here in France, is not a new one. It's common knowledge and there are actually several branches of the bloodline living to this day. Yes, Miyah, you have cousins—although far removed. Nevertheless, we have taken all necessary precautions for your safe journeys here. It's our sworn duty, and one not taken lightly."

"Plus," Michael reminded him, "she has an entire arsenal of guardians you don't even see. You'd never want to encounter the wrath of Nona!"

Tomas laughed and then told Miyah he needed to speak with her privately and asked for them to be excused. They went for a walk to the river and sat on the bench that had become one of their favorite spots to reminisce. Michael could see them from the window and knew they were engaged in an important conversation. Tomas used hand gestures as he spoke and Miyah continually nodded her head yes, understanding his message.

Michael didn't mean to spy, but he was curious as to what Tomas was sharing with her. He trusted Michael enough to tell him he was connected with the Rennes-le-Château secrets, so why couldn't he share the entire story with him? He surmised it had to do with the bloodline, yet he felt left out. After all, wasn't he connected to the bloodline now too? After a while Miyah and Tomas came into the house and went directly to Tomas' room. Miyah motioned for Michael to join them.

Michael sat on a chair in the corner of the room to be out of the way. Tomas walked over to his black priest cloak, kept on a hanger, hung on a nail on the wall of his bedroom, a reminder of his path. He took the hanger off the nail and behind it was an envelope taped to the wall. He gently peeled back the brittle, yellowed tape to remove the envelope, returned the hanger and cloak to its place, and motioned for Miyah to sit beside him on the bed.

"I know all of these secrets are a lot to put on you in one day, but I've been contemplating this and I feel I need to get it all out at one time, so please bear with me." He handed her the envelope.

"Another secret message," he simply said. "Nona gave this to me right before she died. She wanted me to give it to you."

"But why didn't she give it to me herself?" Miyah asked.

"She wanted me to give this to you, but not until you became a mother yourself. I won't be with you in the States when your child is born, so I guess it's OK to give it to you now."

Miyah took the envelope and held it in her hands for awhile before she could bring herself to open it.

"After all the conversations I've had with Nona through the years, why would she leave a mysterious envelope with you? Why couldn't she just tell me, or lead me to it herself."

"Ah. . .but she did lead you to it. I think it was her way of connecting the two of us. You see Miyah, I always knew you would come to me one day. I knew I would see you again."

Miyah slowly opened the envelope. There was a letter and a second, smaller envelope. Before Miyah read its words, she ran her hands over the familiar handwriting of her grandmother. She loved her perfectly scripted penmanship, the way Nona looped her letters and let the 's' and 'e' at the end of a word draw out like a line that led you somewhere distant. Miyah took a deep breath and read the letter out loud.

My dearest Miyah,

By the time you read this you will already know that I have been with you, in my spirit form, watching you grow and guiding you in your work. I am so very proud of you and your dedication to your healing mission.

Now you are a mother and another dimension has been added to your life. I will be there with you, singing lullabies in your baby's ear and helping you teach her, as Junia and I have taught you.

But let me get to the point of this letter. I have a message for you about the first cedar box—the one that was carved for Mariam – Mother Mariam. I told you that we had been searching for it for many years, which was true. What I didn't tell you was that we did locate the general whereabouts of the box and that it hasn't yet been retrieved.

When the last of the Isaac lineage, the keepers of the cedar box, died in Great Britain, they gave the box to a trusted doctor in Scotland who used the box in his practice for many years, until his sudden death. We discovered that his death was no accident. It was a failed attempt to steal the box, which thankfully was hidden away and kept safe. He knew he was in danger before his death, and mailed this key to my mother, Dolores, with an odd poem.

Miyah opened the smaller envelope and a key fell out onto her lap. It looked familiar. She retrieved her own key from her necklace pouch and held the two keys side-by-side. They matched—both her cedar box key and this key were in the shape of an ankh.

"Why are the keys in the shape of an ankh?" Michael asked.

"The ankh is an ancient Egyptian sign for divine life," Miyah explained. "It's often seen in the hands of the gods who were the keepers of life, as we saw on the obelisk in Paris. It's shaped like a key—a key to the unknown future, or even the very secret of life itself."

She unfolded the paper with the poem and read:

. . .the path to box is in the skye
do not attempt until three generations have gone by.
only the faeries can flag the way
among a handled cross they play.
the guardian of gazanias will only let it be
by presenting them the proper key.

"What does that mean?" Miyah asked. Tomas shrugged. She continued to read the letter.

My dear. It is time to tell you that the Scottish doctor was my father. I was only a child when he died. He and my mother, although living on separate continents, were very close. My father, Alyn, was so concerned for our safety that he requested three generations pass by before an attempt was made to locate the box, which is why he didn't even tell my mother where it was hidden. He only left this poem.

Now, three generations have gone by and the birth of your daughter marks the fourth generation since that note. When your daughter is old enough to understand the Touchstone calling, it will be time to reunite the two cedar boxes again. . .

Before she read any further, Miyah stood up and called Nona's name.

"Nona! Nona! I know you're here. Appear now and explain all of this to me. Why the mystery? Why the riddles? Can't you just tell me? Nona!"

Tomas tried to calm her down. "Miyah, I'm sure she didn't mean for you to get yourself all upset over this. . ."

"It's OK, Tomas, I'm here," Nona said, standing behind them.

Miyah turned to face her. "Why is this task being put upon the shoulders of my daughter? I won't have her put in any kind of danger."

"Calm down dear," Nona said, putting a healing hand on her granddaughter's shoulder. "That's precisely why the poem said to wait until three generations had passed, so the mystery of the box would be completely forgotten and there would be no more danger. I would never put any of my family in harms way, you of all people should know that."

"I'm sorry, Nona. I just. . ."

"You're just being protective of your child. It's quite all right, my dear. And this isn't something you need to concern yourself with for several years. You just needed to have the key and the poem in your possession, and to know what lies ahead for your daughter. It'll be very important that the two boxes come together again. It'll mark a change in the destiny of the Touchstone carrier's responsibilities and that directly reflects on the future of your daughter."

"How so?" Miyah asked, concerned, glancing at Michael in the corner.

"Let's just say for now, that it'll be a much easier time for her than it has been for others of the Touchstone line. When the two cedar boxes are reunited, the time will come for the Touchstone story to be known and the pressure of protecting the secret will be released. If your daughter possesses the 'gift' she will still have healing energies, but she will be freed from guarding the bloodline, and can live a normal life. It will be a positive change. Don't worry. Her life will be filled with happiness. This I know."

"What do you mean *if* she has the gift?" Miyah asked.

"Remember that sometimes the selected one skips a generation, even two in some instances. There's no guarantee that your daughter will be gifted as you are."

"I hadn't even considered that," Miyah admitted.

Nona's words comforted both Miyah and Michael, who was doing his best to be silent, although he was amazed to actually be in the presence of Nona. But, upon hearing this, he silently hoped his daughter would be one of the skipped generations. How he would love to have a normal family life with Miyah and his child.

"But this letter means that the two boxes *were* together—reunited with my great-grandparents, Dolores and Alyn, each owning one," Miyah said, trying to put the pieces together.

"Yes, both Dolores and Alyn had boxes. In a sense, it's what brought the two of them together, even though he didn't know about hers at the time. Remember, Alyn's cedar box came to him because there were no more descendents of the Issac family, and he was a trusted friend whom they knew would use the powers of the box to heal wisely. He didn't know the true origin of the box, just that it had healing powers. My mother's cedar box was passed down through generations of the bloodline, and fiercely protected through all those years. Had Alyn lived, I believe she would have told him, and the boxes eventually may have sat side-by-side."

"Why is this being placed before me in such a riddle?" Miyah asked. "Why couldn't you have just told me everything when you told me about Tomas?"

"Because you needed to come here and find some things out for yourself first. Life isn't always easy, Miyah, and sometimes I wonder if we kept you too protected from the world. Look at what a wonderful adventure you've had here with Michael and Tomas. You have amazing gifts and powers, but you're also human and sometimes need to be reminded of that."

"So, are you going to give me the translation of the poem?" Miyah asked abruptly. "Or is that something the human side of me has to figure out?"

"All I will tell you is that you need not worry about deciphering the poem right now. You have a child to birth and raise first. As I've said to you many times, 'when the time is right. . .'"

"Yes, I know, but with all of this mystery. . .how can I not want to know?"

"Because your daughter is the fourth generation. You must wait for her to locate the box. It's meant to be her journey, not yours. . .although nothing says you can't be there to help her. I'll give you this, however. Part of the poem was obvious. . .*do not attempt until three generations have gone by.* And I'll tell you that . . .*the path to box is in the skye,* refers to the Island of Skye in Scotland. The rest must remain unsolved until. . ."

"I know. . .until the time is right," Miyah finished her sentence. Nona gave her granddaughter a hug and taking Tomas' arm the two of them walked together down the hallway.

"Now I have some things to discuss with Tomas," Nona said, as he happily patted her hand.

"Don't go far," Miyah called after her, "I have more questions for you on another matter." She just then realized how natural it looked for the two of them to be together like that. She remembered seeing them many times in her youth, arms linked, walking in conversation. Oh, how she wished Nona could stay in human form.

"Are you OK?" Michael asked as he watched her place the letter, envelope and key between the pages of her diary.

Miyah walked to him and put her arms around him. They stood there together in silence for a few moments. She wanted to feel his protection and strength.

Finally he spoke. "I've seldom seen you so vulnerable. You're usually a rock of confidence."

"I've felt like such a different person lately," she admitted. "I don't know if it's the pregnancy or if it's all this information about family that's suddenly been presented to me. It's a lot to handle after so many years of being alone."

"It's probably a combination of both. But don't worry, you're not alone now. I'll always be here for you. Let *me* be your rock." Michael stood there with his arms around her, holding her. Miyah felt much better.

"You have that healing touch, too," she said, smiling at him. "I can feel it. Thank you. Now, let's go and see what happened to Tomas and Nona."

They found them sitting side-by-side talking in low voices, like teenagers on a first date. Miyah hated to interrupt, but needed to have some questions answered about her own father. Both Miyah and Michael relayed their conversation of the other day, and what they had surmised about the deaths of their parents. Michael also told them about his theory of the bomb shelter. Nona listened intently, as did Tomas. Finally, after Miyah and Michael finished presenting their questions, Nona spoke.

"You're correct in what you're telling us. Michael, your parents were such good friends of both Junia and John. It was very difficult for them to keep secrets, but they also knew they had to do what they thought was best. Junia asked them not to tell John about Miyah because she wasn't sure she could make a commitment to him at that time. He didn't really abandon Junia and you. He always thought he'd come back a rich man and then Junia would never have to work again. John never did know the path of the Touchstone she was on. Time just slipped past him, he was so involved in his treasure hunting. It wasn't long after your father's accident that Junia passed."

"She left me," Miyah said sadly.

"She left you with me. That's different. She knew your path. She knew what lay ahead for you and that it would be better directed under my care.

She was a proud healer, but never wanted to be a carrier of the Touchstone legend. She felt you were eager for that duty and passed the torch to you. She never left you, Miyah. She gifted you with the family secrets and completed her mission here."

Tomas stepped forward. "I felt exactly the same way, Miyah. When Junia left, and again when Nona left, I felt abandoned. It's taken me many years to realize that it had nothing to do with me. It was their path and I had to honor that. Just like coming to France after Nona passed was my destiny. The bond of love has never wavered."

"And the accidents?" Michael asked. "They weren't really accidents were they?" He almost didn't want to hear the answer.

Tomas simply nodded his head. Michael welled up with emotion and turned and walked into the other room. His parents were dead, but knowing they had been murdered made it even more tragic.

"Both of you need to know that you've been led on this journey by your parents. They wanted you to discover these truths together. They always wanted the two of you to be partners when you grew up. I'd say they've had a hand in that too," Nona said.

"And my theory about maps and documents in my dad's safe?" Michael asked, not being able to wait until he got home to discover for himself.

Tomas came forward and handed him a copy of Magazine Mysteria, dated April 1990.

"Read this article," he instructed.

Michael looked at him questionably, then read the highlighted portions out loud.

". . .*after inheriting, in 1920, some books which once belonged to Abbé Boudet, he had found amongst the pages of 'Masison Pittoresque' (by the same author as 'La Vraie Langue Celtique'), a fragment of an act dated March 4, 1747, which mentioned that under the altar of a certain church on the site, there was a crypt containing four tombs and two chests, which held various documents and old books. . . There was a request that the existence of the crypt should remain secret and it mentioned that half of a mysterious parchment was missing. The owner of the first half of that parchment sent out a request to whomever might be in possession of the other half to keep it a secret.*"

Michael looked up at Tomas and then to Nona, and back to Tomas. "Are you telling me that my father found the other half of this parchment and it's in his safe?" he asked, thinking it inconceivable. "He was keeping it a secret in his safe?"

"I don't know, Michael," Tomas replied. "But if it is, it could be very dangerous for both of you. My advice is that if it *is* there, let it rest in peace."

Michael and Miyah stared at each other for a few moments. Neither could respond.

"Secrets. Secrets. Secrets. Are there any more either of you have to share with us?" Miyah finally asked, feeling exhausted.

"Not today," Nona laughed. "I must be going now. I'll be back to see you very soon," she said as she threw them kisses and faded into the vapors.

"What did she mean by that?" Miyah asked.

"Well, I have a little something I want to talk over with Michael tomorrow, so we'll just see," Tomas said as he looked at his watch.

"It's way past my bedtime. Lock up for me, would you? I'm heading to bed." He kissed Miyah on the forehead and patted Michael on the shoulder as he walked by. "Good night my children. Sleep well."

"Yeah, right," Michael said. "Sleep. After a day like this?"

26　The Ceremony

Miyah had a restless night and slept in late the next morning. Michael went downstairs for a glass of juice and found Tomas already awake. Over breakfast Michael asked, "Yesterday you said you had something you wanted to talk with me about. Is this a good time?"

"Let's go for a walk," Tomas suggested. The two men talked about the events that had transpired while Michael and Miyah had been there and about Miyah in general as they walked along the river. They cut into the woods and followed a path, and engrossed in their conversation, unintentionally arrived at the Throne of Isis.

"Have a chair," Tomas motioned to the throne.

"I don't know," Michael replied. "Is it for the queen or for the devil?"

"Whatever you want it to be," Tomas chuckled, settling himself on the ground, leaning his cane against the arm of the stone chair. Instead of perching himself on the cold stone, Michael joined Tomas on the ground.

"I've been meaning to ask you why you and Miyah haven't gotten married," Tomas came right to the point.

"Oh, I've asked her," Michael quickly replied. "She's so committed to the Touchstone that she said she wasn't ready to make another commitment."

"Do you think that after your trip here, and all she's discovered about family and how important our relationships are, even though they aren't mainstream partnerships, she'd reconsider?"

"I'd love it if she would. Funny you mention this because the last morning we were in Paris I went out and bought her a ring. I was going to give it to her on this trip and ask her, again, to marry me, but there's been so much going on, I never found an appropriate time. I thought it would be really romantic to get married in Paris. I even brought my father's wedding band with me, just in case she said yes."

Tomas slapped his hand on Michael's knee. "I'm so happy to hear that!" he exclaimed. "I was afraid you weren't interested in taking your vows with her."

"Quite the opposite," Michael said sadly.

"What would you think of getting married in Rennes-le-Château? It would seem an appropriate place, the bloodline coming home and joining in union on the very site that has held so much of the family's secret past. I could arrange everything."

"I. . .I think it would be wonderful. . .but we're forgetting one key piece here. Miyah. She has to say yes, first."

"Well, what are you waiting for? Just ask her, my boy. See what she says. I think she may feel differently after all she's learned these past couple of months. Just ask her!"

"I will," Michael said. "I'll ask her today. Thank you, Tomas, for accepting me into the family like this. It means a lot to me."

"I was an outsider too, you must remember. Not all the men who've contributed to the bloodline through the ages have had the opportunities to see behind the veil as we have. We're both very fortunate men. Thank you for being so devoted to Miy. She's always been my little angel."

Michael hoped Miyah was still sleeping when he got back. He quickly made her favorite breakfast of oatmeal, wheat toast and fruit topped with yogurt, and arranged it on a tray with a bouquet of wild flowers he picked on his walk. When he got to the bedroom Miyah was just awakening.

"I thought I smelled toast," she said stretching. "What time is it? I really slept soundly."

"You must have needed it," he replied. "You tossed and turned all night. I think you had too many secrets rolling around in your head. Yesterday was quite a revealing day. I hope you're hungry." He put the tray on her lap and propped up her pillows.

"What kind of special treatment is this?" she asked. "I didn't order room service."

"You better get used to breakfast in bed. I'm going to make it my specialty," he said as he gently kissed her forehead.

They talked about what they should do for the day while Miyah ate her breakfast, and had a good laugh when she spilled oatmeal all over her stomach.

"I'll get you a towel," Michael offered, heading to the bathroom. He came back, put the tray on the end of the bed and when she took the towel from him, something fell out of it.

"What's this?" she said, picking up a small box. Michael sat on the bed next to her and said nothing. Miyah slowly untied the ribbon and opened the box to reveal a diamond ring. Her eyes widened in surprise and she let out a little gasp. Michael watched her intently, trying to read her. She just stared at the ring for awhile, trying to gather her thoughts. When she looked at Michael, she had tears in her eyes.

"It's so beautiful," she said, "but. . ."

"But what?" he was on the defensive, fearing another turn down.

". . .but it must have cost a lot of money. You shouldn't have. . ."

"But I wanted to. . .and I want to marry you more than anything. Please, please say yes this time. I love you so much. I want you to be my wife. Miyah, will you marry me?" His voice faltered as he spoke, not knowing if he could bear another rejection.

Miyah was silent for a few moments. She just sat there, looking into his eyes, feeling his emotion as he waited for her answer.

"You know, Michael. . ." she began.

"Shhh," he said, putting his fingers to her lips. "I know. Please just tell me yes or no. . .please just tell me yes. . ."

Miyah loved him so much in that moment that a surge of emotion rushed through her and she couldn't stop her tears.

"Yes. Oh, Michael. Yes, I want to marry you," she whispered as she flung her arms around him and kissed him. "Yes. Yes. Yes!"

Michael couldn't hold back his emotions either, and they clung to each other in tears of joy. Michael kissed her and soon they were swept away in their passion for each other.

The two lovebirds finally came downstairs a few hours later, freshly showered and smiling from ear-to-ear. Tomas knew he would have some arrangements to make.

"Congratulations," he said, walking over and embracing them together in one big hug. "You don't know how happy this makes me. What made you change your mind?"

"I've always wanted to marry Michael, that was never the issue. I just didn't think it was possible to have a solid relationship and do justice to my duties as the Touchstone carrier at the same time. Finding out about you and Nona has changed that."

"I'm so happy for you, my dear. Love is something you shouldn't ignore and a love like you and Michael share doesn't come along very often. I'm so pleased you're going to celebrate that love with marriage."

"Like you and Nona did?" Miyah surprised him with her response. "I saw that Nona had added your name to hers on my birth certificate, when she signed as midwife."

Tomas reacted shyly. "Nona and I said our vows privately. Of course, we couldn't do it through the Church, but in our hearts, our ceremony was just as binding as any official paper could have been. So, yes, we were married, and I'm glad you know that. It's been one of the hardest secrets I've had to keep. I wanted everyone to know that Nona was my wife. My dear wife."

Quickly changing the subject, he added, "So, did Michael tell you of my suggestion regarding Rennes-le-Château? Is that all right with you?"

"It's more than all right, Papa Tom. It's perfect. We didn't talk about a date though. There are a lot of things to consider."

"How about two weeks from tomorrow?" Tomas suggested. "We don't want to waste any time and you don't need to worry about the arrangements. I have plenty of friends to help with the big details. You tell me what you want and I'll take it from there."

"Two weeks! This is so sudden. Give me some time to make a list and think about all of this! One thing I do know is that I don't want a big wedding. I want something simple. It's not the wedding that's important to either of us. It's the vows." She looked at Michael and he put his arms around her.

"You just tell me what to do. I'm at your service," Michael said to both of them. "All I care about is making Miyah my bride. Spare no expense."

The next few days were a whirlwind of planning. Tomas helped Michael expedite the marriage license and Lydia insisted on sewing a wedding dress for Miyah. "You can really do this in two weeks?" Miyah exclaimed. "That's just too much work for you."

"Don't worry your pretty little head," Lydia told her. "I've been sewing all my life. It's an honor to make your dress. You just let me measure you and tell me what style you like. We can go together to pick out the fabric."

"Oh, I don't know. Nothing fluffy, something simple. . .you must know that I am very practical and would like to be able to wear this dress on other occasions. I don't want it to sit in a box after the wedding. Let me make some sketches and see what I can come up with," she suggested.

"Then do it today," Lydia demanded, handing Miyah some paper. "I need to get started right away if I'm to be done in time."

Tomas consulted with Miyah on the plans he was making. After all he had been to hundreds of weddings in his lifetime.

"I don't think there's enough time to do all of this so quickly. We don't have to rush into this. We can wait another month or so. I don't want it to be a burden on you."

"Burden, are you kidding? This is the most exciting thing that has happened around here in a long time. Everyone is wanting to help. *They* want to make this a big event. It is a big event. Don't you understand Miyah? Many of these villagers have been 'in the closet' so to speak for ages, supporting the bloodline in private. Your wedding is bringing them together in a way that's hard to explain. Everyone wants to take part in the celebration. Haven't you noticed how friendly everyone has been to you, both in Rennes-les-Bains and at Rennes-le-Château? You're family to them. They're honored to have you here. Let them have their party. It's not just your wedding they're celebrating. You're giving them the opportunity to openly join together as a community. . .a community of believers and healers."

"I don't want to be a celebrity. Please let them know that. I'm just a person, a daughter of the bloodline, yes, but first I'm a bride like any other. I don't want any special attention."

"Let us give you a beautiful wedding. That's all we ask," Tomas said. "Trust me."

"Yes, I do trust you. And thank you for all you're doing, but I don't want a fuss made over me. I don't like attention drawn to me or my powers."

"Miyah, you'll find that many of the people in the villages here have special powers. You're not alone in that. You have cousins here—family connected through the ages. This is a reunion of the bloodline. So don't worry, I'll see to it that you'll get the attention any bride deserves and nothing more. It'll be a wonderful wedding day for you and Michael."

"One more thing. Please, no gifts. The wedding is gift enough. Please stress that to everyone."

The days that followed went by quickly as word spread and Miyah and Michael got to know the men and women who offered to help with the wedding. They felt like old friends as they gathered to talk about food, flowers, cake and music. This had all come about so suddenly, and Miyah had never thought about a wedding dress before. She made sketch after sketch of dresses and finally settled on a simple design, practical, yet elegant, hoping it wouldn't be too difficult for Lydia to sew.

A couple of days before the wedding Michael presented Miyah with the amber necklace he had purchased in the village earlier, a perfect memento of their stay in Rennes-les-Bains.

"I love it," she said as he placed it around her neck. "It's absolutely beautiful."

"The amber was supposedly mined from the area," he said, and told her the stories the shopkeeper had shared that day. "We'll have to take a closer look at the artwork on the copper beads, though," he added. "They look pretty interesting. The clerk said the necklace was very old."

Miyah's gift to Michael was more personal. She performed a sacred wedding ritual, using spikenard oil she had purchased in the village. By candlelight, she gently and methodically massaged her bridegroom's feet with the oil, and as part of the ritual let her hair brush down against his feet, taking in the aroma of the oil. Michael was in heaven. The foot massage alone was enough to put him into ecstasy, but the thought of this ancient ritual being performed by Miyah, his beautiful Miyah, was overwhelming. It was both tender and erotic at the same time, a wedding gift he would never forget.

~ ~ ~ ~ ~

Tomas held true to his word. The wedding day soon came and the streets of the medieval castle village were filled with pots of colorful flowers set out by residents in front of their homes. Tables with white linen cloths lined the grounds and centerpieces of wildflowers, berries and roses adorned them. The festivities were scheduled to begin around 6:30 p.m., after the tour buses and tourists had left. Tomas may have worked miracles in getting everything arranged so quickly, but he couldn't shut down the town for the wedding. Tourism was their livelihood.

Candled luminaries lined the streets and walkways of the village. Each luminary had a "MM" punched into the bag. The letters shimmered as the light of the candle shone through. Miyah wondered it if stood for Miyah and Michael—or did the initials have a deeper, bloodline meaning?

The streets were filled with residents from the villages, family, neighbors, friends, priests, nuns, and former parishioners of Tomas', milling around in a festive mood. Miyah had no idea where they all came from, but was pleased they had come to celebrate—even though she had requested a small wedding.

A trio of violinists and a flautist began the ceremony with sweet music that drifted out over the valley. Michael and Miyah walked hand-in-hand to the steps that led to the platform connecting the Magdala Tower with the orangery greenhouse. There were 11 steps on each side of a circular well-shaped fountain, and they separated briefly, each taking a flight of stairs—totalling 22 steps. They met at the top and then walked to ascended a winding 22-step spiral staircase to the top of the tower, which was lined with pots of flowers and more luminaries.

Miyah's ankle-length dress was made of flowing white silk with layers of soft crepe de chine, overlaying each other like petals of a flower. Lydia had done a beautiful job with her design, allowing the folds of the dress to lay in a manner so the dress could be worn after the baby was born. The round neckline and edges of the layers were trimmed with small pearl beads, as was the high waistband. Lydia also made a beautiful shawl of the same fabric for evening wear. Miyah wore the amber necklace and also dainty diamond earrings that had belonged to her mother and grandmother. The sides of her hair were pulled back into a long braid that blended in with her thick hair, and interwoven into the braid were small buds of pink, white and red roses picked from Tomas' garden. She was radiant.

Michael was just as handsome in black slacks and a white long sleeved shirt with pearl buttons. Lydia had made him a waistband from the white silk fabric to match Miyah's dress. His skin, tanned from the sun, and his hair pulled back into his usual pony tail, made him look very debonair. He wore the Faith Stone necklace that Miyah had given him when he began his work with the cedar box.

Although retired, Tomas had received special permission to officiate the ceremony. He began with a prayer.

"God, who is above us, around us and inside us, guard over these children of yours who are becoming one today. Hold them in your protective hands and give them guidance while they walk their path together. Help them to always see the positive in life and be an inspiration to each other and to others. Let the light of peace follow them, and surround them with your love. Bless their children, and their children's children, that they too may live in a world of peace, light and love. Bless all of those gathered here today in a reunion of family and friends who celebrate our past and our future on this, the wedding day of Miyah and Michael. Blessed be. Amen"

They stood on the top of the Magdala Tower with the patchwork colors of the valley below them and an orange glowing ball of sun warming them as it slowly made its way toward the horizon. Michael and Miyah looked into each other's eyes as Tomas performed the ceremony. Around the bride and groom, the spirits of the ancestors stood together, proudly witnessing the wedding of their children as the two of them said their wedding vows.

"Michael. Little did I know when I came into your life that you would become my best friend. You are the man who I can trust with my secrets and my desires, the man who accepts me for all that I am and all that I must be. I love your gentleness, your intellect, your humor, your strength when I need it, your caring and giving ways, and I love the way you look at me. My life was empty without you, but I didn't know it. How could I ever live now, without you? You are my family, my friend, my husband. I love you."

She shook as she put the ring on his finger, the wedding ring that had belonged to his father.

"Miyah, you are the light of my life. You gave me back my life, and I vow to always be by your side, to protect you, take care of you, be your best friend and love you forever. The joy, the laughter, the passion, the feeling of elation when I see your smile, is what I live for each day. I never knew what real living was until you came along. Thank you for generously sharing your special gifts and talents. You make the world a better place, just by being here. Now you can rest on me. Let me be your rock. You are my family, my friend, my wife. I love you."

He emotionally wiped tears from his eyes as he placed the ring on her finger. Miyah took a deep breath to retain her composure. Tomas offered another blessing and then announced those final words:

"With the power invested in me, I am proud to pronounce you husband and wife. Michael, you may kiss your bride."

Among cheering from the villagers below, Michael and Miyah kissed, sealing their wedding vows with tears of joy. Miyah tossed her flower bouquet into the crowd and threw kisses to everyone there, thanking them for making this day so special. They practically skipped down the steps and into the crowd of people, who through the process of planning their wedding, had suddenly become good friends, the community Michael had spoken of earlier. And the party began.

The cake, a traditional French *Croquembouche*, decorated with flowers, was the center of attention. The menu was printed on a menu board on the table, in French, but also in English for Miyah and Michael's sake. It read:

Buffet Froid ~ Appetizer (a variety of cold cut meats)
Pause Glacée (Ice cream with alcohol - to reinvigorate your appetite)
Poulet de Bress au vinaigre de framboise et sa garniture printanière
(Chicken breast with a raspberry sauce and vegetables)
Croquante du jardin (Garden salad)
Formages (Cheese)   Café (Coffee)

"The food looks exquisite," Miyah said as she sat down.

"Yes, but it sure reads fancier in French," Michael laughed.

Sweet smelling French breads, cheese, and fresh fruit were also consumed, and wine and champagne flowed freely. There was music, dancing in the streets and Miyah and Michael were introduced to many people who were related in one way or another back through centuries of bloodline links. Miyah and Michael mingled and danced throughout the night until the last guests kissed them on each cheek and wandered back to their homes. Even Tomas forwent his usual early bedtime and stayed with them to the very end.

Before heading back to Rennes-les-Bains, the newlyweds climbed back atop the Magdala Tower and enjoyed a star-studded night, with a full moon looking down over them.

"It couldn't have been better," Miyah said, snuggling into Michael's arms. "Thank you for being persistent. I'm so happy when I'm with you."

"Me too," Michael said. "I love you so much."

"Did you see them?" Miyah asked.

"You mean Joshua and Maryum? Yes! I can hardly believe it!" Michael exclaimed. "What an honor to have them here."

"And did you notice that Tomas didn't use the phrase, 'til death do us part' in the ceremony? He knows that even after death, we don't really part," Miyah noted.

"Hmmm. Nona was here wasn't she?" Michael asked.

"Yes, and so were your parents. . .and Junia. It really was beautiful."

"My parents were here? Why didn't they allow me to see them?"

"Probably because this was our day. They didn't want you to get all emotional over them. But isn't it beautiful that they were all here?"

"Yes, I suppose you're right. I have to say that I did feel their presence a couple of times. I guess maybe I did know they were here all along. It's too bad Elizabeth couldn't have made the trip. I offered to pay her way and everything, but she said she just couldn't get away from work and school. She really seems to be happy. She gives us her blessings though."

"I know. We're very lucky to have such supportive family surrounding us, no matter what the dimension. Speaking of family, we should probably get Tomas home. He has to be so tired after this long day. We need to do something special to thank him for all of this."

"Yes, let's put some thought into that," Michael agreed, and they went to find Tomas.

As quickly as everything had been set up, it was dismantled by the men and women who volunteered. The only traces left of the celebration were memories of laughter and music that continued to echo through the valley in the evening air.

~ ~ ~ ~ ~

Everyone slept in the next morning until almost noon when Lydia arrived with left-over food from the wedding.

"We won't have to go to the market for a while," she said, trying to find a place in the refrigerator for everything.

"You take some of this too," Tomas insisted.

"Oh, don't worry, I got plenty and so did the others who helped. Everyone was so generous. It was such a beautiful wedding."

"And my wedding dress was absolutely perfect," Miyah said, going over to give Lydia a hug. "I can't thank you enough. It'll be one of my most valued treasures."

"I'm so glad you liked it," Lydia said.

"I didn't like it—I loved it!" Miyah exclaimed. "Thank you again."

"There's enough fabric left over to make something else, a blouse or something. I'll bring it by later today."

"Oh, heavens no. You keep that. Make yourself something out of it."

"But it's silk. It was such expensive fabric. . ." Lydia started.

"I want you to have it, please. It's the least I can do. I insist."

"Thank you, Miyah. It'll always be something special to remember you by. I'll cherish it, whatever it turns out to be! I have to get going. I have other stops to make today. Have a wonderful day, and congratulations again to the two of you." She waved as she hurried back to her car.

The three of them hungrily dug into the left-overs, happy they didn't have to cook.

"What's this?" Michael asked when he noticed a nicely wrapped package on the coffee table.

Tomas picked it up and held to his ear.

"What are you doing, listening for a bomb!?" Michael teased.

"That's not so funny," Tomas said. "Stranger things have been known to happen here."

"Ridiculous," Miyah said, taking the package from him. "I thought I said no wedding gifts. Is it from you, Tomas?"

"No, really," he said. "I don't know where it came from. Lydia must have brought it when she delivered the food, or someone dropped it off while we were sleeping."

The three stared at the box for a moment, and then Miyah closed her eyes and tuned in on the package. "It's OK," she finally said. "It's just a wedding gift. Don't do that to me, Tomas. You had us all going there for awhile."

"I'm sorry. I get overly cautious when things like this just appear," he said. "There have been too many mysterious happenings in these villages over the years."

"Well, let's open it and see what it is," Michael said, reaching to help. They unwrapped the box and found a beautiful gold goblet. It was intricately carved, and no doubt very old. Tomas put on his glasses to take a better look.

"This is very exciting!" he finally said. "I believe this could be one of the pieces of the treasure that Saunière found. He gave a lot of the items away to his friends in the village. Whoever gave it to you, it has probably been in their family for several years and they wanted you two to have it. It's very old, very historic. . .and very valuable. That's quite a gift."

"I don't know if we should accept it," Michael said. "Don't you think it should stay here in the village? Maybe you should keep it."

"Oh, no. I think it's perfectly fitting that a piece of secret treasure from the area go home with you. It's a very nice gesture on behalf of someone in the village. It's your wedding gift. You two should cherish it."

"I wish we knew who to thank," Miyah said. "There's no card."

"Oh, believe me. Those who have pieces of the treasure would rather remain anonymous. Just celebrating your wedding and bringing everyone together is probably enough thanks," Tomas said.

"But, as long as we're on the subject, I do have a wedding gift for you," he winked.

"Now Tomas, you've done enough already. Please, no gifts," Miyah pleaded.

"OK then, it's not a wedding gift. It's something I would have given to you anyhow, Is that better?" He went to his desk and brought back a fat envelope of papers with a black ribbon tied around it, and handed it to Miyah.

"I've had my estate signed over to you, Miyah. My land, this house, my car, everything I own is yours. And before you can object, consider this. I'm getting old. I think I still have a few good years left in me, but you're my heir and it makes sense to do this now, rather than go through all the court fiasco after I die. Everything is paid for, so don't worry about that. Both of you are family here and I want you to feel welcome to come back anytime. We have to go in and sign a couple more papers and it's all yours. Just do me a favor, and let me live here until I die, OK?"

"I don't know what to say. I wasn't expecting this."

"Of course you weren't. Just say thank you. That's all I need to hear."

"Thank you, Papa Tom. Thank you. I love you."

"Oh, I like to hear that too," he laughed, hugging her. "I love you too, Miy."

"Goodness, I seem to be crying a lot lately," Miyah apologized, dabbing her tears with her napkin. "It must be the pregnancy."

"Or it could be that you're just happy," Michael said.

~~~~~

Michael and Miyah took Tomas on a weekend trip to Paris as a thank you for all he had done—welcoming them into his home and making all the wedding preparations. They stayed at Hotel Britannique as before and enjoyed the sites, with Tomas as their guide this time. He loved the city and said he used to go there often when he first arrived in France. They returned to the Louvre and examined specific paintings with a scrutinizing eye, looking for clues hidden in the images. Having Tomas' comments and perspective on the art made them see things much clearer than before. They went to St. Sulpice and explored the church while Tomas met with some of his fellow priests. Then they returned to the Church of Mary Magdalene so Tomas could also connect with his friends there.

While they were waiting for Tomas in the church, Miyah spotted the same priest who had given her the first prayer card. She retrieved it from her diary and brought it to the man, handing it back to him as a way to communicate that she knew he was a part of a sacred circle protecting the bloodline, and to thank him for his services. He took the card turned it over, and smiled at her.

"Il est bon. Nous partageons votre secret. Frères dans le besoin ont toujours été bien accueillis et servis dans cette église," he said, and handed the card back to her. *"S'il vous plaît garder cela pour la prochaine fois que vous êtes à Paris. Merci. Dieu vous bénisse."*

"What did he say?" Michael asked, after the priest left.

"He said, 'It is good. We share your secret. Brothers in need have always been welcomed and served in this church.' That's exactly what the second card said. It's a password of sorts," she answered.

"But he gave the card back to you."

"Yes, and he said, 'Please keep this for the next time you are in Paris. Thank you. God bless.'"

She turned to Michael. "Somehow it's so comforting to know there are more people here who know about the bloodline and have carried it as their own Touchstone for centuries. I'm oddly relieved to know that I'm not the only Touchstone carrier."

"It's all a part of your big, extended family, Miyah. I'm so glad we came."

They enjoyed every minute of their Paris weekend with Tomas. They dined at Cafe Rousilion on rue Cler and found their way to the classic Paris bistro, Thoumieux on rue St. Dominique, because Tomas said they had the best *cassoulets* in the city. They strolled along the Avenue Des Champs Elyseses, enjoying the vibrant sights and sounds of Paris. On the Pont d'Lena Bridge, where they had a perfect view of the Eiffel Tower, Tomas broke into song, singing to them in French as people gathered around to listen.

"He should have been on stage instead of behind a pulpit," Michael said as they applauded his theatrical performance.

They stopped in front of the Obelisk again and Miyah had that same sense as before that there was a message hidden somewhere for them. She was glad Michael had photographed it so well the last time they were there. She would be anxious for him to download the photos he had been taking on the trip. She made sure there were plenty of photographs taken of Tomas and of her and Tomas together, and of course of her and Michael as well. He had lent his camera to one of Tomas' friends to photograph at the wedding, so she was just as anxious to see those photos. It had been such a perfect few months. They had no idea they would be staying so long when they came to France.

The next few weeks passed quickly and all three of them knew it was time for Miyah and Michael to return to the States. Tomas tried to convince them to stay and have the baby born in France. Then the baby would have dual citizenship. It was enticing, but Michael really felt they needed to get back home. They, in turn, tried to convince Tomas to come back with them, even if it were just for a visit. He said he was so settled in and that, other than for them, he had no desire to return to the States. He assured them he would stay around long enough to meet his great-granddaughter, and that was what they wanted to hear.

People came by each day to say goodbye and there was a big dance in the town square of Rennes-les-Bains in their honor the night before they left. They were part of the community now and knew people by name. They were going to miss everyone and vowed to come back soon to show off their daughter. They exchanged addresses and emails of friends, and Lydia assured them she would continue to take good care of Tomas. That was the most difficult part. Leaving Papa Tom.

Early in the morning the next day, with Lydia at the wheel, they drove west, past Toulouse to spent a couple of hours touring Lourdes in the foothills of the Pyrenees, on the banks of the Bave River, the meeting point of the Seven Valleys of the Laveda. After all the years Tomas had lived in France, he had never visited Lourdes, but he had done his homework.

"Michael, do you want to get into a numbers game again?" he asked. "Bernadette Soubirous, the young girl who had the 18 apparitions of the Virgin Mary in 1858, which prompted the mass pilgrimages here, was born on January 17!"

"No," Michael exclaimed. "What is it with this January 17 date? Some day I hope we'll figure that one out."

"I have no doubt that she had those apparitions," Miyah was thinking out loud. "After all, look at how Nona can appear to us and how Joshua appears. Those are the Mary stories I love, her appearing and giving messages and healing. That's the beautiful part of the story. And I understand why people want to come here. Look at us. We came here to be in the energy of a place where so many pilgrims travel each year to honor the Holy Mother. But it's so geared to tourism—so commercial. There are over 400 hotels here to accommodate tourists."

"How else could it be, Miyah? With hundreds of thousands of pilgrims flocking to these sites every year, the locals make a good living on it, and yes, so does the Church. The tourists are going to come either way, so they may as well take advantage of it," Tomas tried to explain.

"But do they come now just out of curiosity because it's so promoted as a tourist destination, or do they really come to honor Mother Mary? Are people truly healed here, or is it a big production of the Catholic Church to fill their coffers in an attempt to keep the faith alive?"

"I would imagine it's a mix of all of that," Tomas admitted. "Everyone has their own motives."

"I'm sorry, Tomas. I don't mean to take away from your pilgrimage here. I know it has its own special meaning for you. This is a beautiful place with a lot of meaning. I just hope people come here for the right reasons."

"I hear the artwork and frescos are exquisite," Michael noted as they walked down the esplanade toward the towering steepled church.

They toured the magnificent cathedral with its beautifully detailed, golden frescos and admired the giant gold crown on the top of one of the chapels. They walked through the groomed gardens to the grotto and stood in line to touch the stone of the cave where Mary had appeared, and even bought plastic bottles in the shape of the Virgin Mary to fill with holy water.

"The cathedral and frescos are beautiful, but the grotto isn't at all what I expected," Miyah admitted, referring again to how tourist-driven the site was. She turned on the faucet from a plastic pipe stretched over a trough, to fill her bottle with holy water. "I thought it would be more reverent and not so materialistic."

"Yea," Michael laughed. "The holy water is free, but you have to buy the bottle to put it in!"

"It's such a mix of emotions," Miyah admitted. "This version of Mother Mary who the Catholic Church has romanced is not at all the Mother Mariam I know. I embrace her as an intelligent woman who was a loving daughter, wife and mother, raising a large family and experiencing the everyday joy and pain that go with being a mother. She had hardships and strife in her life, just like any other human—more than many. Putting her on a pedestal as a Queen or a Saint makes her a non-person. It doesn't tell her story as a woman, a powerful woman who healed the sick and helped the poor. Mariam, as well as her mother Anna, have big stories to tell. Where is their human story within the Church?"

"I think those who come to honor her,

Mary in the Grotto at Lourdes, France

must do so in their own way," Tomas offered. "The Church sees her as the Virgin Mother of Jesus. Whether you believe their story or not, at least she is out there, a woman of the Bible, for all to honor and respect. You don't have to agree with the Church to feel her heart beat for the pilgrims who come here, and other places to worship her. Honor her in your own way. You know her story."

They watched people kneel before the crowned virgin statue, saying the rosary, burning candles, drinking from the taps of holy water and following the stations of the cross. They walked through the Grotto of the Apparitions, the Rosary Basilica with the Upper Basilica in the Crypt and the Underground Basilica of St. Pius X.

"They say this underground building can hold 20,000 people!" Michael exclaimed, looking at a posting explaining the area. "I'd be claustrophobic for sure."

Finally, it was Lydia who pointed to her watch and said they must get going to get to the airport in time for their flight. She also noted that Tomas was leaning on his cane a lot, a sign that he was getting tired. Miyah saw the attention Lydia gave to Tomas and knew he was in good hands. She appreciated that he had good people to care for him. It made it a little easier to say goodbye. She quietly sent a wave of healing energy to him and watched as his body straightened and his limp eased.

The good-byes came quickly as they arrived at the airport in Toulouse with little time to check in and get to the gate for their flight to Paris and then on to the States.

"Send me news when my granddaughter arrives," Tomas said as he hugged Miyah farewell, tears swelling in his eyes. "I love you, my sweet Miy. And you, Michael. Take good care of Miy."

Michael felt such a tender spot in his heart for this special man. "I'll take good care of them both," he said. "Don't worry."

"We promise to come back soon," Miyah said as Tomas and Lydia reluctantly waved goodbye. "Thank you both for everything. I love you Papa Tom," she repeated, as he slowly drove away in the big, black Cadillac.

27 Preparations

Miyah had mixed emotions as they stood in front of Michael's house while the driver unloaded their luggage. It had been a long flight, but she wasn't even tempted to use her "powers" to beam them back home. Now she understood what Michael meant when he said he wanted to savor every moment of the journey with her. She, too, didn't want their adventure to end. But now they were back to reality. Back home. It's not that she didn't like living in the States. It's just that she felt such a community, such a sense of family in France, in Rennes.

Elizabeth had been watching for them and bounded out the door as soon as the taxi drove up. She ran into Michael's arms.

"Oh, I've missed you both so much," she cried, reaching out to include Miyah in her embrace. "And look at you!" she exclaimed, putting her hand on Miyah's belly. "I'm so excited! I'm going to be an auntie! How are you feeling? How was the wedding? How was the trip? Were you comfortable enough on your flight home? I want to hear everything. . ." she rattled on as they went into the house.

Michael laughed. He hadn't seen his sister so lively in years.

"Let us get settled in first," he said. "It's been a long day traveling." He brought their luggage upstairs and then joined Miyah and Elizabeth in the kitchen.

"I took some cooking lessons while you were gone, and I might point out—it's all healthy food! I thought you might appreciate something when you got home – salad, pasta with fresh vegetables. I hope you like it."

"You're so thoughtful," Miyah said. "Thank you. It smells delicious."

"I want to hear all about the wedding. I hope you have photos. I know I'll be mad at myself forever for not flying over, but it was so difficult to get away with my new job and classes at school."

They ate dinner and told Elizabeth about the wedding, Paris, and some of the highlights of their trip. They didn't include the family secrets Miyah had unearthed in France, just that she enjoyed visiting her grandfather. And they didn't tell her of Michael's discovery about their parent's accident.

When dinner was finished Elizabeth announced she had a big surprise. She led them upstairs to the guest bedroom and told them to close their eyes. She swung open the door.

"OK. Open your eyes!" she commanded. Both Michael and Miyah were astonished.

"You did all this by yourself?" he asked in amazement.

"Do you like it? I hope you like it," she said in response. Elizabeth had cleared out the room and made it into a nursery for the baby. She had painted the walls white and on half of one wall she'd added thin, pink stripes. A plush, flower-designed rug covered much of the wood floor and sheer pink curtains framed the window. A menagerie of whimsical, pastel animals were stenciled on a section of one wall, with children's poems playfully swirling around them.

"I bought the crib, rocking chair and changing dresser at a yard sale and painted them with a fresh coat of white paint, and got all the other stuff on sale. It was so much fun shopping for the baby. I guess I got a bit carried away!" She was so excited. "It's such a big room, so I left the bed in here in case you need to be in with the baby some nights. I hope you don't mind I did this. I mean, if you had other ideas, you can change it. I won't be offended."

"Oh no!" Miyah exclaimed. "This is perfect. To be honest, I hadn't even thought about a nursery. I can't believe you did all this for us. It's wonderful. I love it all!"

Elizabeth pulled open drawers and showed them some of the cute little outfits she had bought. "And I got a really good deal on this bassinet. You can keep it in your room or use it downstairs."

"We can't thank you enough. It's incredible," Michael said. "I'm going to reimburse you for this," he added. "You spent way too much."

"It's my wedding / baby gift to you. And besides, I've had a blast doing it. I'm glad you stayed away so long so I had time to finish it. It's been a good project for me," Elizabeth replied, grinning from ear to ear. "Besides, that's what family is for."

"Yes, family," Michael said, looking tenderly at the women in his life. It was all about family.

~~~~~

They went to bed that night without unpacking, exhausted from their journey, but happy at the thought of their welcome home efforts by Elizabeth. It meant a lot, especially to Michael.

Elizabeth said she'd be sure not to disturb them when she left for work in the morning and suggested they sleep in. She had a class after work, so wouldn't be home until late. And that is exactly what they did—slept in. It was almost noon before either of them stirred.

After breakfast Michael headed into his library and out to the patio. He was actually looking forward to doing some gardening and, after being outside so much while in France, was appreciative of his spacious back yard.

"Come out with me and sit for awhile," he called to Miyah. "Enjoy the birds singing. I think they're welcoming us home."

"I want to unpack some things first," she replied, opening her carry-on luggage. She set aside the papers and deed that Tomas signed over to her of his property in France, and opened the box and tissue paper that encased the antique goblet, mysteriously given to them as a wedding gift in Rennes. Tomas had been very clever in packaging it to get it through customs. He had a shopkeeper friend of his make a price sticker to attach inside the rim, as if it was something they bought in a gift shop. She also wrapped it and boxed it with her store logo. The security man at the airport had asked Miyah to remove it from her bag and examined it to be sure it wasn't stolen goods or an antiquity. Miyah pointed to the 25-euro price tag. The officer looked at the price tag and shrugged his shoulders, placing it back into the box.

Miyah decided to leave the sticker in place. It was a good diversion just in case someone else questioned the origin of the goblet. She unpacked the rest of her bags and then grabbed the goblet, papers and deed and headed downstairs.

"I think we should put these in your father's safe, if that's OK with you," she suggested to Michael. "I could take the deed and Tomas' papers to RoseVine. I know they would be safe there, but Tomas' property will eventually belong to our daughter, so you should have access to them too."

"I've been itching to take a look in that safe ever since we got home," Michael said, coming inside, locking the patio door behind him. He proceeded to the front and the kitchen doors and locked them also.

"I just want to be sure no one comes into the house when we're in the bomb shelter. Now, more than ever, I feel it necessary to keep it a secret. I hope Liz hasn't told anyone about it. That could be disastrous."

They headed downstairs into the shelter. Michael looked around and said it appeared that everything was the same.

"It doesn't look like Liz has even been down here," he said as he checked the locks and security system. They went into the storage room and Michael slid the clothes aside on the closet rod to reveal the safe. He dialed the combination to unlock it and slowly opened the door.

"I'm not sure if I want to know what's in my dad's papers," he said, hesitating to touch anything. Slowly, he began to empty the safe of its contents, handing things to Miyah to lay out on a table they had cleared. There were long rolls of architectural papers and maps, black notebook journals, a couple of boxes, passports, a pottery jar of foreign money, some jewelry, documents, manuscripts and other papers. There were also two pistols and a box of shells, which Michael left in the safe.

"If you want some privacy to go through these things, I understand," Miyah offered. "I can go upstairs while you sort through them."

"No. I'd rather have you here. You know as much as I do about their work. I could use your help—and emotional support." He picked up the passports and flipped through the pages. "I guess I hadn't realized how much they traveled," he said. "They had to get their passports renewed every ten years so there are four passports each for them, three old and one current, and they're all full, some even have extra pages added to them. They had a good life."

Michael sorted through some of the papers, legal papers for the house, paid off mortgage papers and other documents. He recognized some of the jewelry that had been in the family for a long time—his grandmother's rings, a diamond broach and other pieces.

"I should give these to Liz one of these days," he said. "I just want to be sure she's ready to realize their sentimental value first." He put the jewelry and legal papers back into the safe.

"These look like Dad's field journals. I want to bring these upstairs and read through them," he said, setting aside the notebooks.

"You might want to bring this upstairs to read also," Miyah suggested, handing him a box that contained a manuscript. "It looks like your mother did lot of research while in the Rennes area. You were right when you said you didn't think she could resist writing a mystery novel about the region. It looks like she at least started one—and maybe decided it was better not to have it published just yet."

Michael took the box and turned through the first few pages. "It looks as though it's a draft. I can hardly wait to read through this. She must have thought it pretty controversial to have put it in the safe." He put it with the field journals.

"You might also want to look through this," Miyah said as she spread some of the coins from the jar out on the table. "I think some of these coins might be gold. Some are very old and unusual."

Michael picked up a coin and studied it. "Do you think they could have come from the treasures of the Rennes caves?"

"It's likely. Maybe you'll find out more when you read through your dad's field notes," she suggested.

Slowly Michael reached for the rolled up tubes of paper. He spread them out, one after another and studied them. Some were from archeological digs his father had been on in various parts of the world. They were clearly marked and dated. He carefully rolled each one up and placed it back inside the safe after he examined them.

"There's only one here that isn't identified or dated," he commented. "It looks like a series of hallways or tunnels. I guess it could be anywhere, but it isn't drawn the same as his other drawings." Michael stood silent as he surveyed the diagrams and sketches. Then he looked over the top of his reading glasses at Miyah and he didn't have to say a word.

"It's the cave, isn't it? The cave under Mount Bugarach."

"Yes," he replied.

"It could have been drawn early on, when you were there as a boy," she said.

"No. It couldn't have been. . .because it includes the lake and waterfall, exactly as I remember seeing them. He didn't know about them until I told him I had been there. He must have found his way there too, in order to draw them so accurately. There are other markings here, other caverns and tunnels," Michael pointed. "And look at the cross marks here. They might indicate where they found treasure."

"They look a lot like Templar crosses," Miyah agreed. "This shouldn't really surprise you though, to find this map. He kept maps and sketches of all his digs," she indicated, refering to the other rolls of papers.

"I'm not surprised to find it, I guess. But it might verify what Tomas was telling us about treasures found in the area. Is treasure still there?" Michael tapped his finger on one of the cross marks on the map. Then he noticed a smaller scroll among the tubes and began to unroll it.

"Oh my God," he said before he had completely unrolled the parchment. "This is the document Tomas told us about—the other half of the parchment written about in that magazine article he read to us. So my father really did have it!" Michael carefully examined the words on the brittle paper. "It's in some other language. Can you translate it?" he asked, handing the paper to Miyah. And just as quickly, he pulled it back.

"On the other hand, I don't really know if I want to find out what it has to say. There's been so much tragedy related to this mystery—tragedy that touches home for both you and I. Do you realize this document and treasure map could be very important and could lead to millions of dollars worth of antiquities, and possibly documentation that could expose many dark secrets of the Church?"

"And what do you propose to do with this parchment and map?" Miyah asked.

Michael leaned on the table with both hands and stared at her for a few seconds. Then he rolled up the map and parchment and placed them back into the safe.

"I intend to do nothing," he replied. "Nothing for now, anyhow. If my parents were murdered because of what they knew about these treasures, I would rather have those secrets stay buried with them than take a chance on putting the rest of my family in danger. Sometimes secrets may be better kept hidden. There's a reason the owner of the other half of the parchment requested it not to be revealed. Right now, I think we need to honor that."

"I agree," Miyah said. "I'm proud of you for being so honest. Some day the time will come to reveal this mysterious document, but I think we need to know more about the circumstances first."

"Let's see what else we have here," Michael said, opening one of the boxes and digging through some yellowed tissue paper. Both Michael and Miyah did a double-take when he peeled away the wrapping. She took the box she had brought down to put in the safe and opened it, holding their wedding goblet up next to the goblet Michael had just unwrapped. The cups were a matching set. Miyah and Michael were speechless.

"How could this be?" Michael finally spoke.

"Michael. This could only mean that whoever gave us this goblet must have known about the goblet your father had. Who could have known that? Tomas thought this might have been one of the pieces Saunière gave to a friend, and he was passing it on, but this wasn't a gift given because of my connection with the bloodline. It was given because of your connection—your father's work in the area. Someone in the village must have known or worked with your father and knew about the treasures he found."

"Or knew both of our fathers and the treasures *they* found. There were other people working with them on this project. Miyah, this person, these people, were probably at our wedding! They made friends with us because of their connection to our fathers. And they must have known this would reunite the two goblets."

"Maybe it's a sign, a message that they acknowledge us as offspring of their colleagues and it was their way to pay respects to our fathers. Interesting, isn't it, that in a sense, your parents were also tied to my bloodline—not only by their friendship with my parents, but also through the discovery of some of the Templar treasures, which are woven into the stories of the bloodline."

"I guess our destiny was written long before we even realized it," Michael said. They wrapped the two goblets together in one box and placed the box inside the safe, next to the coins and map. Michael picked up his dad's field journals and hesitantly put them back into the safe next to the goblets.

"I think I should put it all to rest," he said. "It doesn't seem like it's the right time to do this now. I don't know why. My gut feeling is telling me to set it aside. I'll come back to it later. I really do want to read through these documents, but I don't think I'm ready yet to know what they may reveal. Is that OK with you?"

"Of course. You need to honor those feelings. You'll know when you're ready."

Michael took the box containing his mother's manuscript and added it to the treasures inside the safe.

"I never would have, in my wildest dreams, thought I'd have buried treasure right here beneath my own house. Let's hope it rests safely and no further harm comes to any of our future generations because of it."

"Amen," Miyah added. "Amen."

~ ~ ~ ~ ~

Michael spent the rest of the week downloading his photographs from the trip and organizing them into categories—Paris, Obelisk, Churches, Limoux, Alet-les-Baines, Rennes-les-Bains, Rennes-le-Château, Saintes-

Maries-de-la-Mer, Wedding, Tomas, Lourdes, Chartes Cathedral. Then he subcategorized some of the photos: the Louvre, paintings and statues, Church of Mary Magdalene, other churches, etc., so he could locate them easily. Next was the task of naming everything so he would remember which church was which and which village it was in. He burned DVDs of his images to archive them. He loved digital photography and how easy it was to organize everything. He didn't have to worry about sorting through negatives to identify them and find the right ones to make a print. The only downside was that he often didn't make prints from his digital photos and no one saw them but himself. This time he planned to make an actual hard-cover photo book of trip photographs and mementos for them to enjoy when they looked back on their journey.

As he opened one of the images in Photoshop he noticed something unusual. One of the photos of the church in Saintes-Maries-de-la-Mer had large orbs floating around in the church. The photos before and after were OK, so Michael knew it wasn't a camera flare or dust. He zoomed in to take a closer look. Some of the orbs were quite large and clear, others were smaller and faded. Each had a smaller circle in the center with a white ring around it, and distinctive lines, like a bloodshot eyeball, only everything was white and shades of gray.

"Of course there could be ghosts and spirits in the church," he thought. "It was also used as a fort and safe haven during hostile attacks." He smiled at the notion of capturing these spirits on film.

Then he came across another photo in the Opera House in Paris. This one was of a statue and although it didn't have orbs, there was a white blur going across the figure. The statue was in focus, so it wasn't camera movement. It had to be a ghost, he thought. Michael studied the hundreds of photos he took and these were the only two that were unusual. He sorted them into a folder marked, "Ghosts of France."

But it was the wedding photos that he spent most of his time admiring. He had given his camera to one of Tomas' friends to take photos, so he was curious to see the photos of the ceremony. He couldn't wipe the smile off his face as he clicked through picture after picture of that day—the most important day of his life. He noted some photos of them that he wanted to enlarge and frame. Then he looked through the pictures of the people who attended the wedding—new friends and old relatives that Miyah hadn't even known existed. So many people had come to celebrate their wedding. But there was one face that kept popping up in the crowd that didn't seem right to Michael. The man looked familiar, yet he couldn't put a name to him. He knew he had seen him before, but couldn't place where. He was in several photos, mostly standing by himself, looking at others in the crowd, never mingling or talking with anyone. It seemed unsettling to Michael. He put these images in a separate folder to show Miyah and see what her thoughts were. Maybe she would recognize this strange man.

~ ~ ~ ~ ~

Miyah had business to tend to and each day whisked herself away to her own home to take care of things. It really was the best of both worlds. She knew RoseVine would always be safe and taken care of while she was away from it, as it had been for centuries before her. It was part of the magic of her family. She had offered to bring the goblets, maps and other items there for safe keeping, but Michael said they had been safe in his house all these years, just because he knew about them now shouldn't make any difference. Besides, someday he would decide to read his mother's manuscript and his father's field journals. He wanted them nearby.

Miyah had only a few days left before the baby would be born. This day, she prepared a ritual to assure an easy childbirth. She smiled as she recalled how she and Michael had come across a statue of Diana in a small French village on their trip. She had placed a strand of her hair on the base of the statue as an offering.

Before Christian times, Diana, also known as Artemis, was called the Holy Mother. She was the virgin who lived in wild places, had mysterious powers and was worshiped in the moonlight. "Dia Anna" meant "nurturer who does not bear young," however she was called upon in fertility rituals by women who wanted to become pregnant, and also by women asking for easy child birth. Images of this Holy Mother were worshipped everywhere by women: in caves, the woods and trees. She was symbolized by both the Sun, the torch of life, and by the healing powers of the Moon. She was also called the Protector, the Teacher of the Young, Teacher of Knowledge, and Knower of Wisdoms, the Goddess who dealt with women's mysteries.

Miyah thought it was interesting that the ancient Roman celebration of Nemoralia, the Festival of Torches in honor of Diana, August 13-15, had been converted by the Church in the 6th century, into the Festival of Assumption of the Virgin on August 15, in spite of a statement by Saint Epiphanius, Bishop of Salamis (Cypress), in AD 377, admitting that no one actually really knew of the eventual fate of Mother Mary.

Miyah laid out the contents of her medicine bag and removed her diary. She gently turned the pages to an entry that described an ancient ritual to Diana.

"We gathered at a lake, surrounded by shady forests of sacred trees. We brought gifts to honor the Goddess - pieces of woven fabric, colorful thread, and prayers written on flat stones. We hung them on a long fence made from fallen branches. Requests and offerings to Diana are everywhere, including written messages on ribbons tied to the stone altar, and attached to trees. There are also small clay and hardened bread statues baked in the form of body parts that are in need of healing, drawings of mothers with children, and tiny sculptures of animals.

We celebrated with dance and song, and ate apples and other fruit. Before our procession around the lake, we washed our hair in the water and decorated ourselves with blossoms. With wreaths of flowers crowning our heads, we walked barefoot along the sandy shore. The light of our burning torches and candles joined with the light of the full moon, dancing in reflection upon the surface of the water – Diana's Mirror. It is a night of sacred ritual for women."

Miyah placed a photo of Diana in the center of a ring of stones. She added a statue of Mariam, the Holy Mother of Jesus, a photo card of Our Lady of Guadeloupe, and icon cards of Maryum—Mary Magdalene, along with the photo of Nona, Tomas, Junia and herself as a young girl, and a photo of her and Michael. With these she placed other imagery of healers, a Buddha statue, and finally a painting Junia had made years ago of Joshua—her family still preferred to call him Joshua, honoring the original Yeshua pronunciation instead of Jesus, which was the Roman translation of Yeshua. In the painting Joshua was sitting in lotus position and meditating. In his hand he held a globe of the world. It was Miyah's favorite image of him. . .peaceful, content, holding the world in the palm of his hands. Her family had always insisted on only the peaceful, positive images of Joshua—portraits of him with children, performing miracles, or standing with his hands outstretched—images that represented the healing and teaching aspects of his life.

"Why would we want a symbol of his painful ordeal on the cross to remind us of the most traumatic and sorrowful event of his life?" Nona had asked her. "Focus on the triumphs, not the tragedy, the positive, not the negative. We celebrate his life, not his perceived death."

Miyah sprinkled drops of frankincense and myrrh oil onto rose petals scattered among the photographs and statues within her ring of stones. She lit seven candles, citing a prayer as each flame began to burn its fire into the air.

"For protection. For an easy birth for my child and myself. For a healthy baby. For prosperity in her life. For wisdom. For love," and the last candle, "In deep gratitude for all you have given us, and for your continued blessings." Then she sat and meditated on these things, bringing only positive and good things into her life and into the life of her unborn child.

After almost half an hour of deep meditation, Miyah suddenly began to laugh out loud, breaking her pensive mood. Her belly was moving, as if in rhythm to a dance. The baby began to roll and kick until Miyah had to change positions.

"Are you adding your own prayers, little one?" Miyah asked, gently massaging her belly. "It's a good time to start when you're young! They're listening, I'm sure of that."

"Yes we are," a voice came from the shadows.

"Nona! I knew you were here. I could feel you. . .and you too, Mother," Miyah smiled. "I know it's not your mission to come to me as often. I'm always so happy when you're here."

"I feel the same way," Junia replied, walking toward her daughter. "We didn't mean to disturb you."

"Oh, you didn't." Miyah put her hands on her belly. "The little one here decided she wanted to put in her own requests, and I think one of those was for me to move around. She'll have no problems finding her voice when she arrives!"

Miyah got up and welcomed them both with warm embraces. Then the three women got comfortable on pillows on the floor around the stone circle, the light of the candles glowing on their faces.

"I knew you were participating in my safe birthing ritual. Thank you for holding the energy with me."

"I sense you have some questions for us. Am I correct?" Nona asked.

"Of course," Miyah laughed. "I knew you'd be here when I was supposed to receive my answers. It never fails, does it?"

"That's the beauty of our connectedness," Nona replied. "That intuitive knowing."

"What did you want to ask?" Junia questioned. "Could it have to do with a name for your daughter?"

"Of course it does," Miyah laughed again. "You know it does! That and a couple of other things, but let's start with that." She took a drink of water. "Naming my child is important, especially considering our bloodline, and I want to honor both of you in her naming."

"That's very sweet of you, Miyah," Junia said. "But you must choose a name you like, not just for us. What does Michael say about names?"

"Oh, he's very open about it. He liked the name Sera. Of course, he wanted my name in there somewhere, but I told him that any name with an 'M' will be in honor of me and carry on our tradition. He said whatever I choose will be good with him. He knows the name and its meaning is important to me."

"Your name, 'Miyah,' means 'illusion or magic' in Sanskrit," Junia explained. "It's also another name for the Hindu Goddess, Maa Durga

(Mother Durga) who helps in situations of distress. Does that sound familiar? You're always helping someone. Durga is a form of Devi, the supreme Goddess with ten arms, riding a lion or a tiger, carrying weapons and a lotus flower. She always maintains a meditative smile and practices mudras, symbolic hand gestures. Just like you, Miyah. Always peaceful and using your hands to heal."

"I feel like I need ten arms sometimes to multi-task when I'm healing!" Miyah said. "Although since my powers have been reduced with my pregnancy, I sometimes feel like I'm slacking."

"Oh, enjoy your down-time. It won't last much longer!" Junia replied.

"And 'Junia' is derived from the name of the Roman Goddess 'Juno,' who was the wife of Jupiter and the queen of the heavens. She was the protectress of marriage and women, and was also the Goddess of finance."

"Wow, Mother! I didn't know you had such power behind your name!" Miyah exclaimed. "And what about Nona?"

"Well, 'Nona' comes from the Latin word 'nonus' meaning ninth, which refers to the nine months of pregnancy. Nona was also the name of a Roman Goddess of pregnancy. That's probably why I was midwife to so many babies in my lifetime," Nona answered. "But Nona is only a nickname. My given name was Morgan. My middle name was Nona."

"Nona! You always have more secrets in you. How come I never knew that? Morgan. I like that," Miyah contemplated. "It may just solve my 'M' dilemma, because neither Nona or Junia started with 'M.' Morgan June. How does that sound? Then I have both of you. What does the name Morgan mean?"

"Well, I believe it's originally Welch, a Celtic name meaning sea born or circling sea, which is interesting being you want a water birth! It also means great brightness or bright—and I have no doubt that she'll be a bright light in this world!"

"Morgan," Miyah repeated. "I like it."

"I like it too," Junia replied. "And how about the rest of the name? I know you haven't taken Michael's last name yet."

"I'm still trying to figure that out. Again, he's being very patient with me, and of course, would like me to change my last name. But I feel I need to keep my name connection with the bloodline. Nona, you added Tomas' last name before yours, Nona Thornburg Sinclair, and Mom, you added my father's last name before mine, Miyah Maartin Sinclair. I could change my name to Miyah Wilder Sinclair, but then our last names would be different . . .mine Sinclair and the baby's Wilder. Michael wants the baby to have his last name. It's getting difficult."

"Why don't you just add his last name to yours?" Nona suggested. "Miyah Maria Maartin Sinclair Wilder."

"That's a long name!" Miyah exclaimed.

"It is on paper, but you could just go by Miyah Wilder," Junia said. "Nona keeps telling you that big changes are coming. You see for yourself from your travels to France how open everything is about the bloodline. Soon there will be no more bloodline secrets to hold and the Touchstone legacy will no longer be an issue. Your and your daughter's Touchstone calling will be that of continuing your healing work, on whatever level you desire. It'll be so much simpler. We've all been waiting for this time to come. Maybe your name changes are symbolic signs of these times. How do you feel about that?"

"I'm not sure," Miyah replied. "I don't want to let go of what I've known all my life. I don't want to be the one to give up our family naming tradition, yet in another sense it sounds really freeing."

"You wouldn't be giving up our family tradition, Miyah," Nona explained. "Change is inevitable. You just happen to be the generation in its pathway. You're a healer. You'll never give up that family tradition. It'll take a load off your shoulders knowing that our bloodline history, and all the secrets held within it, will be told. Yes, I would think that would be very freeing!"

"Morgan June Sinclair Wilder. I like it," Miyah said. "I'll see what Michael thinks."

"I sense that's not all you wanted to talk about," Nona stated.

"Yes. I have some details about the actual birth to work out. Michael and I have had a lot of discussions about this. I wanted to have the two of you deliver my baby. Heaven knows you've done it hundreds of times during your careers. But Michael points out that you're both, well. . .dead! He doesn't feel comfortable having spirits deliver his child. He has faith in both of you, but it seemed a little too much for him. He wondered if something went wrong, how would we deal with that and all."

"That's a rational human response," Nona replied. "He has a point, even though he underestimates the far reaching abilities of our powers."

"I know. But I also want him to be comfortable. She's his child too. During my pregnancy I've been seeing a midwife, Jonna, who I've worked with many times in my own healing practice. Although she isn't aware of the bloodline, she understands my powers and is a healer herself in many ways. She was trained as a medical doctor, but became frustrated with the system, and learned about herbal remedies and other alternative healing ways. She brings a lot to her midwifery with her physician background and open mind. Her friend, Monica, is an herbalist and a doula, who will be assisting. And my massage therapist, Barbara, will also be there to help me through labor. The three of them work together a lot. They know I want a water birth and that I want to have my baby at home. By at home, I mean here, at RoseVine. I also want both of you here—in physical form, assisting. Is that possible?"

Nona answered. "We can both be here to help, of course. Only you and Michael will be able to see us, though. We can arrange for your team to come behind the veil, to RoseVine, during the birth, but there'll be no follow-up or return visits here. We'll have to erase their memory of place so they won't remember being here."

"I'll be bi-locating to Michael's house afterward, as soon as we're able," Miyah added. "That should take care of any confusion. We can put a spell on Jonna, Monica and Barbara so they think that's where the birth took place and they can check in on me there. It would be easier too, having Michael's address on the birth certificate."

"You know, that's why the big hot tub was installed in the upstairs bathroom shortly before you were born. It was the best thing we ever did to this old house, remodeling that bathroom. Junia insisted on a water birth, too. That's how you came into this world, Miyah, gentle and soothing, not crying and cold. Water birthing isn't a new concept. It's been around for a long time, only many hospitals just let the mother labor in the water and make them get out for the birth."

"The entire process is so much easier on both mother and baby," Junia added. "It'll be OK. We'll make it work. Tell Michael not to worry. You'll be in good hands."

"There is one more thing you're going to have to share with Michael," Nona said.

"He'll only be allowed one more journey with the cedar box for now. He's gone through the healing transformation it offered him, and he's also come to know the secrets the Touchstone holds about our bloodline. His last journey will give him some further information for his writing and a chance to say his farewells to Joshua."

"I knew that would be coming soon," Miyah replied. "It'll be hard on him. He's become almost addicted to those journeys. He knows he hasn't been able to work with the box during my pregnancy because I'm not able to hold the energies for him. That's been tough. Do you know when his last journey will be?"

"Soon," Nona replied. "I'll be there with you to keep the energy levels where they need to be for his safety. Don't worry about that."

"Thank you for doing that. He'll appreciate it too, I'm sure. I'm so happy you both have come here today. I feel more at ease having talked with you about names and about my big day. I'm so ready to have this baby!" Miyah stretched, rubbing her hands along the small of her back. I've been doing a lot of yoga and squats to get in shape for this water birth. It's helped me a lot, but I still get these aches in my back, and my feet sometimes swell. . .I feel like I've been pregnant forever!"

"You won't have to wait much longer, dear," Junia said as she rose and kissed her daughter on the forehead. "We'll see you soon."

"Yes. We'll see you very soon," Nona repeated. "Now we must go. Finish your ritual and go home to your husband. Take a warm bath and relax. Your life will be much busier when you have a baby to take care of. Enjoy these quiet moments while you can."

"I love you both," Miyah said, as Nona and Junia disappeared back into the shadows of the room. "Thank you for your wisdom."

Miyah took Nona's advice. She finished her ritual, blew out the candles and tended to a few more things she needed to do and then "transferred" herself back to Michael's house.

"You've been gone a long time," he said as she walked into his library. "Should I start to worry about you. . .you know. . .being so close to the time and all?"

"You don't need to worry. Nona and Junia will be watching over me to be sure everything is OK. We had a long conversation and got some details worked out. They agree that Jonna, Monica and Barbara should midwife the birth, but they'll still be there, even though the women won't be able to see them."

"And what about the water birth? Honestly Miyah, I don't know about that. It sounds dangerous or something. Couldn't the baby drown?"

"We've been over this, Michael, but let me reassure you again. First of all, water births provide a much less traumatic birth experience for the baby, a much gentler transition from the womb to the outside world, because the warm water resembles the environment the baby has been living inside my body for the past nine months. The warm water also softens the light, colors and noise as the baby leaves my body.

"And secondly, it's going to be so much easier on me. Dealing with the pain of natural childbirth is much easier in the water. The buoyancy of the water is a form of hydrotherapy that'll help with my lower back pain. It's also going to be good for mobility, strength and redistribution of the blood. It's pain management. The squatting posture, rather than having to lay on a bed with my legs up, allows for gravitational pull, which will open and align my pelvis and fully open up the birth canal to allow the baby to descend easily.

"Believe me, Michael, I've been present at plenty of births and have seen the difference in the pain levels for the mothers. The mother in a squatting or sitting position in warm water decreases skin tears and there's usually no episiotomy involved. No cutting. No stitches. And don't worry, there have been no reports of infant deaths due to drowning at birth."

"Isn't squatting for that long of time going to be hard on you?"

"That's why I've been doing so much yoga. It strengthens my body. Remember, I'll be in the water, floating, relaxing in between contractions. I won't be squatting the entire time I'm in labor. Before hospitalized births, and still in many cultures today, women gave birth using the position she found most natural and comfortable – squatting or using a birthing chair."

Miyah added, "Up to the late 1960s, hospital's standard position for childbirth was the mother flat on her back with her feet tied to and held up by stirrups. It's really the worst position for childbirth. It was said that this position originated from a command by French King Louis XIV, back in the 1600s, who wanted to watch one of his mistresses give birth. It made it easier for the doctor and became a trend, so to speak. But most women really hate this position because they have no control over the birth. On your back and with your legs up in the air, you can't move around much and the pressure of the baby's head on your back and tailbone is very painful. The mother has to push her baby against the force of gravity, requiring her to strain and push harder and longer. And in this position, the size of the birth canal can be reduced by up to 30%, so during delivery, the baby is used as a wedge to force open that narrowed birth canal. It's painful and causes unnecessary stress for both the mother and baby.

"Doctors I've talked with said that horizontal births were required with the use of epidurals and anesthesia. Before this horizontal birthing position in Western cultures was adopted, upright birth postures were used. Due to a resurgence of women requesting it, there are now modern birthing chairs and also beds that move into a sitting position."

"I know. I'm sorry to bring it up again. It's just something so foreign to me. I can understand the reasoning behind squatting verses laying flat to give birth. That makes sense. But I really had never heard of a water birth before—not only a water birth, but a home birth and a midwife and doula! No doctor or hospital. No pain medication. You can certainly understand why I'm concerned," Michael lamented.

"My midwife works with the hospital and if there are any concerns she'll have me transferred. She's a licensed doctor, Michael. She was part of a medical clinic and worked in hospitals for years, but she prefers her work as a midwife. That's her practice now. She has a lot of experience. You need to trust her as much as I do. . .and also remember that we have a lot of extra help on our side." She patted him on the arm. "I have a feeling you're going to need more help than I will when the time comes."

Michael put his arms around her and held her close. "I couldn't bear to lose you. That's all," he said. "I love you too much."

"You can never love too much," she said, snuggling into him. "Relax. Everything will be fine. I promise you that."

He looked down into her eyes. "Promise?"

"That's what I said," she replied.

They stood there in each other's arms, savoring the moment.

"I have a surprise for you," Miyah finally said.

"I like surprises. What have you been brewing up?" he asked.

"I'm more the messenger. How would you like to go on another journey with the cedar box?"

"I've been waiting for that," he quickly replied, but then added, "but I didn't think it was possible in your condition because of how much it takes to support me while I'm traveling. I don't want to put you at any risk."

"Don't worry. Nona will be here to help me. She'll be doing all the work. It was her idea."

"In that case, when? How soon? I'm ready anytime. It's been so long."

"Let's plan on tomorrow morning, if that's all right with you," she said.

"Absolutely. I can hardly wait. Thank you, Miyah. I don't know what else to say."

"Thank you is good," she said. "Thank you is always good."

28 The Final Journey

Michael was up early the next morning. He finished some of his writing and then prepared breakfast for Miyah so he'd be ready to travel as soon as possible. At the same time he was a bit nervous, never knowing where he would land, always hoping Joshua would be there and wondering what the purpose of this next journey would be. So much had happened to him in the year since the cedar box had come into his life. It was his connection to an old friend. A friend he had missed these last few months. He was eager to reunite.

Miyah came downstairs refreshed and after a light breakfast they were ready to begin. She suggested they make this journey in Michael's bedroom, the place where he had first experienced the magic of traveling with the box. He agreed, not realizing that Miyah thought it fitting that his first and last journey happened from the same place.

He watched with familiarity as she removed the cedar box from her medicine bag and placed it on the night stand next to his bed. He had pulled the white chair close to the bed from its place by the window for Miyah to sit near him. He remembered those first nights when he watched her sitting in that chair, bathed in moonlight as she repeated mantras for his healing. It seemed so long ago, yet it seemed like yesterday. He laid down on the bed and got comfortable, being sure his Faith Stone was secure around his neck.

Miyah called on Nona to be present and assist in Michael's safe journey and she quickly appeared, nodding a silent greeting to Michael. He smiled at her in return and then turned his attention to the cedar box. Miyah said her ritual prayers and began to hum a familiar, haunting tune. It didn't take long for Michael to see the smooth panel on the box begin to move and take shape . . .to form a landscape that filled his vision and reached out with a rainbow of colors. It grasped ahold of him and pulled him into its mystery.

He went through a shaft of crystallized light and was deposited on a hill overlooking a valley covered with red roses, violets and narcissus. He could smell the scent of sweet herbs and had the feeling he'd been here before. In the distance he saw mountains with snow capped peaks rising over the valley. Michael stood looking down at a village below, with fields of wheat and rice, orchards of apples and other fruits. He was trying to recall why he felt familiar in this place.

"I said you would come back here," a voice behind him said. "Welcome back to Kashmir."

Michael turned to see a very old man, holding onto an olivewood walking staff, sitting on a large rock under a shade tree. He walked toward the man, barely recognizing him. The man was dressed in a white tunic and had long hair and beard. He was thin, but not frail. The wrinkles on his face told of a very old age, yet the man exuded vitality.

"Joshua?" Michael asked.

"Well of course," the man said with a laugh, reaching his hand out to Michael. "Who else would you be expecting!"

"I. . .I didn't recognize you," Michael apologized. "It seems that many years have gone by since we met last."

"Yes. I forget about the time lapse. It's so irrelevant to me. But you are correct. I am well over 100 years old now, and have seen a lot happen in my time. But I'm still here and continue to do my work. It's good to see you, my friend. Let's see. Do you recall where all we have met in our adventures?"

Michael answered, counting on his fingers. "The first time I met with you through the cedar box was in your carpenter's shop. I first met Maryum then, too. The next visit was when you were twelve, carving a cedar box for your mother. The next three times you were in India: Jagannath, Puri; a cave in the Himalayas; then here, in Kashmir. Next I met with you in Scotland. The last time I traveled, Miyah and I were at your wedding feast—and then Miyah and I were honored when you and Maryum attended our wedding in France."

"Ah, very good, Michael," Joshua commended. "I can see these journeys back into ancient times have left an impact on you. I know you have learned much because of these travels."

"More than I ever would have dreamed," Michael replied. "What you've taught me and guided me to find has led me to an altered history of religion I had no idea existed. To say the reality of it is mind-blowing is an understatement. I've been researching and writing and am amazed at how much information is out there already. So many things I would have dismissed before as hearsay, sometimes even blasphemy, but having you as my mentor makes it all so credible.

"I know you've been there, guiding me as I did my research and writing. I could feel your presence. I can't express how grateful I am for all you've shared with me. The legacy of you being a great teacher and prophet stretches beyond the boundaries of time and space and continues to help and heal people today." Michael was feeling emotional as he tried to sum up his gratitude.

"So you understand why all the travels and studies I did when I was a young man were so important. How else could I have gained the knowledge if it wasn't by the collective ancient wisdom of many teachers, sages, gurus, healers and masters. They formed the basis of my own teachings, which I have been able to share with others for over 100 years of my own earthly lifetime, and these teachings have also continued throughout the ages in other forms."

"And you are back here, with the Lost Tribes of Israel."

"Yes. I'm very comfortable here. I no longer feel I have to keep moving and have put down roots here. It's a beautiful place—the mountains, lake, streams, the lushness of the valley, flowers, crops. People here really do consider this to be paradise on earth. Come and let me introduce you to some of my family here." He got up and the two of them started to walk slowly down the hill toward the village.

"Family? Is Maryum here also?" Michael asked.

"No. My beautiful wife and beloved friend, Maryum, left this earth many years ago," he replied with sentiment. "Her life was full, and she also came to be a great teacher, healer and prophet. And, as I believe you discovered while in France, she was well revered for her wisdom, even though it isn't as openly known everywhere. Maryum never really cared about any recognition for her work. Her mission was to heal and to teach. . . the same as my own. Our children grew and prospered and have continued to carry on our family healing traditions—as you well know!"

"Yes," Michael answered. "Miyah."

"Miyah, along with her many cousins and relatives from our bloodline through Sera Tamar, Joseph David and John Martin. Many years after Maryum died, I married again, in Kashmir. My wife, Mirjan—some called her Maryan—and I also had children. But she has also since passed." Joshua watched for Michael's response. "Are you surprised?" he asked.

"Well. . .yes. Just when I think I've learned all your 'secrets' you give me more! So that means there isn't just Miyah's bloodline—the bloodline of you and Maryum, but there is another bloodline of Kashmiri descent!"

"Yes there is and it's important for me to tell you more about them, but first we must talk of other things. Do you remember when I told you that I was leaving writings and messages in places I've traveled to chronicle my life? I also want you to know that traces of my life have been left in other ways. Many of the places I traveled through or taught or healed in have places named after me—like *Yusmarg – Meadow of Jesus*, and *Aishmuqam – Jesus' place of rest*. I'm not telling you this in boast," Joshua added. "Just so you know these places document my life's path."

He continued, "Stories of my life in Kashmir are well documented in several old Persian books including, *Negari-Tan-i-Kashmir*, and *Tarikh-i-Kashmir* written in AD 1413 and tell of my teachings here. There is also a Hindu book written in AD 115 in Sanskrit, called the *Bhavishya Maha Purana*, that gives details of events and my ministry," Joshua related in his gentle tone.

"I doubt if I'll be able to locate any of those books," Michael said. "Can you tell me some of the stories?"

Joshua laughed out loud. "I suppose these details are important to you. It seems so long ago to me. One story relates to repairs to the Throne of Solomon, a temple on the top of Mount Solomon in east Srinagar, that

I helped negotiate. I was 85 years old at the time. On two of the pillars inscriptions were made in Persian about the masons who did the work. But another inscriptions says, '*At this time Yuz Asaf proclaimed his prophethood. Year fifty and four (AD 78). He is Yusu, Prophet of Bani Israel.*' *Yusu* or *Yuz Asaf* is also what they called me. *Yuz* is Hebrew meaning Yeshua and *Asaf* in Hebrew means gatherer. In some places they also called me *Isa Mesih* or Jesus the Messiah.

"A written story that relates to my second marriage was while I was in the Tibetan mountains and I met with my old friend King Shalewahin. He insisted I needed a woman to take care of me and offered to let me choose one from among fifty of his consorts. I told him I didn't want a woman to work for me. If I ever chose a companion again, it would be as my equal, as my beloved Maryum had been. After much consideration I did find such a woman who was gentle and kind. Mirjan was from a shepherd village in the valley of Pahalgam. She was a descendant of Manassé des Bneï's tribe, Israel emigrants of Babylonia. We had several children and descendants. The family of Sahibzada Basharat Saleem, has a genealogical table which traces the ancestry of his family back to me. They called me *Shahzada Nabi Hazrat Yura Asaf.* The structure that houses my tomb is next to Saleem's ancestral home. Family tradition required that the tomb be guarded by the eldest son of each generation. Saleem was one of those eldest sons, and arranged to have the tomb maintained until his death. There is much controversy over my tomb now and it is currently maintained by a Board of Sunni Muslim Directors.

"Muslim?" Michael questioned.

"Yes. This area, when I first came here, was primarily Buddhist, and before that it was a Hindu community. Many of the Lost Tribes had incorporated Buddhist and Hindi traditions into their Jewish culture. Remember, when they came here, Christianity as you know it had not yet developed. Bear with me, because I am talking into the future here, past my lifetime. Buddhism lasted until the 14th century when the valley came under control of Muslim rulers, and later under the influence of the Sikhs. So many of my descendants here through the years, have converted to Islam. It wasn't that difficult for many of them because of some similar beliefs."

"You mean similarities in Islam and Christianity?" Michael asked.

"Muslims believe in one God, translated in Arabic as Allah, the same God of the Christians. The Qur'an describes many biblical prophets and messengers as Muslim: Adam, Noah (Arabic: Nuh), Moses, myself and my apostles. The Qur'an states that they were Muslims because they submitted to God, preached his message and upheld his values. In Surah 3:52 of the Qur'an, it says that my disciples said to me, "We believe in God; and you be our witness that we submit and obey (*wa ashahadu bil-muslim na*)."

"But it seems adverse that your message was of early Christianity and your own Kashmiri descendants didn't stick with that and went instead to become Muslims—especially in today's world, when there are so many Muslim extremists."

"Don't judge all Muslims by the mission of a few," Joshua said sternly. "Imagine judging the Roman Catholics during the Inquisitions as terrorists and saying all Christians were terrorists because of it. You know that wouldn't be true, so don't do injustice to those who are faithful and peaceful Muslims."

Michael's face flushed, as if he had just been scolded.

"You are missing the point, Michael. This is an important part of my story as a true prophet. Jesus is a universal figure throughout many religions, not just Judaism and Christianity. There are 34,000 different sub-groups of Christianity—34,000! And within all those Christian religions, my human life is only biblically referenced in my birth, a short time during my youth and about three years of my adult teachings. But other parts of my life are referenced in Buddhist, Hindu, Gnostic and Islamic holy books and teachings, as well as in ancient history books of Persia, India and other Eastern countries."

Joshua tapped his walking stick on the ground as he spoke to accent his words. "If people could only understand how my life was meant to connect religions instead of seeing them as separate—how the combined story of my life, as told through each of the holy books and ancient scrolls, was meant to unite people, not drive them apart by dogma and power, each saying that their way is the only way to God. I traveled and studied these religions to learn from them, to honor them, and to seed myself within them and their traditions. *I am the link.* I became everyone's prophet, teaching that personal acts involving prayer, self-purification, love, truth, purity of heart and the practice of meditation would bring human beings to God. Sharing, caring, respect. It's that simple. The only way to achieve true peace in the world is by breaking down the barriers of religious boundaries. The mission of my life is the same, no matter which religion tells my story. The end goal is the same. God, *who is within each of us,* is the same."

Joshua halted, as if he were exhausted by his own words. "See, Michael, I, too, get frustrated by the way the world has gone—what it has evolved into in your time. It's so unnecessary. So pointless. . .so destructive."

Michael put his hand on Joshua's thin shoulder. He felt the hopelessness Joshua was experiencing and was surprised to see this side of him.

As if reading his mind, Joshua replied, "I am human, Michael. You forget that. I am a prophet. . .but I am human. . .and now I am also very old."

There was a brief moment of silence. Michael didn't know what to say, how to react. Finally Joshua spoke.

"You talked about your tomb. Where is that?" Michael asked.

"It is called Rozabal, which means the prophet's tomb. It is in Srinagar."

"It seems strange having a conversation about your tomb, when I'm here, talking with you as a live person. But then, I guess nothing should seem strange to me anymore. Especially when it comes to crossing into generational zones of past and present," Michael said.

"I think you will like the village. The word 'Sri' means abundance or wealth and 'Nagar' means city or place—'place of wealth and abundance.' You can see that simply by looking across the valley. There are also many artists here who are known for their handicrafts, weaving of woolen shawls and dress material, and those who do woodcarving. It is truly the promised land."

Joshua stopped talking as they walked. Michael thought maybe he needed a rest. It was a long path from the top of the hill into the village.

But then Joshua said, "I have two things I must show you before your return. Take my arm."

Michael obeyed and they moved within that flash of light he had become accustomed to. When he opened his eyes he was in a place of more modern times—standing under, of all things, a television tower.

"Where are we?" he exclaimed.

"Interesting isn't it?" Joshua responded. This place was called Mari in honor of my mother. Now it is known as Murree. First I must give you some history of why I brought you here." Joshua sat and motioned for Michael to join him.

"As you know, after the crucifixion we left Jerusalem and traveled to Egypt, then on to England and Scotland, among other places. After living and teaching for many years in those lands and being separated from each other at times, we reunited—myself, Maryum and my mother Mariam, and journeyed back to Jerusalem under disguise, for a brief time. Our children, Sera, Joseph and John, were settled with their own families by this time and wished to remain where they were, in France, Italy and England and carry on their healing and teachings. We each had our own missions to fulfill and could always bi-locate to see each other whenever we wanted.

"I was accompanied by several disciples, my mother Mariam, my wife Maryum and my brother Judas Thomas. Thomas is often called my twin because, even though we are 12 years apart, we look much alike, and the name Thomas itself means 'twin' in Aramaic.

"We traveled through Samaria and Galilee to Damascus, Syria. While in Damascus I received a letter from the ruler of Nisibis, also known as Magdonia, a six day journey away, requesting me to come and cure him of an illness. While we were there, around AD 48, King Gopadatta of India requested the King of Magdonia send him a skilled builder to construct a Roman-style palace. I suggested my brother Thomas, who was a mason and a talented carpenter. Thomas and two of my other disciples traveled through Mesopotamia, then went by sea and the Indus River on to Taxila in what is now northern Pakistan. Within six months after arriving, they built the palace.

"The rest of us traveled to Persia, or Iran, and then through Afghanistan and eventually met up with Thomas in Taxila. Here we attended the marriage feast of Abanes, one of our friends who was a former emissary. I should mention that during this time Thomas wrote letters of our travels, and they were sent by an emissary from India to Edessa (Turkey), to Jerusalem and on to Rome. The Acts of Thomas was complied and used, along with the Gospel of Thomas, by all the Christian Churches until the decree of Pope Gelasius, who in AD 495 declared Thomas' writings heretical because they rejected the virgin birth concept, and thus my divinity. The writings also established my physical presence in Taxila, which is now Pakistan, and also here in Kashmir long after the crucifixion and supposed resurrection. They certainly couldn't have that known publicly!

"With Thomas' building work completed we continued our journey and traveled 45 miles from Taxila to this place, in what is now called Murree. Many years had passed since we had begun our journey, and it was very hard on my mother. Even though she was aging, she insisted on going to Kashmir—the land of the Lost Tribes of Israel—The Promised Land. She died before we reached our final destination. It was her time. We buried her in an east-to-west direction in the Jewish burial tradition, here at Pindi Point.

"She rests on this hilltop, on the southern slopes of the Western Himalayan foothills, with a beautiful view ascending to the northeast, toward Kashmir. The tomb became known as '*Mai Mari da Asthan—the resting place of Mother Mary,*' and has been respected by many religions. Hindus came to pray at her tomb, and Muslims, who came into the area later, recognizing that the tomb was of a Jew or a Christian of the Holy Book, also began to honor her and make offerings here. This has continued for generations."

"Until modern civilization came in and completely disrespected the burial site," Michael interjected.

"Yes. In 1898 a defense tower was built at the site for British troops garrisoned on the Afghan frontier. In 1916, the British decided that for security reasons they had to demolish Mother Mary's tomb to keep people from visiting it. The people protested and after an engineer of the British garrison was fatally injured in a tower accident, the British took it as a sign of divine intervention and gave up. In the 1950s the tomb was repaired, and when the defense tower was obsolete and destroyed, this television tower was erected in its place."

"A television tower!" Michael exclaimed. "It seems so disrespectful. Why don't they at least move the tomb into a safer and more respectable place?"

"That would be impossible. It would outrage the people here. They have been caring for this grave, generation after generation, for almost 2,000 years. Prayers and offerings have been made to Mother Mary at this site throughout the ages to bring relief in times of drought. . .and the rains have come."

"I guess you could look at it as a giant erector set headstone, reaching into the heavens. . ." Michael said, looking up the tower. "A mix of ancient and modern combined. At least people wanting to visit her grave won't have any trouble finding it." He was trying to find a positive to the situation.

"Michael. Look at it as a uniting of religions. . .Jewish, Christian, Hindu, Muslim. All have come here to honor her gravesite. Isn't that beautiful? Isn't that what we are trying to do in our teaching? Unite. My mother has accomplished that in her death, in a simple tomb on the top of a hill overlooking the land she so wanted to see. . .the land of the Lost Tribes of Israel. She is bringing religions together as they come to honor her at this grave site."

"Yes. That's a wonderful thought. If only that concept could grow. We'd have a peaceful world, with no more war. I'm glad she at least made it to Kashmir before she died," Michael said.

"Well, she didn't quite reach Kashmir. We are actually in Pakistan, but she did have a view of Kashmir from here, from this hilltop before she died. That made her very happy. That is why she is buried here."

Joshua bent down and picked up three different sized stones and carefully balanced them, one upon another, as a small shrine to honor his mother. Michael did the same.

"You know it's just her body that was buried here. Her spirit is what remains with us and that never dies," Joshua said to Michael. "We may feel sorrow at death, but must rejoice in knowing that life continues in other forms and other dimensions. You have learned this with Nona and Junia."

"And with you. . ." Michael added.

"Yes. And with me," Joshua nodded at his pupil, holding out his arm, indicating it was time to travel on. Michael linked his arm with Joshua's and again they vanished into thin air.

This time they landed inside a rectangular cement structure, underground. A musty aroma filled the air.

"What is this place?" Michael asked, feeling a bit claustrophobic.

"We're in my tomb," Joshua answered.

His reply sent shivers up and down Michael's spine.

"What. . .?" Michael began.

"There is much controversy in your day regarding this place," Joshua explained. "You would most likely not be allowed to travel to Srinagar now, with the political and military problems Kashmir is experiencing. But I wanted to show this to you, so you can see for yourself and know it is so."

Michael observed a small entrance hall that led to a gallery which surrounded an inner chamber. He followed Joshua as they entered this chamber. On the left side there was a wooden tablet with an inscription that said *"Ziarat Yuza Asaf Khanyar."* It had been presented by the Department of Archaeology of the state of Kashmir. The word *ziarat* referred to Jesus as a saint. The rest of the inscription told of him coming to Kashmir centuries ago and preaching the "truth."

There were two tombstones enclosed by wooden framework on the floor of the inner chamber. Joshua pointed to the largest tombstone, at the furthest end of the chamber.

"That's where they say my grave is," he said nonchalantly. "The other grave, near the entrance is a 15th century Muslim saint, Seyed Nasir-ud-Din Rizvi, who was a devotee of mine and requested to be buried next to me."

Michael shivered. This was almost too eerie for him.

Joshua then pointed to something behind the tomb, in the northeast corner of the chamber. A stone block which had been used for burning candles, revealed carvings of human-size footprints with markings of crucifixion wounds on each of the feet.

"The footprints had been completely covered in candle wax from people making offerings, until a few years ago in your time when the wax was cleaned away. They also found a crucifix and a rosary," Joshua explained.

"Do you come here often?" Michael tried to lighten his mood in this dark place.

Joshua smiled. "As with my mother's tomb, people of many different denominations have visited here—Christian priests, Hindu Brahmins, Buddhist monks, heads of states, among them. The people of Kashmir who visit call it the tomb of *Hazrat Yuz Asaf of the Nabi Sahib*, Honorable Jesus of the Lord Prophet, or the *Shahzada Nabi*, the Prince Prophet, or sometimes the tomb of *Hazrat Isa Sahib*, the Honorable Master Jesus.

"But that is not really the true tomb. It is situated north to south, in Muslim burial fashion, like the graves in the cemetery behind the building. My real crypt lies below." Joshua reached out for Michael's arm and in a flash they were underneath the chamber.

"See, the true grave lies aligned to the east-west in Jewish burial tradition," Joshua said, stretching out his hand to make his point. "There used to be a stairway from the outside, but that has been closed."

Michael noticed light streaming through a small window, falling directly onto the tomb. He was compelled to reach out and touch the coffin. Placing his hand on the stone, in the spot where the window light touched the tomb, he felt a warm sensation, almost a tingling feeling on the palm of his hand and fingertips. He had expected the stone to be cold, not warm and comforting.

He suddenly became conscious of the fact that this is where Joshua actually took his last breath of life. He said his tomb had been placed on the very spot where he had died. Michael realized how surreal his situation was at that moment. Here he was in current time, underground, looking at a burial crypt containing the actual bones of Joshua. . .Jesus. . .in Kashmir, no less. Yet he was talking with the very person who was buried there—a 100+ year-old Joshua, who died almost 2,000 years ago! He quickly pulled his hand away and was beginning to feel dizzy trying to comprehend it all.

"Thank you for bringing me here," Michael said. "I don't want to be ungrateful, but can we leave now? I mean, I don't want to go back yet. I'd just like to get out of here."

"I understand." Joshua took his hand, and they were gone in a flash of light.

Michael slowly opened his eyes, hoping he was still in the presence of Joshua and hadn't been sent home. He was relieved to find himself, along with Joshua on the banks of the lake, across from the city.

"It's been a long session for us this time," Joshua said. "I have enjoyed your visits. I won't be on this earth much longer and I must tell you that this may be your last journey to see me in this manner."

Michael was dismayed and didn't want to hear this news, but at the same time he knew it would have to end at some point. He simply nodded his head in acknowledgement.

"My work with you through the cedar box is complete. You are healed and you have learned much about my life during these travels. Now you must go home and fulfill the promise you made to Miyah when she agreed to heal you."

"Promise?" Michael said. He never was quite clear of this promise he had made.

"Yes Michael. You are my messenger. Your mission is to take all of this information you have been given and write it for the world to read. Much is to be revealed. Yes, it has all been presented in one way or another over the years. Like I told you before, we have been sending messengers throughout the ages who have revealed our truths through art, books, films, and also through spiritual teachers. None of what you have learned is completely unknown. But you must put it all together. That is how you will fulfill your promise. To take all of these threads of information, of history, of truth, of ancient wisdom and weave them into a tapestry that can be understood, that can be read and accepted. It may bring about challenges and changes, Michael, but your world is in dire need of change right now."

"I don't know if I'm capable of such a huge undertaking," Michael admitted. "I don't know if I can do justice to what you want me to do."

"All you need to do is have faith," Joshua said. He reached out and lifted Michael's Faith Stone on his necklace. "If you are ever in doubt, remember this. Remember this, and think of me. I, and many others, will be there to help you. Don't doubt. Believe, my friend. Just believe."

"I'll do my best," Michael said. "For you I'll do anything."

"Now I must leave you. I have a celebration to attend. I would invite you, but I think it is time for you to return to your world. You have a baby coming soon. Congratulations! Another generation of my bloodline. . .and the first of yours. I have enjoyed our visits, Michael, and remember that I will always be there when you need me."

Joshua hugged Michael. "I love you son," he said and Michael couldn't hold back his tears. "I love you too," he sobbed.

As Joshua turned to walk away, Michael called after him. "What is the celebration?"

"It's my birthday. I'm 125-years-old!"

Before Michael could wish him a happy birthday, he felt himself whirling into that familiar cedar dizziness with colors and light swirling around him, and in a short time he was back in his own room, resting on his bed. He lay there in silence for some time before he opened his eyes. He felt so much emotion, he didn't know how to handle it. When he finally opened his eyes, Miyah was there at his side. Nona was standing over her, but soon disappeared, greeting his return with a wave of her hand.

"Miyah," he said tenderly, reaching out his hand to take hers. "You know what a journey I've been on, don't you?"

She simply nodded her head.

"It's my last time isn't it? He said it was my last time." Then he somberly added, "He's getting ready to die, isn't he?"

"Yes, Michael. It wasn't long after you visited with him, maybe a few months. But he knew then, and was prepared. He was ready to leave the earth and journey on to his next mission. I have an entry in the diary I want to read to you, if you are clear enough from your re-entry to listen to it."

"Yes, please do," he answered, not bothering to sit up. Miyah turned to the marked pages in her book and began to read.

I have received a letter from my great uncle Judas Thomas, which has traveled for nearly a year to get to me. It brings sorrowful news of the death of my grandfather, Yeshua. This is what Thomas said: - "Yeshua, Yuz Asaf, as we speak of him in this land of Kashmir, called for me, his faithful brother and disciple. I am known as Ba`bad here, and I went to him on his deathbed to hear his last wishes. He said to me, 'My time for departing from this world has come. Carry on your teaching and healing duties properly, my dear brother and friend, and turn not back from truth. Meditate and say your prayers of faith. Do not forget that love is the most powerful of all. Embrace honesty, love one another and all that is around you, and you will be at peace.'

He instructed me in the matters of his last requests, directing me to prepare a tomb for him, placed in the exact spot where he died. Then I helped position him with his head toward the east, and stretching his legs toward the west, he gasped his last breath of air. As he left his earthly body, I saw his spirit peacefully elevate toward the light. It was a beautiful sight to behold. Yeshua's life was long and fruitful. He traveled much, learned much and taught much. He healed and was himself healed. He loved and was himself loved. His life was good. His earthly body now rests in peace.

We have many followers here now to carry on Yeshua's teachings, so I will soon leave this place and travel back to Taxila, then to the mouth of the Indus River. From there I will sail with intentions of landing in the southern tip of India and along the western and eastern coastlines to continue my missionary work. Yeshua was so fond of that land, and I am anxious to continue his gospel of love, truth, and purity of heart to the people. I am also an old man, but I must continue Yeshua's work until I too, take my last breath on this earth.

As he died, Yeshua whispered one last message for me to tell his family and followers. He said not to be sorrowful for him upon his death, but to rejoice with him and to celebrate his long and fruitful life. He lived and loved well and taught the truth as he was taught, and now. . .he peacefully rests as God intended." -

29 The Next Generation

With the nursery set up at Michael's house, ready for the new arrival, Miyah was spending time at RoseVine preparing for the birth of her baby. She wanted everything to be in order when the time came. The large bathroom with the jacuzzi tub was scrubbed spotless and she brought in a favorite lamp to set a more calming, subdued mood and avoid the harshness of an overhead light fixture. She wanted music, something soothing, yet meditative, so she chose a pensive chanting CD by Benedictine monks, and a selection of chanted mantras by Krishna Das. A CD player was placed on a cabinet in the corner of the bathroom with a vase for fresh flowers. She wanted flowers. She also brought in mixtures of herbs made into teas that would help ease the pain of her labor, and if need be, help speed the process along. She set a water pitcher and glasses in the room. She also wanted there to be plenty of juice and food in the kitchen for those who were helping, in case the labor was long.

Miyah knew that Jonna, her midwife, would be bringing everything needed for the baby after the birth, but she made sure there was an area prepared for her to set up what she needed. She had freshly laundered towels and had prepared the bedroom that adjoined the bathroom. She felt confident she had thought of everything.

Now she turned her attention to her family's medicine pouch. It was time to add her own signature to the bag, before her daughter, the next generation, was born. Her mother, many years ago, had told her of the significance of each of the patches and symbols on the bag. Miyah admired the two small roses, one red and one pink, that Junia had embroidered in a corner of the bag. The rose was a feminine symbol of hope, joy and an expression of beauty and grace. She said the pink blossom was for happiness, gentleness and sweetness and the red blossom was a symbol of martyrdom—a sign of the family's Touchstone destiny. Nona's addition to the medicine bag was a small piece of mirror, carefully tucked into the fabric and sewn so there were no sharp edges.

"This is so we always remember to stop and reflect on what our purpose is in the world," she had said. "And to remember that everyone you meet is a mirror image of yourself. What you see in them, is also a part of yourself." Miyah understood this now, more than ever.

She emptied the contents of the medicine bag onto a table in the library. It was the first time she could remember when everything was emptied from the bag—the cedar box with its supply of essential oils and stones, the linen pouch containing her diary, little bags with a variety of crystals and other stones used in her rituals, sage for smudging and other amulets. Wrapped at the bottom of the bag was the larger stone with the lines on it that resembled those of her own palm.

She shook out the bag and held it up to the light. She loved its texture and smell. Holding it to her nose she breathed in aromas of ancient healing oils, trace odors of distance campfires, and the more recent smells of her own magic potions. She turned the fabric of the bag over in her hands, admiring the warm colors of the earth that blended with the bright and bold embroidered symbols, little bells, tiny mirrors, and gemstones that had been embedded into the cloth. Again, she remembered that special day when she was given the bag and told that whenever love is woven into the texture of life, it never wears out.

Miyah had spent many days trying to decide what her symbol should be. She finally sat down and began to make a sketch, surprising herself at what she drew. Undoubtedly influenced by her trip to France and all of the Mary Magdalene imagery they encountered, she found herself drawing a double M, but realized it wasn't only symbolic of Mary Magdalene. The double M also represented Miyah and Michael. She felt their marriage was the beginning of the change Nona kept talking about. Their union marked the beginning of a generation of new Touchstone carriers.

She designed two bold M's, one upright, the other upside down, which formed a diamond in the center, representing their child, and two half diamonds on each side for Michael and herself. She also knew that diamond shapes are symbolic of the sacred union. The blade and the chalice were also honored within her design with two X's forming, and related to Cathar significance as an emblem of enlightenment and an acknowledgment of the bloodline. Wrapped around the M's were vines and roses, symbolic of RoseVine, her family home, illustrating the connection to the vine—the bloodline of Joshua and Maryum. At the top, the vines formed into a heart, representing the love that holds families together in life, as well as in death.

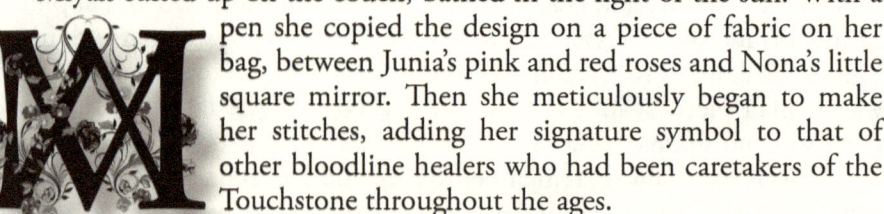

Miyah curled up on the couch, bathed in the light of the sun. With a pen she copied the design on a piece of fabric on her bag, between Junia's pink and red roses and Nona's little square mirror. Then she meticulously began to make her stitches, adding her signature symbol to that of other bloodline healers who had been caretakers of the Touchstone throughout the ages.

~~~~~~

Miyah knew the time was near. She had been having lower back pain for a couple of days. Not wanting to alarm Michael, she dealt with it in her own way—stretching, yoga, walking and deep breathing. Now labor had started, quick and hard.

"Wake up Michael. It's time for this baby to come."

Michael shot out of bed like a cannon. He helped Miyah up and asked what he should do.

"Write a note to Elizabeth and put it on the table. Tell her we went to meet with the midwife, and we'll call her later, so she doesn't worry. And then call Jonna. Her number is on the fridge. Ask her to meet us at RoseVine. She has instruction."

Michael pulled on his trousers and rushed downstairs. "Nona, I hope you are here," he said out loud. "I think I'm not going to be much good at this."

"Don't worry, Michael. I'm taking good care of her," he heard a voice in his head reply. It still didn't calm him.

Rushing back to Miyah, he found her leaning over a chair breathing through a labor pain.

"How far apart are they?" he asked.

When she was able to speak, she told him they were just a few minutes apart and she needed to get into the water to ease her labor pain.

"Jeez, Miyah, why didn't you tell me you were laboring all night. I could have done something, helped you through breathing, just done something."

"Like worry?" she quickly said. "It's OK, Michael. Nona has been here with me. I woke you when I needed you. Are you ready to go?"

He quickly slipped on a T-shirt, grabbed his bag that contained swimming trunks and a toothbrush, and slipped into his sandals.

"Do we need anything else?" he asked.

"Just my medicine bag," she replied. "Everything else is already there and ready."

Michael grabbed the bag off its hook on the wall and took Miyah's arm. She nodded to Nona, and in a flash they were gone, re-materializing at RoseVine where Junia was waiting for them.

While Junia prepared the jacuzzi tub, Michael paced the floor, watching for the delivery team, Jonna, Monica and Barbara to arrive. He opened the door the minute they stepped out of the cab, and welcomed them inside, rushing them upstairs to the bedroom and connecting bathroom where the birth would take place. Miyah had slipped into a warm bathrobe and seemed to be doing all right. Michael was a mess. He went out on the porch to get some fresh air, thinking he might get sick.

"Calm down," Junia said to him, appearing at his side.

"Shouldn't you be upstairs with her?" Michael asked anxiously.

"She's in good hands. Don't be so worried," Junia reached over and put her hand on his shoulder. As if a page had been turned, Michael felt his anxiety disappear. He knew it was Junia's healing touch.

"So they've assigned you to me," he said, trying for a faint laugh.

"Something like that," she replied. "I remember soothing you with mini-healings when you were a little boy, playing with Miyah. Once you fell out of a tree in your backyard. Another time you skinned your knee, riding too fast on your bike. You were always showing off. Your mother had her hands full with you."

Michael jerked his head around and looked into her eyes. He suddenly remembered all those years of his childhood when Junia and his mother, Kat, were friends. Now Junia seemed like an old, familiar friend. He appreciated that she was here with him now. She had always been family.

Meanwhile, Jonna checked Miyah to see how far she had dilated. Miyah had previously prepared her toolbox of oils for the women to use and Barbara was sorting through the fragrant bottles to use in massage and grounding work before the very hard labor began. Monica wound Miyah's curly hair on top of her head to keep her cooler, as she explained the properties of the oils Barbara was choosing.

"Of course, you already know this, but we find it's always good to explain as we go along—it also gets your mind off of what's happening to your body right now!" She continued, "One of the oils Barbara is going to use is thyme. This plant asks what you're open to, so it will know where you are spiritually. We all know the answer to that, but it's a necessary place to start in balancing emotions. Thyme also reduces stress, relieves anxiety and energizes the body."

Using almond oil as a base, Barbara began massaging, starting at Miyah's feet in a grounding ritual, asking the universe to make this an easy birth, and to be sure Miyah's mind stayed totally present in order to cope with her physical reality during this time.

Monica opened the bottles and handed Barbara other oils, explaining their use, as Barbara continued her massage. "We're also using spruce, which helps open and release any emotional blocks you might have and create balance; white fir, to create feelings of empowerment and anchoring; and ylang ylang to increase relaxation and restore your equilibrium. And I'm using a blend of lavender, sage and jasmine to open the uterus and facilitate birth."

"Hmm. It smells so wonderful," Miyah whispered, enjoying the foot and leg massage.

"Do you mind adding some Angelica oil?" she asked. "I know it helps bring memories back to the point of origin before trauma, and I'm sure I'm going to need that before I'm finished here!"

"Of course," Monica said, looking through the box of oils. "Angelica also releases negative feelings and offers protection—it's sometimes called the Oil of Angels," she added.

"Yes, I know," Miyah smiled and closed her eyes, completely enjoying being pampered in this way. Feeling Barbara's healing fingers massaging her tense body she started to relax. . .until suddenly her labor began to get more intense. Her body arched with sharp, shooting pain.

"It looks like my spa treatment is over," she lamented, breathing through the pain. "Thank you so much. It's such a nice, gentle way to begin to work through this process. Don't go away. I'm sure I'll have time yet for more massaging!"

"That's why we're here," Barbara replied. "Don't worry. I'll know when you need me. . .and where!" She put her hands on Miyah's shoulders, moving her fingers in gentle circles as Jonna checked her dilation again. It was time for Miyah to get into the tub to ease her labor. She took off her robe and slipped into the warm water, leaning back so the water almost reached her shoulders. Feeling the gentle waves of water made her more comfortable. Nona had previously turned on the lamp and flipped the light switch off. Music was playing from the CD player and a couple of candles laced with lavender oil had been lit. Monica took over in her doula role and helped ease Miyah through her breathing during the pain episodes, while Barbara continued to massage her shoulders and back. Jonna unpacked her doctor bag of clamps, scissors, and other necessities she would need when the baby arrived.

Now that Michael had calmed down, Junia brought him back upstairs where he changed into his swimming trunks and went in by Miyah to be present during the birth. At first he was a bit embarrassed to come into a room of four women with his wife naked in the tub, but when he saw that being naked was the last thing Miyah cared about, he got over it. Barbara moved, motioned for Michael to take her place, behind Miyah.

"What should I do?" he asked.

"Just sit behind her on the rim of the tub and hold her under the arms, yes, like that. It'll give her support and lessen her straining," Barbara instructed. "Give her water when she needs it. You're her servant right now. Massage her back. Do whatever she needs you to do. She'll let you know."

Jonna could see the concern in Michael's face as he looked at his wife in the pool of water. Her eyes connected with his and she softly said, "I sense you're a bit nervous about this type of birth." She didn't wait for him to answer. "There are many things we're monitoring here—the constant temperature of the water, for one. We'll be sure to keep only a three degree window variance between the temperate inside the mother, 99 degrees, to that of tub water." Even though he was knee deep in the tub as he sat behind Miyah, Michael reached down and felt the warm water with his hand. He nodded his understanding of what Jonna had just told him.

"One of your jobs will be to keep an eye on the thermometer for us, OK?" Jonna pointed to the thermometer bobbing in the water on the edge of the tub.

"I can do that, "Michael agreed, glad to have assignments.

Jonna continued, "Part of the reason water birthing is usually easier is because the pressure inside Mom is different than atmospheric, or outside, pressure. The water pressure is actually closer to where the baby has been living all these months, making the transition easier for the baby."

"I told him not to worry about the baby drowning in the water," Miyah said. "But I'm sure he's still concerned about that." She squeezed his hand.

Jonna smiled. "That's usually the first thing people ask me when they want to know about water births. But you needn't worry. A baby takes the first breath, which sounds more like a gasp, because its central nervous system is reacting to the sudden change in temperature and environment. With the baby birthing into the water—the same temperature as Mommy's womb, that shock isn't there. It's not until we actually take the baby out of the water, into the atmospheric pressure and change in temperature we just talked about, that her system reacts and she begins to breathe. Of course, we'll get her out of the water within seconds. Then we place the baby skin-to-skin against Mommy to keep her warm, and cover her with a soft towel. Does that help ease your worries?" she asked.

"It really does help to hear the scientific reasoning behind it," he replied. "Thanks for explaining." He could feel Miyah's body begin to tense and tightened his arm grip around her.

Miyah was experiencing another labor pain and with Michael supporting her from behind, she began to roll her body back and forth in the water. She closed her eyes and started to moan with the music. It put her into a trance-like state as she worked through the pain.

Between contractions over the next couple of hours they talked, chanted together and even sang songs. At one point Miyah's contractions seemed to have stalled and Barbara used a mixture of geranium and jasmine, drizzling it on her stomach and massaging in a clockwise motion to stimulate the uterus to contract. Miyah was so ready to have this baby.

Then the pain became intense. Miyah moved into a squatting position with Michael holding her, his legs on each side of her for support. Nona and Junia were nearby, watching the familiar scene, only this time they were not the doctors. They were the family. With Monica coaching Miyah to breathe and Barbara massaging her hands, Jonna took charge of the birthing.

About that time, Michael noticed the cedar box on the vanity. He tried not to look at it, knowing he had no willpower when it came to its beckoning. He began to see flashes of light, and didn't know if he should let go of Miyah or what.

"God, what if I bi-locate to some other place and she comes with me in this stage of birth?" he thought. "That would be disastrous!"

He closed his eyes, avoiding looking at the box. But a light seemed to penetrate his mind and in came the moans and screams of hundreds of women—women of the bloodline giving birth throughout the ages. He heard wailing, yelling and hysterical laughter, followed by the cries of hundreds of babies who had been birthed by these women. He felt like he was in a torture chamber with these screams of pain echoing from wall to wall. Junia looked up and realized what was happening. She stepped in front of the cedar box, breaking its hold. The light and noise disappeared and Michael's body relaxed, almost slumping, until he opened his eyes and realized where he was and what was transpiring. He straightened his posture and regained his grip on Miyah's arms, as she loudly moaned in her own pain.

Miyah's doula was ardently coaching her now.

"Take a long, deep breath, now exhale and push. . .push. . .that's right. Again. Breathe, exhale and push. . .good Miyah. . .that's right. You can do it. Once more, breathe, exhale. . .push!"

It seemed like the pain would never end when Miyah heard the midwife say, "Her head is coming, I can see it." Taking another deep breath and exhaling one last, long, hard push. She heard the midwife announce, "She's here, Miyah, she's here. Reach down and pull out your baby!"

Miyah reached down into the water between her legs and felt her baby's head. She literally pulled her baby out the rest of the way from inside her own body. She lifted the slippery, little body out of the water and cradled the baby in her arms, holding her closely against her own naked chest.

Miyah cried out, "Look at her. She's so beautiful. Look at all that hair. She's so beautiful!"

Jonna quickly placed a towel over the baby to keep her warm and proceeded to clear the baby's mouth and passages of amniotic fluid, while Barbara stimulated the baby's breathing by gently rubbing the bottom of her feet.

"She seems too content to cry," Michael said. "Does she have to cry? She's breathing, isn't she?"

"Oh, we want her to cry a little. It clears her lungs of fluid," Barbara replied.

Miyah and Michael held their breath until that small, innocent cry came out, announcing that their daughter had indeed arrived and was now in charge of everyone around her. Michael bent down and cradled his wife and infant in his arms and they both shed tears of joy. Nona and Junia stood by, arms around each other, just as emotional to see a new generation of their bloodline born into this world. Miyah looked up at them with pride.

Several minutes passed as Jonna, Monica and Barbara stepped back to let the couple revel in the miracle of their new daughter.

"Do you want to cut the umbilical cord?" Jonna finally asked Michael.

"Me? Cut the cord?" he responded with apprehension.

Miyah looked at him. "Go ahead," she said. "It's a very special moment."

"I know, but it's her lifeline to you. It seems pretty scary."

"It's not at all scary," Jonna said, "It *was* her lifeline, but now, once the umbilical cord is cut, a number of necessary changes will occur in your baby's lungs and circulatory system. The amniotic fluid will drain, or be absorbed from the respiratory system, and her lungs will inflate, moving oxygen into the bloodstream. By exhaling, carbon dioxide will be removed from her lungs."

Michael reached over and took the scissors from Monica.

"Just cut between the clamps," she instructed.

He opened the scissors, took a deep breath, and cut through the tube that held the veins that had supported his baby inside her mother for the past nine months.

"That felt so weird," he said, handing the scissors back. "Like cutting through the consistency of a tube of thick string cheese." Everyone laughed.

"Can I take your baby for a few minutes, Mommy? I want to clean her up and check her over," Barbara said, gently reaching for the newborn.

"And I have some work to do here with you too," Jonna added, gently massaging so all of the placenta would pass.

"Some people see the placenta as a special part of the birth, since it has been the child's life support for so many months," Barbara noted.

"I'd like to see it," Miyah said. Michael made a face at her.

"Really?" he asked.

"In some cultures, parents plant a tree along with the placenta in honor of the child's birth," Jonna added.

"I like that idea," Miyah replied.

"And in some cultures the placenta is ceremoniously eaten by the newborn's family. In fact, the great majority of animals do this naturally for nutrition," Monica noted.

"OK, let's just plant a tree," Michael quickly responded. "We'll pass on the other."

"Let's get you out of the tub, Miyah, so you can get situated and nurse your baby. We want to be sure she can suckle well. Daddy can hold the baby while you get settled in your bed."

While the trio of women tended to Miyah, Michael clumsily held his newborn daughter in his arms. He put his finger next to her tiny hands and pushed open the blanket to count all her toes. He looked adoringly into her wrinkled face. She opened her dark eyes and seemed to look right at him.

"You are going to be so loved," he said to her. "You just can't imagine how much love there is in this family. Welcome to the world, little one. Welcome into our lives."

When Miyah was situated in her bed and all the medical necessities were taken care of, Michael brought the baby to her. She took her daughter into her arms and snuggled her to her breast. Miyah couldn't take her eyes off her baby.

"Look what we did, Michael," she said. "Look what we made. She's so beautiful."

Michael sat on the bed with his arm around her, staring at their baby. He brushed some damp curls from Miyah's face and watched her first attempt at nursing their baby as this newborn instinctively opened her tiny mouth and suckled her first mother's milk.

"You are so beautiful," he said. "Do you know that you're glowing? I'm so proud of you and all you went through. I couldn't have done it. I couldn't have stood the pain. I'd have had to have a shot or some pills or something. You're so amazing." His emotion was matched by hers and they, together as a family, reveled in the miracle of birth.

"I don't mean to interrupt, but we have a little gift for you," Barbara announced, handing Miyah a neatly ribboned box.

"Seriously? You've done so much already, I didn't expect a gift," Miyah replied.

"We know," Barbara said. "It's some things for the baby. Who can resist all the cute little pink things?"

Miyah opened the box and took out a soft, fluffy, pink blanket with rose designs in the corners. There were also a couple of little sleepers and a sweet, little pink dress with matching bonnet. Tucked in the side of the box were two bottles of essential oils.

"They're frankincense and myrrh," Monica offered. "Use them on the umbilical cord until it falls off. They're good antibacterial, antiseptic and anti-inflammatory oils."

"So the wisemen mentioned in the Bible giving frankincense and myrrh had practical meaning," Michael said. "I didn't know that."

"Myrrh is also good to avoid stretch marks," Monica laughed. "At least it worked for me!"

"Come here. . ." Miyah said, reaching out to give them a group hug.

"You're awesome," Michael said. "I can't thank you enough. I mean it."

"It was our pleasure," Barbara said. "We've all worked with this young lady through the years, and know and appreciate all the healing work she's done for so many people. We're happy to be here for her on this special day. Congratulations to both of you."

"Now it's time to give you some privacy," Jonna said, as they closed the door and went about their business to clean the tub and pack up their equipment.

"We'll see you tomorrow, and don't hesitate to call any of us if you have concerns," Barbara added. Jonna planned on staying the night to keep watch over Miyah and the baby to be sure there were no complications.

"I'm sure I'll be fine," Miyah thanked them again, and then turned to Michael.

"And thank you for being there with me, Michael. It meant a lot to me. I know it made you queasy."

"Of course. I wanted to be with you, although I'm afraid I wasn't much help. I could see Junia there, ready to zap me away if I passed out on top of you or something! But I really felt comforted that both Junia and Nona were there. It's interesting that your doulas and midwife couldn't see them. Those three women were so amazing."

"Oh, I'm sure they sensed their presence. They're very intuitive women. The next time they see me, we'll be in your house. Nona has put a spell on each of them, so they won't know it's a different location. Your address will be on the baby's birth certificate as place of birth. Nona will transfer us there in a little bit. Junia will see to it that everything is taken care of here and Jonna will sleep in the nursery to be sure everything is OK medically for a day or so."

"Speaking of Nona and Junia," Michael said. "Where are they? I thought for sure they'd be right here, oohing and aahing over their grandbaby."

"I think they realize how important a moment this is for us and are giving us our space. We'll see plenty of them, I'm sure. Right now, I just want you here next to me and our daughter."

"I can't believe you're doing so well after what you just went through. I didn't expect that."

"That's because I didn't have any anesthesia or drugs. A lot of times when you see women who are so worn out after childbirth, it's because of the effects of the drugs."

"You're incredible," he repeated, looking at her lovingly.

"Now our work is really going to begin," she said. "Michael, I know you said that whatever I decided to name her was all right with you. But I want to be sure you're OK with the name I've chosen before we put it on paper. We've talked about so many different names. So, how do you feel about Morgan June Sinclair Wilder. Morgan for Nona, that's her real name, June for my mother, Sinclair—my last name, and your last name, Wilder. And I do want to change my married name to Wilder, Sinclair-Wilder."

"Morgan. I like it," Michael replied. "I'm glad you want to add Wilder. I didn't want to put any pressure on you, but I'm very happy about that." He leaned over and gently kissed her on the forehead.

They sat in silence for a few minutes, staring at the miniature bundle in Miyah's arms. Each little movement she made brought smiles to their faces. It was as if the world stood still and the only thing in the entire universe was that tiny baby, that minutes old infant, who already knew how to captivate her world.

"There is something more we need to check," Miyah said, remembering that the first sign of a child of the bloodline having the "gift" of healing was through the lines on the palm of her hands. She carefully unwrapped her baby's tiny hand from the beneath the blanket and uncurled her little fingers. She turned the baby's hand palm up and placing her own hand next to Morgan's, she slowly began to trace the lines on her baby's palm.

"What are you doing?" Michael asked as he watched.

"I'm checking to see if she has the M markings that match the lines on my hand—the Touchstone markings." Miyah slowly concentrated on her task. Both Nona and Junia were watching, leaning in from the shadows, waiting to hear the verdict.

"Do they match?" Michael anxiously asked, straining over her shoulder.

"Do your palms match?

"Is she. . .?"

The Touchstone Diary
Book II

Bloodlines and Promises

1 Living Between the Worlds

Morgan June Sinclair Wilder was a special child. The signs were clearly marked on the palm of her hand. The same life lines that her mother, Miyah, her grandmother, Junia and great-grandmother, Nona, along with other women of the bloodline before her, had inherited. Those of a healer. As if being born into a generational family of healers wasn't enough, the child seemed to have known instinctively the day she was born, that she had a big mission to fulfill.

The years passed quickly as Morgan grew from a cuddly infant to an energetic toddler. Miyah began teaching her, almost from birth, about the mystical side of life. Both Miyah and Michael gave their daughter an early appreciation of nature and the importance of honoring all living creatures. They spent a lot of time in forests and special gardens studying herbs, flowers and the medicinal properties of plants. Learning was a game to Morgan and it came easy, as if she already knew it all from another lifetime.

Oftentimes her grandmothers, Junia and Nona, appeared to the child in spirit form and, in her innocence, Morgan accepted them as everyday reality.

"She reminds me of you," Nona once said to Miyah as she watched a five-year-old Morgan intuitively pick a handful of leaves from a plantain plant in the garden. She proceeded to put them in her mouth, chewed them to mix with her saliva and then applied the poultice of wet leaves to a bee sting she had just gotten, to draw out the toxins and ease the pain.

"Yes," Miyah agreed. "She learns quickly," walking over to examine the extent of the sting and praise her daughter for her quick response. "Does it still hurt?" she asked.

"No, Mama," Morgan replied. "I fixed it."

Things had changed at Michael's house since Morgan was born. Michael's sister, Elizabeth, moved into her own apartment and with her job and friends was enjoying her life. Little was seen of her, and although Michael did miss his younger sister, he was glad she finally had a life of her own. Even though he enjoyed a very large inheritance from his parents, Michael resumed his freelance writing career, which enabled him to work from his office at home. He continued to research information and work on the book he promised Miyah he would write about her bloodline.

Miyah and Michael were good parents and Morgan's childhood was filled with love from many dimensions. They also honored their promise to Miyah's grandfather, Papa Tom, and had returned to France several times each year, proudly showing off Morgan to their friends and relatives in the villages of Rennes-les-bains and Rennes-le-Château. Tomas seemed to have an agelessness, especially when it came to Morgan. He talked to her on the phone several times a week and had already taught her to speak quite a lot of French.

One evening, as Morgan played with a handmade rag doll Tomas had given her, Michael turned to Miyah and asked, "Do you ever think of us having more children?"

This caught Miyah off guard.

"Michael, you must know that isn't possible. My life must be devoted solely to Morgan and her preparation to carry on our legacy of healing. Her lessons are so important now as she grows older."

"I guess I knew the answer, but I thought I would ask," he quietly replied. "I just love that little girl so much, I thought it would be nice if she had a brother."

"Remember, Michael, I said it wouldn't always be easy raising a Touchstone child. And it won't be long before we'll have to leave from time to time to begin Morgan's more advanced teachings."

"Leave? I thought you were teaching her here. Where do you have to go?" he objected.

"You'll have to think of it as Morgan going off to school now and then. There are many levels to her teachings and some of them will need to be done at my family home, at RoseVine—where others can bring their wisdom into her lessons. You've been there and know we'll be safe. You've witnessed first hand how powerful our veil of protection is. You must have patience and faith in us."

Michael watched his daughter playing and wondered if he could bear being away from her. Miyah had warned him many times that raising Morgan meant sacrifices and it would be difficult. He truly didn't know if he was as strong as Miyah thought he was and if he would be able to live up to her expectations of him.

"You're all you must be and more," she said unexpectedly, reading his thoughts. "Never doubt yourself, Michael. You're a very special being. You'll find difficult times ahead, but know that you'll get through them. You'll discover you're stronger than you give yourself credit to be."

Michael never quite got used to Miyah's ability to read his thoughts. Sometimes it irritated him, but more often, he appreciated her positive influence on him.

"God, you're so good for me," he finally said, folding her into his arms, smelling the familiar fragrance of her hair.

"I just never want to lose either of you."

Miyah didn't reply, for she had seen a glimpse of what lay ahead, and knew Michael would need all of his strength to pull himself through. She wished she could change some of what she had seen in her visions, but knew what she foresaw could not be avoided.

"I'm glad you brought it up because I've been meaning to talk to you about these lessons. . .and we'll begin on Monday," she finally said. "Morgan and I will leave early in the morning. You can tell your sister, and anyone who may ask, that we're visiting relatives somewhere, if you must."

"Will you call me?" Michael asked.

"I'll see what I can do," Miyah replied. "We'll enter into a dimension between worlds where time is not a reality. Morgan's education will be accelerated as she's prepared for her role in carrying the Touchstone. To us, there will be no such thing as time, while in your reality it could be days or even weeks. I'll try to make our first lesson short so you can prepare for our absence easier. But, Michael, you'll have to accept this. It has nothing to do with you, or even with me. It's all about Morgan and her future."

"Can I at least come and visit once in awhile?" he asked.

"Of course, I can arrange that, but it has to be done without disrupting her studies."

"You'll have to write down the address for me. Funny, but I've looked for that house before and couldn't find it," he said, remembering the day he frantically went searching for Miyah after he learned she had drawn him to her with a love spell the night before. He was hurt that she didn't know she wouldn't have to use a spell to bring him to her, and he reacted. He later tried to return to her house—but it was no where to be found.

Miyah thought before she answered. "Michael," she began. "Do you think it strange that you've only been to RoseVine twice—the first time we made love and again when Morgan was born?"

"With all the mysteries of your family, I never questioned it. We've been so happy here and I never had reason to think about it much. Why?"

"After the work you've done with the cedar box, traveling into other dimensions and all, I suppose you won't think this any more unusual. . ." she began.

Michael had not forgotten where the journeys through the cedar box had lead him, and he often longed to go back again to the time when he conversed with Joshua in ancient times. It had changed his life.

"Whatever are you talking about?" he asked.

"You've heard me talk about the house being 'behind the veil' and know that few have been invited there. Well," Miyah continued, ". . .the house really doesn't exist in this dimension."

"Of course it does. I was there. Tomas was there. . .even my mother was there when you were born."

"You were there because you were allowed to enter through the veil, into a dimension that exists between the worlds. You've seen how beautiful it is—the gardens, the feeling of being surrounded by pure love. . .this is where we'll be. You can relax knowing Morgan will be safe and happy there, as if she were home."

"So that's why I couldn't find the house when I went looking for you so long ago. There was just an empty lot. Does this mean I won't be able to contact you at all?" Michael said with anxiety.

"Oh, we'll figure out some sort of system for you to get in touch with us," Miyah said, firmly adding. "We'll be there for one reason, and that's for Morgan to learn about her past and her future. She's already grasped a great deal about herbal remedies and such, but there are mystical realms and rituals she must be introduced to and she can't be distracted. To her, it'll seem as if she's only away from you for a day, maybe less. I told you, time won't even exist for us there."

"Will your mother and grandmother be there. . .in spirit, I mean?" he asked.

"Of course. The house will be filled with our ancestors. They're the teachers of today's children."

"I guess it does sound crowded," Michael conceded. "But it doesn't seem fair," his voice trailed off.

"Knowing where you are does help ease my mind, but I'll miss you both terribly. I just want to be with you all the time."

"The first time will be the hardest," Miyah warned. "But it'll get easier each time. You must believe that."

"Each time? How long will this go on?"

"Over the next few years," Miyah answered. "There's much to learn, Michael. You have no idea how much. I've taught Morgan the basics for her age. Now comes the hard work."

"You promise you'll always come back to me?" he asked.

"Yes, we'll both always come back to you, Michael. We promise."

~~~~~

Michael read three storybooks to Morgan Sunday night, before he finally said "no" to her pleas to read another book, a diversion from going to bed that Morgan was quite good at. He finally tucked her in and lingered as her soft, little arms hugged his neck. She gave him a dozen baby kisses on his cheeks, then cradled his face in her tiny hands and said, "I love you Daddy." Michael's heart melted.

"I love you too, Pumpkin," he replied. "I'll miss you when you go off to school tomorrow, but you know I'll always be thinking about you. And be sure every night when you go to bed, you look up at the stars and say good-night to me. I'll be doing the same to you—and our words will meet somewhere in the night sky and explode into a million daddy-daughter kisses."

". . .and I'll scoop them all up and. . .and gobble them down," Morgan said, making piggy noises.

"Hey, be sure you save some for me!" he laughed, tickling her tummy, as she wriggled and giggled.

"Don't worry about us, Daddy," this wise little soul said, suddenly turning serious. "I know this school is important for me, but Mommy will take good care of me. I'll miss you, but you'll be OK by yourself for a little while. I just know it."

Michael hugged her to him, his eyes tearing up. "I know Sweetie. I know. I'll miss you so much."

"But now, you need to get to sleep. It's way past your bedtime." He tucked her in and gave her a kiss on her forehead. "I love you Morgan," he whispered.

"I love you too, Daddy," she said, snuggling in with her teddy bear and rag doll.

Michael turned on the angel night lamp by her bed and switched off the ceiling light. He stood in the doorway for a few seconds, looking at his sweet daughter all cuddled in her blankets. His heart was filled with so much love he thought he would burst.

"God, I hate saying goodbye," he said as he entered his bedroom. Miyah was brushing her hair and looked at his reflection in her mirror.

"I know, dear. We won't be gone long this first time and I'll connect with you as much as possible. You have work to do, just concentrate on that if you can. I don't like good-byes either. I'll make it as easy for you as I can."

Michael went to her and as she stood up, her robe slipped off her shoulders and onto the floor, revealing her naked body.

"You're just as beautiful as the day I met you," he said, taking her into his arms, running his hands down along the curve of her slender back. Holding her close to him and seeing her nakedness in the mirror behind her made his body ache for her even more. He kissed her passionately, first on her lips, then her ears, neck, shoulders and working his way down her body, he gently laid her on the bed and continued his quest, his mouth caressing every inch of her.

"Just lay back," he whispered. "Let me make love to you first. . .let me. . ."

Miyah softly moaned and arched her back to the touch of his wet lips. Her fingers ran through his hair and massaged his head, stimulating him even more as he made her senses go wild. They both let go of any thoughts that were in their minds and were completely obsessed with this moment of sensual pleasure. They were lost in the ecstasy of their lovemaking, as if it were the first and the last time they would ever be together.

~~~~~~

Early the next morning, before the sun came up, Michael awoke and smilingly recalling the night before, he rolled over to embrace his wife and start the day with an encore. Instead he found a note on Miyah's pillow.

Michael,

I awoke early and watched you while you were sleeping. Do you know how handsome you are? I love you so much. You were so peaceful I didn't want to wake you. I know how you hate good-byes, so I decided to leave early to make things easier. There is fresh-squeezed orange juice and plenty of food in the refrigerator. Take care of yourself and don't worry about us. We will return in a few days. We love you.

xxxooo Miyah and Morgan

Michael jumped out of bed and raced downstairs, hoping they hadn't left yet. All he found was a scribbled note, tucked underneath a glass of dandelion flowers.

I love you Daddy, Morgan

He picked up the note and held it to his heart. Slumping down in the chair, he sobbed like a little boy.

"I don't know if I'm strong enough for this, baby," he cried. "I miss you already."

As if he thought he could catch up with them, he pulled on his jeans and a T-shirt and grabbed his car keys. He found the map where he had circled the park the last time he tried to find RoseVine, and headed in that direction. He parked his car along the street across from the empty lot and stood on the sidewalk, staring at the lot. A man jogging by stopped and asked him if he was OK.

"I. . .I thought there was a house there," he stuttered, pointing to the darkness of the empty lot.

"Oh, I think there was a house there ages ago. . .they say it was a grand old house, but that it was haunted by some witches who did all sorts of strange things there. Don't know what happened to it. It's been an empty lot all of my lifetime," he said. "Are you sure you're OK?"

Michael nodded and the man jogged off.

An elderly man, huddled in a topcoat to keep warm, was sitting on the bench in the dimly lit park. Michael sat down next to him and just stared toward the empty lot.

"Where is the house?" he asked. "Where are Miyah and Morgan?"

"Are you talking to me?" the old man asked.

"Ah. . .no," Michael sighed. "I thought there was a house on that lot."

He glanced over at the old man and saw that he was turning something over and over between his fingers.

"Where did you get that stone?" Michael asked. Even by the light of a single street lamp, he recognized it as being the same as the stone Miyah had given him after she cured him of his cancer—his "Faith Stone."

"It was given to me by a woman who healed me after I almost died from a childhood illness. She lived here," the man replied. "I was only ten-years-old at the time and I came here a few times to see her. She'd come out of her house, cross the street to the park, and we'd sit on this very bench for hours. She talked to me, mostly listened I guess, but she helped me through some hard times in my life—not only recovering from the physical illness, but she helped me get through an abusive childhood. I wouldn't have made it without her. And then one day, she told me I was completely well. I'd be able to take care of myself and didn't need her anymore. I remember how strong I felt after she said that, as if I'd really been healed, body and soul. I walked away feeling two feet taller.

"The next time I came here. . .this," he gestured toward the empty lot, "is what I found. I never understood." His voice trailed off. "I tried to tell others about this woman, this angel, who helped me, but they dismissed it, saying I was delirious, that it was an after-effect from the high fever. No one even remembered a house being on this lot. They didn't believe me. But I know it was real. She gave me this stone. I come here once in awhile when I need inspiration. I sit on this bench and just stare at the empty lot," he said, fumbling the stone in his hand as he spoke. "I know it was real."

After a long silence Michael asked, "How long ago was that?"

"Oh, a long time ago. . .I'm 83 now, but I'll never forget. I owe her my life"

The man looked at Michael.

"But didn't you just say you thought there was a house here too?" he asked with hope in his voice.

"Ah, no. I was mistaken," Michael lied, not wanting to share his own story. "It must in the next block over." He wondered if this woman the man was talking about was Miyah's grandmother, Nona, or even Nona's mother, Dolores?

The man lowered his head for a moment. He picked up his cane and as he began to walk away, he stopped and turned toward Michael.

"Don't give up hope," he said. "Don't ever give up hope." He turned and slowly walked down the street into a stream of dewy, dawn light, just as the sun began to appear over the horizon.

"What does that mean?" Michael wondered. Suddenly a ball of fear knotted up in his stomach.

"Oh my God. Is the same thing happening to me? Are they disappearing from my life too? No. Our circumstances are different. Aren't they?" He got up to run after the old man and ask more questions. He needed reassurance that the same fate wouldn't befall him. But when he looked down the street, the man was no where to be found.

He thought, "Was this a messenger—someone sent to prepare me for the worse?"

Michael slipped back into the insecurities of his old self. He ran over to the empty lot, looking for traces of a house. . .rubble. . .anything.

"I've been in the house. I know it exists. She said its 'behind the veil.' What the hell does that mean?" He stumbled into the area where he remembered the back yard to be. Then he saw a familiar site silhouetted by the sunrise—the tree he had hidden behind that night he watched Miyah performing her fire ritual under the full moon. Yes, this was the same tree. He knew it. He put his arms around the tree, closed his eyes and hugging his cheek to the rough bark, crying out in his emotions.

"Miyah! Morgan! Where are you?"

After a few moments, Michael jumped, abruptly opening his eyes. He felt someone lay their hand upon his shoulder. He could clearly feel their presence, but when he turned to look, no one was there. He took a deep breath and felt a calm come over him. He let lose his grip on the trunk of the tree and slumped to the ground, leaning his back against the old oak.

"Miyah," he finally pleaded, regaining his sanity. "If you're here, please give me a sign. You've reached out and helped me through many other dimensions when I traveled into the past. I know you can give me some reassurance now—something to help me adjust."

He closed his eyes for a moment to regain his composure, but soon opened them and looked around, smelling something burning. In the distance he could see movement silhouetted in the sunrise. Squinting, he recognized a form. . .a body dancing around a bonfire—the familiar form of Miyah. But she was not alone this time as she was when he saw her doing her love ritual around the fire many years ago. A ring of naked women accompanied her as the fire flickered and burned its smoke up to the sky. And then, as quickly as it appeared, the image was gone.

"Oh God," Michael sighed. "Thank you for the sign, Miyah. Be patient with me. Please, be patient."

He sat for a long time in this place, watching the sun slowly rise over the horizon. He didn't know if he had the right, or even if they would hear him, but he asked for Joshua, Maryum, Nona, Junia, and the spirits of the powerful women Miyah had told him about, to be with him, to guide him so he would be able to accept his fate as the father of a child of destiny.

~~~~~

Miyah sat at her desk writing in the diary. Hearing a call in the distance, she paused, and walked to the window. Through the curtain she could see Michael in the backyard, struggling in his anxiety over losing her and Morgan to the world beyond the veil.

Reaching out to him, she tried to reassure him that he need not go through all of this anguish, that they will in time return to him, as she had promised. She felt sorry he was feeling so emotional and wondered briefly if she had overestimated him.

"No," she thought. "He'll get through this. So much of our Touchstone legacy wouldn't have been revealed to him if he couldn't carry through. He made it through some pretty incredible circumstances when he traveled back in time to meet with Joshua. He'll survive this too."

"Yes, he will," Nona's voice interrupted Miyah's thoughts. "But love is a powerful thing and this is a most difficult time for Michael. He'll eventually find the self-confidence he needs, but his struggles are necessary lessons for him to appreciate the outcome. You've seen some of what lies ahead, Miyah. You must let it take its course."

"I know you're right, Nona," Miyah replied softly. "It's just difficult to see him suffer."

"It'll only make him stronger," Nona said. "You must also be strong."

"Yes, I know," Miyah said.

She watched Michael for awhile longer, then walked over to a big overstuffed chair where her young daughter played with the doll Papa Tom had given her.

"Was that Daddy?" Morgan intuitively asked.

"Yes, it was," Miyah said, not one bit surprised that Morgan sensed his presence.

"Don't worry about him, Mama," she said. "He'll be alright. I'll tell him that again when we get home."

"You are already so wise," Miyah said, gathering Morgan into her arms. "Come closer, my sweet child, I have a story to tell you. A story you must always remember and share with your own daughter some day. You've inherited our wisdom and have begun to learn of our healing ways, but there's more. Times are about to change and your life will be much simpler than mine and the lives of the women of our bloodline. You'll no longer have to hold our secrets, as they'll soon be revealed to the world. But as a healer, there's more for you to learn and that's why we're here."

"What secrets, Momma?" Morgan asked. "Can I tell Daddy?"

"We'll tell him together," Miyah replied. "But for now, it'll be between you and me, OK?"

Miyah fetched the cedar box on the table next to her and let Morgan run her hands across it, as if the young child already appreciated the workmanship of its carving. Removing a leather strap with an ankh-shaped key from around her neck, Miyah unlocked the cedar box.

Morgan looked to her mother, as if asking permission, and Miyah nodded with a loving smile. Morgan carefully and slowly lifted the lid. It was as if light illuminated the treasured contents of the cedar box as, together, they peered inside.

Miyah said softly, as she reached inside, "It's time you knew of our family Touchstone."

2 Ashes to Ashes

Over the next few days Miyah, Nona and Junia, and other spirit ancestors worked with Morgan. They were amazed at how quickly she grasped the concepts they were teaching her and how easily she accepted everything, asking very deep questions and effortlessly understanding the answers. Occasionally she responded with, "I already know this," and they realized she had been born as a much more advanced soul than they originally perceived.

"I like school. It's easy!" she announced to everyone's delight.

"Can we go home and see Daddy now?" she said late in the afternoon one day.

Miyah glanced at Nona, and then smiled at Morgan. "Yes, I think that's exactly what we should do today. You've worked so hard, you need a little vacation."

"Can we meet Daddy in the park? I want to play on the swings."

Miyah had to keep reminding herself that even though her daughter was wise in so many ways, she was still a little girl—and swings and slides were just what she needed right now.

"I'll get a message to him," Miyah answered.

"But don't tell him we're coming," Morgan pleaded. "I want to surprise him!"

Miyah smiled, thinking of how her curly-haired daughter was already in control.

~~~~~~

Michael had been working at his desk, trying to meet a deadline for an article he was writing for a magazine. One moment he was typing away and the next minute he found himself standing up and stretching.

"I could use a break," he thought and headed to the kitchen for a glass of lemonade. He gulped it down, rinsed his glass and put it in the sink, and decided to go for a little walk to get some exercise.

"Fresh air will do me good," he said out loud, glancing at the clock. He headed to the park across the street, his favorite park in the entire city— partly because it seemed like his own personal playground when he was a boy growing up, but also because it was beautifully landscaped with flower gardens and shaded with tall oak trees. The playground had also been his favorite, with swings, slides, teeter-totters and a round platform that spun. Now a wooden fort-like structure had been added with rope ladders and all sorts of fun things for kids to play on. He strolled on the walking path for awhile, stretching his legs while enjoying the birds and the late afternoon sun. All of a sudden he heard a yell from across the pathway.

"Daddy! Daddy! We're home!"

He spun around and saw Morgan running toward him. She leaped into his arms and smothered him with kisses. "I missed you so much," she said.

"I missed you more," he replied, holding her close. "I'm surprised to see you!"

Miyah came up to him and put her arms around them both.

"How was school?" Michael asked. Morgan babbled on about things she had learned and then squirmed to get down.

"Can I go play on the swings now?" she asked, as Michael put her down. They watched as she ran off to claim one of the empty swings.

"Busy, busy little girl. How was her attention span in your classroom?" he asked as he welcomed his wife home with a hug.

"It's amazing," Miyah replied. "She's so much ahead of a lot of the things I wanted to teach her. It's like she came into this world loaded and ready to go. She makes my job easy."

"Good, because then maybe you won't have to be gone so much," he replied, giving his wife a kiss. "I really missed you both. You know I went looking for your house don't you?"

"Yes, I know. I saw you."

"And you touched me to calm me, didn't you?" he asked, looking into her soft, brown eyes. She nodded.

"Just do me a favor. I know I don't like good-byes, but it nearly killed me to wake up and have you and Morgan gone. I'd rather work through the goodbye next time, OK?"

"OK," Miyah said, stretching up to kiss him. "I missed you too, you know." They sat on a nearby bench and watched their daughter burn up energy running from swing to slide to fort, as any other normal little girl would do. Only they both knew she was far from normal.

~~~~~

The next few days were filled with good family time—playing hide-and-seek in the back yard, reading favorite storybooks, splashy bubble baths and long walks in the park. Michael wanted to spend every moment possible with his girls. Because Morgan turned out to be such an advanced child, Miyah decided she would take Morgan "to school" every weekday, but only during the day and no more overnights until she was older. This made Michael much happier.

A few weeks later, on a Sunday afternoon while the family was sitting down to a late picnic lunch spread out on a blanket in their backyard, Nona appeared.

"Hi Nona," Morgan said, running over to hug her great-grandma, as if a spirit appearing in the middle of the day was an ordinary thing.

"Hello, my sweet girl," Nona replied, hugging Morgan. Miyah

immediately sensed that something was wrong, but before she could ask, Morgan piped up.

"Papa Tom didn't call me this morning. He always calls on Sundays. He's sick, isn't he?" She casually plopped herself back down on the picnic blanket and reached for her plate of food.

Nona kept her eyes fixed on Miyah. "Yes, my dear, he is. How intuitive of you to know. Your mother is doing a great job with your lessons."

Michael watched the two women as they stared at each other, mentally exchanging thoughts. He could tell by the ashen look on Miyah's face that things weren't good.

"It seems that all the females here know what's going on. Can someone fill me in?" he kindly asked.

"I've just come from Tomas and he's near his time to pass over. He's calm and he's ready, but he requested to see the three of you first. I know it's short notice, but do you think you could come back with me today? Now?"

Miyah looked at Michael. "Let me make a couple of phone calls and I'll be ready," he said, getting up and heading to his study. Miyah started to gather up their picnic lunch and asked Nona to watch Morgan while she got some of their things together.

Nona turned to Morgan. "How would you like to go back to France? You remember your house there don't you?"

"Oui, j'aime ma maison en France," Morgan slowly and meticulously replied, using the French Tomas had taught her.

"Oh, you love your house in France! That's good!" Nona exclaimed.

"Oui," Morgan replied with a giggle. Then she somberly asked, "Papa Toma is going to die isn't he?"

"Yes, dear, he is," Nona said.

"He's really old, isn't he?" she asked.

Nona laughed. "Well, yes, I suppose. But he's had a wonderful life and we mustn't be sad for him."

"I know, but can I be sad for Mama—and for myself, because I'm going to miss him? Who'll teach me more French lessons? And, other than Auntie Elizabeth, he's the only person who ever calls me on the telephone."

"Those are good points. We'll have to work on that," Nona replied to Morgan's logical thinking.

"Nona," Morgan said.

"Yes dear."

"Do you think I'll ever get to go to France on an airplane?" she asked. "I've never been on an airplane."

"Well, you have plenty of time for that, and yes, I'm sure you will. Our way of transporting is just so much quicker and more convenient. You'll appreciate it as you get older."

"Is Papa Tom going to be living with you now, in the sky?" Morgan asked.

"Yes, I suppose that's right. He is going to be with me now."

"Then will his spirit be able to appear and come and see me, like you and Junia? He can give me French lessons then," she reasoned.

Again Nona chuckled.

"We'll have to see about that too," she replied. "You never stop thinking do you?"

"Should I?" Morgan asked, looking up at Nona.

"No. Never."

The two of them walked hand-in-hand toward the house.

~ ~ ~ ~ ~ ~

Miyah always loved going to France. As a family they had been able to visit Tomas many times each year and spent several days with him each time. Often, she even "popped" over herself for an hour or so, just to talk with him. He had so many stories to share with her and she enjoyed being in his presence. She also liked visiting with all of her newly discovered cousins, aunts and uncles in the area. She had family there who understood her. Most of them had the same healing abilities and beliefs and she was treated no differently than any of them.

Miyah fondly recalled when Morgan was just weeks old and they brought her to France to meet Papa Tom. He was so delighted. He held the little bundle, his great-granddaughter, and literally danced around the room with her cradled in his arms. He said, "She looks just like Junia when she was a baby—she looks just like you when you were a baby. I'm so happy. Thank you Miyah for bringing her to me."

Papa Tom took part in Morgan's blessing ceremony on that visit. Miyah remembered it vividly. She shut her eyes and could see the entire ceremony play out as if it were only yesterday. . .baby Morgan, Miyah, Michael, Papa Tom, Nona and Junia were at the river behind Tomas' house in Rennes-les-Bains, where he had made a stone circle with a small altar in the center.

Nona had begun the ceremony by saying, "Children are our future and represent the light of the world. Morgan June was sent to earth to help make this world a little better. . . a little more interesting. We honor her and each of us present today to witness this welcoming ceremony and to participate in the parent/baby blessing of Miyah, Michael and Morgan."

Junia took over, "First we wish to honor the earth for her many gifts. We have, in this circle, components of nature—a feather for air, a shell for water, a candle for fire and a stone for earth. We also have fresh flowers—daisies—to represent innocence. Around them, we'll honor the four directions."

Everyone faced East. Junia raised her arms to the sky and began.

"O Great Spirit of the East, invisible Spirit of Air. O vast and boundless

Grandfather Sky, your living breath animates all life. Grant us patience to hear the inner sounds, to welcome change and embrace challenge, to honor the ecstasy of movement and the joy of the dance."

Everyone turned to face South. Nona spoke, raising her arms to the sun.

"O Great Spirit of the South, invisible Spirit of Fire, grant us your heat to warm us and your sunlight to nurture all life. Give us the wisdom to open up to the light, to embrace our shadow, and bring to us awareness, passion and growth."

Turning to the West, Junia continued, motioning to the river.

"O Great Spirit of the West, Spirit of the Great Waters, of rain, rivers, lakes and springs. O Grandmother Ocean, womb of all life, grant us the power to dissolve boundaries and release fear. Give us the privilege to taste and to feel, to cleanse and to heal."

Facing the North with everyone, Nona raised her arms to the woodland beyond.

"O Great Spirit of the North, protector of fertile land, and of all green and growing things, the noble trees and grass. Grandmother Earth, song of nature, great power of nurturing and endurance, grant us your strength to grow and bring forth flowers of the field and fruits of the garden."

Then Nona and Junia had everyone in the circle hold hands and raising their arms to each element, they chanted.

"We honor 'Above' with our arms stretched out in connection; 'Below' with our feet planted firmly on the ground; 'Within' to help us to know that we are unique, precious and powerful and to help us acknowledge the obligation of our own divinity; and 'Without' to connect and care for all creation."

Nona said, "Next we wish to welcome the ancestors. Our lives are the legacies of those who have gone before us. The ancestors of Morgan are as much a part of her community as those of us who are present here today. Morgan, and all children, are the fulfillment of the dreams of many generations. Joshua and Maryum – I call upon all of Morgan's ancestors to be with us now to participate in this protection, blessing and welcoming ceremony.

"Ancestors, surround us with your ever present love and breathe into us your wisdom. Keep us mindful that the miracle of incarnation is both a gift and path back to you. Birth is a reunion. Thank you for your guidance and protection. Thank you for the wisdom to listen when you whisper into our ears. We light our candles in honor of our ancestors. The lighting of these candles also symbolize the light of love."

Everyone picked up a candle, lit it from the flame of a central candle, and placed their candle in the sand near the altar, along with the feather, stone, shell, larger candle and flowers.

Tomas spoke up, "Sweet baby Morgan, as a child of the universe, of

God, has been given many gifts from the Divine so she can light the way for her future. It's important for us to support her and protect her, so that her gifts may blossom. Miyah and Michael, as Morgan's parents, it's also important for you to play with her, make funny faces and noises to make her smile and laugh out loud, send lots of pictures of her to me here in France, spoil her to the best of your ability, feed, clothe and shelter her, teach her to care for the earth and her environment, to have gratitude for all around her and share with her your wisdom and the memories of her ancestors."

Everyone laughed at Tomas' comment about the photos and funny faces. He proceeded with the ritual.

"This holy water came from the sacred pool at Lourdes in France, collected when Miyah, Michael and I were there a few years ago. Well, I guess that Morgan was there too, in her mother's womb," he chuckled. " So, I thought it was appropriate to use this holy water here today."

As he poured some of the water into a bowl of rose petals, Junia explained, "We're using pink rose petals because they stand for grace and perfect happiness."

Tomas walked over to Morgan and her parents and sprinkled the rose water on the top of their heads, making the symbol of a spiral and said, "Miyah, Michael and Morgan, you are connected, protected, loved and blessed by the Divine."

He gently rubbed rose water on their foreheads, making the symbol of a pentagram, the sacred star, and said, "All your senses are blessed, protected, and awakened."

He touched the rose water over their hearts, making a symbol of a circle and said, "Your heart is blessed so you may feel compassion for yourselves and for others."

Next he sprinkled rose water on each of their hands, making the symbol of a triangle, while saying, "Your hands are blessed so you may reach out to the world."

He uncovered Morgan's feet and rubbed rose water on them, making the symbol of a square and then bent down and did the same with Miyah and Michael's feet, announcing, "Your feet are blessed so you may connect with the earth, be grounded and stand your ground in this world."

Morgan was wide awake, laying in Miyah's arms like a little angel, as if she knew this was a special day in her honor. Nona stepped forward, and as the baby grasped hold of her finger, she said, "Morgan, your spirit is strong . . . and so is your grip! This strong spirit will guide you through this life. Know that you have angels to watch over you and you are never alone. Know you are deeply loved and that your presence brings overwhelming joy to your parents and all who are around you, now and always, on this sacred earth."

Junia finished with, "Miyah, my daughter, your spirit is strong and it's guiding you through this life. Know that you have angels who watch over you and you are never alone. And know that you are deeply loved and your presence brings overwhelming joy to Morgan, Michael, and all who are around you, now and always, on this sacred earth."

"Amen," everyone said in unison. It was the most beautiful blessing ceremony Miyah had ever witnessed and she would remember it always as if it were yesterday.

~~~~~~

During Miyah's most recent visit to France, Tomas had talked about his wishes for when he died. He was old and could feel in his bones that his time was near. "I'm ready any time, Miyah, so don't mourn me when I go. I've had a good life. I'll always be your Papa Tom." They both knew the Church would step in and take care of the arrangements so he would have a "proper" Catholic burial as a retired priest, but Tomas had been insistent with his friends in the Church that he wanted to be cremated and some of the ashes were to be given to Miyah to dispose of as he had instructed her. He told everyone; he wrote it and had it notarized; and he put it in a will. It was important to him.

After the church funeral, he wanted a simple ceremony, a celebration of his life with family and close friends at his house—the house he had willed to Miyah. He requested that Miyah spread his ashes in three of the places he loved the most: the Salz River behind his house; from the tower at Rennes-le-Château where Miyah and Michael were married; and in the yard behind RoseVine, back in the States where he was so happy in his younger days with his beloved wife, Nona, his daughter Junia and his granddaughter Miyah. She had promised him she would see to it.

~~~~~~

It didn't take Miyah long to gather a few things for this journey and for her, Michael and Morgan to arrive with Nona at Tomas' house in Rennes-les-Bains. Tomas' housekeeper, Lydia, greeted them at the door with sincere hugs, her face red from crying.

"I somehow hoped he would live forever," she said. "At least another ten years or so. He's such a good man. This entire community will miss him."

"What happened?" Michael asked.

"He caught a cold that quickly went into his chest and turned into pneumonia. He went downhill so fast and accepted it so easily. He simply said it was his time. He was ready. It's just not right," Lydia shook her head. "It's just not right." She hurried them into Tomas' room, diverting Morgan into the kitchen with some cousins until Miyah called for her. A priest, two women and another man from the village were sitting with Tomas. They nodded to Miyah as she entered the room, then quietly left.

Miyah sat down next to the bed and took Tomas' hand. Michael stood at her side. It was an unusual moment for Miyah. All her life she had been called upon to help people with their passing into the next world, or to heal them, whatever she was called to do. In this case, she knew it was time for Tomas to go, yet it was the first time, since her mother Junia and grandmother Nona, that she was close to anyone who was dying. Her emotions were so mixed. She knew that death was just a part of the cycle of life and that one day Tomas' soul would come back into this world for another lifetime, but she had just reunited him not that many years ago and didn't want to lose him again. She was sad at the thought of him passing, yet she was happy he was going to be with Nona, his beloved wife and with Junia, his loving daughter. Miyah knew that Tomas was rejoicing in that. With all the good he had done in the world, there was no doubt he would be received with open arms on the other side. Miyah thought of Joshua, standing there to greet him, this priest of God who understood and preached the truth about the holy family. That made her happy and gave her strength.

"I'm here, Papa Tom. We're all here," she said, bending over to kiss him on the forehead.

Tomas opened his eyes and slowly smiled. His mouth was too dry to speak and he motioned for Miyah to get his water glass. She gently placed the straw in his mouth, so he could sip. His voice was hoarse and weak, but he thanked them for coming and motioned for Miyah to come closer to him. She leaned nearer so he could whisper in her ear.

Michael couldn't hear his words, but knew these last words Tomas spoke to her must be important. He watched Miyah intently listening to everything Tomas was telling her.

"God, she's so brave," he thought. "I don't think I'd be able to hold up." Just watching made his eyes sting with tears, but he knew he had to be strong for her and for Morgan.

When Tomas was finished speaking to Miyah, he reached out for Michael's hand. "I know you'll take good care of Miy for me," he said hoarsely. "You're a good man, Michael. I'm glad you're here."

"Thank you for all you've done for us, Tomas. You know how much we love you," is all Michael could muster up before his voice quivered. He gently squeezed the old man's hand.

"Morgan. Is Morgan here?" Tomas asked weakly. "I need to see how her French lessons are coming." Michael let out a little laugh. It was so like Tomas to divert the attention away from himself and think of someone else, even on his deathbed.

Michael came back into the room with Morgan. She had already been told to be careful around Papa Tom because he was very weak. She walked over to the bed and stared at him for awhile. He didn't say anything to her. He was feeling sad that he wasn't going to see her grow up. He knew how special she was. Then Morgan walked over to the corner of the room, picked up a little stool and carried it over to the bed. She stepped up onto the stool to get herself closer, put her head down on Tomas' chest and innocently said, "You look really tired, Papa Tom. I'm going to miss you, but I'm glad you'll be able to go play with Nona and Junia now. It's their turn to have you with them."

Tomas smiled and replied in a raspy breath, "I'm going to miss you too, my little Morgan. Je t'aime tellement." *(I love you so much.)*

"Je t'aime trop père," she replied. *(I love you too, grandfather.)*

"Oui! Votre Français est très bon!" he said. *(Yes! Your French is very good.)*

"Oui. Merci," she said softly. "Au revoir Papa Tom." *(Yes, thank you. Goodbye Papa Tom.)*

"Au revoir mon petit précieux," he replied. *(Goodbye my precious little one.)*

Then she lifted her head and looked into his eyes. "I asked Nona if you can come back to us, like she does, so we can continue our French lessons. I'll be waiting for you Papa Tom. Don't forget me. I'll be waiting for you to come back." And she reached up and kissed his cheek before she stepped down from the stool and walked back into the other room.

A tear slipped from the corner of Tomas' eye. He glanced at Miyah and Michael, and closed his eyes in an attempt to hide his emotion, but the pain on his face was clear. Miyah reached for his hand and quietly said, "It may be possible, Papa Tom. I'll hold on to that thought. I'll be waiting for you too. Je t'aime plus que moi peux exprimer." *(I love you more than I can express.)*

"Je t'aime aussi, mon cher Miyah, *(I love you too, my dear Miyah.)*" Tomas said, barely able to get the words out. "Goodbye, my sweet Miy."

Michael saw Nona and Junia in the room. Had they been there the entire time, he wondered? Were they waiting for Tomas?

Tomas began to cough and gasp for air. Miyah knew it was time and she put her hand on his forehead to send calming energy to him. He looked directly into her eyes acknowledging that he knew it was his time, but he was not filled with fear, or even sadness. He had a peaceful look on his face and his eyes reflected that.

"It's so beautiful, Miy," he whispered. "They're all here, welcoming me. My Nona, Junia. . .Joshua and Maryum. There are so many of them waiting for me. It's so beautiful." Then he closed his eyes, and gasping for air a few more times, he let go. Miyah left her hand on his forehead for a few moments, then slowly withdrew it. Michael put his arm around her and they stood there, looking at Tomas.

After a few minutes they both saw a glowing light, his soul, rise from his body, linger a few moments and then dissipate into a beam of pure, white light that hovered over him. Then it was gone and the room was still.

"Wow," Michael reacted, speaking softly and reverently. "That was incredible. Seeing his soul rise into the light like that. It was so beautiful."

"Yes, it was," Miyah replied. She had seen this many times in her work, and each time marveled at the power and beauty of that moment.

Michael reached over to pull a blanket over Tomas' face. Miyah gently grabbed his arm and said, "No, wait. Leave him as he is. I want the others to see how peaceful he looks."

They stood there a few minutes and then turned, walking together to tell Morgan and the others that it was done. Papa Tom had died.

~~~~~~

Tomas had been correct in saying that the Church would take over his funeral arrangements. Miyah had assumed it would be in the small church at Rennes-les-Bains where he was parish priest for so many years, but instead it was a big affair at the Church of Mary Magdalene in Paris.

Miyah saw to it that Tomas' wishes of cremation were honored, despite a minor confrontation with one of the older bishops, who didn't believe in cremation. The priest, Father Jacob, who had given Miyah a special prayer card message during her and Michael's first visit to the church many years ago, had stepped forward in her behalf and vouched for Tomas' wishes. He had become a good friend to both Miyah and Michael and helped them throughout the funeral proceedings—"brothers in need are welcomed here," he had always told them.

The church was overflowing with people from Rennes-les-Baines, Rennes-le-Château and the surrounding villages. Tomas had made quite an impact during his life in France. The funeral was also attended by priests and bishops and clergy of many other denominations, a testimonial to his own belief in honoring all religions.

There was a lot of ritual, incense burning, and prayers in Latin. A choir sang hymns that echoed throughout the massive church. Morgan sat quietly, looking around at all of the paintings on the ceiling and at the frescos on the walls. She pointed to the large, white statue of Mary Magdalene surrounded by three angels, behind the altar.

"Oh, she's beautiful," she whispered. She watched as the procession took place and pointed to the priests, bishops and cardinals in their long robes and tall hats. Miyah could only imagine what sort of questions she would ask later. She was glad Morgan was attentive to details and knew she was soaking it all in. Michael was sitting on the other side of Morgan and was also amused at her reactions and observations.

They were seated along one side of the church in the front row, so it was easy for them to observe the crowd of people present for the funeral. At one point, Michael noticed a familiar face in the crowd—the mystery man he had seen in their wedding pictures. Michael saw the man glance their way several times, but turned away when Michael looked back at him. Michael tried to keep his eye on him and when the funeral was finally over, he tried to locate him in the crowd, but the man was elusive.

"Who was this man?" Michael wondered, "If he's just another friend of Tomas, why am I singling him out, and why hasn't he come and introduced himself like the others?" He didn't like the feeling that they had been followed by this man when they were in France years ago, and here he was again. He had to find out who this man was.

Father Jacob and several other priests who were close friends of Tomas, also attended the life celebration at Tomas' house a few days later. Lydia, along with Miyah's relatives, oversaw the food preparation, and neighbors and friends arranged flowers around the house. Miyah had put a photo of Tomas, Nona, Junia and herself on the mantel for others to see how happy he was during that time of his life—when Tomas lived in the States and spent time with them at RoseVine. The funeral definitely was more of a festive atmosphere than Michael had ever seen. Any funeral he had attended consisted of a luncheon in the church basement with church ladies bringing hot dishes, macaroni salads, ham sandwiches and chocolate cake. This array of freshly baked breads, exquisite cheese, slices of meat, fresh fruit, sweet desserts and wine. . . plenty of wine, was reminiscent of their wedding celebration here in France a few years ago. But Michael knew that is exactly what Tomas wanted, and Lydia and the others knew it too. . .a life celebration.

Everyone toasted Tomas. Person after person stood up and told stories of how Tomas had impacted their lives; how he had healed their illnesses; how he had coached them through hard times; how he helped through many a financial crisis; how he was a good friend and priest; and how they all loved him. The stories were touching, a real testimony to the legacy of Tomas' life. Eventually eyes turned to Miyah to speak.

"I'm not sure what to say. Many of you have known Tomas much longer than I, and I can tell by your stories that you knew his humor, as well as his generosity, quite well," she began. "I know he's lived here in France, in this very village, most of his life, but I had the privilege of knowing him first—for the first 18 years of my life, when he was a much younger man and was our family priest back home. But Papa Tom, as I called him when I was a little girl, was much more than that."

She paused, as if deciding if she should share the personal story of their life, but realized that these were the people who were closest to Tomas, and they already knew most of the details. She glanced over and Lydia smiled at her, as if to encourage her to continue.

"You may know that Tomas and my grandmother, Nona, were companions. They loved each other deeply. He was there when my mother Junia, his only daughter, was born. He was there when I was born. He was the only male figure in my life as I was growing up. He was always at our house. He was there for all the events of my life—birthdays, holidays, even our solstice and equinox celebrations. Papa Tom was there for me when my mother, Junia, died and when my grandmother, Nona, died. Only I didn't realize then how hard it must have been for him, because I didn't know how he was connected to my family. . .that he was my grandfather. It wasn't until about seven years ago that I discovered this, and we were reunited.

"I have to admit that at first I was a bit angry that I hadn't been told this in my youth, and felt as if I had been cheated out of all those years without him since Nona died. But we talked at length about this and I understood why it had to be. Besides, who can stay mad at Tomas?"

People lifted their glasses to him. "Here, here," they said.

Miyah proceeded. "Tomas performed our wedding ceremony, which most of you attended, and we later discovered that he had performed the marriage of Michael's parents, Paul and Katrina, and baptized both Michael and his sister Elizabeth. A few years ago he presided over our daughter, his great-granddaughter, Morgan's blessing ceremony. I'm honored to say he was my grandfather. I'm blessed to have known him growing up and to have found him again as an adult. He's opened my heart and brought an entirely new perspective to my life. . .our lives," she motioned to Michael and Morgan.

"But I'm not in mourning for Tomas. Not just because he asked me not to, but because I know he's been reunited with his beloveds, Nona and Junia, and that he's smiling down on us today. I admit that I have mourned for myself, my family, all of you, his friends and neighbors, who loved him from the heart, and who will miss his presence dearly. He's done more good in his lifetime than most, and he'll always be remembered for his charming character, his wit, talents, healing ability, his quick laughter and teasing smile, and for his patience and loving heart. We would have all loved to have him here another ten. . .twenty years. . .but we must be happy that we were all touched by him in one way or another and we must never let go of those memories.

"So. . .here's to Tomas," she said, lifting her wine glass in a toast.

"One more thing," Miyah raised her voice above the clinking of glasses. "I have to say that our time here in France, with Papa Tom and all of you— goodness, until just a few years ago I didn't even know I had other living relatives!—our time here has been some of the happiest of my life. Papa Tom, and all of you, have enriched the lives of my family," she motioned to Michael and Morgan again, "more than you'll ever know and we thank you from the bottom of our hearts."

A few tears were shed and hugs were shared as Miyah made her way through the crowded room. Then, as if it were her cue, and to everyone's surprise, little Morgan bravely stepped forward and climbed atop a chair so she could get everyone's attention. She told a quite detailed story of her and Papa Tom playing hide-and-seek around the Throne of Isis stone chair in the woods nearby, and how he acted like he couldn't find her, but she knew that he really knew where she was all along, curled into a little ball in a corner of the giant throne with his jacket over her.

"He was always being silly like that," she concluded, to everyone's laughter. These stories were touching moments, but for the most part, they were met with laughter and cheers, not tears and sadness. It was truly a celebration of Tomas' life.

Afterward those who wanted to participate walked in procession to the Salz River, behind the house and sang lovely songs and hymns in French, while Miyah and Morgan poured some of the ashes onto the rocks of the gently flowing river. Miyah was glad to hear the songs as the ashes were spread. There really was no need for words. She and Morgan simply looked at each other, understanding how important this moment was to both of them, mother and daughter—granddaughters of Tomas. Miyah and Michael had taken a lot of time to explain to Morgan about dying, funerals, what was happening in the process, and to answer her many questions about death. She seemed to understand, as Miyah knew she would.

The following day, Michael, Miyah and Morgan drove Tomas' old black Cadillac up to Rennes-le-Château and had a private ceremony while spreading Tomas' ashes into the wind from atop the Magdala Tower, and watched them scatter and blow over the valley below.

"This is where Daddy and Mommy got married," Michael said to Morgan. "Right here on top of this tower."

"I know," Morgan replied. "You told me that the last time we were here, remember? Is that why Papa Tom wanted to have ashes left here? Because he liked your wedding?"

"No dear," Miyah replied. "It's because this place was very special to *him*. And because it was *his* special place, we had our wedding here. It was his idea. Our family has a long history in this village and in the village where our house—Papa Tom's house—is. When you get older, I'll share it all with you."

"I'm almost seven," Morgan reminded her. "How much is older?"

Michael laughed. "We'll let you know," he said. "Sometimes I think you must be at least 50! Are you sure you're only six?"

"Daddy," she laughed. "Of course I am. You're so silly."

~~~~~

They stayed in France for an extra week to get everything in order. Lydia's daughter and her new husband had been looking for an apartment and Miyah offered the house to them for the rest of the summer, on the condition that they would keep up the yard work and maintenance. Also Miyah and her family would be coming back now and then and wanted to keep their bedroom private so they would have it available when they visited. Lydia had been Tomas' housekeeper, cook, and friend for many years and Miyah trusted her completely. She had taken good care of Tomas and sincerely mourned his passing.

"He was like a father to me," Lydia said. "I don't know what I'll do without him." Miyah knew Lydia would see to it that the house was taken care of.

Miyah packed away a few of Tomas' things to bring home that she felt were important and personal, including Tomas' priest robe which hung on the wall of his room, but for the most part left much of the rest of the house the same. They hoped to come back as often as they could. After all, it had become their second home and the people of the village were now their friends—and, sad as it was, Michael and Miyah both realized that they really didn't have many close friends at home.

The day before Michael and his family were planning to return to the States, they went to the town square to do some last minute errands and sat down to order a pizza at Pizzaria de la Place. Morgan asked permission to play in the nearby playground while they waited for their food and she ran off to have fun. Michael and Miyah felt safe in the village, but still always kept a close eye on their daughter. Michael noticed she was talking to two other children. The girl was about 12-years-old and the boy, who was small in stature, looked a few years younger. Michael felt a déjà vu moment and wasn't sure why, so he got up and wandered over to hear their conversation.

Morgan was pointing to a brace on the boy's leg and asking questions on how he got hurt and why did he have to wear the brace? The girl, at first, was protective of her brother, saying, "Don't pick on my brother. Leave him alone." But Morgan held her own.

"I'm not picking on him," she said. "I just wonder why nobody healed him."

The girl shrugged her shoulders. "We were in a really bad car accident when we were younger. I had some broken bones and stuff but everything got better. My brother's leg was crushed really bad and at first they thought they would have to cut it off, but then they thought they'd try to fix it with metal pins and things. He's worn this brace ever since and he can't bend his leg."

"Does your leg hurt?" Morgan curiously asked the boy.

"He won't answer you," his sister replied. "He hasn't spoken a word to any of us since the accident, over seven years ago."

"Why?" Morgan asked.

"I think it was because our dad died in the crash and it traumatized him or something. He was jumping around in the back seat of the car and thinks the accident was his fault. But we kept telling him it wasn't. Some guy just ran smack into us."

Morgan observed the boy, who looked back at her with a sad expression.

"I'm sorry about your daddy," she finally said. "Did you know Papa Tom? He just died too. He was my great-grandfather. I loved him a lot, but that doesn't mean I'm not going to talk anymore. He's in heaven with the angels and my grandmothers. I think he's pretty happy. I think your daddy is happy there too and wouldn't want you to be sad and not talk to anyone. You know he can probably see everything you do from up there."

The boy looked down at the ground and didn't respond.

Morgan wasn't about to give up. "If you want me to I can fix your leg," she said with confidence.

"Don't be silly," his sister replied. "He's been to almost every doctor in this country and none of them could help. Why do you think you can? Don't tease him like that."

"I'm not teasing," she said.

"You don't have any medicine. What can you do?"

"My mama says my medicine is in my hands and in my heart," Morgan looked at the girl, "I really can help. It's sort of like magic. But first he has to tell me it's OK, otherwise I can't do it."

Morgan stared at the boy. "If your leg hurts and you want it to stop hurting—if you want to run and play without this old brace, you better tell me or else I'll just have to leave you like this," she put out an ultimatum. The boy didn't answer.

His sister hesitated, and then asked, "Can you really fix him? Can you make a miracle? I've heard of people around here who do that. Maybe I should go get my mom."

"Whatever you want," Morgan said to the boy. "You gotta tell me now."

By this time Miyah had joined Michael and was observing what was going on. The children didn't notice they were standing nearby.

"Should we go get her?" Michael whispered.

"No," Miyah quickly answered. "Just believe in her."

Morgan stood for a while, then turned to leave. "Fine," she said, taking a small step.

"Wait," a faint voice replied.

Morgan spun around to see the boy looking directly into her eyes. His sister was standing with her mouth open, hardly believing that her brother had spoken.

"OK," he slowly said. And that was it.

Morgan rubbed her hands together until they felt warm. Then she knelt down and placed her hands on each side of the boy's leg, between the braces and the scars, and closed her eyes. In her mind she was asking for Joshua, Maryum, Nona, Junia, Papa Tom and all the angels to come and heal this little boy's leg. She asked them to do it through her—to use her to work their magic. She knew they could do it. Her mother had taught her a lot about healing and now was the time to put it to use. She really wanted to help this boy. Her intentions were pure.

Miyah also concentrated all her healing energies into her young daughter.

"Your hands are hot," the boy slowly whispered.

Morgan was concentrating so hard that her closed eyes were squinting and she was almost holding her breath. Then she let out a big sigh and intuitively rubbed her hands up and down his leg, as if she were smoothing the muscles and bones into place.

"Does it still hurt?" she asked. "The pain should be gone now," she said with confidence. It's fixed."

The boy looked at his leg for awhile to gauge if he felt any different and then he looked up at Morgan. He had been living with pain in his leg for years, no matter what medication he took. For the first time, he felt nothing. No dull aching, no sudden twinges, no throbbing. Nothing. He looked at his sister and than back at Morgan.

"Well?" his sister said. "Does it still hurt?"

"No," the boy said. "NO," he almost shouted. "She did it!"

"Your leg is healed. . .and you're talking! I can't believe it!" His sister hugged him and swung him around.

"Take the brace off," he commanded. "Take it off."

"I think you should have your mommy do that," a wise Morgan said. "I know your leg is better. You'll be able to walk, but you should have your mommy take the brace off."

"She's right," his older sister chimed in. "You've had to wear that thing for a long time. You'll probably have to exercise your leg or something before you walk on it. Let's go find Mum."

The boy hesitated. He looked at Morgan again, who was just a few years younger than himself, and shyly said, "Thank you. Thank you for making the pain go away. . .for healing my leg."

"Yes, thank you," his sister said, innocently accepting what had just transpired. "Thank you for the miracle."

Morgan just smiled and said, "You're welcome," and started to walk away.

"Wait," the girl said. "You should wait until my mum sees him. She'll want to thank you too. Wait until the brace is off and see if he can bend his leg. Don't you want to see?"

"No. I already know," Morgan said casually and she ran over to play on the swings, as if healing crippled boys on the playground happened every day in her life.

Miyah and Michael looked at each other in wonderment. If he hadn't been through a healing himself and knew of the powers his wife and her bloodline held, he probably wouldn't have believed it. So this is what Morgan has ahead of her, he thought.

Just then he remembered why this seemed so familiar. These were the same children he observed in the park the first time he was here, when he and Miyah came to reunited with Tomas. This was the little girl in the yellow rubber boots who was jumping around, making her brother laugh until their mother came and picked him up to bring them home. It was the same crippled boy with the brace he had seen those many years ago. How synchronistic, he thought. Miyah read his mind.

"You wondered at that time why no one had healed him," she said. "There were lessons that needed to be learned by his injury. Some were lessons for him, some for his sister, and others for his mother and people around them. Even though he's suffered, he was never given more than he could bear. He'll be much stronger because if it, and their faith will also be strengthened by the miracle that's just happened. God does work in mysterious ways."

Miyah added, "And I can't help but think this is also a lesson for Morgan. Her first healing, and it was with other children. Maybe that'll be her path—to be a healer of children. Just look at her over there on the swing. She's so innocent and nonchalant about what she just did. I guess it's good she doesn't have an ego about it. She's a very special girl, that daughter of ours."

They walked over to get Morgan and decided it might be a good idea to get their pizza to-go, before they attracted attention. That was the last thing they wanted for Morgan at her tender age. They collected their pizza and Miyah quickly zapped them back to their house.

Just as Miyah did their disappearing act, she looked over her shoulder at the children. Their mother was there and the daughter was telling her about the little girl who had just made a miracle and healed her brother's leg. At first she laughed at them and didn't believe them, but then her son said, "Mum, the pain is gone," and when she heard her son speak, she tearfully and joyfully knew something important had just happened. They looked around to find the little healer, but Morgan had already been whisked away. Miyah watched as the mother peeled away the brackets holding the metal brace in place, and when he bent his leg, she grabbed him to her and began to sob, "Thank you, God. Thank you, God."

This is the reason Miyah was a healer. This is why Morgan's mission in life was so important. She, too, was a Touchstone healer.

3 Revealing the Diary

The years passed quickly and Miyah and Morgan stuck to their daily lesson routine while she was growing up. But now the lessons were more advanced and each time they stepped behind the veil of RoseVine for longer periods of time. Michael didn't like their absence, but had reluctantly accepted it, throwing himself into his work when they were gone.

Miyah had been saving the diary until the end of her daughter's teachings. She had referred to it often throughout the years and told of stories recorded in it, but Morgan had never seen these stories and teachings herself.

She was now a teenager and to her, the opening of this sacred diary was like stepping inside a place of initiation—a right of passage—into a world that only the women of her bloodline knew, where their lives, personal joys and tragedies were recorded in the loops and dots of their own handwriting. Their blood, sweat and tears were imprinted in the folds of each page. The smell of their perfume and healing oils were merged with the ink that penned their words. Miyah had told her daughter that opening the diary opened her senses to another dimension. It was as if the voices of these powerful women were there, reading aloud the words they had written throughout the ages, retelling their story over and over again. She never tired hearing their messages. It was *her* story. And now it had become Morgan's story. A new lesson was to begin. A new light would shine. Morgan had earned her graduation papers—the well-worn pages of the diary.

On this day, Miyah motioned for Morgan to sit on the sofa by the window. The last rays of sunlight shone through the glass panes and rested upon Morgan, rimming her with an aura of light. Miyah stood for a moment, looking at her daughter, recalling the day when Junia sat on that same sofa and shared the diary gift with her. Time had passed so quickly. She could see the spirits of Junia and Nona gathered around Morgan, proudly smiling with their approval.

Miyah fetched her medicine bag and sat next to her daughter, catching that same ray of sunlight on her shoulders. She slowly removed the cedar box from the bag and placed it on the wooden table in front of them. This box had been handed down through the generations, along with the diary and medicine bag. It had been carved in ancient times by Joshua as a wedding gift for his beloved, Maryum, who used it to hold her healing stones, oils and herbs. When the time was right, she passed it on to her own daughter, Sera. It traveled through the hands of women of the bloodline, eventually to Nona, Junia and then to Miyah and would some day belong to Morgan.

Miyah laid her hands on the lid and paused a few moments in prayer. She then reached for the worn, washed-leather pouch on the cord around her neck and retrieved a familiar gold ankh-shaped key. Unlocking the lid, she slowly opened the cedar box to reveal a bundle of old cloth, some stones and crystals. She picked up the cloth bundle and unwound the fabric to reveal a large black stone. It was a rounded, long, pyramid shape, embedded with sparkling bits of crystals. She held it up to the light and the tiny crystal specks seemed to bring the stone to life. Miyah handed the stone to Morgan.

"Look carefully at this stone—especially at the lines of the cracks on its surface," she said. "Now look at the palm of your hand and compare it to the lines of this stone."

Morgan put her hand next to the stone. "Wow! That's so cool," she excitedly replied. "The lines are the same." Then she grabbed Miyah's hand and compared it to the stone. "Your palm lines match too!" she exclaimed.

"Yes. The lines on this stone match the palms of Junia, Nona and all the women of our bloodline who were Touchstone carriers. I guess you could say it's our official handprint. This is a very powerful healing stone," she said. "You'll learn to use it wisely in your healing work."

Morgan turned the heavy stone over in her hands, then placed it back into its fabric nest. Next, Miyah carefully removed a simple linen, hand-sewn bag from her medicine pouch, and unwinding its ties, revealed the

thick leather diary inside. An emblem initialed both the corner of the bag and the cover of the book. Running her fingers over the design on the book, she explained to Morgan that the symbol was a talisman, "charged with magical energy," as her grandmother, Nona, had told her.

"This is a family crest, as ancient as the diary itself. Within the design is a double M. Every women in our family has one or two M's somewhere in their name. I've told you about the double M, the symbol I embroidered on the medicine bag and what it symbolizes. It's similar to an alchemy sign for glass," she noted. "I see it as more of an hour glass of our

bloodline—with each generation sifting through the earth cycle. When you turn it over and the next generation continues. . .and so on."

"That's a beautiful analogy," Morgan said.

Miyah got up and moved some books on one of the library shelves and brought back a very old, hand-blown hour glass.

"This has been in the house ever since any of us can remember," Miyah said to her daughter. "I used it nearly every day after my mother died and again when Nona died, to remind me of our powerful connection. It helped get me through some pretty tough times. Sometimes I sat and concentrated on those tiny grains of sand and they brought me into their stories and gave me hope and inspiration. It's very special. Now it's yours."

Morgan carefully took the hour glass from her mother's hands. "Are you sure I'm ready for all of this?" she nervously asked, knowing of the responsibility that came with all of this knowledge.

"You're ready, my dear," replied Miyah, picking up the diary again and sitting next to Morgan.

"We'll read slowly so you can digest every word. Listen to the voices as they speak to you and absorb the wisdom between the lines. Feel the emotions and don't be afraid to express your own. Our women have endured a lot to be the carriers of the Touchstone and they deserve our complete respect and attention. Get to know them, and you'll find how easy it is to receive help whenever you need it, in any phase of your life. They're always with us, here, within the pages of the diary, to assist."

"How old is this diary?" Morgan asked.

"The very first entry is by Anna, grandmother to Joshua, and then by Mariam, the mother of Joshua. That would be over 2,000 years ago. The pages have been treated with sacred oils that keep them from deteriorating, but you still need to handle them with absolute care and gentleness. I recommend saying a prayer of gratitude each time before you open the book. It's truly a gift, having access to the world of our ancestors like this. Read in reverence and you'll be surrounded with so much love, you'll feel like bursting! It's a drug, but a good one that fills you up and makes you want to give back to the world in every way you can. Don't be fearful of its power. You're that strong too, but read only a little at a time in the beginning, or else you'll not be able to absorb all the energy it has to share."

Morgan sat with the book in her lap, running her hands over the worn leather cover, letting her fingers outline the double M design embedded in the corner. She looked up at her mother.

"How will I ever learn to read this. You said it's written in many languages?"

"You will in time, just as I did. You'll be guided by the women who wrote it. But for now, I'll read to you. Don't be afraid to ask questions. That's how we learn."

"Junia and Nona are here with us, aren't they?" Morgan asked. "It's been a long time since they appeared to us in spirit form, but I can feel their presence."

"Yes, they are, and a lot more spirits from our bloodline are excitedly awaiting this moment too. They're the secret behind being able to read the diary. It's through their voices, that the words are translated."

Morgan closed her eyes and thanked all the ancestors who were there. She thanked her mother for her wisdom and she thanked all the women of her lineage for being strong enough to carry this book through the ages to her. She vowed that, in gratitude, she would always take time to honor their stories and the teachings they brought forward. Then she opened her eyes and slowly lifted the cover of the diary.

~~~~

The first entry was short, printed in small letters on the second page of the book. Miyah read:

To my daughter, Mariam, on your wedding day. May your life be long and fruitful, and recorded here for your children to know your journey.

March 8 BC

My love and blessings,
your mother, Anna

Written in the margin of the book was a date, *March 8 BC*. Morgan would find many of these footnotes that others, throughout the years, had taken the liberty to write, updating the diary with modern dates, time lines and other information they didn't want to get lost or overlooked.

Morgan held her breath at the sheer magnitude of the moment. She was about to look into the journey of others who brought the lines of healing and light into her being. She wondered if this was how every woman felt as the diary began to reveal itself to them. She welled up with so much emotion that she wasn't sure if she could go beyond that first entry.

Miyah put her arm around her daughter and gave her a soothing hug.

"Yes," she said, hearing Morgan's question intuitively. "This is a part of accepting the love I was telling you about. Powerful, isn't it? And beautiful. I felt exactly the same emotions the first time I opened the diary."

Miyah continued, "Perhaps I should tell you a little about the times of Mariam before we read further. Bear with me on this, OK? It's a lot to consume at one time.

"Mother Mariam had brown eyes and light hair. She was a Jew, but her racial family was made of Syrian, Hittite, Phoenician, Greek and Egyptian heritage. The diary begins with Mariam, but among her lineage of ancestors were well-known women—Annon, Tamar, Ruth, Bathsheba, Ansie, Cloa, Eve, Enta and Ratta.

"This was a time in history when the entire Mediterranean world was a unified empire with Roman political and social systems. Greek culture and language, along with Aramaic and Hebrew, existed with the influence of Jewish religious and moral teachings. There were good roads connecting cities. The seas were clear of pirates and trade and travel was common.

"Since the age of three, Mariam had grown up in the temple, where she said she was often visited by angels. This was the temple at Mount Carmel, where the original school of the prophets was located. Students studied astrology, numerology and other subjects like reincarnation and healing with herbs, under Essene teachers. Mariam's mother, Anna, was a well-known Essene priestess and young Mariam was chosen to be raised and educated as one of the twelve temple maidens. She was twelve-years-old when she left the temple to return to her parent's home."

"Who were the other maidens and what became of them?" Morgan asked.

"Some of their names were Andra, Sophia, Shelmar, Sofa, Clana, Josie, and Edithia, who Mariam mentions in this diary as attending the birth of Joshua. And Mary, who became the wife of James, the son of Zebedee," Miyah responded.

"A man named Yosuf was employed by Mariam's father, Joachim, in building an addition to his house. His ancestors were builders, carpenters, masons and smiths. He was actually Mariam's cousin, the youngest son of Joachim's brother Jacob and his wife, Lois. Yosuf had also been raised in the spirit of the Essenes, so the two knew each from the temple. When Mariam, who was almost 13-years-old at the time, brought Yosuf a cup of water during a noontime meal, the courtship of the pair began. Mariam and Yosuf married in March 8 BC, accordance with Jewish custom, at Mount Carmel in a sacred Essene ceremony. Yosuf was old for marriage, 32. Mariam was 15. This marriage took place after a normal courtship of almost two years."

"But why was there such an age difference? That must have been weird to marry someone as old as your own father." Morgan made a face.

"He was chosen by the priests as a man of honor who could care for her," Miyah simply said. "He also had good bloodlines.

"Yosuf had deep, black eyes and was a brunet. He had many non-Jewish ancestors through the female lines of his ancestry, which went back to the days of Abraham, and to earlier lines of the Sumerians and Nodites. Mariam had a true Davidic ancestry. Yosuf was not of the original line of King David. However, six generations prior, Yosuf's paternal ancestor, who was an orphan, was adopted by Zadok, a direct descendant of David. That meant that future generations, like Yosuf, were also counted in the House of David. I know this all sounds confusing, but back then lineage was important."

"I know I won't remember all this now, but thanks for setting the scene for me, Mom," Morgan smiled.

"OK," Miyah laughed, gently turning the page. "The first entries of Mariam's story begin after her wedding and settling into their new home."

Morgan noticed the penmanship on the parchment paper of the old diary, written as if a young Mariam carefully formed her words. She wrote in exact detail. Miyah read the paragraph aloud:

> _ Not long after our marriage, my husband Yosuf and I moved into our new home, built by Yosuf and two of his brothers, in the northern part of Nazareth. The house is near the foot of a high hill, overlooking the surrounding countryside, on the outskirts of the city. The top of the nearby highland is the highest of all

the hills of southern Galilee, except Mount Tabor range to the east, and the hill of Nain, which looks about the same height. I walk there when I want to be alone. The view is vast and I feel at peace. Our house is located a little to the southeast of the hill, about midway to the road leading out of Nazareth. A narrow trail winds around the base of the hill in a northeasterly direction, to a point where it joins the road to Sepphorisis.

With such detailed description of her new home, Mariam must have realized the importance of record keeping for future generations. Miyah read on:

_ Our home is a one-room, stone building with a flat roof and an adjoining shelter for housing animals. Yosuf made all of our furniture — a low stone table, a lantern stand and several small stools. I brought with me earthenware dishes and pots, and my loom for weaving. We have mats for sleeping on the stone floor. For evening meals the table is lighted by a small, flat, clay lamp, filled with olive oil. In the back yard, near the animal hut, is a shelter that covers the oven and the mill for grinding grain. It requires both of us to operate the mill, one to grind and another to feed the grain.

The next entry was earmarked by a note in the margin, November, 8 BC.

November 8 BC

_ I had a vision last night. I must not tell anyone, but can't contain myself, so will spill my dream into this diary. An angel appeared to me. He announced that I had conceived a son, who was blessed by heaven. He said I should name him Yeshua, and that he would be a great leader among men, teaching a message of love and truth. He said many things to me about this special child, which I find hard to believe. I was told not to speak of this except to my husband, Yosuf, and to my kinswoman, Elizabeth, to whom he had also appeared. He told Elizabeth that she would also bear a son who would prepare the way for my son, and that she would name him Elias John.

The next entry began:

_ After many weeks, I am certain I am with child. When I finally told Yosuf of my vision and of my condition, and that our child was destined to be the great teacher, he was troubled and could not sleep for many nights. At first he doubted the angel's visitation. Then when he finally accepted that I had really heard the voice and believed it to be a divine messenger, he was still torn and wondered how such things could be. How could the offspring of human beings be a child of divine destiny? But after several weeks of conversation, we have accepted that we have been chosen to become parents of such a leader and healer who was chosen by God to teach his people. I have persuaded Yosuf to let me journey four miles west of Jerusalem, in the hills, to visit my cousin Elizabeth.

"Mariam remained with Elizabeth for three weeks, comparing

experiences and talking over the future of their sons. Her next entry was written somewhat later."

> – I have just returned from traveling to Mount Carmel to visit my mother Anna and father Joachim. Although well versed in the etherial beliefs of the Essene traditions, they, along with my brothers and sisters, don't believe my story about the divine mission of my unborn son to unite the world. They think I am going a little insane because of my condition. I have not told them of my visit from the angel. My husband, Yosuf, is a mild-mannered man and in every way faithful to the religious practices of his people. He talks little, but thinks much. As a youth, among his eight brothers and sisters, he had been more cheerful, but lately he has been subject to periods of mild spiritual discouragement.

"A later entry speaks about a dream of her husband, Yosuf."

> – Yosuf said a brilliant celestial messenger appeared to him last night and told him many things, and that our son would become a great light in the world to all races and peoples. The messenger told him that at first his own people will barely receive him, but to those who would, he would reveal that they are all the children of God – all a part of God. After this dream, Yosuf believed.

Morgan impatiently waited while Miyah got up to make a pot of tea. She was already consumed with the diary. She ran her fingers over the words as if they were in braille, studying the style of lettering. Settling back, next to Morgan with a hot cup of herbal tea for each of them, Miyah continued.

> – The month we were married, Caesar Augustus announced that all inhabitants of the Roman Empire be numbered and a census be made. However a census was not made in the Palestinian Kingdom of Herod until now, a year later. It is not necessary that I go to Bethlehem for enrollment, as Yosuf is authorized to register our family, but I have insisted upon accompanying him. I don't want our child to be born while Yosuf is away. I also hope to visit my kinswoman Elizabeth on this journey. Her son was born March 25, and has already been circumcised, the traditional eight days after, and was formally named Elias John. I would so like to see them. I have packed food for three or four days and we are set to depart at the break of day, August 18. My mother Anna will accompany us, as well as others from the Mount Carmel community.

Dates were recorded in different time language in biblical days, so Miyah translated them into current era time to make it easier for Morgan to understand. 7 BC. was written in different ink in the margin of the diary.

> – Because of my condition, I will ride in a blanket-laden cart pulled by our donkey, along with the provisions, and Yosuf must

walk, even though he is not as fit as usual. He has worked hard building our new house, along with all the furnishings. His father has recently been disabled so Yosuf also contributes to the support of his parents. It has taken a toll on him. I'm glad I'm making this trip with him, although I am certain he is worrying about me traveling at this late time of my pregnancy. My hand maiden, Sophia (Josie) also travels with us and I am grateful for her attention. We joined with several others who had carts, rode donkeys, camels or walked. They brought musical instruments, food and tents, and we sang as we traveled and told stories around the campfires at night.

Mariam continued her diary entry a few days later.

_ Our first day of travel brought us around the foothills of Mount Gilboa, where we camped for the night by the river Jordan. Early the next morning we continued our journey and partook of our noontide meal at the foot of Mount Sartaba, overlooking the Jordan Valley. We journeyed on, making Jericho for the night, where we stopped at an inn on the road on the outskirts of the city. Following our evening meal we engaged in much discussion with other travelers at the inn, concerning the oppressiveness of Roman rule, Herod, and the census enrollment. Some compared the influence of Jerusalem and Alexandria as centers of Jewish learning and culture. After such deep conversation, we retired for the night, ready for a good sleep.

_ We arose early the next morning and reached Jerusalem before noon. On the outskirts of the city the roads widened and became paved with stones, cut and laid by Roman slaves. Aquaducts and deep wells along the way supplied us with water. After visiting the temple, we continued on to Bethlehem and arrived by mid-afternoon. We set up our camp with some others in a valley watered by a small spring, near Etam, just beyond Bethlehem, where we took refuge away from the noise of the overcrowded village. The city was filled with people arriving to register for the census. Roman soldiers were everywhere, their swords and spears shining in the sunlight, as they smacked their whips upon the backs of slaves who moved too slowly.

_ All of the inns were filled and even Yosuf's distant relatives had no extra room. Sophia is a friend of the innkeeper and has arranged for several of our group to stay in a caravan stable, hewn out of the side of a rock, situated just below the inn. It had been cleared of animals and cleaned up for the overflow of lodgers. Leaving our donkey and cart in the courtyard, Yosuf carried our provisions on his shoulders and we descended the stone steps into the cave. It was beginning to fill up with other travelers, but we found space in what

7BC

had been a grain storage room to the front of the stalls and mangers. Tent curtains were hung to separate spaces, and we counted ourselves fortunate to have such quarters. Yosuf wanted me to rest and he was going to go out and enroll, but I felt very uncomfortable and asked him to stay with me and register instead the next day. It had been a long journey. He stayed by my side.

_ The shelter was crowded, damp and noisy and I was grateful when my mother Anna found a place for us to stay outside of the village, with Elizabeth, in a small house owned by Zacharias. Yosuf loaded our belongings and we traveled a short distance to new lodging. We entered through a hallway from an inner courtyard, which connected three other dwellings owned by Zacharias' brother Zenos. The room was small, an upper room above a stable that opened to fenced pens and hillside caves, used for animals and storage, but there was room for all of us to sleep and I was more comfortable in the presence of family. Yosuf found a small wooden crib, used to feed sheep and goats in the stable below. He washed it and filled it with fresh straw, then it was lined with sheep's fleece and covered with folded sheets of soft Egyptian cotton. This is to be our son's cradle for many months to come.

There were three small droplets of blood dotting the top of the next page, which looked as if they had deliberately been dripped onto the page, as a talisman of sorts for the pain Mariam had endured. There was also a gap in the writing and a darken stain on the page, as if something that had been placed there ages ago had either simply disintegrated, or had slipped out of the pages. Miyah had been told that Mariam had pressed a piece of her baby's umbilical cord there, between the pages of her diary, as a symbol of good luck and long life. August 21, 7 BC was written in the margin of the diary.

_ I was so restless and uncomfortable, I fear I kept everyone awake all night. By the break of day the pain of childbirth was strong. Elizabeth sent for Sodaphe, the wife of the innkeeper. Her two daughters, Edithia and Sarapha, also came to help, bringing cotton sheets and urns of water. It was a very difficult time for me and my laboring lasted until after midnight. Anna gave me a root to chew to lessen the pain and repeated mantras with me to calm my breathing.

_ Our son, Yeshua ben Yosuf, was finally born – his head covered with curly, auburn-golden hair. I was joyous, but fatigued from childbirth. Anna placed my placenta into preservative oils in a container to later be ceremoniously buried. I weakly gazed at my son, Yeshua laying upon my belly while the umbilical cord was cut and tied and he was taken by my mother Anna to be washed. She was the first of our family to proudly hold my son, her new

August 21, 7 BC

grandson, whom she had just helped deliver. Then Sarapha, only a year younger than myself, wrapped my newborn babe in the cloth I had brought from home, and pressing her lips to his brow, she presented him to me.

- I held him to my breast and he immediately began to suckle. With my newborn near to me on my mat, I slept like I never had before, content that I had given birth to a healthy baby, which was all that was important to me at that moment. Let it be recorded that my son was born about an hour after midnight on the twenty-first day in the time of Elul, according to our Jewish calendar.

Mariam's next entry was made several weeks later and gives a recap of the events following the birth of her son.

- The next day, while making his census enrollment, Yosuf met with one of the men we had debated with at the inn in Jericho. He introduced Yosuf to a wealthy friend of his, who when he heard that I had just given birth, offered us his room at the inn. There was more space for us, Anna and Josie, so after a few days we moved to the inn and lived there for almost three weeks, until we found lodging in the home of a distant relative of Yosuf. During that time, according to Jewish practice, our son was circumcised and formally named Yeshua ben Yosuf.

- The following week Yosuf conferred with Zacharius, as both he and Elizabeth believed that Yeshua was to become the Jewish Messiah, and that their son, John, was to be his ally, as the angel had prophesied. Elizabeth and I bonded even closer with the prospect of our sons' divine futures and I have convinced Yosuf to let us remain in Bethlehem, the City of David, for at least a year so that Yeshua might grow up to become the successor of David on the throne of all Israel. Yosuf has already found some carpentry work in the city.

Miyah, herself, had many questions regarding the holy birth story as she was growing up. She was confused with the version told in Christian churches—that Yeshua/Joshua/Jesus was conceived of a virgin, born on December 25, instead of August 21; and what about the star that the three wise men followed?

The virgin part was easily explained by Miyah's mother, Junia. Many Old Testament sayings were distorted in translation—the passage, "a maiden shall bear a son," was changed to read, "a virgin shall bear a son." There were many "maiden/virgin births" reported in biblical times, perhaps based on all the virgin births in Greek mythology. In the ancient world, the word "virgin" or maiden, referred to a woman who had not yet given birth, so the first born was referred to as a virgin birth. Miyah accepted that as a sensible explanation.

As for the shepherds and wisemen, Junia had explained to Miyah what the women of her ancestry had shared with her when she asked the same questions. That no shepherds or other creatures came to see the newborn baby until the arrival of Mesopotamian priests from Ur, a city near Babylon, when Yeshua was more than three-weeks-old. A spiritual teacher of Ur had a dream in which he was told that "the light of life" was about to appear on earth as a baby among the Jews. The three Magi, wisemen, went looking for this "light of life" and after many weeks of searching in Jerusalem, they were ready to return to their country. Zacharias heard of them and told them that he believed Yeshua was this child. There was no star to guide them, just the road to Bethlehem, where they found Mariam and her baby and they bestowed them with gifts. The Magi weren't kings, as made out to be in 6th century writings, but were expert astronomers, versed in magical practices.

There were also many other wisemen who traveled to see the baby over the course of the next years—they came from Persia, India, Egypt and also from the Chaldea, Gobi, or the Indo-Tao Land. Some were Buddhist lamas, in search of their next holy leader.

"Then what about the beautiful legend of the Star of Bethlehem?" Miyah's mother had asked as a child. Nona had an answer waiting for her, as told to her by ancestors.

"It does have to do with the stars," she had said, "but this can be explained through astrology. An extraordinary conjunction of Jupiter and Saturn in the constellation of Pisces occurred in 7 BC, resulting in a nova, or a new star. Everyone who saw this was impressed by the sight of the two planets so close that they appeared in the night sky as a double star of great light. Such an encounter of this sign of the Zodiac occurs only every 794 years.

"The legend of the Star of Bethlehem was applied to these extraordinary, natural events and the Magi story followed, resembling the path of the priests from Ur. As knowledge was passed throughout generations, myths became traditions and were eventually accepted as fact, adjusted to the time frame of the birth. The stellar conjunction of the planets still makes a beautiful Star of Bethlehem story, it just has little to do with the birth of Yeshua, except for its timing."

Morgan was full of questions and she receive the same answers that Miyah had gotten from her mother regarding the birth story and the mis-celebration of it at Christmas time.

Miyah took a deep breath. "I think you'll find this interesting, although it'll be a lot for you to apprehend," she said. "It has to do with Mithra. It's said that the god Mithra was born on December 25 as an offspring of the Sun. He was represented as a beautiful youth, a great traveling teacher and master with twelve companions, and he performed miracles. Mithra was called 'the good shepherd, the way, the truth and the light, the redeemer, a savior, the Messiah.' He was identified with both the lion and the lamb."

"Wait," said Morgan. "Aren't you talking about Jesus?"

"You would think so, wouldn't you," Miyah replied, walking over to search the bookshelves, which spanned across an entire wall of the room.

"But the religion of Mithra preceded Christianity by roughly six hundred years. Mithraic worship at one time covered a large portion of the ancient world. It flourished as late as the second century. The idea of a Messiah supposedly originated in ancient Persia and this is where Christian concepts of a Savior came from—Mithras, the sun god—Yeshua, the son of God.

"As far as pin-pointing an actual birth, early Christians didn't actually celebrate Jesus' birth, only his resurrection. Their focus was on the Son of God, not the Son of Man. By the 4th century the Church decided to begin celebrating Jesus' birth to reinforce his humanity, but by then the date of his actual birth was unknown. Since the birthday of Mithras was already a widely observed holy day, the Church simply declared December 25 to be the 'Feast Day of the Nativity.' The feast day of the S U N soon became the feast day of the S O N."

Miyah selected a handful of books from the bookshelf and handed "The International Encyclopedia" to Morgan. "Read this," she said, unmarking a page.

Morgan read, "Mithras seems to have owed his fame to the belief that he was the source of life and could also redeem the souls of the dead into the better world. The ceremonies included a baptism to remove sins, anointing, and a sacred meal of bread and a consecrated wine, believed to possess wonderful power."

Miyah opened a marked page on the "Chambers Encyclopedia" and read, "The most important of Mithras' many festivals was his birthday, celebrated on the 25th of December, the day subsequently fixed—against all evidence—as the birthday of Christ. The worship of Mithras early found its way into Rome and the mysteries of Mithras, which fell in the spring equinox, were famous even among the many Roman festivals. The ceremonies observed in the initiation to these mysteries—symbolical of the struggle between Ahriman and Ormuzd (the Good and the Evil)—were most extraordinary, and to a certain degree were dangerous in character. Baptism and the partaking of a mystical liquid, consisting of flour and water, to be drunk with the utterance of sacred formulas, were among the inauguration acts."

Morgan picked up the copy of "The Catholic Encyclopedia" and read that the early Church Fathers found this religion of Mithras very disturbing, as there are so many similarities between the two religions.

"Listen to this!" she exclaimed, finding another reference. "This is unbelievable!

#1 – Hundreds of years before Jesus, according to the Mithraic religion, three wisemen of Persia came to visit the baby savior-god Mithra, bringing him gifts of gold, myrrh and frankincense.

#2 – Mithra was born on December 25, recorded in the "Great Religions of the World." '…it was the winter solstice celebrated by ancients as the birthday of the Mithras sun god.'

#3 – Before Mithra died on a cross, he celebrated a 'Last Supper' with his twelve disciples, who represented the twelve signs of the zodiac.

#4 – After the death of Mithra, his body was laid to rest in a rock tomb.

#5 – Mithra had a celibate priesthood . . .

Morgan looked up at Miyah, "Well, we know that one wasn't the same," she said with a smile. "But here, there's one more.

#6 – Mithra ascended into heaven during the spring (Passover) equinox, the time when the sun crosses the equator making night and day of equal length.

"I can't believe no one ever talks about this!" Morgan exclaimed.

"Oh, there's been plenty of debate over the centuries. The Church prefers to suppress it because it suggests that Christianity took many of its elements from this earlier 'pagan' religion and they became intertwined as their own Jesus story. There's a lot of material evidence in Mithraic temples and artifacts that archaeologists have found scattered throughout the Roman Empire. The temples were built underground in caves, filled with elaborate icons. A relic was also preserved in the catacombs at Rome. It was a painting of the infant, Mithra, seated in the lap of his virgin mother, while on their knees before him were Persian Magi adoring him and offering gifts.

"So you see, Mithra was one of the major religions of the Roman Empire, prominent especially among the military because Mithra was also the god of war, battle, justice and faith. Romans celebrated the birthday of Mithra, and when they began to shape Christianity, this festival was converted into a Christian celebration instead, honoring the birthday of Jesus, not Mithros— as December 25."

Morgan picked up another of the books Miyah had placed on the table. She read about other deities and legends who had been born of virgins: Augustus (his father was the god Apollo), Agdistis, Attis, Adonis, Buddha, Dionysus, Korybas, Krishna, Osirus, Perseus, Romulus and Remus, Tammuz, Zoroaster—all men, she noted.

Morgan had never really believed in the virgin concept from the beginning, so that was easy to dispel. It made sense that the word virgin meant a woman who hadn't yet given birth. But it really made her think when she got to a chapter that listed accounts of pagan gods from many different cultures, who had the same attributes that Christians claimed of Jesus. She read:

APOLLONIUS OF TYANA: Apollonius the Nazarene was born in Asia Minor, his birth was heralded by a spirit, born on December 25. He was able to exorcise demons, cure the sick, forecast the future and brought people back from the dead. He was put on trial by the Romans, died on a cross, appeared in ghostly form to two followers in a cave and appeared to his apostles after his death, to teach.

ATTIS of PHRYGIA: Born of the Virgin Nana on December 25. He was both the Father and the Divine Son. He was a savior, crucified on a tree for the salvation of mankind. He was buried, but on the third day the priests found the tomb empty. He had arisen from the dead (on March 25). His followers were baptized in blood, thereby washing away their sins, after which they declared themselves "born again." His followers ate a sacred meal of bread, which they believed became the body of the savior.

BUDDHA – INDIA: Born of the virgin Maya on December 25. He was announced by a star and attended by wisemen presenting costly gifts. At birth, angels sang heavenly songs. He taught in the temple at age 12, and was tempted by Mara, the Evil One (Satan), while fasting. He was baptized in water with the Spirit of God present. Buddha healed the sick and fed 500 from a small basket of cakes, and he walked on water. He came to fulfill the law and preached the establishment of a kingdom of righteousness and obliged followers of poverty who renounced the world. He transfigured on a mount, died, was buried, but arose again after the tomb opened by supernatural powers and ascended into heaven (Nirvana). Buddha was called: "Good Shepherd," "Alpha and Omega," "Sin Bearer," "Master," "Light of the World," "Redeemer," etc.

DIONYSUS - GREECE: Born of a virgin on December 25 and placed in a manger. He was a traveling teacher who performed many miracles, including turning water into wine. His followers ate a sacred meal that became the body of the god. He rose from the dead March 25. He is identified with the ram and lambs, and was called "King of Kings," "Only Begotten Son," "Savior," "Redeemer," "Sin Bearer," "Anointed One," the "Alpha and Omega."

HERCULES – GREECE: Born around winter solstice of a virgin, he was sacrificed at the spring equinox. He was called "Savior," "Only Begotten," "Prince of Peace," "Son of Righteousness."

KRISHNA - INDIA: Krishna was born while his foster-father Nanda was in the city to pay his tax to the king. His nativity was heralded by a star. Krishna was born of the virgin Devaki in a cave, which at the time of his birth was miraculously illuminated. The cow herds adored his birth. King Kansa sought the life of the Indian Christ by ordering the massacre of all male children born during the same night as he. Krishna traveled widely, performing miracles, raising the dead, healing lepers, the deaf and the blind. The crucified Krishna is pictured on the cross with arms extended. Pierced by an arrow while hanging on the cross, Krishna died, but descended into Hell from which he rose again on the third day and ascended into Heaven. Krishna is one of the Hindu trinity.

OSIRIS – EGYPT: He came to fulfill the law, and was called "KRST," the "Anointed One." Born of the virgin Isis-Meri on December 25 in a cave/manger, with his birth announced by a star, and attended by three wisemen. His earthly father was named "Seb," which translates to "Yosuf." At age 12 he was a child teacher in the Temple. He vanished for 18 years and at the age of 30 he was baptized in the river Larutana—the river Jordan—by "Anup the Baptizer," who was beheaded. (Anup translates to John.) He performed miracles, exorcised demons, raised El-Osiris from the dead, walked on water, and was betrayed by Typhon. He was crucified between two thieves on the 17th day of the month of Athyr, buried in a tomb from which he arose on the third day, 19th Athyr, and was resurrected. His suffering, death, and resurrection was celebrated each year by his disciples on the Vernal Equinox—Easter. He was called "The Way, The Truth, The Light," "Messiah," "God's Anointed Son,' the "Son of Man," the "Word Made Flesh," the "Word of Truth." He was expected to reign a thousand years.

. . .and then there was

MITHRAS – PERSIA: He was born on December 25 of the Sun God and a virgin mother, called "the Mother of God." He was a symbol of justice, truth and loyalty. He was considered the saviour of humankind and stories tell of his healing the sick, raising the dead and performing miracles (making the blind see and the lame walk). Throughout his lifetime, he was seen as a protector of human souls, a mediator between heaven and earth and was associated with a holy trinity. He remained celibate, until the age of 64, and throughout his life he preached the virtues of ethics, moral behavior, and good will.

A footnote about Mithras written on a piece of paper in the book stated: *"Mithraism came into the ancient Roman world about 75 BC, and later ranked as a principal competitor of Christianity for 200 years. Paul was born and raised in the city of Tarsus, a region in SE Asia-Minor, now called Turkey, where Mithras was well known. Many biblical scholars now believe that Paul, the alleged author of 13 out of the 27 (maybe more) books of the New Testament, was influenced in his writings by this strong religion of Mithraism, as a profound likeness between Mithraism and Christianity can be seen. Mithraism was so popular in Rome, the pagan Emperor Constantine, who believed in the sun god Mithras, designated a certain day of the week to him—Sunday, which means the day of the sun."*

Morgan flipped the book shut and tossed it on the floor.

"So basically, all the pagan religions were alike, including Christianity. It just happens that one of them became the most powerful, and did its best to wipe out all the others," she said sarcastically. "No wonder why you don't claim a name for your spirituality. How ironic."

"It is ironic, isn't it, coming from the roots of our lineage," her mother replied.

"But wait. Doesn't that have some bearing on OUR story?" Morgan asked, confused. "Was the beginning of our bloodline also born out of myth?"

"No, Morgan. It's not myth. Many events occurred as stated in biblical tales, but some of them were intertwined with Mithra legends. The base of the story is there, it's just been elaborated upon. You'll know the difference when we read the diary. You've already read how common the birth of Yeshua was in comparison to what was written several hundred years after the event.

"The thing you must remember is that when we speak of Yeshua/Joshua/Jesus as a link in our bloodline, we're speaking of the life of Jesus, the Jew, who we knew as a great man, a healer and prophet, not the Gentile Jesus who became a symbol for the Romans as they developed their Christian story. You'll see many similarities in beginning pages of the diary, as in those of Mariam's writings, but as you read on you'll find details and a much different story unfold through the words of the women of the bloodline. We're fortunate to have this record. That's why I guard this sacred diary with my very soul. It's not just the Touchstone of our lineage—it holds the truth of our people's spiritual mission throughout life."

Morgan sat silent. This isn't what she had expected to find when she began today's lessons. It isn't something she really wanted to hear either. It changed the way she looked at religion. She never felt she needed a name for her spirituality either, and just like her mother, she embraced all religions and a belief in one God. But this had to do with history at its core and the real lives of her people throughout history. It was what her bloodline was all about. It made for a confusing mix of theology that seemed to distort the original, simple and plain teachings of Jesus into political convenience, accelerated by the persecution and suppression of any who tried to support the "old" ways.

"Some religion," she mumbled, wondering if she even wanted to continue reading the diary.

Miyah placed the diary back on Morgan's lap and sat down next to her.

"Let's continue," she said. "It'll restore your faith."

Morgan reluctantly removed the marker she had placed in the diary pages, and Miyah began to read.

> _ Moses taught the Jews that every first-born son belongs to the Lord and in many customs must be sacrificed. Newer laws say that in place of death, an offering or redemption can be made to a priest. So instead of sacrificing our first born son, we will redeem him by making a payment of five shekels to a priest. Yosuf and I are taking Yeshua to the temple in

Jerusalem to present him to the priests for his redemption and at the same time to make a proper sacrifice of two young pigeons for my purification. According to Mosaic laws, I must present myself at the temple for ceremonial purification from the uncleanliness of childbirth.

The scribbled handwriting of the next entry indicated it was written quickly, not having the time, but urgently wanting to record events.

_ We returned from Jerusalem safely, but we have learned that Herod has tried to find and question the three priests from Ur who visited us in Bethlehem. I have heard they have returned to their homeland, but he is upset to hear that our little Yeshua is being called a King among the people. Two of Zacharia's friends, Simeon, a singer, and Anna a poetess, performed a song for Yeshua's redemption, announcing him as the God of Israel. Yosuf and I were disturbed by this early salutation of the prophetic mission of our son and now fear for his safety. We have been forced to hide him in secret with Yosuf's relatives. Even Zacharia and Elizabeth remain out of sight. Yosuf is afraid to seek work and our small savings are disappearing.

"What happened?" Morgan asked her mother.

"After more than a year of searching Herod had still not located Yeshua, but thought he was in Bethlehem. He was obsessed and ordered a search of every house in Bethlehem and that all boy babies under two-years of age be killed, so any child who might become King of the Jews would be destroyed. In one day sixteen boy babies died, including Herod's own first-born son. The massacre of these infants happened in the middle of October, when Jesus was a little over a year old.

_ I am in such anguish, I cannot bear it. Is it my fault these babies have been slaughtered? The son of my friends, Ruth and Jacobinus, is dead. Am I to blame because I believe my son to be the deliverer and boasted it to others? How can this happen? Zacharias was told of Herod's plans and dispatched a messenger to Yosuf. My friend, Mateal offered us her beasts so we could flee to Egypt away from Herod. Many others have also left. By nightfall we departed Bethlehem with our son, for Alexandria, to avoid attracting attention. We are traveling by Hebron to Beersheba, and from there will cross the desert to the Mediterranean. Zacharias provided us with funds for the journey. Even he and Elizabeth have left Bethlehem. We will stay with relatives of Yosuf. My heart is so filled with sadness I cannot bear the thought of those parents losing their children. God forgive me.

Morgan could feel the pain in the pages as Miyah read.

"They stayed in Alexandria for two full years, not returning until after the death of Herod," said Miyah. "At that time there were over a million

Jews in Egypt, living in colonies with synagogues and schools. There were also many viharas, Buddhist missionary schools, and Yeshua was introduced to the wisdom of Eastern philosophy at a very young age, by Essene teachers and Buddhist scholars in Alexandria."

"How do you know all this, mother? Is it written in the diary?" Morgan asked.

"Some of it is, but there are also very complete records left by the Essenes and other scholars from that time period. Many of these sacred documents had been hidden to keep them safe and have only recently been discovered and translated, like the Nag Hamadi Library and the Dead Sea Scrolls. Only four gospels are included in the Bible. Twenty-six gospels were excluded—The Gospel of Thomas, the Gospel according to the Hebrews, the Gospel according to the Egyptians, the Gospel of Peter, the Gospel of the Ebionites, the Gospel of Judas, the Gospel of Barnabas, the Gospel of Mary Magdalene, and the Gospel of James, to mention a few. The Gnostic Gospels are a collection of writings about the teachings of Jesus, written from the 2nd - 4th century. There are also a lot of apocryphal books, like the Book of Enoch."

"What does apocryphal mean?" Morgan asked.

"Well, the modern term to the ancient "apocrypha" would be 'top secret government documents,'" Miyah laughed, glad her daughter was absorbed in all of these confusing, new revelations. "Apocrypha was applied to writings kept secret because they contained knowledge considered too sacred to be disclosed to anyone other than the initiated. But in some cases they were books and teachings the early Roman Church rejected because it didn't fit their means.

"There's also much to learn from books of other religions, the Torah—the sacred writings of Judaism; The Holy Qur'an—the holy book of Islam; the Bhagavad Gita—meaning "Song of God," one of the most important Hindu scriptures. Judaism and Islam also trace their beginnings back to Abraham, so their writings contain common threads of origin. There are many practices, teachings and customs that cross-pollinate with Buddhism."

She stopped to observed her daughter. "Is this too much to teach you now? We have a lot of time for these lessons. I know in all the years you were home-schooled, you didn't seem too interested in history."

"No, please go on, Mother," Morgan said. "I may not be able to absorb it all now, but I want to hear it. I've never heard any of this before."

"I know," Miyah replied. "I wanted to wait to share this until you were older, so you would understand it better. I admit, it can get pretty confusing—and is even more confusing with so many version of religious teachings. But this is our story that has been handed down through the ages."

Miyah continued. "In the Christian Bible there's no record of Yeshua/

Jesus from after age 12 until he reappears around age 30 and is baptized by John the Baptist. I always thought that strange, so when I was a young girl, I began to research and ask a lot of questions on my own—this was before I had *my* diary lesson. I found it was not difficult to find information about those lost years—especially with the huge library, strategically placed, right here at my fingertips." Miyah pointed to the floor-to-ceiling bookshelf, filled with books on religions subjects.

"I know you've never had an interest in reading these books," she said, "but maybe now you'll feel differently. They're all yours," adding, "be sure to read about a Jewish historian named Flavius Yosufus, who 50-70 years after the crucifixion wrote about the Essene healers of his time. Writings have also been discovered in monasteries in Nepal, Tibet and India that give detailed records about the travels of Jesus and his life throughout those 'lost' years. If you can't find what you are looking for, just ask Junia or Nona, they'll search it out for you. Books have been known to literally fall off the shelves!"

Both laughed, knowing full well that whenever either of them needed something, Junia and Nona were always there to help. . .and sometimes to challenge them to find their own answers.

Morgan admitted that now she was actually anxious to explore their personal library. "It's hard to believe there's so much written about all of this, yet it seems that so few people know about it," she said. "I bet I could also do a lot of research on my computer," she added with enthusiasm.

"Yes, that's possible," her mother replied. "But be sure to cross-reference everything you find. There's a lot out there that's also purposely deceiving."

Morgan let out a sigh as if to acknowledge the big lessons ahead of her, and she turned the page to the next entry in the diary. Miyah continued to read.

_ Our time in Alexandria has been good. Except for with a few relatives and friends, we have chosen not to talk of Yeshua being a child of promise. I keep him close to me, lest anything befall him, but he is healthy and growing. We have stayed in many places while in Egypt, including Mataria, on the right bank of the Nile River, Al-Moharraq, and the monasteries of Wadi-el-Natrun, also known as the "Herbal Garden" because of its unique fruits and flowers.

_There are well over 4,000 living in the monastery, and our Essene brothers have provided shelter for us, as well as shared their teachings and meditations. They wear white garments and do not partake of eating the flesh of animals. I am learning more from them about the healing properties of herbs and stones. Yeshua is also quick to learn their gentle ways and even at his young age, I find him listening to their teachings. He is learning the language of birds and of beasts, the healing powers of trees, herbs and flowers, and the hidden secrets of precious stones. He has learned the motions of the Sun and the

Moon and the stars.

Mariam left spaces between her diary entries, indicating that time had passed. Sometimes it seemed time between writings was only a few days, yet in other instances, it appeared that years had passed. It was difficult to obtain an exact time line because of this, but Morgan soon realized it was the personal content of the diary that was of utmost importance to the writer, and not so much the date events occurred, unless relating to births, deaths and occasional ceremonial events.

– We have spent time with my brother Isaac and his wife Tabitha in Heliopolis and have traveled much to temples along the Nile, to the great pyramids of the Giza Plateau. They are truly amazing sites. It is nearing our time to journey home. Upon hearing of our plans to return to Palestine, my young son was presented with a complete copy of the Greek translations of the Hebrew scriptures. Surely a sign that he is meant for greatness.

– As we return to our home, we are making a pilgrimage with many of our family, following the same path Moses took with the Israelites across the desert to Etham. We have journeyed south to a narrow strip of land that bordered the Red Sea on the west and a range of mountains on the east to Mount Sinai. Traveling on a boat belonging to our friend, Ezraeon, bound for Joppa, we celebrate Yeshua's birthday. We traveled overland to Bethlehem, and counseled with relatives as to the current safety of the city since Herod's death.

– Yosuf has doubts that our son is destined to become a kingly deliverer of Israel and can see no reason to stay here in the City of David. He wants to return to our home in Nazareth of Galilee, so after 30 days in Bethlehem, we are leaving at dawn. Five of Yosuf's kinsmen will accompany us on our journey and in four days we shall be back in the home where we began our marriage. It has been more than three years since we left Yosuf's brother and his family in care of our home. He has convinced me that it would be unwise to spread the word of the future prophecy of our son, for his own safety. My husband is anxious to return home.

The next entry in the diary was shorter, as Mariam must have had little time for writing. A date in the margin was written as April 2, 3 BC.

April 2, 3 BC

– We have been blessed with a second son, James. Yeshua is happy to have a baby brother. Yosuf has built a small workshop close to the village spring, and near the caravan tarrying lot, where he can do carpentry work with two of his brothers. He has a good business making yokes and plows. They are also working in leather, rope and canvas cloth.

Another short entry appeared many months later. 2 BC was noted on the page.

2 BC _ Our daughter, Mirium, was born on the date of July 11. I am blessed with another healthy child. Yeshua is of great help to me with the younger children and he never ceases to inquire the nature of all sorts of things. He has already learned much about area vines and plants for medicine and healing. We have made a shallow box of sand for him to draw maps and practice his writing in the Galilean dialect of Aramaic. He is learning Greek from the copy of the translated scroll that was given to him in Egypt. We have been told there is only one other complete copy of the Scriptures in Greek in all of Nazareth.

It seemed that Mariam could only manage one entry a year for quite some time. Her life was filled with the everyday hard work of raising a family. The margin of the next entry indicated her next writing was made in AD1.

AD 1 _ My kinswoman Elizabeth and her priest husband Zacharias have come to visit us with their son John for two days. How I longed to see her and hear news of their lives since we last met. Yeshua, James and John are bonding as friends. They do not know of the predictions of the two boys' greatness and are content to draw maps in the sand. Yosuf is working as a builder and we are no longer struggling to feed and clothe our growing family. His work travels him to Cana, Magdala, Nain, Sepphoris, Capernaum and Endor, as well as building work closer to home. James is able to help me with little Mirium, so Yeshua often travels to help his father. They sometimes spend months at a time at Mount Carmel and Qumran where Yosuf has work and Yeshua is able to study.

_ Yeshua also travels for long periods of time with my brother, Yosef of Arimathea to Britannia, Gaul and other lands. Yet, Yeshua still takes time to study flowers and plants and also the stars at night. We have a dovecote on top of the animal shelter, adjoining the house and use profits from the sale of our doves as a charity fund, which Yeshua administers to the needy, after he has made the tithe to the synagogue.

_ We were blessed with our fourth child, a son, Yosuf, March 16.

The next entry did not have a date and had spaces in between paragraphs, which seemed to indicate that it was written to catch up events that had happened over a period of time. Mariam wrote often about her children and little about her own life, which was probably because her children consumed her life. Miyah read the entries about all Mariam's children, but Morgan paid special attention to the notes about Yeshua.

_ Yeshua continues his formal studies in the synagogue school.

Yosuf has already taught him Aramaic and Greek. He has learned to read and write and to speak Hebrew. Yosuf and Yeshua often work in Bethany, near the eastern slopes of Olivet, and stay with the family of Lazarus, Martha and Maryum. They have become steadfast friends.

_ Yosuf and I take our children on walks to the top of the hill where we can see a view of Galilee and can make out the shapes of sailing vessels on the distant Mediterranean. On clear days we can see the long ridge of Mount Carmel running down to the sea, and to the north we see Mount Hermon's snowy peaks. From all directions we can see caravan trains as they wind their way in and out of Nazareth. People from many places travel through here on their trade routes and Yeshua and James always want to hear stories of other lands. Yeshua has traveled much with his uncle, Yosef of Arimathea, and I fear he desires to continue his travels to lands even farther away from his home.

_ My sons help me with milking the cow, caring for the animals and the making of cheese. They have learned much working on the farm of Yosuf's brother. Yeshua spends much time with his uncle fishing on the shores of the sea of Galilee, near Magdala. He has learned to weave and also has mastered the harp, exchanging dairy products for lessons.

AD 2 _ Our son, Simon, was born on April 14.

AD 3 _ Our 2nd daughter, Martha came to us on September 13.

AD 5 _ Our seventh child, Judas Thomas, was born to us on June 24, with many complications. I was ill for a long time and Yosuf has been at my side. The children have been very helpful. Yeshua has taken on the tasks of his father, running errands and tending to the building business.

AD 7 _ Another son, Amos, was born on January 9, with more ease to me than his brother Thomas. There was snow on the mountains and it was unusually cold that day. Water in our buckets turned to ice. Our family is growing large, but the children are much help to care for each other and our household. Yeshua graduated from his course of training at the synagogue school and, as is traditional with the first-born, was pronounced a son of the commandment, a child of the Most High and a servant of the Lord of all the earth. We have told him of the prophecy of his future as the Messiah, the deliverer of the people. He is spending more time speaking with travelers from the caravans and is yearning to explore further. He makes a plea to Yosuf and myself to allow him to travel to these far away lands with them. He argues that if he is to fulfill some great mission on earth, he must know more about the land and its people. His travels with my brother Yosef has left him yearning for more.

_ Yeshua is thirteen years of age, the time, according to

our Jewish tradition, when a son should begin preparations to marry, especially if he is to become an important rabbi. Already fathers have approached us, who believe he would make a good husband for their daughters, but Yeshua is adamant in his desires to travel and says he has no interest in betrothing at this young age. I fear we must let him go the next time the caravans pass through. His future has already been determined and he is wise beyond his years. Yosuf tells me we should not stand in his way. It saddens me to the bone. We have asked him to wait until the rainy season has ceased to depart from us. He, his cousins and uncle Jacob will be joining the caravans soon.

"These entries were made AD 1, 2, 3, 5 and 7. There is a long gap in diary entries and I assume it's because Mariam was busy with her large family. Then there are only two entries, and another long span of time before she wrote again, in AD 8." Miyah explained and continued to read.

AD 8 _ Tragedy has entered our lives and in my sorrow I cannot properly put the words to paper. On September 25, a runner from Sepphoris brought news that Yosuf had been injured by a fall while working on the governor's residence. My son James, now eleven-years-old, accompanied me to Sepphoris, but my beloved Yosuf had already left this earth by the time James and I arrived. We brought his body back to Nazareth, where he was laid to rest with his forefathers. We have had no direct word from Yeshua for more than a year, but caravan merchants tell us he has traveled far, into the East. I have asked the caravan travelers to carry the news of Yosuf's death, in hopes that it reaches the ears of Yeshua. I am left with seven young children in my home to care for, and am again with child. Yosuf's family has been helpful, and even though I try to remain strong in the face of my children, I am a broken woman inside and my heart aches. I pray for the strength to carry on and raise my children in good health and in good faith."

Miyah stopped reading for a moment. Morgan was somber and said nothing.

"Yosuf was 48-years-old. Mariam was almost 31 and would give birth to a total of nine children." A lump swelled in Morgan's throat and she dare not speak. The next entry was short. AD 9 was noted in the margin. It read:

AD 9 _ The child I bore was a daughter. I named her Ruth. She came to me on April 17 in Capernaum. I felt the presence of Yosuf with me while I labored. Elizabeth was here to help me and as her son, John, has also taken to the caravans, she will stay with me for a time to help with my family. I am grateful to my brother Yosef of Arimathea, who has taken on our guardianship and will help with the needs of my family.

Miyah read other entries made through a span of time about the everyday life of Mariam, as she struggled emotionally to survive. But there was no mention of Yeshua until many years later, in AD 22.

AD 22

_ I am saddened by news of the death of my cousin Elizabeth, who unexpectedly left us this day. Ten years have passed since her husband, Zacharias' horrible death. John returned after his father's death to care for his mother and they journeyed to my home months after. They visited again two years later and we broke bread. John refused to accept Zacharias' priest allowance due him from the temple funds and Elizabeth announced that she and John would travel south to the wilderness of Judea and make their home near Hebron, near Engedi on the Dead Sea. This is where John had taken his formal Nazarite life vow when he was at age 14. I begged her to stay and live with me here in Nazareth, but John was determined to move and they left the summer of his twenty-first birth date. John supported them these past years by raising sheep and goats, but I have heard that upon Elizabeth's death, he has presented his flocks to the brotherhood and has detached himself to fast and pray. At 28, he is the same in age as my Yeshua.

Miyah placed a marker in the diary and closed the book.

"We'll read more another time," she said. "Sometimes my brain scrambles from translating while I read. I need a break and you, my dear, have had quite a history lesson to absorb for one day."

"No, Mother, don't stop now," Morgan begged. "I want to hear more."

Miyah looked at her daughter kindly, understanding her fever for more. She recalled the same scene many years ago when she begged Junia not to stop reading.

"OK, just a couple more entries and then I must rest my eyes. You'll know what I mean when you learn to read the diary for yourself." She scanned through some of the writings and then continued.

_ I rejoice that my first-born son, Yeshua has returned to us. It has been many years since his departure and I often feared that he would never come back to his family. He tells us of great lands he traveled to—India, Tibet, Nepal and Greece. He was saddened to hear of the death of his father, long years past, but takes pride in his brothers and sisters and how they have cared for me and each other in his absence. He spoke of the teachings he has received from many cultures, and it is easy to see why people gather around him to hear him teach. If his father, Yosuf could only be here to see the prophecy made true. My son left us a boy and has returned a man.

_ Yeshua's return has affected my family in ways I did not foresee. As the second oldest son, James has remained faithful to the family and taken on much responsibility in his brother's absence. Yeshua is not interested in stepping back *into the role of the eldest son and receives much attention with his tales of adventure. I sense that James is resenting him. My youngest child, Ruth, now nearing fifteen years, has never known her brother Yeshua. James has been her father-figure, being my husband, Yosuf died before her birth. Many people hold Yeshua in awe because of the new insights and wisdom he gained in his studies in the East, but others say many unkind things about him, that he is a Jewish revolutionary and an agitator. Ruth does not understand why the words he teaches are of such controversy. Ruth is very beautiful and a Roman, named Philoas, an examiner of taxes, has taken an interest in her.*

– I am hopeful Yeshua will seek a wife. He spends much time at the home of his childhood friends Lazarus, Martha and Maryum.

– It is difficult to understand the life of Yeshua. He is home, yet he is not. He says he must go out and teach the people and he cannot do his work staying here with me. I know he is right, but I long to keep my son in my home. Soon after he returned, he traveled to Phoenicia and Cornwall, the birthplace of my mother, Anna, with my brother, Yosef of Arimathea, who owns a fleet of ships and is an importer in the tin trade. Yosef, a well respected Essene and counselor to the Jewish Sanhedrin, is also guardian to Yeshua. Yeshua stayed for some length of time in a small house of mud and wattles, for study, prayer and meditation. He told of studying with Druid tribes in their universities of philosophy, astronomy, numbers, geometry, medicine, poetry and ritual. He said these Druids have a trinity of three golden rays as their Celtic symbol and he also said that they continue to exalt my mother, Anna, from the time she spent there as one of their priestesses.

– Yeshua is away much of the time. He has also returned to Egypt with my brother Yosef, and it is here where he passed the seven tests of the seven Essene sages.

Miyah paused. "I should tell you a little about Mariam's brother, Yosef of Arimathea. He played a very important role in the life of Joshua. Yosef, an Essene elder, was a very rich and influential man in both the Jewish and Roman societies. He was an importer of cloth, copper and tin. Tin was as valuable as gold in those days, the chief metal used in the production of bronze. The tin trade existed as early as 1500 BC, and was mined and refined in Britain—sometimes called 'The Tin Island.' There was a great demand for it and Yosef was the man who controlled the tin and copper industry because of his many mines.

"At that time, the world's major amount of tin was mined in Cornwall, smelted into ingots, or molds, and exported throughout the world, mainly in Yosef's ships. He also owned one of the largest merchant shipping fleets that traded in ports of the known world. This is one of the reasons Yeshua had such wide access to travel. Working on these trading missions exposed him to many parts of the world and to other cultures. The Druids of Glastonbury, which Mariam mentions in her writing, are believed to be an offshoot of Essene Jews who settled there in ancient times. They had a mystery school rooted in the Kaballah, which also taught the subjects Yeshua said he studied. So traveling with Yosef gave Yeshua an opportunity to learn about other beliefs and to further his education, which was encouraged by his uncle."

Miyah closed the diary and looked at her daughter.

"You can't stop now. It's not that late. Can we continue for just a little longer? Please, Mother. I want to hear more," Morgan pleaded again.

"Yes, and you'll always want more," she replied. "There's plenty of time, Morgan. I need to rest my eyes. Remember, I'm translating these words as I read. Why don't you browse through some of these other books and familiarize yourself with the history and religions of the time. It'll give you a better understanding of our story. There's so much yet to learn. I'm going to finish my tea and go to bed."

Morgan, not ready to give up the diary just yet, curled up on the sofa with the book cradled tightly in her arms. She laid her head on a pillow and closed her eyes. She whispered a prayer of thankfulness to Anna and Mariam, and all those yet unread, for leaving this legacy of her ancestral sisters. She wanted them to know that all the hard work they had done, and all the sacrifices and suffering they had endured was not in vain, and that generations of their kinswomen and kinsmen throughout the ages had gained from the sharing of their story and the passing of the diary. And that she, Morgan, was humbly grateful for being among this elite group of women whose lives were interconnected. She could feel their love beating through the cover of the diary and she smiled at the thought of being surrounded by the spirits of these women.

Miyah came back into the room a while later and found Morgan sound asleep, content in her dreams. She gently kissed her daughter on the forehead and covered her with a blanket, leaving the diary in the folds of her arms.

"Sleep well, my child," she said. "There's much more to come. . .so much more."

~~~~~

Miyah changed into her nightgown, knowing she would need a good night's sleep, for tomorrow there would be more deep lessons to share with Morgan. Sitting in front of her mirror, she brushed through her hair with long strokes. When she was finished brushing she lit a candle in a bowl on the dresser, cleaned the hair from her brush and rolled it into a small nest, which she placed into the fire. She expected to see the hair flame up into a golden light—a sign of long life. Instead, the hair smoldered away, withering into the smoke. Miyah gasped. She had not expected this omen of ill health. She had a lot of work to do with Morgan and needed her health and strength for these lessons.

"What does this mean?" she asked, calling out for Junia and Nona. "Tell me what this omen means," she demanded.

There was nothing but silence.

"I'm sorry, I didn't mean to be so demanding," Miyah recanted. "Please, appear to me and advise me," she humbly asked. "I'm not finished with my work here, yet."

Nona and Junia gathered around Miyah and held her in their loving energy.

"No, my dear daughter," Junia responded. "You're not finished. You have time to complete your mission."

Nona added, "You've seen what is written for the future of Morgan. She must find her healing strength through her own abilities. Don't you know that's why Junia and I left the earth at an early time in your life, so you, the next generation of Touchstone carriers, could fulfill your mission in your own power?"

Miyah's heart was heavy. "Is this omen for me, or one of my family?" she finally questioned.

Nona replied. "There are events in the distant future that will shape what is to come. Accept these events, as they were written into your lifebook when you were born. Enjoy your daughter and continue her lessons. Don't blame, don't judge. Forgiveness will be part of your own lessons."

"Our love is always with you Miyah," Junia said. "But I must also tell you that I'll no longer be appearing to you in spirit. I've chosen a body in which to reincarnate and will be birthing into the earth realm once more. As we know, our souls gather back each time in circles of family and friends, our red thread of destiny, so our paths will cross again in this lifetime. Watch for me, my dear. Be happy for me, as I'm anxious to return for another lifetime of lessons."

Miyah didn't know what to say at first. She hadn't thought about her mother, or grandmother, ever leaving the spirit world and returning to earth.

"Will I know you, Mother?" she asked.

"You will know me, my dear," Junia said giving her daughter a hug. "I will always love you."

Miyah felt sadness, yet joy at the same time. "Good-bye Mother. I love you," she called out as the ancestors faded into the shadows.

Miyah turned off the light and sat in the darkness of the room for a long time, watching the candle flicker and finally burn itself out. She smelled the ending smoke as it permeated the room and knew that, like a candle, all life only burns for a short time. It's how bright that light shines while it's burning that's important.

4 Lessons

Elizabeth watched Michael as he paced back and forth across the floor of his library, mumbling to himself. She knew Miyah was taking Morgan away to some special school for long periods of time now and staying there with her, and she also knew her brother didn't like it at all. She missed them too. But each year Michael seemed to grow more and more irritated by it. He accepted it at first because they were only gone a few days at a time. But as Morgan grew older and her lessons advanced, they were gone longer and longer—including weekends. Miyah had always managed to send him messages to reassure him, but lately this wasn't enough. He felt shut out of their lives. Elizabeth felt sorry for Michael. Morgan was his daughter too, and he had every right to have a say in her future.

"Don't you think she should live a normal life?" she had heard them argue. "That's what you said you wanted for her when she was born. She needs friends and should be doing what teenage girls do at this age."

"And just what is that, Michael?" Miyah would ask. "Go to the mall? Have a boyfriend? Have you asked her if she feels she's missing out on life? Don't you realize that she knows what her destiny as a healer is and that she accepts it willingly? Believe me, I know. I went through the same thing. We're so lucky she understands that she's gifted and looks forward to her future. It's her own choice now. Elizabeth didn't understand a lot of their conversation and had tried to talk with Miyah, expressing that she thought it was unfair to Michael, but Miyah just told her she didn't understand all the circumstances.

Elizabeth tried to get Michael out of the house and spend time with him when Miyah and Morgan were gone, but lately he was in such a bad mood, she didn't even want to be around him. She was reminiscent of those days when he was sick and how moody he had been. It was easier to stay away and just phone him every day to check in. He never said much on the phone, but she still wanted him to know she was there if he needed her.

Miyah had hoped it would never come to this. Michael was a good father and she knew he reacted this way because he missed Morgan. They had always had such a happy marriage, but the last few months he was irritated and they seemed to be arguing a lot. Sometimes he seemed to forget the circumstances that brought them together in the first place. She kept telling him that things will change and Morgan's role in the Touchstone legacy will be the most important ever, but he was tired of hearing this.

"When will it change?" he wanted to know. "When will these trips end so we can get back to being a family? I can't stand the loneliness I feel when you're away. I just want us to be together."

"I'm sorry, but you know as well as I do how important this is. You knew it from the very beginning. In respect for you, I put off starting Morgan's formal teachings until she was six," Miyah stressed, reminding him that she was much younger when she began her studies with Junia and Nona.

"But that was different," he shot back at her. "Your father didn't have a chance to know you. Hell, he didn't even know you existed when he died. Don't you ever feel like your family legacy has left a wake of men who would have liked to have known they had children? I feel as if they've been cheated—that I'm being cheated and I *know* my daughter?"

Miyah was silent.

"I'm sorry. I didn't mean to be so harsh. I shouldn't have said that. But isn't there another way?" he asked, softening his voice. "You can't just keep taking my daughter away, disappearing into the vapors like ghosts, when I have no idea when you'll return."

"Michael," Miyah reminded him with an even tone, "you knew there would be challenges when you accepted the responsibility of fatherhood. Haven't I told you over and over all these years what to expect? You have to trust me when I tell you that it all ties in with the promise you made on your deathbed."

"Oh, the promise again. That damnable promise. Sometimes I wish I had never made it," he shouted at her. "If I were dead now I wouldn't be going through this hell."

"Be careful what you wish for, Michael," Miyah warned, raising her voice. "Be careful what you say. Remember, this isn't just about you. You're thinking only of yourself. You must understand that Morgan is most important here. You should be proud, not condemning. We've come a long way to get to this place in our legacy. It's Morgan's birthright to take her place among our sisterhood, and it was a choice she agreed to even before her conception. She was brought into this world with a very special purpose and you know that. You have to trust me on this," she stressed again.

"Trust?" Michael spewed the word, not being able to get over his anger. "Trust you like the night Morgan was conceived—when you made your witch's potion and drew me to the garden with your spell. Is that what you mean about trust?"

Miyah turned away from him and bit her lip. Tears burned her eyes, as she well remembered that night. But she remembered it with love in her heart, not the bitterness of betrayal.

"I'm sorry," Michael quickly said, reaching out for her. "I didn't mean that. I don't know what's gotten into me. Sometimes I feel like a mad man, I miss you both so much. I feel excluded from your lives and the bitterness inside me is growing into a disease I can't control—it's consuming my life like the cancer I had when I first met you. I'm so sorry, Miyah. I hate arguing with you. Is there some sort of compromise we can come up with that works for all of us? We have to try something," he stressed.

Miyah looked at him, understanding the torment he was feeling. Other than his research, family was all he had. She had tried to encourage him to find a hobby, golf, fish, take up running, something he could get out and enjoy, and maybe meet other people. They really did have a pretty secluded life. She at least had her healer friends—Jonna, Monica and Barbara, who she continued to worked with and occasionally got together with socially. Jonna's daughter, Jennifer, and Monica's daughter, Cassandra, had become good friends with Morgan. Barbara's son, Taylor, who was a few years younger than the girls, also hung around them a lot. So Morgan wasn't without friends. These kids were also home schooled and their mothers were healers in their own ways, so they actually had a lot in common. No, she didn't feel Morgan was missing out on anything. But he was right. It was Michael who was missing out.

She walked over and gave him a hug. "You're right. We need to do something. I hate it when we fight like this."

He reached out and held her, remembering all the times of their past when things were so wonderful, so much easier.

"How about this," Miyah suggested. "Give me one more session with Morgan—two or three weeks, and then I'll see if we can go back to a daily schedule. We're just now getting into some very important work and I don't want her to be distracted. We can work this out. I don't like seeing you so distraught either."

"That would be better," he replied. "I suppose I can make it through another few weeks knowing it'll be different afterward. I'm sorry I feel so strongly about this. And I'm really sorry I said those things. You know I don't mean it. Maybe I'm being selfish, I don't know. I just can't help it. I do understand how important all of this is, Miyah. It's hard, that's all. . .it's just so hard."

~ ~ ~ ~ ~

Two weeks had passed with only a few messages from Miyah and Morgan. Elizabeth stopped by one afternoon to find Michael in another stormy mood.

"Are you OK?" she asked. "You don't quite seem yourself today."

"Damn her for always getting her way," Michael suddenly said as he paced back and forth in his library. He picked up a book and slammed it onto the desk.

"You don't mean that," Elizabeth said as she watched him. "I understand how you feel, but getting mad and cursing isn't going to help. You need to stop thinking about it so much and put your energy into something productive."

"Now you sound just like her," Michael shouted.

"Come on Michael. I know the two of you love each. Why are you making yourself go through this agony? It isn't going to last forever. They're at school, for Christ's sake. Your situation with Miyah has always been a little odd, as far as I can see, so why are you making such a big deal of this now? I miss them too, but they'll be back soon. You're overreacting. Are you sure you're feeling all right? You look a little thin."

"Oh, I'm fine," he replied. "I'll be fine."

"Let's go out on the patio and soak up some sunshine. Maybe fresh air will help your mood. You stay cooped up inside here too much. You need to get out more. How's the garden coming along?" she tried to get his mind off of his misery.

Michael reluctantly followed her to the patio.

"Wow, this place is really looking overgrown," Elizabeth said with surprise. "When were you out here last?"

"I don't know," Michael replied, looking around. "I guess I have neglected the yard and gardens lately."

Elizabeth rolled up her sleeves. "Well, then I think I have just the perfect therapy for you. . .and for me. Remember how much fun we used to have working in the yard? There wasn't a weed in the place and the flowers were always so beautiful. Why are you standing there? Get the tools!" she commanded.

Michael looked at her and was about to object, but he too, knew that this would be a good deviation from his depression. He managed a small smile.

"It's good to have you here, Sis," he replied. "You're always taking care of me." He turned and headed toward the shed to retrieve some yard tools.

The two of them worked side-by-side most of the afternoon, weeding flowers and plants, mowing and trimming the yard. Elizabeth sprayed him with the water hose, trying to bring out the old, playful brother she knew. Finally they sat under the shade of the oak trees to admire their work.

"I've always loved this garden," Michael finally said. "I can't believe I neglected it for so long. Thanks for coming over. Liz. This has been great therapy."

"See, all you have to do is keep yourself busy and the time will go by faster. I know Miyah keeps the house spotless, but there must be a million other things you could do around here."

"Yeah, there have been a couple of things swirling around in my head. I guess I just need to stop feeling sorry for myself and start a project. My last freelance job is finished and my work has been slow on Miyah's book."

"Miyah's book? Is that what you've been doing all the research on for the past 100 years," she teased. "What's it about anyhow?"

"Oh. . .it's just some family history stuff I'm working on for her," he said, avoiding giving any more detail. "But how about you?" he diverted the conversation. "I never ask you what's going on in your life. I'm not a very good brother, am I?"

"Oh, you're the best," she said, giving him a smile.

"You're getting up there in age. Don't you think you should find a husband and settle down?" He winked at her.

"Oh, look who's talking, Mr. Single-until-he-was-in-his-forties!" she exclaimed. "I've had plenty of boyfriends over the years, but guess I've just been so career oriented that I never took any of them serious. I do have a date this weekend though."

"I'll be waiting for a report," Michael replied.

"Oh, so now all of a sudden you're going to screen my dates again. It's a little late for that!"

"I know. I trust your judgement. The years. Where have they gone? One moment I'm a new father and suddenly I have a teenage daughter who is hardly ever home. When she's not studying with Miyah she's off with her friends."

"Well, that's pretty normal," Elizabeth replied. "That's what teenage girls do. You should be grateful she's such a good girl. There's some pretty scary stuff going on out there. Believe me, I know."

"Yeah, I should be grateful," he said slowly. "Anyhow, I'm glad you came by today."

"Thanks, but now I've got to get going. I'm meeting some friends for a movie tonight. I'd invite you to join us, but you'd say no anyhow." She kissed him on the forehead and headed toward the house. "I'll call you tomorrow."

"Sure, leave me to put everything away and clean up!" he called out, stretching his aching back as he stood. "I'm not getting any younger," he mumbled to himself, feeling aging pains.

"You've got nothing else to do," she shouted over her shoulder.

"Humph," he replied, thinking of the stacks of work piled up on his desk.

Michael finished his work in the yard and cleaned up, then went into the house to make dinner. He stood with the fridge door open when he suddenly got this strange feeling, like someone was calling him. He straightened up and shut the refrigerator door. For some reason he had an overpowering urge to take a walk. Forgetting his hunger, he went outside. His footsteps guided him like a magnet, and he headed toward the park. . .the park across from RoseVine.

"I hope everything's OK," his thoughts were buzzing. When he arrived at the park he first glanced at the empty lot where he knew Miyah's house was "behind the veil," as she always referred to it. A feeling of anxiety arose from his stomach and he turned to search the park. Suddenly, a girl jumped out from behind a tree and started running toward him.

"It worked," she yelled. "Hi Daddy! It worked!" She almost knocked him over as she threw her arms around him.

"Morgan!" he yelled, picking her up and swinging her around in the air. "What a surprise! What do you mean it worked? What worked?"

She took his hand and led him to the park bench.

"It's something Mom has been teaching me—using the power of the mind to contact others and send messages. It's so exciting. I just kept thinking of you and of how much I wanted to see you. Then I thought of the park and wanted us to meet here—and here we are!"

"It sounds a bit like mind control," he said.

"Oh believe me, Mom and I have been over and over the proper use of this and if I ever use this power for anything but for healing or for good, it will be taken away from me. Isn't it great though? Here you are!"

"Where's your mother?" Michael asked, looking around.

"She's bringing dinner over so we can have a picnic. It was my idea. I've missed you so much."

Michael kissed her forehead and hugged her to him. "I've missed you more, baby," he said.

Michael glanced at the empty lot. A car approached on the road and just as it drove past, Miyah appeared on the other side of the street, a picnic basket on her arm and a blanket thrown over her shoulder. She waved and hurried across to join them in the park. Morgan took the blanket and spread it out on the grass while her parents embraced.

"I don't even care what's in that basket," he said. "I'm just so happy to be here with the two of you."

"I thought you'd feel that way," Miyah replied, not telling him she had picked up on his earlier emotional relapse. "Morgan and I agree that we should do this often. We should have thought of it sooner."

"Yeah, that would have been nice," he mumbled, helping her unpack the basket. "It looks like she's really progressing in her studies. She bent my mind in a flash."

Miyah laughed. "She's so amazing. She makes my job pretty easy."

The family ate their dinner and talked until the sun started going down.

"It's getting dark," Miyah finally said. "You should probably get going."

"Oh, come on. You could just zap me home or I could have Morgan 'call' me a taxi if it gets too late," Michael joked.

"Great idea," Morgan piped in. "Can I Mom? I need to practice."

Miyah looked over her teacup at Michael.

"Awe, come on, Mom. I'm not ready to go yet anyhow. Can't we stay longer, please, please." Michael sounded like a begging child. Morgan laughed to see the playful side of her dad and joined in.

"Pleeeeeease, Mom."

"Looks like I'm overruled here," she grinned. "Just let Morgan know when you're ready, sir, and your royal coach will appear."

As eager as Morgan was to practice her newly learned powers again, she was more content to spend as much time with her dad as she could. Even though she knew she'd be finished with this long period of studies in about a week, she knew how much this visit meant to him.

The trio walked across the street to RoseVine and disappeared behind the veil of protection that shrouded the house. It was almost midnight before Morgan concentrated her will and "called" a taxi for Michael. She was excited that her call had worked so effortlessly.

"Great," Michael joked. "Now I'll have two women telling me what to do! I wonder if this mind thing is something I could learn," he said to Miyah as he kissed her goodbye. "Then I could call the two of you to me any time I wanted to see you. Now that would be good magic."

He turned to Morgan. "Keep practicing. Call me anytime and I'll be here."

"Love you Dad," she said, blowing him a kiss. "See you again soon."

"Love you too," he replied, getting into the taxi. Michael looked back at the house, and before the cab driver could ask, "Where to?" Miyah and Morgan were both gone, whisked away, back into the vapors of life in between the worlds at RoseVine.

5 Women of the Diary

Michael joined his wife and daughter every day for lunch or dinner after that and was happy to be a part of their day. It gave him more focus on his own work, just knowing he would see them.

Miyah continued to read the diary to Morgan, stopping to answer questions and to add her own thoughts to some of the entries.

Some women wrote a page or two, or just a paragraph or a signature, simply to have a record counted among the Touchstone carriers. It was difficult to know who penned many of the entries, as there were also recipes for potions, spells and prayers written without a signature author.

Weather spell to call the sun - First, light a gold-colored candle. On a piece of paper, draw a map of the area where you want the sun to shine. You can draw a detailed map or simply write the name of a place. Put your intentions into the paper as you draw. Then move the map counter-clockwise, circling it around the flame of the candle three times. Imagine the flame is the sun. Then burn the map in the flame while chanting: "Sun, shine your light upon this place you see. Cover it with your warming rays, honoring this request for me." Pluck one of your hairs and burn it in the flame to seal your spell.

Many notations had been made in the margins in several different handwritings, which only added to the mysterious nature of the journal. As Miyah read the diary, it gave Morgan a better sense of what the lives of these women were like throughout the ages. Most of what has been recorded in religious studies refers to the masculine viewpoint of historic events. The diary revealed the emotions of the feminine as told by women in everyday lives.

Morgan was also surprised to read notations about 12 women disciples—something she had never thought about before. She made a list:

Mariam - the mother of Joshua

Maryum - Joshua's wife (Mary Magdalene)

Helena Salome - Joshua's aunt and the wife of Maryum's brother, Lazarus

Mary Jacoby - Joshua's aunt and the wife of Clopas

Martha of Bethany - Maryum's sister

Abigail - Joshua's cousin and daughter of Mary Jacoby and Clopas

Ruth - sister of Joshua

Mary - the mother of James

Marium Joanna, Sara, Lois Salome and Susannah Mary - Joshua's cousins.

Important holy women were also talked about in the dairy: Rahab, an influential woman in the Jewish and early church traditions; Salome, the wife of Zebedee and mother to James and John; Joanna, the wife of Herod's steward Chuza; Bathsheba, the wife of Uriah; Junia, a prominent apostle who had been imprisoned for her dedication; Prisca; Ruth; Susanna; Tamar; Persis; Euodia; Syntyche; and Julia. Many worked and traveled as disciples in pairs with their husbands or brothers. Often, it seemed they were not well received:

_ Some public inns are now refusing to serve food and lodging to our people because they attract too much attention and the owners do not want to clash with the authorities. Myself, Saraphia, Johanna Chusa, Susanna, Mary Marcus and Martha have established private inns to supply the disciples and Yeshua with their needs. We are advised in advance where the travelers will be and when they will arrive. We have created almost twenty inns to accommodate them along their way. Some of the properties belong to Lazarus and other relatives of families, and these inns are scattered all over the country and have become known as the disciples' inns.

_ Saraphia is in charge of the inn to the north of Mount Calvary on the northwest side of Jerusalem. She has an old chalice which she bought from the temple. Yeshua and the disciples use it for the sacraments. When old items are no longer used in the temple they are melted down and remolded into other useful items. This chalice was meant to be melted in the fires. Saraphia does not know what metal it is made of, but it resisted the heat and would not melt, so was sold to her instead. It is shaped like a pear and is quite large, with two handles. It has a spoon hidden in the foot and is brown, overlaid with gold. There are also eight smaller cups that complete the set. Saraphia claims the chalice is holy and that it belonged to Moses at one time, and that is why it didn't melt in the fires.

It wasn't clear whether every journal entry was written exclusively by her own bloodline of women, but it didn't matter. The writing gave insight into the lives of the women of that time who obviously knew her family well enough to be entrusted with making an entry in the journal, and someone who perhaps realized the importance of recording their messages for others.

_ My friend Naomi, is close to me in age. I describe her as having a complexion that is fair, gray eyes and dark brown hair. She is a gentle person, a good cook and a good housekeeper. With her beautiful voice, she is always asked to sing for us. When we were younger her family lived outside of Jerusalem, near Bethany, including her brothers, James who is older and John who is younger. Now, as she ages, she is drawn between the training of her mother in the holy activities of the Essenes, or dedicating herself to the faith of her father and brothers. She has a position in the Jewish faith, yet she also has connections among the Romans. Naomi is educated in schools and has Essene teachers from Carmel, yet she is connected to the Sisters of the orders known as the Church, and to the orthodox activities of the Sisters of Mercy among some Jewish sects. Choosing her path has been confusing to her and we discuss it at length. This is a crucial point in her life. She confided to me last night that she has come to her decision. She has heard the teachings of Elias, and has decided to join with those of the Essene group. This man teaches that women are equal and can dedicate their lives as well as men.

"Elias was John the Baptist, right?" Morgan asked. "Tell me again about the Essenes."

"Yes, Elias was John the Baptist. The Essenes were the most enlightened of Jewish Hebrews, tracing their origins back to the ancient mystery schools of Moses, Akhenaten and even further," Miyah explained. "'Esse' means being, and 'ene' means source. So Essene translates as 'Source of Being,' or 'Holy One.' Primarily of Hebrew descent, their main language was Aramaic."

Miyah could see that Morgan needed more, so without getting into too much detail, she continued.

"Essenes were known to be a cross-pollination of many wisdom teachings. They were as knowledgeable about Krishna, Isis, Osiris in ancient times as they were about Buddha and Moses. Their eclectic traditions allowed them to accept and appreciate many different cultures and beliefs that were used to honor the same God/Goddess. You'll read a lot about the Essenes in the lives of the women in the early years. It was that perspective of honoring many different spiritual ideals that shaped the lives and belief systems of our family thousands of years ago, and even today. We'll talk more about that later," she offered, anxious to continue her reading. Miyah chose another entry from the diary.

_Martha is weaving a robe with the assistance of her older sister, Esdrela. It is woven in one piece with a hole in the top for the head and cords to bind it around the waist. The color is pearl-gray, with selvage woven around the neck and edge. Woven into the selvage portion of the bottom is

the Thummin and Urim, Hebrew holy symbols. Martha
said the robe is meant to be presented to Yeshua.

Miyah read through generations of entries, stopping only to answer
Morgan's questions. Many of the entries were written to record simple
moments and emotions, with the author not realizing what an impact these
words would have as they related to what are now considered to be historic
events. Morgan was most interested in the early entries of the women,
partially because their lives were so foreign to her.

"I still don't understand why the marriage of Maryum and Joshua had to
be suppressed," Morgan said. "I know in the later years of the Church it had
to do with control and women's issues, but was it also hidden at the time?"

"No, it wasn't hidden in the circles of people who knew them," Miyah
replied. "But the marriage had dynastic importance, uniting the families of
two friends, David, son of Jesse, and Jonathan, son of Saul. Their friendship
was a story that had been told for centuries in every Jewish home. Maryum's
marriage to Joshua was also political—to fulfill a prophecy that God would
send them a Davidic Messiah who would deliver the nation from the tyranny
of Rome and bring about an era of peace and prosperity promised by the
Hebrew prophets, Micah and Isaiah.

"Joshua, the Messianic Son of David, had the correct genealogy and
was also a worker of miracles. He healed the sick and brought enlightened
teachings to others. Maryum was a royal daughter of the Tribe of Benjamin,
whose ancestral heritage covered the land surrounding the Holy City of
David—she was very rich, an heiress of the lands bordering Jerusalem.

"Israel's first anointed, King Saul, was of the Tribe of Benjamin and his
daughter, Maacah or Michal, widow of Uriah the Hittite, was a wife of King
David, event hough he is most known for his wife, Bathsheba. Through
the history of the Tribes of Israel, the Tribes of Judah and Benjamin were
the closest and most loyal of allies. Their destinies were intertwined, so a
dynastic marriage between a Benjamite heiress to the lands surrounding the
Holy City of Jerusalem and the Messianic Son of David would have been
seen as a sign of hope and a blessing."

Morgan had a confused look on her face. Miyah explained further.

"To answer your question simply, it was necessary to keep the marriage
quiet for political reasons—so Herod Antipas would not discover that an
heiress of Benjamin had been united in marriage to an heir of David."

Morgan was silent, pondering all of this, but she was spilling over with
questions and couldn't keep still for long.

"You said the diary began with Anna giving it to Mariam as a wedding
gift. But where did she get it? Was it her diary first?"

"That's a very good question," Miyah replied, amused at her daughter's
unending curiosity.

"Anna was an educated woman, and influenced by the great library at Mount Carmel, kept a personal journal, so maybe that's where she got the idea to gift Mariam with a diary. This leads us to learn a little more about Anna. She was a very powerful woman and we'll spend some time learning about her life. Anna was a prophetess and highly regarded in the Essene community. She was knowledgeable in higher alchemy, astrology, numerology and the sages' mysteries. She was also head mistress of the Essene spiritual community at Mount Carmel, the secret School of the Prophets, which is why her daughter Mariam was inducted into the community as one of the 12 maidens when she was a child."

"Did we talk about this before?" Morgan asked. "I recall something about 12 maidens."

"Yes, we did, and I know it's really difficult to remember everything, but don't worry, you will in time."

Miyah continued, "At that time people of Anna's community were tuned into the spirits of plants, minerals, fire, water and air. They had an understanding of herbs, simple raw foods and gardened to sustain themselves through the seasons. They also honored the cycles of the seasons, Mother Earth and Father Sky, through songs, dances and feasts."

"Sounds a bit Native American to me," Morgan responded.

"Yes, indeed. They're the people who haven't forgotten humanity's basic roots. We can all learn lessons from them." Miyah continued, "Anna and her first husband, Mathias, had two children, Yosef in 57 BC and Martha in 55 BC. Yosef later became known as Yosef/Joseph of Arimathea when he married Eunice Salome, the daughter of a Hasmonean prince, named Arimathea. Eventually Joseph owned as many as 12 ships and became a wealthy importer of tin, copper and goods, which allowed the family to travel extensively. Anna, who was living in the Essene community at Carmel, and Mathias later disolved their marriage and he moved to the Essene community at Qumram."

"Isn't that where the Dead Sea Scrolls were discovered?" Morgan asked.

"Yes, and Anna and her family were instrumental in saving many of the manuscripts during that time period. Scrolls were hidden in Ephesus, in France and as far away as Britain, in attempts to preserve ancient records. We'll get to that in our studies. But let's continue with Anna. . .

"She continued her work in Mount Carmel and also traveled to Egypt to receive further teachings. Later she married Joachim and from 49 BC to 33 BC they had 12 children: Ruth, twins Isaac and Andrew, twins Mariamne and Jacob, Josephus, twins Nathan and Luke, Rebekah, Ezekial, and Noah. Their twelfth child, Mariam, or some say Mary Anna, was born in Ephesus, which is in what is now known as Turkey."

"Are you serious?" Morgan exclaimed. "That's a total of 14 kids in two marriages and having babies over a 37 year period! Insane! That poor woman."

"Oh, she was anything but poor," Miyah quickly replied. "As I said, she was a priestess in the Essene tradition and a high teacher in esoteric studies where they worked with high frequencies in their minds and bodies. They used astral travel and bi-location methods taught by masters from other parts of the world, and even from other dimensions. She was much more than a saint."

"Oh, that's right. The Church calls her Saint Anne. At least they acknowledge her," Morgan said.

"Yes. But it would be so wonderful to have her life as a priestess revealed," Miyah responded. "She was a great woman."

"It looks like there were a lot of women who received little attention for their greatness, according to what you've read to me from the diary so far. That must be a small handful. . .we haven't even gotten through all the generations."

"We will in time, Morgan. There's so much to cover. When you're able to read through the languages for yourself you'll go over and over these pages, as I have, and each time discover something new. So now you understand why this diary is so important to our heritage. It'll always be safe at RoseVine. When it's yours, you must treasure and take good care of it."

Morgan reached over and lightly ran her fingers over the hand-written words on the thin pages of the diary, as if to honor and thank these words for coming to life for them.

"I'll guard it with my life," she said softly. They were both grateful they had this diary to bring them back into the lives of their bloodline—their roots—and to be able to receive the insights it offered.

"You've done so well in your lessons, Morgan. I think you're ready for another phase."

"What do you mean?"

"You've traveled through space, bi-locating with us to France and other places when we visited Papa Tom years ago, but now I want to take you on a journey into the past to experience first hand the lives of some of our ancestors."

"Like what Dad has done with the cedar box?" she asked anxiously. "I've always been a little jealous of that and wondered when it would be my turn."

"I think it's time. But we don't need the cedar box for you to venture back. It's built into your DNA to be able to do these things. I just needed to be sure it was the right time to teach you."

"Do you know where we're going or will it be a surprise like it was for Dad? Each time he 'traveled' he said he had no idea where he would end up."

"I'll guide you on how to control your destination, but again, we'll go through the long list of rules for using these powers. It's imperative that you abide by our strict code of practice or you'll lose your privileges. Do you understand? I can't stress this enough."

"Yes, Mother. I do understand and swear I'll never dishonor the bloodline. I know we've been chosen to carry out important work. . .and I'm honored to be a part of that. I'll never let you down. Honest."

~~~~~~

Morgan watched closely as her mother prepared for them to time travel. She lit a candle and chanted words that Morgan tried to remember. Then she blew out the flame and while the smoke was still permeating the air, she waved a white feather through the smoke, weaving it into a circle, three times counter-clockwise and then fanned it up into the ethers.

"I'm performing this ritual for protection," Miyah explained. "Normally there would be someone here, holding the energy for us while we're gone, and I could call upon Nona to do that for us. But there is another way, and I want you to be aware of the rituals and practices that call upon others for protection in these cases. As I'm performing this ritual I'm also setting a tone of intention of where I want to go and what I want to accomplish while there. That is very important. It's how you control your destination. I also ask for a safe return to this same place and time frame and give thanks for all that I have and for what is to come."

She added, "It helps to know that no matter where I am or what I'm doing, Nona has vowed to take care of me. . .and you too."

Morgan nodded in a gesture of understanding.

"Are you ready?" Miyah asked, and not waiting for an answer, she took Morgan's hand and they were whisked away into a swirling fog of light and air. Morgan felt like she was in a tunnel of clouds with a bright light at the end, guiding them and swirling around them at the same time.

"This is awesome!" she thought, yet she squeezed her mother's hand a little tighter, for reassurance.

When the fog cleared they were standing on solid ground.

"Where are we?" Morgan said as she looked around the unfamiliar landscape.

"I want you to meet some of your ancestors," Miyah replied with a distinct note of happiness in her voice.

Morgan exclaimed, "What do I do? How do I act? I'll be so nervous."

Miyah put a calming hand on Morgan's arm. "Just be yourself, dear. Be polite, be friendly. That's all you need to do. And don't expect to see halos or holy signs over their heads! They're just people—like you and me. They'll love you for exactly who you are. You shouldn't have worries at all about our visit. All I ask is that you pay close attention to details. These things you'll always want to remember. With your inquisitive mind, that should be easy."

"But where exactly are we?" Morgan asked.

"We're on the Aegean west coast, in Ephesus, which, in the time we've come back to, is the capitol of the Roman province of Asia. You'll find it in your current geography books as located in Turkey. Ephesus had a population of more than 250,000, which made it the second largest city in the Roman Empire, and the world at that time."

"What was the largest city?" Morgan asked.

"Rome," her mother replied. "While in Ephesus, I want to show you the Temple of Artemis. It was originally a Greek temple dedicated to the worship of the Mother Goddess—and later was also known as the Temple of Diana. You'll notice it looks in structure a lot like the Church of Mary Magdalene you've visited in Paris, which was fashioned after this temple.

"Take a good look, because this temple, which was completed around 550 BC, was one of the Seven Wonders of the Ancient World. It had been partially destroyed many times over the centuries and reconstructed. Unfortunately, it met its final demise in AD 401 in a riot led by a priest during the destruction of what the Church considered pagan symbols and places of worship—which included the Temple of Artemis. It's sad the Church was so threatened by it that they had to destroy it and its art. . ." Miyah sighed.

"It had taken more than 120 years to build this temple. But at least parts of it live on, because many of the stones were carried off and used in construction of other buildings. Some of the columns in the Hagia Sophia Temple in Istanbul originally belonged to the Temple of Artemis. And several of the statues and other decorative pieces were used in construction of buildings throughout Constantinople—which is now called Istanbul."

Miyah turned to Morgan. "I want you to appreciate this peek into the past. In our time period only foundations and sculptural fragments of this temple remain."

Located at an economically robust region of the country, the temple drew merchants and travelers from all over Asia Minor, including pilgrims, peasants and artisans. Miyah conveniently made Morgan and herself invisible to the others who milled around the temple so Morgan's lessons wouldn't be interrupted.

Morgan was in awe standing in front of the Temple of Artemis. The entire building was made of marble, except for the roof. Stretching 377 feet long and 180 feet wide, its area was about three times as large as the Parthenon in Athens. The temple was enclosed in colonnades of 127 Ionic columns, each 60 feet high that made a wide ceremonial passage around the temple. The two women felt dwarfed as they climbed the steps and stood among the carved reliefs that had been worked into the temple's columns.

"The Temple of Artemis," Morgan said under her breath. "Who was Artemis?"

"She was a Greek Goddess, the virgin huntress and twin of Apollo.

Don't you remember? We talked about her in our studies. The Ephesians mainly worshiped the goddess Cybele, who represented the fertile Earth. She was a goddess of caves and mountains, walls and fortresses, nature and wild animals—especially lions and bees. Many people's ancient beliefs in Cybele were incorporated into the worship of Artemis. The temple attracted thousands of worshippers from far-off lands. Cybele/Artemis's Roman counterpart was Diana. That's why the Temple was also later called the Temple of Diana.

Once inside there was no need for words. Columns boasted the richness of the temple with gilding of gold and silver. Morgan admired the works of art, paintings and sculptures that adorned the temple. She directed her gaze to sculptures of women that were enormous in size.

"Who were these sculpted after?" she asked. "Amazons!"

"Yes! You're right," Miyah laughed. "The Amazons were said to have founded the city of Ephesus. They were a nation of all-female warriors in Greek mythology. As you can see, the temple was influenced by many beliefs and is a symbol of faith for many cultures."

Morgan pointed to a statue of a goddess just east of the open-air altar.

"Artemis," Miyah said. The image was intricately carved and decorated with a multitude of jewelry and drilled amber tear-shaped drops with elliptical cross-sections. Similar to an Egyptian deity, her body and legs were enclosed within a tapering pillar-like column, from which her feet protruded. Morgan examined the carving closely, reaching up to touch the bold lines of the statue.

"What's happened to these beautiful pieces of art?" she asked.

"Amazingly, some have survived and are housed in museums. This piece, 'The Lady of Ephesus,' is in the Museum of Efes, in Turkey. Others are in the British Museum. The fact that they survived after all these centuries, I find simply incredible."

Morgan walked over to examine another life-sized, white marble sculpture of a woman driving a chariot pulled by two large lions. She looked at her mother inquisitively.

"Cybele," Miyah said, picking up a coin from the floor. After turning it over to examine it, she handed it to Morgan. It was an image of Cybele, minted at Ephesus. The many-breasted goddess wore a mural crown and rested her arm on a staff formed of a serpent with its tail in its mouth—the symbol of eternal life.

"They made coins with her on it?" Morgan was surprised. "She must have really been important!"

"Yes. All of these Goddesses were important in different phases of history. You mustn't forget them. But, we need to get going. I just didn't want you to miss the opportunity to visit this important icon of the past."

"Thanks Mom," Morgan replied as she placed the coin near the base of the statue. "This beats a history book any time!"

Miyah and Morgan stood on the steps outside and looked over the bustling marbled city. Beyond the Temple of Artemis, along the north side, facing the road, was a basilica which housed the law courts. The two women walked south, through the city, past the acropolis and the stadium, past a giant outdoor amphitheater, the Grand Theater, built into the hillside, with seating for 24,000, and the Library of Celsus. The harbor was down from the library with a wide columned avenue paved in elaborate mosaics and lined with shops behind enormous columns. Porticoes of pedestrian walkways were open between the shops and columns and at night they were lit by 50 large torches. The harbor was filled with tall-masted sailing ships from all over the world.

The two women faced the triple-arched Mithridates Gate that lead into the city's marketplace, housing rows of shops. Morgan tugged at Miyah's sleeve to urge her to let them explore what was available in the shops.

"You know we can't bring anything back with us," she reminded her daughter.

"I know, but it can't hurt to take a peek," she pleaded. "We can just window shop, can't we? It's educational!" she added.

Miyah chuckled and gave in to her daughter's logic. They strolled through a street with freshly baked bread and an assortment of vegetables, fruits and grains arranged in bins. Fly-ridden meat hung from poles and smelly fish glittered in the sun. The odor of penned or tied live animals turned them away toward another street where they found olive oil, wine, honey, salt and Arabian herbs and spices.

"Don't they have other stuff–like clothes and things?" Morgan asked, enjoying seeing what people of that era had to eat, but not that interested. They found an area where copper kitchenware, bronze tables, marble bowls and carved statues, ceramics, glassware, stools, dishes and oil lamps were sold. They also found silks, perfume, and jewelry made of precious stones.

"Now that's more like what I was looking for," Morgan said, as she gazed at some colorful silk fabric. "It's too bad we can't do just a little shopping!"

Miyah laughed and steered her daughter back onto the main street where they continued through the city. She pointed out marble statues lining the streets and porticos paved with mosaics that led to private residences on the right, and to public buildings on the left. This included a brothel, three-story public bathhouse and the public bathrooms, where toilets were cut into marble benches arranged along each of the walls.

The women marveled at the mosaic detail of birds, fish, flowers and designs paving the street. Before walking through the impressive eight marble columns of the Prytaneioun, Miyah pointed out the eternal flame of Ephesus, which burned day and night. After they crossed the large public square, the State Agora, which was surrounded by administrative buildings, they left the bustle of the greatest city of the East and its massive stone walls, and walked to the outer edges of the compound and through a grove of fig trees. The land met a flowing river that curved to the east, where a small settlement of houses nestled into the side of Nightingale Mountain.

"I had no idea that kind of luxury existed back in those days," Morgan said, turning to take another look at the city. "This must have been an incredible place to live!"

"Ephesus was, without a doubt, one of the most progressive cities in the world. Many of our family traveled here and stayed for a time. Many came and went frequently on ships to other ports. Joseph of Arimathea had a home here and he was very generous hosting others to stay in his villa when he was traveling, which was pretty much all of the time. That's where we're heading now, to his home."

They picked up their pace and followed a narrow road up the side of the mountain. Both women were panting and had to stop to get their breath.

"I don't know how they did it," Morgan whined. "I thought I was in pretty good shape, but I'm beat. I haven't walked this much in. . .ever!"

"They didn't know much else, other than walking," Miyah said. "They had donkeys and carts, but most of their traveling was done on foot. Come on, we're almost there," she urged her daughter on after they caught their breath.

"Can't you just zap us there?" Morgan asked, honestly wondering if she could walk any further.

"I want you to know how it was for them in this time period. Things aren't always easy," her mom replied. Just then Miyah saw a familiar figure in the distance waving to them.

"Look, we're already here," she said anxiously, waving back. "There's our welcoming committee."

"You mean people can see us now?" Morgan asked. "We're not invisible anymore?"

"These people can," Miyah replied.

Morgan wiped the sweat from her forehead with her sleeve and wondered if she looked OK, fidgeting with her hair. Miyah knew Morgan wanted to make a good impression, but her daughter didn't realize that how her hair looked or if she had her makeup on right didn't make one bit of difference to anyone. It was what was "inside" that made the impression. Miyah knew her daughter would be fine. She was anxious to introduce her and show her off to her ancestors.

"We've been waiting for your arrival," a young woman greeter excitedly said as she met them with a broad smile and warm hugs.

"Have you been enjoying your tour through Ephesus? It's much different than our homeland." She pointed to the vista down the mountain. "From here you can view both the city of Ephesus and the sea. It's so beautiful, don't you agree?"

Not waiting for an answer, she took them both by the hand and led them a short distance to the villa.

"We must get you out of the sun and into a place where you can rest," she said. When they were in the shade of the courtyard, and had freshened themselves from the cool water of the statued fountain, Maryum came in and brought a tray of refreshments. She greeted and embraced Miyah. Then she took Morgan at arms length and stood looking at her. Morgan couldn't stop smiling.

"You're the image of your mother," Maryum finally said. "I'm so proud to have you as a new generation of Touchstone carriers. Welcome granddaughter. Welcome." She gave the girl a long, strong hug and Morgan could feel a warm energy permeate her being. Her tired body was revitalized and the beads of sweat on her forehead disappeared.

"Thank you," she said almost tearfully. "I'm so honored to be here."

Miyah made the formal introductions. "Morgan, this is Maryum, one of our grandmothers. We've dispensed with the great-great-great-etc. grandmother formalities and simply honor all of our grandmothers equally," she explained to her daughter.

"Maryum is married to Joshua," she continued. Two more women entered the courtyard and Miyah ran over to meet them. They embraced and greeted each other with laughter and talked for a few moments, then walked arm-in-arm back to Morgan and Maryum.

"Morgan, this is your grandmother, Mariam, Joshua's mother," she gestured to the other woman. "And this is her mother, Anna."

Each of the women embraced Morgan and commented on her beauty. Morgan blushed and said she was proud to meet them. She noticed their clothing, tunics made from a mixture of cotton and silk, dyed in colors of blue, violet and saffron yellow. The dresses were long, made of two pieces of cloth, worn one on top of the other and belted at the waist.

After the formalities were over, a rush of conversation began and didn't stop until much later, when an older woman came in and said that lunch was ready.

"This is my handmaiden and my friend, Josie," Mariam said as she squeezed Josie's hand. "We've been together for a very long time. Josie, this is my newest granddaughter, Morgan, and you know her mother, Miyah."

Josie politely greeted them both and Miyah walked over and hugged her. This strong woman had been through a lot with Mariam in her lifetime and Miyah had always felt a warm spot in her heart for her.

"It's so nice to see you again," Miyah said honestly.

"You haven't been back to see us in a long time," Josie commented. "We've missed your visits."

"I have my hands full teaching our family secrets to Morgan," Miyah laughed. "Maybe now that you've all met Morgan, you'll see more of us. Soon she'll be able to come back to visit you on her own for further teachings, so I'm sure you'll see a lot more of her."

Morgan beamed. This was something she had never thought about—that she would continue her lessons on another level with the women who actually comprised the lineage of her family. First hand history at her fingertips. That was an amazing concept. Her mother was right. She felt completely comfortable with her grandmothers. All of them.

They left their sandals in the entrance hall and were given a quick tour of the house at Morgan's timid request. The house was three stories, built around the central courtyard, which was surrounded by marble columns and colored frescoes. The main floor held a dining hall, living room with a grand fireplace, library and a main hall for large gatherings. All of the floors were covered with intricate mosaics; some were geometric patterned, some boasted figures and flowers. The top floor housed many bedrooms that were sparsely furnished with large beds, chests and tables, and had open doors to the courtyard with an outer balcony that connected the rooms. Elaborate silk curtains that were lined to conceal the light, decorated the courtyard side of each room, and beautiful paintings and artwork from Yosef's travels around the world adorned the walls and tabletops. The rooms were simple, yet elegant with their shining marble floors and artwork.

The bottom level, which was just as elegant, housed the servants quarters, the kitchen, the baths and a room with toilets and wash basins. All the floors were covered with detailed mosaics. Morgan noticed how neat and clean everything was.

"You have servants?" she asked with surprise.

Josie answered, "We're more like friends than servants and Yosef pays us very well. I feel fortunate to be living in such luxury. We each have our jobs, but are all treated as part of the family. Mariam is my best friend," she added.

Anna was proud of her son's house and all of its amenities. She stated, "We have a fresh water spring that runs down the mountain, alongside the villa. The house also has its own well and cistern, as well as municipal running water and is centrally heated with a system they call hypocausis." She explained, "There's a furnace near the sweat room in the baths, where water is boiled in large cauldrons. The steam and hot air is carried through ceramic pipes that have been placed in the walls and under the floors of the rooms. It's amazingly comfortable in the cold seasons."

"Where is Yosef? Is he traveling?" Morgan asked.

"Yes, he has a cargo of copper to transport from his mines. He won't return here for several weeks."

"And where is Joshua?" Morgan was so hoping so meet him on this journey.

"He's preparing for our journey to the East and will arrive with Yosef on his ship," Maryum replied. "Don't worry. You'll have other opportunities to meet. We thought this first meeting would be best as a gathering of your ancestral grandmothers and cousins."

"Thank you so much," Morgan was sincere. "I'll never forget this day."

The women ended their tour and retreated to the dining room, seating themselves at a long, finely fashioned copper-top table. Glasses of wine were poured and served.

"Can I drink the wine?" Morgan whispered to her mother.

"Yes, it's OK," Miyah whispered back. "It's a mixture of wine and honey that aides in digestion. The honey bee is the ancient symbol of Ephesus and a sacred symbol for the priestess. It even appears on some of their denarius—silver coins."

An array of beetroot, cabbage, leeks, mushrooms, lettuce, salted fish and fruit filled the center of the table. A small silver bowl was filled with sea salt and Miyah explained that salt was considered to be very important. Even the poorest of families would be sure they had a bowl of salt at their table.

Anna nodded her head and everyone at the table held hands, forming a circle for the blessing. Morgan was seated next to Maryum on one side and Anna on the other.

They closed their eyes and Anna began. "Thank you for the earth that gave us this bountiful crop of vegetables and fruit for our table; for the sun whose rays warmed the earth and the seeds within; for the rain that nurtured the plants; and the insects that replenished the soil. Thank you for the waters that gave us the fish and for the sea that produced the salt which preserves our food."

Then Mariam, to the right of Anna added, "Thank you for the farmers who harvested the crops, the fishermen who caught the fish, those who transported this food, and to the workers in the market who sold us their wares."

To her right was Josie, who always ate her meals with the family. "Thank you for the cooks who prepared this meal and for friends around us." Mariam squeezed her hand.

Next was Miyah. "Thank you for the family gathered here and for the love we all feel as we partake in this meal together. And thank you for the dedication of the women of the bloodline throughout each generation."

Maryum prayed, "Thank you for Yosef and his generosity in providing this house to all family and friends, and seeing to our comfort while we're here—and for the safe return of Yosef and Joshua and all who travel with them."

It was Morgan's turn. Remembering what her mother had just told her, Morgan added, "Thank you for the vine and the grapes that produced the wine, and the bees that gave us the honey."

Anna smiled with approval and said, "Amen," which everyone repeated.

As the women relaxed and ate their lunch they quizzed Morgan on her studies: what she had learned about the use of herbs and potions; what she had learned so far about the bloodline women; had she performed any healing acts? Morgan didn't know, but this was, in a sense, her graduation exam. She answered their questions without hesitation and with enthusiasm to be able to speak so openly about her powers. When the conversation slowed Morgan felt comfortable enough to ask a few questions of her own. She started with the easy ones, like, "What do you put in your hair to make it so shiny?" and "How do you keep your skin so nice," things that every teenager notices. Then she asked some deeper questions.

"How do you feel about the Temple of Artemis that honors the goddess? I mean, aren't people around you leaning toward Christianity now?"

Mariam responded to her. "First of all, we are Jews. The city's government has a wide band of religious tolerance and there are no laws pertaining to religion. Goddesses have been honored at the temple here for ages, so in this time, it's common. We attend the synagogue here, but also go to honor the goddesses at the temple. They're connected with the earth and the heavens in many ways, other than just myth. We'll bring you to the temple with us and teach you more about that on your next visit."

Maryum said, "Ephesus is a very progressive city in this time. Because of the harbor and shipping industry we have every kind of food, clothing and household goods. Houses have running water and heat, the public baths are free to all, as well as the hot rooms and massages. Even the Grand Theatre has free musical concerts, poetry recitals and performances for those who can't afford to pay. There's a fair tax system to balance the rich and poor, and the poor receive child benefits, as well as free wheat and vegetables. It's a perfect balance for a healthy community."

Anna added, "Roman Christianity, as you know it, really hasn't been adapted here yet, in this time. Remember child, we did not choose to be known as martyrs and saints. It wasn't until much after our time, in AD 431, as you mark time, that the Third Ecumenical Council proclaimed our Mariam as Mary, Queen of Heaven. By that time they had renamed the largest building here in Ephesus as the Church of the Virgin Mary, and it is there that the proclamation was made. They even named the roadway approaching Ephesus The Virgin Mary Road!"

Morgan looked at Mariam—the "Virgin Mary." She was just shaking her head back and forth.

"These things didn't happen during our lifetime. Thank God!" she exclaimed, to everyone's laughter. "But I've seen into that future and know they've taken away my human side and made my image into icons, statues, church bells, glass windows in cathedrals and even candles. I've passed into the hands of the Renaissance masters and ended up on their canvases and in their sculptures. They've made me into a symbol, not a woman—someone whom I do not recognize." She solemnly shook her head again.

"But wasn't Christianity getting organized in this time period?" Morgan asked.

"Yes, but Jerusalem Christianity was a much simpler version of what later progressed," Maryum responded. "Joshua's teachings were based on a way of life, living with a pure heart, compassion and respect. His main message was of love. Most of the concepts of your time were later incorporated by the Church, making it much more complicated, political—making the followers dependent on the Church for their salvation. Joshua taught that each person is responsible for themselves, based on the way they live their lives. Only you can save yourself. His teachings were purposely misconstrued by the early Church to gain control of the masses. You must know all of this from your studies?"

"Yes, but it seems clearer coming directly from you. People in my time are taught something much, much different than what you're telling me."

"It is so, child. Just remember that much of it is not our original teachings," Maryum added. "We didn't seek to control or implement a fear-based religion. Rather our mission was to unite the people, to heal and to educate with simple truths."

Morgan would have kept quizzing them if Miyah hadn't intercepted.

"My daughter is very curious," she said. "Her questions will never end."

"That is good, Miyah!" Anna replied. "How else will she learn, if she doesn't ask questions? Don't worry, we'll let her know if we grow weary of her inquiries."

The women continued conversing most of the afternoon, taking long walks along the gardens. They were joined by other women of the family: Maryum and Joshua's daughter, Sera Tamar Maria; her cousin Sara, the daughter of Sera's brother John; and Sara's daughter Sara Bernice, who all lived in France. The women had traveled together on one of Yosef's ships to spend a season with their family. Ruth, the youngest daughter of Mariam was also visiting. Many other grandmothers, aunts and cousins joined the reunion and introduced themselves to Morgan.

She talked with each of them and had so many questions about their lives, especially Sera, who was the next direct woman from Maryum in her bloodline. But there wasn't enough time and she was assured she'd have many more opportunities to have these conversations. She was overwhelmed, but loved every minute of it. She truly felt a sense of belonging and was happy to feel such a close family connection to all these women.

The day went by quickly and the mood grew more somber after most of the women had returned to their lodging in the city, or retreated to their rooms in the house.

"This house was built by my son, Yosef of Arimathea, but it's really a family home," Anna said. "Family is always welcome here. I believe I'll be buried here when it's my time to leave the earth."

Morgan calculated that Anna must be in her 90s or older.

"I was born here in Ephesus and I hope for my bones to be buried here, also," Mariam added. "But I'll be traveling soon with Joshua, Maryum and some of their disciples to the far East. I'm aging and I've seen it in the smoke of the candle that I may not return. We have such a luxurious life here, thanks to Yosef, but I choose to travel with my son, Joshua, and witness his ministry to the Lost Tribes of Israel."

Morgan stared at her grandmothers for a few moments and thought about how casually they spoke of their own deaths.

Reading her mind, Mariam offered, "Death is a part of life, child. It's a cycle. Everyone will experience the death of loved ones around them. That is unavoidable. Instead of mourning the loss of a life, remember always to celebrate that life. In that way it isn't really lost to you." Mariam glanced toward Miyah as she spoke.

"Also remember that each life returns time after time to complete their lessons on the earth. I look forward to the completion of this life and to returning again. I also have much to learn."

"Speaking of lessons," Miyah interjected, "I think this has been a wonderful classroom for Morgan, to be here with all of you today. I thank you from the bottom of my heart for welcoming me home, and for welcoming my daughter, but I think it's time for us to return now."

"Ah, Mom," Morgan began. "Do we have to go? Can't we stay just a little longer?"

The women laughed and Morgan found herself embarrassed that she had begged like a child.

"I'm sorry. I know we have to go," she immediately retaliated. "This has been the best day of my life. I mean it! I'm so honored to be here with all of you. I don't have words to express my gratitude."

"Just think of us when you're doing your studies," Maryum said. "Think of us as real women, humans, whose blood flows through your veins. You are of our bloodline and we're proud to know you. You have our complete blessings." All three women nodded to Miyah, a silent gesture that meant Morgan had "passed" their generational testing and that she was ready to go on to continue her studies. It was like graduating into Touchstone college.

Morgan hugged each of them with lingering embraces. Her tears flowed freely and she wasn't ashamed of that.

"We'll be here for you. Return soon," Maryum whispered as she held her granddaughter in her arms. "Thank you for coming."

Miyah also embraced her family with emotion. "I love you all so much," she said.

"And we love you," Maryum replied.

Miyah reached for Morgan's hand and looking over their shoulders to savor the last glimpses of their loved ones, they walked toward the city and into a familiar glow of fog that lifted them into a swirling eddy of light and brought them back to their own home.

~~~~~

"Wow! That was awesome!" Morgan exclaimed when they arrived back in the library of RoseVine. "That was incredible! When can we go back? I have so many questions—I forgot to ask about the diary and I can't believe I didn't ask them about the cedar box, and. . ."

"Oh you'll have many opportunities to travel back to them now that you've been introduced," Miyah assured her. "I wanted your first travel into the past for meeting some of the early women of our bloodline in a peaceful time, but we must pace your journeys there, and remember that things won't always be the same when you return. A few years after the time period of our visit, Saint Paul arrived in Ephesus with evangelical Christianity and in a few years things changed drastically. He was eventually run out of Ephesus and went to Macedonia, but he had already stirred things up. Saints Luke, Mark, Peter, Philip and others, came to preach in Ephesus and it became known as the Cradle of Christianity. Saint John later become the head of the Christian Church in Ephesus."

"So you're saying that the peaceful city we just visited, along with the worship of Goddesses, didn't stay that way for long," Morgan reiterated.

Miyah replied, "It didn't take long and 165 Christian churches grew up in Ephesus and the surrounding area. There were 77 Christian churches recorded in Italy and only 24 recorded in the Holy Land. By the time Christianity became the official religion of the Roman Empire, in AD 381, Ephesus was becoming known as the birthplace of Christianity."

"I have just one more question," Morgan said. "Mariam said she wanted to be buried in Ephesus. Earlier we talked about her dying and being buried near Kashmir, India."

"Well, in a sense both are true," Miyah answered. "She died on the way to Kashmir and was buried in Pakistan. Some of her bones were later removed and carried back to Ephesus. So technically, both can claim the burial site of Mariam. The same is true of Maryum. Her bones were also brought from Kashmir to Ephesus to be reburied, although early writings referred to Constantinople, which would be Istanbul. Anna died in Ephesus and was also buried there, as she requested. So you could say that the bones of the grandmother, mother, and the wife of Joshua rest in Ephesus, the city they all loved.

"But the Church wouldn't allow these women to rest. Some bones of Maryum were later removed and are now in the Church of St. Mary

Magdalene in Paris, in Vezelay, St. Baume, and other parts of France. There's a small stone house close to Joseph's villa in Ephesus, with a hearth and two altars. It was used by women of all religions for ritual, prayer and meditation. It's now 'officially' claimed by the Church to be the house of Mariam, called Panaghia Capouli or 'The Door of the Holiest.' They claim it's the place where she died and ascended to heaven."

Miyah continued. "In 1891, the Pope declared the little stone house a shrine and within one month over a thousand pilgrims had visited the site to see the house and hoped to be cured by drinking water from the nearby spring. Over a million people a year now make the pilgrimage. The roads have been paved, they brought in electricity, reconstructed the house, planted olive trees, added a bronze statue and lined the street with souvenir shops. It's now another church tourist attraction, which draws not only Christians, but also Muslims. It's interesting to note that Mother Mariam is mentioned in their holy book, the Koran, more times than she is in the Christian Bible. The house even has verses from the Koran relating to Mariam, framed on the wall."

"Is that because of Joshua's life in Kashmir" Morgan asked.

"That may have something to do with it," Miyah answered. "Muslim pilgrims go to the site and perform *namaz*, or prayers, in the house and then outside attach little pieces of cloth along the wall with prayers they hope to be answered.

"At least, because the Church claims that Mariam ascended into heaven, no one has sought the actual burial site of her bones. That is a blessing. May her bones, as well as those of Anna and Maryum, rest in peace."

"They're still at Joseph's house in Ephesus, aren't they? The real graves, I mean?" Morgan questioned.

Miyah sighed and changed the subject.

"We really had a wonderful day, didn't we?" she said, lovingly stroking her daughters thick hair. She knew Morgan would return often to the arms of her grandmothers. They had much to teach her.

"Thank you so much, Mom, for taking me there. I loved all of it. And I love all of them. I'm so happy right now!"

Morgan kissed her mom on the cheek and clung to her for an emotional moment.

"When can we do another journey?" she finally asked. "Where are you taking me next?" She was excited about this new privilege.

"We'll do another trip soon, but you must remember that we're only capable of traveling back through our own bloodline. There are rules. You can't go back to spy on people—to see what your friends were doing last night, or for that matter go forward to see what the stock market will do. This only relates to our own ancestry."

"So, can I go forward to see what the future will hold for me and my life?" Morgan asked.

"That's possible, but not recommended, and it has to be cleared through the council. In very rare instances it has been allowed. There are other ways of foreseeing the future that you'll learn." Miyah had a sudden flash of when she placed her hair from the brush into the flame and watched it fizzle and smoke. She shuddered.

"Are you alright, Mom?" Morgan picked up on her change in energy.

"Oh. . .yes, I was just thinking of something else," Miyah answered. She attempted to shake off her premonition. "Let's break for some ice tea before we continue," she suggested, heading toward the kitchen. "I'll be right back. Are you hungry? We get so involved in our work that we forget to eat."

"No, I just want to continue. I'll be right here waiting for you," Morgan replied.

Miyah came back a few minutes later with a pitcher of raspberry ice tea, a tray of egg salad sandwiches and a big spinach salad topped with walnuts and fresh strawberries.

"We have to remember to take breaks and stretch and eat," she laughed. "We have to keep up our strength."

Morgan dove into the tray of food and ate heartily. Partly because she realized that she really was hungry, but mostly to get the food out of the way so they could continue her lessons.

6 Witches of the Past

"Before we do another journey," Miyah informed her daughter, "I want you to know that sometimes personal and emotional adjustments have to be made after you've witnessed some of the past. It's not all fun and games. You have to be prepared for what you don't expect. I'm not quite ready for you to go solo on your time traveling yet, but when you do, you'll have to remember to always be cautious and follow the rules. Your best source to start will be to choose writings from the diary and enter into them to get a clearer picture of what the woman who penned the story was experiencing. This will also bring you closer to the true content of the diary and its powerful messages. You also have to promise not to 'be gone' too much. I remember when I first started this, all I wanted to do was to travel back. Nona took my privileges away for a few weeks until I learned to monitor myself."

"You mean you were grounded!" Morgan teased. "That's awesome! I never thought of you ever getting grounded. . .I mean grounded in the sense of being reprimanded," she added.

"What? I'm human," Miyah laughed, then added, ". . .and you do not have my permission to go back into events of my current life. Understand?"

"Aww, Mom. No fair," Morgan laughed.

"So let's get started, and this time I want you to do the protection ritual by yourself. It's important to do it correctly. I've written the words for the chant on a piece of paper. Once you have it memorized, burn it in the flame of the candle. If you should forget it later, it's written in the dairy."

A bit nervous, Morgan took the paper from her mother's hand. They gathered around the candle and Morgan lit the wick with a fireplace match.

"But what should my intention be? Where do we want to go?" she asked, remembering to set her destination.

"I want you to set an intention of going back into a time of difficulty for women. Normally you will have targeted destinations, but until you have a place and era that you want to pinpoint, this will do. Your travels may not always be pleasant and you'll need to be able to adjust to that when you return."

Feeling a little reluctant after hearing the last of her mother's words, Morgan knew she would need to concentrate even harder. Trying to remember all of the steps Miyah had done, she placed two stones, one for each of the travelers, near the base of the candle. She looked at the neat loop of her mother's handwriting on the paper and slowly, yet with command, read each line aloud.

"I call upon all who guard over us to protect us from negative powers. Safely guide our steps, our voices, our thoughts and our energies to the place I have chosen. Let us be greeted with respect and love and allow us to understand the lessons we are meant to receive from our ancestors. Provide us with safe passage back to the place where this journey began. With great gratitude I thank you for your guidance. Amen. So be it."

Morgan blew out the flame of the candle and while the smoke filled the air, she waved a white feather through the vapors, weaving it into a circle, three times counter-clockwise, and then fanned it up into the ethers. She reached over and took Miyah by the hand and they were off to another journey through time.

~~~~~~

"What's that awful stench?" Morgan asked as the swirling light that carried them into another world dissipated and they found themselves in the night streets of a busy city. Judging by the clothing of the people bustling around them and the buildings surrounding the plaza on which they stood, Morgan guessed they were somewhere in Europe.

She had a feeling of foreboding and grasped her mother's arm.

"Don't worry, dear. I've put a spell out so we can't be seen. You aren't in any danger."

Morgan didn't lessen her grip. Fear sank into her being, as she looked toward a platform with people gathered around. Not far from the stage was a smoldering bonfire and next to it another, yet unlit, stacked with branches. Several woman were bound and stood on the platform.

"Here is an eye witness," a man proclaimed, gesturing to a young altar boy at his side. "He saw with his own two eyes, this woman hiding bread given out during communion, and he dutifully reported this to his priest."

"I only took the bread to feed it to my cow," the woman shouted back in tears, "so it will give more milk for my children."

"Silence witch!" the man in charge yelled, raising his hand as if to strike her. "We know you were going to use the bread in your witch's potions. Who were you intending to harm—the priest who fed you? You steal, you lie and you have intent to harm others!"

"No. No. It's not true," the woman objected, but was soon silenced when a guard stepped up and hit her on the face with the flat of his fist.

A man bravely stepped forward in the crowd, his voice strong and unwavering.

"These women who you torture into confessions are innocent! Why do you search for sorcerers? Take the Capuchins, the Jesuits, all the religious orders, and torture them as you do these women and children—they too will confess. Should a few still be obstinate, keep on torturing, as you do to these innocent people—and they too will give in. If you want more, take the Canons, the Doctors, the Bishops of the Church—they too will confess. . ."

The man did not have a chance to finish his speech.

"Arrest that man! He defends the witches—he surely must be one of them. Arrest him and bring him here to me!"

Before those who stood guard over the woman on the stage could wind their way into the crowd, the man had disappeared into the shadows of the night. Some in the crowd pulled at his coat and his body as he ran, but others stepped aside and cleared the way.

Many of the crowd gathered were intentionally placed there to feed the fire—to get the crowd riled up and justify the deed that was about to be done. Some came out of curiosity, and yet others—friends and relatives of those accused—hoped that at the last moment a miracle would happen and these women would be spared.

"If they're witches as they're accused," Morgan whispered to her mother, "why wouldn't they use their magic to save themselves?"

"Exactly. . ." Miyah replied. "Most of the women were innocent bystanders. But others were healers, holy women, shaman. Some of them, these witches, these good witches, were our ancestors."

Morgan looked at her mother aghast. Of course. She remembered Miyah telling her that she would only be allowed to travel into the lives of their bloodline. Relatives or not, she couldn't bear to watch what was about to happen. She was grateful her mother had made them invisible, because she knew that she too, like the brave man who had just spoken, would have stepped forward in defense of these women. Where was the justice?

"*Tace pro pace*—be silent and live in peace," Miyah said quietly, reading her daughter's thoughts.

"Test her! Test her to see if she has the mark of the devil!" a man yelled from the crowd.

"What does he mean?" Morgan asked.

"They claim that when a witch makes a pact with the devil he touches her and leaves a mark on her body. The mark is insensitive to pain. One test is to prick her body with a blade. If she doesn't flinch or bleed when pricked on that mark, they claim it's evidence that she's a witch."

"A mark, what sort of mark?"

"Anything—a mole, a past scar, a birthmark, and if they can't find anything they'll claim that the devil made it invisible. It really doesn't matter. It's just an excuse to torture them."

One of the guards stepped forward and stripped the clothing from the woman, her nakedness open to the world. He ran his hands over her body, looking for a mark. With a lusty, toothless grin, he took pleasure in his quest. His hand rested on the side of her breast, eagerly massaging her.

"A mark!" he shouted. "She has the mark." Not bothering to show his find to anyone else, he pierced her breast with his knife. The woman screamed in pain.

Morgan hid her eyes, hearing the woman's agony.

"But doesn't that mean she's innocent?" she asked under her breath. "She felt the pain."

"This woman cries out in false pain," the leader of the mob shouted. "She mocks us. Guilty! I say 'guilty' to the witch!"

Morgan looked around and saw that someone in the crowd began to chant and others joined in.

"She made my crops fail!"

"She made my horse go lame and my cows go dry!" they shouted, blaming anything that was bad in their lives on spells made by this woman. It was becoming a riot. Yet others huddled together, men attempting to protect their women and children from witnessing the sight. Children were crying, afraid and horrified at what was happening.

"Why are they here—why don't they leave?" Morgan asked, in a pleading voice. "The children shouldn't be here!"

"They won't give up hope that something may happen at the last minute and someone will be released. It has happened. Sometimes one or two of the accused women are burned at the stake and the others are let go. It's an example of control and fear."

"Control. . .by who?"

"We've stepped into a time in history when all Christians—Protestants and Catholics—are expected to help the Dominican monks, whom the Pope placed in charge, to convict people 'in association with Satan,' who are accused of causing disease, ruining harvest, harming cattle and other crimes. Here, in France, they placed boxes in every church and parishioners were advised to put names of persons they suspected of witchcraft. Anyone they didn't like could be accused. Torture during criminal interrogations was accepted, including the torture of children to force them to testify against their parents."

"Can't you stop this? Can't you just take them out of here?" Morgan pleaded, shutting her eyes.

"We're not allowed to tamper with history, Morgan. You know that. Events that occurred here had a domino effect on many lives at that time and in the future. And remember, these women, men and children, who suffered during this time, have all come back into other lifetimes. There have been lessons learned from each phase of their lives—and yes, some of these lessons have been very hard. Six generations of children watched as their mothers were burned at the stake."

Morgan uncovered her eyes long enough to catch another glimpse of the three women who had been declared guilty of witchcraft. They were tied, naked, in a circle to a central pole with kindling and branches piled around them. Torches were passed and the kindling flared. Surrounded by flames, with their hair already singed, the women's eyes were dilated by fear.

Only their screams carried their innocence into the crowd. The sound of the wailing women and cries of their families in the crowd, the excited brutality of the masses couldn't drown out the crackle of the flames as it consumed the frail bodies of its victims. The smell of flesh burning was overwhelming. . . only matched by the final haunting silence of the women. . .

"Can we leave now?" Morgan begged. "I don't think I can stand this." She began to swoon.

~ ~ ~ ~ ~ ~

When Morgan came to her senses she was back home. She reached over and clung to Miyah, sobbing with abandonment.

"Why did you make me witness that?" she asked accusingly. "I can't believe you brought me there!"

"Was your experience worse than that of the people who actually went through it?" Miyah asked, almost coldly. "This wasn't about you, Morgan. It was to show you the reality of the horrors that happened in the span of centuries. Having access to this window of the past, you'll experience both the highs and the lows. You need to know that when you travel back in time it may not always be a bed of roses. History can be brutal."

Morgan felt a little sheepish. "I'm sorry. I know it's not about me. I just didn't expect that. It was so horrible. I feel so sorry for those innocent women and their families. It's hard to believe that witchcraft trials, torture and executions like that really happened."

"It's ironic because, as we talked before, belief in magic was universal before those times. Almost all cultures believed in supernatural means to help in hunting, to make crops grow better, or to make humans and animals more fertile. Magic was used to heal the sick, and for the majority of people who lived before the 18th century, magic through plants, potions and other means of healing was an ordinary part of everyday life."

"What changed?"

"It was a religious holocaust. 85% of the nine million people who were tortured and murdered were women. The sanctioning of witch trials occurred over a period of about three centuries and grew when Pope Innocent VIII alleged, in 1484, that many men and women were in collusion with the devil—mostly women, because their relationship to nature, goddesses, spirits and rituals to honor the earth. These women were midwives, healers, herbalists, councilors and holders of wisdom. The patriarchy of the Church didn't like the attention or gratitude given to women and in a sense declared war on them. They held too much power and if people had a direct pipeline to their spiritual source, they didn't need the authority of the Church. They needed to suppress women. Husbands were advised from the pulpit to beat their wives, not out of rage, but out of 'charity for her soul.' The simple earth-honoring beliefs of paganism were turned into devil worship, and folk culture into heresy. Christian churches mandated witch trials and the burning of live human beings. It was a legal act, a law. They even had a handbook for interrogation, 'The Hammer Against Witches.'"

"It's so barbaric! I can't believe it was actually a law ordered and carried out by the Church! What kind of religion is that? " Morgan asked.

"Theologians and religious scholars don't deny what happened and the wrong-doing of the Church, yet Church archives on witchcraft trials still remain closed, even to academic scholars."

"How did they stop it? Did the priests finally realize this was not very 'Christian'—that the Church was terribly wrong?" Morgan questioned.

"It took a long time," Miyah answered. "The last legal execution for witchcraft in England was in 1684—in Switzerland it wasn't until 1782. Eventually educated people gradually stopped believing in witches and magic, and during the 18th century witchcraft was regarded as just a superstition. Attitudes had changed so much that laws against witchcraft were repealed in England and replaced by a law that simply made it illegal to 'pretend' to cast spells or tell fortunes."

"As horrible as it was, Mom, I'm glad you brought me there. It gives me a new perspective to what sacrifices were made, willingly or not, in the name of healing and supernatural beliefs. I also realize that many of those people weren't even healers and were accused randomly. I'm sure glad I didn't live during that time period."

"How do you know you didn't?" Miyah asked.

7 Riddle in Skye

Miyah and Morgan were both ready for a break after their intense studies and looked forward to returning to some semblance of a normal life with Michael. The hardest part for Morgan was that she wouldn't be able to share the excitement of her "travels" with her friends. It was made clear that it was strictly against the rules.

They prepared for their return and as Miyah packed up her medicine bag, a folded piece of paper slipped from the diary. Morgan picked up the note and read:

> ". . .the path to box is in the skye
> do not attempt until three generations have gone by.
> only the faeries can flag the way
> among a handled cross they play.
> the guardian of gazanias will only let it be
> by presenting them the proper key."

"That's an odd poem. What does it mean?" she asked her mother. "How did it get in the diary?"

Miyah took the paper from her daughter's hand and a memory flashed through her mind of the day she was given the poem and the letter written by Nona. She opened the diary and took out an envelope she had pressed between the last pages of the book.

"This is a letter Nona wrote to me many years ago," Miyah said. "It was meant to be given to me upon your birth. At the time I was a bit upset with it, but now I understand its reasoning. The fact that the poem just happened to fall out of the diary now and present itself to us, I think, is an omen that it's time to for us to give this matter our attention."

Miyah opened the envelope, unfolded the letter and began to read.

My dearest Miyah,

By the time you read this you will already know that I have been with you, in my spirit form, watching you grow and guiding you in your work. I am so very proud of you and your dedication to your healing mission. Now you are a mother and another dimension has been added to your life. I will be there with you, singing lullabies in her ear and helping you teach your daughter, as Junia and I have taught you.

But let me get to the point of this letter. I have a message for you about the first cedar box—the one that was carved for Mariam—Mother Mariam. I told you that we had been searching for it for many years, which was true. What I didn't tell you was that we did locate the general whereabouts of the box and that it hasn't yet been retrieved.

When the last of the Isaac lineage, the keepers of the cedar box, died in Great Britain, they gave the box to a trusted doctor in Scotland who used the box in his practice for many years, until his sudden death. We discovered that his death was no accident. It was a failed attempt to steal the box, which thankfully was hidden away and kept safe. He knew he was in danger before his death, and mailed this key to my mother, Dolores, with an odd poem.

I know this will be a difficult time for you and when you call upon me, I will explain further. But for now, you must not put any more energy into this until the time comes when you and your daughter are drawn back to solving the riddle and venture to retrieve the missing cedar box. When the two cedar boxes are reunited and safe, the time will be right for the entire Touchstone story to be known. Your daughter will be freed from guarding the bloodline secrets and, although she will retain her healing abilities and connections to our ancestors, she will be the first generation to live a life free from safeguarding our family secrets. For at that time, these secrets will be made known to the world, the truth of our ancestry will be told, and we will at last be free.

I love you now and forever.
Your grandmother, Nona

Miyah stood looking at the letter in her hand. At the time it was given to her she was so upset that she didn't finish reading the entire letter. It seemed much clearer to her now as she re-read the contents.

Morgan didn't know what to say. It took a while for this to sink in. This letter pertained to her future. Did this mean that all the things she was learning now about her ancestry would be available to everyone? She no longer would have to school in the shadow of RoseVine and bite her tongue when she wanted to discuss with her friends the things she'd discovered in her studies? In the life of a teenager, this was huge—in the life of a Touchstone carrier, this was huge.

"Wow!" she said. "So, if this was going to happen, why have I been on such a strict study regimen? Why have I needed to learn all of this family history and all of these details?"

"Oh, you don't quite understand," Miyah quickly responded. "This doesn't mean you'll no longer be a part of the Touchstone carriers. It simply means that your mission will be different. Instead of guarding these secrets, as we've done throughout the ages, you'll become a teacher of our true history. You, Morgan, will be a family historian who knows and has experienced much of our family's lives first-hand. That's a great honor."

"That sounds like a big job," Morgan replied.

"Oh, you won't be alone," her mother assured her. "Your cousins in France and Britain and in other places of the world are also being prepared as teachers—and I suppose there are also many here in the States we don't even know about yet. You'll have good company. For a long time I thought I was the only Touchstone carrier. When your father and I first went to France to meet with Tomas, Papa Tom, we met many of my relatives and discovered there are many of us cousins, all descendants of the bloodline, who are charged with the same responsibility."

"But will people believe this? I can't imagine it'll be easily accepted," she stated. "Our family story pretty much goes against everything people have been taught about their religious background."

"It'll happen gradually. It's time for changes to be made in our world, time to give people hope for a future without the guilt of sin and the fear of God's wrath that has been put upon their shoulders for generations. This movement will be about love, compassion, healing, acceptance, respect, sharing, caring, honor, truth, equality and peace. All the things Joshua taught before his mission was misrepresented and quoted out of context. Many churches are already in tune with this and aren't as concerned with dogma, corporate wealth, power, and control of the Church. So you see, there is already a start, a movement of hope."

"But what about the Church?" Morgan asked. "They aren't going to like this new Bible story. It contradicts everything they're based upon."

"Don't worry. The Church will survive. It always has. There may have to be major alterations made in some cases—and believe me, all of this information, the secrets we've been guarding over all this time, are already known by the Church. Records are hidden within their vaults that reveal all of these truths. There will come a time when these records will be 'mysteriously' rediscovered and the Church will reinvent itself, apologize for their oversight and continue on. Even the appearance of the Dead Sea Scrolls has begun some of this controversy. Most people need some semblance of Church, no matter where they worship. The Church provides a sense of community for them and for some it's the only place they can feel spiritual. That will never go away. My hope is that this will unite all religions, and will eventually put an end to religious wars. It's the only true path to peace on this earth. It's a big program, Morgan. No doubt about that."

"Whew. I don't think I can live up to what's expected of me," she sighed. "Sounds like I'm supposed to save the entire world!"

Miyah laughed. "Not at all. What this will mark is just the beginning of a new era. As I said, it'll happen gradually. Your life isn't really going to change much for now. We need to keep up with your studies so all the wisdom of your elders will be transferred to you. But you'll see, little by little, pieces of our true history appearing in conversations, public forums, in movies and books. . ."

"Is that what Dad has been working on ever since I was little?" Morgan always saw her dad sitting behind his desk with stacks of religious and history books, typing notes into his computer.

"Yes, dear. That's a big part of this shift. Your father's book will compile much of what you and I have learned. That's why he was given access to his time travels and also to the diary. The day will come when he actually begins to put all of this together—when he begins to write our story. That will mark a big phase of this shift—when our family will be revealed in all of its truth in the series of books your father is working on."

"Does he know this?" Morgan asked, wide-eyed.

"Not entirely," Miyah admitted. "I've asked him to write what has been revealed to him about our family, but he doesn't quite realize the impact it'll have. He'll discover that in time. I want him to write it from his own perspective so not to be tainted by the outcome. Another reason you and I have been doing your studying away from him, is so he can concentrate on his research. Nona and the ancestors have been helping him behind the scenes, leading him to the right information, helping him to compile his data, but he doesn't realize that either. He was chosen for this particular job for many reasons, and they will all be revealed to him in their own sequence. I'm not even fully aware of all the details."

"See, that's something else I still don't understand about this family. If we have all of these 'gifts,' why can't we just access everything? Why can't you just look ahead and see how Dad will be involved in our story. Why couldn't Nona just ask where the second cedar box is and be given that information?"

"You're asking why we don't know everything," Miyah said. "We just don't. Everything we need to know is revealed to us in the time we're supposed to know it. That's the way it is. When we're able to access information, it's only because it's proper for us to do so at that time. Sometimes it's because there are lessons to be learned in the process of the discovery. Remember, I told you there are rules."

Morgan responded with a big sigh and took the letter from her mother.

"So what's this about a key?"

Miyah shook out the remaining contents of the envelope to reveal a small key. She retrieved her own key from the pouch in the necklace around her neck and held the two keys up, side-by-side. They matched. Both were in the shape of an ankh at one end. Miyah handed the key to Morgan.

"When the other cedar box is found, this key will belong to you, as well as the box. For now I'll put it on the chain with my key for safe-keeping."

Morgan turned the key over in her hands, studying the markings on the curved portions of the ankh. Then she handed it back to her mother.

"Twice in their history the two boxes have been together: when Mother Mariam lived with Joshua and Maryum and the two women used them to hold their healing oils and herbs, and again when my great-grandparents— Nona's parents, Dr. Alyn and Dolores Harris—each owned one," Miyah explained. "Nona's father, Dr. Alyn, was entrusted with his cedar box when there were no more descendents of the Issac family. He was a faithful friend whom they knew would use the powers of the box wisely. Dr. Alyn didn't know the true origin of the box, that it was carved by Joshua when he was 12-years-old for his mother, Mariam. He just knew that it assisted him in healing people. The other cedar box passed down to Dolores, Nona's mother, was also carved by Joshua, as a wedding gift for his bride, Maryum, and has been passed down through generations of the bloodline. It's the box I have today."

"But I don't understand what the two boxes being reunited has to do with the timing of the release of the family secrets," Morgan questioned.

"There are many reasons, Morgan. One is to keep them in a safe place so they remain in our family. These cedar boxes, because of their origin, contain powerful healing energy and should never fall into the hands of someone who would only use them for power or to promote themselves for material gain. When the two boxes are together in our family, it's a guarantee that they'll only be used for the good of healing. It's important that we locate the other box, so they remain in the family. . .together. Remember, before he was murdered, Dr. Alyn hid the cedar box because someone was trying to steal it, so someone must have known about the powers of the box at that time. That's why he wanted it hidden for four generations, hoping it would be forgotten by would-be-thieves and their future generations."

"What would happen if someone tried to use one of the boxes to gain power for themselves?" Morgan asked. "Could they use the box to go back in history like Dad has done?"

"Your father was able to do that through my supervision and with permission of the council," Miyah said. "As far as someone else, these are questions I can't answer, Morgan. I don't know. I'd like to think there is a spiritual safety shield connected with each of them. I asked these same questions of Joshua years ago. As the carver of both of the boxes, I thought he'd be the one to go to for those answers. He just smiled at me, shrugged his shoulders and said nothing. Let's hope we never have to find out."

Miyah added, "Think about this. These cedar boxes are over 2,000 years old. Even if no one realized the powers they hold, historians, museums and religious institutions—even countries, would want to claim them for their archives as antiquities. They may even fight over their right to claim them."

"But how would anyone know about them?" Morgan wondered.

"There are stories throughout the ages that refer to the mysterious healings that occurred with the use of a pair of simply carved cedar boxes dating from the time of the holy family. Many of them have been recorded in diaries, ancient scrolls, inscriptions, even in early religious books. Once people become aware of a new holy family story, they'll start to pay attention to these details and will begin searching."

"Like they have been for the Ark of the Covenant, Noah's Ark. . .the

Silver Chalice," Morgan added.

"Exactly."

"OK, I understand that, but what does it have to do with. . ."

Miyah interrupted, "I know what you're asking. The timing. Part of it is simply a sign. The reuniting of the cedar boxes signals a time when religious unity needs to begin, and for that to happen new truths must be revealed."

". . .like the true events of our family—the continuing life of Joshua after the crucifixion and the fact that he didn't die on the cross, the acknowledgment of his wife, children and their generations, his life in India and studies with Buddhist and Hindu teachers, that he's buried in Srinagar, Kashmir and all of that?" Morgan responded.

"Yes, all of that and more," her mother said. "The world has gone out of balance and a new cycle of peace needs to plant itself in order for the future of humankind to survive. It's that important. This cycle begins with the breaking down and rebuilding of many religious beliefs. Beliefs that, as we said before, offer a new light of hope to the world. The fact that Joshua continued to teach his message of love and how to live a peaceful life, and that he continued to heal those who needed him until he was 125 years old—and that Maryum's teaching and healing mission, especially her work throughout France as Mary Magdalene, was just as important—it's a beautiful story, an inspiring story.

"That box has been hidden for generations, safely, I hope, and its retrieval has been charged to you. Your father and I are allowed to help in your search, but the ultimate discovery has to be by you."

Miyah smiled. "I know what you're thinking, Morgan, and it doesn't work that way."

"Whaaat. . ." Morgan said, caught in her thoughts. "Why not? Why can't we just go back into the time when Nona's father hid the box and see where he put it? He's part of our bloodline—a grandfather—so we should have access into his past. Why can't we just do that?"

"Remember, I told you that part of the process is the discoveries you make along the way. There's a reason you've been chosen to locate the box, so there must be some lessons involved that you need to learn. You should look at this as a challenge, a mystery for you to solve. You have this riddle to unravel that should lead you to your treasure."

Morgan took another look at the poem. "So the first line of the poem is about the cedar box," she stated.

"*The path to box is in the skye*" means that the trail to find the box is. . .in the sky?"

"The answer to that clue was given to me by Nona. She said it's in the Isle of Skye, in Scotland," Miyah offered.

"Scotland! I never would have guessed that. OK, that tells us where to start." Morgan continued, "*do not attempt until three generations have gone by."* Well, that's clear. And the last line, *"by presenting them the proper key"* has to do with the key you found with the letter, so we must have to show the key to someone. The rest of it doesn't make much sense."

"I don't know either. But I do know one thing. . .we better pack our bags."

"You mean we're going to Scotland?" Morgan exclaimed!

"We should talk to your father first, but I have a feeling he'll be just as anxious to go. He has his own special connection to that land from his travels back in time to visit Joshua and Joseph of Arimathea's tin mines when they were building the first abbey in the area. I'm sure he's told you about it."

~ ~ ~ ~ ~

Morgan hardly gulped for air as she relayed all that had happened to her on both of her journeys into the past. Because he knew first hand the excitement of these time travel adventures, Michael was just as excited for her and listened intently, asking questions and taking notes as his daughter spoke of her observations at the witch trial and of her adventures with her grandmothers.

"Did you see Joshua?" he eagerly asked.

"No, he was away with Joseph somewhere, but Maryum said I would meet him the next time I returned. Wouldn't it be cool, Dad, if we could all go back next time as a family? That would really be a great reunion!"

"Yes, it would be," Michael replied, smiling at Miyah, agreeing that it would indeed be a very special journey. He was glad to have his girls back home, and even happier to hear that Morgan was finished with her daily studies for awhile.

"Mom showed me the poem and letter from Nona that was given to her when Papa Tom was alive," Morgan said, producing the poem for him to read.

"Oh, I remember this," Michael said, looking over the poem, and then the letter.

"Mom said that the 'skye' part of the poem referred to the Isle of Skye in Scotland. . ." Morgan said, leaving her sentence dangle.

"I see where this is going," Michael said, slowly looking from Morgan to Miyah and back. Morgan held her breath.

He finally spoke. "Well, when do we go?" Morgan jumped in the air and clung to him, kissing his cheek over and over.

"Yes! This will be so much fun. We haven't taken a family trip in years. I can hardly wait!" she squealed.

That night the family celebrated the end of the formal school program and the promise of Scotland with Morgan's choice of dinner—pizza, delivered.

Plans progressed quickly for the trip to Scotland. As a family, they made a list of places they wanted to visit, including the modern day version of places Michael had previously journeyed to through the cedar box, or sites that Joshua had told him about: Glastonbury—the fabled Avalon; The Isle of Iona; and Eilean Isa—"The Island of Jesus." He wanted to see how the centuries had changed these places, if they even still existed.

Miyah was hoping to visit Rosslyn Chapel south of Edinburgh where she knew there was more family history. She also wanted to visit a church she had heard about that housed a stained glass window of Joshua and a pregnant Maryum—Kilmore Church in Dervaig on the Isle of Mull. But most of all, her goal was to retrieve the family's cedar box, their number one priority.

Morgan wanted to visit castles. It all sounded quite romantic to her, but she knew, too, that she had an important task to accomplish and put a lot of thought into decoding the poem. She was taking her mission seriously.

Agreeing to travel the traditional way, as Morgan had never actually traveled by airplane before, Michael made the arrangements. Conveniently, one of his old writer friends, who lived in the States, had generously offered the use of a house he owned on the Isle of Skye.

The family flew into Glasgow and rented a car. Mapping their way 180 miles north, they connected with A 82 and then to A 87, crossing from the Kyle of Lochalsh on the Skye Bridge, heading toward their destination. Getting there was an adventure—first trying to understand the rich Scottish dialect, and then driving on the opposite side of the road. With the steering wheel on the right, instead of the left, Michael could never remember which side of the car to get into.

They laughed when they read the "Rules of the Road" in a road guide, but soon discovered that it was no laughing matter. When a road sign said "Use passing places to permit overtaking," it meant you were on a narrow one-car road with passing places on each side every 100 yards or so. Michael had to pull over every time he met a car, or they would pull over depending on which side the passing place was on. A wave of the hand as a polite thank you gesture and they were on their way again.

Another hazard was presented by sheep. The guidebook warned, *"they are not to be regarded as cuddly, friendly, woolly jumpers. Treat them as devious, plotting assassins hired by some crooked breakdown merchant to force cars off the road. They are a menace. They have absolutely no road sense and as a result of years of roadside breeding, are chronically oblivious to car horns and flashing lights."* Michael found that to also be a true observance.

Gaelic sign posts pointed the way as they drove, keeping the song and language of the land alive throughout the island. Driving through the country they enjoyed the scenery and noticed its changes from alpine peaks and waterfalls to rolling farmland, bleak moorland, wooded valleys and cliffs dotted with mysterious caves. Michael was itching to get his camera out, but knew there would be plenty of time for that.

The drive proved to take much longer than anticipated because of the roads and a heavy rain. They finally stopped in Portree, the capitol of the island, for groceries at a co-op food store and a much-needed break. They had been traveling for over 24 hours since they left home and were anxious to arrive at the writer's house. It would suit them well for a base while they were deciphering the poem and exploring where Morgan thought the clues led.

"It says here that the entire population of the island is only 9,000," Morgan read in a guide book she bought at the store. "The island is only about 50 miles from end to end, and varies from six miles to 25 miles in width. I should think that would make our treasure hunting easier," she commented with confidence.

They continued their journey and Miyah, who had navigator duty, finally directed Michael to turn right onto a narrow, winding dirt road.

"Are you sure this is right," Morgan asked. "We're in the middle of no-man's-land. There are sheep on the road! Where are the stores and the houses?"

Michael drove slowly for about a mile among flocks of sheep on the narrow, grassy, winding road and finally stopped in front of a closed gate.

"This must be it," Miyah announced.

"You're kidding?" Morgan said leaning forward from the back seat to look at the big, white house at the end of the road. Spread out in front of it was the wavy waters of the loch, an extension of the sea.

"It's beautiful," she said, adding, "I wonder if the house is haunted?"

"Morgan!" Michael laughed. "I'm surprised you'd say that with your family background! You're not afraid are you?"

"How long are we staying here?" she asked, avoiding his question, knowing not all spirits are good.

Miyah got out and opened the gate and after Michael drove through, she securely re-latched it. They had been forewarned that an open gate welcomed the neighbor's sheep into the garden, and these animals were quite smart in avoiding being herded back to their own side of the fence. Miyah took a deep breath and could almost taste the fresh, salt air.

Michael had a key and they went inside the house.

"Wow!" Morgan exclaimed. "It's nothing like I expected. I thought it would be old. . .dark and creepy!"

"I know," Miyah agreed. "It's so beautiful."

"I guess I forgot to tell you that after Mark bought the house he had it completely gutted and remodeled. Everything in the place is new, from the heated slate floors and this modern kitchen to the dishes and the bath towels! Pretty great, huh."

"We'll have to do something special to thank him," Miyah said. "This is like having our own hotel!"

Mark had given Michael a very detailed list, numbered 1 through 30, of how to navigate around the house—everything from how to light the AGA, a boxlike iron cook stove, to the best places to dine and shop in the area. They were very grateful for his list.

Morgan carried in the groceries they had bought in Portree and Miyah checked out the facilities in the kitchen, while Michael brought in the rest of their luggage from the car. Morgan couldn't wait to explore the huge house. She quickly made a swing through the main floor and then went upstairs to check out the other two stories of the house.

"There are SIX bedrooms up here," she called out. Michael and Miyah smiled at each other at their daughter's enthusiasm and climbed the steps to look around the inviting rooms. Miyah immediately felt drawn to one of the bedrooms on the west side with a view toward the loch. It had a king-size bed with a fluffy down comforter. Michael put their suitcases inside the door to stake their claim. Morgan looked through each of the rooms and decided, just in case it was a little spooky during the night, that she would feel safer in the room right next to her parents. Plus, it also had an excellent view of the rolling hills and plenty of room for her to spread out her belongings. She knew she could never be confined to a suitcase.

Michael was in heaven when he discovered the library. It was two stories with entrances from each level of the house and the floors were connected by a spiral staircase inside the library itself. Large windows brought in natural sunlight and offered a spectacular view of the loch with layered hills in the distance, boasting wind generators to harness the wind to take advantage of the everyday, wild winds of Skye. The windows on the east side of the library offered a serene and picturesque view of a green pasture dotted with white, fluffy sheep surrounded by a long, curving stone fence. A fireplace warmed the room, top and bottom floors. There was a desk on each level and fine artwork. Bookshelves lined the walls and the local Skye information books would be helpful to understand and navigate the area.

They continued to familiarize themselves with the house and then walked around the grounds outside to take in the breathtaking view of the inlet and the vista beyond. They had plenty of time. Daylight would last until almost midnight. It would be the night sky they would miss when they wanted a signal that it was time to go to sleep.

"Mark said to use anything we'd like from his garden," Michael said to Miyah. "His neighbors take care of the place when no one is here and he says there's always an abundance of vegetables."

Michael found a basket in the garage and they picked tomatoes, spinach, green beans, zucchini, onions and some herbs to start with. Miyah eyed the eggplant and peppers, ripe on the vine, and was already planning ahead for her next meal. She was going to love having this big garden at her fingertips.

After dinner, they sat around the table and, bringing out their wish-list of places to see, they agreed to make a plan. Their number one priority was the cedar box.

"I know this trip came up suddenly and none of us had a chance to really do any research, so let's take the guide books and other info we brought with us and see if we can brainstorm this," Miyah said.

"I want to do some research on the internet," Morgan replied, taking out her laptop. "I bet the old doctor didn't know that we'd have something as handy as the internet when he left his clues."

"There's something about the internet on Mark's list," Michael said, getting up to retrieve the paper. "Ah, yes, here it is. . . he says it's very slow and has problems going through walls."

Morgan laughed. "I can understand that. These walls are as thick as my arms are long!"

"He says it works much better on the west side of the house, which is where our bedrooms are, so that's convenient. You might want to try it there if it doesn't work anywhere else in the house."

Morgan first tried the library/study and couldn't get a signal, so she headed upstairs to her bedroom and got a connection. All three of them spent the next few hours going over possible sites. Miyah and Michael used their guide books and spread maps out on the long dinning room table, studying the island for clues, although they often got sidetracked, talking over interesting information that didn't really pertain to their goal. They also reminded themselves that this was Morgan's mission, and although it was of utmost importance that they locate the box, it was also made clear to them that they were only there to assist her, not to do the work for her. Along with the retrieval of the box, it was also a sort of initiation for Morgan—a chance for her to take charge and be in control of the situation. She'd have plenty of times ahead of her when she'd need this kind of confidence.

All of a sudden, they heard yelling coming from upstairs as if someone had just seen a ghost. They ran up to Morgan's room, only to find her jumping up and down.

"Are you OK? What's the matter?" Michael asked, reaching for her.

"I'm fine!" she said, trying to calm down. "I think I've figured out the location!" She showed her parents a map she had drawn of the island, dissecting it into quarters. She already knew the answer to the first two lines of the poem.

. . .the path to box is in the skye
do not attempt until three generations have gone by.

They were already in Skye and she was the fourth generation, so she concentrated on the third line, which related to faeries.

only the faeries can flag the way

In each quarter of her map she marked where the castles and sites were that she found might relate to faeries. There were a lot of them, as faerie lore had always been a part of the legends of the island. From there she had crossed off the sites she thought could be eliminated for one reason or another, leaving only a handful of sites for them to search out. Then she had made a list of those sites and the information she researched about each one.

"When I first read the poem it didn't make any sense. But when I break it down, and cross reference it, I think I already have a pretty good idea of the general area," she said excitedly.

Both Michael and Miyah were impressed how Morgan had tackled her assignment. Knowing it wasn't a game, rather it was a very important mission, she had taken it seriously and put her logic to mind.

"Let's see your list," Miyah said. Morgan had places numbered, but said they weren't in sequence of importance, just written as she discovered them. Miyah read out loud:

"1. Faerie Pools
2. Faerie Waterfall
3. Faerie Glen
4. Faerie Bridge
5. Ferry flags. But I see you've already crossed that off."

"Yes, I thought that maybe 'faerie' was purposely misspelled and it could refer to a clan flag on one of the ferries. But then I discovered #6. . .and I think this might be it!"

Miyah looked at Morgan's next choice.

"6. Faerie Flag," she read. "Well, faerie flag does tie in with the poem.

. . .*only the <u>faeries</u> can <u>flag</u> the way.*

"Isn't that exciting! Can it be this easy?"

"We haven't found it yet," Michael reminded her. "What's the story behind the faerie flag?"

"It's in a glass case in Dunvegan Castle on the northwest side of the island. It's the oldest inhabited castle in Scotland and even has a faerie tower! Dunvegan has been the home of the chiefs of the MacLeod clan for over 700 years and has a lot of clan relics. The Faerie Flag ties in with the Faerie Bridge, #4 on my list. Listen to this. . ." Morgan opened her notebook and read from some information she had copied.

"The old bridge got its name from the time in Clan MacLeod history when the fourth chief married a faerie. They had a baby son but the faerie wife was only allowed to stay on the human plain for twenty years and then had to return to her own folk. Her husband walked with her toward the bridge, three miles from Dunvegan, sad that she had to leave, but knowing he couldn't do anything about it. As they reached the bridge, the faerie rose slowly into the sky and dropped a piece of silk fabric she had torn from her dress. 'Keep this flag' she said 'and unfurl it to the wind whenever a crisis hits and the Faerie Folk will come to your aid. It will save you and your clan twice, but woe betide you if you unfurl it a third time.'"

Morgan looked up with a twinkle in her eye. "Don't you just love faerie tales?" she laughed. "I read that the flag has already been used on two occasions to save the clan. Once when the MacLeods were on the edge of defeat from a surprise attack in Waternish in 1520. The flag supposedly made the MacLeod forces appear like giants and the enemy fled, leaving the MacLeods victorious. Another time the flag was said to have stopped a plague that attacked all the cattle on the island."

"So we could look at the Faerie Bridge or Dunvegan Castle," Michael said.

"Yes, but there is another tale that might also give us some clues. It says that during the celebration after the birth of a MacLeod heir, the nurse left the baby uncovered, and when she went back to check on him, she found him wrapped in the Faerie Flag. She showed the bundled-up child to the clansmen and it was said that faerie voices were heard singing of the magical powers of the flag. Another story said the faeries wrapped a MacLeod infant in the flag when he was sick and at the point of death and the baby recovered. Maybe there's a nursery room we could check out at the castle."

"We won't know exactly where to look until we go there," Miyah said. "I think we've just made our plans for our first search. Great work Morgan. At least you've narrowed it down."

Morgan beamed.

"Hopefully the next two clues will be as easy," she said. ". . . *among a handled cross they play, the guardian of gazanias will only let it be. . .*neither of these lines make much sense to me."

"Well, your mother is right. I don't think we'll understand them until we get there. I know it's still light outside, but it's almost midnight. I think we could all use some sleep. I hear it doesn't stay dark very long these nights."

"Oh, I'm not worried," Morgan said, fetching something from her carry on bag. "I have these," she said, holding up the eye blinds she got on the airplane.

Her parents laughed, wishing they had thought of that.

~~~~~~~~

Early the next day a neighbor, Willie, came by and offered to show them where some stone circles were on the property. He wasn't sure of their origin. Some thought they were from the Viking era, others said they were grave markers. Miyah intuitively felt they were more than that and they eagerly agreed to accept his escort to the area.

They walked through the pasture, along a stone fence, through at least four gates that had to be opened and closed to keep the sheep out (or in) and then cut across the boggy, heather-laded landscape. Miyah was glad they wore their rubber Wellies. After awhile Willy stopped and pointed to the top of a tall hill.

"We have to go up now," he said, nonchalantly. Miyah and Michael looked at each other with a "you've got to be kidding" glance, but neither of them were about to give up now. Morgan, always ready for an adventure, was already part way up the hill. Michael needed to grab hold of the heather clumps and branches to help pull himself up the hill and keep his footing. But it was worth the climb. The view at the top was breathtaking.

They could see lochs (inlet lakes) that flowed out to the sea in the distance and a fishing village that was three miles away by road seemed to be just over the hill. They found there were actually two stone circles. The larger one, the one Willie brought them to see, was more square than round, and that's why he thought it might be a gravesite. One of the taller corner stones had markings on it, an "X" with other lines. It looked like it might be a rune symbol.

They sat quietly for a few moments, taking in the energy of the place, and soon both Miyah and Morgan were drawn to the smaller stone circle a few yards below. From their viewpoint it had a tall headstone-shaped rock in the center with nine large stones circled around it, although some of the stone had been dislodged from their original place, it was still obvious that they had once formed a part of the circle.

They hiked down to the site and upon closer investigation, Miyah noticed there were small, round holes that had apparently been somehow drilled into the rock. She poked her finger into each of the finger-sized holes but couldn't tell how deep they were. Two were directly across from each other, about a foot apart. A third hole was about two feet lower and drawing a line from one to the other formed an odd-shaped triangle. One more hole was discovered on the side of the stone, almost level with the lowest hole on the front side. Michael examined them closely, but didn't have any ideas as to what they could have been used for.

"They don't go all the way through," he observed. "This place might have been used for ceremony or ritual." Miyah and Morgan simultaneously placed a hand on the stone, near the bored-out holes, and each said a silent prayer of gratitude for whatever part in history this place held. Michael thought of the Druids, but Miyah was thinking it had a connection to the Vikings, maybe even the Knights Tempar.

Willie had gone off to have a smoke and hadn't noticed their little ritual, but he probably would have appreciated it. He had told Miyah that he wished that he had taken time when he was a boy to ask the elderly people questions about the old days and learned more about the folklore of the place. He knew where some of the Druid sacred places were on the island, but had never explored them himself. He did know this land was special, though. He respected the island and it was obvious he was proud to show her off to them that day.

Portree – Boats in the bay
Isle of Skye

Portree – water reflections
in blue, pinks and green

Quiraing Loop shoreline
Isle of Skye

Sunrays and sheep of the
loc, Isle of Skye

Sheep are everywhere!

Stone fence and landscape
Isle of Skye

8 Faerie Tales

The family felt comfortable in the house and it didn't take Miyah long to familiarize herself with the kitchen. She was in awe of the AGA—the big cast iron stove. It was lit when they arrived, courtesy of George, the caretaker, and at first she wasn't sure how to use it. It had three ovens in the front and two round "grills" on top with hinged, domed lids. She soon discovered that it held a constant temperature, and that one of the top grills was a boiling burner and the other a simmering burner. Frying eggs or boiling soup, she would never have to turn the stove on…just raise the dome lid, put the kettle on and cook away. She would, however, discover how easy it was to forget things, like warming muffins in the oven and burning them. The AGA contained and circulated its heat so no odors went into the kitchen. Miyah was accustomed to smelling her food as it baked or cooked so if she didn't set a timer, sometimes with the AGA, dinner had to be rethought.

While Miyah prepared breakfast on the AGA the next morning, Michael thought he'd test his women's beliefs in faeries, since the subject was so prominent in their recent conversations.

"So, Morgan," he started. "I don't know much about faeries. Do you think anyone has actually seen one, or are these just fanciful legends?"

Miyah gasped at his doubt, until she saw him wink at her and realized he wanted to see where Morgan would go with this.

"Unfortunately, Dad, faeries have been seen less and less since the 18th century," she retaliated with some historic facts. "I know that in most of the former Celtic countries, like here in Scotland, and in Ireland, Wales, Britain and Germany, faeries were a pretty common sight for centuries. But now, people don't see them as often and they think faeries may be in decline and will eventually disappear—*because* so many people no longer believe in them." She stared at him with an accusing glare.

"What?" he said. "I believe! I believe in faeries! I was just asking!"

Miyah joined in the conversation. "There's a famous story, and Michael, you'll appreciate this, 'The Faeries of Cottingley Glen' refers to a series of five photographs made by young cousins, Frances Griffiths and Elsie Wright. They lived in Cottingley, near Bradford, England, when the photographs were taken. The first two photos were made in 1917 and were publicized in 1920 when "The Strand" newspaper published a piece by Sir Arthur Conan Doyle, showing the photographs. The photos actually showed faeries as small humans with period style haircuts, dressed in filmy gowns with large wings on their backs. The fifth photograph, which wasn't published at the time, showed faeries sunbathing. Doyle accepted these photographs as evidence that faeries existed. He even wrote a book called 'The Coming of the Faeries,' about the Cottingley Faeries."

Michael's photography background kicked. "Not to be a doubter," he nodded toward Morgan, "but you know how things can be manipulated in a darkroom. They actually thought these photos were legitimate?"

Miyah responded, "Yes, a man named Harold Snelling, an expert in fake photography, noted that the dancing figures in the photograph weren't made of paper or any fabric and weren't painted on a photographic background or altered in a darkroom. He also pointed out that the faerie figures hadn't moved during the exposure, but he indicated the blurred motion of their moving wings. The two men and other experts who examined the photos said the girls were too young and inexperienced to be able to create such a hoax and they all agreed the photographs weren't fake."

"What happened to the two girls," Morgan asked.

"Until her death as an elderly woman, Frances Griffiths continued to claim they really did see faeries," Miyah answered.

"I read about the faeries of Skye last night," Morgan said. "There are a lot of faerie stories, which makes me not so sure Dunvegan is our treasure spot. There are so many possibilities."

"Like what?" her dad asked.

"The faeries of Skye are supposed to own herds of cattle and deer. The cattle are red and speckled and can swim across the sea. There are only ten places in the whole island where they'll graze. One of them is a field near Portree where faeries supposedly make the grasses wave in the breeze to *flag* the best grazing pastures."

"Hmmmm, that could be a difficult place to find," Michael agreed.

"And faeries seldom have horses, but sometimes borrow horses belonging to mortals and ride them across the country at top-speed, making their gowns blow in the wind like flags. Again, a reference to faeries and flags."

"But that reference has no tangible place," Miyah noted. "I think we should still begin our search at Dunvegan. That was your first gut feeling."

"Yes, you're right. I pinpointed that when I did my map. Let's start there. Oh, and this has nothing to do with faerie flags, but did you know that faerie dogs are green with a lighter shade of green toward their feet, and that sometimes their tails are long and braided and coiled on their backs?!"

"Now you're pulling my leg," Michael laughed.

"No really. . .that's what they say," Morgan smiled. "So if you see any green dogs, you'll know the faeries are nearby!"

"I'll watch for them," Michael teased. "Green dogs, indeed."

They finished their breakfast and set out for the Faerie Bridge and Dunvegan Castle, less than an hour drive away.

"What have you learned about Dunvegan Castle," Michael asked as they drove along through the countryside. "What exactly will we be looking for?"

"I'm not sure," Morgan admitted. "I guess we just have to ask questions."

"We have to ask questions without revealing our goal," Miyah was quick to remind them. "Be sure you don't mention the poem or the cedar box."

"If we have to, maybe we can say we're on a treasure hunt," Morgan suggested, adding, "that's not really a lie."

"Let's give out as little information as possible," Miyah warned. "I'm sure all tourists ask questions about the Faerie Flag and faerie legends if they're so popular on the island. We don't want to send out any red 'flags!'"

"Oh, bad pun, Mom. Bad pun," Morgan laughed.

The road to Faerie Bridge was off the main road to Dunvegan and being it was no longer used, was blocked off to traffic with large rocks. The three adventurers parked the car and walked slowly over the bridge with an odd sense of fantasy rushing in their veins.

"It seems kind of weird," Morgan said standing atop the old stone bridge. "As if I'm walking over a bridge into a land of fairytales."

Miyah nodded to her, understanding how she felt. She too, had a light, almost whimsical sensation. They climbed down the soft grassy incline toward the stream flowing under the bridge to examine the stones along the archway, the cracks between the stones and the foundation of the old bridge itself. Michael pulled out his camera and took several photos at different angles as they searched.

"It would help if we knew what we're looking for," Morgan said.

"Well, the next clue alludes to a handled cross," Miyah said. "I'm not sure what 'handled' means. My first thought would be a Celtic cross, but I can't configure a handle within that design. Do either of you see anything that looks like a cross?"

The trio searched around and under the bridge and found nothing they thought related to the clues on the poem, nothing that could hide a treasure.

"I can't imagine the cedar box would be hidden out in the open like this with no protection from the elements," Miyah finally said. "I think we can cross the Faerie Bridge off your list for now."

Everyone agreed and got in the car. They drove three miles down the road to the village of Dunvegan. They couldn't resist a stop at Jann's Organic Cake Shop, across from the museum in Dunvegan. Her sign enticed them with handmade cakes, breads, handcrafted truffles and Belgian chocolates, along with homemade soup and sandwiches. They made their purchases of sweets and talked with Jann, the owner, garnering more information about the area before they headed down the road to Dunvegan Castle. Its massive grey towers and battlements stood impressively against a background of sky and tall trees. The defense fortress was built on a rock, 30 feet up, arising from the receding shores of Loch Dunvegan.

"It's amazing," Morgan finally said. "It's a real fortress castle. I can hardly wait to go inside!"

They parked in the lot across from the gate. Michael paid £9.00 each for their entrance tickets and they walked the wide path through hedges that lead to the castle, crossing a little ravine, which most likely was spanned by a drawbridge in the olden days. They approached the main door and entered a square hall with stairs leading to wooden galleries above. The MacLeod banner of white with the family legend and Coate of Arms in crimson embroidery, hung from the beams as if to welcome them to the estate.

"Good morning, folks," a friendly man greeted them. "Hugh MacLeod, the 30th MacLeod Chief, sometimes welcomes visitors to Dunvegan Castle and MacLeod Estate, but he's preoccupied this morning, so you'll have to settle for me as your personal guide." He continued, "My name is Henry, and you three seem to be my only charges this morning. Lucky you! Ask all the questions you want. I'll do my best to give you an answer and promise I won't make anything up!" He gave a jolly belly laugh.

As he walked them through the hallway, he explained, "Originally designed to keep people out, our historic Dunvegan Castle was first opened to the public in 1933. Over the years, we've given a warm Highland welcome to visitors, who have included Sir Walter Scott and Queen Elizabeth II. Dunvegan Castle is regarded as one of the most important historic castles in Scotland and represents an unbroken line of occupancy for over 850 years. It's survived clan battles, the extremes of feast and famine and profound social, political and economic changes."

Morgan found herself leaning forward, trying to understand his words through his thick accent, as he continued.

"Of course, throughout time each generation has changed the castle architecturally to meet their own requirements. Today the castle has a more unified design with Victorian dummy pepper-pots and defensive battlements running the whole length of the roof line. This restoration was carried out by the 25th Chief between 1840 and 1850 at a cost of £8,000. Underneath this outer skin, however, there remains a series of complete buildings, each of a different date. That's why the massive exterior combines six separate buildings, of which you can visit five. The sixth building and the upper floors are administrative and domestic offices."

They explored the buildings with Henry, visually taking in every detail, from period furnishings and elaborate decor to the exquisite art on the walls, and discretely asked him questions to see if they could garner any clues to lead them to the whereabouts of the cedar box, or at least to something that resembled a handled cross. Nothing seemed to resonate.

Finally, they stood in front of the glass case protecting the Faerie Flag. After relaying the history of the flag and the MacLeod legends with faeries, Henry admitted, "I know there are a lot of negative stories, but faeries never really steal anything, only the substance of it. For some, there was always fear that faeries would come to steal a little baby and if they did succeed in carrying it off, in its place they would leave a dwarfed old man with an alarmingly large appetite. That proved false here at Dunvegan, as the faeries were always known to protect the children of the MacLeod bloodline.

"Even if faeries stole cattle or food, they always left something in its place, so it was more of a trade," he added, in their defense.

Henry gestured toward the glass case on the wall. "Not much is left of the Faerie Flag, I'm afraid. There were many small pieces cut from it about the size of postage stamps when MacLeod pilots went into battle during WWII. Some of them took bits of the flag for magical protection, and those who had pieces of the flag with them, I might add, did return from the war alive. Alas, I believe that if an occasion ever arose to unfurl the flag again, the delicate fabric is bound to turn to dust."

They looked at what was left of the yellowed flag, preserved under glass.

"As for legends," Henry nodded at Morgan and said, "Bagpipe music has been heard coming from the drawing room where the flag was stored. No source of the music can be found, but it's believed to come from the faeries, the first ghosts of Dunvegan Castle, who still protect the flag."

"What kind of fabric do you think it's made of?" Morgan asked.

"Oh, they've tested it, they have," Henry said. "The Faerie Flag was analyzed by the South Kensington Museum at the request of Sir Reginald MacLeod who was the 27th Clan Chief. The results revealed that the material was silk that had been woven in either Syria or Rhodes sometime between the 4th and 7th centuries, and may have been brought to the Isle of Skye from the Crusades.

"I'll also tell you the first legend of the Faerie Flag. A member of the MacLeod clan was once sheltered by a hermit during the Holy Land Crusade. The hermit warned him about the evil spirit of a woman who lived in a mountain pass that MacLeod had to cross to return home. As he passed through the area, he confronted the spirit, who turned out not to be evil. Before she disappeared, she revealed to him the future of the MacLeod clan and told him to make a banner from her robe and to carve a spear out of her staff, and bind them to form a flag for protection against evil spirits as he traveled through the land. Now, we don't know what became of the spear, but many believe this piece of fabric is from that flag. Of course, the spirit of the woman, was really a faerie," Henry added, defending the name "Faerie Flag."

"That would connect the results of the analysis of the fabric back to the Crusades," Michael logically concluded, wondering if the cross symbol of the early crusaders had anything to do with the handled cross of the poem.

"And what about the Faerie Tower," Miyah asked, searching for clues.

"Ahh, that's our next stop," Henry announced.

They climbed up the many steps of a narrow, spiral, stone stairway in an ancient tower until they came into a chamber with enormously thick walls and windows that provided a spectacular view of the blue loch below and the bold Skye headland beyond.

"Legend has it that each future bride of a MacLeod had to pass one night alone in this room so the faeries had an opportunity to inspect her and approve of her worthiness."

"Is that still true with today's generations?" Morgan asked.

"Only if they're willing to do so themselves," Henry answered. "Things have changed a bit around here since the olden days."

The trio of treasure hunters looked around for signs, but the barren tower room gave up no clues that related to the poem or the cedar box.

Descending the stairway, they walked down the hallway and passed the entrance to a small room with a hatch door in the floor, dropping to a dark dungeon below. Miyah immediately felt a coldness and a deep, heart-heavy feeling of sadness, taking in emotions of the men and women who had been imprisoned there over the centuries of Scotland's history of war and tribulation. She could actually hear their torturous screams and anguished moans of torment. Whatever their crimes, they had been humans and felt suffering and pain in the same way as their accusers. She stopped momentarily and sent a wave of healing to the spirits of those who remained, and offered a message of release, telling them they could escape the ties that kept them bound to their dungeon graves, simply by going toward the light.

"Silence your mind, open your eyes and your heart, and go toward the light," she whispered three times. "You'll find your peace and the love of the angels who await you." She held her fisted hand to her heart, nodded her head, and said, "Go now. Follow the light," repeating it three times as a beam of light flashed into the darkness.

Michael had gone ahead with Henry and didn't notice the women lagged behind, but Morgan stopped with her mother and witnessed this powerful release of compassion. She too had felt the same emotions and heard the same sounds as her mother. Goose-bumps swelled on her arms as she watched and could actually see the darkness through the arched stone entrance come aglow with light and could feel the movement of spirits as they reached out and listened to Miyah's message of hope.

"Go now. Follow the light." The screaming and moaning slowly thinned . . . and finally stopped, as these spirits released themselves and gradually sifted into the light before it disappeared and darkness again engulfed the dungeon—but now the darkness of the damp stone cell was silent. That feeling of foreboding was gone.

Miyah looked into her daughter's eyes and Morgan could feel the healing energy that Miyah had just released into the corners of the terrifying dungeon. Nothing needed to be said. Morgan had witnessed first-hand that Miyah's role as a healer went beyond herbs and tinctures and that her powers were compassionately unleashed whenever she felt summoned. This spontaneous act of healing was an enormous lesson for Morgan. One she would always remember. Miyah silently took her daughter's hand and the two of them caught up with Michael and Henry to continue their tour. Morgan realized that this most likely was a common occurrence in her mother's everyday life. She performed silent miracles that no one but herself knew were happening all the time. This gave Morgan a new respect for another aspect of the life she was expected to lead—that of a silent healer, whenever she was summoned to do so. She had big shoes to fill.

When they caught up with the men, Henry led them to another of the fabled objects of Dunvegan Castle and Morgan tried her best to shake off what had just occurred and get back into the mode of a tourist. Luckily Henry kept up his flow of information so her mood was unnoticed.

"Here be Rory Mor's drinking horn," he proudly stated, referring to a drinking horn, tipped with silver. He explained, "It's named after a MacLeod Chief, Sir Rory Mor, and was made in the year 1493. Each chief, upon coming of age, must fill this horn to the brim and drain it at one draught."

"It doesn't look like it holds much," Morgan leaned over to examine it.

"Aye, that's because most of the inside has been filled in. Originally the cup would have held two or even three bottles of wine. The chief's drink now is only a moderate one. Ah, change, change," Henry bemoaned, shaking his head, as if he had actually lived in those early centuries.

Michael noticed the ornate Dunvegan Cup nearby and examined the giant goblet through the glass case. It was made of oak and stood on four short silver footed legs. Rounded at the bottom and square on top, it was embossed with silver in which, Henry said was once studded with precious stones, but only a few bits of coral remained. It was ornately carved with design and lettering and Michael looked for something that might offer up a clue.

"Because you seem so interested in faeries, I'll tell you of the cup's faerie history," Henry said. Morgan looked at her father. Could this be the lead they were looking for?

"In the days of the third MacLeod chief, a cattle-herder, named Lurran Casinreach was present at a strange faerie feast. He believed the faeries had done him some harm and as a means of revenge Lurran stole their cup as it was being passed around the table. Eventually it came into possession of the lairds of Dunvegan Castle."

"Why would the faeries have such a giant cup?" Morgan asked, disappointed that she could relate no clue to this story.

"A faerie tale is a faerie tale," Henry smiled, not really answering her.

"And that, my dear folks, is the end of our tour today. We normally end with a walk through our beautiful gardens, but as you can see, it's pouring rain outside. I'll initial your tickets, so you can return at your leisure to explore our gardens. I have no control over the weather!"

They thanked Henry for his interesting insights during the tour as he marked their tickets for a future return and they headed back toward home.

"I love that castle," Morgan said, "but am a little disappointed that we didn't find any references there that could point us toward our treasure."

"This is only our first day of hunting, dear," Miyah tried to be positive. "We still have a lot of area to cover. At least we had a wonderful day and learned a lot of history. Maybe there were other reasons we were drawn to that castle," she said, winking at her daughter. Morgan understood what her mother meant, referring to their experience with the dungeon. She sat back in the car, suddenly feeling a sense of complete satisfaction of their day's journey.

~~~~~~

Over the next few days the family explored other places on Morgan's list—the Faerie Pools, a series of rapids flowing over the rocks of a small ravine in the shadow of the Cuillin Mountains; and the Faerie Waterfall. Neither produced any clues. They also took time for Michael to photograph the pinnacles of the Old Man of Storr, a rock formation looming 160 feet above the forest. They saw Kilt Rock, Columban Chapel at Skeabost, one of the earliest Celtic churches built on the island. On the Quiraing loop on the northernmost part of the island they visited the Skye Museum of Island Life at Kilmuir, showing highland life from over a century ago. They stopped along the barren highway to "make a phone call" at a lonely red British-style phone booth, standing by itself on the bend of the road, surrounded only by windy landscape and sheep.

At Morgan's insistence, they stopped at the Staffin Museum to see the first dinosaur fossils found in Scotland that were from Jurassic rocks in the Staffin area. They zig-zagged throughout the countryside, stopping at Skein Village, Skye's oldest 18th century inn, and went to spend time on Coral Beach, one of the few beaches on Skye with a great view of the highest sea cliffs, Dunvegan Head.

They visited the Neist Point Lighthouse on the westerly point of the island and looped down to Broadford for Morgan to buy some art supplies. She was looking for oil crayons and there was a slightly used box in the gallery, but no new boxes for sale. The gallery keeper told her to take them with her and use them. When they pass by that way again she could return them. Now that was island hospitality!

Now they were off to explore Faerie Glen. They first drove to the village of Uig to pick up some picnic supplies. A tourist there offered information he had heard about the faeries.

"Are you going to Faerie Glen?" he asked. "I heard that if a mortal goes to visit the faeries in their green knolls, they should stick a knife into the ground near the entrance to enable their escape. They say that iron is the greatest protection against faeries, but you could also consider oatmeal."

"Oatmeal!" Morgan laughed.

"It's true. If a boy is going any distance after dark, his mother sometimes fills his pockets with oatmeal, which prevents him from seeing any 'guide people.' You should also know that it's unlucky for mortals to wear green because it's the favorite color of the faeries," he added, pointing to Morgan's green rain jacket.

"Thank you for your advice," Michael said to the man, who made his purchase and left the store. "We'll keep it in mind."

Morgan looked down at her green jacket and decided it would be a sign of good luck to her. If the faeries like green, they may be attracted to her. She'd give anything to see a real faerie!

The storekeeper gave a chuckle as the man left. "There are so many legends and tales around here, you never know what you might hear." Not to be outdone by a non-local, he added his own flavor to the storytelling.

"Now the most told tale about this area is that if you need help, are in despair, want to fall in love, want to harm someone, seek revenge, whatever, you go to the Faerie Glen, recite your wish and leave an offering."

"What kind of offering?" Morgan curiously asked.

"Oh, money, food, jewelry, a picture or something that represents you. The offering should be left underneath a rock or a collection of rocks. Once you leave the glen, the faeries will collect your offering and if it's worthy of your request, your wish will be granted. Be warned, however, if you go to the glen and take something that doesn't belong to you, the faeries will haunt you until you return whatever you took."

"You seem to know a lot about faeries," Morgan said, already thinking about what she could leave as an offering.

"I've lived here all my life," the storekeeper said. "Faeries are all over this land and live extremely long lives. They have magical powers and can cast spells. We island folk have a lot of respect for them. Back in pagan times people called the faeries 'The Mothers,' and honored them as little gods and goddesses. They weave in and out of the heavens, the earth and the underworld, but are mostly found in wooded groves, like Faerie Glen. You should look for a small enclosed meadow there, believed to be a meeting place for faeries."

"How about what that man said about an iron knife or oatmeal for protection?" Morgan asked.

"I've never heard that one before," he admitted, "but I don't think you'll need protection. Humans don't often see the faeries because of the division of the worlds." He saw the disappointment on Morgan's face, and added, "But every now and again people might get a glimpse of them. Mostly at twilight when the veil of the worlds is thin and briefly open." As an afterthought he added, "But you might want to look out for the wee green men. They'll chase you and bite your tires." He laughed.

They made their purchases and thanked the clerk for sharing his knowledge and drove a few miles to Faerie Glen. The area seemed otherworldly. Covered with many strangely-shaped conical hills rising from six to 30 feet in height, it was overgrown with thick, mossy grass, littered with bleating sheep and animal droppings. Morgan saw some strange, yellow mushrooms and felt like Alice, stepping into Wonderland. The small lake held the reflection of one of the hills, adding another mystical element to the scenery. They hiked to explore some castle ruins that were so overgrown with grass they could actually walk up to the top of what was once a tower. After a while they settled with their picnic basket near a small circle of stones, shaped like a spiral, to eat their lunch. Other than the sound of the wind and of water cascading over the rocks of a brook nearby, it was very peaceful.

Michael noticed that Morgan was unusually quiet. "What are you thinking, Morgan? You aren't afraid are you?"

"Oh, no, not at all. I'm trying to concentrate to call the faeries to me. I so badly want to see one," she replied. "I'm hoping they *like* my green jacket and come near to see it."

"Are you thinking of leaving an offering?" Miyah asked.

"Yes, I am. I think I'll leave my charm bracelet. There are a lot of shiny, dangling things on there they should like."

"That's a pretty expensive offering. You've been collecting those charms for a long time," Michael was surprised. "Are you sure?"

"As much as I love my bracelet and don't want to give it up, it seems to be a good sacrifice as an offering. I know the faeries will think it a worthy exchange for granting my wish."

"Can you share your wish?" her dad asked.

"Of course, but you already know. I want them to lead us to the cedar box and help us retrieve it safely," she replied. Both Michael and Miyah smiled and nodded their heads in approval.

"We can use all the help we can get," Michael replied. "That's a very worthy offering and a worthy wish."

Morgan finished her lunch and wandered a short distance to an open meadow. There were several large rocks scattered along a stone wall and some other stone foundations. She stacked three rocks on top of each other and, holding the bracelet up so the faeries could see its worth, she said out loud, "Faeries, I know you're watching me. I can feel your presence. My wish is to find, and keep safe, an old cedar box that has been in our family for centuries. We can use your help and will be grateful for your guidance."

She then placed the bracelet beneath the middle rock and smiled, saying, "I just want you to know that green is my favorite color too!" She felt like she needed to seal her wish with something, so she blew three kisses toward the stack of rocks and walked back to her parents.

"You know what I love about this land?" she asked. "I love that we can openly talk about things like faeries with people in public and not be laughed at. That we can leave gifts for the faeries without feeling silly and really believe they'll help us. That's just too cool!"

Miyah and Michael agreed with their daughter that it was very cool.

As they picked up their picnic basket and headed back toward the car, Morgan looked over her shoulder and stopped in her tracks. She swore she could see the outline of a band of faeries hovering over the pile of rocks she had just stacked. The movement of their wings glistened in the light of the twilight sun and little bits of laughter filtered into the air. It was that time of day the storekeeper spoke of, when the veil between faerie and human worlds was thin. Morgan tapped her mom and dad on the shoulder and motioned toward the stone pile so they too, could experience this rare occurrence. They stood silently, watching and listening and Morgan thought one of the cute, little creatures looked directly at them, as if to let them know they were accepted and also privileged to catch sight of the band of faeries. A few years ago Michael would have not believed this possible. But now, he believed anything was possible—even faeries.

They watched and after a few moments visions of the faeries disappeared. Morgan jumped in the air and gave out an excited hoot as they finally turned back toward their car. And as they walked away, the stack of three rocks, rolled apart. . .and the charm bracelet Morgan had left, disappeared.

It was indeed a worthy offering.

Dunvegan Castle
Isle of Skye

Isle of Skye - Landscape
of Old Man of Storr

Eilean Donan Castle
Scotland

Landscape at Faerie Glen
Isle of Skye

9 The Guardian of Gazanias

Toward sunrise the next morning Morgan was awakened by loud screeching noises and the sound of something banging against her window. She jumped up and ran into her parent's bedroom and got into bed between them.

"There's something trying to get into my room!" she cried, pulling the down comforter all the way up to her eyes. Shaken awake from their sleepiness, both Miyah and Michael could hear the noise. Michael looked at his girls and bravely said, "I'll go see what it is." He was grateful when Miyah piped in and said, "I'll go with you."

"You're not going anywhere without me!" Morgan said, and the three got out of the bed, huddled together and slowly crept toward the next room. On the way Michael unplugged a heavy, brass lamp from the dresser, the only defense weapon he could see nearby. The noise grew louder. Michael was glad to have Miyah next to him, knowing her powers may come in handy if the situation got out of hand. Sheltering the women behind him, he was the first to peer inside the doorway. He looked left and right and saw nothing. Then the thumping noise sounded again. Michael's posture straightened and his grip on the lamp relaxed. He stepped inside the room.

"Crows," he said. "It's the crows."

"What?" said Morgan, letting out a sigh of relief and following him into the room. "Crows? Why would they be trying to get into my room? That's creepy."

"That I don't know, but they seem to be hitting your window and then flying back to their perch in the trees. They must be trying to get your attention," Michael said.

"Wherever crows are, there's magic," Miyah piped in. "They're symbols of spiritual strength that remind us to look for opportunities to manifest our own magic."

"Well that certainly could relate to my mission," Morgan said.

"I seem to remember something in the Bible about the prophet Elijah being fed by crows when he was hiding in the wilderness," Michael said.

"That very well could be. Crows are messengers that call us to look for the magic in our everyday world," Miyah added, looking at her daughter. "They're trying to draw your attention to something. Something around you that most likely seems pretty common to you."

"But what could that be?" Morgan asked.

"I think they're trying to tell you to be aware of everything around you. Your answers may be found in the simplest of places."

"I wonder if the faeries sent them," Morgan mused. "That would be awesome."

"Well, at least we know your noises weren't ghosts," Michael concluded as he went to get dressed. "I guess we get an early start today. I, for one, don't think I can go back to sleep after all this excitement."

"Same here," Miyah agreed. "I'll get dressed and start breakfast. How about you Morgan?"

"I'm not staying up here without you guys," she quickly replied. "I'll help with breakfast."

Michael got wood from the shed for the fireplace and Miyah and Morgan headed to the garden to pick some vegetables to add to an omelet. As they were picking, the grounds keeper, George, whom they had meet the first day they arrived, came by to see if they needed anything. He laughed when he heard about the crows waking them so early.

"It seems this house is the only place nearby that occasionally has a problem with hooded crows," he said. "They won't hurt you, they're just noisy and a bit of a nuisance."

George asked where they had been on the island so far and Morgan gave him the rundown of their day trips.

"Did you walk through the gardens at Dunvegan?" he asked when he heard they had visited the castle.

"No, we got rained out, but were given a rain check, literally, to go back," Miyah replied.

"You really should make the trip back there. The castle gardens are worth a visit," George noted. "They were landscaped in the 18th century and have paths through the woodland that wind past pools and streams fed by a cascading waterfall. It's a hidden oasis with species of plants and trees that have only survived at the estate. I go there often, just to enjoy the beauty of the grounds, especially the formal round garden. It's filled with many varieties of Rhododendrons."

"You must be an avid gardener," Miyah observed, listening to him talk about the castle gardens.

"Yea, I enjoy gardening and flowers," George admitted. He gestured to Morgan, who had just picked an armful of multistar-shaped flowers from the edge of the garden.

"You'll find the biggest garden of those gazanias there too," he casually stated. "They close up when the weather is dull so are sometimes called Scotland's treasure flower."

Morgan stopped in motion when she heard George's words. She looked directly at her mother. Gazanias! The treasure flower! How much clearer could it be? —*the guardian of gazanias*—they were flowers!

"Well, I'll be on my way," the friendly Scotsman announced. "I was just stopping by to be sure everything was OK with you folks. I'll be seeing you again I hope."

"Thank you for stopping," Miyah replied. "And thanks for the tips on the Dunvegan gardens. We'll be sure to go back and check them out."

Morgan could barely wait until George left and closed the gate behind him. She ran over to Miyah, jumping up and down.

"Did you hear that?!" she exclaimed. "*Gazania!* It's a flower! A *treasure* flower! I must have spelled it wrong when I googled it. How could I have missed that?"

"If the castle has the largest gardens of gazanias, Dunvegan might still be our target. Plus, we've checked off everything else on your list," Miyah stated.

"The *guardian of gazanias* must be the gardener, or the caretaker of the grounds!" Morgan exclaimed, putting one of the treasure flowers in her hair. "Let's hurry up with breakfast. The castle opens to the public at 10 a.m. We should be waiting at the gate!"

Morgan ran to the house, calling for her dad to tell him the news. Miyah picked up her basket of vegetables and gazanias and followed her, looking up at a row of squawking hooded crows sitting on a tree limb.

"Something around us that seems pretty common, huh?" she said, repeating the words she had said to Morgan. "Thanks for your morning nudge. We might have missed George if you guys hadn't knocked on Morgan's window so early."

She chuckled at the sequence of events that always seem to fall into place when the timing is right, and looked forward to going back to Dunvegan. They'd have a busy day ahead of them.

~ ~ ~ ~ ~ ~

They looked everywhere as they entered the gardens. Morgan had made a sketch of one of the flowers so she would be sure to recognize it in the gardens.

"We'll walk the entire grounds, if we have to," Morgan firmly stated. "We're so close. I just know it's here."

Miyah had to agree. She felt it from the beginning, but knew she had to step back and allow Morgan to solve this mystery and locate the box herself—and to do it without using her powers. That alone was a difficult task.

"We need to go back to the fourth line of the poem," Morgan reasoned. "*among a handled cross they play. . .* what could a handled cross be?" She looked for some resemblance of a cross.

"Maybe it has something to do with a Celtic cross, like you suggested before. But I don't see Celtic crosses anywhere?"

Morgan showed her parents the sketch of the flower and they recognized clusters of gazanias which were abundant in the gardens. For more than three hours they walked the entire wooded pathway and explored along the pond, around the waterfall and the central gardens, examining every statue and sculpture they found for references to a cross.

The five acres of formal gardens were a hidden oasis of eclectic mixes of plants, woodland glades, shimmering pools fed by waterfalls and streams flowing down to the sea. They looked through the water garden, with its bridges and islands of rich and colorful plant varieties and searched around the Formal Round Garden and its box-wood Parterre centerpiece. The Walled Garden, formerly known as the castle's vegetable gardens, had a diverse range of plants and flowers, including a water lily pond and Larch Pergola. They searched everywhere, including the Standing Stone, raised stone pool and the 18th century wooden bridge.

It was getting late in the day, but they kept up their search. Wandering deeper into the woodland, they came across a small gardener's house that was surrounded by an iron fence with a closed gate, indicating it was off limits to tourists. They decided to circle back and started down the path they had come, when both Miyah and Morgan stopped in their tracks. They turned around in unison and stared at the fence. Lining the grass inside the fence were rows of colorful flowers—multistar-shaped gazanias with the distinctive pink stripes down the center of each petal. Miyah retrieved the necklace from around her neck and removed the key from the pouch. She held it at arms length, lining it up with the design of the iron fence. The tops of each of the poles were formed in the shape of an ankh, matching the shape of the top of her key. And placed among the gazanias below, were statues of cherubs and faeries. . .*among the handled cross they play.*

"I don't believe it!" Morgan exclaimed. "Now what do we do?"

"I guess we see if anyone's home," Miyah answered.

They opened the creaky gate and approached the house. Morgan bravely knocked on the door and waited. No one answered, so she knocked again, louder. She was impatient.

"The caretaker is probably working somewhere on the grounds," Michael suggested. "We could ask for him at the castle. . ."

Just then the door opened a crack and an uncertain, gruff voice asked, "What do you want?"

Morgan slowly said, "We've been sent here on a mission. . .a treasure hunt, and think maybe you can help us."

"Does this mean anything to you?" Miyah asked, holding up the ankh-shaped key.

"No," the man in the house replied. "I don't think I can help you."

Not accepting "no" for an answer, Morgan stated, "My great-grandfather may have left a package here for me many years ago and I've come to retrieve it." Michael touched her shoulder, indicating that maybe they should leave.

Morgan stood fast. "If you'll just let us come in, we can tell you more."

The door slowly creaked open and the three visitors entered the room. The light was dim and the cabin was small, but the place was clean inside.

The caretaker gestured for them to sit on the couch next to the stone fireplace. He sat across from them and waited for them to speak. There was an awkward moment and finally Michael spoke.

"We should introduce ourselves. My name is Michael Wilder. This is my wife, Miyah and our daughter, Morgan."

The man nodded.

"My grandfather was Dr. Alyn Harris. Does that name sound familiar to you," Miyah asked.

"Can't say that it does," the elderly man answered in a thick Scottish brogue. "I've lived here all my life and don't recall that name. What's this about a package your daughter mentioned?" he asked.

Morgan responded. "I believe that many years ago, maybe as long as 70 years ago, my great-grandfather, Dr. Alyn, left a box here for safe keeping."

"Seventy years is a long time. What makes you think your package is here?" the man questioned her.

"He left a paper with clues on it for me to follow. They led us to your house. This has to be the place," she almost pleaded. "We've traveled a long way to retrieve it."

The man was silent for a moment.

"What's in this package you be looking for?" he asked.

Morgan hesitated. Miyah nodded for her to answer.

"It's just an old box that was carved by someone in our family years ago."

"What's in the box?" the man repeated.

"Nothing. I mean, I think it's empty."

"Then why is it so important to ye?" the old man asked.

"It means a lot to me as a family heirloom," Morgan truthfully replied. "My great-grandfather wanted me to have it."

Again the man sat in silence. The family patiently waited for him to respond.

"I vaguely recall, many years ago, when I was a wee lad, a man came by once in awhile, an acquaintance of my father. The last time he was here he asked my father to watch over a package for safe keeping, until he came back to fetch it." Morgan's heart was racing.

"When he didn't return after a few years, my father opened the package to be sure it wasn't anything illegal. It was just an old box. We couldn't get it open, but shook it and it was empty. My father stowed it away. Let me see if I can remember where he put it," the man said. "It was a long time ago."

Miyah squeezed Michael's hand as they waited for the old man to ponder the location of the box. He sat for the longest time, sorting through a cobweb of memories in his head.

Finally he got up and taking a chair from around the table, he motioned for Michael to follow him. They went into a back bedroom and the man set the chair near an outside wall.

"I'm too old to stand on chairs. I'd probably fall and break my neck," he said. "Hoist yerself up there and take a look in those rafters. If we didn't burn it for firewood, it should still be up there somewhere."

Michael stepped onto the chair and peered across the open rafters of the room. The man handed him a flashlight and he slowly scanned across the beams. Morgan and Miyah watched with anticipation from the doorway. Other than strands of cobwebs, Michael didn't see anything. Then he made a second sweep with his flashlight and brought the light back to the opposite corner of the room. He got down and moved his chair over to the wall nearest the door, and stepping back up, he shined the light into a deep corner, where the beams crossed. Reaching cautiously into the darkness, his fingertips felt something solid. It was covered with cobwebs, like a blanket of protection. He tried to knock some of the cobwebs away with the flashlight, glancing around, hoping the web-maker wasn't lurking nearby, and winced as he reached in deeper. He grasped hold of something and pulled it from its hiding place.

Trying to keep his excitement from showing, he immediately recognized the box—the same cedar box he had seen Joshua carve for his mother, Mariam, on her birthday. He had a vivid flashback to that day and actually could smell the scent of fresh cedar. He saw the young boy turning a small oblong box without nail or peg, over and over in his hands, running his fingers along its sides and joints to be sure there were no imperfections. The sides and bottom all dovetailed into one another and pride shown on the boy's face. Michael remembered his early visit back to Joshua as if it were yesterday.

His hands were shaking when he stepped off the chair and, trying to brush away the cobwebs, he handed the cedar box to Morgan.

"I believe this is for you," he said, hardly able to contain himself.

"Not so fast," the man stepped up, reaching for the box. "How can you prove this box is yours?"

Miyah handed the ankh key to Morgan.

"By presenting you the proper key," Morgan replied, repeating the last verse of the poem. She put the key into the hole and opened the box. It was empty, as anticipated, but Morgan knew that the treasure within its emptiness was invaluable.

"Well, I'll be," the man said, peering inside. "I guess the old box is yours."

"Thank you," Morgan said and she walked over and gave the man a kiss on the cheek.

"Thank you. This means so much to me, you'll never know."

The man faltered and blushed. It had been a long time since a beautiful young woman kissed him. It made him smile involuntarily.

"Thank you," Miyah added, taking his hand in hers. He felt a warm sensation go up his arm and into his body, suddenly making him feel almost youthful again. The chronic pain in his back disappeared. He gave her an odd look and then softened.

"Forgive my manners," he apologized. "I don't get many visitors here. I retired from my caretaker duties long ago and the MacLeods were kind enough to let me stay in our old family house here in the woodland." He was trying to make conversation and it was obvious he had lived alone for a long time.

"Where did you say you come from? I should have offered you some tea."

"Thanks for the offer," Michael responded, avoiding his question while he put the chair back by the table. "We've taken up enough of your time." He reached out to shake the man's hand. "We really must be going. Thank you for helping my daughter in her treasure hunt. Is there any compensation . . .err . . .do you want us to give you anything for stowing the box all these years?" Michael offered, reaching for his wallet.

"Oh no," the man answered. "I'd forgotten all about it. Twas no bother to me. It was my father who was doing the favor, as I said, to some friend of his. Why do you suppose he brought it here? Was he in some sort of trouble or something?" The man was suddenly curious.

"I don't think so," Miyah responded. "My grandfather loved riddles and games. I think he just wanted to see if we'd be able to unwind his clues. I wish he were still alive to see that we found it," she added.

"As you see, the box is empty so there's no monetary treasure to be gained. It's just sentimental," Morgan said. "Thank you."

"Yes, thank you again," Miyah said and they left the house.

The man stood in the doorway, watching them head down the pathway before he went back into the house and closed the door, retreating back into his solitude. Watching them through the window, he went to his telephone and tracing his finger down a line of faded names and numbers on a piece of paper taped to the wall, he slowly dialed a number. . .

Miyah happened to turn and saw him through the window. She had an uneasy feeling.

"We didn't even ask his name," Michael commented.

As soon as they were out of sight, Morgan jumped up and down, hugging the box to her chest. She put her hand over her mouth so anyone nearby couldn't hear her screams of joy. Miyah and Michael felt the same way and released their joy in hugs of laughter. When they were finally able to calm down, Morgan examined the box carefully, turning it over in her hands.

"It looks just like yours, Mother," she said as she handed it to Miyah.

"I really want to spend more time with this, but would rather do it after we're back home and it's safe," Morgan said, "Can you scamper away for a little while and put this in a safe place?" she politely asked Miyah, looking around. "I don't feel comfortable with it here."

"Safe with my cedar box back at RoseVine," Miyah responded.

"Yes," Morgan said. "Can you do that? I don't want to worry about having it with us the rest of our trip. I couldn't stand it if anything happened to it now, after all these years of being hidden. I can hardly believe we found it!"

"That's a very good idea, dear," Miyah said, proud of her daughter's reasoning.

"Before you do that," Michael said. "Can I take a look at it?"

"Of course," Morgan said, handing the cedar box to him.

Michael handled it as if it were glass. Emotions welled up as he ran his hands over the smooth cedar sides, rounding each corner. Miyah watched as he opened the lid and traced his fingers over the letters in the corner that held the signature of a young Joshua. *'Ayin (a), vav (oo), shin (sh), yod (y).'* Hebrew is read right to left, so you get 'yshooa', Yeshua, or Joshua. This moment was powerful for him in other ways. After all, of the three of them, Michael was the only one who had actually seen this box before—in his "travels" back into ancient time. He stood there, staring at the box, running his hands over the surface, remembering his travels with Joshua. He brought the box up to his face and took a long, deep smell of it.

"You can still smell the cedar after all these years," he reverently whispered, recalling that the smell of cedar was key to his entering the vortex of mystery within the cedar box.

Morgan and Miyah knew how special this was to Michael. They told him to take his time and walked down the path a ways to leave him alone with his thoughts. He finally handed the box to Miyah. She reached over and kissed her husband, knowing what an important time this was for him—for all of them.

"We'll celebrate this properly when we get home," she said, tapping the top of the cedar box. "But Morgan's right. We need to get it safe at RoseVine as soon as possible. Nona will take care of it there. Don't go anywhere, I'll be right back." Miyah dematerialized before their eyes.

"I can hardly wait until I'm allowed to do that on my own," Morgan said casually, as if every girl's mother could disappear at will.

Michael laughed and hugged his daughter to him.

"What an incredible day," he said. "I guess the faeries liked your sacrificial bracelet and granted your wish after all."

The two of them found a comfortable log off the side of the pathway and sat down to wait for Miyah's return, discussing what the recovery of the cedar box meant to them. Michael told her of his visit when he first saw the box being carved by Joshua when he traveled back in time, and about the signature inside. He was happy to share this with his daughter.

"And now the box is yours," he said. "It's touched many lives on its path to get to you. If it could only tell us stories of all its journeys."

Morgan put her head on her father's shoulder, feeling a closer bond to him than she had ever realized before. "It's touched each of our lives," she said. "We're all connected with it in ways we probably don't even yet realize. I'll think of your story, your connection with the cedar box, every time I use it. I can hardly wait to put my herbs and oils in it. I think it'll be so happy to be used again. Do you think it has the same power to draw people back into the past as Mother's cedar box?"

"I was wondering the same thing," Michael admitted. "I suppose we'll find out someday, if. . ."

". . .if we're supposed to," Morgan finished his sentence.

When Miyah returned a short time later, they happily continued their walk back to the car, chatting and enjoying the sunlight on the gardens. But when they arrived at the parking lot their pleasant afternoon was halted as they were approached by a guard from the castle.

"I'm afraid I need to search the three of you," he stated with authority.

"Now just a minute," Michael stepped forward. "We haven't done anything. We're tourists, enjoying your gardens. Here, see, we have our tickets."

"It's illegal to take anything off the castle grounds," the guard warned.

"We didn't pick any flowers or anything," Morgan said. "Honest." She was glad she had made a sketch of the gazania instead of bringing one from their garden at the house.

"I'm just doing my job. Let me have a look in your bags," he demanded.

Morgan handed him the small backpack she was carrying and he rifled through it. Finding nothing he handed it back to her.

Michael held up his hands. "I have no bag," he said, and the man proceeded to pat down his pockets.

"How about that one," he said to Miyah, gesturing to her bag. She was relieved that she hadn't carried her medicine pouch on this little venture, and she handed the guard her shoulder bag.

"Looks like you have something big in there." He sorted through her belongings and pulled out a wooden box from the bottom of the bag.

Morgan gasped.

"Where did you get this?" the guard asked.

No one answered. Morgan looked at her mother with disbelief.

"Just as I expected," he said. "We got a call that someone was trying to take an antique off the property. This looks pretty old."

"No!" Morgan exclaimed. "This was a gift from my great-grandfather. It's mine. It doesn't belong to the estate. It's mine!"

"If you got it here, it belongs here," the guard firmly stated, glaring at her. "I could arrest all three of you for stealing."

Michael stared at the box and then looked at Miyah. She said nothing.

Morgan began to protest again and Michael put his hand on her arm to stop her.

"We mean no harm," he said to the man. "We were on a mission, a little family treasure hunt to retrieve this box, and that's what we did. As you can see, it's empty and has no real value, other than it's sentimental to us. As my daughter said, it was a gift to her. But if you insist on keeping it, we won't protest. We have satisfaction in knowing that we were able to solve our little mystery hunt."

"Mom!" Morgan shouted, starring at her mother. "Can't you stop him?"

Miyah simply shook her head. Michael tightened his grip on Morgan's arm.

"Please," Michael said. "We meant no harm. Take the box if you must."

The guard stood there for a few seconds, looking over the three suspects. Finally he said, "I guess you look harmless enough, so I'll let you go. But I have to keep this box. Nothing from the estate is to leave the property. It's my job, nothing personal to you folks," he said, almost apologetic.

"Understood," Michael said. "Thank you."

He put his hands on Morgan's shoulders and practically pushed her into the car. Miyah and Michael got in the car and Miyah immediately turned around and put her finger to her lips, a motion for Morgan to be quiet. Morgan reacted with tears and a heavy, loud sigh, but obeyed her mother. As they drove away, Miyah closed her eyes and mentally scanned the car to be sure no one had "bugged" it. She didn't know if there were others watching them. When she was confident they were clear she opened her eyes and looked at Michael.

"Very clever," he said to her.

"Clever!" Morgan shot from the back seat. "What's so clever? I thought you were going to bring the box home where it would be safe. I can't believe this happened. Get it back. You can get it back can't you?" She was distraught. "How can you both be so calm?"

Michael maneuvered past the road that led to the Faerie Bridge and headed back toward the writer's house.

"Your mother is very clever. How did you know they would come after the box, Miyah?" he asked.

"I saw the old man on the phone as we left the cabin. It just didn't feel right," Miyah replied. "Don't worry Morgan. *Our* box *is* safe at home. I replaced it with another wooden box, an old jewelry box I had. Our cedar box has been hidden for all those years, so they have no idea what it looked like. The old man didn't even touch it, so I'm sure he won't know either. They'll probably put it on a shelf somewhere in the estate and no one will know the difference."

"You mean. . .you switched boxes! Why didn't you tell me? I was horrified!"

"That's exactly why I couldn't tell you, dear. You needed to react in a natural way. We couldn't give it up without any resistance."

"Then how did you know, Dad?"

"Morgan, I've spent personal time with our cedar box. I knew as soon as I saw the other box what your mother had done. If you hadn't been so upset, you probably would have noticed too. So don't worry. We didn't get arrested. We have our cedar box. They have a box. All is well," Michael reasoned.

Even though he was reassuring his daughter, Michael and Miyah looked at each other with the same thoughts. . .could a new generation of the people who tried to steal the box from Dr. Alyn be searching for it? They both hoped this incident was as simple as the castle just guarding its belongings and that no one knew about the box and its path. . .and the family's true mission. Miyah shook her head, as if to dispel any more negative thoughts. They had the cedar box. It was safe back at RoseVine. To be sure all was OK, she imagined a protective veil around the three of them. They were also safe. They would be protected on the rest of their journey.

To lighten the mood on the drive back they discussed what they should do now that their goal was achieved. Would they be able to continue their trip and turn it into a relaxing vacation, or would they be too consumed with elation that they would want to return home immediately to celebrate the reunion of the cedar boxes?

Miyah received a strong message in her mind that she knew was from Nona. The message said, "Stay, relax, enjoy your family time together while you can, and have some fun." Miyah smiled to herself. She knew the word "fun" was not often in her vocabulary.

"I'll take care of things here," Nona beamed her. "All of you deserve a reward for recovering Mariam's healing box. I'll be here when you return. The box is safe with me. Good job."

She relayed her "message" from Nona to her family, and they agreed it was good advice. Besides, now they could enjoy the other sites they wanted to see. Morgan knew that what she had already learned on this trip, and what she was yet bound to learn, was the best education she could ever hope for.

10 The Isle of Iona

The family did relax and enjoyed the rest of their vacation. Other than trips to France to visit when Tomas was alive, and later to keep in touch with friends and relatives in Rennes-les-Bains, they had never traveled together. Casually planning their days now, they each made lists of places they wanted to see and Michael routed their intended excursions out on a map. Each day they journeyed out for an adventure.

They drove back toward Dunvegan Castle and took a boat across Dunvegan Bay to the Island of Isay, which in earlier times was called Eilean Isa, the Island of Jesus. Michael was sure this was one of the islands Joshua told him about visiting when studying in Scotland with the Druid priests and priestesses. He could feel Joshua's energy and felt like he was walking in his footprints as they explored the island.

Back on Skye they went to an oak forest between Tokavaig and Org, to visit an ancient site, The Grove of the Druids, that was a sacred meeting place of the Druid priests. On the road from Broadford to Elgol, they stopped at the Well of the Druids. Another day they traveled to see stone circles and discovered the remains of castles and old estates. They explored Mealt Waterfall—dropping 300 feet to the sea, the water blew away with the wind before it even reached the sea below. Morgan got her fill of castles: the ruins of the Knock Castle or Caisteal Chamuis, haunted by the "green lady"; Duntulm Castle; Armadale Castle; and just over the Skye Bridge, the famous Eilean Donan Castle, which turned out to be her favorite.

They had become fond of the writer's house, but decided they would travel to other points as they began their journey back to Glasgow, so they spent a day cleaning it from top to bottom, wanting to leave it as it was when they arrived. Miyah smiled as she folded laundry, noting a small stack of unmatched socks on the shelf above the dryer. Even here, at the far reaches of the world, the washing machine housed hungry monsters that had an appetite for eating up single socks.

Morgan left a couple of sketches she had made of their travels as a thank you gift for Mark, the owner, when he would return later that month. They visited one last time with the neighbors and thanked them for their hospitality and, closing the gate behind them, they said goodbye to the house, the AGA, the bountiful garden, the neighbor's sheep. . .and the hooded crows.

They crossed back over the Skye Bridge and retraced their route until they turned south on their way to Oban, where they drove onto the ferry bound for Craignure on the Isle of Mull. One of the places Miyah wanted to visit was Kilmore Church (Church of Mary) in the small village of Dervaig, on the western side of the Isle of Mull. Built in 1905 on an earlier religious site, it had an unusual architectural style and was constructed with a distinctive round tower, possibly in reference to the tower usually associated with Mary Magdalene. The church had seven stained glass windows, one of which Miyah was particularly interested in. Dating from 1906, one year after the construction of the church, the window was created by a leading Scottish stained glass artist, Stephen Adam, who died in 1910. It isn't known who commissioned the design, but its symbolic representation is an unusual portrayal to be found in a church.

While Michael took photos of the famous stained glass window, Miyah reverently studied the figure of a man who the Church recognizes as a young Jesus, detailed with the traditional Nazarite central parting of the hair and a halo surrounding his head. He was holding hands with a pregnant woman, his wife Mary, her auburn hair flowing from beneath her head scarf. Her sash or belt was placed below her abdomen rather than around her waist, accenting her swollen belly. A gospel text appeared below her. Miyah read it aloud, *"Mary hath chosen that good part, which shall not be taken away from her."* It was a quote from Jesus in the Gospel of Luke, ch.10, v42.

"What a revealing piece of art to find in a church," Morgan stated, standing next to her mother, viewing the family portrait. "It really does look a lot like Maryum, and Joshua too. It's a beautiful portrayal of them."

Miyah pointed out other symbols included within the design of the window—the twin towers on each side, symbolic with Mary Magdalene; the faces and wings of two childlike faces in the arch of the window, their wings forming a protective arch over a symbol that resembled the Star of David; noting that the "star" was placed directly above the "New Jerusalem" Temple, with a golden deer on the apex.

"The golden deer is used in Buddhist symbolism," Miyah explained, offering yet another dimension to the window's significance. On the tall pillars were symbols of pomegranates, roses and oak leaves, and the figures of Jesus and Mary stood in front of a large "M" archway.

As they left the church Miyah told Morgan about some of the revealing stained glass windows she and Michael had visited in France years ago. "But this. . .this I believe, is the most revealing and powerful of them all," she added. "I hope you got a lot of good photographs, Michael. I want to frame this one."

They spent the day exploring castles and sites on The Isle of Mull. They had

Jesus and pregnant Mary M. window in Kilmore church - Isle of IMull

decided to spend a few nights on the nearby Isle of Iona and booked rooms at the Argyll Hotel, a small family-run hotel that had been in business for 140 years. Cars weren't allowed on Iona, unless you were a resident, so they parked their rental car at Fionnphort and took the ferry across. The entire island was only a mile at its narrowest and two miles at its widest points and less than five miles long, so they planned to either walk or take the island's taxi to their destinations.

All three of them were excited to visit the Isle of Iona. Morgan was happy because there were white, sandy beaches; Michael, because he knew that is where Joshua did most of his studies with the Druids and he wanted to feel that presence. He had read that Iona was actually a misspelling of Iova, which means "Yew Island," in reference to an important sacred tree. But even before that time, the island was referred to as "Innis nam Druidneach," the Isle of Druids. Old records told stories of St. Columba and his followers fighting to overtake the local Druid holy men, when they landed to conquer the Druids and take possession of the island, boasting Christianity over Celticism. Even that new religion was not the same Christianity as is known today. Michael was interested in the history of the island, pre-Columba— the time of the Druids.

Miyah was anxious to spend time on Iona because she had an intuitive feeling. She wasn't quite sure what it meant, but felt that a lot of her family history lie within the boundaries of this small island. Her diary told of their travels to Cambrea, later named Eilean Isa—Isle of Jesus—and then to Innis nam Druidneach, Island of the Druids. Later named Isle of Iona, it was the birthplace of Joshua and Maryum's youngest son. Maryum had written in the diary:

— Mother Mariam, Yeshua and I, along with some of the disciples, have traveled with Yosef across the lands of Mariam's ancestors and have been welcomed with open hearts.
Cambrea – Eilean Isa, Island of Jesus
It is on the Island of <u>Cambrea</u> where we stayed with the Druid monks for a time, as I was heavy with child and unable to travel far. Then we sailed to a nearby island that had a larger Druid community so I could receive better care, and our son John was born there, on <u>Innis nam Druidneach</u>. When the baby and I are strong enough we will travel again to where Yosef of Arimathea has business with the royal family, who are related to him and Yeshua, but for now, I am content on this beautiful island with our new friends.
Island of the Druids – the Isle of Iona

Miyah also knew from her diary, that at one time young John and his older brother Joseph had stayed with Joshua in Scotland to study with the Druids, while Maryum and his sister Sera returned to France for Sera's formal Isis training.

Glastonbury

We have settled here among family and friends for many years now and I do love this beautiful land. Our sons Yosef David and John are growing in the likeness of their father and Sera is in her twelfth year. It is time for her to expand her knowledge and receive her priestess initiation into the mysteries of the Temple of Isis, so we will begin a journey back to Gaul. Yeshua, Joseph and John will remain here for a time so they can receive required teachings from their father as they grow. They will return to the Isle of Iona *Innis nam Druidneach for further teachings with the Druid priests. Our sons' education is of utmost importance. I know they will be well cared for, but my heart aches to leave my young sons and my husband. Yeshua assures me we will be reunited again and reminds me that the future of our children lies in cultivating their own wisdom.*

Miyah was aware of the history of a John Martin, who was believed, even in early Christian times, to be the son of Jesus and Mary Magdalene, born on Iona. Curiously, the holy Isle of Iona had also been known as the Isle of John at one time. Miyah knew that in early history the Martin name had spread throughout Scotland: Crossmartin, Martinhope, Inchmartin, Ecclesmartin, Eglismartene, St. Martin's parish, St. Martin's Acre, Strathmartin, the St. Martin's Stone, St. Martin's Church, St. Martin's Well, St. Martin's Den, and there were many more. In Mull there was an ancient church site known as Kilmartin, and the origins of the Scottish Clan MacMartin were known to date at least as far back as the Middle Ages.

Miyah was aware from her diary that Joshua and Maryum's youngest son, John, had married and his wife died while giving birth to their daughter Sara, named after John's sister, Sera. John later married again and they had two sons, Thomas and Germane. Thomas had a son named Simon, who went by the name of Simon of Merian, in honor of his great-grandmother, Maryum and his great-great-grandmother, Mariam. But what had become of these children—the descendents of John Martin? Miyah was looking to connect some of the dots. She was certain that the St. Martin who was celebrated on this island must be descended from the son of Joshua and Maryum, who in turn would make him her relative. Could Miyah have cousins still living here? She was anxious to explore her roots on this island. Iona was considered to be one of the most holy places in the world.

Michael and his family settled their suitcases into their three-room suite at the hotel and eagerly set out to explore. Their sightseeing list began with regular tourist sites, starting with the early thirteenth century ruins of the nunnery. Miyah was surprised at the steady stream of tourists who filed through, meeting the daily ferry schedules. She wondered how much of the true nature of the island they got, coming and going so quickly from place to place. She was glad her family was staying on the island for a few days so they could feel the energy of the 3.4 square mile island. Iona was often described as a "thin place, where the material and spiritual worlds seem separated only by the thinnest of veils." This, Miyah understood.

At the nunnery they discovered a marble likeness of the tomb of Anna MacLean, the last prioress of the nunnery, who died in 1543. Her tombstone had a carved image of herself at one end, and foot-to-foot with her was a figure of a woman and child that contained an inscribed dedication to "St. Maria." This woman had long hair and her body was flanked by twin towers, both medieval symbols to indicate Mary Magdalene. Above St. Maria were images of the sun and a half moon. This ancient effigy to Mary Magdalene had much significance relating to the stories of her life on this island, as Miyah would soon discover.

Next they walked 1/4 mile down the road toward the pink stone abbey rising out of the fields beyond them. By the roadside, standing tall at the junction of three medieval streets, between the abbey and the nunnery, they found MacLean's Cross. Carved from a single stone slab, the ornate disc-headed cross was carved on both sides. The east side, which faced the road, greeted travelers with a cross-head decorated with two animals. A crucifixion scene was on the other side. Michael walked around and ran his fingers over the soldier on horseback carved on the foot of the shaft, trying to get a sense of the inscription, but the words were no longer legible.

They continued their walk, and in front of the abbey stood another carved cross honoring Saint Martin. This is the cross that caught Miyah's eye. This fourth-century bishop surely must have been a

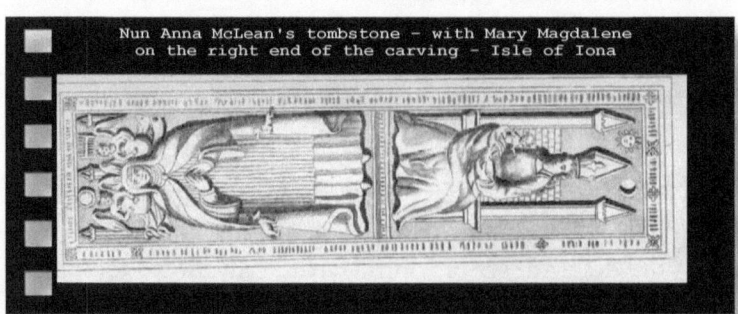

Nun Anna McLean's tombstone - with Mary Magdalene on the right end of the carving - Isle of Iona

descendant of John Martin. The impressive 14-foot-tall cross, a relic from the early Celtic period was one of the high crosses, all dating from the middle or late 8th century. Miyah ran her hands over the carvings, trying to pick-up on its energy. The sculptures were badly weathered, but she could identify many of the scenes and figures: Daniel in the lions' den, Abraham and Isaac, David with musicians, and a scene of a man about to anoint another man.

Miyah recalled St. Martin's Church where she and Michael visited in the south of France and the story of a Roman soldier who, one cold winter night, cut his military cloak (capella) in half and gave half to a disabled person, who turned out to be Jesus disguised as a pauper. St. Martin died in AD 397, at age 80, and was buried November 11—a day that was later associated with peace-making and reconciliation.

Miyah knew that sometimes crosses were erected at entrances to burial grounds, which were considered to be cosmic entrance and exit points where the material and spiritual world come into close contact. She felt a spiritual connection with St. John's Cross, another of the high crosses. The original St. John's Cross had been moved into the abbey museum many years ago, but an exact replica stood in front of the abbey. Miyah examined the surface of St. John's cross, which was ornamented with Celtic interlace, along with serpent and patterns. Always documenting, Michael was busy photographing the fine carvings and details of the crosses nearby.

St. John's Cross - (original in the museum) Isle of Iona

St. Martin's Cross Isle of Iona

Miyah was especially interested in the Celtic pattern of woven vine points intertwining heaven and earth—the ring, a prominent feature of Celtic crosses, which originated on Iona and then spread to Ireland. There were other references to Ireland on the island also. Monks left the island in the middle of the ninth century and moved to the monastery at Kells, Ireland. *The Book of Kells*, now at Trinity College in Dublin was begun by the monks on Iona between 790 and 830 and taken to Kells a few years later.

The family wandered into the museum and viewed other fragments of crosses, along with grave markers, some carved with Norse runes, dating from the 10th or 11th century. Outside, they looked for the cloistral building, but found that only two pillars on the west side of the cloisters remained from the original Benedictine building. On the east side of the pillars were sculptures of plants of the Bible; on the north, plants of Iona; on the south, birds of Iona; and on the west flowers of Britain. It was a good history lesson for Morgan and she made notes in her journal.

Entering the Abbey, St. Mary's Cathedral, a volunteer in the reception area handed them a leaflet and Michael put some money in the donation box for the Iona Cathedral Trustees, the committee responsible for the upkeep of the buildings. Out of the corner of his eye, as he glanced through the abbey doors, he thought he saw a familiar person walk past.

"That can't be," he thought. "Who would I know here?" He decided he was mistaken, but still, it jolted his memory.

He caught up with his wife and daughter and they walked through the abbey, enjoying its simple beauty. Only fragments remained of the original church with additions and restorations spread over many centuries. Listening to the information at the end of a guided tour, they learned how historic this little island was, in that unworked flint from Mesolithic times had been unearthed near the abbey, evidence of communities working the land as early as 3,500 BC. On the west side of the island were remains of the ramparts of a small Iron Age hill fort used by northern Celtic tribes.

"The island was quite self sufficient," the tour guide commented. "Even the communion table here in the abbey was made of marble excavated from the island." Michael listened intently, but his eyes couldn't help but wander through the crowd—searching for the mystery man he had just seen.

Someone in the tour group asked about the current community of only 135 inhabitants on the island and their spiritual beliefs.

"We have a healthy approach to worship that promotes peace and social justice," the guide replied, her words echoing among the thick walls.

"We're a community that supports causes of the poor and exploited; promotes political activity that combats racism; and engages with environmental and constitutional issues. We also have a commitment to strengthening interdenominational understanding—an integral approach to inter-faith spirituality and development of the ministry of healing."

The woman who asked the question was expecting a much simpler answer and she stuttered a small thank-you as she stepped back into the crowd. Miyah smiled. With those few words, she had just fallen in love with the people of this island. . .and she especially resonated to the reference of promoting "inter-faith spirituality" and "the ministry of healing." This, to her, was another reference of the steadfastness of the work Joshua and Maryum were known to carry on during the time they lived on Iona. She was so proud to hear that their work and beliefs continue to be honored in this place.

Miyah followed Morgan and Michael outside to continue their own tour. They wandered, laughing and talking, through other highlights of the island, enjoying the day and eventually made their way back to the pier. Stopping to post a card to Elizabeth back home, Michael caught a glimpse of the mysterious man again, talking with some of the local islanders. Michael started toward him. He needed to know why this man was so familiar, but when a ferry-load of tourists filtered onto the island, Michael lost sight of him again. It was as if he had disappeared completely.

"Is something wrong?" Miyah asked him, laying her hand on his arm.

"No," Michael replied. "I just thought I recognized someone."

"It's that man you keep seeing, isn't it?" she asked.

Michael looked at her, not recalling he had mentioned it to her, but resigning himself to Miyah's super perceptive talents.

"Yes," he admitted. "I can't place him, but I know he looks familiar."

"He sounds pretty elusive," she mused. "Do you think he's avoiding you?"

"That's just it," Michael admitted. "I don't think he's even seen us, or knows we're here. Maybe he'd come over and say hello and solve the mystery if he recognized us."

"Well, there you go," she confirmed. "I'm sure we'll connect sooner or later."

"Maybe," Michael said doubtfully. Of one thing he was certain–this reoccurring sighting of this man was no coincidence.

The Abbey
Isle of Iona

Sheep and Castle

11 The Mystery Man of Iona

The next evening Morgan wanted to stay in the hotel and catch up on her journal instead of going out for dinner with her parents. They said they'd bring her something from the restaurant and Michael teased his daughter about him taking her mother out on a date.

"I'll try to have her home by midnight," he said. "And sober!"

"Yeah, like I'd worry about that," Morgan laughed.

Michael and Miyah walked out, hand-in-hand. Morgan liked the thought of her parents going out on a date. They seldom got away alone together.

Michael and Miyah chose a nice restaurant on the island and they soaked in the ambiance over a couple glasses of wine. Taking their time eating dinner, they enjoyed conversation about their success in finding the cedar box and of their Scotland adventure in general.

"Funny," Michael said, reaching for Miyah's hand. "After all these years, we never run out of good conversation. Do you know how much I love you?"

"Yes. . .as much as I love you," she replied. To anyone observing, they looked like two lovebirds on their honeymoon.

Nearby, a man who appeared to be in his late sixties or so, was sitting at a table with a group of people when he casually glanced over and saw Miyah and Michael seated across the room. His face went ashen. He excused himself from his friends and began to head toward the door. At that moment Michael had excused himself to go to the men's room and he caught a glimpse of the man—the same man he had been seeing around the island—the mystery man. Michael caught up with him and grabbed the man's arm, swinging him around to face him. It *was* the man he had seen before—the same man who had followed them in France.

"Do we know you?" Michael asked abruptly. Not wanting to cause a scene, he slowly ushered the man over to a table on the patio where no one else was seated. Miyah saw the encounter and joined them.

"Is everything OK?" she asked. Thinking perhaps the man was feeling ill, she pulled out a chair for him and he sat down.

"Are you all right?" she asked. Miyah sat down across from him. Michael stood by her side. No one spoke. The man looked at Michael trying to decide if he should get up and run, or face his assailant. Then he looked over at Miyah. He couldn't stop staring at her. Finally, his shoulders slumped, he put his hands over his eyes and began to sob. She patted him on the shoulder, trying to soothe him.

"I'm sorry," he said. "I'm sorry."

They gave him a moment to compose himself and Michael asked him again why he had been following them.

"I knew I had seen you before," Michael said. "You're older now, but I recognize you. I have pictures of you in the background at our wedding, and I know I saw you at the church for Father Tomas' funeral. Who are you? Why were you following us?"

The man wiped his tears with a napkin from the table and stared at Miyah. He finally spoke. "My name is John Martin."

"John Martin," Miyah repeated. "Are you related to the Martins of the island, a descendent of John Martin perhaps?" she said light heartedly, wondering if he was one of the cousins she'd been hoping to discover.

"No, the name is just an odd coincidence. . .Miyah," he said slowly.

Miyah stiffened. "How do you know my name?"

The man stammered. "Because. . .I knew your mother. . .Junia. . ." he stopped, waiting for a reaction.

Miyah was dumbfounded. It was like a cannonball had been hurled at her. Did he mean. . .

"What do you mean, you knew her mother?" Michael asked, being protective of his wife.

"And I also knew your father. . .Michael," the man responded, looking Michael in the eye.

Now it was Michael's turn to feel his gut tighten. He sat down on the chair next to Miyah. Who is this man?

"I never wanted this to happen. Especially not this way. I never expected you would end up on this island, of all places," the man babbled. "Miyah. I don't ever expect you to forgive me," he paused. "But. . .I'm John Martin. John Maartin. . . your father."

Miyah gasped. "That can't be," she said. "My father died in a car accident in France years ago. You must have me mistaken for someone else."

"And the body was never found," the man reminded her.

"Is this some cruel joke?" she replied. "How dare you play on our emotions with your lies." She started to get up to leave, grasping Michael's arm for support.

The man, John, reached out and touched her arm. "Please sit down and let me explain. I have a lot to explain to both of you," he said with a pained expression on his face. "As long as we're all here, just give me a chance to tell you my story. . .please," he begged. "You too, Michael. Your father was my best friend and my business partner. I have a lot to tell you, too. Just give me a chance to explain," he begged.

Michael and Miyah looked at each other in disbelief. Finally Miyah sat back down and folded her hands in front of her on the table. Michael sat next to her and put his arm around her, as if their connection would give them both strength. He had only seen Miyah upset a few times in their life together and they were mostly related to discovering hidden secrets about her family. Now he understood those feelings, because he had the same emotions surging through him. They stared at this man, waiting for him to speak.

"I don't quite know where to begin," he said. "I wasn't prepared for this."

"Why you abandoned my mother might be a good place to start," Miyah boldly suggested. "And if you knew you had a daughter all these years, why didn't you contact me? Those would be good places to begin," she said, feeling anger, an emotion she rarely experienced, welling up inside her. At that same time, she stopped and took a couple deep breaths to control her emotions and hear his story. It didn't affect just her. Michael's family was also involved. They needed to find out what this man, who claimed to be her father, had to say.

John took a deep breath and let out a long sigh. He began. "First of all you need to know that I loved your mother very much. She meant more to me than anything. When I started working with Michael's father, Paul, in France, my intentions were to make enough money to ask Junia to marry me. I thought I had to have a bankroll and financial security before we could take that step. Oh, I know Junia didn't care about that, but I guess it was my pride. I needed money to feel I could take care of her properly. And when I saw how successful Paul was and how happy he and Kat were. . .I wanted the same things. He taught me so much. . .your father," John said turning to Michael. "He was a generous man and I loved him like a brother." John lowered his head for a few moments to compose himself. "I'm so sorry about their death . . . their accident."

"How did you know about that?" Michael quickly asked.

"I kept track of them. . .and of you, Miyah, through the years. But it was important to keep my distance."

"Because everyone thought you were dead," Miyah said flatly.

"Yes, because of that. . .but mainly for protection. . .to protect you Miyah. Even you, Michael."

"So, you're saying you played dead to protect us?!" Michael exclaimed, standing up. "That's bullshit!"

John was silent. He slowly continued, "I don't expect either of you to believe me and I certainly don't expect you to forgive me or understand any of this, but now that we're here, I need to at least tell you my side of the story."

Miyah touched Michael's arm and gestured for him to sit down. She really did want to know why he was absent in her life. He owed her that.

"Miyah, when I first went to France to work with Paul I was elated to be working on a real archaeological dig. It had always been my dream. I had taken courses in college, but never finished my degree. This was my first real job in the field, and Paul was a master. We had been friends for several years.

Junia and I spent a lot of time with Paul and Kat."

John looked into the distance. "Those were some of the best years of my life. When I left for France, your mother and I wrote letters and I had only intended to stay a few months and then return to get her. I begged her to come to France to visit me, but she always said she couldn't leave her midwife duties. She was always busy helping others. Sometimes I thought her job was more important than me, and I was. . .well, I was jealous. I admit it was stupid of me, but I was young and in love and wanted the world to revolve around me. I guess I just wanted her to love me more than anything else.

"Then Paul and I made an important discovery in our research and I committed myself to staying and seeing it through. I did go back home once, in another attempt to beg Junia to join me in France, but she said it wasn't possible. So I returned to France brokenhearted and threw myself into the work we were doing, which I won't go into now, but it turned out to be very controversial, shall we say. There were forces out there that didn't want us to discover some of the things we were finding."

"Are you talking about the caves under Mount Bugarach?" Michael questioned.

John gasped, looking around as if to be sure no one else was listening. "How do you know about that?"

"We probably know more than you think," Michael responded, deciding not to tell him of the maps and gold coins he and Miyah had discovered in his father's safe.

"And I'd like to know even more, since it involved my father," he added. "Remember, I was there when I was a boy and you and my father were working in the caves. I got lost for an entire day under the mountain and made a few discoveries myself. After that day, Dad never let me go back and Mom and I always stayed in Paris or nearby villages when we accompanied him on his work trips."

"Ah, now that you mention it, I do remember that. We were worried to death about losing you in the labyrinth of caves. You were such a curious little boy, I thought for sure you'd follow in your father's footsteps some day."

"Why did you stop your work at Bugarach?" Michael asked, getting back on subject.

John didn't want to reveal too much, and said, "For now, let's just say that we were forced to halt our research and close the dig."

"Was it after one of your co-workers was murdered in a 'mysterious' accident?"

John looked at Michael with surprise, wondering how much he knew and how much to reveal to him.

"Look, Michael, I know I owe it to you. . .to both of you. . .to tell you about what happened there. I can't give you details now, but I will tell you that all of our lives were threatened. . .and there was more than one mysterious accident with our crew during those Bugarach years. That's why your father left the site and returned to the U.S., so you would all be safe. He said it wasn't worth the lives of his family. I had planned on going back too. Then my car accident happened. Someone cut my brake line and I lost control. My car went over a cliff and burned. It was assumed I was cremated in the fire. But I had been thrown from the car and was laying in the long grasses along the slope of the hill. Shortly after the crash, a car pulled up to the edge of the road. I was about to call out for help, when I heard their conversation and realized it was not an accident. I was targeted. I had no choice but to remain silent. Dead.

"Through some of the priests in the village I was able to obtain a new identify and I laid low. I thought things would blow over after a while and I could reappear, but it didn't happen. With the site we were working on closed down, I thought the best thing for me was to remain in the shadows so there would be no more danger to anyone else. The only other person still living who knew about our latest discoveries was Paul. With me gone, and after Paul announced his retirement from the project, I thought he and Kat would be safe back in the States.

"Whether you believe it or not, it was very difficult for me not to let Paul know I was alive. He and Kat had been my connection to Junia when she was still alive, telling me how she was, bringing me photographs. Now I had lost them all—everyone I had loved. We just got in too deep." John shook his head. "Too deep. . ."

"With whom? Who was threatening you?" Michael asked.

"It doesn't matter anymore," John said. "I've been over and over this, and there is no use fighting them. All I can say is they're bigger than us. . . bigger than anything. It's not worth the loss of lives. It's just not worth it."

John looked back at Michael. "Why do you think your parents built the secret room under your swimming pool? It was for their own safety— the safety of your family." Michael was stunned that John knew about the hidden rooms.

John continued, "I thought that after all these years they were safe. I couldn't believe it when I heard they were in a fatal car accident. I just couldn't believe it."

"So you know they were murdered too?" Michael asked.

John looked down at the table. He didn't need to answer.

"How did you know they were in an accident?" Michael interrogated.

"I have connections," he repeated. "It's the same way I kept track of Miyah over the years."

Miyah had been silent all of this time, listening to the conversation. This man knew too many details about both their families. Was he really her father? She was still stunned at the thought. His looks had changed a lot since the photographs she had were taken. His explanation about keeping silent for safety reasons all these years made some semblance of sense, she supposed, but it still didn't explain why he hadn't contacted her before his accident. She was young when he supposedly died, but surely he must have known he had a daughter. Didn't he just say he kept track of her? And why didn't he ever return to Junia? Why did he break-up with her mother?

"Why did you leave my mother. . .and just when did you know you had a daughter?" she bluntly asked.

"At first I stayed away from Junia because I was upset that she had rejected me. She wouldn't join me in France. I assumed she didn't really love me after all. We had some great years together. . .happy years. . .but I really thought she deserved more. She was always helping others. She was such a good woman. I was selfish. I didn't blame her for not wanting to be with me. The best I could do was let her be free to move on," he answered defensively. "I honestly didn't know that you existed, Miyah, until Junia's death.

"I was there at her funeral. Of course, I was disguised. I couldn't take a chance on being recognized. But I saw a photo of myself and Junia on a photo board and then I saw you. I did the math and realized that you must be my daughter. At first I was angry with Paul and Kat for not telling me. I had all I could do to keep from approaching them. How could they keep that from me? It would have changed everything. I saw how they were with their children and I would have loved to have a family of my own. I was angry at myself for staying away from Junia, thinking she'd be better off without me, being a stupid martyr. I missed out on so much and it was my own fault. Then I realized that Junia must have sworn them to secrecy—and worse yet, I thought she just didn't want me to be a father to her child. I was rejected again. I didn't deserve to be a father. If Junia didn't want me to be your father when she was alive, then I was better off staying dead to you after her death too." John's voice cracked as he poured out his story. He never thought this day would come. He expected to live out his life with his secrets hidden deep within the hole in his heart.

"I'm sorry," he sobbed, lowering his head to hide his tears. "I never thought I'd have to tell you this. I'm so sorry."

Miyah didn't know what to do. She felt compassion for this man, yet she was also angry with him. She looked at Michael and could see he was feeling the same emotions.

She reached over and patted his shoulder, consoling him. After all, isn't that what she was trained to do. . .to be a healer. It just never seemed to be as easy in her own personal life.

"I don't expect you to forgive me," John said, putting his hand on top of hers. "I just hope you'll understand why I did what I did. I was wrong. I know that. But at the time, I thought it was the right thing to do. I've made big mistakes in my life. . .sometimes I wish I really did die in that car crash. It would have eliminated a lot of misery for all of us."

"Don't say that," she instinctively soothed. "You were given a second chance for a reason—a second life to use wisely. I'm sure you've made better choices because of it."

She spoke slowly, choosing her words. "Michael mentioned photos of you in the background in our wedding pictures. And he saw you at Papa Tom's funeral. Did you know Tomas? How did you know about our wedding?"

John shifted in his chair, regaining his composure. "I knew Father Tomas from when Junia and I were together. He was a close friend of both families. I always thought he'd be the priest to marry us some day. So I was surprised to discover that he had ended up in the south of France. After my accident, I was protected by some of the priests. They jokingly called themselves 'renegade priests.' Curiously, they also knew about, and encouraged, the work we were doing under the mountain. I had undergone some pretty serious surgery for facial injuries caused during the crash and my face was altered quite a bit. Although he didn't know it was me, Father Tomas was one of those men who helped. He didn't recognize me, and why would he? It had been many years since I had seen him and I looked different now.

"That's also how I was able to keep track of you later, Miyah—through a channel of these priests, who for some reason kept watch over you throughout the years. They never questioned why I wanted to know. I just said I was a friend of the family. Maybe some of them knew the truth." He continued, "I never understood completely where the information came from, except that I knew Father Tomas was a close friend of your family, and I assumed that information was from him.

"Yes, I was at his funeral, and I was at your wedding. You were the most beautiful bride I had ever seen and I was so proud of you. . .of both of you. My daughter was marrying the son of my best friend. It was the best day I had in years." John's face lit up, remembering the day. "I was afraid to approach you, that I might give myself away and spoil your wedding."

"And did you by any chance leave a gift for us at Tomas' house the next day?" Miyah asked.

John hesitated. "Uh, yes I did. I thought the two of you should have it. It was one of the goblets Paul and I found on our dig. I saw it as a gift from your fathers. It probably wasn't very wise of me. I should have at least put a note on it asking you not to show it around. It's quite valuable to the people who know its origin."

"Don't worry," Michael said. "We surmised its worth. And thank you for that. It was a nice gesture—a gift from our fathers. It has more value to us now because of that. We also have a matching goblet of my father's and they are both in a save place," he added.

"I'm curious, but you never married?" Michael asked, knowing Miyah would want to know.

"No. I never did. I could never love anyone as much as I loved Junia," he said, looking directly at Miyah. "You must believe that."

"How did you end up here on Iona?" Michael asked, deciding he kind of liked this man after all.

"I wandered around for a long time, doing odd jobs and traveling to keep from being noticed. Eventually I made my way to Scotland and I heard someone talking about this island—this tiny, holy island where Jesus and Mary Magdalene lived for a time and where their son, John, was born. That blew me away, but at the same time, it coincided with some of the things we learned while digging under Mount Bugarach. I had to come here. To hear there was a history that was talked about as matter-of-factly as a page in a schoolbook, was unbelievable! And then when I heard that the name John Martin was as common as John Doe, I saw that as a sign. I changed my name to John Martin, minus one "a" in our original spelling of Maartin, and was interestingly accepted on the island as one of the many lines of John Martin cousins, hundreds of times removed. A needle in a haystack. I blended in and have ended up loving the open spiritual beliefs, the politics of the island and the people here. I've been here for many years and finally have found a place where I belong—where, until today, I thought my secrets would forever be buried."

Miyah and Michael looked at each other, not surprised by his comments of Jesus and Mary Magdalene, yet realizing that he knew nothing of Miyah's genealogy on her mother's side.

"You don't have to worry about that," Michael assured him. "We won't expose your secrets. I think it's better for everyone involved that you remain anonymous. We also have a daughter to protect. You must know you have a granddaughter."

"Yes, I saw her at Father Tomas' funeral and a few times in Paris. She's a beautiful child. Is she here with you? I hope I can see her. . .meet her. . .you don't have to tell her who I am. I'd just like to meet her."

"She's not a child any more," Miyah replied. "Maybe we can arrange for you to meet, but you have to give us time to process all of this."

Michael piped in, "Do you think there's still any danger of whoever you were hiding from? We don't want to put her in harm's way."

"It's been years. No one here knows who I was before I came to the island. But I'll leave it up to you if you want to reveal who I am to her or not. It's not for me to say, I know that," John said.

"You just have to give us some time," Miyah repeated. "This is quite a shock to both of us."

"And to me as well," John said honestly. "I never expected to see you here, not in a million years. This has to be some weird coincidence."

"There are no coincidences," Miyah said, thinking she needed to have a council with Nona as soon as they were done with this conversation. She must be behind this chance meeting. She had a lot of explaining to do.

"Our waiter must think we skipped out on our bill," Michael said, standing up, signaling it was time to end this conversation.

"Oh, let me get it," John said, reaching for his wallet.

"No thank you," Miyah quickly responded. "We'll take care of our own bill."

"We'll be here for a few days," Michael said. "Is there a place where we can contact you?"

"Let me give you my card," John said, retrieving a business card from his wallet and handing it to Michael.

"Island Tours and Truths," Michael read. "So you're a tour guide?"

"That's what I do now," John lightened his tone. "I provide private tours of Iona and the surrounding islands. It gives me a chance to use some of the things I learned from my archeology days. Did you know that some of the rocks on Iona are around 2,700 million years old?" he said, unable to resist.

"And in case you're interested in a tour, every Tuesday there's an organized pilgrimage around Iona, starting 10:15 at St. Martin's Cross in front of the Abbey, ending at St. Oran's Chapel around 3:30. Or I can give you a private tour anytime."

Miyah could tell by his tone that he had a very charming side to him and was probably good with people, but she still wasn't sure what to think of this revelation. She watched as John offered a handshake to Michael. John respectfully looked at Miyah and she awkwardly reached out to shake his hand.

"It's been a revealing evening, but it was nice to meet you. . .John Martin," she said. It all seemed so formal, but she wasn't ready for a hug or a kiss on the cheek. She had accepted his story, his explanation of why he had abandoned her and her mother, but she wasn't sure if she could forgive him just yet.

"Good night, Miyah," he said, wanting so badly to hug the daughter he had never held before—the daughter he had never rocked or soothed as a baby. But he held back, knowing he had no right to expect anything from her. Did he even deserve to know his daughter after all these years? Yet, his heart felt lighter than it had for years, just being able to face Miyah and tell her the truth he had hidden behind a face of deception for so long. Whether she decided to accept him as her father or not, he had unloaded his burden, and his soul felt free.

Miyah watched him walk away and had mixed emotions about this man, her father, a person totally unknown to her throughout her entire life. She had a lot to think about.

Michael paid their dinner bill and they walked back toward the hotel in silence, both of them processing what had just happened, an unexpected turn of events. Finally Michael suggested they go sit on the beach for a while and work through this.

"What do you think?" he said as they settled themselves on a couple of boulders. Miyah took off her shoes and sunk her feet into the sand, digging down deep through heat left from the sun.

She spoke slowly. "My first response was disbelief, and then anger. Not only at him, but at my mother and grandmother for not telling me this. How could they have kept it from me?"

"What do you mean? It sounds like John didn't have any interaction with them after he left," Michael said.

She looked directly at him. "But they must have known somehow, at least after they crossed over. They must have known then. They see things. They know things. Why didn't they tell me?"

"Did you ever ask them questions about your father?" Michael wondered.

"I don't know. I must have. Nona's the one who told me about his supposed accident. She could have told me everything then."

"Yes, I could have, my child," a voice suddenly came out of the darkness, as the misty form of Nona appeared next to her. "And I would have if you had pursued it. But you didn't, so I assumed the timing wasn't right. These things happen in a rhythm that neither you nor I understand. We must trust that the sequence of time is laid out in a manner that is most beneficial for each of us."

Miyah was usually so glad to see her grandmother, but this time she just stared at her. She knew what Nona said was right, but she still felt betrayed.

"First it was my grandfather, Papa Tom, that I found out was alive after all these years, and now my father! Is there more? What more could there be? Do I have siblings hidden somewhere too? I feel like I'm a player in a long-running version of 'This is Your Life Miyah Maria Maartin Sinclair Wilder.'"

"Miyah, life isn't a game," Nona said sternly. "And this isn't just about you, or even Michael. It's also about John's feelings and emotions. He's gone through a lot of hell over the past years."

"Why are you defending him?" Miyah questioned.

"Think about it. He knows he made mistakes, giving up on Junia and not telling you he was your father when he found out. He was a broken man and felt he didn't deserve to complicate your life. Think how hard it was for him to find you and then give you up. But he did keep track of you, Miyah. He was at a lot of your life events when you didn't even realize it, he even went to your wedding. He loves you Miyah. He loves you as much as he loved your mother and he gave you both up because he thought it was the best thing to do. John and Junia's lack of communication caused a lot of grief in both of their lives and they each suffered for it. Life isn't always easy. Even if we have insight into these things, it's not our place to meddle. It's just information. I thought I taught you that years ago," Nona added.

"You could have at least given me some warning," she sulked.

"There were signs," Nona replied.

"Like when we kept seeing this mystery man reappear at events," Michael said. "I guess I should have investigated that somehow over the years. I knew it was strange, but it was such an on-again-off-again thing, I didn't follow up."

"How could you have put that together?" Miyah said. "It's pretty far-fetched to think the mystery man you kept seeing was my father!"

She thought for a few moments. "All right, Nona, I get it. It's just such a shock. I don't mean to act like a spoiled child, but, really, these are big things. My grandfather, and now my father. After you died I was so alone. And now, so many years later I find that I had family I could have connected with. I don't understand why I had to be so isolated. I know I threw myself into my work, but it wasn't always easy. I felt abandoned when my mother died when I was so young, and again when you died and left me alone. . .then later, learning about Tomas. And even he left me and moved to France, knowing I was his granddaughter. And now I find out that John, my father, left me too. Is this a sacrifice I've had to make for the Touchstone? Abandonment? It seems so unfair."

Michael reached over and took her hand in a reassuring gesture that he would never leave her.

"It's not so much about the Touchstone, Miyah, rather it has everything to do with life. Other than your ancestral background and healing abilities, you're no different than anyone else. Everyone's lives are complicated. This has been the path you chose when you came into the world. It's all about learning lessons.

"Just think of how many people you helped during that period. You were an instrument of healing, my dear. You must never trivialize that. Your work was. . .is. . . important. Now you have your own family and you're still working. Every day you send healing energy to others in many ways. You could think of those years when you were alone and so focused, as your college years. You learned and you worked hard, with compassion and intent. I don't pretend to understand why things happen the way they do, but I'm wise enough to accept the fact that everything happens for a reason. Now you have a lovely family. You're still helping others, maybe not with the same intensity, but you've earned that. Maybe you need to send some of that healing energy to yourself. Forgive. Accept. Believe."

Miyah sat there, looking at her grandmother's spirit. Finally her body relaxed somewhat and she let out a big sigh.

"Thank you, Nona. You always know exactly what I need." Her tone softened. "I shouldn't wallow in self-pity. I should be glad for what I have. . . no matter when it comes to me. I shouldn't just think about myself. Mother died, broken hearted, thinking that John was dead. How did she feel when she crossed over and discovered he was still on earth?"

"Feelings, as you describe them, don't really exist in this realm, Miyah. It's just information. . .facts. Of course we have compassion and love, but it's a different type of emotion. Although she never appeared to John, she watched over him for all those years, trying to guide him. Remember, he has his own life's path and it's not our place to change that. I'm sure he felt her presence. Maybe that's why he never married, I don't know. But now that she's reincarnated and is no longer in spirit, you might find things to be different in his life too. Give him a chance, Miyah. Get to know him and I think you'll be pleased to see where his path has led him."

Miyah sighed again.

"I must leave you now. I love you, dear—and your wonderful family."

Miyah always hated to see Nona leave, especially because as the years went on, she had appeared to her less often. Miyah knew that she was privileged for each visit.

"I love you too, Nona. Thank you," she called after the vapors of Nona's spirit as she dissipated into the mist above the sea.

Michael reached over and put his arms around his wife, hugging her to him. He was touched by her admittance of feeling abandoned, and of her vulnerability, a side of her not often shown. Suddenly Miyah unleashed her emotions and began to cry, something he never witnessed.

"It's OK," he soothed. "Crying is good. Just let it all out. I'm here for you, Miyah. I'll never leave you. You need to know that. I'm here."

She felt comforted, rocking back and forth in his arms. She felt safe, yet she couldn't stop the tears that needed to be released—tears that had been stored away since she was a young girl, accumulated over many years of wondering why people in her life always left her. She needed to release that pain of abandonment. She was grateful Michael was there. He was her rock, as he had said in their wedding vows. And Michael cried with her, feeling her pain and releasing some of his own pain around the death. . .murder. . . of his parents. This had also been an emotional day for him.

~~~~~

It wasn't until the early morning hours that they finally made their way back to the hotel. Morgan was waiting for them.

"Where the hell have you been?" she asked, like an angry parent. "I've been up half the night worrying about you. I didn't know if I should wake everyone up on the island and start a search or what!" She was clearly upset.

Michael and Miyah were caught off guard. They looked at each other and then began to laugh.

"It looks like you forgot to bring me some dinner too!"

Miyah shrugged. It was the last thing from her mind last night.

"What? Are you both drunk or something?" Morgan yelled. Their laughter making her even more crazy with angst.

"No. Not at all," her father replied. "We just didn't expect to get scolded like delinquent teenagers when we came through the door. I'm sorry. Neither of us realized it was so late or we would have been back sooner or something," he feebly made an excuse.

Miyah went over to hug her reluctant daughter. It was then that Morgan noticed her mother had been crying, her eyes still red and puffy from her outbreak.

"Are you OK, Mother? Is something wrong?" Morgan quickly changed her attitude.

"Oh, things are fine now," Miyah said, taking her daughter's hand. "Your father and I have just spent the night talking about some important things. Things we need to share with you. But, honestly, I'm exhausted. Can we wait until later and we'll tell you all about it?"

"What! You come in here after 3 a.m., you've been crying and say there's something important you need to say, and then tell me to go back to sleep until morning! How can I sleep? Tell me now. I'll never get back to sleep," she loudly objected.

Michael had already headed toward the bedroom. The emotions of the evening had taken its toll on both of them.

"Yes, honey," he called over his shoulder to his daughter. "It's important, but it's not life threatening. You must be tired too if you were up all night worrying about us." He walked back into the room and kissed his daughter on the forehead. "Hit the sack and we'll have a nice family conference later over breakfast."

Morgan began to object again, but could see the strain on her father's face. She realized this must really be important and gave in to them.

"All right, but I know I won't sleep well. . .and you know how crabby I am in the morning when I don't get my sleep," she warned.

"Then we'll wait until lunchtime to talk," Miyah quickly retorted as she closed their bedroom door.

Morgan shrugged and retreated to her room, wondering what the mystery could possibly be.

It didn't take long for all three of them to fall sound asleep.

~~~~~~

It was after 10 a.m. before anyone awoke. Morgan was up first and she quickly knocked on her parent's bedroom door and let herself in. She crawled into bed between them, just as she used to when she was a little girl, and wriggled and squirmed until they both awoke with smiles on their face, recalling her familiar childhood antics.

"It's morning Mom and Dad. Aren't you ever going to get up?" she said as if she had been up for hours herself.

"I guess you must have gotten your beauty sleep," her father teased as he got up and headed to the shower. "You seem to be in a much better mood this morning." He added, "Did you make coffee too?"

"Coming right up," she said as she jumped out of bed. "Now get moving! I want to hear your story from last night." She hustled off to the sitting room of their suite to get the coffee maker going. "This better be good," she called back to them.

Miyah stretched and wished she could just stay in their cozy bed all day. Telling Morgan she had a grandfather on the island would be big news, but meeting with her father again would also be challenging. In a way she dreaded it, yet in another way, she was anxious to talk with him again. She thought about what Nona had told her and realized that his life had not been easy either. It wasn't all about her. It affected Michael too. He had a great relationship with his parents until his late 30s when they suddenly died. He missed them dearly. John was a present-day link to them, to his own past. Michael was actually anxious to talk more with John about his parents and about his dad's work in France. If this man was Paul's good friend, he couldn't be all bad. His dad was a very good judge of character.

They agreed the night before that to tell Morgan of her grandfather was the right thing to do. Miyah didn't want her to be a victim of family secrets like she had been. Morgan would have to deal with it in her own way and whatever she decided, to meet him or not, would be fine with them. At least she would know the truth.

Morgan was waiting at the table with three cups of steaming coffee and some left-over bagels and honey nut cream cheese.

"OK," she said. "I want to hear all about your date last night. It must have really been something."

Miyah curled her hands around her coffee cup, as if the warmth would help her find the words. She knew from her own experience how it felt when she found out about Papa Tom. She was happy, but felt betrayed. Yet, this was different. Morgan's grandfather—Miyah's father—was a man neither of them knew or had ever met. How ironic that Michael was the person in the family who had actually known John years ago. How twisted Miyah's fate seemed when it came to family.

Michael sensed his wife's hesitancy and set down his coffee mug.

"We ran into a man last night. A former colleague of my father, whom I met when I was a young boy," he began.

"That's cool," Morgan said. "Did he remember you? What a coincidence!"

"Yes. A coincidence," Michael repeated, adding, "No. It was more like fate."

"I don't understand," Morgan said, curiously.

"Well, the man was more than just a business partner and friend of my father. . ." Michael began.

"The man. . .his name is John. . .also was a friend of my mother, Junia," Miyah said. "In fact, he was a very good friend." Miyah stopped and looked her daughter in the eyes.

"This man, John, was in love with Junia. They were together for many years until he left for France to work with Michael's father. Junia thought he died in a car crash after a time. . ."

"But that sounds like your story of. . ." Morgan stopped in mid sentence. "That sounds like the story of your father," she said, under her breath.

"Yes. It does. . .yes, it is. . ." Miyah sighed. "John is my father. It seems he didn't die in the car accident like everyone thought. It's a long story and we'll share it with you, but right now, what's important is that we want you to know that you have a living grandfather and he is right here on this island."

"No way!" Morgan said, not knowing quite what to think. "No way," she repeated.

"Way," Michael said dryly.

There was a moment of silence. Morgan was processing this, just as her mother had the night before. A million thoughts were running through her head. She wasn't sure if the fact that she had a grandfather would really have much impact on her life. She had two wonderful parents she adored. It's not like she needed another parent figure, like her mother did when she found out Papa Tom was her grandfather. Miyah had been alone all those years and Papa Tom proved to be an important person in her life. No, Morgan was completely content with her family as it was. Mostly she was thinking about her mother and how this must be affecting her. No wonder she was so distraught when she came in last night.

Finally Morgan got up and stood behind Miyah. She leaned over and wrapped her arms around her from behind and just held her mother. Eyes closed, faces side-by-side, framed by Morgan's wild hair, they seemed like one mind—Miyah flashed memories of Junia, Nona, of childhood loneliness, and then of Papa Tom. Morgan flashed back memories of pure love—of Junia, Nona, Papa Tom, Michael and herself, in a role-reversal, like a mother reassuring her child of how much she is loved.

Michael emotionally watched them for awhile and then got up and joined the circle. Embracing them both with his long arms, he began to sway gently back and forth, as if he were rocking babies in a cradle. It was a tender moment and all three became serene in their cocoon of unconditional love.

Finally Miyah broke their trance with a deep sigh of contentment, all her anxiety about her father and telling Morgan had been rocked away in a wellspring of love.

"This isn't at all how I expected it would be," she said. "I was concerned how you would react, Morgan. About your feelings. I expected a strong reaction from you, maybe a little ranting and raving! And here you are, mothering me, protecting my emotions like I was your child."

Miyah kissed her daughter on the cheek and then, as the layer of arms and bodies unfolded, she kissed Michael too. "And you, my rock," she said to him, "thank you for your compassion and strength. I love you both so much."

She touched Morgan's hand. "So you're all right with this? Do you want to meet him. . .to meet John. . .your grandfather?"

Morgan didn't hesitate. She knew it all had to be completed now. Everything needed to be out in the open.

"Of course I want to meet him. He's your father. He can't be all bad!" she said lightly.

Michael and Miyah proceeded to tell Morgan all they had learned the night before—everything John had told them about why he stayed away and lived in the shadows, of why he hadn't claimed Miyah as his daughter when Junia died. Michael filled in parts about him being at their wedding, and at Tomas' funeral and even following them in Paris. It seemed almost like therapy as Miyah told John's story, as if she was working it out in her mind, finding logic in his actions, and even finding it in her heart to forgive him for his mistakes.

Morgan decided that even if she hated John, her grandfather, when she met him, she'd never convey that to her mother. She was bigger than that. No, she would meet him and be polite. . .but he would still have to prove himself to her for putting her mother through so much anguish.

12   Bella

It was arranged. They met at a small cafe on the island. It was owned by a friend of John's, who had offered to be open during off hours so they could have privacy. The owner, a woman named Margo, scurried around placing tantalizing dishes of food in the center of the table, family style, making sure everyone was satisfied with her choice of entrees. Miyah wondered if she was hovering so she could hear their conversation. It had to be almost scandalous news of the day for this small hamlet.

To Morgan's surprise, she found that she liked this man. . .her grandfather, almost from the start. He politely nodded to her and gently shook her hand when they were introduced, not wanting to seem too forward. He told her how beautiful she was, just like her mother. That, of course, made points with both of them. But she knew he sincerely meant it.

There was a glint of sadness in his eyes, but overriding that was a sense of pride, deep pride, in his daughter, his granddaughter and even in Michael. John joyfully told stories of Michael when he was a boy traveling in France with his parents, Paul and Kat. John talked a lot about Paul and Kat, Morgan's grandparents, whom she hadn't known. He talked about Nona and his life with Junia. He told tales Morgan had never heard before and she loved the stories. They all did. He knew more about her grandparents than Morgan did—maybe even more than Miyah or Michael. It melded their relationship somehow—made John really seem like family.

She had expected someone much older looking. He certainly had taken good care of himself and looked healthy and vibrant. It must be the island living, she thought, or maybe it was just because he seemed so pleased to have the truth out and have his daughter, his family, here with him. He seemed genuinely happy about that. It was obvious.

They spent the better part of the afternoon talking and enjoying their meal. Margo was picking up some of the dishes when a little girl, almost three-years-old bounded into the dining room.

"Nana! Nana," she squealed, running toward Margo with open arms. Margo quickly set the dishes down and scooped up her granddaughter into her arms.

"Bella! Whatever are you doing here?" Margo asked, pleased to see the little girl, yet trying to usher her out of the room so as not to interrupt John's guests.

"Mama said I could come," she said with a big smile. Her dark brown eyes were gleaming with mischief.

"Oh, let her stay in here with us," John said, reaching out his hands to the little girl. "Come here Bella and see Uncle John!" He looked at Miyah. "No relation. But I tell her to call me Uncle John."

Bella jumped up on John's lap and began to pick at his plate of food. "Goodness. Doesn't your mother ever feed you?" he laughed.

Miyah watched and wondered if this is what John would have been like with her as a child had he been around, or with Morgan, his own granddaughter. She didn't feel jealous, rather she was enjoying how this little child brought such light to John's life. Miyah realized that he had made a big sacrifice in not revealing himself all those years. It was a sacrifice for all of them. But those days were behind them and John fit the role of an uncle well.

"John has helped with my granddaughter so much," Margo explained. "My daughter lost her husband shortly after Bella was born and John has been a God-send to all of us," she admirably looked over at him. "He's Uncle John to a lot of people on this island, always helping with this and that."

"Now, Margo, that's enough," John said humbly. "Everyone helps each other here. I'm no different."

But Miyah could see that he was different, and she could see that Margo thought so too. She wondered if John had seen the spark in Margo's eye when she looked at him. Miyah smiled at the thought that there were more reasons than helping with her daughter and Bella that Margo wanted him around.

Suddenly Bella slipped off Uncle John's lap and walked over and stood in front of Miyah. She reached up and put her hands on each of Miyah's cheeks and cradled her face in her tiny fingers.

"You look just like I remember you," she whispered, and reached out and gave Miyah a clinging hug. Miyah held her, tears stinging her eyes, as in that moment she realized that Bella wasn't just a little neighborhood child. Bella was the incarnate soul of Junia. . .of her own mother. Miyah knew it and the innocence of the child Bella, knew it too.

"I love you," Bella said softly and then as quickly as she had arrived, she happily skipped off into the other room to find Nana's cat who had three-week-old kittens.

"Where are the kitties, Nana?" she called, as if nothing had just occurred. It was simply a passing moment in time.

Everyone was staring at Miyah. "I've never seen her do that before," John said. "I don't know what got into her."

"I do," Miyah replied softly. "Do you believe in reincarnation, John?" She couldn't bring herself to call him Dad or Father, so John would suffice.

"Yes, I guess I do," he answered. "But who. . ."

Before he could ask, Miyah said, "Bella. . .sweet little Bella carries the soul of someone you loved deeply. She's the incarnate of my mother—of Junia. No wonder you two are so dear to each other."

John was dumbfounded. He didn't know what to say.

"That's really beautiful," Morgan piped in. "Of course. It's Junia. I sensed something familiar. I love it. I love it." Morgan got up and went out looking for Bella. She had loved her Grandmom Junia so much, even though she had only known her in spirit. She missed her "appearances," which stopped when she told them she was preparing to reincarnate into another body on earth. It wasn't long before Morgan and Bella were walking hand-in-hand around the back yard, laughing together and looking for kittens.

"Whew," John finally spewed out. "I don't know what to say. It seems kind of weird."

"Why?" Miyah asked. "That she found you? That Junia came back to you? Souls always come back into the same groups they've lived with before. Sometimes a daughter is the mother or the father. Sometimes the mother is the son. We come back to our family and friends, into the circles of those who loved us or touched our lives. Some cultures call it the red thread of destiny. So don't be surprised. Junia found a way to be with you, to be playful with you and bring out that child inside you that you buried years ago. As Bella, she found a way to crack your shell and allow you to love again. Who can resist the innocent love of a child? She's brought you laughter and life. Embrace that."

Miyah nodded toward Margo, busy stacking dishes in the kitchen. "And I think she's brought you someone to share your life with in this stage of your being. Do you see how Margo looks at you?" she teased.

"Oh come on. We're just friends," John replied, feeling a blush of red creep into his cheeks. "That would really seem weird anyhow, if Bella was really Junia. It would be like I was two-timing her." He glanced toward Margo in the kitchen, happily singing as she did her chores.

Miyah laughed. "No, John. That's not it at all. Bella and Junia's soul are one, but they're two different people. Bella is a child. . .she is Bella. Trust me on this. Junia has no doubt orchestrated this from the beginning of her incarnation. She's trying to tell you that it's OK to love again. You both made mistakes, but through the passage of time you've forgiven each other. She wants you to be happy. Bella approached me in a brief instance of soul remembrance. She doesn't really know she was Junia. She's just a child. A very special child. You missed out on my childhood, and Morgan's childhood. Now you have the chance to make it up. . .to see what it's like to be a father, a grandfather. . .an uncle. Don't miss out again."

"How do you know all of this," John asked.

"It's in my genes," Miyah said. Michael put his arm around her and smiled.

~~~~~

The next couple of days went by quickly and most of the time was spent with family. John had explored every inch of the island and was happy to share his knowledge of the land and its elusive history with this eager audience. Miyah listened intently as her father, who knew nothing of the family Touchstone, talked about how he truly believed that Jesus and his wife, Mary Magdalene and their children, Sera Tamar Maria and Joseph David lived on this island, and that their son, John Martin was born here.

"Many of the islanders know this," he said matter-of-factly. "It's a factual part of our history."

Conversation never seemed to end. There were questions, answers and more stories. Michael pressed John about his parents and his dad's work. He seemed satisfied to find out more about his father's many projects and enterprises they had worked on together. It gave him a deeper understanding of his own father, and even though it often made him sad because he missed them so, it also brought him joy to know that both his father and his mother lived their lives to the fullest, with no regrets. He was surprised at how much John knew about them, and how much he admired them.

Dinners were at John's house, who made sure that little Bella was always there, and of course her grandmother Margo was present to care for her. They met Bella's mother and other friends of John's on the island. He proudly introduced his daughter, granddaughter and son-in-law to everyone and Miyah could see that the community had deep respect for this man. . . her father. He tried to convince them to stay on Iona with him.

"It's a special corner of the world," he assured them. Morgan thought it was a great idea, but her parents' only commitment was to visit often and to invite him to the States to visit them.

"The world is much smaller today with all the technology available," Michael told him. "We'll keep in touch."

John could barely contain himself as he bid farewell to his newly rediscovered family on the last night of their trip. He had never felt so much love, giving and receiving, in his entire life. He didn't know about Miyah's powers, or even about the legacy of her family bloodline, but he did know that she was a special woman, a special woman just like her mother. He would hold her in his heart forever and cherish their reunion. In some ways the days they spent together seemed like a lifetime.

It was indeed bittersweet at dinner the last night as they all sat outdoors, under the stars, listening to the waves lap onto the shore. The events of a few days had changed the lives of many and had touched the hearts of a family destined to meet again in this land they say is a "thin place, where the material and spiritual worlds are separated only by the thinnest of veils."

As they enjoyed their dinner, John couldn't help but notice the amber and copper necklace Miyah wore. Finally he asked where she got it.

Michael answered, "I bought it for her as a wedding gift. Why?"

John hesitated. "It looks familiar," he replied. "Years ago, while working in the Languedoc region of France, on the Mount Bugarach job, I bought some local amber from a merchant and brought it to an artist to make a necklace for Junia. The amber in Miyah's necklace looks the same."

Michael responded. "There were many amber necklaces in the shop where I bought this. How could you recognize this amber?"

"Yes, but were there others with copper beads?" John asked. "Did you by any chance purchase this in France?"

"Yes. I bought it in a small shop in Rennes-les-Bains. The shopkeeper said it was from locally mined amber and that the copper beads were very old. She didn't know much else about it, except that it was made by a local artist. Come to think of it, I didn't see any others with copper beads."

"That's because I also brought the copper beads to the artist. They came from our discoveries under the mountain, part of the treasure we uncovered, along with the goblets you now have. I can hardly believe it!" John exclaimed. "That you'd end up with this necklace. That's such an incredible coincidence."

Miyah smiled, knowing there are no real coincidences. "What do you think their origin is?" she asked, fingering the beads on her neck.

"Judging by the quality and alchemy of the copper we determined they were very ancient. Perhaps as old as biblical times," he added.

"Joseph of Arimathea was a well known copper merchant and miner at that time. Is there a possibility they could be from his era?" she quizzed.

"Anything is possible," John responded. "They definitely predated anything else we found in the line of copper beads."

"But if you had it made for my mother, why didn't you give it to her?" Miyah questioned. "How did they end up in that shop?"

John looked at her. "I had intended on picking them up right before my accident. There was no way I could return and let it be known that I was still alive. And, I have to admit, that as traumatic as that time was for me, I really forgot about it. They must have held the necklace for a while and then put it up for sale. Thank God you have good taste, Michael. It's so ironic that after all these years, Miyah has ended up with her mother's intended necklace."

"Ironic indeed," Miyah mused. She knew she must take special care of this necklace and also sit in meditation with it to find if it really was a connection, through the copper beads, to her bloodline past. She had always felt an odd sensation whenever she wore the necklace and instinctively felt it was special beyond the fact that Michael had given it to her as a wedding gift. Could the copper in these beads actually have come from Joseph's mines in Scotland? The very mines that Joshua worked as a youth? It wouldn't surprise her in the least. There was a reason she was now the caretaker of this jewelry, and Miyah recognized Michael's perception in listening to the voices that lead him to purchasing it.

"What else did you and my father keep from the mountain?" Michael asked.

"You might be surprised, but the goblets and those few beads are about it. We weren't looking for gold and material treasure, Michael. We were searching for ancient documents we knew existed. I promise I'll tell you more about them later. For now, just know that our intention was never to pillage the mountain of her treasures. But, believe me, there's a lot hidden there, I've seen it with my own eyes. I'll admit that it was a challenge not to get caught up in the lustful desire of the treasures we found. We talked about it at length and agreed it wasn't our place to disturb the relics. Many of the villagers from the area had pieces that had been found through the ages and they were careful to keep it secret. Otherwise the Church, or government, would have stepped in and confiscated the items, asking a lot of questions that no one wanted to answer."

"Then how come you decided on the two goblets and the beads?" Michael asked.

"It's a funny thing, but it's as if they rolled in front of us, begging to be rescued. Both goblets sort of fell from their place and landed at our feet, and the copper beads spilled out of one of the chalices. Paul and I agreed to each take one goblet and divided the beads, so I wouldn't be surprised if you find some of the copper beads in his belongings, Michael, just as you did the goblet. You probably just never knew how precious they were."

~ ~ ~ ~ ~ ~

On the last morning before they were to leave the island, Michael, Miyah and Morgan walked to the highest point on the hill, Dun I. They sat in a triangle and Miyah and Morgan did their morning meditation. Michael had never quite gotten into the practice of meditation. He couldn't quiet his mind long enough, but he did know that his attempts relaxed him and he often joined his wife and daughter in their meditations. He sat in lotus position and looked out over the bay, breathing in the smell of the earth and listening to the rhythm of the sea below. He closed his eyes and felt completely at peace.

Soon he heard the distant sound of chanting. It became louder and louder as it neared. It was as if the rhythmic tones were surrounding them in their circle atop the hill and he didn't want to open his eyes. Not because he was fearful of what he might see, but because it was so beautiful and peaceful, he was afraid it would end. Then, through his closed eyelids, he saw a vision of a circle of monks, Druid monks, surrounding them and chanting ancient Gaelic scriptures. He could make out the features of one of the men under the shadow of his hooded robe. It was Joshua. The man lifted his eyes and looked directly at Michael and in those deep brown eyes he saw a warmth that welcomed him to this holy place, this holy island, this very spot on Dun I, a spiritual site of the Druid priests and priestesses. Next to Joshua were his sons, Joseph and John who also acknowledged the family meditating in the center of their sacred grounds. Michael nodded his head, in a silent exchange of recognition and deep gratitude and smiled at the thought of connecting with the deep, holy spirit of this land.

The Druid priests and priestesses then continued chanting as they unwound the circle that enclosed them and formed a line. Heading down the hill and out of sight, their chants becoming a whisper in the wind. Michael still had his eyes closed. He knew it wasn't a dream. He was becoming accustomed to things like this happening and felt so honored that he was offered this vision.

After a while he opened his eyes and both Miyah and Morgan were sitting there smiling and watching him.

"It looks like you've mastered the art of meditation after all, Dad," Morgan said. "I thought you'd never come back."

"How do you feel?" Miyah asked, as usual, knowing what had just transpired for him.

"Peaceful," Michael replied. "And happy. I've found what I was hoping for on this island. We'll have to come back here again," he added as they got up to walk back to the hotel to collect their belongings in time to catch the ferry back to the Isle of Mull. He couldn't wipe the grin off his face. He was so pleased.

"We'll have to come back here often," he repeated.

"Yes, often," Miyah softly agreed, looking thoughtfully out over the beach into the deep, blue waves of the sea. She had come here hoping to find some long, lost cousins, relatives of Joshua's son, John. But she had found so much more. . .not a distant cousin, or even a relative of that lineage. She had found John Maartin. Her father.

13 Rosslyn

Before heading back to the airport, the family drove an hour past Glasgow on A8, and near Edinburgh they turned and headed toward the village of Roslin. Miyah wanted to visit 15th century medieval Rosslyn Chapel before they left Scotland. The Chapel was built in 1446 by Sir William St. Clair, an ancestor of Miyah's, the third and last prince of Orkney.

They knew this would be a quick trip and they would return at a later time to get the full impact of this beautiful chapel. Michael was anxious to see the church too. World renowned for its famous stone carvings, some of the finest in Europe, many related to symbolism of the Old Testament, Freemasonry and non-biblical writings. Rosslyn Chapel was part of what was intended to be a larger cross-shaped building with a tower at its center. Though incomplete, it took 40 years to build. After Sir William died in 1484, he was buried in the unfinished chapel. The larger building he intended to build was never completed.

"Rosslyn Chapel has the largest number, around 100, of Green Man carvings of any other medieval chapel in Europe," Michael told Morgan.

She wrinkled her nose and looked at him. "Green Man! What's that?"

He knew he'd get a rise out of her on that one. "A Green Man is a pagan figure—a sculpture or drawing of a face that's surrounded by leaves. You'll see branches or vines sprouting from the nose, mouth, nostrils or other parts of the face and these shoots sometimes have flowers or fruit."

Green Man – Rosslyn Chapel

Rosslyn Chapel

"Sounds scary," she responded.

"Not at all. They're works of art. I'm sure you'll recognize that you've seen a Green Man before, once you see these."

"Visiting here reminds me of the Cathar history in France," Michael said to Miyah as they approached the grounds. "I suppose it's because of the mystery of the Knights Templar associated with Rosslyn Chapel."

"Yes," Miyah agreed. "There are supposedly many references

to them in the chapel. It's also been rumored that many artifacts may be hidden here, or at least clues as to where to find them."

"What kind of artifacts?" Morgan asked.

"Important biblical texts, the lost Scrolls of the Temple, the Ark of the Covenant, Templar treasures. . ." Michael answered.

"Sounds like an old 'Raiders of the Lost Ark' movie," she laughed.

"Could be. . ." Michael mused. "Could be."

"Tell me about these Knights Templar," Morgan requested.

Michael quickly obliged, always eager to share knowledge. "The Knights Templar were the best-known military crusading order of the Middle Ages. The Order of the Temple was founded in 1118 with the duty of protecting pilgrims going to and from Jerusalem, but at the same time they were also searching for hidden treasures under the long destroyed Temple of Solomon in Jerusalem. They eventually developed into one of the richest and most powerful organizations in the medieval world, and had a large network throughout Europe and the Middle East. In addition to fighting in the Crusades and assisting pilgrims, they became the bankers to kings and originated our modern-day concept of a letter of credit."

"What happened to them?" Morgan asked.

Michael continued his narrative. "The Templar Order lasted for nearly two hundred years, before both the French king and Pope Clement V attempted to put an end to their power. The first effort was sudden and brutal—on Friday the 13th."

"Is that where Friday the 13th gets its reputation?" Morgan asked.

"It may have something to do with it. In the early hours of Friday, October 13, 1307, Templars were arrested by the officials of King Philip IV in the name of the Inquisition, and their property was confiscated. The Templars were arrested, tortured, charged with heresy, brought to trial and burned at the stake."

"They were all murdered?" Morgan asked.

"There's speculation that many survived and traveled to the Americas wtih the Vikings," Michael answered, as a memory of the caves below Mount Bugarach and his dad's work there flashed through his mind. "Some fled to Scotland, but the real question is where the Templars hid their treasure and whether it will ever be found?"

"They say that Rosslyn Chapel has something to do with that?" Morgan questioned. "That's awesome. Another treasure hunt!"

"Well, there is a village nearby named Temple," Michael noted. "And a plantation, Temple Wood, that's in the shape of the splayed Templar cross."

"I don't think we'll be doing any treasure hunting today," Miyah laughed. "Just enjoy the chapel. It really is a spectacular piece of art."

"It's beautiful!" Morgan exclaimed shortly after, as they approached the grounds. She was even more amazed when they entered into the chapel itself.

Stretching 69 feet in length and standing nearly 42 feet high, practically every surface of Rosslyn Chapel was intricately carved in outstanding craftsmanship. There were literally hundreds of individual figures and scenes carved around the insides of the entire church. Michael pointed to a knight on horseback with a figure of a woman riding behind him, holding a cross. Not a cross as Christians know today with the base longer than the crossbar, rather it was a Templar cross, with even portions, as Miyah and Michael had seen in their journeys to France before Morgan was born.

There were double roses, lilies, stars, a unicorn, lions, angels, the moon, sun, doves and other symbols covering every inch of the building. It was a place where pagan and Christian traditions freely mixed. That was refreshing. Miyah noticed the five-star carvings, a dove in flight carrying an olive branch, the foliated cross and the artichoke, all said to have Templar associations.

Surrounding a window were carvings of maize or Indian corn, which seemed to challenge history, as the presence of this plant carving in the chapel raised many questions. Corn, or maze, was considered an exotic plant that originated from the Americas, a country traditionally thought to have been discovered by Columbus in 1492, almost 50 years *after* Rosslyn Chapel was built. It's now believed that Henry, the 1st Prince of Orkney actually landed in the Americas nearly a hundred years *before* Christopher Columbus.

There was so much to absorb, but Morgan easily recognized the Green Man carvings her father told her about as she stood in front of one of the many carvings, admiring its detail.

"The vines sprouting from his mouth represent nature's growth and fertility," Miyah explained. "They show the unity between humankind and nature. Every single one of these carvings hold some sort of symbolic detail. It's a giant book, whose pages will most likely never be fully deciphered."

Michael motioned them to an area of carved cubes that protruded from the arches of the Lady Chapel wing. Each one of the cubes was unique, carved with individual symbols made up of lines and dots.

"They look like they could be musical notes," Miyah said, turning her head side-to-side to get a better angle.

"Or. . ." Morgan surmised. "They could be keys to a secret code!"

"Morgan!" Miyah exclaimed. "We didn't bring you here for a treasure hunt. Just enjoy the artistry. This is a very special place."

"I know Mom. Just kidding. . ." Morgan replied, but she knew she was going to do some serious research on the Knights Templar and their treasures when she returned home. She'd make it her own extra-credit history assignment. After all, the St. Clairs of Rosslyn were related to them in a distant way—St. Clair, Sinclair. She was also very curious about the

Knights Templar /America connection. That was history worth exploring.

They went down the stairs into a basement portion of the chapel that had two small rooms on the side of a main room. There were unique drawings on one wall, said to possibly be ancient architectural blueprints scratched in stone. Miyah was drawn to them and felt they held a deeper meaning. She reached out and put her hand on the cold stone, tracing the lines, and suddenly she felt dizzy. Standing behind her, Michael caught her as she swayed.

"Are you alright?" he asked anxiously.

"I'm OK," she replied. "There's some type of energy down here. It's very strong. I'd like to have the time to sit with it awhile."

"Only if I'm by your side. I don't want you passing out on us," he said. "But, I'll tell you that I feel something too. I don't know what it is, but it gives me goosebumps."

Just then the lights flickered off and back on. The guide called down to them that they were closing. Disappointed they didn't have more time, Miyah took one more look at the drawings on the wall. "Are they blueprints, or a map to some other site?" she said to Michael. "And what was that strange energy that made me dizzy? That's never happened to me before."

"I don't know," Michael said as he steered his wife back up the stairs. "And I don't really care to find out right now." He was glad they had to leave.

On the way to the car Morgan again mentioned the treasures said to be hidden at Rosslyn Chapel. She couldn't get the idea of Templar treasure out of her head. She knew she'd have to return to Rosslyn Chapel some day to find out more.

"The guide said they aren't doing any type of exploration here for treasure," Michael replied to Morgan as they left Rosslyn Chapel to head back to Glasgow. "The chapel itself is a great treasure and they're focusing their work on restoration and maintenance of the building."

"But, after all these years, I'm sure they must know where or what the treasure is," Morgan responded, not wanting to let the subject go.

"Speaking of treasure and mystery, there is one more place I'd like to visit after we return the rental car at the airport," Michael said, changing the subject. "I was wondering if you could whisk us away on a little detour?" He questioningly looked at Miyah.

"It's Mount Bugarach, isn't it?" she asked. Michael seldom requested her to use her powers to travel in this dimension, so she knew it was important to him.

"Yes. How come I knew you would pick up on that?" he said with a chuckle.

"We were in sync with that idea," she said. "How do you know you weren't picking up on my thoughts?"

"Maybe your magic is rubbing off on me after all these years," he smiled.

"Or maybe you're just pulling up your own magic from inside of you," she suggested.

"Yeah, Dad," Morgan chimed in. "I like that idea. We'd make a pretty intense super-family!"

"I just thought going to Mount Bugarach would be a good way to honor both our fathers," Michael came back to the subject. "I feel I need some sort of closure of what Dad was doing there, of why he left, who was threatening them, why someone tried to kill John? Were my parents really killed because of discoveries on the mountain? What could have been so important? For some reason I feel it calling me—calling us."

"I don't know if we'll find any of the answers to your questions, Michael, but I agree that we're being called to the mountain," she said and they prepared for an impromptu side journey to France.

Inside upper Rosslyn Chapel

The Apprentice Pillar, Rosslyn Chapel

Lady Chapel Wing Rosslyn Chapel

Inside the crypt downstairs Rosslyn Chapel

14   Bugarach Farewell

"Where are we?" Michael asked when the mist cleared. "This doesn't look like I remembered. Where's the caves and the waterfall beneath the mountain?"

"I think it's because we're on the mountain. Our fathers' work was on the ground level and under the mountain. We landed here for a reason. Let's see what's going on."

Miyah noticed a group of people nearby who seemed to be gathering for some sort of ceremony or ritual. They were making their way up the rocky terrain, which looked challenging, but elderly women and barefoot peasants seemed to relentlessly be making the pilgrimage. Someone motioned for Michael, Miyah and Morgan to follow them, which they did, and the group ended their climb in a shrub-lined area at the top of the mountain. Here, on this large plateau, they joined others who were forming a circle. An abundance of food—fresh baked bread, cheese, fruit, dates, couscous—was placed in the center for a community meal. Someone had even carried bottles of wine up the mountain.

Thankful for the invitation, but not wanting to intrude, Michael, Miyah and Morgan continued on a trail that led up to another part of the mountain. It was rocky and the trail narrowed as they climbed. They finally stood at the highest point of the mountain on a small, flat boulder, overlooking the valley below. The wind was fierce, but the temperature hadn't dropped and their body heat was high from the strenuous climb.

After they caught their breath, Michael watched as Miyah and Morgan spontaneously began to move into yoga postures, the wind blowing their hair, and the sun brimming their bodies. He thought it amazing that they were changing postures, and couldn't see each other, but were synchronizing into the same positions. Their minds and bodies were in sync. It was a beautiful sight. . .a graceful mother-daughter dance, honoring the raw elements of the mountain itself.

When they were finished they each chose stones from the ground and stacked three stones atop each other, saying prayers to honor family who had passed over—Paul, Kat, Junia, Nona, Papa Tom. It was a fitting memorial, a good release for each of them, especially Miyah and Michael.

As they walked back down the path, they were joined by three young travelers with small backpacks, who had come up from the other side of the mountain.

"Are you here for the World Peace Meditation?" one of the hikers asked.

"I didn't know about it," Michael responded.

"You're welcome to join in if you like," the young man said. "The mountain is known locally as Pech de Thauze or Crossroads of the Four Winds. It's a powerful vortex," he added as they continued on their way.

"World Peace Meditation," Morgan repeated, liking the sound of it. "As long as we're here, I think we should join in."

Not waiting for her parents to answer, she followed the three hikers down the path.

Arriving back at the plateau they noticed that the crowd of people filled the grassland. Tents had been set up and firewood was gathered. The sun was setting and a circle of pilgrims around the fire was growing larger, with people holding hands and saying prayers aloud in each of their native languages.

The family joined the group, linking hands, and Morgan realized there were people from all different countries in this prayer circle. Songs were sung and prayers were called out—all at the same time in many different tongues. Michael, Miyah and Morgan offered their prayers along with the others. Prayers for Mother Earth, for the planet, prayers for loved ones, for those who are in need, for those who are in war, for all beings, all animals. . .and for peace among nations, religions, governments, communities, families, and for peace within. The energy was high and full of joy and light. The prayers and singing went on for hours and the smoke of the fire carried their words up into the heavens.

As the night wore on, some people began to disperse into their tents or to find their way back down the mountain. The fire continued to roar, but was eventually coaxed into a more manageable flame, and a small group of people moved into lotus posture to meditate for world peace, chanting and singing within the circle around the campfire for the remainder of the night. Michael, Miyah and Morgan were among them. It was so peaceful. None of them wanted to leave.

It was getting cold and a fog set in. Moussa, a barefoot Gypsy in the crowd, set off into the fog to get more firewood. Michael stirred the flames and huddled close to his family to generate body heat. Miyah was meditating and working to raise "tummo," heat in her body, so she could easily bear the cold. Michael could feel the warmth emanating from her body.

The light of the flames danced a warm glow on the faces of the peacekeepers around the circle. Behind them, shadows were cast from the fire onto the wall of fog. Morgan watched her shadow self, larger than life, looming at a distance and dancing along with the flames, while she tried to stay in the light.

She was able to generate tummo for a short amount of time, but then opened her eyes. There was still singing in the distance and so much going on, she couldn't concentrate. Everyone around the fire was meditating, or were they sleeping sitting up?

The group had gotten smaller. . .less than ten people still sitting and the fire was going out. Michael and Miyah seemed content in their peaceful stage, but Morgan wasn't comfortable and wondered if she should nudge her folks and suggest they leave. Finally Moussa, the Gypsy, returned from the darkness with firewood and the chill was thwarted as the flames and the heat renewed.

Michael opened his eyes and noticed that Christo, one of the other hikers who was sitting next to him, was awake too. He quietly asked him who they were and where they came from. Michael didn't understand Christo's answer.

"We are 'the key.' If you have any questions, now is the time to ask," Christo said.

Michael wanted to repeat the questions he already had asked, who are you and where did you come from? But he didn't think that was the kind of question Christo meant.

Instead, he said, "If you are the key, I want to go through the door."

Christo answered, "You can't go through the door at this time because your mind is too clouded and there is still work you need to do."

Michael looked at him, confused. Christo closed his eyes and the trinity of hikers sat in peaceful meditation by the fire, wrapped in their warm blankets, eyes closed, in perfect posture.

Michael already knew his mind was too clouded to meditate. He wondered what Christo meant by there is still work for him to do. He sat, taking in the sights around him and snuggled closer to Miyah to keep warm. She was in a deep state of mediation and didn't seem to feel the cold. He looked over at Morgan. She was shivering and couldn't concentrate on meditating either. The ground was cold, damp, and hard. He motioned for her to move closer to them and wrapped her in the blanket that some kind soul had just given them. If they couldn't concentrate on meditation, maybe they could stay warm together with their body heat and at least sleep.

They awoke in the early morning hours covered in soot and moisture. Someone had laid a chunk of cheese and some dates on a blanket for them and others came by and shared more food. Morgan's body finally began to warm as the sun began to shine. Michael got up to help put another load of wood on the fire, stirring the ashes until they flamed again. Miyah yawned and stretched as if she had just crawled out of a cozy comforter.

"Weren't you freezing last night?" Morgan asked her. "I almost asked you if we could leave. I was so cold!"

"Hey. You're the one who wanted to join in the celebration. I thought you were sitting in meditation for world peace with us all night. I didn't feel the cold. I thought it was a beautiful night."

"You're kidding me, right?" Morgan scoffed. "I guess we need to go over this tummo lesson a few more times, because I sure couldn't get it to work for me last night."

"It takes practice," Miyah laughed. "Surely you must have gotten something out of your experience last night."

"Of course. I thought it was beautiful. . .all the singing and praying, the dancing. I just didn't expect it would last all night."

"It doesn't hurt for you to be uncomfortable once in awhile," Michael chimed in. "Then you appreciate what you have a little more."

"Sounds like something a parent would say," Morgan moaned.

"Well, I hope our meditations had some affect on the world. I'm so pleased to see groups of people from all walks of life gathering like this to pray for peace. There's strength in numbers and in the power of prayer."

"We're heading down to the lake to continue our peace prayers," one of the younger peacemakers called to Morgan as she whisked by.

"Join us. It'll be warmer down there!"

"As long as we're here. . .I think we should," Michael said winking at Morgan. "We're part of the group now. We should see this through, don't you think? I know I'm enjoying it."

Morgan shrugged, but followed them. "As long as it's warmer down there," she mumbled.

As soon as they reached the lake, Morgan's mood changed. The sandy beach welcomed them and people clustered into small circles to continue their songs and prayers. Everyone was joyous and generous, sharing peace necklaces, food and stones with prayers written on them. Morgan joined a meditation group that was already sitting in posture, as did Miyah.

Michael was thinking about what Christo had said to him. He decided this might be a good time to learn more about meditation. Everyone else was doing it, so he didn't feel out of place, after all, he'd had some experience on Iona. He got into position and Christo came around and corrected his alignment, stretching his spine and pulling his shoulders back and his head up. He hadn't realized how important body posture was and how much better he felt in the proper position.

Then Christo curiously said to him, "Since it's the anniversary of your birth, you must throw your eyes into the water, and then throw your body into the water, and then throw your mind into the water. You must release attachments to this world and to memories that cling to you."

"How did you know. . ." Michael began to ask how he knew it was his birthday—and how he knew he was struggling with the memories of his parents and their death. But the man put his fingers to his lips and then gestured for him to begin his meditation. It was clear what to do.

Michael sat, eyes closed. At first thoughts of his dad working under the mountain filled his mind with memories, and then the questions

Mount Bugarach, Languedoc Region, southern France

came—Did this lake connect to the lake under the mountain? What was so important inside the caves of this mountain that people were murdered for its secrets? Will the treasures ever be discovered again? Have they already been found and whisked away so know one will know the truth? More questions fought to fill his mind. He could feel his body slump, but he remembered his posture and straightened his back,. He felt like his father was sending him a message to release his anxiety about the mountain, that he shouldn't waste precious energy on the past. He should make peace with the deeds that occurred regarding the mountain, move on, and rejoice in the moment. This made it easier for Michael to clear his mind and concentrate on his breathing. Soon, he felt himself being guided and his energy being held by strong, spiritual beings. He could feel the light of Joshua beaming through him, guiding him into a deeper and deeper state of meditation. It was as if Joshua was sitting next to him, above him, all around him, within him, in lotus position, generating this peaceful energy.

The light penetrated a stream of water, glistening, almost blinding from the reflections. Michael threw his eyes into the water, his ears, his hands, his body, his mind. . .his everything into the water. He could feel his body stirred into energy and for the first time he felt his being dissolve into pure nothingness. Emptiness. The particles of his body vibrated into pure light and he became one with all there is. It was extraordinary and perfect. It was pure peaceful energy, and yet nothing at the same time. The light of the entire universe filled his being and he was that light.

It was hours before Michael finally came back into his body. He opened his eyes and looked over at Miyah, sitting next to him. He now understood why her daily meditation practice was so important and how she had made it through last night in such peacefulness—how all those people on the mountain raised their vibration to pray for peace throughout the cold night. Miyah had always told him when he was ready he would find how enlightening meditation was—how it "fills your soul," she said. Their prayers for world peace had certainly touched his heart and filled his soul—and he had found peace with the mountain.

He excitedly looked around for Christo, having a strong feeling that he and Joshua were one in the same, and that he had experienced yet another dimension of Joshua's teachings, but he could not see him anywhere.

Michael just smiled. "It's my birthday," he said. "I feel like I've just been born!"

"I know," Miyah hugged her husband, and as if everyone had been waiting for him to come to the party, someone opened a bottle of champagne and the bubbles flowed into cups while they celebrated. These strangers, peacemakers, sang "happy birthday" to Michael in half a dozen different languages at the same time.

"How did they know?" he asked, looking at Miyah and then Morgan.

They just shook their heads.

"We didn't tell anyone!" the women said in unison. They hadn't.

Then the peacemakers held hands and ran down to the water together and swam out into the lake—some fully clothed, some shedding their clothing along the way. No one really cared. It was a celebration.

It ended up being such a special day, a birthday Michael would always remember, a fitting farewell to release the anxiety he had over his father's life on Bugarach. And as they prepared to leave the mountain later that night, lights of a chateau across the lake cast a long glow, shining the numbers 11:11—a symbol of the doorway of destiny—onto the waters that stretched out to thank the peacemakers for all of their prayers.

Michael had found the key. He was at peace.

15 *The Confrontation*

"Whew, it's good to be home," Miyah said when Elizabeth picked them up at the airport.

"I know," she replied. "It seems like you've been gone forever! You'll have to tell me all about your travels. I got your postcards. Paris looked amazing, and it looked like it was beautiful on that island. I hope I make it there some day."

"Oh, we intend to go back," Michael replied. "And we'd love to have you go with us, that is if we can ever tear you away from here. You always seem to have something going on, or some reason to stay home."

Elizabeth laughed. "I know. I guess I'm just a home-body. I really am content to travel vicariously though the three of you!"

Morgan talked most of the way home, filling Elizabeth in on their adventures, carefully avoiding the "family secret" parts that she knew were meant for no one other than herself and her parents. She talked about castles, the faeries, the beaches and vacation highlights a "normal" family would have experienced.

When they arrived home, Elizabeth had a nice meal waiting for them. She also had news and could hardly wait to share.

"A few exciting things happened around here while you were gone," she finally blurted out. She waited until after dinner when the dishes had been cleared, so she wouldn't have too much explaining to do. "I have a new. . . well, really an old, boyfriend in my life."

"Hmmm, an old boyfriend," Michael mused. "Let's see. . .could it be Todd or Justin? Or is it Jim. . .Danny. . .oh, maybe Marcus?" he teased.

"Oh come on. I haven't had that many boyfriends," she said. "Well, maybe," she laughed.

"It's about time you got serious and settled down, Liz. You're not getting any younger," he taunted.

Miyah gave him a jab in the ribs. "She's just fine, Michael. There's no age-time on love. You, of all people, ought to know that!"

Elizabeth continued, "I dated this man a long time ago. We had some problems, but he's changed a lot. . .matured. It's all good. You'll see."

"Are you going to keep us in the dark, or do you have some grand revelation planned?" Michael asked.

Miyah suddenly felt a twinge of doubt in her bones. It couldn't be. . . she thought. Before she could ask, Elizabeth said, "You probably don't even remember him, it's been such a long time. He's coming over tomorrow to say hello to everyone."

"Well," Miyah asked. "Does he have a name?"

"Bob. His name is Bob," she said. Michael shrugged his shoulders.

"See, I said you wouldn't remember him. I'm heading to bed. You guys must be exhausted too. I'll see you at breakfast," she announced. "It's good to have you back," she called over her shoulder.

Morgan was right behind her. "I'm checking out too," she said. "I'm beat. See you in the morning." She gave them each a kiss and followed Elizabeth upstairs.

"Good night dear," Miyah said. "Sweet dreams."

"Hmmm," Michael said as she left. "Bob. She's right, I don't remember a Bob."

Miyah was silent.

"I detect that you do remember this Bob fellow," he said, noticing her suddenly sullen mood.

"I don't know," Miyah said slowly. "I guess we'll find out tomorrow."

~ ~ ~ ~ ~

The day passed quickly. Morgan headed out to be with her friends. Michael downloaded his photographs, then spent time in the yard. He had missed his gardening while they were gone and was anxious to reconnect with the soil of his own land.

Miyah conversed with Barbara, Jonna and Monica about patients they had been working with while she was gone: births, illnesses and how her services would be needed. She, too, missed her healing work and was anxious to get back into the stream of things. Since Morgan was born she had joined with these three gifted women to form a healing circle, so to speak. It made it easier for her to explain herself, now that she was a mom and in the community. Working with a massage therapist, midwife, doula and herbalist was a good transition, making her work seem less mysterious. She was grateful that society was so much more accepting of alternative healing that it had been years ago. It made it easier on all those who truly wanted to help others in their mission to heal with alternative methods.

When the doorbell rang that evening, Elizabeth gleefully announced her re-discovered boyfriend. Michael and Miyah went to the foyer to meet this new beau and they stopped in their tracks. Michael couldn't have been more dumbfounded and Miyah's worst suspicions were realized.

"Hello, Robert," she said coldly. "I never expected to see you back here again."

"Hello Miyah. . .Michael," he said politely. "I was afraid you'd remember the worst of me. That was a long time ago. Times have changed. I've grown up. Surely you can let bygones be bygones."

The silence was awkward. "You're not still mad because he called you a witch once, ages ago?" Elizabeth asked innocently. She had never really known what transpired that day when Robert tried to steal the cedar box. She always thought Robert had left because she told him she never wanted to see him again.

"No, of course not," Miyah replied honestly, looking intently at Robert. "That was minor in comparison. . ." She stopped her sentence short, yet wanted him to know that she did remember how he lusted after her cedar box and healing powers.

"I told you I've changed," Robert reiterated. "Friends?" He held out his hand. Miyah shook his hand, but with an intentionally strong grip to remind him that she was a powerful woman not to be reckoned with.

"Even calling him Bob now, seems strange," Elizabeth said, cuddling up to his side, suddenly recalling how smitten he had been with Miyah all those years ago. "It's a part of his new image."

Michael couldn't stomach it and said he thought his cell phone was ringing. He turned and headed toward his library and picked up his phone from his desk for a non-existent call. The last thing he wanted to do was to alienate his sister again. He needed time to get a grip on this.

"I trust the two of you, and your daughter, had a lovely trip," Robert said. "Liz has told me so much about Morgan. The pictures I've seen of her are beautiful. She's a replica of her mother. I suppose she's following your footsteps too in your medical. . .ahhh. . .healing practice." He was clearly fishing. "Is she home? I'd love to meet her."

Miyah flinched. "No, she's out for the evening."

"You can meet her later, Bob," Elizabeth stepped in. "We're going to be late if we don't leave in a minute." She turned to Miyah. "We're meeting friends to plan an engagement party. Don't worry," she added with a giggle. "It's not ours! It's for our friends Jim and Kari. Come on, Bob. We really need to get going."

"OK, dear. Whatever you say," he said with a smile. "It was good to see you again, Miyah. You too Michael," he called through the arched doors of the library. Michael simply nodded his head and waved as if he were in deep conversation.

"What a coward!" Miyah said when they left. "I mean you!"

Michael put his phone down. "I know. I'm a coward. I couldn't help it. If I stayed in the room with that man I would have said things I would no doubt regret later and I can't bear to put that wedge between Liz and myself again. I had to step away to figure out how to deal with this."

"I know," Miyah said softly, putting her arms around her husband. "You're not a coward. You're a very smart man."

Michael replied. "The thought of that man in my house, probably most of the time we were gone, is unbearable! He probably went through all our stuff. I don't believe he's changed. I think he still has ulterior motives."

"I agree completely," Miyah said. "I'd like to think that for Elizabeth's sake, he really does love her and that's why he came back, but a voice in my head says to beware."

"I hear the same voice," Michael said. "It's shouting loud and clear."

He added, "The way I see it we have two choices. Concede, so Liz is happy with us and hope for the best, or play along until we can figure out a way to see if he's sincere or not."

"You mean set a trap for him?" Miyah asked.

"Maybe. Liz would never listen to us. The only way is for her to find out for herself what a scoundrel he really is."

"Those are harsh words."

"Oh, come on. You know your gut is warning you, too," Michael said. "I think you need to call in your troupes for this one."

Miyah knew he was right. She had a feeling it would take a bit of time to work through this, and knew they would need an immense amount of patience. Patience and strength. She also knew that she didn't want Morgan involved in any way and was formulating a plan to protect her. She knew they had just returned from a lengthy trip, but maybe it was time for that "language immersion" program Morgan always wanted to do to fine-tune her French. They could send her to France to stay with relatives for a few weeks. She would be safe there. Miyah could "pop in" once in awhile to check on her. Morgan loved the little house at Rennes-les-Bains and all of her cousins there. They could join her, and maybe bring Elizabeth, when all of this was over. Michael agreed it was a good plan. They just needed to act soon, before Robert dug his way into the family any deeper.

~~~~~

Morgan was thrilled with the news of France and was eager to extend her adventurous travels. Without giving many details, she was also told that Elizabeth, and everyone else, would think she was in Australia on a study abroad program. Morgan, ever intuitive, asked few questions, knowing her parents always had the best intentions for her, whatever their reason. Used to the mysteries that shrouded her family, she trusted them completely. Family warmheartedly awaited her arrival in France and she felt good knowing she belonged to a large community of aunts, uncles and cousins who shared her same gifts and wisdom. . .people she could actually talk with about healing and family history. It promised to be a great summer.

Back home, things weren't so rosy. Michael and Miyah were forcefully polite whenever Robert came around, but avoided lengthy conversations with him. They listened to Elizabeth in her love-struck stage, gushing about him, but held their tongues when it came to giving advice. Miyah tactfully counseled her whenever Elizabeth asked for input, but was careful not to express her own concerns. She and Michael had agreed to give Robert the benefit of the doubt for now. Perhaps, just perhaps, he had really changed and no longer had an interest in the cedar box and the powers he thought were beneath its cover. It was doubtful, but they agreed to give him a chance.

It didn't take long for him to show his true colors. After a few weeks of niceties, Robert abruptly got to the point. Michael was in the garden and Elizabeth was in the kitchen making tea. Miyah was sitting at her desk writing when Robert approached her.

"So, whatever happened to that old box you used to have?" he bluntly asked. "Liz always said you protected it with your life. It must hold some pretty powerful medicine."

Miyah put her pen down and looked him in the eye. "Whatever brought that up?" she asked. "What interest could you possibly have in that 'old' box, as you put it?"

"Oh, don't play dumb with me, Miyah," he said. "We both know that box is somehow connected to those healings you became so famous for. I just want to know what the secret is. . .what kind of magic is inside. . .what kind of witchcraft it holds?"

"No, Robert. What you really want is to find out how you can get your hands on the box so you can use its powers too," she boldly said.

"Why not?" he admitted. "Why should you be the only one to do good in the world? Can't you share some of the glory with others? I just want to help people too. I want to be a healer too."

"You want to be powerful and famous, Robert. It doesn't work that way. The power isn't in the box. . .it's in the hands of the healer," she replied.

"Yeah, yeah, that's what you say, but I've never met anyone who has the abilities you do, and you're the only one I know with a box like that, so I've put two and two together and surmise that it has more to do with just your ability. It's got to be the box."

He added, "Hell, it's got to be pretty old. It's worth something just for that."

Miyah glared at him. "You'll never know," she said.

Just then Elizabeth came into the room with a tray of tea. Miyah excused herself and went out into the garden to join Michael. It made Robert uneasy to see them talking. He knew she was telling him that he asked about the box. It didn't matter. He would do whatever it took to get his hands on that magic box. He thought he could make millions with it.

Michael made a fist as Miyah relayed her conversation with Robert. He glanced toward the sitting room and had all he could do to hold himself back.

"It's time to set our trap," Michael said. "Let him expose himself."

~~~~~~

It was a simple plan. Leave the box out in view, so Robert could easily attempt to steal it, but it was key to have Elizabeth present so she could see what his real motives were. It may seem like a cruel scheme to involve her in, but it was the only way she would believe his motives.

Miyah emptied Morgan's cedar box, the one they recovered from Scotland, of its contents and placed the herbs, stones, crystals and other items into her own cedar box, which she carefully whisked away to the safety of RoseVine. As an extra measure of security, she called on Nona to be present, in case work "behind the scenes" had to be implemented. She was taking no chance of losing either of the cedar boxes again.

Meanwhile, Michael had been doing some research and discovered that Robert had a criminal record of theft and bribery. He had served time in prison. This explained where he was part of those years when his sister had lost track of him. Michael didn't intend to show this to Liz unless it was the last resort, but he did want to have the information handy just in case the police had to get involved. He hoped it wouldn't come to that.

It was late in the day and Elizabeth had invited Robert over to watch movies and spend the night. While they watched their movie in the front sitting room, Michael and Miyah would spend the evening in their usual place, the library/study. All the lamps were on and the library's glass-paned French doors from the hallway were closed, but were uncurtained, so a clear view into the room was possible if anyone walked by. Michael sat at his computer, writing, and Miyah was curled up on the couch reading an herbal book and making some notes. In front of her, on the coffee table, was her empty medicine pouch and placed on top of that was the cedar box. She had a few stones and essential oils set around and a couple of small bags of herbs to make it look like she was preparing a potion or at least consulting for a new brew.

Robert walked past several times on his way to the bathroom or the kitchen, peering in from the dark hallway to see what they were doing. Of course he noticed the cedar box right away.

It was getting late and Michael poked his head into the front sitting room to say he was going to bed. "Miyah's still up, but she's calling it quits soon too," he announced. "Good night."

"Good night," Elizabeth and Robert said in unison. He was trying to act as casual as possible.

It wasn't long and they heard Michael call down from upstairs, "Miyah, can you come up here for a minute?" She obliged, heading up to their room, leaving her box and medicines on the table. They heard the bedroom door close behind her and Robert made some snide remark about Michael getting a little tonight before hitting the sack. Elizabeth didn't comment, thinking he was being a bit crude and it was none of his business.

Robert could hardly stand it. He waited and waited, but Miyah didn't come back downstairs. "She must have fallen asleep," he thought.

"I'm going to make some tea," he finally said and headed toward the kitchen. Elizabeth was half asleep and mumbled, "OK."

Robert went straight to the library. The library door was ajar and the lamp by the sofa was still on, casting shadows from the box onto the table.

"She must have thought she'd be coming right back down," he mused. "The dirty devil must have tired her out," he whispered with a wicked smile.

He quietly slipped into the room and bent over the cedar box. He hesitated, almost afraid to touch it at first. Then he slowly ran his fingertips over the top. He picked it up, eye level, and turned it over and around to view each side.

"It's just a plain, crude box," he said under his breath. "Nothing fancy about it." Still, he believed it had special powers and it was his turn to see what it could do for him. He tucked it under his arm and headed toward the front door. Stepping into the sitting room, he grabbed his jacket and slung it over his shoulder to hide the box. Elizabeth stirred and he bent down and kissed her on the forehead.

"I'm going to head home," he said. "You're tired anyhow."

"Oh, no, don't go," she said, waking up drowsily. "Let's go up to bed. I'm not that tired."

"No, it's OK. I think I'm coming down with a cold or something. I'll call you tomorrow."

"Are you sure?" she said, yawning.

"Yeah. Later, Babe," he said. Looking at her there on the couch he thought it was a pity he'd never see her again. He had actually grown to like her. But now, he had what he came for, what he'd patiently stuck around for all these weeks, and he could barely wait to get out of there. He turned to leave and suddenly the hall light flipped on.

"You're not leaving already, are you?" Michael asked. "It's early."

"I, ah...I think I'm coming down with a cold. Don't want to get everyone else sick. See you tomorrow," he mumbled as he headed toward the door.

"Not so fast," Michael raised his voice in confrontation. The noise brought Elizabeth into the hallway.

"What's the matter?" she asked sleepily.

"I think your boyfriend might want to answer that," Miyah piped up from the shadows.

Seeing her, brought back that image of the last time he attempted to steal the box, when she morphed into a giant shadowing poltergeist with faceless spirits surrounding her. He shuddered at the thought and bolted toward the door, holding tightly to the box beneath his jacket.

"No problems," he said. "I was just leaving."

Michael grabbed his arm and swung him around. His jacket fell to the floor, exposing the box tucked under his arm.

"What?" Elizabeth said. "What are you doing with that?"

"I was just going to borrow it and polish it up for Miyah. . .it, it looks like it's in pretty bad shape. . .I was going to surprise her," he stumbled on his words.

Elizabeth looked doubtful. "Oh, Bob," she said in disappointment. "What have you done?"

"He's stealing my cedar box!" Miyah exclaimed. "Don't let him get away!"

Robert pulled away from Michael's grip and ran out into the street. Elizabeth ran outside and watched him disappear into the darkness of the night. She started after him, calling his name in disbelief, but she tripped and fell into a thorny hedge. She was sobbing uncontrollably. Michael and Miyah stopped to help her. A whirlwind of mist whizzed past them as Miyah saw the spirit of Nona shoot down the street to follow after Robert.

Robert ran as fast and as far as he could and seeing no one behind him he finally retreated into a dark alley. He crouched behind a garbage can, panting to catch his breath. He thought he was safe and took the box out from under his arm and held it eye level again.

"You're mine now!" he yelled in excitement. "Now you'll answer when I beckon and do my deeds. I'm going to be rich!"

Unable to wait any longer, he slowly opened the lid of the box to see what magic potions it held inside.

"It's empty!" he spat. "Damn. It's empty!" Then, he ran his hands inside the box to see if he might have missed something. He felt letters engraved in the corner of the wood.

"This must do something," he said, rubbing his fingers over the letters, hoping to unlock some secret code.

"That won't do you any good," a voice above him said. Robert jumped up and hugged the box to his body in a frantic state. He was spooked and looked all around. No one was there.

"Who's there?" he shouted.

"Oh Robert. We're so disappointed in you," the voice replied. Nona let a cold, clammy finger of mist reach out and touch his face.

Robert jumped and swatted at his face. He turned in circles, looking on all sides. He backed against a brick wall, clinging to it, as if it would protect him. He looked down at the box, lid still open, cradled in his arms.

"Is it coming from inside the box?" he asked. "Is someone inside the box?"

"Don't you know this box is only to be used for good—for healing?" the voice asked.

"I don't know anything," he shouted. "Who are you? Where are you? Leave me alone!" His heart was pounding so wildly he thought he would have a heart attack. "Go away!" he yelled and looked frantically for an escape from the dead end alley he had pinned himself into.

"Very well. You've chosen your fate," the voice replied.

"What? What fate?!" he yelled back.

Just then Robert saw Michael, Miyah and Elizabeth walking toward him from the street side of the alley.

"It's you, witch!" he said, pointing to Miyah. "You're making this box talk to me! You've cursed it!"

"No, Robert. It's you who has brought on the curse," Miyah replied. "You and your evil intentions."

"Here, take the damn thing," he said, attempting to throw the box toward them. But the box stayed in his hands like glue. "Here," he repeated, trying to thrust the box away again and again.

"Take it! Take it!" he cried in hysteria.

Miyah lifted her hand and the box fell onto the pavement in between them and Robert. He stood there for a moment and hearing police sirens somewhere in the distance, he panicked and tried to run past them, back into the street, into the cover of darkness. But as he moved, his foot caught the edge of the cedar box on the ground in front of him and the smell of cedar permeated the air. His body became a murky vapor of dark clouds, funneling and swirling into the side panel of the box—into an abyss of dark figures and shadows, moving in sync, taking him into their fold. . .into the dark hell of a world unknown. His screams for help could be heard, loudly at first and then diminishing to a tiny high-pitched voice, and then there was nothing. In an instant it was done. The smell of cedar disappeared and the box sat empty on the black surface of the pavement, rimmed by the dim light of a single, distant street lamp.

Michael had grabbed his shrieking sister and holding her to him, he sheltered her eyes from the sight. He stared at this box. . .a partner to the cedar box he had safely traveled through many times. He was in awe of what had just transpired. This was not typical of the cedar box Michael knew. Where did Robert go? Would he ever return? Was he dead? Michael looked to Miyah for answers. She shrugged and looked to Nona, standing over the cedar box. Nona nodded her head and disappeared into the night.

Miyah gingerly picked up the cedar box and looked it over. It didn't appear to be damaged. She said some words over it in a language Michael didn't recognize, made hand motions and touched it gently, lovingly. She was clearing the box of dark energies and anything negative that may have lingered. When Miyah was finished with her ritual, the box took on a new sheen, a healthy, spiritual glow, indicating it was again an instrument of peace, healing and love as it was meant to be.

Morgan had once asked her if there was a "safety" feature built into the cedar box if someone attempted to use it for evil purposes. This answered her question.

There was one more detail to take care of. . .Elizabeth. Still sobbing, she was clinging to her brother. Not wanting to say anything out loud, Miyah "beamed" a message to Michael, who immediately responded with a nod. Miyah would have to erase Elizabeth's memory of what had just transpired, and maybe her memories of Robert all together. It was the only way to ease her trauma and emotional pain. They had to re-write the ending, and Elizabeth and Robert's relationship.

With the wave of her hand and a few chosen words, they were back at the house. Michael and Miyah were in the library. Michael was at his computer writing and Miyah was curled up on the couch reading an herbal book and making some notes. In front of her, on the coffee table, was her empty medicine pouch, and placed on top of that was the cedar box. Elizabeth and her boyfriend, Bob, were in the sitting room, watching a movie.

Michael turned off his computer and Miyah packed up her cedar box and potions and placed them back into her medicine bag. They turned off the lamps and went, together, to say goodnight to Elizabeth and Bob.

The couple was curled up on the couch under a quilt that Michael's grandmother had made. Both were sound asleep. Michael turned off the TV and bent down and kissed his younger sister on the forehead. Bob's arms were curled around her and they both had contented looks on their faces. Bob Alexander, a tall, good-looking blonde from New Hampshire, who was studying to become a lawyer, had just met Elizabeth a few months ago for the first time, and they had instantly been attracted to each other. His parents and siblings loved Elizabeth and she was crazy about them. She had an entire family to love, and to love her back. It was a match, shall we say, made in heaven.

And the man named Robert. . .he was just a diminished memory of an old boyfriend she used to know. . .many years ago.

16 *The Wilder Side*

Life seemed to move ahead smoothly. Morgan came back from France filled with stories of her cousins and new friends, announcing that she wanted to spend every summer there.

"It's hard to explain, but I feel like I *belong*," she said. "I don't have to hide who I am and what I know." Miyah completely understood and was happy her daughter was so passionate about family, but she also stressed to Morgan that she wasn't finished with her studies yet.

"Just because you're home-schooled doesn't mean you can ignore your formal education," she reminded her.

"I know that, Mom. But look at how much I learned while I was there. Mon Français est à l'aise, oui?" she retorted.

"Yes, dear, your French is excellent," Miyah said, finally agreeing they would spend more time at their house in Rennes-les-Bains in the future. It was a promise she was anxious to keep. She also wanted to return to the Isle of Iona. Even though Miyah still couldn't bring herself to call him, "Dad," she did keep in contact with John Maartin. Because of his past with both her and Michael's family, he was still linked to them in more ways than just being her father.

It was their visit to Iona that had piqued Michael's interest in finding out more about his own father's work. He didn't know if it was something John had said, or if that connection spurred him to dig a little deeper. He was spending a lot of time in the "bomb shelter," sorting through his father's papers and examining his belongings in the safe.

He spread out the maps his father and John had drawn and studied them for hours with a magnifying glass. Along with his work on Bugarach, there were several other "treasure maps," some were areas closer to home, in North America and Nova Scotia. He wondered if they were connected to each other in any way, and knew the only way he would find out was to get John here to go over the maps with him. As he rolled the documents and maps back up he left sticky notes on the ones that most interested him. Surely John would be able to provide answers to some of his questions.

As he was returning items to the safe, he noticed the box that held a manuscript his mother had been working on before she died. He thought her main focus was children and teen mystery books, but he discovered this manuscript went much deeper than that. It was the beginning of a book carved out of real life—their life in France.

The beginning chapters wove a story about a young family exploring the region and enjoying weekend sabbaticals from the father's job as an archeologist working on a top secret dig. She had an outline and pages of notes, but the manuscript was far from completion. Michael nostalgically read through the pages as if he had written them himself about his own life. It *was* his life. . .his family's life. . .even Miyah's family was included with references to their friends. Of course the names were different, but the characters were unmistakable.

The story was also laced with intrigue and danger. Was it fiction or was it real? It certainly sounded like it could be detailing some of the events that surrounded their own dismantled Bugarach project. Michael thought he had released his anxiety over his parent's death, but thoughts kept coming to the surface. He found that he still didn't quite have the closure he needed. He was looking for facts, names, for more information that might disclose who had threatened and ultimately killed his parents and the others who had mysteriously died. Who had attempted to kill Miyah's father? Surely there must be some clues.

To his dismay, the writing stopped abruptly after a few chapters, with little or nothing for him to grab onto that could lead to resolving their mysterious deaths. Yet, there was something in one of the chapters that seemed almost out of place in the family story he knew. She wrote about a woman, whom Michael assumed was Junia, and her soul connection to her, as a "cousin" from an ancient bloodline. She talked about the two women occasionally working together in a healing practice. . .and even detailed the birth of the other woman's daughter—Miyah. What did she mean. . .a soul cousin? He didn't understand and when he presented it to Miyah, she didn't understand it either.

"Are there more secrets Nona hasn't told us?" he accused.

"Let's remember that our mothers were very close, that Kat no doubt knew of mother's powers and evidently of her bloodline, which is interesting, being few people were given that knowledge. Also remember, Michael, that she wrote fiction. Maybe she was intrigued by mother's situation and this was her way of including it into her story."

Michael reluctantly agreed. "I just thought it strange the way it was written," he said. "I suppose you could be right. It's fiction based on some personal facts. It's a novel. At least it gives me a lot of good details I can use in writing my. . .err. . .*your* story," he added.

"Yes," Miyah reiterated, although intuitively she, herself, was not completely convinced that what Kat had written should be dismissed so easily. Something told her there was more to Kat's story.

17 Blood Runs Deep

Morgan kept her herbs, stones and essential oils in her cedar box, the one a young Joshua lovingly carved for his mother, Mariam. The two boxes sat side-by-side when not in use, just as they had done in ancient times when Mother Mariam and Maryum possessed them. Morgan had graduated to the level of mastering "materializing" from place to place, and with that freedom, along with a vow to adhere to a strict code of ethics, she was able to travel to RoseVine by herself to access the vast library and to council with the wisdom of the spirits who were there for her teachings. She had also made excursions back to visit with her "grandmothers," learning more about their personal lives, connecting the string of bloodline women to their entries in the diary.

"I'm so proud of you," Miyah said to her daughter one day. "I believe I've taught you almost everything I know! You're an excellent student. . .and sometimes, I find, you're the teacher! I've also learned a lot from you, too," she laughed. "There's one more important exercise I know you're ready for," she said as she placed both cedar boxes on the coffee table in front of them. "Come. Sit by me and let's talk."

"What is it, Mother?" Morgan was intrigued.

"Our cedar boxes are used for more than storing our healing tools," she began. "Used in the proper way, they provide a passageway to healing on many levels—physical, emotional, spiritual."

Morgan anxiously asked, "I've been waiting for this day. We haven't journeyed together in such a long time! Where are we going? What are we going to see?"

"Hold on there," Miyah laughed. "We're not going anywhere. You've materialized to other time frames so you could learn from our ancestors. Now it's time to learn how to use the box to benefit others, for their healing."

"Do you mean like when Dad traveled back into the past?" Morgan asked.

"Exactly," Miyah replied. "He's agreed to do so again, only this time with you holding the energy for him."

"He trusts ME to do that?" Morgan said, with some doubt. "But what if. . ."

"Shhh. Don't even think those things, Morgan. If I didn't think you were ready, I wouldn't be approaching this now. You must have confidence in yourself. I'm here. Nona will be here. And your dad is really anxious to travel again. It's been a long time since his last journey."

"Yes," Michael said, coming in from the kitchen, holding up the Faith Stone that Miyah had given him years before. "I thought my time journeying with the cedar box was finished. I'm really anxious. . .honored. . .for another chance."

Morgan sat looking at her dad. Why did this scare her? What if. . .

"Don't worry, Morgan. I trust you and your abilities completely. You won't lose me in the abyss of time. Your mother will see to that!" he joked, adding questionably, "Won't you dear?"

"Of course! As I said, we wouldn't be doing this unless I, and our spirit council, thought she was ready. How about it Morgan?"

"I wish I had as much confidence as everyone else," she started. . .

"Well, then, you need to sit for a bit and meditate on that," her mother said quickly. "You can't go into something like this with doubt in your mind. Get positive. Believe in yourself. Why don't you go out into the garden for awhile and contemplate this and come back when you're ready. We'll wait."

Morgan found a favorite spot under the shade of a tall oak tree in the back yard and sat lotus style. Closing her eyes, she focused on only positive outcomes. . .on having confidence in herself and of what it meant for her to be a child of the Touchstone bloodline. As she meditated, her back straightened, her breath calmed and she quickly gained that inner faith, the self-assuredness and balance she needed to carry out the work she'd been trained to do, in whatever level or form it took. She had never faltered at any of the other assignments she had been given, why should this be any different? She asked for guidance and wisdom from her elders.

"OK," she said, returning to the library. "I'm ready if you are."

Michael was already stretched out on the sofa, his Faith Stone on a leather string around his neck.

"I've taught you the prayers and chants for clearing the box and asking for right actions, productive journeys and safe returns," Miyah said. "And if you care to add anything to your prayers, you're free to do so. Your words must come from your heart." She added, "For you, it'll seem like watching through a crystal ball. You'll be able to see all of Dad's journeys as they occur. Your only duty is to hold the energy of the box, so the stream of power isn't broken. And don't worry, I'll be here with you, as well as Nona, who'll be lingering around here somewhere!" Miyah said, looking around. Nona rarely appeared these days, yet both Miyah and Morgan could feel her presence and knew she was there, helping them behind the scenes. They felt her spirit and her love.

"Thanks Mom. Thanks Nona," Morgan said. "And thanks Dad for being my guinea pig!"

"Guinea pig, lab rat. . .I'm all yours!" Michael laughed.

Miyah took her medicine bag and covered her own cedar box. "You're going to use your box for this," she explained. "I previously took the liberty of 'testing' it to see if it truly did maintain the same positive healing powers of my box, and am happy to report that it's identical."

"What else would you have expected?" Morgan asked.

"I don't know, but I needed to be sure it was still pure. It was lost for so long." Miyah also remembered the day when the box absorbed the dark energy of Robert into its shadows. She needed to know the box was clear of that energy and hadn't assimilated any of that negativity into its fabric. With the assistance of Nona, she was positive the box was back to its original character – that of a healing tool. No trace of Robert or his dark energy had been found. Wherever he "landed" in the abyss was a mystery that no one was interested in unraveling.

Morgan walked over and kissed her father on the forehead and then sat on a chair next to him.

"I love you, Dad," she said.

"Love you too, Sweetie," he replied. "Don't worry. You can do this," he said in encouragement.

"I know," she said with confidence this time. "Yes I can."

She leaned over and rubbed her hands respectfully on the lid of the box and began to chant the prayers her mother had taught her, slowly at first, and then she closed her eyes and let her senses take over. Her prayers flowed like a poem and her hands nearly glowed with the warmth she felt.

Even though it had been a long time, Michael was not at all apprehensive about his pending journey. He had put out an intention of his own and was hoping some important questions would be answered on this time travel. He watched intently and, like mother like daughter, it was as if Miyah were sitting there performing the ritual. Soon the strong smell of cedar permeated his consciousness and he saw the side of Morgan's cedar box begin to move as a theatre of people and landscapes drew across the panel in a performance that was beckoning him in. . .and he was gone, pulled back into the mists of time.

~~~~~

The glow from a few candles threw shadows on the wall of a mud house and people scurried around in the dim light of the room. As Michael's eyes grew accustomed to the subdued light, he realized the focus of attention was a woman across the room. She was thrashing and groaning and a maiden wiped the sweat from her brow as the woman's breathing quickened and she finally gave out a loud, long cry of pain. Suddenly Michael heard the innocent cry of a baby, quivering in the arms of the midwife hovering over the woman.

"You have a son," she said. "A healthy son." She covered the child and placed him in his mother's arms. A man, the father, who had been by her side, helping in the delivery, reached over and tenderly touched his newborn son. The happy family seemed oblivious to anything else going on around them and Michael felt a bit intrusive. He quietly opened the door behind him and stepped outside.

"Where am I?" he wondered as he scanned the landscape. Suddenly he realized this place was familiar to him. He had been here before. He knew the land. He walked toward the sound of the waves clashing on the shore and stood before the sea, feeling as if he had just returned home from a long journey. Behind him were green, grassy knolls and large boulders. Beyond, along the horizon, was the outline of another island. He knew this place.

"Welcome home Michael!" a voice behind him said, clapping his hand on Michael's shoulder.

A startled Michael jumped and turned around. It was the man who had just attended the birth of his son.

"Joshua!" Michael exclaimed. "I'm so happy to see you again!" He joyfully embraced his friend, saying, "I hope I'm not intruding. I see you have a new son. Congratulations!"

"Thank you," Joshua said with pride. "Both the boy and Maryum are doing fine. She needs to rest now."

Michael's head was spinning. He had hoped to reconnect with Joshua, but was taken off guard with the birth and was trying to recall his history to pinpoint this time and place. After all, the last time he saw Joshua, he was a much older man. . .125-years-old. . .and he was dying. In fact, he died.

"It's confusing, isn't it?" Joshua offered, reading his thoughts. "You are obviously back into an earlier time of my life. You are on Innis nam Druidneach, the Island of the Druids, or as you know it, the Isle of Iona. You visited here before."

Joshua continued, "And you have just witnessed the birth of our son, John, or as he will come to be known, John Martin.

"This really is déjà vu," Michael stated. "We, my family, were just there, here, on Iona a few months ago on vacation. We learned a lot about John Martin and his generations of family on this island."

"Yes, I know," Joshua replied. "I saw you in meditation on the crest of Dun I hill, when my sons and I were in ritual with the Druid priests. Remember? I'm sorry for bouncing back and forth with you between time frames, Michael. Sometimes it's easier to explain things out of sequence. But here you are and you must have some questions to sort through. Come, sit down," Joshua motioned toward a cluster of large boulders edging the sea. "How can I help you?"

Michael followed him and sat down. He wasn't sure what to say. Usually Joshua did the talking and Michael's mission was to listen and learn.

Joshua noted his hesitation. "First let me tell you that I've been keeping an eye on you, Michael, you and your family—my lovely Miyah—and Morgan. She's making her ancestors proud. You've come a long way from the first visit we had all those years ago. I'm proud of you too, for your strength and your fortitude. I know you've been working on a special project and you still have a big job ahead of you, compiling all we have revealed to you throughout the years. I want you to know that it's time."

"Time? Time for what?" Michael asked.

"It's time for you to put your notes together and complete that book you've been working on. You've been preparing, outlining and researching, but now you must get serious and begin. Just write. There is much to say and your world is finally ready. It's time to fulfill the promise you made to Miyah when she first came to you, when she sent you to us for healing. That shall be your task when you return to your home. Write that book."

Michael knew he would have to put all his research together sooner or later. He had written chapters here and there of events that happened, but nothing cohesive enough to be put into book form. He'd have his work cut out for him. He knew he could no longer procrastinate. He did make a promise. . . one he intended to fulfill.

"What if no one wants to read it?" he asked sheepishly.

"You don't worry about that," Joshua laughed. "Your job is just to write it. Get it on paper, record it. The rest will be taken care of."

"Now that I have given you this message, I sense there's something you would like to know. It seems you set an intention for yourself before you journeyed back here today," Joshua intuitively asked.

"I don't know if this is appropriate or not," Michael started. "But I still have so many unanswered questions around the death of my parents. Why did someone kill them? Who? Can you tell me?"

"One of my most important teachings, Michael, is about forgiveness. Death is part of the cycle of life. It doesn't really matter now how your parents died, or even who was responsible. Would you seek revenge if you knew? Would you harbor hatred? Find solace in knowing that those people's actions will find justice in their own karma. It is beyond you. You must forgive and let it go. There's nothing to be gained by holding on to the past. I thought you learned that on Mt. Bugarach. It's difficult, I know, but in order for you to find peace, you must forgive. Your parents are with you in spirit. They love you. They had full, loving lives while on earth during this reincarnation. Find comfort in that. Even though you think there are still unanswered questions, they had completed their mission. Their work was finished. They raised two wonderful children, you and your sister. Both your parents had successful careers that made a difference and influenced people's lives, even if they may not have realize it, and your father did some very important work that is destined to continue in other ways that you will understand some day."

Michael sat silently and listened to the rhythm of the waves. This was not the answer he was hoping for.

"I do have some information I believe you'll be interested in, Michael." Joshua said softly. "It's about your own bloodline."

"My bloodline?" Michael questioned. "I don't know much beyond my parents and grandparents. It never occurred to me to do a genealogy." He stood and shifted his feet into the white sand.

"Well, that isn't necessary," Joshua replied. "All you really need to know is where your deepest roots come from. Have you ever wondered why you were given privileges into my life the way you have—beyond your documentation and research?"

"Yes. All the time. I've felt so honored," Michael quickly responded. "But I thought it was so I could write the story of your bloodline."

Joshua chose his words carefully. "You just witnessed the birth of my son, John. Why do you suppose that is so?"

"I don't know what you're getting at, Joshua" Michael replied, a bit confused. He had gotten many revelations from Joshua in the past, but he didn't understand what he was alluding to this time.

"Michael. John, my son John, is *your* ancestor. You are from his bloodline."

Michael was dumbfounded. "But," he stammered. "But that would mean that I. . .I am of. . .of your bloodline. How is that possible? Miyah. Miyah is of your bloodline. . ." he could barely get the words out before he had to sit back down on the boulder. "Miyah and I are related?" he blurted out!

"Why are you so shocked? Miyah is from the lineage of our daughter Sera, as you are from the line of our son John."

"But doesn't that make us cousins or something?" Michael was grasping for reality.

"If you consider cousins, 2,000 years removed. . .which would make practically everyone in these times related one way or another. Don't worry, Michael. There is no incest here. You and Miyah loved each other as my children and throughout the ages you have been connected in many lifetimes. Now, generations later, you have found each other again and love each other in your union as husband and wife. It's as it was meant to be. You are connected by the bloodline and also by the red thread of destiny. You are soulmates."

"How. . .how. . .?" Michael began to ask and then paused. "That might explain why my mother wrote about her and Junia being soul cousins. She must have known! My God, she must have known and never told me! Did she have the same healing gifts as Junia's family?" He turned to Joshua.

"Your mother came from the bloodline of John, the masculine side of the family. Junia is of the bloodline of Sera, the feminine side. It was mainly the descendents of that feminine side who worked with the Touchstone energies. Your mother healed in many other ways—through her words and deeds. She made children laugh with the children's books she wrote. She made people think and use their wit in her mystery novels. Everything was layered in a message. Healing comes in many forms, Michael. You are a healer, too, following the footsteps of your mother, using words to soothe, encourage and inspire. Just think back on the subjects of all the articles you've written over the past years and you'll find a thread of healing woven into every one of them. Don't disregard your abilities, Michael. Your talents come from a long line of healers too. We all carry our own gifts within us."

Joshua watched Michael to be sure he was absorbing all this. "What you need to understand is how important this is to the children. . .the child of your union–Morgan. Coming from a double line of my offspring, her ties to our Touchstone of healers is stronger than most. You and Miyah were chosen for this child and you have both taught her well. The world in your time, in all its turmoil, will need her strength as a healer and a leader. She, along with her Touchstone cousins, will be a public voice for our story when new spiritual truths are revealed. She is strong. She will prevail."

Michael had no words.

Joshua stood up. "I should be getting back to Maryum and my new son. We are fortunate to have traveled here to this island for the birth. His legacy will be carried on here far into the future. . .as you well know."

Michael realized why he had been drawn to this tiny island and had such an urge to return. It's where his roots were. . .as a generational son of John, who was born here. . .and as a grandson of Joshua. How could he, Michael, ever be so deserving?

"Wait, Joshua," Michael called after him. "Does Miyah know this? She's always said how important a role Morgan would have in the future. Does she know?"

"She does now," Joshua said with a smile, knowing her vision was clear and she was seeing all that had transpired. "Both Miyah and Morgan."

"Wait!" Michael called again, running after him.

"I. . .I just want to thank you. . .and to tell you how much I love you," he stuttered.

Joshua wrapped his arms around Michael like a father and replied, "I love you too, Michael. I always will. And, although you may not realize it, you have some very special intuitive 'gifts' yourself. You might start allowing them to come through. You are, after all, my grandson."

Michael's head was swirling. He had a hard time putting this in context. He was of Joshua's bloodline! He, Michael! Just like Miyah. He watched as Joshua walked back to the hut where his family awaited him. He wanted to run after him and join him and stay with him longer. He had such an overwhelming feeling of being loved that he thought he would burst. And within that feeling of elation, came reality, as the mist from the sea enshrouded him and he returned to a familiar world.

~~~~~~

Michael lay on the sofa, not moving. When he finally opened his eyes, he rolled over slowly and saw both Miyah and Morgan staring at him, wide-eyed. No one said a word.

"You didn't know?" he finally said to Miyah as he sat up, the blood rushing to his head. "I can't believe it."

Morgan could no longer hold back her emotions. She got up and practically knocked her father over as she embraced him. "You're back! I heard it all! All that Joshua just said to you! What incredible news, Dad," she said. "We really are a trio of healers!"

"I. . .I guess so," Michael answered, keeping his eyes on Miyah for her reaction. She was just as stunned as he had been.

"No wonder we had such an immediate connection," she finally said, joining her family on the sofa. "I knew that first night when I came to heal you that we were connected somehow. Never did I dream that we were of the same bloodline! Welcome to the Touchstone family, Michael. I guess you've already been properly inducted! No wonder you were able to stick with me through all these years and accept all of my. . .of our," she motioned to Morgan, ". . .our demands, which I know at times might have seemed overbearing. Because you are one of us. You are. . .have always been . . . family." She lovingly put her arms around him.

Michael sat there, still a bit dumbfounded, shaking his head. "That's part of the reason my mother was allowed behind the veil at RoseVine. Why she was there when you were born. They knew they were related, so to speak. Mom knew she was of the bloodline, just like Junia. It's so complicated," he muttered.

"Yes," Miyah responded with a smile. "Complicated has always been a good way to describe our family."

"Ahhh, did you happen to notice that I—and my cedar box—got you back safely, Dad?" Morgan said, gently patting the top of her healing box.

"You did great," Miyah praised. "You've earned your graduation papers with flying colors. But don't think that anything you heard just now will get you any extra privileges around here," she added lightheartedly. "We've always known you were special."

"Yeah," Michael said with a grin. "We just didn't know how special."

18 *Morgan's Miracle*

Time seemed to go by quickly and the family settled in to a normal life, as normal as a Touchstone family could expect. Each kept busy with their own work, but found plenty of family time. They also worked on the "bucket list" they had made, doing things they said they would do some day, including going back to visit family and friends in France and Scotland several times. Elizabeth even made the journey with them once to see what Rennes-les-Bains was like, after hearing so much about their lives and family there. They were all happier than they had ever been.

After many phone conversations, John was finally convinced that he was ready to return to visit the States and those tough memories of the past. He decided it was time. Michael had reminded him to think only of the good memories he shared there with Paul, Kat and Junia. He also told him he was anxious to share the contents of his father's safe with him to find out more about their discoveries when they worked together. John wasn't sure if that's why he wanted to return, or if that was keeping him away. It was Margo, who had become more than just a friend to John, who finally convinced him that he should go and get to know his daughter better. Margo knew how important family was. She had obtained sole custody over her granddaughter, Bella. Bella's father had died when she was a baby and her mother recently died of a brain hemorage It was a sad situation, but John stepped in to help Margo with the child and their lives were truly blessed by the circumstances.

John insisted that Margo and Bella join him on his month-plus vacation. It had been a good visit and Miyah realized that she enjoyed getting to know her father. At first peeling away those layers of mistrust was a bit difficult, but after awhile, she found that he was a lot more sensitive and loving than she had expected. She wondered if his relationship with Margo had anything to do with it. It must have been difficult for him to let down his barriers and allow himself to love again. Of course, Miyah knew that little Bella most likely had a lot to do it.

Michael and John spent a lot of time in the bomb shelter going over the maps and artifacts Michael's father, Paul, had protected in his safe. John had stories about each item and Michael eagerly took notes, grateful for the information John was able to share with him. John had worked on archeological digs with Michael's father a lot more than Michael realized, not just the project at Mt. Bugarach. Michael also discussed the other maps with John and they made plans to possibly re-explore some of these regions in the near future. Even though John told Michael that being there and going over all of these memories of the past with him was almost like being with Paul again, there was still a lot of mystery. Most of it shrouded around the Bugarach treasure map. Michael felt that John wasn't telling all he knew. Was he still protecting his family from possible danger? Michael hoped that in time, John would spill it all out so he could collect all the puzzle pieces that perplexed him around the life. . .and the death of his parents.

Each day of their visit was filled with laughter. The entire family made day-trips to area attractions, spent lazy days rowing boats across a lake, enjoyed daily walks and playtime in the park across the street. They visited a traveling carnival, and made a couple of trips to ride the intricately hand-carved horses, giraffes and other animals on a nearby carousel. Morgan felt like she had a little sister and enjoyed revisiting all these places her parents had taken her to when she was a child. John and his new family extended their vacation and stayed longer than originally planned. Life seemed almost too perfect.

~~~~~

Miyah sat at the edge of her bed, combing through her long, silky hair. "My hair seems to be thinning a little with age," she said. "Maybe I should cut it all off, short," she mused. "It sure would be easier to care for."

"Don't you dare," Michael, laying next to her, raised himself up on his elbow. "I love your hair. Here, let me brush it," he said as he took the brush from her hand and gently ran it through the strands of her hair, down to the middle of her back.

"Don't worry. When you're too old to take care of it, I'll do it for you," he laughed. "I love brushing your hair. . .just don't tell anyone else that!" he added, reaching over to kiss the nape of her neck.

"I knew this would lead to more than hair grooming," Miyah said playfully, turning around to get his full attention. She teased, letting her robe slip off her shoulders. "You should do this. . .brush my hair, every night." Soon the brush was set aside and they were lost in playful passion, something neither of them had grown too old for. Quite the opposite. It was as if their passion had increased with the years and they were more in love than ever.

Michael sighed, resting next to her naked body. "You're just as beautiful as the day I met you. Have I ever told you that?"

"Yes, dear. All the time. . .but don't ever stop," she laughed. "I'll never tire of hearing it!"

"I want this to last forever," he said, running his finger between her breasts and onto her stomach. "Promise me," he whispered as his kisses followed the trail he had just made. "Promise we'll be together forever," he repeated.

"I'll always be with you," Miyah answered, arching her back in response to his touch. "I'll always be with you," she repeated, knowing that "forever" was an impossible word. Michael lost himself in her and they made love passionately into the night, and then slept peacefully in each other's arms.

The next morning Miyah awoke before Michael. She rolled over and watched him sleep for awhile, gently caressing his forehead. She loved this man so much that tears stung her eyes.

Quietly slipping out of bed, she picked her hairbrush up from the floor where it had ended up the night before. She ran the brush quickly through her hair, cleaned the brush out and rolled the wad of hair into a little ball. She pulled her hair back into a pony tail, put on a pair of jeans and a sweater and headed downstairs. She had a lot of things she wanted to do today.

Miyah headed out to the garden. Morgan was there to greet her. It had become their ritual each morning to meet in the garden and meditate together. It was a good way to begin the day.

"Are the others awake yet?" she asked her daughter.

"I don't think anyone is up, but I already have the teapot on," Morgan replied, as they got comfortable on their cushions and into position for their morning ritual.

Before Miyah began, she took the little puff of hair she had retrieved from her hairbrush and threw it out into the yard for the songbirds to use in their nests. Immediately a magpie, flying from right to left, swooped down and collected her gift, flying it up to a distant nest. Miyah gasped. It was believed that if a magpie built a nest with a person's hair, that person would meet an untimely death. Was this an omen or a mere coincidence? Miyah shuddered and recalled years ago when she had burned some of her hair in a candle ritual. The smoke grew dark as the candle faded—another bad omen. But it had been years and everything was good. She remembered Michael's request of "forever" from the night before.

Morgan, too, saw what had transpired and silently watched her mother's reaction. She recognized the bad omen and hoped she could counter it with some special prayers in her meditation.

"How is time measured?" Miyah inwardly questioned, purposely shrugging off these warnings.

Time had indeed been good to them. Morgan continued to prove herself as an exceptional young woman. She had joined Miyah and her friends in their healing practice and was making quite a reputation for herself. She mastered using the cedar box to unleash its healing powers, even though, since that day with her father, she had never "sent" anyone back into the past to meet with Joshua. It was as if access to that domain was no longer required. Michael had been privileged because of his genealogy, but now the energy of Morgan's cedar box was all that was needed to obtain results, that and the healing powers of its owner.

Michael had tackled his writing with zest and even though he knew it would take time to put all of his research, notes and personal experiences together, he was determined to stay the course, anxious for the day when his book would come together in real chapters and make some semblance of sense.

Elizabeth and Bob had married, and after a honeymoon in the south of France, settled in New Hampshire near his family. Michael missed his sister, but was glad that she had a full and happy life. They kept in touch.

And now they had reconnected with Miyah's father—with John and his new family, Margo and Bella.

Yes, time had been good to all of them.

~~~~~~

Other than the magpie incident earlier that morning, everything was perfect. Everyone stirred and rallied for a big family breakfast, followed by a morning of gardening and grooming the yard. It didn't take long to complete their task with everyone helping, and they were soon sitting in the shade with tall glasses of lemonade, admiring their handiwork.

"I always marveled at how Kat landscaped this garden for minimal maintenance," John commented. "Yet, they both loved to be out here working with the plants and the flowers. I think it was good therapy for them."

"It was good therapy for the entire family," Michael added. "As kids, I can't remember Lizzy or I ever complaining about helping with the gardening. It was a good family project."

"Just like today," Morgan added.

"Yes, just like today," Michael said, reaching over to pat her hand. "Thanks for your help. All of you. Thanks."

"It was fun," John admitted, adding, ". . .working together as a family."

"Can we go to the park now?" a voice said from behind his lawn chair. Bella, with a smudge of dirt on her face, was patiently waiting for her daily jaunt to the playground in the park across the street.

"Everything looks really pretty," she added, looking around.

"Yes! How could we forget the park?" John said, jumping up to take her hand.

"First, let's get that smudge washed off your face. I'll go with you too," Margo said, getting up to join her little family.

"Yippee!" Bella squealed as she ran toward the house. "Let's go to the park!"

"Wait for me!" Morgan called out, following behind them.

"You go ahead," Michael said, getting up from his chair. "I have some emails and things I need to check. I'll see you all later."

"I think I'm going to go for a jog around the park while they're at the playground," Miyah said.

"We're so lucky to have that park right across the street from us. It's always been like our private stomping ground," Michael chuckled.

Miyah gave her husband a hug and he responded with a tender kiss. "I love you," he said spontaneously.

"You too," she said as she went in to change her shoes. "Join us when you're done with your work."

"Will do," he replied.

~~~~~~

The sound of children's laughter always made Miyah smile. As she ran her laps around the two acre park, she could hear the squeals and joyful screams of the children flying high on the swings, twirling dizzily on the go-round, or sliding fast down the giant, tunnel slide. How could anyone not respond with joy to that melodious miracle of innocent laughter?

She slowed her pace as she neared the playground. Kids were always running across the jogging path as they played, or chasing after get-away balls. John and Margo sat on a bench watching Bella and they waved to Miyah as she neared.

Nearby a few older kids were playing with a big, red kickball. One of the boys aggressively kicked the ball and it flew into the air, over the top of the swings and out into the street. Miyah saw, out of the corner of her eye, a young girl jump down off her swing seat and run to retrieve the ball for the boys. She didn't want the red ball to get away and was clearly on a mission to save it.

Then it was as if everything happened in s l o w m o t i o n. . .

Miyah saw a car speeding down the street. She could see the boy behind the wheel, a young teenager, was not paying attention to his driving. His radio was blasting loud rock music with the bass vibrating into the air with a wild drumbeat. And the teen was looking down. . .texting a message to his friends. Miyah knew what was about to happen and projected herself to the scene. She sent out a message of "Stop!" to the driver and his car came to a screeching halt. But it was too late. He looked up just as he heard a thump connect with his front bumper.

A shrill cry came from the little girl as she found herself on the other side of the street, scraped and bleeding from her fall. Crowds quickly gathered from the park and John ran over and scooped Bella up into his arms.

"Is she OK?" Margo's shaking voice asked. "Is anything broken?" she cried. "Oh, baby, are you OK? Please God, let her be OK."

Bella put her arms around John's neck and clung to him, shaking and sobbing. She cried as she asked, "Is she dead? She pushed me away. She saved me. Is she dead?"

John and Margo had been so focused on Bella that they hadn't noticed anything else around them. They looked behind them to where Bella was pointing and saw the crowd gathered around a woman on the ground in a pool of blood.

"Oh God," John said, handing Bella to her grandmother. "God. No!"

"Don't touch her," someone yelled. "Don't move her," but Michael was already there, bending over his wife, cradling Miyah in his lap, rocking back and forth. He had been on his way to the park when he saw the accident play out—the red ball rolling into the street and Bella right behind it, in line with the car as it sped toward her, and suddenly the form of Miyah, flying in from nowhere, into Bella's place, pushing her away from disaster.

"Do something, Morgan," Michael begged. "Fix her. Pleeeeease. Morgan, Nona. . .please. . ." he pleaded between his sobs. "This can't be happening. Miyah don't die. You can't die. . .Miyah!"

Morgan knelt down next to her mother and put her hands on her head. She forced herself to shake away her own state of shock and pulled together all the energy she could. She summoned her cedar box and it appeared, like magic, in front of her. She was suddenly aware of the crowd of children and adults surrounding them, and with the wave of her hand, she froze them in time. It was only herself and her father moving in real time in the spaces between the minutes. Morgan tended to her mother, who was breathing shallowly as she fought for her life, her broken body spread out on the hot pavement.

Morgan passed her hands over Miyah's broken leg and a bone, which had been exposed, melded itself back into place and her leg straightened from its angled position. She scanned her hands over other parts of Miyah's body and her frame shifted, as if the bones in her spine and her hip bones that had been crushed during the impact, seemed to miraculously go back into place and mend themselves. Morgan held her hand to her mother's heart, saying prayers that came out of thin air, over and over again. . .prayers of healing, of love, of hope, of desperation.

"Nona, Joshua, Maryum. Spirits, ancestors, guides, power animals, all be here now. Heal the broken body of Miyah. Make her well. Please, don't take her away. You can't take her away. I summon all of you. Help her, help me to heal her. Help us. . ." She opened her cedar box and it was as if she was frantically scooping something out of it and rubbing it over her mother's body. She put her hand on Miyah's forehead and covered her face with the invisible healing energy.

"Make this a miracle. She has so much yet to do on this earth. I need her. We need her. Heal her. Give me the wisdom and the strength to make her well. I'll do whatever you want, just, please, save her. Help me! Help me!" Morgan was shaking.

"Nona! Joshua!" Michael called out. "Help Morgan. Help Miyah. Please save her. Don't let her go!" He wept. "Forever, Miyah. We said we'd be together forever. Don't leave me. Don't leave me."

Through the blur, Miyah saw her husband and daughter hovering over her and could hear their frantic calls. She saw Morgan moving her hands around her and could feel the healing energy permeate her body like a warm blanket. She no longer felt any pain.

She saw Nona, Joshua and Maryum standing at her feet, holding their hands out to her, serenely smiling, welcoming her. A beam of light extended from their fingertips toward her, waiting for her to connect with them.

Miyah could hear the desperate prayers and the attempts to heal her coming from her daughter, and the sobs of Michael as he rocked her in his arms. She felt so loved on both sides. She wasn't sure what to do.

"Is this the way it ends?" she asked Joshua, reaching into the stream of light to take his hand. "Is my time on earth finished? Is my Touchstone journey at an end?"

"You have a lot of questions for one in such a position," he answered. "You, of all people, who has led a life of helping others cross over, are questioning your own time?"

"I. . .I just wanted to do so much more," she said, looking back lovingly at her family. "I know there's more for me to accomplish. . .so much more for me to do. . ."

"Do I understand you're asking for that second chance you have so often brought to others?" Joshua asked.

"Look at Morgan," Nona said, nodding back at the image playing out below them. "She's working so hard. She's doing everything right. Your teachings with her are complete, Miyah. You're free to let go, if you so choose."

"If I so choose," Miyah repeated.

"It's so beautiful," she said, looking around her. "It's so peaceful and loving here."

"The journey of a soul is woven with choices and free will," Joshua said. "You have lived a life of a good Samaritan. Your heart is pure, your passage of years on earth has been filled with enlightenment. But you have completed your life's purpose at this time."

Miyah looked into Joshua's compassionate eyes with understanding.

"You know the veil between our worlds is thin and the window of time open to you for choosing is now. You can surrender to the light and stay with us at this time, or you can return to your world."

Visions of Joshua, Maryum and Nona brightened as Miyah felt their love glowing all around her. She looked at Michael and Morgan below her, feverishly working to revive her depleted body. She loved them both so much, yet she felt no regrets, no sadness or pain. . .just love. . .pure love.

"I said I'd never leave him," she said to Nona, seeing the anguish on Michael's face.

"You can be with him, and with Morgan, in many ways," Nona replied. "You know that from your own experiences."

Miyah smiled. She was so peaceful in that moment.

~ ~ ~ ~ ~ ~

For Michael and Morgan, those moments, frozen in time, seemed like an eternity. Morgan pulled in every spell, every positive thought, every prayer, every healing ritual she knew. She called on the healing powers of the cedar box to work a miracle.

Michael prayed, calling to Joshua to come to them and help. He didn't know Joshua was answering his calls—but he was there for other reasons. He was there to bring his daughter home. Sometimes prayers are answered, but the answer might be not be what you expected.

The crowd, still fixed in a state of limbo, seemed black and white to Michael's vision. Suddenly a large, red ball came rolling through the crowd, stopping next to him. Following it was a little girl in a blue and yellow sundress with bloody scrapes on her elbows and knees. Bella knelt down next to Michael, across from Morgan. She stared at Miyah, limply cradled in Michael's arms.

"Is she dead?" Bella innocently whispered.

Michael lowered his head and sobbed uncontrollably.

Bella moved closer and put her hands on Miyah's face. Michael reached out to brush her away, but Morgan intuitively put her hand out for him to let her be.

"Miyah," Bella said. "Miyah are you there? It should have been me, not you. I'm sorry the car hit you. You saved my life. You have to wake up so I can thank you. I want you to wake up. . .and so does Junia," she said, placing the doll she had been carrying onto Miyah's chest. It was the old doll that Papa Tom had given Morgan as a child, but when Morgan gifted Bella with the doll, Bella had named it Junia, unaware of its namesake.

Michael stared at her. He knew this child was incarnate of Junia's soul, but he understood that there would be no trace of Junia's past life in her. Were the family ties so strong that the soul of Junia was also calling out to heal her daughter? Michael held on to every thread of possibility he could.

Completely spent of emotion, Morgan put her head on her mother's breathless chest and clutching the doll in her hands, she cried. "I love you Mommy, I love you. Wake up," she sobbed. "I'm sorry I failed you. I healed your broken bones, but I can't save you. Why can't I save you? Please wake up. It can't be your time. It can't be. I need you!"

While Michael and Morgan mourned, Bella kept her eyes fixed on Miyah. She was too young to understand death, and still believed her "Auntie Miyah" would awaken. She kept patting Miyah's face gently, as if to revive her from her sleep.

Suddenly Morgan raised her head and put her hand on her mother's chest. She thought she could feel her body moving up and down, slightly, but enough to indicate that she might be breathing. Morgan began sending positive healing energy into her mother's body, concentrating on maintaining her breathing and bringing her back to consciousness.

"She's waking up, isn't she?" Bella said excitedly. "I knew she would wake up! I haven't thanked her yet."

Michael raised his head and wiped the tears from his eyes. He realized that Morgan had resumed her healing work on Miyah and saw that she had begun to breath again.

"What can I do?" he shouted. "Tell me what to do!"

"Just hold her, Dad. Hold her and send her love. Send her enough love to bring her back. That's all we can do right now. . .just send her all your love."

Michael held his wife in his arms, rocking her back and forth and he thought he could physically feel the warmth and life gradually coming back into her body.

"Come back Miyah. That's right, come back to us. We love you. We love you. Come back," he said over and over again.

Miyah's body twitched.

"Just lay still, Miyah. Just lay still. We're here," Michael said. "Morgan is taking care of you. You're going to be OK," he repeated, stroking her hair with his hand. "We love you. You're going to be OK."

Miyah weakly opened her eyes and her vision began to slowly clear as she saw the faces of Michael and Morgan looking over her. She could feel their love, trying to draw her back into their world.

"It's a miracle!" Bella shouted. "Morgan made a miracle!"

Then she whispered, bending close to Miyah's face to be sure she heard her words. "Thank you Auntie Miyah. Thank you for saving my life,"

"Bella," Miyah managed to reply, each word an effort. "I'm. . .glad. . .you're safe."

"I'm sorry you got hurt," Bella said sadly. "It was because of me."

"It's. . . not your. . . fault."

Her gaze returned to Michael and Morgan. "I. . . love you both. . .so much," she whispered to them. "I'll always. . .be with you. Forever. . .in my heart."

"I love you too," Michael and Morgan said in unison.

"Stay with us. Don't leave again," Michael said trying not to sound panicky, as he felt the slightness in her breath.

"I saw you. . .working on me. . .Morgan," she whispered. "I'm so. . . proud of you." Her voice faltered. "I love you," she repeated. "I love you all . . .so much. Forever. . .Michael. . .forever," she whispered. "The light it's. . .

so beautiful. . .so peaceful. . ."

"Come on Mom. We need you here. Be strong. You can do this. Stay with us!" Morgan cried with anxiety—all the while knowing in her heart that her mother had just come back to say goodbye.

Miyah's eyes fluttered and she drew her last breath, lying there in Michael's arms.

Everything was still for just a moment, as Michael and Morgan looked at each other in hopelessness and grief. And then, as if on cue, the crowd around them came back to life, from black and white to color, and the street was busy with the sound of people asking what had happened. The whine of a siren drowned out the chatter as an ambulance neared the scene. John pushed through the crowd and knelt at Miyah's side.

"Oh God, is she alive?" he anxiously asked. "Is my daughter alive?"

Bella put her hand on her Uncle John's shoulder.

"Morgan made a miracle and Auntie Miyah woke up," she announced. "I told her thank you for saving my life before she went to sleep again. She said she loved us. I know she meant you too, Uncle John. I know she meant she loved you too."

19 Treasuring the Magic

The next few days were a blur. Elizabeth and Bob immediately flew in from New Hampshire and took charge of arrangements that had to be made—the cremation, a "celebration of life" gathering for their small circle of friends and friends of Morgan's, as well as contacting family in France and organizing a family farewell in Rennes-les-Bains at a future date.

Margo helped with household duties and tried to keep Bella busy so she wouldn't be too traumatized by what had happened. As soon as the funeral was finished, Margo planned to return to Scotland with Bella. She knew she'd need to use all her mothering skills, loving the child so much that she wouldn't be emotionally scarred. She didn't realize how resilient children are, and that Bella was probably the most stable of the entire group right now. John was pretty much useless, he was in so much agony. He disappeared into the bomb shelter and only came up when necessary. He couldn't deal with any of this.

Michael was grateful for everyone's help as he was in such deep mourning, he couldn't think straight.

"I can't believe this happened," he lamented.

"We made love that last night," he said to Morgan as they huddled together on the sofa in the library, wanting to be alone in their grief. "I told her I wanted our lives together to last forever. She said she'd always be with me. *She said she'd always be with me...*"he stressed in a trance-like state. "Do you think she knew this was going to happen?"

Morgan was just as lost, holding on to her dad for strength. "I don't think so. We had plans to meet Barbara and Monica that evening to prepare some herbs," her voice trailed off.

"The magpie!" She suddenly jumped up. "The magpie!"

"What?" Michael responded. "What magpie?"

"When we were getting ready to meditate that morning, a magpie swooped down and took a ball of Mother's hair and tucked it into its nest," Morgan said, running out into the back yard.

"I don't understand what that has to do with anything," Michael said, following her, wondering if his daughter was delirious from her anguish.

"Don't you see? It was an omen. A bad omen. I knew it and so did Mother. I even meditated on it to reverse the negative energy. Mother seemed to ignore it, as if she didn't want to face any messages it might be bringing."

Morgan picked up some stones from the garden and frantically started throwing them at the nest. A magpie flapped its wings and flew from its perch on a nearby branch, squawking in protest.

"Give it back!" she shouted. "Give my mother's hair back!" She kept throwing rocks, hysterically trying to dislodge the bird nest.

Michael ran over and grabbed her, attempting to pin her arms to her side. "Calm down Morgan. You can't believe that your mother died because a magpie put some of her hair in its nest. Surely the bird couldn't have caused that accident."

Morgan, suddenly aware of her emotional outburst, just stood there, staring at her dad. He gradually loosened his grip.

"No, you're right. The bird didn't cause the accident. It was just warning her that something bad was coming. She chose to ignore it. She didn't want to face it."

"Would things have been any different if she had?" he asked.

"I don't know," Morgan replied, "I really want to believe so. . ."

Then Morgan, who thought she didn't have any tears left in her, began to cry uncontrollably.

"I failed! Don't you see? I failed," she cried. "Dad! I couldn't save her! It's my fault. I couldn't save her! I'm not a healer. I couldn't even save my own mother!"

Michael held her to him. "Shhh," he said. "Morgan. Shhh. You know that's not true. You did everything you could. I saw you mending those broken bones, putting them back in place and I saw you healing other parts of her, taking away her pain. How can you doubt yourself?"

"How?" Morgan was almost in hysterics. "Dad! Because she died! That's how! She died! Don't you understand? I couldn't save her!"

"And why, Morgan, do you think you have the power over life and death of another person's being?" a voice from behind them asked. Both Morgan and Michael turned to see Joshua standing beneath the big oak tree in the center of the yard.

"Joshua!" Michael called out and the two of them ran toward him, as if he were there to bring Miyah back to them. But there were no welcoming hugs, or even a familiar smile.

"Morgan," Joshua repeated, waiting for an answer. "Why do you think it was your choice to save her?"

"I. . .I'm a healer. I should have been able to save her," Morgan replied.

"But what about the *will* of your mother? Have you considered that?"

"You mean she wanted to die? She wanted to leave us?" Morgan questioned with doubt.

"You know as well as I do that she didn't *want* to leave you," Joshua said sternly. "I'm surprised at you, Morgan, with all the lessons you've had—and you too, Michael, with all the teachings you've received, that you are both in such denial about death when it touches your own lives. Do you forget that Miyah spent a lifetime helping others cross over to the other side? Yes, she helped offer second chances, as with you Michael, but those second chances weren't for her to decide. The choice was to be made by each individual being.

"Miyah didn't need a second chance, because she had already fulfilled her life's purpose on earth and it was her time to leave. . .to return to our dimension. It's that simple. It was her time. You are a healer, Morgan. Don't ever doubt yourself. You healed Miyah's body and took away her pain, but her soul wasn't yours to keep. I know you both miss her because you love her, but instead of mourning your loss, celebrate the life of Miyah, knowing she ended her time on earth offering the ultimate sacrifice—saving the life of another. It may seem tragic and traumatic to you, but it was an honorable death.

"Celebrate the hundreds, thousands of people Miyah touched—healed, helped and inspired during her lifetime. Smile when you think of her and be happy for her commitment to life. Rejoice in how much she loved and how the light of her soul warmed the hearts of so many."

Joshua kept talking. "Everyone dies. It's the cycle of life. You know Miyah would want you both to go on and live your own lives to the fullest. You each have commitments to fulfill, your own life's purpose. Get on with it. Make her proud. Love Miyah, but celebrate her, don't waste the precious minutes of your lives feeling sorry for yourselves because she's not here. She'll always be with you. . ."

Michael interrupted. "That's what she said! 'I'll always be with you.' That's what she said to us. Does that mean she'll be able to appear to us like you are now?" he asked with hope.

"Like Nona does?" Morgan added.

"She may, but not until after a transition period. She has just shed her earthly body and must adjust to her spirit form. It will take some time, but she'll make herself known to you when it's appropriate. Even if you can't see her now, you'll feel her with you. Allow yourself to feel. Don't close down in your grief. You have each other, you have family and your own healthy bodies. Both of your parents have crossed over, Michael, and you must have felt their presence from time to time."

"Yes," Michael slowly replied, recalling how he knew his parents were there on his and Miyah's wedding day. "Yes, I have," he simply said. "Thank you Joshua," he conceded.

"I know that grieving is a natural part of losing a loved one," Joshua admitted. "But most people grieve for themselves—for no longer having the person they love there to hold and to talk with. Grieve for yourselves if you must, but keep it brief. I don't mean to sound harsh, but life must move along and nothing will be gained by your depression. Most of all, don't grieve for Miyah. Her life was remarkable. I'm so proud of her. Be proud of her too." he said.

"I am," Michael quickly responded.

"I am too," Morgan said. "Of course you're right. I know all of this. It's just so much harder when it happens in your own life. I miss her so much already."

"That's OK," Joshua replied. "Miss her. You're allowed. Love her. Honor her. Remember her—every part of her being, every part of your lives together. But let that bring you joy, not grief. She wants you to remember her in joyfulness, not in sadness. Do you understand this?" he asked.

"Yes," they replied.

"Then come, my children," Joshua said, stretching out his arms to embrace them. "Feel the love I have for you and the love Miyah is sending to you this very moment. Celebrate her life with me in these blessings."

Joshua closed his eyes and held both Michael and Morgan in his arms for moments that seemed like an eternity. A warm glow of love permeated their bodies and a peacefulness came over both of them, a healing calmness. When they opened their eyes, they felt as if they had awakened from a deep sleep, a sleep which had revived and restored their bodies. . .their very souls.

"Farewell, my children," Joshua said as he began to vanish. "Celebrate Miyah. She so deserves a celebration."

~~~~~

Morgan hadn't been to RoseVine many times without her mother, but today she went alone. She wanted to retrieve an antique vase for use as an urn to hold Miyah's ashes. It had been a favorite of Miyah's, a treasure she bought on one of their many trips to Paris. Morgan pensively walked around the house, lingering with her memories. It seemed so empty without her mother. Morgan's footsteps seemed to echo in the hallways, reaffirming her desolate feeling. She slowly collected photographs and other things she wanted to place on the altar for the ceremony. Included were some small, ornate, hand-blown glass perfume bottles from Egypt. None had ever held perfume and Morgan wasn't sure who had actually collected them, but they were favorites of her mother's and Morgan had plans for them.

"It's so quiet," she thought. "It's as if the spirits in this old house are honoring mother with their silence." Or, she reflected, "maybe they're preparing to welcome her home." The thought of Miyah's spirit joining the wise ancestors of RoseVine who had taught her, taught them both, and continued to work their healing magic through the veils of time, gave Morgan solace. It was a beautiful thought and she actually smiled as she vanished to return home with her collection of mementos.

~~~~~~~~

Joshua's visit was on the minds of both Michael and Morgan as an informal celebration was about to get underway in the garden at Michael's house a few days later.

Miyah and Michael didn't have a very large circle of friends, so the service celebration was to include John, Margo and Bella, Monica, Barbara, Jonna and their children, friends of Morgan. A couple of longtime neighbors who knew Michael's parents, had asked to attend out of respect for his family and they brought other neighbors with them, the community Michael talked about, but didn't realize existed in his own neighborhood. Elizabeth and Bob were there, as well as Bob's family from New Hampshire, who insisted on being there to support their daughter-in-law and her family. Michael wanted it to be a celebration of Miyah's life, as Joshua had suggested, but he also wanted it to be brief and informal. He thought Miyah would have preferred it that way.

A few chairs had been set out under the shade trees in the back yard and an area of the garden was arranged with an "altar," holding the vase of Miyah's ashes, her medicine bag containing the cedar box and her diary, the healing stone and other meaningful items. Photographs were placed on a nearby table. Included was a childhood picture of Miyah, Junia, Nona and Papa Tom, and other photos of Miyah that Michael had taken in Paris and on their travels. He had spent hours sorting through his photos deciding which to print. He wanted them all there, all the memories. . .but knew he could only choose a few. Two photos of Miyah and Michael's wedding were included. One of just the two of them and another with the two of them and a man, Miyah's father, John, watching them proudly in the background. There were several family photos of Miyah, Michael, Morgan and Elizabeth. Morgan had also added the old photo from Miyah's diary of Kat, Paul, Junia and John—her grandparents, to the row of memories.

Just as Michael stepped forward to say a few words, he heard the side gate squeak and clang open. He looked up and saw person after person filing into the back yard. Soon, the entire yard was full of people. . .and priests, Michael had never seen before. Each reverently bowed his or her head toward Michael as they entered, finding a place to stand in the now crowded yard.

Michael was perplexed until he heard a voice in his head, the voice of Nona. "It's some of the people Miyah has healed over the years," she explained. "They've come to pay their respects."

Michael was so overwhelmed, he had to blink back the tears.

"Welcome," he said. "Welcome friends of Miyah."

He looked at his brief notes and realized that it wasn't enough. All these people were here to honor Miyah. How did they know? As soon as everyone was settled, he put down his notes and spoke from his heart.

"Miyah came to me years ago when I was dying of cancer. I wasn't a very nice person then. I was angry and self-absorbed—which my sister, Liz, will no doubt, confirm," he gestured to Elizabeth and she smiled slightly, shaking her head at his comment.

"I know I was a challenge, but Miyah saw things in me that I didn't know existed. It didn't take me long to fall in love with her. What surprised me, was that she loved me back. She not only healed my cancer, but she took me on a journey that I never would have imagined possible. A journey of life that could only play out with Miyah at my side. She was beautiful, gifted, compassionate, honest, humorous, playful, loving, giving. . .she was amazing. Words aren't adequate enough to describe Miyah. She was my best friend."

Michael paused, clearing his throat, fighting to hold back his tears.

"A wise man told me not to mourn for Miyah, but rather to celebrate her. So I don't mourn for Miyah today. She had a blessed life. She gave of herself and her healing talents to anyone who needed her and she did it without hesitation, with love. . . so much love. I mourn for myself because I'm lost without her by my side. There's a hole in my heart," Michael's voice faltered, "but all around that hole pulsates the memories I have of Miyah and of our precious life together—and in those happy memories I find peace. She gave me many gifts—good health, strength, confidence, inspiration, eyes to see the world and beyond. . .and she gave me love. But the most important gift she ever gave me. . .is our daughter Morgan." Michael reached out for Morgan's hand and she joined him by the altar.

"Miyah touched, healed and inspired many," Michael continued. "Her life was truly filled with magic. Miyah was the magic.

"Thank you all for coming here today to honor Miyah. Thank you from my heart," Michael concluded, touching his fisted hand to his chest and bowing his head to the crowd gathered.

Morgan cleared her throat. She was touched by her father's words. "My father just said it all. The memory of my mother will never die. Her magic lives on in each of you. . .those she touched with her life and her healing. I only hope I can live up to her standards and make her proud of me. I love you, Mom," she said, looking up to the sky. "We all love you."

Morgan walked over and picked up an antique hourglass from the altar. "My mother gave me this," she said. "She told me it represented the hourglass of our family bloodline, with each generation sifting through the earth's cycle."

She turned the glass over and watched the tiny grains of sand filter through the narrow passage to blend again on the other side. "She used it to bring her peace when her mother, Junia, and her grandmother, Nona, died. And like these grains of sand, she said the next generation will always continue. . .and the next, and the next. . ."

Morgan placed the hourglass back on top of the medicine bag. She lingered a moment as her fingers traced the emblem Miyah had embroidered on the corner of the bag, the two joined M's that formed a diamond in the center for Morgan and the heart above, surrounded by roses and vines.

Then together, father and daughter opened the lid on the cremation vase and spread some of Miyah's ashes in her favorite flower bed, among the rows of gazanias Miyah had transplanted from Scotland. They returned the vase to the altar and each picked a gazania and placed them on the altar next to a photo of Miyah.

Elizabeth had planned on saying a few words, but she was so filled with emotion, she couldn't speak. Barbara, Monica and Jonna stepped forward together and talked about how they were honored to work with Miyah through the years and attested to the powerful healing abilities she possessed. They also told Morgan that they had no doubt she could fill her mother's shoes and they were there for her in every way.

Thinking the tributes were finished, Michael was ready to motion for everyone to join them for lemonade, but before he had a chance, a man from the crowd stepped forward.

"I came here today out of respect for Miyah. She healed me of leukemia, over ten years ago," he reverently said, nodding toward the altar and then went back to his place in the crowd, holding up a healing stone that Miyah had given him after he was healed.

One after another, men, women and children stepped forward, holding up their healing stones like a candle, and briefly gave their respects, relaying their connection with Miyah.

"Miyah saved me from a depressive suicide."

"She birthed all of my children."

"She saved my baby."

"She helped me through an abusive relationship."

"She healed my cancer."

"She restored my faith in God, in Jesus' true message, and I am honored – we are honored," he gestured to other priests in the crowded yard, "to be given insight into the bloodline and to have offered ourselves as family guardians."

All sat mesmerized at the lives Miyah had touched, realizing this was just a handful. When the last testimony was finally finished, John stood up. He had not intended to speak today because he was still in so much pain, but he was inspired by what he had just heard.

"I, ahh, I didn't really know my daughter, Miyah, until a short time ago, but I'm so grateful to have found her and, ahh, to have spent time with her recently. She was the best thing that ever happened in my life. I only regret, deeply regret, that I hadn't known her sooner. I, ahh, lost out on so much by not being in her life as she grew up," John said sadly, looking down at the ground.

He raised his head, "But listening to all of you here today, makes me know my daughter a little better, and I'm grateful for that. She was a remarkable woman, I know that. But you've just shared parts of her life that I didn't know much about. Thank you for your kind words and for the love we share of Miyah."

It was brief, but John needed to express himself. He sat back down next to Bella.

Bella looked up at her Uncle John. She reached over and patted his hand. Then she stood and slowly walked up in front of the crowd, as if it were her duty to add to the testimonials.

"It's my fault Auntie Miyah died," she said bluntly. "She died because she saved me from that car running over me. I know it's my fault." Everyone was silent.

Margo gasped and started to get up to stop her granddaughter from talking, but Morgan motioned to let her be.

Bella continued. "I felt bad because I really loved Auntie Miyah and I felt like I had known her for a long, long time. I didn't want her to die. But Morgan told me not to be sad. She said that everyone has to die sometime and she didn't think it was really my fault, it was just Auntie Miyah's time to die. She said I should instead be proud of her because she sacrificed herself for someone else. For saving me. So I want to promise that I'll be a really good girl until it's my time to die, because Auntie Miyah is an angel now, looking down at me. I want her to be proud of me and not to be sorry that she died to save me."

Bella walked over and pulled at a pink rose until it let go from its vine and she reached up to place it on the altar—a pink rose, Junia's favorite flower—the rose, a symbol of hope and an expression of beauty and grace. Pink for happiness, gentleness and sweetness. All that was Miyah.

With that, Bella sat back down between Margo and John and folded her hands. She'd said her piece. There wasn't a dry eye in the place.

Michael finally broke the silence. He thanked Bella, all those who had come forward to share their stories of Miyah, and everyone for coming. He directed them toward the patio for lemonade and lunch. Margo looked nervously at the meager sandwiches, salad, and fruit bowl she had prepared for only a few people. Michael glanced toward Morgan and she understood his message. With a wave of her hand, the buffet of food and pitchers of lemonade multiplied to miraculously feed everyone who had gathered in Miyah's honor.

Morgan looked back into the garden and smiled at Joshua and Maryum, standing near the altar. Joshua nodded to her in approval.

"That's my girl," he said proudly.

20 Final Tributes

John and his family returned to the Isle of Iona in Scotland shortly after the ceremony and Michael and Morgan joined them. It was only for a few days, but John, and especially Bella, were glad they had accompanied them.

Morgan had a few of the Egyptian perfume bottles filled with some of Miyah's ashes to be spread in places they knew she would approve of. Before they left, Michael spread ashes at RoseVine in the garden where they had first made love under the full moon of her spell, and said his own painful good-byes. Morgan placed a bottle of her mother's ashes among the books in the library at RoseVine and knew the spirits of her ancestors were welcoming her. Somehow she took solace in knowing that her mother would be with the spirits at RoseVine, among the teachers that had guided her in her Touchstone lessons.

But on the Isle of Iona there were no community tributes or ceremonies, only father and daughter privately saying their own prayers as they spread Miyah's ashes into the wind atop Dun I, the highest point on the island, an ancient site where Joshua had once studied with the Druid priests and priestesses. They stayed with John on the Isle of Iona only a few days and then traveled on to complete their mission.

Next they traveled to Paris, one of Miyah's favorite cities, where the family had often visited. Together Michael and Morgan went to the Church of Mary Magdalene, The Louvre and other sites that were meaningful to Miyah. And at night, as the Eiffel Tower blinked its lights in a silent tribute, they spread her ashes in the Seine River from the Ponte Alexandre Bridge, under the glow of globed lights, with gilded cherubs and winged horses looking on.

A huge family gathering awaited them in Rennes-les-Bains and Michael was amazed at all of the extended cousins, aunts and uncles who attended, along with friends the couple had made over the years. There were also many priests, some quite elderly. Michael smiled as he recalled the name "renegade priests," those who were sworn protectors of the family secrets. It was truly a celebration of life, more of a party, but Michael knew Miyah would have approved. It reminded him somewhat of Tomas' funeral, when people came to celebrate life, not to mourn death.

Morgan, having spent many of her summers here, was completely at home. Michael noticed that she wore the amber and copper beaded necklace he bought Miyah the first time they were in Rennes-les-Bains. He remembered Miyah wearing it on their wedding day and was glad that now Morgan cherished it as much as her mother had. She looked so much like Miyah. As he watched her milling through the crowd that came to pay their respects, the image of Miyah on their wedding day flashed through his mind and he felt Miyah's spirit there too, proudly watching their daughter. It made him dizzy with memories and he brought his hand to his heart as if to hold her there within him.

Michael saw how Morgan fit in here and knew it wouldn't be long before he would see less and less of her. He knew she belonged here too, with her peers, with her family of healers.

While in Rennes-les-Bains, Michael and Morgan had their own rituals, sprinkling Miyah's ashes in the Salz River behind Papa Tom's house, and then in the woods at the base of Throne of Isis, where Michael told Morgan of the visions her mother had there years ago.

"I know," Morgan said after he finished his story.

"Then why did you wait until I was finished to tell me?" he laughed.

"I love that story. Mom wrote it in her diary."

Michael was a bit surprised. He hadn't thought a lot about Miyah's own diary entries.

"What else did she write in the diary?" he asked.

"Oh, you already know everything, I'm sure," Morgan answered. "I can share it with you, but I'm not ready to read back through it right now. You understand, don't you?"

"Of course," Michael replied. "Of course I understand. I'm glad she added her own story to the legacy of the diary authors. She had so much wisdom to share."

Morgan got up into the seat of the stone chair, the Throne of Isis, and patted the cold rock beside her. Michael sat next to her and they spent the afternoon, sitting in the arms of Isis, sharing their own stories about Miyah. Sharing the love.

～～～～～

The next day Michael fired up Tomas' old black Cadillac and they drove up the hill to Rennes-le-Château. He had one more place he wanted to spread some of Miyah's earthly remains. This wasn't as much about the ashes themselves, as it was about cherishing places they had shared together, honoring important milestones of their lives.

Morgan knew this was a very personal mission for her dad, so she sat beneath the shade of a tree and watched from a distance as Michael slowly and reminiscently climbed the staircase of Magdala Tower, to the place where his and Miyah's wedding ceremony had taken place. He walked to the edge and stood for the longest time on top of the stone building, a patchwork of colors spread out over the valley below him. He reached back and pulled the binder out of his pony tail and let his hair blow with the wind. Miyah loved his long hair and had asked him never to cut it off. She said he reminded her of Joshua when it was down. After all, they were related.

Michael stretched out his arms and with all his might, shouted out the wedding vow he made to Miyah when they were married in this very place, almost twenty years ago.

"Miyah! You are the light of my life! You gave me back my life and I vowed to always be by your side, to protect you, take care of you, be your best friend and love you forever. The joy, the laughter, the passion, the feeling of elation when I saw your smile, is what I lived for each day."

His voice softened in the wind as his words choked. "I never knew what real living was until you came along. Thank you for generously sharing your special gifts and talents. You made the world a better place, just by being here."

His voice broke and he paused for a moment, resuming his vows in a quieter tone. "You rested on me. I was your rock. You are my family, my friend, my wife. I love you."

Then he added, "I will always love you. Forever, Miyah. I will never leave you."

He stood for a while with his eyes closed, the wind blowing through his hair, then he turned and poured some ashes on the spot where they actually said their vows. The wind didn't take them. They settled instead into the lines of the massive stone floor, as if to welcome a daughter of the bloodline home into the historic cracks of the old tower.

Morgan had been watching tearfully and put her arm around her father as he came down the steps. Wrapped up in their emotions, they were both surprised to see an elderly priest round the corner and silently motion them to come inside the tower. He didn't say anything to them, but led them to a shadowed wall, where he reached up and removed a flat, half stone from the wall, revealing a small open space behind it. The priest silently indicated for Michael to place the glass bottle of Miyah's remaining ashes into the "safe" in the wall. Michael hesitated.

Then the priest reached into his robe and produced a prayer card, handing it to Michael. He recognized it immediately. It was the same as the card given to them on their first Paris visit when they went to meet Papa Tom and were welcomed by the priests at the Church of Mary Magdalene, who told them they were always welcome there in time of need. On one side was a picture of Jesus in the garden with Mary Magdalene kneeling in front of him, and a crypt with the stone rolled away. Michael turned the card over to see a hand written note on the back, written in French. He knew what it said, but Morgan stepped forward to translate. *"Brothers in need have always been welcomed and served in this church. . ."*

"It's just like the card in Mother's diary," she said.

"Yes," the priest said, taking the card from her and placing it in the small, secret, stone vault.

"Let her ashes come home to rest with her bloodline."

Michael understood. He placed the Egyptian perfume bottle containing Miyah's ashes into the space in the wall. He wanted to add more to this small crypt—his Faith Stone, his wedding ring, a photo, but the priest quickly replaced the stone, brushed over the wall with his hands so no trace of residue would remain to give away its secret. Michael quickly realized it wasn't about him. It was Miyah's place.

"It is good. Bless you, my children," the priest said as he placed his hand on each of their heads. Then he turned and walked away.

Michael watched him leave. Looking back at the wall he, himself, couldn't tell which stone protected the ashes of Miyah. He wondered how many other stones in these walls held the secret remains of the bloodline, the DNA of Miyah's bloodline. Ashes, not bones, of Miyah's holy ancestors.

Magdala Tower
Rennes-les-Chateau, France

21   *Ending the Touchstone*

"It is as it shall be," Miyah had often said to Michael. Yet he so wanted to write parts of the story differently, hoping that segment of his life would re-write itself—that Miyah still lived and their lives continued happily ever after. But he knew that truth lay between the lines and this story was not his. He was only the messenger filling in the pages. The story was much bigger than he.

Michael eased his loneliness by committing himself to fulfilling his promise to Miyah. The spirits of the tribe of ancestors gathered around him each day as he worked on his book. They inspired him telepathically and discreetly provided more and more material for him to discover. They prompted him to continue working, knowing that when the information in his book was revealed, the pressure of being the guardian of the Touchstone would be lifted for all who carried its secrets.

Miyah's journey, Junia and Nona's journey and that of all their sisterhood, and Morgan and Michael's journeys as well, were all bound together by blood—the bloodline of Joshua and Maryum—and would be told in the folds of the pages Michael was preparing. Morgan's life marked the beginning of a new generation of Touchstone healers, a generation who lived the truth out loud, rather than seeking to conceal or protect it, so all would be revealed to the world. The spirits of the Touchstone ancestors mingled around, almost festively, as Michael, completely aware of their presence, worked away on their story.

~~~~~

One afternoon, Morgan stopped by her dad's library office for a chat.

"I'm really busy, honey," Michael said as he shuffled papers. "Can we talk later? Just give me one hour."

"I know, Dad," she responded. "But this is important, and I think it'll be a great help for your book."

"What is it?" he asked, looking up at his daughter. For a moment it was as if he were looking into Miyah's eyes, and a pang of loneliness rushed over him.

Morgan gently laid the worn medicine bag on Michael's desk. Reaching inside the bag, she pulled out both cedar boxes and laid them on top of the fabric.

Getting right to the point, she said, "I've decided to keep mother's cedar box to use in my own healing work. It's been handed down through the ages to women of the bloodline. But, I want you to have Mother Mariam's cedar box. It's the first box Joshua carved, and you were instrumental in helping Mom and I find it. It's often been kept through the ages within masculine energy, so I think you should be its next keeper. After all, you *are* a part of the bloodline." She added, "But, please take good care of it. You know how precious it is."

Michael hesitated, then slowly reached out to stroke each cedar box.

"I know you've been keeping them safe at RoseVine," he said with emotion. "I wondered if I'd ever see them again. Thank you Morgan. Just having this by my side will inspire me."

"I know," she said sincerely. "In some ways I think mother's cedar box is more yours than anyone's. You spent a lot of time, had a lot of adventures with it. But I have meditated on this and I know I'm meant to carry on her tradition with it."

She continued, "My great-grandfather, Nona's father, Dr. Alyn was the last person who used Mother Mariam's cedar box in his healing practice, so I think it fitting that it's passed down to the male side of the family—to another healer. You, Dad—another descendant of Joshua and Maryum."

Morgan reached back into the medicine pouch and brought out a necklace with an ankh shaped key. She placed it around her father's neck.

"I'm officially making you the keeper of Mariam's cedar box," she said, tucking the necklace under his shirt. His hand grasped the key and held it to his heart.

Morgan flipped her long, dark hair over her shoulder and Michael noticed the familiar thin strand of leather around her neck. Attached to it was the pouch that held the key to her cedar box. He recalled when he first saw Miyah open her cedar box and he wondered then what could be so important about an old box, a book, a few stones, and a heap of shredded fabric. Now he knew. They were perhaps the most valuable items in the world when it came to spiritual history. He'd come a long way in the past few years, from his deathbed to a new life—a truly born-again life, and he would never see things in the same light.

"The box is empty, but you might want to put some of your and Mom's photos or special memories in it for the time being. There are many ways to heal," she added. "I can only use one cedar box at a time in my work and it's a shame to keep it hidden away. I think it's been calling for you."

Michael looked at her, a bit startled.

Morgan laughed. "Oh. I don't mean calling you like the smell of cedar did when it took you back into ancient times to meet with Joshua. It won't make you disappear into distant lands like when you did the healing work with Mother and her cedar box. Nona and I put a 'lock' of protection on it so its traveling days are at rest for the time being. I just mean it should be in your presence, like an old friend."

"Like an old friend," Michael repeated.

There was a long silence.

"I miss her too," Morgan said. She walked behind his chair, wrapped her arms around her father's shoulders and gave him a tender hug.

"Do you know how many times she said she was so happy she had you in her life? Sometimes she talked about how lonely her life was after Nona died and how the only thing she ever knew was her healing practice. That is, until you came along. She loved you so much Dad, and often said what a good father you were. She knew I would be taken care of, that I'd have you to see me through the tough times."

"And vice versa," Michael solemnly replied, patting her hand.

"And she probably also knew that I would keep pushing you until you finished this project you've been working on ever since I can remember!"

"It's complicated. . ." Michael began.

"Yes, I know!" Morgan laughed. "Believe me, I know! I also know that when the time is right, as Mom always used to say, everything will fall into place."

"Yeah," Michael said, "We've already waited 2,000 years, what's a few more!"

"We *had* to wait until the world had evolved enough spiritually to question the old ways without being burned at the stake as a heretic—until people were open to new translations and the discovery of hidden texts and other treasures," she responded with a serious tone.

"Just think of it, Dad. In a sense it's like the coming of Christ in the prophecy. Only the coming is not a physical being. It's a new version of an old story. And that story isn't of fear, or of a vengeful God, or of sins and repentance. It's the story Joshua and Maryum, Jesus and Mary Magdalene, taught to the masses themselves, for over 100 years—a story of love, compassion, family and life—of teaching others appreciation of nature and our environment, of prophecy and everyday miracles. The world will know that there should be no judgements by the Church or others, that there are no real mistakes or being born with sin—that everything is about learning lessons, experiencing all that life has to offer, about growth. Each person is equal. Everyone will know that Joshua's lessons were all about love. That by keeping love and compassion in our hearts, we'll always be joyful. It's so simple, yet the Church made it so complicated."

"You're so wise," Michael said proudly, looking at her. "Just like your mother."

"And didn't she tell you it wouldn't always be easy? Now, we need to look ahead, Dad, and you have your promise to fulfill—writing the story of *our* bloodline. That's monumental in itself and you wouldn't be able to do it if you hadn't experienced all that you did. Think of those wonderful adventures with Joshua in ancient times. It also helps that *you*, yourself, are part of the bloodline too! You and Mom coming together like you did was pure destiny—the 'Red Thread of Destiny' she always spoke of."

"Yes, it's a beautiful story and I feel blessed that I was given all those opportunities to learn from Joshua in his time. I've already put a lot of that into words. The only part I would change is about losing Miyah. I miss her so much." Michael took a deep breath.

"I miss her too, but she knew intuitively what was foreseen, Dad, and she couldn't stop it. Her destiny was written when she was born. And I know she wanted you to be here for me. I need you and love you as much as she did. I hope you know that."

"Yes, I do know that," Michael said, smiling at his daughter.

"Dad, just look what you helped accomplish. The two cedar boxes are reunited, as they were meant to be. That's a milestone in itself. And we know that Mom is always around us, watching over and guiding us on our way. I can feel her every day and am looking forward to the time when she appears to us, just like Nona and Junia have. Our Touchstone journey isn't quite over yet."

"Listen to you," Michael replied. "I should be saying these things to you. Who's the parent here?" They both laughed.

"We still have a lot of loose ends to tie up—some mysteries to solve that you and Mom just touched on, like the old parchment half-letter, treasure maps, notes and other secrets in your safe and. . ."

"Slow down. Let's take one step at a time," Michael said. "Let me finish *this* book before we start on the next one!"

"Sorry. You know how I love a mystery!" she grinned.

"I have one more thing to loan you to help with the details of your writing," Morgan said. "Don't let this out of your sight. It's an important connection to Mom."

She reached into the medicine bag and produced Miyah's diary. She removed it from its linen pouch and absentmindedly let her fingers trace the lines of the family emblem on the cover, the MM that followed the names of the women of her sisterhood throughout the ages. Her own name, Morgan, was included in that tradition of having one or two M's in their name.

Michael's heart skipped a few beats. "Are you sure you want to leave this with me?" he asked. "You know I can't read most of it."

"I know," Morgan replied. "But some of it is in English, and you can read Mom's entries. I'll be back and can help you with the rest. I have an idea of some of the passages you may want to hear."

Michael recalled the days when Miyah used to sit and read portions of the diary to him. Now, just the thought of seeing, touching, the words that Miyah had written in her own hand was almost overwhelming.

"I'd like that," he said pensively. "I'd like that a lot."

"Well, you'll never finish this book if I don't leave you alone," Morgan said, kissing him on the cheek. "I have more work I need to do today, but

I'll be home for dinner. Now get to work!" she called over her shoulder as she headed for the door, slinging the medicine pouch over her shoulder, just like Miyah used to do.

Michael remembered what Nona had told Miyah about the family medicine bag many years ago. "It was sewn with magic and love, and whenever love is woven into the texture of life, it never wears out."

Love and magic had truly been woven into the texture of Michael's life. He was eternally grateful.

~~~~~

"Why has all this been revealed to me?" Michael once asked Miyah long before her death.

"Perhaps," she had replied thoughtfully, "It's simply because you're a writer and it's time for this story to be revealed to the world. Perhaps it's time. . ." her words had trailed into a soft sigh. Michael couldn't detect if it was a sigh of relief that she no longer would have to be the protectress of the cedar box, the keeper of the healing stones and the guardian of such a powerful secret, passed through generations of the daughters of her lineage, or if he sensed an edge of uncertainty and even a slight feeling of fear, as she looked ahead at a prediction of what was to come.

He wondered if humanity had really evolved enough to absorb the spiritual light that had been hovering over decades, waiting to reveal this story of enlightenment, healing, unconditional love and living in complete, untainted faith, rather than in fear—a much different, even contradictory story, to what much of organized religion had been teaching.

Yet, wasn't it a more compelling story to know that our great prophet lived on to teach his wisdom throughout the land for over a hundred years, that his beloved wife was also a spiritual prophet who healed and taught alongside him, and together they left a legacy of ancestors behind them to carry on their healing work? It was a beautiful story. A gentler story. Was he, Michael, prepared to be the messenger of this news?

Michael was feeling his age. He sat at his desk and stared at his computer screen for nearly an hour. His promise to Miyah was no easy task. He thought about the old park across from the empty lot where he knew RoseVine stood, shrouded behind the veil of another dimension. He knew she would be there with her ancestors, working their healing magic for everyone who needed them. He often went back to the park and sat, turning his Faith Stone over and over between his fingers and reminiscing of the years they had together—just like the old man he met there many years ago. But unlike that old man, Michael had proof that the house did exist—that Miyah existed. More proof than a flat, worn stone. He had Morgan.

Michael sat for a while, gazing out the window, watching Morgan drive away. He felt blessed to have her in his life. Her words gave him almost a sense of urgency to finish this story. It wasn't only about the promise he had made to Miyah in exchange for her curing his cancer—the promise to reveal the family story. That seemed so long ago and it was just the engine that started everything in motion. Now it was more out of a sense of obligation to Joshua, Maryum and the entire bloodline, his bloodline. Michael felt a surge of pride. It was an honor to be chosen to do this work. He was family.

Miyah, in her spirit form, stood next to her husband and watched Morgan drive away. She sighed with a sense of pride at seeing the woman her daughter had become. It had been a long journey for all of them. She was working hard on the "other side" to be able to materialize and appear to her family, as Nona and Junia had appeared to her throughout her life. She knew it would just be a matter of time and every day she made progress. For now, she was satisfied to be able to be with them in the vapors between the worlds. Even though they couldn't see her, she could still be with them.

Michael returned to his computer and started to type, but soon he paused, searching for the right words. He knew what he wanted to say but just couldn't quite remember all the details clearly. Miyah knew that what he was searching for was something that was written in her diary, a prayer she had used for healing. With the nod of her head, a gentle wind blew in from the window. The diary pages unfurled and opened to the exact page Michael needed to complete his paragraph.

He watched the pages flip and excitedly acknowledged the "magic" with a broad smile, knowing that Miyah was there with him. His heart fluttered and he lifted his eyes to look at photographs of Miyah on his desk.

"Thank you Miyah," he said out loud, gently touching the opened diary pages.

"I knew you would help me. I can feel your presence stronger every day. God, I miss you," he said solemnly.

"I need all the help you and your Touchstone tribe can give me."

Suddenly Michael thought he saw a faint shadow of Miyah in the room. "Are you ready to appear in our world, like Nona?" he asked with excitement. "God, I wait for that day to come. Keep working on it. You can do it. We're waiting for you. I need you now as much as ever. . ."

22 *Fulfilling the Promise*

Brilliant orange and pink hues of the sun winked through the oaks outside his window and Michael watched as a half-circle of sun slipped into the night. He had made great progress on the book, and was almost finished, but had been stuck for days with his memories. Was it writer's block, or the fact that he just didn't want to relive those emotional last days with Miyah at the end of her life?

He dug through a mix of emotions. Some came from the memories that were evoked as they found themselves vulnerable on paper, and yet other emotions arose because by sharing Miyah's story, he was also exposing their private life together. Perhaps he was having trouble writing because he felt a reluctance to reveal himself. He finally realized why it had taken him so long to write this book. He didn't want it to end. He didn't want *their* story to end.

Yet, did the story really have an ending? There were still more discoveries to be made and he had vowed to help Morgan in her quest to learn more, always more, just like her "grandfather" Joshua when he was young. There would be more books to write, more adventures to record, more mysteries to solve. Of this he was sure.

Michael knew he must no longer procrastinate. He needed to finish this book of bloodlines and promises—Miyah's story. . .their story. He finally gave in, took a deep breath, and feeling an unexpected burst of energy, he closed his eyes and just as it had been when he was lying next to the cedar box, he began to see a "movie" play out in the darkness of his vision.

He began to type. . .slowly at first, but as he gained momentum, his fingers flew over the keys and he couldn't stop. He wrote throughout the night, revealing page after page of his final journey with Miyah. He wrote with feverish abandonment, eyes closed, as if he were in a deep sleep, yet his mind, his fingers, wouldn't rest. They wrote. And strangely, he felt at peace with his words, even though they recorded the events of Miyah's tragic end. The process of writing the words gave him a sense of closure to release his own wounds. He knew that Miyah, the love of his life, would always be in his heart.

In the morning, without exhaustion, Michael stopped writing. He opened his eyes, stood up and stretched, needing to step away from this book that was almost complete. He brewed a fresh cup of tea, wrapped his hands around the hot mug, enjoying the warmth that soothed these hands that had been working throughout the night. He went back to his computer for one more page—a title page for this revealing story.

Michael sat down and thought for a while about a name that would bind these pages together. He thought of Miyah and how she gently guided him through his healing and brought him into a revelation of light and peace.

It had to be about Miyah. He said the words out loud to see how they sounded, "Miyah's Journey." Yes, it had been all about Miyah's journey—her story. His fingers typed "Miyah's Journey" in large letters in the center of a new page.

But that's not what appeared on the computer screen.

Michael looked down at the keys to be sure his fingers were in the proper place on the keyboard. They were.

After what he had been through these past years, nothing should have surprised him. But he continued to be amazed at the layers of the universe that were revealed when least expected. He looked at the computer screen and pushed his chair back, rolling himself across the floor.

Michael looked up into the abyss above his head and said, "I know. It's *your* book. I'm just your messenger. Miyah, Joshua, Maryum, all of you! Name it whatever you wish!"

Michael laughed out loud with almost insane candor.

"Thank you, all of you, for allowing me to be your emissary. . ."

Then he looked back across the room at the letters illuminated across his computer screen—the title of his manuscript.

It was not "Miyah's Journey," as he had typed.

Instead, the bold letters typed in the center of his page read—

"The Touchstone Diary"

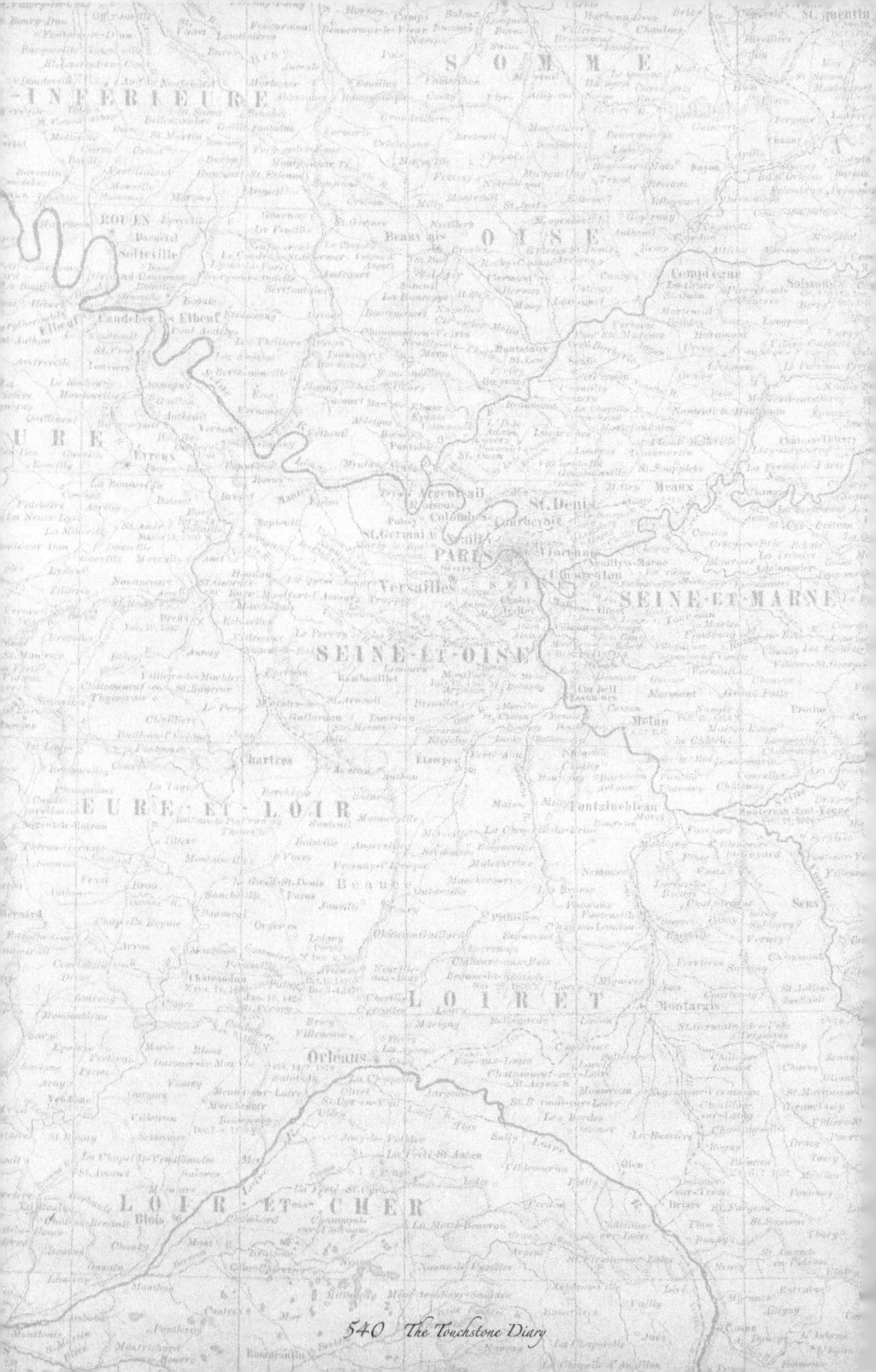

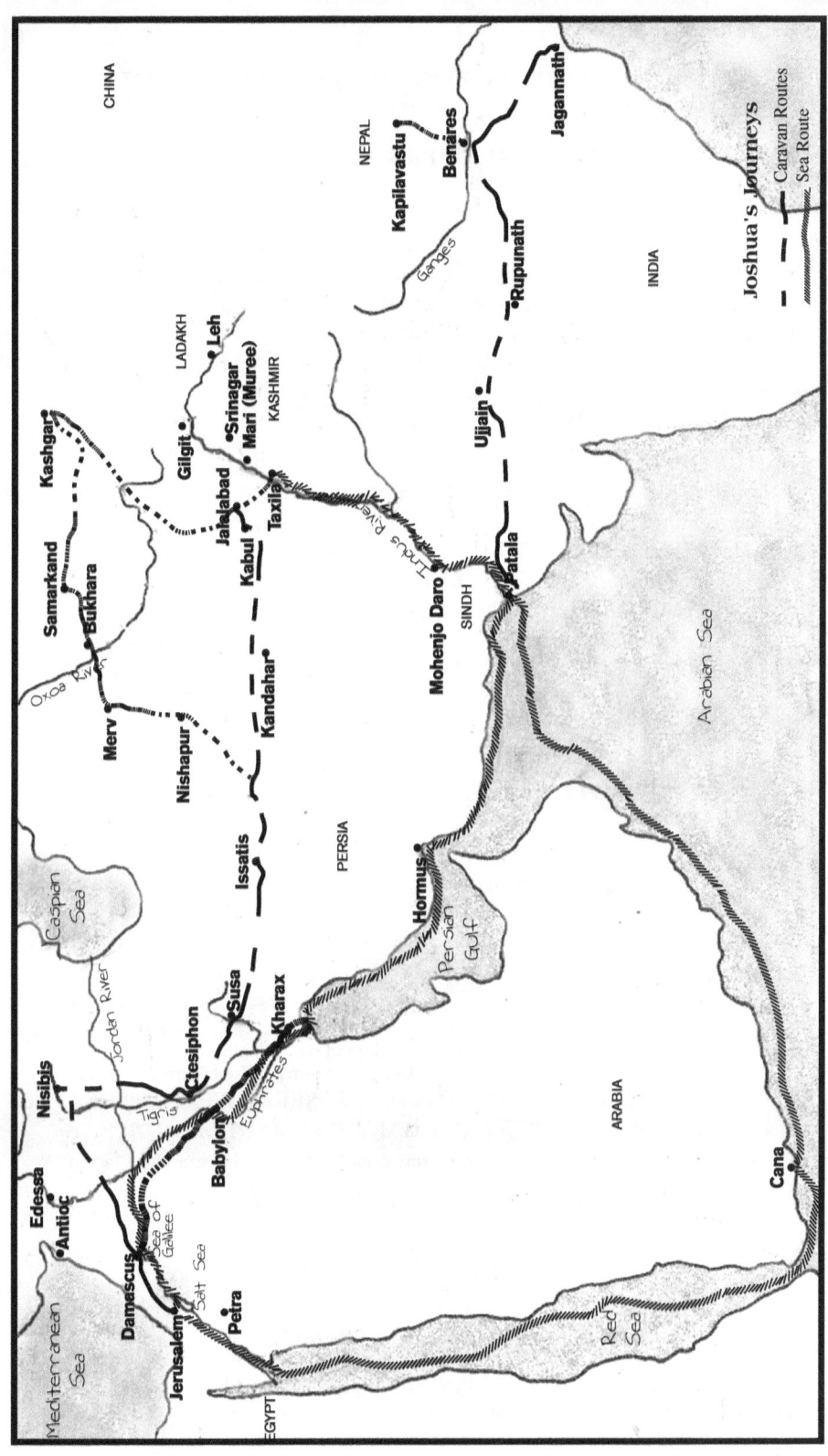

PARTIAL GENEOLOGY OF THE FAMILIES OF
JOSHUA (JESUS) AND MARYUM (MARY MAGDALENE)

KING DAVID - KING OF JUDAH (1008 BC) **AND ISRAEL** (1001 BC)
(wife 1) Bathsheba
- Solomon (Jedidiah), King of Israel and Judah 968-926 BC, *(Mother Mary's ancestors through her mother, Anna and grandmother Elmyra (Estha)'s - lineage)*
(wife 2) Maacah (Michal), daughter of King Talmai of Geshur, and widow of Uriah the Hittite, *(Joseph's ancestors)*. Bathsheba's grandson Rehoboan (Roboam), King of Judah (928-911 BC) and Maacah's granddaughter, Micaiah Melka) married, *making the line a double connection for descendants* - both being direct grandchildren of King David. Their descendants reigned as Kings of Judah, Prince-priests, high priests and eventually Kings of surrounding lands - Asia, Britain, Wales, Scotland, France.

JOSHUA (JESUS) FAMILY

Joiadah (a high priest) - married Elmyra (Estha) - Joiadah's mother was Heline, a descendent of Helen of Troy
1) Elizabeth married Zachaiah the Zadok
- John the Baptist the Zadok
2) HANNAH (ANNA), was born in Fortingal, Scotland
- Anna (1) married Mathias
  - 1) Joseph (married Eunice Salome, daughter of Arimathea, a Hasmonean prince, so Joseph was known as Joseph of Arimathea.)
  - 2) Martha
- Anna (2) married JOACHIM - (his brother Zachariah the Zadok, married Anna's sister, Elizabeth; his brother Jacob married Lois - their son was Joseph (Jesus' father) and he had eight siblings)
  - 1)   Ruth
  - 2-3) Issac and Andrew (twins) Issac married Tabitha
    - Tabitha's daughter - Sara/ husband Phillip
  - 4-5) Miriamne and Jacob (twins)   - 6)   Josephus
  - 7-8) Nathan and Luke (twins)   - 9)   Rebekah
  - 10) Ezekial   - 11) Noah
  - 12) MARIAM/MARY (born in Ephesus) married JOSEPH AB HELI, son of Jacob and Lois, (six generations prior, Joseph's paternal ancestor was adopted by Zadok, a direct descendant of David, counting future generations in the House of David.)
    - **-1) YESHUA BEN YOSEF - JOSHUA/JESUS** - 7 BC
      married MARYUM - MARY MAGDALENE
      (whose brother and sister were Lazarus and Martha)
      1 - Sera Tamara Maria
      2 - Joseph David
      3 - John Martin
    - 2) James   - 3) Mirium   - 4) Yosuf
    - 5) Simon   - 6) Martha   - 7) Judas Thomas
    - 8) Amos   - 9) Ruth

Note: It is documented in Kashmir that YESHUA later married a woman named Mirjan, and had additional descendants of his bloodline with a Kashmiri lineage. There are claims of a genealogical table in the family of Sahibzada Basharat Saleem.

MARYUM - MARY MAGDALENE'S FAMILY

"Maryum was a royal daughter of the Tribe of Benjamin, whose ancestral heritage covered the land surrounding the Holy City of David—she was a rich woman, an heiress of the lands bordering Jerusalem." Mary Magdalene's maternal descent was from the royalty of Judaea, her paternal heritage was of the kingly nobility of Syria. Descended from the Hasmonaean House of the Maccabees (ruling dynasty of Judea and surrounding regions, BC174 to BC37 with generations of Prince-priests.)

Judas of Gamla, (chief scribe), son of Hezekiah, was a brother to Joiadah (high priest), the father of Anna (maternal grandmother to Jesus).

- 1) Menahem the Essene, (Issac Patriarch) founded West Manasseh Magians
    - 1) Judas the Galilean, Founder of Zealots (Chief Scribe)
        - Judas
            - Menahern
        - Simon
    - 2) Simon Magus (Lazarus Zebedee) married Salome (Helena) - their granddaughter Anna, married Brian the Blessed, Archdruid of Siluria, with descendants in Britain, Wales and North Britain, trickling down to include High King Arthur, AD559-603 - no heir by his wife Gwenyfawr of Brittany, but had a child, Modred, (d603) with a 2nd high priestess. These bloodlines connect with the Welsh Kings descending into the Sceneschals (rulers or governors of medieval great houses) of Bretons and Scots.
    - 3) Martha
    - 4) Eucharis married Chief Priest, Syrus the Jairus, (his father, Jonathan Annas, was a high priest AD37 - The Jairus Priest had been a hereditary position from the time of King David and was handed down only through the descendants of Jair.)
        - 1) Lazarus
        - 2) Martha
        - 3) **MARYUM - MARY MAGDALENE** born in Syria 10 BC
            married YESHUA BEN JOSEPH (Joshua/Jesus)
            1) Sera Tamar Maria (Sera - Israelite title meaning princess)
            2) Joseph David - (one of his descendants, Aminadab,
                married Eargen of the "Fisher King" lineage (a long line
                charged with keeping the Holy Grail) - family of King Coel
                I of Camulot (Colchester), and King Lucius. The last of
                their children married a Princess of the Sicambrian Franks,
                which led into the lineage of the Merovingian Kings of
                the Franks, and Queen Viviane I and II of Avalion, which
                traces down to Lancelot, his wife Elaine, and their son
                Galahad. This lineage also connects with King Arthur on
                the maternal side.
            3) John Martin
                - Sera
                    - Sara Bernice
                - Thomas
                    - Simon (Simon of Merian)
                - Germane

Miyah's Partial Family Tree

Dolores Sinclair married Dr. Alyn Harris
1 - Morgan "Nona" Sinclair married Father Tomas Thornburg
1 - Junia Marie Sinclair and her partner, John Charles Maartin
1 - MIYAH MARIA MAARTIN SINCLAIR
married MICHAEL PAUL WILDER
1 - MORGAN JUNE SINCLAIR WILDER

Michael's Partial Family Tree

Paul Wilder married Katrina McKnight
1 - MICHAEL PAUL WILDER
married MIYAH MARIA MAARTIN SINCLAIR
1 - MORGAN JUNE SINCLAIR WILDER
2 - Elizabeth married Bob Alexander

Continue with the adventures and healing magic
of Morgan and her father, Michael,
(along with the spirits of Miyah and their ancestors to guide them)
as they use the power of the cedar box and
messages in the ancient family diary
to unravel clues hidden
in the contents of Michael's father's safe.

Discover a path to mysterious links
of Vikings, Knights Templar, pirate ships
and bloodline secrets that crossed oceans
to become hidden treasure in the Americas.

The Touchstone Diary
Book III

Next in the series - due 2014/2015

About the Author

**Connie Bickman with camera—her career was
destined at age two!**

Connie Bickman has been a writer and photographer since she can remember, and notes that she still has the old Brownie camera her parents gave her as a child.

Connie's passion for travel has brought her to over 40, mostly third world, countries. She packed along her journals and camera as these photojournalist-based travels brought her to far corners of the earth in search of adventure and the opportunity to document native cultures, the environment, and humanitarian issues.

It was through these journeys that she realized misconceptions she had about the foundation of organized religion and how oftentimes people in other countries and cultures had much different perspectives on not only Christianity and conflicting biblical translations, but also on the original concept of the Christ story itself. This began years of research and scrutiny to satisfy her own uncertainties, which brought her to disclose her findings in "The Touchstone Diary," a "fiction-based-on-historical-events" series.

Writing and photography are in her blood, referring to 15 years of owning a portrait studio, and a 30+ year newspaper career. This includes an eleven year period where she was the co-owner/publisher/editor of Turtle River Press, a publication of spiritual and creative energy.

Connie has been published internationally in books and magazines, and has won regional and international awards for her photography and writing. Her book, "Tribe of Women" (republished by New World Library) received a Jeanette Fair Tau State Minnesota Women's Writer Award.

Mother of three daughters, six grandgirls and one great-grandgirl, Connie currently lives Woodstock, NY.

Also by Connie Bickman:

• **"Tribe of Women"** published by New World Library, 2001, focusing on the spiritual aspect of Bickman's journeys, including photography and

excerpts from her journals on encounters with bush doctors in Belize, shaman in the Amazon jungles of Peru, witch doctors in Africa and Aboriginal elders in Australia. ISBN 1-57731-130-2

• **"Through the Eyes of Children"** published by Rock Bottom Books, Abdo and Daughter, a series of ten educational children's books for schools and libraries on the everyday lifestyles of children around the world, which includes photography from travels to Australia, Tanzania, Russia, Mexico, Israel, Peru, Turkey, Egypt, Nepal and Equador.

Author, Connie Bickman, in front of the abbey on the Isle of Iona, Scotland. – photo by Kelli Bickman

Page index of photographs ©Connie Bickman
from "Book I - The Red Thread"

Page index of photographs ©Connie Bickman
from "Book II - Bloodlines and Promises"

Mary Magdalene statue
Rolin Museum
– holding her diary?

Station IV – statue
Jesus and Mary Magdalene

SUGGESTED READING

- **Anna, Grandmother of Jesus**, A Message of Wisdom and Love - Claire Heartsong
- **A Search for the Historical Jesus** - from Apocryphal, Buddhist, Islamic & Sanskrit Sources - Professor Fida Hassnain
- **Bloodline of The Holy Grail** - The Hidden Lineage of Jesus Revealed - Laurence Gardner
- **Holy Blood Holy Grail** - Michael Baigent, Richard Leigh, Henry Lincoln
- **How the Great Religions Began** - Joseph Gaer
- **Jesus and the Lost Goddess**, The Secret Teaching of the Original Christians - Timothy Freke and Peter Gandy
- **Jesus Christ: A Fiction Founded Upon the Life of Apollonius of Tyana** - 1883 Professor Michael Faraday
- **Jesus in Heaven on Earth**, Journey of Jesus to Kashmir, His Preachings to the Lost Tribes of Israel and Death and Burial in Srinagar - Khwaja Nazir Ahmad
- **Jesus Lived in India** - His unknown life before and after the crucifixion - Holger Kersten
- **Jesus Tomb in India**, Debate on His Death and Resurrection - Paul C. Pappas
- **Life and Teaching of the Masters of the Far East**, 5 volume set- David T. Spalding
- **Life of Saint Issa** - Nicholas Notovitch (published 1890)
- **Magdalene's Lost Legacy,** Symbolic Numbers and the Sacred Union in Christianity - Margaret Starbird
- **Paganism and Christianity 100-425 CE,** - Ramsay MacMullen and Eugene N. Lane
- **Philostratus - Apollonius of Tyana**, books 1-3 - Translated by Christopher P. Jones
- **Rabbi Jesus** an Intimate Biography, The Jewish Life and Teachings That Inspired Christianity - Bruce Chilton
- **Rozabal, The Tomb of Jesus** - Fida Hassnain, Suzanne Olsson
- **Saving the Savior,** Did Christ Survive the Crucifixion? - Abubakr Ben Ishmael Salahuddin
- **St. Mary Magdalene,** The Gnostic Tradition of the Holy Bride - Tau Malachi
- **The Church of Mary Magdalene,** The Sacred Feminine and the Treasure of Rennes-Le-Château - Jean Markale
- **The Essene Gospel of Peace,** Translation of the Third Century Aramaic Manuscript and Old Slavonic Texts - Edmond Bordeáux Szckely (books 1-4)
- **The Gnostics** - Tobias Churton
- **The Goddess in the Gospels**, Reclaiming the Scared Feminine - Margaret Starbird
- **The Gospel of Mary Magdalene** - Jean-Yves LeLoup
- **The Gospel of Mary Magdalene** - Karen L. King
- **The Gospel of The Essenes,** The Unknown Book of the Essene Lost Scrolls of the Essene Brotherhood - translated from original Hebrew and Aramaic texts by Edmond Bordeáux Szckely
- **The Gospel of Thomas,** The Gnostic Wisdom of Jesus - Jean-Yves LeLoup
- **Jesus and the Essenes** - Dolores Cannon
- **The Historical Mary,** Revealing the Pagan Identity of the Virgin Mother - Michael Jordan
- **The Holy Land of Scotland**, Jesus in Scotland & The Gospel of the Grail - Barry Dunford
- **The Holy Women Around Jesus** - Carol Haenni, Ph.D
- **The Jesus Mystery of Lost Years and Unknown Travels** - Janet Bock
- **The Nag Hammadi Library,** The Definitive New Translation of the Gnostic Scriptures - James M. Robinson
- **The Priory of Sion Dossiers** - Compiled by Bruce Burgess, René Barnett, Robert Howells
- **The Secret Teachings of Jesus,** Four Gnostic Gospels: The Secret Book of James • The Gospel of Thomas • The Book of Thomas • The Secret Book of John - translated by Marvin W. Meyer
- **The Urantia Book** - The Urantia Foundation, 1955
- **The Woman with the Alabaster Jar**, Mary Magdalene and the Holy Grail - Margaret Starbird

www.ingramcontent.com/pod-product-compliance
Lightning Source LLC
Chambersburg PA
CBHW030841030726
47495CB00005B/1321